PILGRIM'S STORM BROODING

Volume 2

DAMIEN BLACK

CONTENTS

ISBN:

978-0-9954928-9-9 [paperback]
978-0-9954928-7-5 [ePub]
978-0-9954928-8-2 [Mobi]

MAPS OF THE KNOWN WORLD

For detailed map graphics, please visit facebook.com/
brokenstonemaps or simply Google: @brokenstonemaps

Northern Principalities
Mercenary Kingdoms
Steppes of Nath
Steppes of Kala
The Empire
Free Kingdoms
The Great Inland Sea
Vergan Islands
The Great Western Ocean
Sultanate of Nexbaraba
Hierocracy of Sendag
Vindar River
Zhose Desert
The Arid Kingdoms
600 miles

PART I

CHAPTER 1
A NEW ROAD IN SPRING

The highway stretched ahead as far as the eye could see, a steady stream of white stone bisecting the green fields. Adelko was grateful for it; thanks to the age-old craft of the Thalamians, he didn't have any more potholed roads to contend with. They had been on the road but barely a week out of Rima, and already they were riding through the verdant pastures of Pangonia's southern Vania province. A few more days, Horskram had told them, and they would reach the great cityport of Montrevellyn.

The journeyman gazed about him as the five of them pressed on, their freshly shod horses' hooves clattering monotonously against the vast triangular flagstones of the highway. This far south, spring came early, and already the clustered copses dotted about were leafing under cobalt skies. He'd never seen such trees before, only read about them: elms, hornbeams, beeches and alders. The natural verdancy of southern Pangonia made for a pleasant distraction, stopping him brooding on things past – and things to come.

It felt strange not to have Vaskrian at his side. He found the damsels even more standoffish these days, and truth be told their class and sex still intimidated him. Their heathen bodyguard was even less approachable, and as for his mentor... well, Horskram was Horskram. He missed Vaskrian. He hoped his squire friend was alive and well, though you could never guarantee that of a hothead like him.

Reflecting on that, Adelko realised it was a year since he and Horskram had set out from Ulfang on their mission to Rima. Had it really only been a year ago? It felt more like a century.

Centuries had come and gone since the Thalamian Empire had crumbled back into the dust from which it was wrought, as all empires must. Horskram had told him that the great roads built by them had fallen into disrepair, until the advent of the Pilgrim Wars had motivated the southern overlords to start maintaining them better. The latest rash of that fool's war had been declared by Cyprian shortly before they left Rima; already they had passed clutches of crusader contingents on the road, heading the same way. Horskram hadn't been keen to fall in with such zealots, and no one in their company had complained when the adept steered them deftly past.

What will all the holy wars in the world do for your lot, Adelko wondered, staring at the bent-backed serfs hunched over the fields, sowing the rye and barley and wheat that would let them eke out another miserable year. The farther south one went in Pangonia, the more pious men were said to become; but he hadn't seen much evidence of Palomedian charity either here in Vania, or Morvaine and Narbo through which they had passed. *My countrymen have the right of this,* he thought. *The Pilgrim Wars are a folly, a waste of coin and life.*

And yet that was where they journeyed to now: the Pilgrim Kingdoms of Sassania, crucible of the crusades. Adelko couldn't deny the thought of looking on the Redeemer's birthplace excited him, but theirs was a pilgrimage tinged with darkness. If they failed in their mission, the Redeemer's name might never be spoken again.

That got him thinking back to his ordination as journeyman, two months ago. Dressed in naught but a sackcloth, Adelko had felt the cold dawn air keenly as it hummed through the monastery, and done his best not to shiver. Thanks to Edemus, he had less fat to insulate him nowadays, though he wouldn't hold that against his taskmaster. The hoarfrosted clay of the courtyard had felt clammy against the soles of his feet as he'd approached the chapel.

As he'd entered its draughty precinct, the monks flanking him had begun chanting the Litany of Ascension, the rest of the chapter kneeling on pallets around the statue of St Argo. Adelko had shut his eyes and felt rather than heard the sacred words, spiralling up through the colonnade towards the chapel's entablatured ceiling:

Staff of iron and rood of silver,
    The soul sword weighs heavy in my hand:

My spirit awakens, my sleep is done

No more a child, but now a man,
Set on the path of the outer world:
My spirit awakens, my sleep is done

Clothed in flesh, the fire that never dies,
Manna from above to cleanse below:
My spirit awakens, my sleep is done

Till the Final Hour, we keep vigil,
Watching for the Second Coming:
My spirit awakens, my sleep is done

My spirit awakens, the night is gone,
My spirit awakens, Thy will be done!

Over and over they had repeated the litany, as Adelko drew level with the statue and knelt. Hannequin and Horskram had been there, together with the rest of the High Circle – or what was left of it. The Grand Master had stepped forward as Adamantus presented a ceramic bowl. Dipping his fingers into it, Hannequin had anointed the novice's head with oil, and intoned the formal induction:

· · ·

St Argo guard thee, St Alysius guide thee,
   Seven Seraphim inbue thee,
   Palom be thy grace,
   As Reus Almighty sees all

'Arise, Adelko, journeyman of the Order,' the Grand Master had finished. The choral chanting had risen to a final crescendo, all voices seeming to converge at the apex of the chapel. Adelko had felt a wave of wellbeing wash over him, as the conjoined elan of his brethren bathed his animus. But he had felt a shadow at its fringes, too.

That had been a topic of conversation during his last night with Hargus and Arik, old friends so briefly rediscovered. Their faces had seemed childlike in the candlelight as he gave them their final briefing; Adelko did not honestly know what two lowly novices could accomplish in his absence, but he felt more secure knowing someone at the monastery he could fully trust shared his secret.

For all his difficult thoughts, his ordination had proceeded smoothly enough. Horskram had stepped forwards, the folded grey habit of a journeyman in his arms. Getting to his feet, Adelko had stood while two monks had taken the habit and put it on him, fastening it at the waist with a length of hemp cord. The grey wool had felt pleasant against his skin, and not just for sensuous reasons.

It still did, though he was grateful for the cool breeze that offset the noon sunlight as they rode along the road.

A journeyman at fifteen, he thought and not for the first time. *Father, I hope this much makes you proud at least.*

Taking him by the shoulders, Hannequin had gently turned him to face the congregation.

'Give thanks to St Argo and the archangel Ushira, for bringing us this new disciple,' the Grand Master had intoned. 'Adelko of Narvik, initiate of the principles, has joined our brotherhood.'

'Welcome to the fold, Adelko of Narvik, be ye like the saints in reckoning, and serve the Order body and soul, till thine hour cometh.'

It was a simple formal response from the congregation, though he'd scarce been able to believe the words were addressed to him. Hannequin had presented him with his quarterstaff, rood and prayer book. They were the same ones he'd carried throughout his travels, but Argolians were sticklers for tradition and ritual. The formalities done, the monks had filed out of the chapel to go about their daily duties. Were it not for the shadow on his sixth sense, Adelko would have felt almost underwhelmed by the experience.

Not long after, Hannequin had taken down his written testimony against Johann. He hoped that wasn't the only reason for his early promotion. The rest of his time at the monastery had been spent training with Edemus and studying. Adelko had sensed that his taskmaster did not approve of the decision to send him back into danger, or his early ordination. But he'd held his peace.

He hoped the months of hard training would stand him in good stead. He and his mentor had even grown accustomed to speaking to one another in the Sassanic tongue, to ensure his readiness for the foreign land that now beckoned. His body was toned and well-muscled; the rigours of the road no longer challenged him physically as they had once done.

He'd never felt so potent, yet still he feared the way ahead.

Beneath her shawl, Adhelina gazed upon the sunlit kingdom with moody eyes. They'd already passed half a dozen castles the size of Graukolos on their journey from the capital, each one seemingly more elegant than the last. But not all the whitewashed buttresses and spiring pinnacles in the Free Kingdoms could erase her memories of the corrupt court lying at the heart of this vaunted realm.

Pangonia thy fruits are poison, she thought to herself as she gazed upon the piteous peasants toiling in the spring sunshine.

Not all her experiences in the capital had been bad, she reflected philosophically as they rode five abreast along the expansive highway. During their winter sojourn at the *Paradise,* she'd grown more than fond of the girls she had looked after, and just as fond of the babe she'd helped to deliver (not all doxies were willing to choose the Root). What a bastard-born son of a whore would have to look forward to in life, she didn't like to think, but Adhelina supposed a life was better than none at all.

Or was it? She couldn't help but wonder, looking at Vania's sore-taxed peasantry. Much of her life she'd railed at her situation, but could she really complain justly? That was a question she had asked herself many times since leaving the brothel. The women there were treated far worse than she had ever been, used by strange men before being tossed aside like scraps for the hounds in her father's feasting hall. In fairness, not all the clients had been horrid. She'd even had to persuade Layla that Luviah's Teet was an aphrodisiac to be given to patrons, not used to help one enjoy the charms of a particularly handsome customer. The petite pretty blonde had remonstrated poutingly at the time, but been the first to burst into tears when she'd learned Helene was leaving, never to return. Adhelina had shed more than a few herself: common prostitutes were among the most decent people she had ever met, a lot more decent than half the high-born men and ladies she'd grown up around.

Her thoughts turned to the future. It was one she'd already had glimpses of – the second sight had come on her sporadically in the past couple of months. The most terrifying vision had been of a motley crew of strange sailors – some of whom were familiar and some of whom weren't – *flying* above desert sands, red castles dotted across a shifting brown skin like bloody pinpricks. Ahead in the distance had been a great mountain range, its cerulean peaks looming up towards them. A mighty fortress of dark stone seemed to grow from the slopes, beckoning them on...

Adhelina shuddered at the memory, though she wasn't even sure the vision had pertained to her directly. As with her visions of the battle of Linden, sometimes she saw glimpses of things that might happen to people she cared about. Other visions had been less frightful, although the dream she'd had of two grey-garbed monks languishing in a cell did not bode well.

I'm supposed to help them, even when they don't realise it, she reminded herself. *Hopefully the old mystic woman's faith in me won't prove misplaced.*

She glanced over at Anupe, riding next to her. The outlander had said little of late; Adhelina wondered what she was thinking.

Anupe caught the white walls of the next castle, glaring in the bright rays. On a hilltop beyond it, a much older building tottered on its foundations, the shattered obelisks and square colonnades of a ruined Thalamian villa. That and the highway put her in mind of the latter-day empire she had called home for a while; the Chalcedonians who ruled from the mighty city of Illyrium had built theirs on the bones of that much older civilisation. But now she doubted she'd see its red walls again.

Though she was glad to be getting out of the Free Kingdoms, her sense of foreboding had gradually increased. It was obvious they were caught up in a larger destiny – what the northerners called Wyrd and the priestesses of Hamazos called the Godsgame. Now Adhelina had acquired powers of farsight, and spoke in hushed tones of her fate being bound up with that of the monks.

Anupe knew enough of the Godsgame to realise that meant she was bound up in it, too: they hadn't shared so many adventures by chance, of that she was sure.

Perhaps this turn of events was fortuitous, she told herself. Her plan to return to the Empire had probably been a foolish one, she'd decided. Even if she made it back there, she would have to answer charges of deserting. The penalties were less severe for foreign mercenaries like her, but she'd have some explaining to do.

My superior officer ordered me to kill women and children, she thought bitterly. *What more explanation is needed?* Something told her the martial court of the Imperial Legion's Outland Brigade wouldn't see it quite that way.

Yes, a change of direction might be a good thing indeed. After their business was done in the Pilgrim Kingdoms she could head farther south, seek work as a soldier of fortune in the Sassanian Sultanates, or even journey beyond to Sendhé or the Arid Kingdoms... The world was hers to wander at will, yet she felt weary of it just the same. She still yearned for her homeland. But she would scarce be welcome there either, not after killing the elder Yula in a duel of love. Her people had long and unforgiving memories.

She sighed irritably as they passed a group of pilgrims, tugging absent-mindedly at the hood she felt obliged to wear again. *Small need to worry about the future anyway,* she told herself. *Chances are we'll meet our end in the Pilgrim Kingdoms.*

Perhaps the monks thought that didn't much matter; that they were guaranteed a place in their fictitious afterlife. But Anupe knew better. The Harijans alone of the earth's peoples understood: the gods had not seen fit to share the gift of immortality with their fickle frail creations. All that awaited dead men and women was the smothering blackness of the Long Silence.

They drew level with the crumbling Thalamian edifice.

It crowned a hill overlooking the highway; they passed beneath the shadow of its fractured hexagonal walls, the ash-grey stones telling a mournful tale of bygone glory.

Anupe's lip curled in a wry smile.

Let us look upon the mighty works of men, and despair.

Hettie glowered as they pushed deeper into the belt of hills, the land rising with the heat. She wasn't in good spirits. Already she missed the comforts of the *Paradise*; it had been a sordid place of refuge, but one she had grown used to. She missed playing cards with Tyla and Reia. She missed fleecing the brothel's wealthier clientele even more.

At least I've earned enough coin to keep us alive in the Pilgrim Kingdoms, she thought. *Someone has to keep an eye on practicalities, after all.* Not much chance of that with Adhelina, who now seemed convinced she was on a mission from the Almighty Himself.

Our situation gets more absurd by the day. We're off to who knows where when our country is on the brink of being invaded. Word of a muster had filtered back to them the week before they left Rima: the King was assembling a mighty army at the foothills of the Orne ranges. The spring would soon be awash with the blood of their countrymen. *And we'll be hundreds of leagues away, on some madcap quest to avert an ancient evil.* What did they need to go bothering about ancient evils for? There were enough present ones to keep anyone occupied.

But there wasn't much a pair of stray damsels could do

about a war, in any case: they didn't even belong in Dulsinor anymore, never mind Vorstlund. She wondered how many of the folk she had grown up with were still alive. Had Graukolos fallen to the Lanraks?

So many questions that it pained her to think about, all the more because she had no answers.

The pilgrims behind had broken into joyous song. *What are they so bloody cheerful about? Judging by the crusaders we've passed, the Blessed Realm will be just another battlefield before long.*

Horskram nudged his horse from an amble to a canter as the pilgrims started singing. Pious dolts were the last thing he wanted to hear right now. The others must have felt likewise, for they urged their steeds alongside him.

In the folds of his habit he carried a letter of introduction from Hannequin. He wasn't pleased about its intended recipient. He knew Brother Sir Tobin of Dancy by reputation alone. The Grand Master of the Knights Bethler was famed for being a gifted swordsman, tactician and horserider... and infamous for being one of the most ruthless fanatics to disgrace the Pilgrim Kingdoms. But Hannequin had insisted. The Argolians might not share the Bethlers' love of shedding heathen blood, but they did share their interest in Sassanian loremastery: Hannequin had himself lodged with them on several visits to the Blessed Realm during his long service to the Order.

'For decades now, the Knights Bethler have given us

succour when we have sought the mysteries of the Blessed Realm and beyond,' Hannequin had pointed out. 'I can't risk jeopardising that relationship because of your personal history with crusading, Horskram. And besides, you'll be safer at the Bethler preceptory than any other place in Ushalayim. Sir Tobin is overly zealous when it comes to heathens, but he respects Palomedians well enough.'

Horskram hadn't felt too sure of that.

'Sir Tobin respects Palomedians as long as they kill Sha'abatians,' he'd replied.

'The Bethlers have contacts all over the Sassanian world,' Hannequin had insisted. 'They've taken advantage of the Great Schism to cultivate allies among rebel warlords in the sultanates, and know every eminent scholar in the Pilgrim Kingdoms. If Tobin can help us fathom the whereabouts of the fourth fragment, he will.'

'You mean to tell him of our mission?'

'I will allude to it in the letter,' was all Hannequin had said to that. 'Your sixth sense will tell you how far Grand Master Tobin can be trusted.'

Something tells me not that far. I hope you know what you're doing, Hannequin.

He had written the letter with Horskram looking over his shoulder. It was cleverly worded, alluding to an artefact of great importance in the age-old struggle against the Fallen One's servants, without actually specifying its ghastly provenance. But all the same, Horskram still wasn't sure he agreed with Hannequin's plan.

Though the Grand Master had been right about one

thing – Horskram did have a personal history with the Pilgrim Kingdoms. And it wasn't one he cherished.

Memories of that region brought back painful recollections, of prisoners put to the sword and women and children driven shrieking from burning villages. And of worse still... though at least he'd had enough sense to renounce crusading when those atrocities started. But he'd done little to prevent them, and even after all these years, his sins weighed heavily on his soul.

Almighty, Thy will be done, he silently intoned. *May my lifelong penance find some small consideration in Thine all-seeing eyes.*

A cool breeze ruffled the belt of lightly wooded hills they rode through; it was a welcome antidote to Horskram's uncomfortable thoughts about hellfire, but the old fear did not leave him.

CHAPTER 2
UNWELCOME TIDINGS

The keep walls kept a blustery spring day at bay, but the weather was the last thing on Utha's mind. What concerned the Princess Consort far more than that (and her husband Leopold's frail health) was the news her spies had brought back to Westenlund more than a fortnight ago. Initially no one at court had taken the rumours all that seriously. A Pangonian invasion? Their admittedly powerful neighbours were far too busy fretting over their colonies in Sassania and intriguing against one another to bother with the northerly Free Kingdoms. Such views had been exposed as wishful thinking, when reports of an army thousands strong mustering south of the Ornes had been brought back.

Gazing about the garishly opulent hall, festooned with costly silks brought from the Hot South and hanging triangular banners depicting the House of Drüler's coat of arms, Utha resisted the urge to curl her lip in disgust. She almost wished her husband had taken ill years before – Leopold's court was a disgrace, she needed more time to lick it into shape. More than a hundred knights and nobles lolled about the arassed semicircular chamber, leaning idly against fluted colonnades as they feasted on roast boar and hedgehog, braised venison, grilled lampreys with ginger and carum, egg frumenty pottage, beaver pie, and various other dainties the harried cooks of Westerburg Point's kitchens had been ordered to conjure up.

Such gluttony, she thought disapprovingly. *And it's barely past noon.*

But put a stop to it, and she'd have a full-blown revolt on her hands. Or so the Royal High Seneschal, Fraustus, had assured her. It was part of Vorstlending custom to feast often, and Westenlund was the richest barony in the realm. That part of what he'd said was true enough. But whereas the northern nobility kept themselves trim with melees and hunts and skirmishes, the scions of Westerburg had grown fat and lazy.

We've been at peace for far too long, she thought as the herald stepped forward to announce the new arrivals at court. *We don't even test our chivalry in melees, not since my other half thought fit to imitate the Pangonians and abolish them. Those same Pangonians now set to rape and plunder our country.*

'Sir Ruttgur and Sir Agravine, knights of Dulsinor, seek audience with Her Royal Highness, the Most Noble Princess Utha, Acting Protectress of-'

Princess Utha cleared her throat loudly and raised a silencing hand. 'Yes, thank you dear, that will do. You can dispense with the formalities, I know full well what my title entails, and I'm sure our guests do as well.'

Nodding curtly, the liveried herald ushered the two knights forwards. They bore signs of having travelled a rough road; dirty and soiled, and nursing injuries to boot. She'd heard of their arrival that morning, and their injured companion who'd been admitted to the infirmary straight away.

So the rumours of civil war up north aren't just rumours either, she thought glumly. *The troubles of the realm multiply, it seems.*

The knights took a knee. Hers sniggered into their brimful winecups at their dishevelled appearance, but Utha knew better. *Two such hardy warriors are worth more than all of you hangers-on put together.*

'Arise, northern kinsmen, and find yourselves welcome in our hall,' she said pleasantly. 'Pray tell, what brings Dulsinians so far south?'

Sir Ruttgur spoke first. 'You will have heard of the war between us and the Stornelendings,' he said in a flat voice that did little to betray the gravity of the situation. 'We've been sent here to sue for His Highness Prince Leopold's help against our treacherous neighbours.'

He gets to the point this one, I'll give him that.

'I see,' she replied, the pleasant tone not leaving her voice, 'and why would Westenlund do such a thing?'

'We were sent by Sir Urist, Marshal of Graukolos,' put in Sir Agravine. 'With the Eorl dead and his sole heir missing, he is empowered to make you the following offer.'

Ruttgur proffered a scroll. A tatty shred of parchment that wasn't sealed, but tied awkwardly with some twine. Utha beckoned for a page boy to bring it to her, thoughts awhirl. Curious rumours had filtered back to the castle some time ago, from the bustling cityport it overlooked. Somebody looking suspiciously like the heiress of Dulsinor had been sighted, months ago... but by the time the rumours had reached Prince Leopold's ears, Adhelina – if indeed it was her – had been long gone.

Utha's pulse quickened as she read the scroll. The writing was a semi-literate scrawl and clearly written by Urist himself, but its meaning was clear enough.

'Sir Urist would bind Dulsinor to Westenlund, in return for deliverance from the Lanraks?' She could scarce believe the words as they came out of her mouth. Gasps went up around the hall. Her corpulent courtiers suddenly began to take the new arrivals seriously.

'We have little choice, ma'am,' said Ruttgur bluntly. 'For months now, the Stornelendings have besieged Graukolos and laid waste to the lands about. We were part of a sortie of surviving knights led by Sir Urist, but doubtless' – for the first time the stoical knight's voice cracked with emotion – 'they too will have laid down their lives by now.'

'Only winter and the walls of Graukolos have kept the Lanraks from victory,' added Agravine. 'The one is over, and as for the other... not even the castle Goriath built can hope to hold out forever.'

The Princess Consort pursed her lips, tapping the marble throne she had assumed with skittish fingers. Goriath. The master mason's name was well known down south: the very castle she presided over had been the first in the region to emulate his preternatural handicraft. Perched on a promontory of cliff that gave it a bird's eye view of

Westerburg, its semicircular keep stretched the height of forty men above the lip of rock that supported it. The foundations went deep under it, cavernous cellars replete with wine and cured meats and other goods: few would think of starving out Westerburg Point, even if they were mad enough to brave the curtain wall that hugged the cliff edge before doubling back on itself to form a vast triangular courtyard. Its three points were guarded with drum turrets scarcely smaller than the donjon; the eyes of Westerburg Point saw far across both land and sea.

But for all that, Pangonia was mightiest of the Free Kingdoms.

'Our defences are due to be tested, too,' said Utha, echoing Ruttgur's bluntness. 'King Carolus is marshalling an army, and plans to invade Vorstlund. So it would seem our causes dovetail.' She tapped her pudgy fingers on the throne again, leaving both knights to exchange meaningful glances as they registered the news. Her courtiers quaffed their drinks moodily. Even now, many of them were in denial about the pending invasion.

Heaven forfend an actual war should interfere with their merry-making.

A shooting pain through her entrails reminded Utha that her husband wasn't the only one to suffer maladies related to food and drink. But then she'd been living with the Bowel Pestilence for years, and was used to it: men lay low and groaned abed, while women got on with what needed to be done.

Hiding her discomfort (it wouldn't do to show it in front of the entire court, and important guests to boot), she said:

'As you will understand, we can't very well be marshalling a force to march north at such perilous time. But what we can do is send an entourage of emissary, to warn the other barons of Vorstlund that the Pangonians are coming. Judging by the army they are mustering, I sincerely doubt they intend to stop at our principality.'

Ruttgur seemed of better mettle than his companion, though Agravine was clearly quicker on the uptake. 'You mean to call a Council of the Nine?'

'The first in generations,' confirmed the Princess Consort, nodding. 'I seriously doubt even that oaf Hengist will want to continue his petty war with Dulsinor, once he learns of this threat. In the meantime, the Principality of Westenlund accepts your gracious offer. Dulsinor and all its lands will be taken in ward under our royal protection. Once the Pangonians are dealt with, full details of suzerainty will be finalised. Fraustus, see our guests properly quartered and victualled, their wounds tended to. Herald, where is Clothar?'

'I believe he's a'hawking, ma'am.'

'Yes he would be, wouldn't he?' she commented dryly. 'Send for him immediately. Time I reminded him he's still Marshal of Westerburg Point.'

Everyone thinks us so strong, yet few realise how complacent and lax we have become.

Utha waited for Fraustus to usher the knights out, before adding: 'And when we send out the entourage of emissary, add a message to my son in Asberg. It's high time Franz returned home.'

Something she had been meaning to do anyway. Her son

was little like his father. Prince Leopold had been a wise peacetime ruler, but too soft. Soft on the peasantry, soft on the nobility, soft on the merchants, soft on the guilds. Amazingly, that softness had worked after a fashion – Westenlund had increased its wealth under his five and twenty years of princeship, trading itself into ever greater prosperity with half a dozen nations. He'd been well worthy of the coat of arms that fluttered in myriad about the whitestone hall; a red carrack on a yellow sunburst backed by a field of green.

A good trader and farmer, that's my Leopold. Just too, after his own fashion. But he's no warrior-king.

Their only surviving son, the Crown Prince of Westenlund, on the other hand, was cut from a different cloth. Half the reason Franz had insisted on sojourning with the House of Hessé in the Eorldom of Aslund was that they hadn't abolished melees there. Her boy had a feel for battle and a flair for tactics.

Ezekiel knows, we'll need both right soon. My other half couldn't lead us in this war even if he was hale.

Only once before had the castle been taken. Several centuries ago. Rathgar of Dreylund had bribed his way into it after months of siege, only to meet his end by poisoning. The ensuing power struggle had been exploited by the resurgent Westlending army, who turned besiegers into besieged when they attacked their own castle. They'd known about the secret tunnels joining the shoreline to the cellars and storerooms below the keep, and found their work much the easier for it, but Leopold's ancestor Castanmere had ordered them blocked up after their existence became widely known.

Aethelbert the Reckless had tried his luck not long after, but not even the King of Vorstlund could succeed in taking Westerburg Point. He'd died on campaign, and his successor Aethelred of the Purple Heart had agreed a peace with Castanmere, who bent the knee to the House of Bede in return for increase to his holdings.

Westerburg Point had briefly even been the seat of the erstwhile kingdom of Vorstlund, during the Partition Wars when another of Leopold's ancestors, Weregrim the Ill-Fated, had seized the crown. His short-lived spell as monarch had been abruptly ended by a spear in the gut, but that hadn't stopped his descendants stubbornly retaining the title of prince long after the kingdom's demise.

Always, we have found a way to survive and prosper. And so must we again.

Presently, Sir Clothar appeared. A flustered-looking man of middling height and more than middling girth, bald and lop-sided of gait, he'd been a great warrior... decades ago, before the Wasting Sickness nearly killed him.

My Leopold is far too loyal to his own. He should have dismissed Sir Clothar his post as soon as he took ill. Soft, soft to the core – and it will be our undoing, if we are not careful.

'Sir Clothar,' she asked patiently. 'Have you ordered the weapontake I commanded?'

The sexagenarian looked sheepishly at the plushly carpeted floor. 'I must confess, ma'am, I have not,' he mumbled. 'Quite slipped my mind.'

Hoots of laughter were silenced by another imperious wave of the hand. 'Clothar, given that we now have confirmation of a pending invasion, the like none of us has seen in our lifetimes, perhaps you could be persuaded to carry out my order? I'd like to know how many able men we can put in the field.'

'Mm, hmm, why yes, ma'am,' mumbled Clothar. 'Of course, I shall see it done, hmm, yes.'

Utha rolled her eyes to the ceiling. It was covered with a lively fresco depicting Castanmere's victories over the Hessians and the Dreylunders in colours that were vibrantly gory, though she hardly appreciated such art now.

If I don't get rid of this buffoon, the ceiling will be painted in real blood before long. That old sickness did for half his mind too, the poor wretch.

'See to it that you do,' she said. 'And in the meantime, you can also set up regular drills in the courtyard.' She raised her voice pointedly. 'Every man in this room trained to arms is to take part in daily exercises from now on. And we're cutting back on the feasting, too – from today we're placing ourselves on a war footing. Herald, call back Fraustus, I'll give him details of the rationing.'

She didn't know what provoked the ripple of indignant spluttering more – her order that the board would be reduced, or that her court knights would actually have to start working for it.

'Thank you, noblemen,' she said calmly, once the angry chorus had died down. 'You lot have had it easy for long enough, I think. It's high time you earned your places at court, all of you.' She swept the hall with a gaze that was suddenly flinty. 'Because mark my words, if this threat is not anticipated, there won't be a court for much longer.'

That silenced most of them. The ones sober enough to appreciate the realities she was pointing out, anyway.

'Well now, get to it, hmm?' stuttered Clothar, finally finding some form. 'You heard Her Royal Highness, it's harness and the training grounds for all of you. Hmm, yes!'

Sir Clothar tottered out to fulfil her other order (after Utha gently reminded him that he had been given more than one task). Reluctantly the courtiers followed him, some daring to favour her with sour looks.

Left alone with sentries and page boys, Princess Utha shook her head and grimaced as she felt her bowels convulse again. She could only hope the countryside chivalry had kept themselves in better nick than their court cousins.

Franz, my beloved son, hurry home – you've no idea how much we need you now.

CHAPTER 3
A PILGRIM'S PROGRESS

Adelko's nose wrinkled in disgust. Montrevellyn was an evil-smelling place. It looked imposing enough from the crest of hills through which the highway zigzagged towards it; a sprawl of ochre buildings encrusting the coastline, its teeming harbour lashed by the foaming waves of the Sundering Sea. From here the first crusaders had launched the Pilgrim Wars, sailing to the Blessed Realm to make bloody war on the heathen Sassanians more than a century ago. Since those days the port's fortunes had thrived, with pilgrim ships and trading sloops passing through it by the hundreds.

But drawing closer to the cityport, Adelko had found something offensive about the meanness with which its long low buildings squatted alongside its dirt-strewn alleyways; dilapidated tenements that were a far cry from the rich town houses of the burghers that crowned the hills overlooking them. Ragged traders hawked paltry wares from overturned wayns, ignoring the cripples that lolled drunkenly in the sun-drenched streets; fly-ridden beggars called out forlornly as the five wayfarers passed among dingy-looking brothels with half-starved girls leering from their crooked windows.

'Be assured, where wealth is allowed to flourish unbridled, poverty shall lie ruinous in its wake,' Horskram had told him, quoting the Redeemer. 'The port thrives and the merchants prosper in their mansions – everything else between crawls in the muck.'

It hadn't taken Adelko long to adopt his mentor's dislike for the place.

As they drew through the warren of streets towards the harbourside, he welcomed the distraction provided by the orange walls of the barbican, topped with mighty statues each the size of several men. The petrified images of the first crusader lords loomed proudly above its crenelated walls, wheel motifs embossed on kite shields; swords drawn and pointing in a south-easterly direction towards Ushalayim, the city they had conquered. Yet for all their vaunted grandeur, they paled before the Athos Colossi that the Thalamians had built. Adelko recalled his mentor's tutelage, a seeming age ago, when they had cowered in a cave overlooking the Brenning Wold.

From Platinum Age, to Golden, to Silver... the world isn't getting any better with time.

That reflection did little to comfort Adelko as they emerged into Montrevellyn's main square, which abutted directly on to the harbour. The place was a riot of colour, festooned with ships' flags that waved lazily in the tangy breeze rolling in off the sea. It was approaching noon, but already the square was a bustle of pilgrims haggling with the ships' scribes, ensconced in their booths by the pennons, bargaining for a good price to be taken across the waves and purify their souls. The pilgrims wore wheel motifs sewn into their hats and carried crude staves; a cruder amount of dirt was streaked across their unwashed bodies. Some wore chains of penance, while others scratched and itched beneath horsehair shirts.

Scribes accosted them as they traversed the crowded square, reeking with the stink of sweating men and beasts.

'Bound for the Blessed Realm, sirrahs? For ten gold doublons apiece I shall take you there!'

'Don't be robbed by this old scoundrel, o wise friars! I will grant safe passage for a mere five each!'

'Why be fleeced by scoundrels old or young? I'll do it for-
'

The last of these was silenced by a hard stare from Horskram's sapphire eyes. The other scribes took the hint as well.

A statue of Rayonde the Scourge, First King of Ushalayim, loomed over them forebodingly as they nudged their steeds towards the enclosed docks. Taking in the stern patrician's rudely etched face, cruel and bearded beneath his half helm, Adelko wondered which of the Redeemer's lessons – if any – that bygone warlord had taken to heart.

'Very few,' Horskram replied when he voiced that question. 'Make no mistake, the Pilgrim Kingdoms are founded on greed, venality and bloodshed. The Holy City is a fair jewel, grasped by conniving men who lust after its power and riches.'

'So much for going on holy pilgrimage, Master Horskram,' sighed Adelko.

And yet a pilgrim ship was just what they were here to find. Adelko supposed they wouldn't want for protection on the high seas at least – the first couple of vessels they passed were war galleys, loading destriers via side hatches in their hulls. Their masters were strong knights, dressed in full armour and clad in white surcoats sporting a blood-red wheel motif. As they supervised their squires, a perfect clad in white and black intoned a prayer for their souls, punctuating his blessings with a small bronze bell that he rang as he pronounced the hallowed words.

What's so holy about war, Adelko wondered as they passed by, sparing a glance for the stout swords and sharp spears being loaded below decks with the horses.

'This one should do,' Horskram said after they had traversed the water's edge for a minute or two. Carracks, cogs, galleys and sloops of all provenances and sizes clustered like a man-made forest along the length of the harbour. But none was so big as the one his mentor had selected. Even the warships looked of a mean size in comparison.

Adelko gawped at *The Pilgrim's Passage* as they dismounted in its shadow. He had never in all his life dreamed of a ship so big, never mind seen one. It towered from its berth, a veritable castle of oak and cedar; the taffrail stood the height of several men above the waterline, and from bow to stern the deck was larger than a bailey. Two great masts each as tall as a turret sprouted from it, reaching for the clouds far above. The furled sails flapped moodily about the edges, as if yearning to be released.

'Is that thing really going to carry us all the way to the Blessed Realm?' he gulped. Glancing over, he saw the damsels were eyeing it suspiciously as well. He fancied Hettie had turned a paler shade in the last few seconds. Anupe went cowled, so he couldn't see her expression, but his sixth sense told him she was tenser than usual.

'Oh yes,' Horskram reassured him. 'Us, and a thousand pilgrims.'

Adelko groaned inwardly. He'd experienced enough of sailing to fathom how unpleasant this was going to be.

Horskram hailed a scabby sailor, supervising a couple of subordinates as they hauled supplies up one of the ship's three gangplanks.

'Ahoy there, sirrah! I would have words with the captain of the *Passage*, if you will.'

The sailor stopped barking at his subalterns and fixed Horskram with a suspicious glare. 'You can talk to me if you will – I'm the first mate.'

Horskram smiled affably and stepped up to him, producing a hefty money purse. 'I'd like to secure passage to Ushalayim for myself and four companions.'

The mate scowled, his scabs looking none the nicer for it. 'That's what the booth on the square is for – and I hardly need remind a man of the cloth that women are forbidden aboard pilgrim ships.'

Adhelina chose that moment to speak up. 'I've found that rules are made to be broken, and nothing breaks rules like heavy gold.' She smiled sweetly at him.

Adelko had to laugh. His mentor and the high-born lady were already practised at dealing with truculent Pangonian sailors.

'And we'll be wanting transportation for yon steeds, too,' added Horskram. 'Private spaces in the hold close to them would also be agreeable.'

'Private!' The mate chuckled at that, spitting into the sloughing sea for good measure. 'Not for a hundred golden doublons could we get you such a thing.'

'Oh really?' came back Horskram, emptying the purse into his hand to reveal bright gleaming coins. 'I've another purse just like this one ...'

It didn't take long to buy off the captain and mate. The former soon found time to come above decks, his second hollering for him no sooner had he clapped eyes on Horskram's bounty. Ramon was a stocky man with a bulbous head disfigured by some old disease. This gave his eyes a bulging staring look that Adelko liked even less than Montrevellyn; his mean black irises looked fit to burst from his skull, as Horskram dangled two replete purses under his mottled nose.

'Of course, of course!' he declared. 'And forgive my churlish mate's frosty reception. You shall have the finest fare – braised duck and seared kingfisher, blue-rennet cheeses from Thringia and Jura, sweet heavenly wine such as will make you believe you've already set foot in the Blessed R-'

Horskram raised a hand to silence him. 'Spare me your scribe's pitch, captain – I've travelled long enough to know what awaits us aboard the *Passage*. Sailor's biscuit soaked in vinegary wine, a handful of beans and a strip of salt pork daily. It will have to do, for our business takes us to Usha-layim, like it or not. Now, if you'll show us to our pallet spaces...'

Adelko felt his heart nestle gloomily at the bottom of the Sundering Sea. He might have known this would be what to expect. Glancing at the damsels, he could see they shared his dismay.

His mentor must have sensed their gloom, for as the mate led them up the gangplank, he said: 'Be of some cheer – my coin has purchased us twice the usual ration each. We must keep up our strength, after all.'

'Sometimes I really think you enjoy doing this,' muttered Adelko.

'Enjoy what?' asked Horskram, arching an eyebrow.

'Tormenting us,' sighed the journeyman.

Horskram smiled again. 'It is only for your benefit, Adelko. For exigency tests our–'

'–fortitude like nothing else,' Adelko finished for him. 'Yes, Master Horskram, I'm familiar with that passage of scripture. I'm just not that keen on hearing it right now.'

His mentor said nothing further to that, but merely chuckled as they stepped on to the *Passage's* vasty deck.

The ship seemed even larger once you were aboard. Adelko fancied half a dozen Torguns could lie head to toe across its width at the beam, and when he stared up at the crow's nest affixed to the antenna he felt dizzy. The mate, who introduced himself as Claris, led them into the cavernous hold. It was only half full, but already hundreds of unwashed pilgrims lay curled up before chests holding their meagre possessions.

'We bring flesh to the Blessed Realm, and return bearing its bounties,' cackled Claris. 'Nice little earner this. Don't worry about the crew though – any trouble out o' them and they lose an ear! We pay 'em handsomely for their discipline.'

'Yes, thank you,' said Horskram. 'I'm well aware of the strict regime that applies to crews of pilgrim vessels. If only it applied to the passengers as well.'

Gazing about him, Adelko saw it was true. Sprinkled amongst the hair-shirted pilgrims was the odd knave and prostitute.

'So much for not allowing women aboard,' muttered Anupe.

'Ah well, you're not the only ones who pay over the odds for special treatment,' grinned Claris, before doing a double take as the Harijan pulled her hood down.

She caught his eyes. 'I am not as most other women,' she said, laying a hand pointedly on the hilt of her falchion. 'I trust these fellows will keep their hands to themselves.'

Claris spluttered. 'Of course! These are holy devotees – they wouldn't dream of doing anything inappropriate!' But the first mate was leering as he spoke. Just then a grunting sound told of at least one devotee who had succumbed to temptation, and taken up a doxy on her offer of business.

'Are we seriously going to spend four weeks living in such conditions?' demanded Adhelina.

'No,' replied Horskram crisply. 'We're going to spend *six* weeks living in such conditions. Pilgrim ships don't travel quickly, and we'll be stopping over at Panya for a week or so to take on more pilgrims.'

If there was a place below the Sundering Sea, Adelko had no doubt his sinking heart would find it soon enough.

The mate showed them to a section of the hold, marked out in serried ranks with chalked spaces, each one barely the size of a man.

'Well, yer coin's secured you extra spaces all around ye, so there's yer privacy taken care of,' Claris chuckled. He leered again, but didn't dare meet Adhelina's outraged stare. 'And ye're next to the enclosure we use for steeds,' he added, indicating the adjoining portion of space fenced off for that purpose. 'We'll bring horses down last o' course – animals get rightly skittish amidships.'

'Surely not just animals,' said Hettie glumly.

'Now then, be of some cheer,' said the mate as they deposited their belongings in the chests allocated to them. 'We sail at sunrise tomorrow, and tonight the cap'n means to feast the entire ship, in right fine style. Perhaps you'll lead us in dusk prayers for a safe journey to the Blessed Realm?'

'I shall do that gladly,' replied Horskram. 'And look forward to enjoying our last decent meal for many weeks.' The embarkation feast was customary, and a good way of persuading hapless pilgrims they had just got a good deal for their coin. Adelko felt his spirits stir a little from their unhappy resting place beneath the waves.

Princess Hjala tensed as she watched the cloaked riders approaching through the mist. After the long winter, Varmonath had not brought the warmth its name promised, as was so often the case this far north. Glancing fretfully up at the densely packed clouds, she yearned for a ray of sunlight to warm her.

Or calm my nerves, more like.

At least the spot they had chosen for their secretive rendezvous was fairly secluded. Located in the hills over-looking Lake Strom, the glade afforded slivered views of that glassy body of water through its budding rowan trees. Next to her, Sir Manfry and her brother Prince Thorsvald sat tensely ahorse, their faces set grim in the wan morning light. Princess Walsa wore her own dun brown hood and cloak to conceal her face, though her aunt did not seem nervous.

Always so confident that being in the right, all will be well. If only I could be as sure of that myself.

The four figures wended their way slowly up the trail towards the glade.

Well, I don't see any signs of an ambush party. So far so good.

She clutched the reins of her light grey mare more tightly, wishing the day's events could be done and dusted.

The new arrivals entered the glade. When the lead figure pulled down its hood, she could see it was Lord Ulnor. So the plan had worked out this far at least.

The Royal Seneschal's cloudy blue eyes betrayed not a flicker of emotion as he surveyed the four of them impassively. The three sturdy men with him did not remove their hoods, though Hjala could see they were dressed in byrnies and armed with swords.

Three to two, if it comes to a fight – unless of course Ulnor is planning any surprises.

She had taken a big risk in sending word to him a month ago. They had debated it in Manfry's manor house for weeks, patiently awaiting the thawing of the snows while they determined what to do. At last she had persuaded the timorous menfolk of the validity of her plan. They'd decided to leave Lord Wilfred out of it, just to be on the safe side – as Jarl of Stromlund, he was too pressured by leal duty to be counted upon. Walsa had been right behind her the whole way through. Hjala had to admire her aunt's courage. Did Thorsvald and Manfry really imagine the menfolk would be the only ones to lose their heads if this went awry? Sometimes the naivety of mankind astonished her.

'Well, here we are,' said Ulnor dryly. 'A fine morning for a pleasure ride. So you were in Stromlund, after all. It seems my nephew Wilfred has conflicted loyalties.'

Hjala took a deep breath. She'd taken an even bigger risk sending Ulnor a follow-up message when he'd replied to her first, suggesting where to meet. The princess knew she couldn't risk a longer journey, which would increase their chances of being apprehended by the White Valravyn. This was staking all on a single throw of the dice. But then on such bold moves did the fates of kingdoms so often turn.

'The House of Canwolde has ever been loyal to the crown,' ventured Hjala. 'So much so that its foremost scion has seen the wisdom of our suit.'

'Really?' replied Ulnor tightly. 'I don't see Lord Wilfred here.'

'We thought it best to leave your kin out of this business as much as possible.'

Ulnor snorted. It was a delicate sound, but one full of contempt.

'Your concern for my family's reputation is touching,' said the seneschal.

Hjala decide to ignore his sarcasm. 'Our thanks for not turning us over to the White Valravyn,' she said.

If indeed that isn't precisely what you've done. But something told her Ulnor hadn't – if so, the chances were they would have been arrested more than a tenday ago.

'I won't lie, Your Highness,' replied Ulnor, still unsmiling. 'I was sorely tempted. But something in your words... gave me pause.'

'Every one I wrote was true,' insisted the princess. 'Prince Thorsvald's sailors are loyal and true – the news of the fleet in the Frozen Wastes is no falsehood. This threat from our north-eastern flank must be dealt with, the plan to invade Thraxia abandoned.'

Ulnor pursed his lips as he shifted his weight in the saddle. 'And what makes you think the Northlanders can conquer us? They never have, and with good reason – without siegecraft, I don't see how they can take our castles.'

Linden, Blakelock and Rookhammer had been repaired since the war, though they were lightly garrisoned. Many of the new knights created to take on southron lands annexed to the King's Dominions after Thule's uprising were still being blooded, putting down stubborn remnants of resistance from younger relatives of the executed and disinherited nobles.

'You know full well the realm is stretched across itself,' said Hjala, giving voice to these thoughts. 'Do you really believe a ruler canny enough to unite the Ice Thegns for the first time in a hundred years plans on launching a foolish attack? She'll concentrate her forces on one portion of the realm, most like.'

'It could be but a raid she is planning,' said Ulnor.

Thorsvald shook his head. 'Not with a fleet that size. I know a naval invasion when I hear of one, Lord Ulnor – I knew my business well enough, before my brother saw fit to attaint me.'

Hjala could almost taste the bitterness in his voice. Thorsvald hadn't taken that bit of news well.

'He's right, Lord Ulnor,' she pressed. 'This Shield Queen plans to carve out a mainland colony here – the first in hundreds of years. If she comes at us when the realm's forces are scattered hither and yon and looking in the wrong direction, her plan could work.'

'You know all this anyway, you stubborn old coot,' was Walsa's contribution to the parlay. 'So stop playing your fool games, Lord Ulnor. You haven't come here to arrest us, you've come here to plot with us. You don't like Wolfram's lunacy any more than we do. It's bad for the realm.'

Ulnor's face hardened, but he sounded calm enough when he replied: 'I must confess, I had not counted on Wolfram to be quite so... unruly in rule.'

Which is something we tried to warn you of all along, you prideful idiot, Hjala thought. But she knew tact better than her aunt. 'From what we've heard, his raving fits aren't getting any better, and my father has one foot in the Heavenly Halls already,' was what she chose to say.

Ulnor's face betrayed a softer kind of emotion. 'Aye,' he said sadly. 'That, and the other. His Majesty passed yesterday afternoon. Word should spread soon enough.'

Hjala felt a jolt at that. Glancing at her brother, she could see Thorsvald struggling with his own emotions. Manfry made the sign and bowed his head, but Walsa remained as keen-minded as ever.

'That means Wolfram will be crowned King in short order,' she said. 'So we haven't any time to lose. We need to have him declared mad, and Thorsvald instated as regent in his place.'

Ulnor blanched at that. The three hooded knights shifted uncomfortably on their horses. Hjala supposed they were kinsmen, sworn swords of House Canwolde who rendered the seneschal personal service. Their loyalties wouldn't be so conflicted as Wilfred's. She took another deep breath.

'Just face facts, Ulnor,' Walsa continued implacably. 'You backed the wrong horse. You allowed your stubborn sense of protocol to get the better of your wisdom.'

'Wolfram is the rightful heir,' Ulnor said tightly, clinging to his stubbornness.

'Then in Heaven's name man, why are you here?' said Walsa. 'The monarch commands loyalty because he *is* the realm – but if we continue on this path, we may not have a realm much longer!'

'And you know full well what I was hinting at in my first letter,' added Hjala. 'These Northlanders are being manipulated by the Sea Wizard. I need not remind you what that could mean.'

'Yes well, what you both say is true enough,' said Ulnor. 'But you think too much of my influence. Do you think I'd even be here if I still had any? It's Lorthar who commands the King's ear now, not me.' A trace of bitterness entered his own voice now. 'The Arch Perfect, who speaks of the One-Eyed King foretold in scripture. His Majesty's vanity has been well and truly piqued.'

Hjala felt her heart stiffen. Of course. Lorthar. Probably all too keen to be revenged on the king who had clapped him in irons, by controlling his realm through his own son.

'Lorthar has him convinced that he cannot lose in war,' Ulnor went on. 'As long as the Arch Perfect remains in place, His Majesty will continue with his plans for an invasion of Thraxia. Not even a threat from the Northlanders will give him pause. As like as not, he'll simply divide his forces and fight on two fronts.'

The three of them exchanged uneasy glances.

'Then His Highness really has lost his mind,' muttered Walsa.

Hjala ignored her aunt, turning over the information in her mind. Then she allowed herself a cold smile, as the most obvious course of action presented itself to her.

'In that case,' she said. 'Our first task will be straightforward at least, if not entirely easy.'

The others turned to look at her.

'We must remove Lorthar,' said Hjala. 'Permanently.'

CHAPTER 5
A TRAGIC HOMECOMING

Lord Braxus wept as he looked upon the ruins of his ancestral home. Castle Gaellen had been reduced to a cindered husk, its once proud turrets and keep gutted by the vengeful fires of war. The stone structure still stood and would be rebuilt, but the tapestried halls and frescoed chambers he had grown up in were a thing of the past. It shamed him to admit it, but that sight troubled him more than the razed villages and desolated fields they had passed on their steady march north. Perhaps even more than the unrecognisable remains of men, women and children they had encountered in their hundreds, many of them tortured to death by Slánga's brutal highlanders.

What is left to reconquer, he asked himself and not for the first time. *A thousand men at my back, and too late to save my people. All that remains is to complete my revenge.*

The highlanders stationed at Ongist had certainly paid the blood price for their depredations. Of the two thousand quartered in and around the capital, barely a fifth had escaped alive with their leaders. Slánga, Tíerchan and the rest of the survivors had fled back to their highland homes, knowing full well what was coming for them. That had meant relinquishing all the lands they had gained, but then survival put such things into sharp perspective.

His erstwhile companions he'd left down south, to charter a ship that would carry them to Skulla when the northern ices finally broke. Hopefully they'd succeed in their mission, and put an end to that evil. But his part in their story was done. Now it fell to Lord Braxus to assume his responsibility as First Man of Clan Fitzrow. He knew it wouldn't be a joyous one.

Why did they even bother invading? The plough and the fence has never been the highland way. They came here to conquer a land they don't even know how to settle.

'It's a sorry sight, Lord Braxus, and no mistake,' said Lord Cael, not unkindly. 'But crops can be resown, castles restored and furnished anew, young knights trained and dubbed. And not all your common folk were slain – new bairns will grow to be strong of limb and work your fields. Besides that, even Slánga's savages had the sense not to slaughter all your livestock. Where there's life, there's hope.'

Braxus had to quash a bitter laugh. Lord Cael was a stout man in early middling years. His bluff demeanour suggested a man who had seen it all, but this was a wildly optimistic view of the rapine that Gaellentir had been subjected to. More than half his peasantry were dead, the other half broken by tragedy and suffering. None of his knights had been spared, nor their sons and younger brothers. Their womenfolk had been dishonoured half a hundred times, age be damned: a priory for women would be the fate of many now.

But Cael was right about one thing: at least Dreuth was reconquered. King Cadwy had sent two expedition forces north as soon as the snows melted. One to take back Daxtir and drive Tíerchan through the Whaelen Hills and back up into the Hyrkrainians; with Lord Cael of Varrogh, Braxus had led the other through ravaged Gaellentir, in pursuit of Slánga. By now he'd be holed up in his homeland in the Brekkens, where a warren of highland trails and caves would put any invading army at a sore disadvantage. If Braxus was going to act, it would have to be now. He couldn't afford Slánga the chance of regrouping.

Wheeling his horse around, the First Man of Clan Fitzrow squared off against the hundreds of knights, archers and men-at-arms Cadwy had sent with him.

'Now hear this,' he cried, his melodious voice seeming to bounce off the tarnished skies and reverberate across fields that still smoked in places. 'A fortnight you've ridden with me, and you've all seen for yourselves the havoc Slánga has wreaked on my blameless people. I've a hundred demesnes to rebuild, and no one to hold those lands from me. So this I say, to every bachelor in this company not beholden to Lord Cael of Varrogh – ride north with me, and I'll make you a landed vassal once this thing is done.' He raked the meaner soldiers in the company with a hard-eyed stare. 'To every common serjeant and man-at-arms, a knighthood and a place on the floor of my hall – once it's been rebuilt – and a seat at my board daily. A position of honour and a decent living! Your families too shall be catered for. I mean to rebuild the Ward of Gaellentir – and I mean to rebuild it on the corpses of an extinguished people!'

Lord Cael arched an eyebrow. The last part of Braxus' statement he hadn't expected. The young lord ignored him and went on: 'Mark my words, this will be no chivalrous campaign of heroics! Slánga's fighting men are sorely depleted, now is the time to strike! I mean to see the highland threat dealt with, once and for all.'

He felt a dark, cold rage clutch his heart then. It would never let go, and it would change him forever.

'For we'll not just be putting Slánga's last screamers to the sword when we ferret them out of their holes in the Brekkens! Their women too we'll slay, aye and their bairns! Come next winter, I mean to see that not one highland savage defiles those hills with their stinking feet! We'll show them no more mercy than they showed my kith and kin – like diseased cattle, I mean to slaughter them, EVERY LAST ONE!'

The cold rage intensified as he drew his blade for emphasis. It spread upwards from his chest, filling the back of his throat with a sickly sweet taste. The thought of wantonly killing highlanders intoxicated him, as wine does a man who cannot live without it.

'Anyone not for this task, and the rewards it offers, is free to return whence he came.' Spurring his horse forwards, Braxus flung his sword point downwards into the earth, where it came to a quivering halt as he brought up his whinneying steed. 'Those of you who accept my offer – step forwards, and swear an oath upon my sword!'

Lord Cael found the presence of mind to speak up. 'Lord

Braxus, this is most irregular,' he remonstrated. 'The King said-'

'The King said I was to have any and all aid he could spare in retaking my lands,' Braxus cut him off. 'If we leave the highlanders as they are, they'll breed and multiply again like the vermin they are. I mean to secure my ward once and for all.'

'It's too dangerous,' hissed Lord Cael, trying a different tack. 'Once you're in those blasted hills-'

'Spare me your talk of highland tactics, Lord Cael,' sneered Braxus. 'I've been fighting them half my life, I know full well how devious the bastards are. But I've a small army at my back, thanks to the King, and I'll not squander an opportunity when I see one.' He turned diamond-hard eyes on his fellow lord. 'My thanks for your help, Lord Cael, but as you can see, it wasn't needed in any case – Slánga and his savages have fled like the cowards they are. This is my fight, and I would do right by my people, what's left of them. Just keep your men garrisoned on my lands a while, as we discussed – a ravaged realm is a lawless place.'

Lord Cael pursed his lips. Then he sighed. 'If you cannot be dissuaded in this matter, then so be it,' he nodded. 'And perhaps there is virtue in what you say – for too long have these pagan idolators been a thorn in our side.'

Braxus smiled grimly at that, and turning to the assembled host, he repeated his offer.

Some of them paused, but not many. When knighthoods and vassalages were up for grabs, bloody deeds didn't seem quite so shameful. Braxus smiled grimly again when they were done. He had seven hundred men sworn to his cause now, many of them knights and mounted serjeants.

'We'll not waste any time,' he declared. 'Lord Cael, if you would be so kind as to remain here – His Majesty will be sending craftsmen and field workers to help rebuild my ward. The rest of you, we camp here and march at first light!'

Lord Cael's brooding expression matched the darkening skies as they watched the men set up camp. His squire brought them each a horn of mead while they sat ahorse, but the sweet liquid was sour on Braxus' tongue. He would fain drink highland blood instead.

'I understand your thirst for revenge,' sighed the ageing lord, 'but I like this not. Many of those men you take with you will not emerge from the Brekkens.'

'Then their deaths shall not be in vain,' said Braxus stubbornly. 'And you're forgetting one thing. Abrexta had the best of Slánga's warriors stationed in the capital for her invasion of the Westerling Isles. Once the King and his men recovered their senses, they were able to harry most of them unto the death. My guess is Slánga won't have many more fighting men than I do, perhaps even fewer.'

'But what he does have is treacherous terrain that he has called home all his life,' countered Cael. 'The Brekkens have never been conquered, for good reason.'

'Aye, what you say is true – but what choice do I have?' asked Braxus, growing sad again. 'I can't let this go unpunished, Lord Cael. When I'm abed at night... they come and visit me. My father, Sir Vertrix, Sir Regan and all the rest. The shades of the dead demand retribution from the Heavenly Halls.'

Lord Cael frowned at him over the rim of his horn. The hustle and bustle of the inchoate camp suddenly seemed far away in the gloaming. 'That's a pious way of putting it,' he said. 'You've seen a lot this past year, haven't you?'

'Aye, more than I'd care to discuss,' said Braxus. 'And after all the things I've survived, I'll be damned if I let a bunch of rapacious highlanders give me pause.' He tossed aside his empty horn. 'They're going to die, Lord Cael, every last one of them. I'll not rest until it's so.'

Without another word, he nudged his horse towards where his new squire was setting up his pavilion. Beyond it Castle Gaellen loomed, a burnt-out husk silhouetted against the reddening skies. Its frayed contours seemed to cut the horizon angrily, and Braxus swallowed back bile as he dismounted next to his tent.

The dark hunger for blood stayed with him until he slept. But the ghosts of his lost friends and family didn't visit that night. No further need of demands from beyond the grave – they would have justice, and that right soon.

CHAPTER 6
A DANGEROUS STOPOVER

The blue-walled, orange-roofed buildings of Panya were a welcome sight to Adelko's eyes. For more than a fortnight, they had traversed the spring tides, skirting the isles of Curuco and Crenolo as they passed through the Sargossian Straits, a choppy corridor of waves that separated the kingdom of Mercadia from the sultanate of Murad. That had been bad enough. Adelko had taken to reciting psalms to ward off the inevitable seasickness, spurning the filthy hold to stand glued to the taffrail. But he'd soon found far better reasons to recite holy words.

The straits fed into the Sundering Sea, passing through the Dragon's Teeth: two ruined watchtowers of the Elder Wizards that stood at promontories of land on the tips of Mercadia and Murad. Their blasphemous shattered frames seemed to claw at the very seas through which they passed, the ruins sending black greasy fumes spiralling into the air from a perpetual fire that no earthly hand would ever quench. That defiled stretch of water had taken on an eerie sheen in the bright sunlight, and a strange drawn-out groan had bubbled up from beneath the waves as they traversed it. The pilgrims had cowered below decks during that part of the trip, whilst the sailors went about their duties with ashen faces and white-knuckled fingers. Their escort of war galleys had seemed no less perturbed, tabarded crusaders appearing on deck to kneel in prayer, led by the perfect shepherding them to war. Once past the Dragon's Teeth, the sea had mercifully returned to normal, though Adelko could well believe it when his mentor said few dared brave that passage at night.

Now they were back in civilisation again, sails heaving in a brisk wind as they drew ever closer to Panya. The foremost city of Mercadia commanded a fortunate position on the northern fringes of the Sundering Sea, one that had allowed its great merchant houses to control much of the trade passing to and fro, from Montrevellyn, Shazram, and the great cities that the Thalamians had built along the northern coasts of Sassania.

'Save perhaps for Aratheny on the shores of the Great Inland Sea, you will not find a richer trading port,' said Horskram as they stood on the forecastle, watching the pretty buildings grow larger. It didn't seem such a large city after Rima, though already Adelko could tell it had done a better job of sharing its prosperity than Montrevellyn. A series of squat sandstone forts topped the sparse rocky hills that cradled the cityport, seemingly at odds with the elegant conurbation they guarded. As the *Pilgrim's Progress* pulled in towards its semi-circular commercial harbour, Adelko could make out a variety of brightly coloured pennants depicting the sigils of the wealthiest merchant families.

'Mercadia is different to the rest of the Free Kingdoms,' Horskram explained. 'Though the Royal House of Haranya holds sway, it is the merchant princes, not the barons, on whom the Queen relies. Mercadia is a maritime trading power, her ships will take most of the crusaders to the Pilgrim Kingdoms.'

As they drew ever closer, Adelko saw it was true. The harbour they approached abutted onto a vast circle of enclosed docks; poking above their fortified ramparts he could see the tripartite masts of dozens of war galleys, stabbing the cobalt skies with pine fingers. He could just about discern the furled white and red sails that denoted crusader ships.

'The fortunes of the merchant princes have only been improved by the Pilgrim Wars,' Horskram went on. 'Much coin do they extract for escorting pilgrims and warriors to the Holy City, and supplying the ports of the Blessed Realm in times of war.'

Adhelina smiled sardonically. 'You don't sound as though you approve, Master Horskram,' she said.

'I don't,' replied the adept. 'Merchants are a despicable lot, ever ready to turn a tidy profit. Those that do such from war are more despicable still – and those that do such from war in the Redeemer's name are the worst of all.' He made the sign. Adelko could swear his mentor was more perturbed by Panyan greed than he had been by the Dragon's Teeth.

'Well, I don't know about politics,' said Hettie, 'but I for one will be right glad to get on dry land again for a little while.'

'Except we aren't going ashore,' Adhelina reminded her. 'Not here at any rate. I don't trust Queen Edelmira not to apprehend us at King Carolus's request.'

Hettie rolled her eyes, but kept her peace. Adelko frowned. Something about the lady-in-waiting's demeanour told him not all was as it seemed, though he sensed nothing from Adhelina. What could Hettie know that her mistress didn't? He glanced at Horskram, but the adept gave an imperceptible shrug of the shoulders. He supposed it didn't really matter, it was their choice what route they took after all, but...

'It does seem a long way around to get to the Empire,' Adelko ventured. 'Going all the way to Ushalayim first, I mean.'

'I've seen enough intrigue at the Riman court to be convinced the Pangonians will stop at nothing to get what they want,' said Adhelina, shaking her head stubbornly. 'And I'll not take any risks with our freedom after all we've been through. We stay aboard ship until we reach the Blessed Realm. It's safer that way.'

Hettie scoffed at that. 'Safer? Are you sure? How many of those filthy idiots have already tried to have their wicked way with us down in the hold?'

'Don't concern yourself with that,' said Anupe, stroking the hilt of her dirk. 'Need I remind you the first one that tried this lost a finger, the second lost something... much more precious to a man. They are slow to learn, but they learn all the same.'

They exchanged grim glances at the reminder. Adelko had tried his best to forget the blood-curdling scream that had awoken him in the middle of the night: a man suddenly bereft of his member made a sound as petrifying as the demon that had pursued them in Northalde. The more lecherous knaves aboard the *Progress* had indeed learned well enough after that to stick to their vows, or the harlots who welcomed such groping attentions (for a price). It wasn't the only episode of violence they had seen aboard the ship. One week out of Montrevellyn, a sailor had been caught stealing from the galley stores. The captain had made good on his promise and cut off an ear, and incidences of pilfering had dropped sharply to nothing after that. Aside from that, it had been... an unpleasant journey anyway. The food was every bit as foul as Horskram had predicted it would be, and the stench of hundreds of unwashed bodies crammed in the airless hold was almost as sickening as the lurching sea.

And now, it was about to get even worse.

'Oh yes, we're barely more than half capacity,' Horskram confirmed when Adelko asked in a despairing voice. 'In a week's time, when we set out again, this ship will be laden with a thousand pilgrims.'

Hettie sighed and shook her head. 'Better keep your dirk handy, Anupe.'

'Of course,' replied the Harijan with an icy smile. 'This is, after all, what you pay me for.'

'Well, it certainly isn't your gallows humour,' said Adhelina.

A great chain of iron barred the entrance to the main harbour. This was lowered upon the new arrivals being identified, and sea marshals waved them in. Hettie gawped. The harbour's hemicircular docks were dotted with ships great and small. She tried to number them all... and lost count at over a hundred. As the sailors steered the *Progress* into its allotted dock, she caught the glint of sunlight on polished steel. She felt her misgivings grow as she registered a dozen men, dressed in rounded helms that tapered to conical points and wearing leather jerkins and vambraces covered with splints and studs. The armour was foreign, but she recognised watchmen when she saw them. These were eyeing them keenly. One of them leaned in and muttered something to a man with a plume cresting his helm. Evidently the captain. He nodded and muttered something back.

'I thought that story about being apprehended was just a ruse?' she hissed at Adhelina.

'It was!' Adhelina whispered back. 'But the reason why it worked is because it might well be true!'

Hettie's heart sank.

It took a while longer for the ship to dock, as sea marshals helped to steer the mighty vessel into place using great wooden contraptions designed for the purpose. By then Horskram was alerted to the presence of the watchmen, too.

'It looks as though you were right to be cautious,' he told

Adhelina in a low voice. 'You'd best go below decks. Don't be too hasty about it.'

'I am coming with you,' said Anupe, switching her hand from dirk to falchion. 'Just in case those rogues below get any stupid ideas.'

Hettie scarcely listened as they took the stairs leading down off the forecastle. Right now it wasn't licentious pilgrims she was worried about.

Horskram smiled his most affable smile as the watch came up the gangplank. Next to him stood Captain Ramon, shuffling nervously and licking his lips. The watchmen drew level and their leader began addressing the sea captain in Merkish. It was a staccato tongue, a mishmash of Panglian, Decorlangue and Sassanian – Mercadia had been a province of the short-lived Muradi Empire four centuries ago, though they didn't care to be reminded of that heritage.

Ramon turned to Horskram. 'He says-'

Horskram raised a hand. 'I speak Merkish perfectly well,' he said. 'I understand the captain wishes to search this ship.' Turning to face him, he asked: 'May I inquire why?'

'Her Majesty's orders,' replied the captain, his face unsmiling beneath the trimmed black beard that dusted his swarthy features.

'I see,' replied Horskram, still smiling. 'And who might you be, to invoke her authority?'

'I am Captain Gustavas of the Cityport Watch,' said the

guardsman sternly. 'And here at harbour, I invoke Her Majesty's authority *at all times*.'

The watchmen fingered the short swords at their belts. Horskram didn't need his sixth sense to tell him they would use them, if provoked.

He was just about to reply when he was alerted to someone coming up the stairs. Turning he saw it was Hettie, a rather flustered looking Adhelina in tow.

'I told her not to do it,' she said angrily, but Hettie ignored her.

Stepping up to stand beside Horskram, the damsel stared at the watch captain. 'It's us he's after, isn't it?' she said, addressing the adept. 'I don't speak Merkish. Would you mind translating?'

Horskram was about to demur, but his sixth sense told him to play along.

'Of course,' he said carefully.

'This man has orders to take two high-born women of Vorstlending provenance into custody, is that correct?'

Horskram translated. As he did, Anupe stepped up to join them. Her hands were planted firmly on the hilts of both falchion and dirk. Even Adelko's fingers were reaching surreptitiously for the quarterstaff slung across his back. He was rarely without it nowadays – Edemus had trained him well.

Gustavas looked surprised. Hettie's frankness had caught him off guard. 'Yes,' he allowed after a brief pause. 'Those were my orders.'

'Ask him how much he gets paid a week, and his men,' pressed Hettie.

Horskram arched an eyebrow. Adhelina grabbed her friend by the wrist. 'Hettie, are you mad? What foolishness is this?'

'Shut up,' Hettie told her, shaking her arm free. 'Go on, ask him.'

Horskram sighed and translated the question.

Gustavas stared at the damsel. Then his rudely handsome face cracked a grin and he chuckled. Behind him, his men were doing the same. But Horskram had caught the greedy glint in their eyes as they exchanged bemused glances.

Clever, he had to allow. *She's been here five minutes, and already she fathoms the national character.*

Hettie produced a bulging purse.

'I'm willing to bet it doesn't run to fifty gold doublons,' she said. The chink of coin could barely be heard above the bustle of the mighty port, so she opened it for them. Bright gold caught the afternoon sunlight with a glorious glimmer.

Gustavas peered at the gold pieces. Then he muttered something to Horskram.

'He says those are Pangonian doublons,' he sighed, 'and not as big as the cruzados of his native country. The greed of Mercadia knows no bounds,' he added, for Hettie's benefit.

'Oh well, if he isn't interested,' said Hettie with a forced air of nonchalance, tucking the purse back into the folds of her cloak.

Gustavas eyed the vanishing purse with avaricious eyes. Then he spoke again.

'He asks what is to stop him simply taking the money and both of you as well?' Horskram translated.

This had better be good, Hettie.

Hettie flicked a glance sideways at Anupe. Without moving forwards, the Harijan half drew her falchion, letting them see its razor edge.

To Horskram's surprise, she wasn't alone. A soft whooshing sound told him Adelko had armed himself too, and was squaring off against the watch. The pudgy youth was gone; a stocky but sturdy young man stood in his place. The flinty hardness in his eyes matched Anupe's.

Horskram cleared his throat hurriedly as the guards drew their swords.

'Think on it, Captain Gustavas,' he said. 'Fight us, and you and several of your men shall surely die before we do. A report shall have to be made, and doubtless word of the coin the damsels carry will reach your superiors. Meaning, no extra money for those of you who do survive. I'm sure you'd all agree, that isn't the best outcome – for any of us.'

Horskram held his breath. He was bluffing, they all were. Would the captain call it?

A few seconds passed by. They felt a lot longer. The city-port went about its business down below, oblivious, though Ramon and several nearby sailors looked on with tremulous eyes.

Gustavas raised a hand. His men returned blades to scabbards. Extending his other hand for the pouch, he said flatly: 'See that they stay below decks, for as long as they remain here. If I catch them anywhere in the city, I'll arrest them on the spot – you as well.'

Horskram nodded, doing his best not to show his relief. 'It will be as you say, Captain Gustavas.'

Hettie pressed the purse into the watch captain's hand, and it swiftly disappeared. With a curt nod, Gustavas filed his men off the ship.

'What in all the saints was that about?' gasped Ramon. 'I can't be having fugitives aboard my ship-'

Horskram pushed his face into the sea captain's, so it was barely an inch away. 'Your passengers are riddled with women of vice, and knaves who'd dishonour and thieve their way through the entire journey, if they could get away with it. We've paid for your services already, and handsomely – so I'll thank you to keep quiet and stay out of our way!' He put a hand to his own staff. 'And don't even think about reporting what you've seen here, understood?'

Ramon wasn't a brave man, but then it didn't take an Argolian long to spot a coward. Blanching, he nodded like a chastened bairn. 'Same goes for your crew,' said Horskram, eyeing the timorous sailors venomously.

Ramon nodded again. 'Just keep to yourselves,' he stuttered, moving off. 'And don't cause any trouble.'

'Trouble?' Horskram laughed at the captain's retreating back. 'Since when have we been folk to cause trouble?'

TO THE EDGE OF THE WORLD

Wrackwulf eyed the sloop suspiciously. It was first light, and the dirty grey ripples of the Rundle eddied around the diminutive vessel, as if daring it to cast off from Ongist's deserted harbour.

'Are you sure this thing will get us to the Westerling Isles?' He didn't know much of seacraft, but he could hardly imagine the single-master, barely four paces wide at the beam, taking them all the way to Skulla. Never mind the haunted straits that journey entailed.

Garhan beamed at him, revealing a broken cluster of teeth, some of which were silver and studded with semi-precious gemstones. It made him look like a rich lordling's mannequin, rather than the scurrilous pirate he was. 'Never ye fear, brave knight! Bin doin' this fer most o' me loif, man an' boy – a better coxswain ye'll not foind outsoid o' Cobia!' The iron-haired sea dog, wiry as a whippet and no less lithe, fairly brimmed with pride at mention of his homeland. Wrackwulf couldn't think why – so far as he knew, most

Cobians were thieving salty types who'd sell their own mothers for a few gold regums.

Garhan had been contracted to lead Abrexta's fleet of conquest to the Westerling Isles; now that plan had died with its architect, he'd been pressed into similar employment by the King who had survived her.

Similar, and yet very different. The half dozen Cobian scallywags who would be accompanying them hardly made for a mighty navy.

'I'm sure your... credentials bespeak you well,' sighed Torgun, ruefully casting his eyes up the pewter road of water that beckoned them on to the next stage of their mission. 'I think it's more the size of the boat that concerns my trusty colleague.'

'Little need to be afraid there either,' interjected Morcant. 'The smaller the ship, the less... angered the spirits and ghosts will be by its presence. More grief do bigger boats come to, on the Tyrnian Straits.'

Wrackwulf's mood matched the drizzly morning. Another foray into haunted reaches: few if any living in latter days cared to brave the preternatural stretch of waters that had guarded the Westerling Isles for millennia. And he'd been enjoying the comforts of the palace so much: a wash of wine, mead, wenches and meat had borne him on a blissful tide towards full recuperation. And the castle troubadours had even praised his baritone.

That said, perhaps he should be glad to be getting out of Thraxia for a while. Though Abrexta was dead, the country was still in a right mess as far as he could tell: the Crimson League had refused to disband, calling for concessions for saving the realm. The bewildered loyalists had been put on the back foot by that – until one of them suggested that Lady Rowena and her cohorts were still technically traitors. In the midst of this imbroglio were the King, his master of coin Caratacus, and a handful of other trustworthy advisers who'd been freed from the dungeons, trying to make sense of it all and placate everyone.

The sound of creaking footfalls on the boardwalk alerted them to the arrival of Joram.

Yet more cheer to light the brand new day, thought Wrack-wulf. *This one's about as much fun as a doxy with no teets.*

'Good morning,' said the monk, clearly thinking it anything but. 'I trust all is ready for our voyage?' He threw a piercing glance at the tarpaulin that covered their supplies.

'Aye aye, cap'n!' beamed Garhan cordially, exchanging knowing glances with his compatriots. 'And we'll be right glad ter 'ave a man o' the cloth with us on this dangerous journey, for we'll not be relishing joining old comrades in the Seakindred's Locker any time soon!'

Joram snorted at that. 'You'd be lucky. Most who perish on the Tyrnian Straits never see the sea bottom – they remain trapped forever in its accursed waves.'

That wiped the smiles off the pirates' faces. If they'd done a good job of masking their fear, they no longer did so. They were being very well paid for their work; the only thing that could possibly have enticed them to take up such a dangerous voyage.

'Of better courage be,' said Morcant, trying to mollify the crew. 'I know the way ahead as well as any... With luck, the spirits of the sea shall be more kindly disposed to an islander returning home.'

Morcant flinched as Joram pulled a phial free of his grey habit and favoured him with an arcing dash of consecrated water. 'There's for your pagan ways,' he muttered wryly. 'May it bring you closer to the Redeemer, you arrant rascal.'

Wrackwulf and Torgun exchanged glances of their own. A curious relationship had developed between mage and monk since their strange adventure. It was almost as though they had bonded somewhat... whilst still despising each other.

A bizarre companionship, thought Wrackwulf. *But then what isn't bizarre about this whole bloody business?*

The new year had brought changes for others in their party. Sir Braxus – or rather Lord Braxus – was off to reclaim his lands, while Sir Vaskrian had gone back down south to rejoin his liege lady. They'd fairly had to force him onto his brand new charger, telling him it was his duty to obey Lady Rowena (they'd even stinted on the bawdy jokes this time). He'd looked thoroughly miserable as he set off on the long road back to Liathnoc, a bored-looking squire and several horses in tow. He'd even muttered something about a prophecy and being destined to come with them, but Sir Torgun was having none of it: the Northlending did things by the code, and an oath of loyalty was an oath of loyalty. Truth to tell, Wrackwulf was glad of it. The lad was too young for such things, already at eighteen summers he'd seen far too much of the Other Side.

Some normalcy will suit him well, prophecies be hanged.

'Well then, let's to it,' said Joram, interrupting his reverie. 'Hie aboard! I'll intone a blessing before we set off.'

'Perhaps you'd like me to accompany you,' suggested Morcant. 'Seeing as our powers have proved so... compatible of late.' Something in Morcant's pale eyes told Wrackwulf he wasn't just trying to goad the monk for fun any more. Joram's response was a flinty stare, but at least he'd stopped hitting the sorcerer – though he had insisted on keeping him shackled again for most of the winter.

The creaking sloop tottered like a drunkard as Wrackwulf stepped aboard gingerly. He wasn't overly fond of sailing at the best of times, but right now he couldn't imagine a worse voyage to undertake.

'I still don't see why we couldn't have just walked across the seas when they were frozen,' he grumbled, steadying himself against the lurching mast and nearly knocking a pirate into the water.

'You wouldn't like the Straits in winter,' Morcant assured him. 'If you thought the ice devils on the Fern were bad...' He let his voice trail off meaningfully.

'And I suppose I'll like them well enough in spring?' retorted the freelancer. 'If you can call this spring.' He cast his eyes to the mean spitting skies. 'Does the sun never shine in this wretched country?'

'Not usually,' replied Joram. 'And it's only going to get worse where we're going.'

'Wonderful,' said Wrackwulf, plonking himself down in the stern as Garhan and his men cast off. 'Where's that blasted mead we packed?'

The freelancer ignored the irritating chuckle that came

from Morcant as he fumbled under the tarpaulin for the mead. The mage had parked himself just before the head-sail, beyond which the river waters were slowly being trans-muted to a tarnished quicksilver by the weakly rising sun. Joram began intoning a psalm, the words sounding cold and monotonous in his flat voice. Torgun brought out the Circifix of St Argo and kissed it.

'Ah, here we are,' said Wrackwulf, finding a stout ceramic bottle in a wicker casket and pulling it free.

Morcant glanced at him and smiled, before returning his eyes to the waters they now sculled across.

'Oh yes, mead – a right good idea,' said the wizard. 'You'll be needing some Thraxian courage before long, be sure of that!'

'Fine,' growled the knight, uncorking the bottle with his teeth. 'Any sort will do where we're headed, I suppose.'

The first few days were oddly mundane. The only thing that had the crew spooked was the sight of cursed Tarnelion, a blackened island clinging to the Bruin Estuary some leagues north of the Rundle. Something about its ebon crags looked altogether queer; they were malformed into shapes that weren't quite natural, and bereft of any sort of greenery. Joram pronounced the place cursed, telling tales of druiding folk who had turned to the Left Hand Path, sacrificing victims inside a great stone idol said to represent one of the Elder Wizards. That had been in days long before the Middle Time, shortly after the Exiled Clans were banished from the Westerling Isles. Morcant had said little to that, commenting that not all who settled the mainland after the Wars of Kith and Kin had been good people, and looked on smouldering Tarnelion with eyes that were sad and reproachful.

Wrackwulf wasn't bothered: he took a pragmatic approach to all forms of danger, preternatural or otherwise. If they had been headed *to* Tarnelion, he would have paid more attention to the tales, and perhaps been afraid. As things stood, they weren't: by the sounds of it there'd be plenty to fear where they were headed, so why waste time worrying about another haunted place? They had enough of that on their trenchers already.

As they skirted the Caercilly Islands on their fourth day out of Ongist, a more immediate danger presented itself, when the strange folk of those windswept isles came at them in a series of long low barques. Even at this distance, their squat misshapen forms were distinctive. Were those *bones* they were wearing in their long unkempt hair?

Truly we've come to the outskirts of civilisation.

The Caercilly tribesmen were headed towards them, rowing steadily. Squinting at them, Wrackwulf fancied he could also make out the glint of weak sunlight on polished stone.

These boys are no better than the highlanders we fought — they haven't even learned how to smelt.

'Have no fear of Caercilly folk!' said Garhan, flashing them a glittering smile with his jewelled teeth. 'A Cobian sloop will outrun their useless floating logs every time!' He barked an order and the crew tacked sharply to the left, catching a convenient south-easterly wind and picking up knots. The rough-looking Caercilly rowers threw a few rocks and curses their way as the Cobians flanked them expertly, but were powerless to stop the agile sloop outrunning them.

'A rough, primitive people,' sneered Joram. 'Barely even know how to build boats. They never embraced the light of the Creed, and so chose to languish in pagan darkness.'

'The Westerling Kingdoms of the Old Time would put yours to shame,' was what Morcant said to that. 'The pride of the world our galleons once were, and traded we did with nations far and wide. The Moon Goddess was a light in our "pagan darkness", as you call it.'

Joram snorted. 'Fairy tales! We'll be seeing the splendour of Westerling civilisation soon enough, mark my words.'

A shadow crossed the warlock's face. 'True it is, the fruit has fallen from the bough,' he allowed. 'But like to see I would where Thraxia will be three thousand years from now.'

'Writhing in bondage to the Fallen One and all his servants, if our mission doesn't succeed,' said Joram, watching the barques and their rude occupants disappear from sight.

'And what is our mission, exactly?' pressed Morcant. 'You don't really think you can persuade my kinsmen to part with what they have guarded for so long, do you?'

'I have my intentions, but will not speak of them here,' said Joram, indicating the pirates with a nod of the head.

Wrackwulf took another swig of mead, proffering it to Torgun. The other knight shook his head sullenly. He looked as bored and downcast as Wrackwulf felt. This was no work for honest fighting men.

Another couple of days came and went, borne on the lashing surf. Wrackwulf found his sea legs during that time; at least that meant he could drink his mead without being ill, though by now seasickness and savages were the least of his worries.

They saw the first ghosts on their sixth day out at sea. Joram had been right: the leering faces seemed part of the waves, blanched white and apparently made from naught but foam and salt; briny fingers reached for them as the Tyrnian Straits took their small vessel in its pitiless grasp. The pirates – hardly a pious bunch – clung to Joram's prayers as a drowning man clutches driftwood, but not even the friar's psalmody could alleviate the pall of fear that descended on the ten voyagers.

Wrackwulf could see not all the ghosts had been human. Shades of Seakindred, merfolk belonging to the ocean deeps, writhed on the tides, along with stranger looking creatures, whose horrible toad-like forms were no less frightening for being ghostly. Joram told him these had once been Tritons, made in mockery of the merfolk long before even the Elder Wizards rose to conquer land and sea. At times the shades seemed to blend into one another, becoming conjoined apparitions that looked even more ghastly as they undulated together in a sick parody of the waves. The sight made the freelancer feel more queasy than any seasickness could, and he was sick over the side of the hull again.

But when they started hearing the voices, it was even worse.

'So sickly and frail!' came the disembodied words, sussurant and full of malice. 'Why cleave to thy rotting wood? Dive deep in and roll at leisure with us forever!' A winsome mermaid of rippling wine-dark water winked and beckoned to Wrackwulf as he was being sick, her ample bosom heaving in time to the rising waves. He blinked and met her foamy eyes, glaucous and malevolent. An iron grip on his shoulder brought him back to reality. Sir Torgun, his face pale and grim, was standing over him unsteadily as the ship rocked to and fro in the strengthening wind.

'Come away from the side,' he said in a taut voice. 'It isn't safe.'

It was shortly after that when they lost their first man. One of Garhan's pirates went mad, casting himself screaming into the roiling seas, which sucked the hapless sailor under with a hideous speed that defied mortal ken. It wasn't the last they saw of him. About an hour later, his undulant form could be discerned amongst the others, face blanched and foamy as he begged them to join him.

As bad as that day was, the night that followed was yet more terrifying.

They knew something was wrong as soon as the last of the sun disappeared over the haunted horizon. The waves suddenly stopped moving: it was as if their boat sat a vast glossy lake in the dusking light. The sloop was instantly becalmed; the wind had disappeared altogether. Hesitantly

Morcant conjured up a light, bathing them in a pale silvery sheen that made Wrackwulf think of moonlight.

The moon itself was not as it should have been. It was too big, its livid colour all wrong; the craters that pockmarked its surface took alien shapes he had never seen before. It made him think of a face contorted in anger. As if afraid of it, not a single cloud or star could be seen in the darkening skies.

'The Moon Goddess is angry,' said Morcant. 'She likes not strangers venturing to her lands.'

'I thought you said she wouldn't mind because you're here?' demanded Wrackwulf.

'Wrong I was, alas,' said the warlock glumly. Wrackwulf bit down on the insult that wanted to escape his lips.

'Kaia is an un-angel,' said Joram. 'Neither of the angels nor demonkind. She is mistress of all aspects of nature, good and bad, and cannot be trusted. Only paganers would worship such a capricious entity.' Before Morcant could say anything to that, the adept turned to Torgun and said: 'Present the relic of our sacred Order – I shall implore the Almighty's aid through the Redeemer's agency. She shall not be able to abjure His power.'

But when Joram intoned the prayer, the words fell flat, seemingly absorbed by the transmuted sea's impossibly smooth surface. The rood in Torgun's hand seemed to shine a little brighter, but that was all.

It was then that Kaia registered her displeasure.

The sickly moon's light suddenly burned as bright as a dozen suns. A horrid shrieking tore at Wrackwulf's eardrums, sounding like the wailing of a hundred banshees as it set invisible nails clawing at his heart; he was barely aware of doubling up in agony and clamping gauntleted hands to his head. Not even the Palace of Bending Branches had seemed so terrifying. The sound and light intensified to an excruciating pitch, and Wrackwulf felt himself falling away from his own body, as his spirit sought a watery release...

Abruptly both sound and light ceased. Morcant's spell was snuffed out like a candle; Joram's prayers died in his throat. Looking up and blinking, Wrackwulf could see nothing but stygian blackness all around him.

But something had changed. The boat was gently rocking, he could hear the waves lapping against the hull...

And voices, too. Like the ones that afternoon, only many times more numerous, speaking in half a hundred tongues, some long dead and utterly foreign to the ear. Wrackwulf heard a scream among them, this one decidedly human. Morcant managed to mumble a fresh spell, and a wan sick light revealed another of Garhan's men, quivering spasmodically as he drove a dirk into his belly, again and again and again.

'This cursed sea will drive us all to torment and madness!' Wrackwulf cried. 'You must be able to do something!'

Garhan's surviving crew were gibbering and trembling as the Moon Goddess's lunacy took them. Screwing his eyes tightly shut, Wrackwulf forced himself to remember things he'd enjoyed in his life: tournaments, skirmishes, duels of honour, feasting, carousing, wassailing and roistering... anything normal, to stop the madness from taking him. He dimly recalled an old mystic woman had once told him Kaia had the power to drive men mad. He could well believe that tale now.

Opening his eyes, he saw the dying sailor had expired in a heap in the bow. A sick smile was printed on his waxy face, and his eyes seemed to gaze adoringly up at the moon, now hidden in the shrouded skies.

Morcant had begun intoning another enchantment; it sounded similar to when he'd first summoned his familiar. He hadn't seen the wily fox since they settled in at Ongist for the winter.

Perhaps Scratcher would have saved us, Wrackwulf found time to think wryly. At least the humour in that thought might keep the madness at bay a little longer.

The waves became more frenetic, the voices increasing in fervour. They sounded bubbly and eerie. It was worse not being able to see anything. Morcant continued to mutter in a quavering voice; perhaps it wasn't a spell after all, just the paganer's idea of a prayer.

But it was a prayer that was destined to be answered.

Moon and stars suddenly winked into being again, their lucent forms crisscrossed with dark tendrils of blackness that told of clouds. It all looked reassuringly normal. But the voices hadn't dissipated. On the contrary, they now coagulated into a single chorus, one that repeated itself over and over.

Wrackwulf had the sense that they were all being addressed in their native tongues. He couldn't have sworn it was Vorstlending he heard, but he understood the words well enough:

.   .   .

Interlopers, interlopers, come from mainland shores
What brings ye faithless to our hallowed bourne?
Two lives has the goddess claimed, in toll of mortal blood
One more shall she have, else ye perish in the flood!

A clammy coldness settled on the voyagers as the meaning of the words sank in.

'A sacrifice she demands,' said Morcant, giving voice to their darkest thoughts. 'Or else all of us she'll swallow on the tides!'

As if to give emphasis to his words, the seas became choppier, the sloop bobbing up and down manically on the hardening waves.

'I'll not pander to an un-angel,' snarled Joram. 'If it be the Almighty's will that we die, then so be it!' But a pained look crossed his brutish face as he spoke, as though some inner conflict wracked him.

'He has the right of it,' cried Torgun above the roaring waves. 'We can't do as she says, it's our souls if we do!'

'I'm not sure I care about my soul just now,' yelled Wrackwulf, 'it's my skin I'm set on saving!'

One of the sailors was near enough to shove overboard. He was grappling with the larboard outrigger and trying to keep the ship afloat. Perhaps not a good time to kill a man, when he was doing his level best to keep you alive. Besides that, the freelancer didn't feel good about this either. But if the warlock's strange god spoke true, what choice did they have?

He was chewing his lip and clinging to the foremast while he pondered his dilemma, when he caught a flash of movement to his right. Another pirate went shrieking into the sea, to be swallowed up instantly. All eyes turned to the man's killer. The pirate gazed defiantly at his captain.

'Gathrod, you cur!' snarled Garhan. 'I'll have your hide for that, for 'twas ill done!' He couldn't do anything because he was manning the tiller of the boat. Gathrod took up his dead comrade's place on the starboard outrigger, but did not take surly eyes off his captain.

'It was him or us, cap'n,' he yelled above the salty surf, now spraying across the deck as the ship lurched sharply to the right. 'And a reward split three ways is a lot more n' a reward split four! Besides, I never did like the filthy swyver. Always cheated at dice, and ne'er bought 'is share o' ale when we went ashore!'

Garhan spat overboard, but Wrackwulf noticed neither surviving crewman disagreed.

The starboard side was close to being enveloped by the waves now. Everyone was clinging on for dear life. Wrackwulf could hear the planking of the sloop groan beneath its caulking. If the goddess was going to repay their sacrifice, now would be the time.

It went on like that for an interminable length of time. The seas rose and fell, tugging the little vessel this way and that. It seemed that all Garhan and his decimated crew could do now was keep the thing from capsizing; a higher power seemed to move them along according to its will. The seas continued to lash and spray their waterlogged vessel as the night deepened, and all four passengers had to take turns bailing. It was still nearly pitch dark beyond Morcant's feeble light, but at least the bubbling voices had stopped. Wrackwulf felt himself rocked slowly into a strange trance as he hugged the mast; its sodden surface felt rich and grainy beneath his bearded cheek...

Three more days and nights they continued like that. No one spoke now. When not bailing water or snatching a morsel, Wrackwulf found himself slumped lazily in his place at the stern, watching the leaden skies carpeting the firmament with the monotonous hues of the graveyard. At night he drifted into half-waking slumber, and dreamed dreams of watery spectres that dragged him down to the deeps of the ocean to cavort and play. A lambent moon glimmered just above the seabed, the rippling underwater current giving it a peculiar tinge...

'LAND AHOY!'

Garhan's cry jerked him into wakefulness. Sitting up, he saw it was another iron-grey afternoon. Drizzle was falling persistently on the tumid seas, but everything about them seemed normal.

The land they closed towards was anything but.

High and sheer the cliffs of Skulla rose, blotting out the skies with great gnarled fingers that might have belonged to a deformed giant. Their highest point tapered to a single broad promontory of rock, atop which rested half a dozen mighty monoliths of jet-black obsidian. Even at this distance, Wrackwulf could make out strange symbols carved into their surfaces, each one larger than a man. Albatrosses cartwheeled to and fro, their cawing shrieks hanging heavy in the air: the first signs of life in days.

'Malhavern's Point,' said Morcant, reverence in his voice. 'Aurgelmir's Teeth after the Father of Giants the Northlanders called those menhirs, when first they came to make war on us in the Latter Time. But we know better! 'Twas our ancestors who wrought the Druiding Stones, long millennia ago, in honour of the Moon Goddess's coming to our barren shores.' The mage knelt unsteadily in the rocking boat, and intoned a prayer.

A wind that was surprisingly gentle now steered them to the port side, skirting Malhavern's Point and leaving it to the east as the boat rounded its sharp triangular promontory, which cut the straits like some mad god's sword. Dotting the other side of the towering cliff face was an expansive grotto of dozens of caves. This close it seemed impossibly high, the height of many castles; Wrackwulf felt dizzy as he craned his neck to look at its rocky zenith, while the surviving pirates muttered prayers of their own. Many of the caves burned with coruscating lights of myriad hues, somehow unaffected by their exposure to the elements; in the gathering gloom, the grottoed cliff face looked like a second sky filled with multicoloured stars. Its light illumined a bay to the west, where a jumbled hotchpotch of flinty structures passed for what must be a large town.

'Yonder town is Kell, but 'tis the Great Library and Workshops of Skelnaervon that you see in yon cliff face where our true power lies,' said Morcant. A tear streaked his uncomely face as he looked upon Skelnaervon, mingling with the rain and salt spray. 'So long away I was,' he sighed.

Ringing the port town on the other side of Malhavern's Point was a vast curtain wall of flint. Its jagged glittering stones put Wrackwulf in mind of Liathnoc castle in Tul Aeren. Great towers lurched upward from the wall at several points, though he could see these were ruined in many places.

'Alas, never did we fully relearn the craft of our forebears,' said Morcant sadly. 'Magwych Fada-Radharc must we thank for that, for he it was that dabbled in forbidden rites, setting us all on the path to the Wars of Kith and Kin that saw Curufin and Orbegon exiled to the mainland. Yet perhaps theirs was the lighter punishment, for once that war was done our power here waned, and the Moon Goddess punished us with the Nine Pestilences, and for five hundred years we languished in the Second Age of Darkness. In time, our old tomes and parchments and artefacts we rediscovered in yon caves you look upon now. But the highest knowledge was lost to us forever.'

'Justly so,' interjected Joram. Yet an odd sadness was in the monk's tone... was that another look of conflict on his rough features?

Where do your loyalties truly lie? Wrackwulf wondered.

Morcant seemed too caught up in his storytelling to notice anything this time. 'The Westerling *Chronicle* tells that yon curtain wall was once twice as high, when Kell of old was many times its present-day size. In those days, our ancestors could conjure fruit and wheat from bough and soil at will, and the old Westerling Kingdoms both populous and prosperous were.' A wistful dreamy expression had stolen over the mage's pallid face now.

'Much as I hate to interrupt yer,' called Garhan from his place at the tiller, 'but wherebouts would we be dockin' exactly? I don't see much in the way o' a harbour.'

What he said was true enough. The long low buildings that fronted Kell ran down to the water's edge. This close Wrackwulf could see these were built on stilts, to keep them propped up above the lapping shores. Boathouses perhaps?

But Morcant shook his head. 'We won't be docking at the town,' he said. No sooner had he said that than a brisk westerly wind fairly spun their sloop around.

'Tack, you barnacles!' cried Garhan, but his commands were unnecessary.

'The Druiding Council will know of our arrival,' said Morcant. 'Their Thaumaturgy it is that guides us now.'

Joram made the sign, but it was a half-hearted effort and lacked conviction. Wrackwulf could hardly fault him for that. Out here on the edge of the Known World, who could expect the Almighty to answer prayers?

'We're headed straight towards yonder grotto,' said Torgun, still clutching the Circifx of St Argo. 'Are you sure this is the right way?'

'Quite sure I am!' Morcant smiled back at him, his tasselled braids flapping in the wind like a gorgon's snakes. 'For we dock our ships in the very bowels of Malhavern!'

As they drew closer, Wrackwulf could make out a series of coves, lining the bottom of the cliff face like serried archways. More glimmering lights peeped eerily from these entrances. Wrackwulf suppressed a shiver as the sussurant waves hauled them inexorably towards them. Passing under one, he could see a blue-green phosphorescence clinging to the caverns beyond, which appeared to be vaulted in many places with great columns of basalt. These made for naturally occurring docks, in many of which boats similar to their own were moored with thick ropes.

'Seldom do we have cause to venture far on stormy seas nowadays,' said Morcant. 'Sloops and skiffs are all the island folk wright.'

'Oi'll be buggered,' breathed Garhan, his jewelled teeth catching the light in a way that made him look ghastly. 'Thought 'twas just us Cobians who crafted such vessels.'

'The envy of the world our shipcraft once was, as before I did tell you,' said Morcant. 'The high seas we sailed, in ships not even the Thalamians learned to make. Some say we found lands across the Great Western Ocean, where the earth's compass was once thought to be reached.'

As the ship sculled in amongst the underground docks, following a stretch of water that wended its way between them, they could see the boats were lashed together to form a web of intersecting pontoons. Their own glid to a halt in an empty berth, and the crew lost no time in making their vessel fast, using lengths of rope hanging from a great hook above their berth.

'You're organised after your own fashion, I'll give you that,' growled Wrackwulf. Still he didn't like the feel of the place, though he was glad to be safely across the Tyrnian Straits. If you could call this safe.

'The shore is this way,' said Morcant, pointing to the boat

next theirs, the waters lapping its hull looking slick and oily in the subterrene light of the phosphorescence. Now they were closer Wrackwulf could see it looked like some sort of glowing seaweed clinging to the rock of the cavern.

Following the mage, they clambered over one boat after the next. They had traversed about a dozen when Wrackwulf saw the cavern's edge. A long strand of sickly looking sand hugged its lip. Beyond that, he could make out a myriad tunnelways dotting the cavern wall.

Torgun gripped his sword hilt agitatedly. 'This place puts me in mind of the Earth Witch's bower,' he muttered. 'I like it not.'

They stepped off the last of the boats and onto the snaking strand. A welcoming party some twenty strong had emerged from one of the larger tunnels, and now stood before them.

Wrackwulf had seen highlanders aplenty in Thraxia. Killed a fair few of them too, when they'd taken back Ongist. It was said the Westerlings had fathered their ancestors long ago, but there was something altogether different about the stocky men that faced them now. They seemed more venerable than the mainland highlanders, wiser and sadder and prouder too. Many had dyed their red hair and beards bright blue and corn yellow, colours matched by the tattoos that covered their bodies. The quilted furs they wore were fashioned in bizarre patterns, and appeared to be held fast with needles of bone. Their noses and hair buns likewise sported such decorations. Their faces were pale like Morcant's, though they were much more robust of feature: if the mage resembled a fish, these fellows looked more like bulls. Very peculiar bulls at that.

'The Marcher Lords have sent warriors to escort us,' breathed Morcant. 'Best let me do the talking,' he added, looking pointedly at Joram. The monk shrugged offhandedly, though he kept his hands tightly about his iron-shod quarterstaff.

Stepping forwards, the mage prostrated himself on the sands before the Westerling clansmen. He addressed them in a strange tongue; it sounded like a distant cousin of Thrax to Wrackwulf, though he could not follow a word.

They waited in silence while Morcant spoke, exchanging sullen stares with the Westerlings and fingering hilts and hafts of weapons. For their part, the marchers carried broad blunt-pointed swords of silver, their pommels set with topaz and amethysts. Wrackwulf didn't doubt their keen edges, or the strength of the men who wielded them. *A hardy folk indeed*, he thought, taking in their knotted thews. *Bearing the weather up here must be a fight for survival in itself.*

Presently, Morcant picked himself up off the sand and turned to face his companions. 'Not happy about us being here are the Marcher Lords,' he said. 'The Festival of Spring's Awakening is on us, and no business is done at this time.'

'I wondered why the place was deserted,' muttered Wrackwulf.

'And what of your druidic masters?' enquired Joram. 'You said they would be aware of our mission.'

Morcant glanced uneasily at the marchers. 'They say if it was up to them they'd disembowel us right now and throw us into the sea. But swayed them on the matter the Druiding Council has – they've called an emergency All-Meet! Disarm we must before they take us to the summit.'

Wrackwulf eyed the pagan warriors suspiciously. 'Disarm? I don't think so.' He made a point of slowly drawing his double-headed war axe, hefting it in both hands but not letting it go. Besides him he heard a slithering of steel as Torgun drew his own blade. Garhan and his pirates had already produced long knives.

As one, the Westerlings fanned out to flank them, their cold silver swords catching the glow from the luminescent seaweed that clutched the cavern walls.

'I wouldn't, if I were you,' said Morcant. 'Three men have we lost to get this far! Lose no more, I say.'

Wrackwulf arched an eyebrow. 'Why so concerned for our welfare?' he inquired sharply. 'With us out of the way, you're free.'

But the warlock shook his head. 'Under suspicion I am, too! I was gone so long, and scrying home has been difficult. Better that we all live to tell our tale together.'

'A compromise then,' proposed Joram. 'We'll not divest ourselves of weapons, but consent to keep them sheathed on pain of death.' He spared a sardonic glance at the marchers. 'After all, they outnumber us – surely the brave pagan warriors aren't afraid?'

Morcant chewed his lip nervously and translated. The marchers muttered dourly to one another, some shaking their heads. But eventually they voiced their assent.

'They've agreed,' said the wizard. 'But mind you keep to your troth – all our heads it'll be if you don't!'

Reluctantly they sheathed their weapons. The warriors closed in around them, swords still in hand, and steered them over towards one of the bigger tunnels. The ghostly light of the glowing seaweed cast their own shadows in twisted forms across the cavern wall as they crossed the strand. Wrackwulf didn't like the situation they were in, but what choice did they have? They had come this far in their mad mission: now they had to see it through.

He was beginning to wonder if leaving the tourney circuit had been such a good idea after all.

CHAPTER 8
SINS OF THE PAST

The rutted highway meandered before him, reluctantly threading its way through wretched countryside that looked on the verge of turning into full-blown marshland. At times there wasn't even a road, just a boggy ditch or a waterlogged crater. Sir Vaskrian sighed as he steered his dun-brown charger around yet another murky pool. Thraxian roads were the worst he'd seen yet; he almost wished he were ploughing through the winter snows on foot again. The lands of the King's Fold had been reborn under touch of spring; when he'd set off on his reluctant journey from Ongist, virescent leaves had wavered in a steady breeze under a pale blue sky strewn with tassels of cloud. Now he was traversing a rougher patch of land; the bright greens had deepened to sullen browns, and leaves had given way to brambles. At least he wasn't freezing his backside off anymore.

The young knight turned in the saddle to see how his new squire was faring. So fat he could barely sit his courser,

Ibbon wore the same befuddled look he always did (except when he was eating).

'No, look,' said Vaskrian irately, bringing his horse to a halt with a light squeeze of his lower legs before tugging on the reins gently. 'You're not holding the sumpter's reins properly, I showed you already twice.'

At least Ibbon spoke Decorlangue, allowing them to communicate. He was a minor vassal's son, so he'd been expected to learn it. At fifteen summers, he was already more corpulent than many an aged knight; Vaskrian felt sure the Thraxian King had been only too glad to get rid of the feckless youth.

What a squire to bequeath a knight who'd helped to save your kingdom. But, he supposed, you could only expect so much gratitude from a foreigner. At least the gilded mail Cadwy had gifted him was first-rate quality, imported from Pangonia, and his new charger was ferocious and well-built, a good fifteen hands high. It was a little too ferocious though – less than five years old, it was still a young and impetuous beast, yet to get fully used to its new owner.

'You take the sumpter in your left and my palfrey in your right, like this,' he admonished, clutching the reins for both horses without pulling on the bridle of either. 'Because the pack horse is the slower one, right? Less likely to buck the reins, so use your good hand to keep a grip on the palfrey, it's the more skittish of the two, see?'

Ibbon nodded dumbly and struggled to rearrange himself and the horses. It was a painful sight.

And I thought I was bad at squiring, Vaskrian thought as he waited impatiently in the road. Glancing around, half hoping for trouble to take his mind off things, he found no signs of it. Still, you couldn't be too careful: the kingdom was in a restive state. Cadwy was struggling to reassert his authority, and Lady Rowena and the rest of the Crimson League were clamouring for more autonomy and exemption from taxes.

Rowena. His liege lady and mistress. The woman he rode to now. He'd put her off as many times as he could, pleading injury and bad weather. Thrice she'd sent for him, and the third time Sir Torgun had gently but firmly insisted he respond. Vaskrian knew his hero was right, but he hated to leave his friends. The thought of them going off into danger without him appalled. Braxus too, riding north to reclaim his lands, without a single one of them by his side. It just didn't seem right.

And what will I do, a foreign bachelor in a broken kingdom? he asked himself, as Ibbon finished rearranging the horses with a heroic effort. Not even the thought of warming Rowena's bed again appealed that much. It had seemed exciting at the time, bedding a noblewoman, but when it came down to it... she looked, felt and tasted just like any other woman. And it wasn't Rowena he'd found himself thinking of when he lay with the palace wenches in Ongist over the winter. It had been Hettie.

Waste of time that, thinking about her, he thought as they started up the highway again. *She'll be long gone her own way.*

But thoughts of her nagged him nonetheless.

'How long until we reach the Royne then, master?' asked Ibbon after they had ridden a while.

'Getting saddle sore already?' asked Vaskrian, barely

masking his contempt. 'And don't you even know your own country?'

'I've never been this far south in Umbria, sire,' stuttered the squire. His fat head was closely cropped at the sides and topped with a tuft of auburn curls. It was supposed to be some new fashion, but to Vaskrian it just made Ibbon look like the idiot he was. A real man of arms should wear his hair long.

'Well, you won't even be in Umbria before long,' replied the young knight. Though truth to tell, he wasn't entirely sure himself how far the river was. Everything about the countryside looked different now it wasn't blanketed in snow, and he was scarcely more than a stranger to these lands himself.

'These Thraxian roads of yours are bloody dreadful,' he continued, 'so I reckon a couple more days' ride should do it. Then we'll be in Garth.'

That was still occupied territory, so far as he knew. The Crimson League had refused to withdraw the garrisons holding its castles, even moving fresh contingents into the province once the snows had thawed.

Collateral to make sure the King delivers on their demands, he thought. *With any luck, at least that means there'll be more fighting before long.*

Killing Thraxians made no odds to him, the only one he'd really liked apart from Rowena was Braxus. Let them have another civil war, the things seemed to be all the rage nowadays. Last he'd heard, Northalde was at peace, though King Freidheim was rumoured to be grievous sick. His son

Wolfram seemed a good sort, though: he'd secure the realm all right.

Northalde. He missed it more with every passing day. Hard to believe he hadn't seen his homeland in close on a year. King Cadwy's freed courtiers hadn't treated him with anything friendlier than curt respect, never mind that if it wasn't for him they'd still be enthralled or languishing in a dungeon cell. Cadwy's best knights, the ones Abrexta had ensorcelled, hadn't acknowledged him once during his stay at the palace. If it hadn't been for his friends, Lady Rowena wouldn't have needed to send for him even once.

Thraxians. It was true what his own folk said about them. They were feckless and untrustworthy. And now he was stuck here among them, for who knew how long.

The road continued to meander, Sir Vaskrian's thoughts along with it. Perhaps he could sue to be released from service, so he could return to his homeland. But it was unlikely his mistress would agree to that. He could always flee anyway... but that would be deeply dishonourable, most likely Sir Torgun would never speak to him again if he did that. Perhaps his fate wasn't so bad after all: he'd learned Decorlangue tolerably well, maybe if he made the effort to learn the native language too...

But try as he might, he just couldn't convince himself to be happy. Then again, when had he ever been?

Later that afternoon the road entered a copse of tall pine trees, the terrain having cleared up a bit. That hardly brought Vaskrian any comfort: the young knight repressed a shudder as the scaly brown boles embraced them.

It's just a normal wood, he told himself. *Nothing to be afraid of, no Fays here.*

The tree branches were densely packed, forming a canopy of bark and leaf overhead that nearly blocked out the sunlight entirely.

They're just normal trees, you idiot, he reproached himself as another shiver caressed his spine. The rutted road twisted and wound on, the broken sunlight forming latticed patterns of pale yellow across its pockmarked surface.

Rounding a bend, knight and squire came upon an unexpected sight. A covered wayn lay lopsided in the road, one of its front wheels stuck in a groove half the size of a man. Crouching next to it, a heavy-set blond fellow dressed in plain garb was cursing as he tried in vain to heave the cart out of the rut.

It wasn't until he'd drawn almost level with him that Vaskrian realised he was cursing in Northlending.

'You're a long way from home,' he said in their native tongue. Secretly he was overjoyed to meet a compatriot, though it paid to be cautious in such lawless country. Sir Vaskrian casually rested a gauntleted hand on his sword hilt as the man looked up from his unenviable task.

'So are you, by the sounds of it,' he said. 'Begging yer pardon, sir knight,' he added swiftly, tugging a forelock as he noticed Sir Vaskrian's fine armour and tabard.

A commoner then. As I once was.

'Fortunes of war have taken me far and wide,' said Vaskrian, glancing at the trees on either side of the wayn. No signs of an ambush. 'And what brings you west of the Hyrkrainian mountains?'

'Trade,' said the man, indicating the covered wayn as he stood and stretched his back gratefully. 'I've bales of wool and good Northlending iron to sell.'

Vaskrian frowned. 'Trade? Last I heard, Thraxia and Northalde did little trade.' He glanced again towards the trees. Still nothing.

'Last ye heard, ye'd 'ave been right,' replied the trader, scratching his broad, stubbly chin. He wore a short sword belted at his side. Travelling alone, he seemed a rough man for a trader. 'But war changes many a thing, sirrah. Prince Wolfram rules as Regent in Strongholm now. He wants to open up commerce between the two kingdoms, now Thraxia's problems are at an end.'

'Don't be too sure they're over,' replied Vaskrian. 'So Freidheim isn't fit to rule any more? That's a shame. I met him once, he's a great man.'

'Really?' replied the trader, fixing him with keen blue eyes. 'Impressive, sirrah – you must be a man of high birth, to keep such company.'

Vaskrian allowed himself a wry smile at that. He was doing his best to put on his haughty voice; it hadn't got him very far in the pecking order when he was in service to Lord Fenrig at Hroghar, but now he had the spurs it seemed to come much more naturally.

'I wouldn't put it quite like that,' he hedged, deciding to try for some modesty. 'Anyway, you're stuck, by the looks of things.' He flicked a glance back at his squire. There was a narrow gap between the trees and the wayn: Vaskrian supposed he could nudge his charger through it, but didn't fancy Ibbon's chances of leading two horses single file.

'All right,' he sighed. 'Can't have you blocking up the highway, I suppose. Just how much iron do you have in there?'

The trader went to uncover the wayn, but Vaskrian shook his head. 'Don't bother showing me, I haven't got all day.'

'More wool than iron, to be honest,' grinned the trader. 'We could both lift it if we hauled together.'

Vaskrian's eyes narrowed as he leaned down in the saddle to glare at the impudent trader. 'You do realise I'm a knight, don't you?' Perhaps his posh voice wasn't working after all.

The trader shrugged helplessly. 'If ye won't consent to help me, sirrah, what can I do?'

Vaskrian sighed impatiently. 'Ibbon! Get down off that horse and make yourself useful. Help yon trader lift his cart out of the rut.'

Ibbon blinked stupidly, before sliding off his horse clumsily.

Let's hope you've got some muscle under all that fat, he thought. To make up for your lack of wit.

As it happened, Ibbon was stronger than he looked. Vaskrian kept close eyes on the trader as the pair of them heaved together. It took them a minute or so, but eventually they had the wheel set back on the road properly. Vaskrian took advantage of the distraction to check the trees around him again, risking a glance backwards up the road for good measure. Still nothing.

'My thanks, sirrah,' said the trader, stretching his back muscles again and looking at Ibbon, who was leaning against the cart and panting. 'If it wasn't for you good souls-'

He struck as he was speaking the words, pulling the sword from his belt in one swift motion and driving it into Ibbon's side with an expert thrust. The squire fell screaming, his entrails bubbling between fat fingers as he struggled to stop them spilling on to the road.

In an instant, Vaskrian's sword was out of its scabbard. He kicked his horse towards the vagabond, who had whirled to face him, a keen light in his eyes as he crouched and waited, clutching his bloodied sword.

Try to come low under my guard, eh? We'll see about that-

He didn't hear the rustling in the high branches overhead until it was too late. The net fell, its thick ropes swaddling Vaskrian as the leaden weights pulled it tightly around him. The young knight tried to struggle, but that only made it worse; his temperamental charger whinneyed and reared, throwing him from the saddle. Unable to use his arms to break his fall, he landed on his side with a painful thud. His sword slipped from his hand with a jolt.

As he thrashed around on the ground, he was dimly aware of the vagabond striding over towards him. Something else, too: more figures erupting from the wayn, casting aside the heavy tarpaulin that had concealed them. By now the net had him in a tight embrace, pinning his arms to his sides and forcibly joining his legs together at the knee. The weight of his hauberk didn't help matters.

The highwayman – for surely that was what he was – knelt down to face him. At least he hadn't killed him yet.

'All right,' he said, turning to address someone else. 'He fits the description we were given in Ongist, but it's you that knows him – time to earn yer keep and confirm his identity.'

Another face poked down towards him. Vaskrian was still lying on his side and the net obscured his vision, but all the same he knew he'd seen it somewhere before. A thick bullish face, ugly and crude...

'Yeah, it's him all right. He's a lot uglier than when I last saw him, an' better dressed too, but it's Vaskrian.'

It took him a second to register who it was, and even then he could scarcely believe his eyes and ears.

Edric...?

His old rival from Hroghar stood up and kicked him in the face. An explosion of pain burst across Vaskrian's mouth as he tasted his own blood.

'Enough of that,' growled the other. 'You'll get yer chance for revenge, once we're back on the other side o' the border. C'mon lads, lift him up and get him in the cart. Our trusty knight's about to go on a little journey.'

Vaskrian could hardly believe what was happening as he felt strong hands lift him clear of the ground. He thrashed like the Great World Serpent, but all that got him was a sword pommel in the ribs.

'Don't be trying any of that again,' warned the blond man once they'd dumped him in the back of the cart. 'Ye're going back to Hroghar, end of story. We can do it the easy way, or the hard way.'

'Hroghar?' Two burly men, Northlendings too by the looks of it, were lashing the net to the side of the wayn. 'Who are you?'

'I'm the best bounty hunter on either side o' the Hyrkrainians, that's who I am,' said the blond man, getting up on to the cart's seat and grasping the reins. 'But that needn't concern ye – it's who sent us you might want to be thinking of.' Turning in his seat, he barked another order to his henchmen. 'Take his horses and supplies, that'll be a nice little bonus for us. And drag that fat idiot's carcass off the road. The crows can have him.'

Edric jumped into the back of the cart besides Vaskrian as the others obeyed. Fixing Vaskrian with a broken-toothed grin, he pointed to his broken nose. 'D'yer remember givin' this to me in Kaupstad? Been waitin' a long time to get even for that.'

'If you didn't want a broken nose you should have learned how to fight better,' snarled Vaskrian. Even now his old fighting spirit hadn't left him, though he was still stunned by the turn of events. So much had happened since he'd brawled with Edric in the stableyard of the *Crossroads Inn*.

Edric sneered. 'Oh yes, quite the fighter you turned out to be, eh? Sir Anrod of Dalton and his squire Derrick, murdered in the wilderness. Lord Fenrig weren't too impressed by that when he learned of it. Felt a right fool for letting you bugger off to Thraxia with that foreign lordling when he found out. Even then, he was minded to let it go, but then word got around that you'd done fer Sir Branas in the wilderness too – so you could cover up yer crimes.'

'That's a damned lie!' spluttered the young knight. 'Branas died in... on a quest. And Anrod and Derrick we killed in a duel of honour.'

'Try tellin' that to their kinfolk. You made quite a lot of enemies back home, Vaskrian. It was Rutgar wot spread the rumour you killed Branas. I'm sure you remember *him*.'

Vaskrian's heart sank as the realisation dawned on him. Rutgar. Of course. The haughty young knight who'd been his nemesis back in Hroghar. How long ago that seemed now.

'But he's a coward!' protested Vaskrian as the bounty hunter jerked the cart forwards with a flick of the reins. 'He was attainted after fleeing the Battle of Linden!'

'That's right, he was,' said Edric with a nasty laugh. 'But Fenrig gave him a second chance. Took away his holding and demoted him to bachelor. Said he'd give him a year and day to prove his worth, for the sake of his family name. Took him a while to stir things up at court, but he did it in the end. That's four families includin' his payin' out on a fat bounty so you can face justice.'

'You're to return to Hroghar to stand trial for your crimes,' said the bounty hunter over his shoulder, as the wayn trundled on. 'Took us a while to catch up with you, I must say. Even had to shelve the job once we heard you'd gone to Pangonia, you were too far away. Then we got word you were in Thraxia, something about you bein' a war hero.'

'Done quite well for yerself, 'aven't you Vaskrian,' laughed Edric.

'That's right, I have!' he yelled back. 'That's *Sir* Vaskrian to you – I'm a belted knight now, in service to Lady Rowena of Tul Aeren. You have to let me go!'

'Ah now,' said the bounty hunter. 'Problem right there, sir knight. You're in service to the enemy, which makes you a traitor. Doubt that'll go well for ye, but the bounty said alive not dead. I'll give him his due – he's a fair man, Lord Fenrig. Firm, but fair.'

'The enemy? What in the Known World are you talking about?'

'Ah, you wouldn't have heard, would ye?' said the bounty hunter. 'Prince Wolfram plans on going to war against the Thraxians. I'd say that puts you in a rather sticky situation, all told.'

'You've still no right do this, I'm a knight! Unhand me, you – you churls!' But his own words sounded ridiculous to his ears.

'Churls, is it?' barked the bounty hunter. 'I think this one's talked long enough. Right Edric, you wanted some revenge. Kick some silence into him – but don't go too far or I'll cut your throat, ye hear me?'

'Of course sir,' replied Edric. Even now, he knew when to knuckle under.

A few well placed kicks to the face had Vaskrian seeing stars and tasting more blood. When he was done, Edric hauled the tarpaulin over him, blocking out the light. He stamped on his head once for good measure, and when the pool of inky blackness opened up beneath him, Vaskrian dived into it gratefully.

CHAPTER 9
A CITY BAPTISED IN BLOOD

Liquid fire. That was what Ushalayim appeared to be made of. No longer just a word in a tome, the mighty metropolis beckoned to Adelko with golden arms across sapphire waters as their ship pulled towards it. Ignoring the gaggle of excited pilgrims crowding the forecastle with him, the journeyman craned his neck so he could take in more of it. Set on the gently rising slopes of the Tauran Heights that overlooked the harbour bay, its more imposing buildings could be seen for miles around: dazzling minarets that stroked the heavens with graceful fingers, and gold-leafed domes beaming in the bright sun, their bejewelled turrets refracting its light in an explosion of colour. Older buildings there were, too: Thalamian obelisks of warm sandstone, marbled pinnacles of russet red built by the Assurians before them. The less pious called the city The Porcupine, and with good reason.

A rich jewel coveted by greedy men, that was what Horskram had called Ushalayim. And yet there was something undeniably holy about the place: Adelko's sixth sense registered a warm inner glow as the *Pilgrim's Passage* sailed towards it. The Redeemer had been born here, a few generations after the First Prophet had ascended to heaven from the summit of the city. Gazing upon the Shrine of the Ascension, the colonnaded temple from where Sha'abat had left the Known World in a coruscating shaft of light, Adelko felt a first shadow cross his elated spirits. Its resplendent rose-pink precinct had also been the scene of a massacre, when the First Crusaders had cut a bloody swathe through the entire city, wading knee deep in the bodies of the infidels.

The site was also a place they would call home for a time, for that was where the Knights Bethler had chosen to build their fortress headquarters. Adelko could make out the serried teeth of the preceptory's whitestone battlements, jealously clutching the temple its masters had reconsecrated in the Redeemer's name. A bloody benediction, if ever he'd heard of one.

'Adelko!' His mentor's familiar voice. 'Quit your blasted sightseeing, and come below and help us with our things. We'll be docking within the hour, for Reus' sake!'

Six weeks at sea had not improved Horskram's temper. It hadn't done Adelko's the world of good either. The hold had been crammed to the freeboard with reeking bodies once they'd taken on more pilgrims at Panya; he almost wished they had been arrested by the port watch after all, for surely a Mercadian gaol would have been more comfortable. A couple of passengers had died of food poisoning; another had been killed in a knife brawl below decks; the captain had keelhauled a sailor for disobeying orders. The food had gotten more miserable with every bite: Adelko hoped the Bethlers ate as well as they drank.

Pushing his way back through the crowd, he descended the stairway and wove through sailors and pilgrims on the main deck to where Horskram stood waiting at the hatch. At least he'd got his sea legs; the waves no longer held the same terror for him as they once had.

'Come along,' barked Horskram. 'We haven't got all day.'

Adelko knew better than to argue with him in this mood. At least the hold had lost some of its stink now that most of the pilgrims were crowded above decks, weeping and praying at their first sight of the Holy City. Skirting over-flowing buckets of watery faeces with a distasteful grimace, Adelko found the others already busy packing their horses. They had passed the time aboard ship well enough, learning Sassanic from the two monks. Or at least, Anupe and Adhelina had. Hettie had simply looked bored much of the time, and ruefully glanced at her dwindled money purse more than once. He'd tried thanking her for bribing them out of trouble at Panya, but she wasn't having any of it, muttering only that stupid adventures cost far more than they were worth.

He couldn't help but wonder if that was true, in many senses.

The five of them finished packing the horses, emptying their chests of belongings and checking everything was ready. Even the former heiress of Dulsinor had learned to cast aside her ladylike ways, lending a hand with the loading. But then a wretched sea journey was enough to destroy all airs and graces, Adelko supposed.

Perhaps that's what the Almighty wants us to experience – a little more humility, he thought. *If a pilgrim ship doesn't do it, I can't think what else would. Appropriate, I suppose.*

Humility or no, Adelko wasn't looking forward to the return journey. Assuming they lived to make it.

Their work done, the journeyman gratefully made his way back up to the deck. The mate Claris had closed off the forecastle, now full to bursting with joyous pilgrims. Contenting himself with a place at the taffrail, Adelko leaned over it and watched as the three mighty walls of Ushalayim – arranged in a half-hexagonal shape abutting on the Tauran Ranges – gradually filled his vision. The Neck, a fortified walkway that rose at a steady incline towards those walls, connected the city proper to the harbour, where a myriad ships forested the wharf with masts and rigging and sails. A huge barbican offered a second line of protection: statues of saints and crusaders graced its battlements, each the height of many men. Montrevellyn's statuary seemed mean by comparison.

'The portside is ruled by the Merchant Princes of Panya,' Horskram informed Adelko as he jostled his way to stand beside him. 'So don't expect your first experience of Ushalayim to be an edifying one!'

'Will we visit the Holy Sepulchre, Master Horskram?' Adelko knew from his studies in the library that the city was controlled by competing interest groups: while the Mercadians held the lower city where they would dock, the Temple ran the Western Quarter containing the magnificent temple built upon the Redeemer's birthplace. In amongst the myriad spines of the Porcupine, he recognised the Holy Sepulchre's lavish domed exterior, the heavily statued white walls at odds with the elegant Sassanian architecture and the angular structures of Old Thalamy.

'In good time, if our mission permits it,' replied Horskram. 'I would not deny you the opportunity to visit our saviour's birthplace.' He made the sign piously. 'But you know well enough what darker business brings us here.'

'At least we should be protected from the Fallen One's servants while we're here... shouldn't we?'

Horskram nodded. 'Be assured that this place would be the last to fall, should our mission prove unsuccessful,' said the adept grimly. 'But Ushalayim has long been prey to other more worldly forces. Demonkind might have pause before its sacred walls, but not men of arms hell-bent on laying a siege to capture its riches.'

Adelko mulled that over as the ship glid inexorably closer to the harbour. 'Sometimes I get to thinking that mortalkind are the deadliest of the Fallen One's servants, Master Horskram.'

There was a glint of approval in the older monk's eyes as he said: 'At last my tutelage seems to find its way to you. A journeyman of the Order, indeed!'

Adelko couldn't tell if he was being sarcastic or not.

Hettie shooed away a cluster of swarthy beggars as they waited on the bustling wharf for the crew to unload their horses. They were a ravaged and filthy lot, seeming even poorer than the ones back home. Some were hideously deformed, with skins like melted wax.

'Lepers,' supplied Anupe. 'It is a common disease in these climes.'

One particularly enterprising fellow missing an eye and a leg managed to limp close enough to snatch at Hettie's purse... But in an instant Anupe was on him, dirk flashing as she menaced the beggar away.

Hettie scowled and took a deep breath, inhaling the mingled scents of the city: incense and spices wreathed invisibly together with cooking meats and *shisham* in her nostrils. There was plenty to draw the eye and ear, too. The capacious waterfront was festooned with brightly coloured awnings, beneath which traders hawked their wares in loud voices – dark-skinned Sassanians wearing silk turbans and voluminous robes vied with paler Urovians in northern dress, as hundreds of citizens tried to beg, earn or steal a coin. The sultry heat was like no other Hettie had experienced: a late spring day here felt like high summer back home.

'Oh for cool shade and a bath,' she sighed.

'Have no fear,' smiled the Harijan. 'We'll soon get both, for these folk are more cleanly than yours – the bath houses of Sassania are legendary! From what I hear, even your kind take to washing once they have lived here long enough.'

'I'm hardly surprised,' said Hettie, twitching uncomfortably as she felt her body drenching in a torrent of sweat. 'This heat is unbearable. At least we had a sea breeze on the *Passage.*'

Surveying the dirt trails that threaded through teeming stalls, she had to admit Ushalayim was an intoxicating sight. Carpets and hangings slung about the markets sported abstract and beautiful patterns picked out in gold thread and dotted with silver sequins, semi-precious gems and other finery. She wondered how one crafted such luxurious articles: it put her own efforts at embroidery to shame. Lithe-looking cats – curious creatures that were rare in Urovia but seemed commonplace here – slunk from one stall to the next, in search of a titbit from the food vendors; likewise swarms of hornets and flies had taken up residence on some of the sweatier shanks of meat hanging from hooks. She even spotted what looked like the odd lizard, crawling between the feet of shoppers here and there. Adhelina had showed her pictures of exotic creatures in a book once; at the time, she'd scarce believed such things could exist. Now she knew better.

'Well, it smells better than the ship,' said Hettie. 'And the tales I've heard about the wondrous south weren't exaggerated either.'

'Why do you think your folk came here to conquer this land?' asked Anupe, with a wicked grin. 'Surely not for your peace-loving god?'

Hettie was about to reply when Adhelina bustled over.

'Right, our horses are here,' she announced, loosening her shawl about her head to allow more air to circulate. 'It's time for us to bid farewell to our companions and find ourselves a place to stay.'

Her peremptory tone irritated Hettie. 'Yes, it's you we've been waiting for, Adhelina,' she said, none too kindly. 'Perhaps this time we could find some place that isn't a brothel. Mind you, I've lost most of the coin I won bribing those idiot guards in Panya, so maybe we can't be too choosy.'

Adhelina's face went sourer than the pails of milk being sold by a scrawny dark-skinned youth nearby.

'Well there's no need to be quite so rude about it,' she snapped. 'I'm sorry our journey wasn't a smooth one.'

'When has it ever been?' asked Hettie pointedly.

'Ladies, please!' said Anupe, raising her calloused hands. 'I've been on board that damned floating castle for more than forty days, guarding your virtue! I want a cool, clean place and some decent food and wine, yes? You can bicker all you like when we're settled in somewhere.'

'For once I agree with the outlander,' said Horskram crisply, coming up with his horse in tow. A scab-encrusted beggar made to importune him, but the adept shot him such a fierce look he thought better of it immediately. 'The sooner you get to a safe haven, the better. I'll show you to the *Hallowed Sojourn* – it's a hospice for pilgrims, of better quality than most. An old crusading friend of mine runs it. He'll take good care of you, at a reasonable price.'

'We'll be needing one,' muttered Hettie, but Adhelina ignored her. 'My thanks for all your help, Master Horskram,' she said.

'No need, my lady,' he replied. 'Our duty was to see you here safely. Rest a while after our long journey, and visit holy sanctuary in the Temple Quarter – then you can think about getting passage on a merchantman to Khronos.'

If only you knew, thought Hettie sardonically. Adhelina merely smiled uneasily.

'Now let us all away up the Neck,' said the monk, oblivious. 'And watch out for the cutpurses here – some of them are very adept at slitting saddlebags, too!'

They jostled their mounts through the gaggle of people and passed under the Barbican Gate, nudging their way along the triangular paving stones of the Neck's steep incline. Adelko had thought Urovian cities noisy enough, but here the mishmash of different tongues was a deafening clamour. Peculiar beasts that looked like distended hunchbacked horses (surely the fabled camels of the Hot South?) plodded up an avenue flanked with cypress trees that hugged the towering walls, a splash of green and brown on ochre stone. The stalls did not dissipate but became more regular, as merchants took advantage of the shade these provided. Adelko gaped at the variety of things on offer: brass pots and pans that gleamed red in the sunlight, dazzling arrays of gold and silver trinkets, curved daggers and swords of ornate design, silken garments that looked light as a feather, curious fruit that he had never seen before let alone eaten. But it was the tawny men with dyed purple beards dressed in flowing robes who demonstrated flashing powders of myriad hues that really caught his eye.

'Fireworks, they call them,' supplied Horskram. 'An idle distraction, fit only for a decadent nobility.'

'I think I've seen enough real fireworks on our travels, Master Horskram,' muttered Adelko.

'Precisely,' replied his mentor. 'But this is a complex city, of many different faiths and cultures. For more than a hundred years the House of Arjean has held sway here, since Rayonde the Scourge carved out the Kingdom of Ushalayim during the First Pilgrim War. He was a ruthless warlord, but wise enough to see that he would have to tolerate other religions and sects if he wanted to rule a peaceful realm that could prosper.'

Adelko gazed about him as they made their way steadily up the Neck, towards where the buttressed Sea Gate yawned wide, enticing pilgrims into the city proper. The current of faces coming to and fro were indeed a multitude, though many more were tanned than pale.

'Most of the people here are Sassanian,' he observed. 'I suppose it makes sense to keep them happy.'

'Don't be fooled,' said Horskram quickly. 'Many of the original inhabitants were massacred under Rayonde's orders after he took this city. Sassanians are tolerated because of the wealth they bring, and even then they must pay heavy tithes and taxes to do business here.'

'War makes little sense to me, Master Horskram,' sighed Adelko. 'Kings and barons kill and destroy wantonly, then they build palaces and temples and call themselves peacemakers.'

'You'll remember I once told you wars are seldom founded on good ideas,' replied the adept wearily. 'Well, they aren't a good foundation for ideas either. Twice the Princes of Palom have had to go to war again, to keep the Sassanians from taking back what they regard as rightfully theirs – and before long they'll be fighting another.'

A sudden thought occurred to Adelko. 'Do you think they could ever win it back? The Sassanians, I mean?'

'I've been hearing that the Nazharyans have finally ceased their own squabbling and united behind a new sultan. That could make the Fourth Pilgrim War a very different affair from its predecessors, especially if the sultanate of Kallandhar attacks the other Pilgrim Kingdoms to the west of here. Doubtless our gracious host will have plenty to say on that matter.'

'Grand Master Tobin sounds like a dangerous man,' said Adelko. 'Are we really wise to take up with him?'

'I'm afraid the Bethlers are our best chance of an ally here,' sighed Horskram. 'Ushalayim is ruled jointly by the Court of Council. A third of its seats are held by the Bethlers, a third by the King and his nobles, and a third by the Temple – with the Mercadians holding the lion's share of trading privileges and tax exemptions. Frankly, I don't trust any of them, but for our purposes the Bethlers are probably the best of a bad bunch.'

'Why is that, Master Horskram? I thought you said they were fanatics – and didn't they try to have us killed in Vorstlund?'

'We don't know yet how deeply they were involved – Prior Johann has remained tight-lipped under interrogation. He could have simply duped a single chapter into commissioning freeswords to attack us. But the Bethlers are warrior-monks, better versed in hermetic arts than most. Some even say they learned mystic disciplines not unlike our own, from the Sufieli sect.'

That surprised Adelko. 'But the Sufielis are Sha'abatians, aren't they?'

'Yes, they are,' Horskram confirmed. 'But the Faith has been riven by schism for many generations. The sultans and satraps of Nazharya and Kallandhar mostly cleave to the Orthodox interpretation. Those kingdoms have been sworn enemies of the Creed since the Pilgrim Wars started, but in truth they despise heresy even more – which of course makes Unorthodox Sha'abatians natural allies of the crusaders. The Sufielis are regarded as having a foot in either camp, only tolerated and preserved from pogrom by their ability to fight the denizens of the Other Side.'

That sent a shiver through Adelko despite the heat. He didn't need to have the obvious parallel pointed out to him. The journeyman shook his head as they passed under the welcome shade of the Sea Gate. Sunk in his reverie, he almost missed the fanciful carvings of a robed savant taming serpents that curled about its lintel. He guessed it was meant to represent the Sassanian prophet Sha'abat, who had advocated harmonious living with all beasts of the earth, even the foulest ones.

'And I thought Urovian politics were complicated,' he sighed.

Horskram allowed himself a wry chuckle at that. 'My dear boy, you haven't seen anything yet.'

Adhelina let her eyes drink it all in, as Horskram took them through the warren of covered streets that wove a web of brick and tarpaulin through the heart of Ushalayim. Sweating porters, robed perfects, strutting freeswords, patrolling serjeants, veiled women, lurking footpads, fat merchants, scrawny dogs, stringy cats, half-starved mystics, blind soothsayers... the city had it all. She'd once read that it numbered a hundred and fifty thousand souls, and she could well believe it. In area it was at least twice the size of Rima, with double its poverty and opulence to match – small wonder men of different ages had warred against its walls for more than two millennia.

And I used to think Graukolos an incitement to conquest, she thought ruefully.

Her thoughts were interrupted by Horskram pointing along another winding street, which snaked off the ascending road they were following.

'The Street of Caravanserai,' the adept informed her. 'You'll find the *Hallowed Sojourn* along the left-hand side. Ask for Sir Amalric of Bodain when you get there – and tell him I sent you.'

Adhelina pursed her lips. 'Wouldn't it just be easier if you introduced us?'

Horskram shook his head. 'We're late enough as it is – as you can see, traffic doesn't move fast in Ushalayim! Have no fear, Sir Amalric will take care of you. I'll try to look in on you, if I get a chance. May the Prophet watch over your footsteps, and the Almighty guide you always.'

Adhelina feigned consternation. It was better to let the adept think she doubted they would meet again.

'Very well,' she said. 'And may He bless your... endeavours.'

Without a backwards glance, she turned and nudged her horse up the side-street, Hettie and Anupe falling in beside her.

'So, now we can rest – and then you can tell us all about your master plan,' said the Harijan.

'What master plan?' Adhelina didn't care for Anupe's teasing quips. She wasn't enjoying the cloying heat, or the dust that clogged her nostrils.

'I was hoping you'd tell us that,' said the freesword. 'Seeing as how you intend to help Horskram save the world.'

'Very funny,' replied Adhelina. 'Right now, I just want to save myself from dying of heatstroke and thirst.'

Anupe chuckled. 'On that, I'm sure we can all agree,' she said.

The Bethler headquarters loomed above them, its vast single bailey shining hotly in the sun. Adelko felt his sixth sense tingle slightly. They were in the Eastern Quarter of the city now, controlled by the Order they had come to petition. Here the streets were much more orderly, the people better kept and less numerous. Most of them were clearly Urovian, too: the journeyman guessed natives weren't welcome in this part of Ushalayim, though he spotted the odd Sha'abatian pilgrim. These also looked well-to-do.

'They only tolerate Sassanians they can extort from,' he said to Horskram as they struck up the road winding through prosperous town houses towards the fortress. 'But isn't that the very reason why the first crusaders went to war? To stop the Sultan overcharging our pilgrims?'

'That was the justification cited by the preacher Xamiel, and the Supreme Perfect who sanctioned the First Pilgrim War at his insistence. But you'll recall that some in our Order believe that Xamiel was none other than a puppet demon, controlled by another whose name I have uttered before but will not speak here. Likewise, the vizier who put Sultan Jehan the Deceived up to extorting our pilgrims in the first place was also said to be a similar entity.'

'So you and Grand Master Hannequin told me,' said Adelko, recalling the uncomfortable conversation in the Grand Master's study. 'And despite knowing all of that, we're really going to ask the Knights Bethler to help us?'

Horskram sighed. 'Just leave me to do the talking, as usual. Hannequin's letter won't divulge all the details of our mission. The story we shall present Grand Master Tobin is that we are seeking a relic of great import, one that will aid us in the eternal fight against evil.'

Adelko stared at him. 'You're really going to tell him that, Master Horskram? And then what?'

'I will try to persuade him of the need for a guard, to take us to... a warlock I have mentioned before.'

'Let me see if I've understood you correctly,' said Adelko as they edged past a patrol of white-clad Bethler serjeants led by a single knight on horseback. 'You're going to ask a ruthless fanatic to help us seek out the most notorious black magician in the region? So he can help us find a relic that he *just so happens to know about?*'

'Something like that,' frowned Horskram.

Almighty help us, thought Adelko.

His sixth sense was still tingling as the serjeant-at-arms ushered them through the gatehouse and into the bailey. But mingled with that, he could sense the presence of something sacred: it didn't take him long to work out what it was. Flush to the far wall stood a mighty dais – atop it an elegant minaret spiralled up towards the cobalt skies, its slender form encircled with graven serpents of silver and gold. Beneath its jewelled dome, the Shrine of the Ascension terminated in a belfry carved of rose-pink stone, its mosaicked pillars depicting stylised snakes that looked more like abstract patterns than creatures of the animal kingdom. From here the First Prophet had reached for the heavens – and found them. A cobra fashioned of solid gold reared from the crest of the dome, its giant ruby eyes gazing down on them with a blood-red stare.

Surprising that the Bethlers never destroyed such a blasphemous monstrosity, he thought with some irony. *But then their kind are said to worship gold over god, as often as not.*

The temple was enclosed by a sort of inner bailey, guarded by two unsmiling Bethler serjeants. Sassanian pilgrims filed into its precinct, mounting the dais stairs reverentially and wailing the poetic *shuras* of the Faith with every step. Just beyond the open gateway, at the foot of the broad marble steps of the dais, stood another serjeant. This one looked more cheerful than most, and Adelko could see why: he clearly enjoyed extorting his religious rivals, who pressed fat purses into his hand before being allowed entry.

Gold over god, indeed.

The bronze statues that lined the walls of the keep made Adelko feel more uneasy still. Rather than invoking the warrior saints of the Creed, the Bethlers had simply chosen to portray the Redeemer in his earlier incarnation: towering figures clad in carapace armour, wielding sword and shield, loomed over the precinct in differing poses. The Redeemer had been an officer in the Iron Legions before turning rebel against the Thalamian Empire, but that part of his life wasn't talked about much in the wider Temple. Apparently the Bethlers had found the perfect justification to shed blood in Palom's name: the warrior-prophet they worshipped had done just the same during his time on earth.

'I really don't think this is a good idea, Master Horskram,' he hissed, as the serjeant escorting them bade them wait and stalked across the courtyard, to where a group of knights was drilling. 'These are hardly the kind of people that-'

'Be silent!' snapped the adept. 'I told you already to leave this to me. You're a journeyman not an adept, need I remind you? I'm in charge of this mission.'

Adelko chewed his lip resentfully as they dismounted and handed their steeds to an ostler. Taking orders from Horskram was less palatable by the day. How many times on their adventures had his mentor got it wrong? Who said Horskram was the wisest of his kind?

Question everything. Adelko sighed inwardly – that was all he ever seemed to do, nowadays.

His sense moved up a notch as the serjeant returned with another man. Grand Master Tobin was tall for a Pangonian, powerfully built with broad shoulders. But the most striking thing about him was his pate – shorn of all locks, it tapered to a point. His tombstone features did little to inspire confidence in Adelko; his cold, sharp eyes unsettled him all the more. There was a flat certitude in those dark irises, which told of a man who would brook no argument on anything.

'Good day, sirrah,' he said in Decorlangue, making the sign by clapping a hand to his chest in the manner of a military salute. 'I am told you seek lodgings at the Bethler Headquarters. Pray what brings an Argolian so far from home? We have not seen any of your kind here in a while.'

The voice was monotonous, bereft of all emotion. Adelko had half expected another firebrand zealot, but so far the Grand Master of the Knights Bethler seemed nothing like that.

'The Order of St Argo salutes the Most Valiant Knights of the Holy Order of the Bethel of Our Saviour,' replied Horskram, returning the sign as he drew on protocol in a manner that seemed unctuous to Adelko. 'I, Horskram of Vilno, adept of Ulfang chapter, bring letter of introduction from Grand Master Hannequin in Rima. And may I present my second, Adelko of Narvik, journeyman of the Order.'

Tobin turned stony eyes on Adelko, who could not help flinching despite his years of training. 'This one looks over young to rise so high in the Order, methinks.' Without waiting for a response, he motioned curtly for Horskram to present him with the letter.

'Pray be quick about it,' he said, the voice still monotonous. 'As you can see, I have men to train, ahead of our blessed coming crusade.' Behind him knights mounted on agile Kallandhari chargers tilted at serried quintains; others on foot sparred with two-handed swords.

'But of course, Your Eminence,' replied Horskram, producing the letter.

'A strange request indeed,' said the Bethler, returning his flint gaze to Horskram after he had scanned its contents. 'You seek a relic of the Creed, and believe it is being held by the most powerful black magician in Near Sassania. Not with an entire chapter of Argolian adepts could you hope to wrest it from him – knowest thou not that Abdel Sha'arza dwells in the accursed tower that the blasphemous Elder Ones built?'

'Of course, Your Eminence,' said Horskram, forcing a smile. 'That is why we intend to... bargain with him for the thing we seek.'

Tobin's face went from stony to steely in an instant. 'You would parlay with a sorcerer?' The voice remained flat, but his tanned face suddenly looked a shade paler.

'Sometimes a lesser evil must be done to avert the greater, as the Prophet sayeth,' hedged Horskram. 'This relic is of great importance in the eternal struggle against the servants of the Fallen One.' The adept made the sign again for good measure, but Adelko didn't need his sense to tell him the Grand Master was far from convinced.

'Curious that I have never heard of such a thing being

kept by Sha'arza, of all people,' he said, his voice still neutral. 'And this letter from Grand Master Hannequin requests that I help you as much as I can. In what way might the Knights Bethler assist you, I wonder?'

'The journey to Sha'arza's tower is one of many leagues across dangerous Nazharyan country,' said Horskram. 'We could use a bodyguard.'

Another man in the Grand Master's position might have laughed scornfully at that suggestion. Instead Tobin just continued to stare expressionlessly at Horskram, as he replied: 'On the eve of the Fourth Pilgrim War, you expect me to give up valuable paladins, to help you in a quest that seems mysterious – to say the least. And what have the Argolians ever done to help us in return, pray tell?'

'Our orders have ever been friends to one another in the search for knowledge,' said Horskram. 'For though we don't endorse the pilgrim wars, we nevertheless stand shoulder to shoulder in the age-old fight against the Fallen One.'

Tobin's eyes appeared to acquire another layer of frost. Adelko couldn't fathom the man: during their conversation with the Grand Master his sixth sense had fallen off, growing oddly numb. Perhaps it was true what they said about the Bethlers having spiritual powers of their own.

'Knowledge is a two-edged sword,' replied the Grand Master darkly. 'I will consider your request, and pray to the Redeemer for guidance on the matter. Join us for sunset prayers in the chapel – we take the evening meal after devotions here in the Bethel.' He beckoned curtly to the serjeant. 'Show our guests to quarters,' he instructed. 'Doubtless they will wish to rest after their long journey.'

The serjeant took them past drilling knights and soldiers towards another building flush to the eastern bailey wall. It was a domed, multistoreyed edifice, made of the same rose-pink stone as the shrine, curiously at odds with the fortress's plain efficient architecture.

'One of the former sultan's many palaces,' explained Horskram as they entered its beautiful partitioned gardens. 'Annexed by his conquerors, a hundred years ago.'

'I thought the Bethlers decried luxury,' whispered Adelko as they made their way through the riot of colour. He only recognised some of the blooms from illuminations in manuscripts; others he didn't know at all.

'They do,' replied Horskram. 'You will find them sleeping in the barracks as any common serjeant would, on straw mattresses and blankets of horsehair. The opulence you see here is reserved for honoured guests like us.'

'Well that's something at least,' muttered Adelko, as the serjeant took them into a shaded vestibule. Its pointed arches were strange to his eye; likewise the scent of incense sticks that burned in holders was foreign to his sense of smell. The palace was undeniably beautiful, though – the Sassanians differed from them in beliefs, but clearly these were a people to be reckoned with. The serjeant took them up a flight of stairs flanked by an ornately latticed balustrade and onto a landing. They arrived at a set of double doors, inlaid with abstract serpent motifs that flour-ished with wild abandon across their polished teak surface. The serjeant flung these open and bade them enter with a curt nod, before leaving without a single word spoken.

Stepping into the chamber, Adelko felt his spirits rise a

little. The chamber was large and semi-partitioned by an elaborate screen that repeated the serpent motifs. The mid-section of the walls was covered with a series of panels fashioned from a rich veined white material; each one featured a scene from the life of the First Prophet.

'It's made of ivory,' supplied Horskram when Adelko quizzed him. 'Taken from the tusks of the elephant of the Far South.'

'A wonder the Bethlers didn't destroy it,' murmured Adelko, inspecting the intricate panelling as he wandered about the chamber. 'It celebrates the Sha'abatian religion in such detail.' Several divans that would presumably serve as their bedding lined a wall of the first section of the room. The second was given over to a large mosaicked basin, a bath he supposed.

'You forget that the First Prophet is acknowledged in the Creed,' said Horskram, 'though only as a divine inspiration to ours. More importantly than that, Sassanian art is extremely valuable.'

'Gold over god,' sighed Adelko, dumping his pack and staff next to a divan covered with richly embroidered silk cushions. 'Well, it puts Strongholm palace to shame for comfort.'

'Don't get too used to it,' said Horskram, dumping his own things next to a divan beside Adelko's. 'If I have my way, we won't be here longer than a few days. Time is of the essence.'

'I know,' said the journeyman, only half listening as he stepped over to the far end of the chamber. A series of horseshoe-arched doorways gave onto a green-tiled veranda; stepping out onto this, Adelko could see it over-looked the eastern wall of the fortress. Beyond its crenela-tions he could see the city, bathed in the sun's fading glow. The reddening light caught the clustered domes and spires, making them blaze anew with lustrous hues that almost hurt the eye.

'It's a beautiful city, Master Horskram,' he said. 'I can see why so many warlords have fought over it.'

'Yes,' said Horskram, joining him at the terrace. 'All that beautiful bloodshed. The very building you stand in was blanketed with corpses when the First Crusaders sacked Ushalayim.'

Adelko repressed a shudder. Human horror seemed increasingly worse to him than all the preternatural monsters they had faced.

'What made you do it?' he asked after a silent pause. 'Go on crusade, I mean.'

His mentor sighed deeply. 'I was misguided,' he said. 'The perfects tell us our duty is to fight for our liege lords, but that we will go to Gehenna for killing wantonly. The Supreme Perfect offered us a simple way out – fight in the Redeemer's name, and buy back our souls with the blood of heathens.'

The adept could not hide the bitterness in his voice. Adelko felt a twinge of pity for the old monk.

'They lie to us, don't they, Master Horskram?' he asked. 'Always they lie to us, so we'll do their dirty work.'

'Aye,' said Horskram. 'Men of power always find a way to get other men to do their killing for them. Then, when the blood has been spilled, they step across it and steep their lily-white hands in gold.'

Another awkward pause. Somewhere off in the distance, the sound of a flute drifted across the glimmering spires.

'The flautist calls the Sha'abatian faithful to prayer,' said Horskram. 'At least Nexus V is sensible enough to allow the natives their own faith. In the neighbouring Kingdom of Kerala, such liberties are rewarded with the sword.'

Adelko felt his heart lie heavy in his breast. The flautist's plangent notes were beauteous, a melody he had not heard the like of before.

'Even if we succeed,' he faltered, 'the world won't be a peaceful place, will it Master Horskram?'

Horskram smiled sadly, not taking his eyes away from the darkening cityscape. 'No, Adelko, it won't.' They listened to the fluted notes ghost across the dusky skies for a little while longer. Then Horskram turned from the balcony.

'Come,' he said. 'We have prayers of our own to attend to.'

Without another word, Adelko followed him back into the opulent chamber, the sacred notes lingering on his conscience as they receded from his ear.

CHAPTER 10
THE REAVER QUEEN SAILS

A hundred and fifty longships, packed to the freeboards with ten thousand fighting men and women: Magnhilda felt her heart swell with pride as she watched them bobbing on the waves, sea horses ready to be ridden across the sail road to war. All the lords of the Frozen Wastes had answered her call: Bjorg and Vilm, the thegns she had created, even timid Asmund had come from far-away Utgard to pay due fealty. Besides them some twenty jarls, all of them bringing made men to the coming conflict.

From the mighty deck of *Valhalla's Serpent,* the Magna of the Frozen Wastes began to address her fleet. She drew the Twin Furies, allowing the cold morning sunlight to glint on their ensorcelled blades. She had taken Hjalmbitr and Lind-brotna from Guldebrand after she had slain him: soon they would taste the blood of mainlanders.

'Seacarls and shieldmen and berserkers!' she cried, her voice not less predatory than the cawing of seagulls and cormorants that wheeled about the harbour of Landarök.

'Today we plough a bloody furrow across the skin of Valhalla! In one week's time, we shall bring weather of weapons to our cousins' shores! Strongholm we shall invest, and with hook and grapnel we'll take her down-'

A dark bird smudged the flurry of white gulls, wheeling down towards her ship before breaking apart and stretching out into an impossible shape. It turned from black to bluey-green as it coagulated into the form of Ragnar.

'About time,' she hissed, ignoring the superstitious mutterings of the two hundred warriors crammed onto her ship. 'You cut your arrival fine, brother – and interrupted my speech! Your sorceries we shall need to carry heavy loads across the Valhalla.'

'Your war talk interests me not,' replied the elementalist dismissively. 'And as for my sorceries, of such would I speak with you, for I have need of your help in bolstering them.'

Magnhilda struggled to master her growing irritation, which she could feel hardening towards an ugly core of rage.

'I barely hear word of you for weeks, and now you choose the time to make this request of me?' Behind Ragnar, Canute stirred and fingered the haft of his poleaxe. Valkyria, her chief berserker, glared at the warlock with dark eyes. The jet-haired warrior woman had just recently arrived on the coast of Gautlund, from the mountain shrine to Tyrnor she called home in the fastnesses of northern Scandia. She had also been Magnhilda's sometime lover, when the pair of them had served as berserkers together, and was fiercely protective of her liege. Magnhilda only loved Valkyria the more for it, but that wasn't on her mind right now.

'I have been... distracted,' said Ragnar. 'Great powers I am delving into, they tax a wizard to within an inch of his life. I was not well enough to come ere now.'

Looking closer, she saw he wasn't lying. Her half-brother had always been pale-skinned, but now there was a pallor about him that spoke of the grave. The Shield Queen suppressed a shudder as he went on: 'To continue my work, I need... assistants. You will bring them back for me, from the mainland.'

Magnhilda felt trepidation mingle with her rising anger. It wasn't a mixture she cared for. 'What do you speak of, brother?' she demanded tersely. 'Surely you don't need more slaves.'

Ragnar's frosted eye looked nacreous and wicked in the light, as he replied: 'Yes, more slaves. You shall take them from the Northlending coastlands, and bring them back to the Skjel Islands for me. As many as you can manage.'

Magnhilda felt her beringed eyebrows lift a notch. 'What?! This is an invasion not a raid, for Tyrnor's sake! We've made no provision for carrying back slaves.'

'Yes, but you have made provision for supplies, including ropes and ladders for a siege,' replied Ragnar. 'Well have you studied the ways of the mainlanders... but then I was most helpful informing you as to how they make war. As I will be helpful in mastering the waves, so that you can bring so many warriors to Northalde's shores. Now it is time for you to repay me for my assistance.' His sightless eye seemed to take on a luminous tinge.

A metallic sussuration, as Valkyria slowly drew her blade. 'My Shield Queen, let me teach your half-brother some respect for his liege.' Both sides of her pate were cropped, leaving a slender tuft of black hair down the middle and giving her an outlandishly fearsome aspect, even by Northland standards.

Magnhilda raised a hand to stay her. Canute loosened his grip on the poleaxe, though he plainly looked as unhappy as the berserker.

'Very well, brother,' she said patiently. 'Tell me what you have in mind exactly.'

Ragnar smiled thinly as he said: 'You will divide the fleet. A hundred ships will beach at the Strang Estuary as planned, and proceed with the assault on Strongholm. The other fifty shall make for the coasts directly south and disembark their men at Stromlund. Half of those shall march north to join the main attack – the other half shall raid coastal villages and bring me back my slaves.'

'This is foolishness,' growled the Mountainside, tightening his grip on the axe again. 'We'll need every warrior we have to take Strongholm.'

'And once you take it, what then?' shot back Ragnar, favouring the myrmidon with an icy glance. Did even Canute flinch before it? 'Think you that the Northlendings will be content to let reavers menace and ravage their capital unchecked?'

'The Northlendings are divided and weakened, as you yourself have reported,' said Canute, quickly recovering himself. 'Too busy pacifying their southlands and preparing for a land war to the west. Once we have their chief city and slay their king, the rest of Northalde shall fall easily enough.'

'So you like to think,' sneered Ragnar. 'But our mainland cousins have ever proved resilient. Do as I bid, and I would turn a possible conquest into a certain one.'

'Now you speak like a skald,' said Magnhilda disapprovingly. 'Out with it, and break words cleanly, brother!'

The smile did not leave Ragnar's gaunt face as he said: 'By all means, invest the capital. Take it and hold it, if you can. But mark my words, so long as your second expedition proves successful, Northalde's days will be numbered.'

'Still you speak with poet's riddling words,' sighed Magnhilda. 'What use will taking villagers as slaves be in our war?'

Her brother's answer chilled her to the marrow.

'You shall bring them back to me, and I will throw them down the Serpent's Maw, to the heart of the world,' he said. 'With shouted incantation, I will dedicate their lives to He Who Must Not Be Disturbed. Then his servants shall awaken from the inky deeps, and answer to my call. Ten thousand Tritons and more shall emerge from Sjórkunan's bourne, to rape Northlending shore with trident and harpoon.'

Valkyria gaped. 'You would harness the power of the Great World Serpent? That is blasphemy!'

'No, sister of the sword,' said Ragnar, turning on her implacably. 'That is victory. For not even the hardy mainlanders shall be able to resist such an army, when married to our own.'

The chill had not left Magnhilda as she pondered her brother's words. The Tritons were little more than a fabled race, but her grandam's fireside tales of the horrible toad-like creatures had left their mark upon her as a bairn. Could Ragnar really control such monsters?

'You speak of what has not been done since the Wytch Kings ruled the ocean deeps,' said Valkyria, her studded lips curled in disgust. 'I said no good would come of taking up with a demonolator like you!'

'Valkyria has the right of this,' boomed Canute, hefting his axe and treading across the gently rocking beams in a way that was anything but gentle. 'Your Majesty, let me give this devil-worshipper a steel farewell!'

Ragnar inhaled deeply, gesturing towards the axe as he incanted the language of magick. The Mountainside stopped dead in his tracks, as he found himself clutching a weapon made of ice.

'That is but a taste of my powers,' said the apostate priest, brandishing his trident. 'Take one more step, if you wish to feast on them – I guarantee they shall be your last supper!'

If Canute had hid his fear well before, he didn't now. His face went nearly as pale as Ragnar's as he struggled to release the frosty axe, which now burned itself into his palms. Valkyria pulled up short, muttering a prayer to Tyrnor, while behind them the rest of the warriors edged backwards, causing the longship to heave.

Magnhilda turned her eyes back to her brother. She could see how drawn he was: even this trifling sorcerous effort had hurt him. Yet she also sensed he had the power to push past that psychic pain, if further provoked. Just what infernal rites had he been practising in Narborg? Clearly they had boosted his elan – she was a hedge witch herself at best, but knew enough of sorcery to sense her brother was now a master warlock.

'All right, brother,' she said, 'I'll do as you say. But this will sit ill with our host.'

'Just let them be thankful I am sacrificing mainlanders,' snarled Ragnar. 'Am I not showing consideration for your seacarls' property?'

'I gave you more than a hundred slaves from my own lands,' Magnhilda reminded him. The last time she had heard from Ragnar had been when he had sent the request, more than a month ago. She felt a sickness curl into life inside her gut, as she realised what use they had been put to. Not even slaves deserved such a fate.

'And a hundred more shall I take from your personal stock while you are gone,' said Ragnar mercilessly. 'But the World Serpent is hungry – much greater sacrifice does He require before giving me command of the Tritons, who worship Him in salty kingdoms far below the sail road.'

Many of the warriors aboard her ship were openly speaking out now. Fearing a mutiny, Magnhilda called for silence. Across the bows, she could see their consternation had spread to the nearest longships. Clearly the host sensed some dispute was in progress. She had to act quickly, restore order.

'SILENCE!' she cried again, clashing the Furies together. 'The White Eye has not failed us yet, and he is my kin. Let us give him a chance to make good on his promises of swift conquest.' She could sense Ragnar's psychic presence with her own limited elan, though she knew enough of counter-enchantment that he would not try to enthral her.

Even so, she had the distinct feeling that she was being manipulated.

'It isn't right,' said one of her seacarls, braver than most. 'More and more do we rely on sorcery to turn the tide of battle. This bodes ill – not for nothing is this priest named after the world's ending!'

Several throaty *jas* showed the warrior was not alone in his sentiments.

'It will be the Northlendings' world that ends,' said Ragnar smoothly, rewarding the seacarl with a vulpine smile for his bravery. 'Surely you can see that?'

The seacarl blanched and looked away hurriedly.

'I still like this not,' pressed Magnhilda. 'Dividing the fleet doesn't sound like a good idea to me. The walls of Strongholm are high.'

'And not so well defended,' rejoined Ragnar. 'Only a rump of the White Valravyn remains to defend it, along with the city watch. The rest of the King's army is spread to the south and west. And more news I bring – but lately, I have spied the Northlending navy making northwards. They presumably plan to sail around the Pincers and come at the Thraxians unawares. So you see, now is a good time to strike.'

That mollified Magnhilda considerably. Her half-brother's powers of farsight were undeniably useful.

'Very well,' she said, nodding as her confidence returned. 'We'll deploy ourselves as you wish us to. But these... reinforcements of yours had better materialise.' She lowered her voice to a hiss. 'And be controllable, brother.'

The smile did not leave Ragnar's face as he replied: 'Oh

have no fear, sister. Bring me enough slaves, and they shall be bound by one of the greatest powers in the mortal vale.'

Magnhilda ignored the shudder that jolted her spine as she barked the order to Canute: 'Send word to Ravek – half the Skjel fleet are going home, via Stromlund.'

'Excellent,' said Ragnar. 'You shall not regret this, sister.' Without another word, he transformed himself back into a raven and flew south towards the Skjel Islands, leaving a chorus of disapproving murmurings in his wake.

Magnhilda watched him go, her misgivings growing with every beat of the raven's wings.

'You don't have to do this,' growled Canute. 'You are Magna of the Frozen Wastes, not he.'

She weighed her right-hand man's words, as Ragnar's avian form was gradually subsumed by the cloud-patched skies. Her fighting force of ten thousand was mighty indeed: with the Northlendings in disarray, her chances of conquest were already good. But without Ragnar's magicks, she would be able to carry scarce half that number across the seas.

Her brother was right. She owed him. And the warlock hadn't let her down yet.

'No, we'll do as he wishes – for now,' she said reluctantly. 'Let us see which way Logi's dice tumble, so far the Trickster God has favoured our cause.'

'The Trickster God favours no one's cause but his own,' Valkyria reminded her. 'Your brother may be kith, but for too long he has courted profane powers. What does he mean to do with this unnatural army of the ocean deeps?

The Farseers of Norn predicted such a one would come, and herald the world's ending!'

'Valkyria has the right of this, Your Majesty,' insisted the Mountainside. He had finally managed to divest himself of the useless ice axe, which had left ugly chill burns on his hands. 'It is obvious the White Eye's ambitions won't stop at Northalde – and I doubt he means to share power forever.'

The mighty seacarl fixed her with clear blue eyes. They told an even clearer story of his suspicions.

'Yes well, you let me worry about my brother,' she said, hiding her trepidation. 'For now, we need his help. Cast off! Let's get this war under way.'

She turned to face the roiling sail road as her made men scrambled to follow her orders. As she gazed across the *Serpent*'s figurehead, daubed in garish red and blue hues, she suppressed another shudder as she thought of Ragnar in unholy communion with the real thing. From far and wide, the seas beckoned her to a bloody destiny.

CHAPTER 11
A DESPERATE DEFENCE

'Ezekiel help us.' The Crown Prince of Westenlund shook his head despairingly as he surveyed the dismal efforts of the knights he was supposed to be leading into battle. 'We used to be a force to be reckoned with,' sighed Franz, as he watched the corpulent nobles tilting ineptly at quintains. The white walls of Westerburg, the city they would soon have to defend against Pangonia, loomed behind the two hundred knights, many of whom would have been shamed by their squires.

'Yes, my dear boy,' said his mother Utha sadly. 'We did. Too much trade and not enough war has made us weak and lazy. I'd say the Pangonian King has picked an excellent time to invade.'

He had indeed. Word had come of an army fifteen thousand strong crossing the Ornes just days after Franz arrived at court, spurring a lathered courser into the castle ward in answer to her summons. Now they were said to be making swift headway through the southern reaches, pinning castles while they ravaged the countryside. War had come to the principality; Azazel had spread his tainted wings across its villages and manors, and the shadow of conflict had engulfed their blameless folk. The Princess Consort hated to think of her poor people being put to the twin swords – one of cold steel, the other of hard flesh. Already the slaughterings and dishonourings would be taking place.

To make matters worse, twenty war galleys had blockaded Westerburg. There again, Prince Leopold had invested heavily in trade but not war: too many cogs and too few galleys meant their navy was unable to give more than piecemeal resistance. There would be no relief by sea.

What on earth was my husband thinking? she asked herself yet again. *It's a wonder we weren't invaded long before now.*

'Dammit, how long has it been since these men tilted properly?' cried Franz in exasperation. So far, he hadn't been relishing his appointment to Acting Marshal of Westenlund. His mother could hardly fault him for that.

'At least you had the sense to get rid of that idiot Clothar,' said Agravine. 'I must say, ma'am, the worst marshal I've ever seen. I wouldn't trust him to run a tournament melee.'

Even stoical Ruttgur had to crack a grin at that. But Utha was in no mood for japes. Tourneys were one thing; a real war was no laughing matter.

'Incompetent or not, Clothar is of a good family,' she said, rounding on Agravine and his two fellow Dulsinians. 'And you three are here as guests, whom it behoves to be civil, need I remind you?'

Agravine was about to reply when a yell turned their

attention back towards the fields. One of the nearest knights had been sent hurtling forwards over the pommel of his saddle as a quintain sack caught him full in the back. Cursing, Franz stalked over to reprimand him, as he languished in the dirt wincing and clutching his shoulder.

'We're guests, aye,' said Agravine with a smirk. 'Ones who would fain impart your bachelors with some northern mettle.'

'Yes, I'm sure you would,' sighed Utha. Like it or not, she needed that northern mettle now more than ever. 'Which is why I'd appreciate it if you'd concentrate on helping my son, rather than mocking his predecessor.'

'It shall be done, ma'am,' interjected Ruttgur, shooting a disapproving glance at Agravine. 'Rest assured, we'll have your court nobility licked into shape by the time the Barons' Council is convened.'

'Or something resembling it anyway,' deadpanned Agravine, exchanging wry glances with the third Dulsinian knight, Sir Borwine. The young vassal had recovered from his head wound, though their other comrade, Sir Rufius, had not been so lucky. Freeswords from the Frozen Wastes had pursued the four knights, slaying Rufius in the Blattwood before they managed to make good their escape from Dulsinor – clearly Lord Hengist was hell bent on eliminating his rivals to a man.

Would he even answer to the summons, Princess Utha wondered? All the other high lords of Vorstlund had responded to her messengers directly, but the Herzog of Stornelund had refused to answer immediately, sending her envoy back none the wiser.

He'd better get a blasted move on, and let us know if he's coming, she thought irritably. *The council is in two days, and not a day too soon.* Even now, she expected to hear fresh news of the southern reaches being overrun. At least her border vassals were made of sterner stuff, and thanks to the realm's prosperity the castles Altkass, Vizvant and Howfaste were well victualled: provided her castellans remained stout of heart, they should hold out against the Pangonians for a long time.

Pin us down will you, Carolus? That tactic works both ways.

Except, of course, that the Pangonian King's forces outnumbered theirs – he could afford to expend men where she could not.

This council must bear fruit. It's the dungeon cells and ransoming for us all if it doesn't. And that's if we're lucky.

She knew all too well that none of her yeomanry would enjoy such fortune in the event of a conquest. The twin swords of war always fell most heavily on the common folk.

She turned to Fraustus. 'I trust the lords Bjornwulf and Eadgar have been well settled?' The Herzog of Lower Thulia and the Eorl of Dreylund had been the first to arrive, but then their baronies lay nearest.

'They have, ma'am,' replied the seneschal. 'I've victualled them modestly, in accordance with your wishes.' She could sense Fraustus still disapproved of such temperance. It went against all Vorstlending customs of hospitality.

She nodded curtly, choosing to ignore his obvious misgivings. 'Lord Wenfold,' she said, addressing the tall skinny noble beside him, 'you've been most reticent this morning. Have you succeeded in engaging freeswords in the city?'

Wenfold had a protruding mouth and pointy chin at odds with his small snub nose, and watery eyes that belied a keen intellect. The former creased into the semblance of a smile, as he purred: 'I have indeed, Your Highness – nigh two hundred have we now in service. Might I add, I drove a hard bargain too, pointing out that mercenaries stranded at port are hardly in a position to drive one of their own.'

He twiddled his tentacular fingers in that manner he favoured whenever he was saving the Prince's money. Utha sighed. This was typical of her Master of Coin, though she could not deny he was good at his job. 'Coin is one thing we do not lack for, Lord Wenfold, and I'd rather have loyal freeswords than cheap ones. Perhaps you could work in an... offer of extra reward, for exemplary service in the field?'

She beamed at him and Wenfold winced. He did so hate to part with His Royal Highness's treasure – anyone would think he actually owned the laden coffers kept in the rock below Westerburg Point. 'It shall be as you say, ma'am,' he said, with a half-bow that did nothing to hide his pained expression.

Franz was walking back towards them, complaining non-stop about what a useless, bibulous, good-for-nothing bunch of sots the castle chivalry were. His mother felt sure she would have admired him even if he wasn't her son and heir. He wasn't particularly tall or handsome, but a better-made man she could not have asked for. His muscles were honed from endless practice in the field, his curly blond hair and mustachios well groomed. More than that, he was an honourable man and believed in the Code of Chivalry. Even the common folk appeared to like him, rather than just fearing him. That would make him a great ruler one day – if his birthright wasn't ripped away from him by Azazel's claws.

'They're in terrible shape, but they were active squires once,' Franz was saying. 'Ezekiel willing, they haven't completely forgotten everything their fathers taught them. I've instructed them to start dressing like proper Vorstlendings, too – none of this effeminate southern finery, it makes me sick to see good knights dress like popinjays.'

Franz himself was dressed in gambeson and simple tunic, hose and cloak; he carried his father's sword at his side. That was how he proposed to dress at all times, even when off duty. The only change would be when he put on full armour to tilt himself.

'Lord Rothstein of Aslund should arrive today,' her son went on. 'He'll bring a stout retinue, never fear, mother – we'll see these southern devils off our land.' He grasped her shoulders in strong hands, fixed her with keen grey eyes.

Reus bless him, but he really believed... Utha could only pray her son was right.

A clarion call came from the sentry on the gatehouse ramparts. A lone messenger hoved into view, spurring a swift courser along the highway towards the city. He carried a small pennon that bore a stylised dove taking flight on a vair field of vert and gules: the white, green and red heraldry of House Hessé, the family that ruled in Aslund. Franz's smile dropped as he realised the Aslunding messenger was travelling alone. Espying their own standard, the envoy spurred his horse towards them. He had the look of a man who has ridden long and hard for several days. He also had the look of a man who has ridden from grave peril.

Dismounting, the young knight bowed. 'Sir Altan of Danrik, at your service,' he said, in the thick accent of the eastern marches. 'I bring news from Lord Rothstein, and I fear to tell it is not good.'

Franz ground his teeth. 'Bad news is best broken sooner not later,' he said. 'Have out with it.'

'I regret to say that my liege will not be attending the council,' said Sir Altan. 'We are under attack ourselves.'

That caught mother and son off guard. The Dulsinian knights exchanged uneasy glances.

'By whom?' asked Utha.

'The Thalamians,' replied Altan. 'They marched an army through Wulfric's Pass a tenday ago, at least five thousand strong according to our outriders. Pushed through the Breitrand and invested castle Ostanwach. Last we heard, they're marching on Asberg.'

'They're using the same tactics as the Pangonians,' said Franz. 'Pinning your castles under siege while they make for your capital.'

'Of course,' said Utha, 'King Carolus is connected to the Thalamian King by his marriage to Isolte... Reus dammit, why didn't we see this coming? They've made an alliance.'

'And that means our worst fears have been realised,' said Franz. 'This isn't just about Westenlund – it's a full-blown assault on Vorstlund.'

'It also means you can forget about the Eorl of Ostveldt turning up,' put in Agravine. 'He'll be like to make common cause with his neighbour now, in light of a Thalamian invasion.'

Sir Altan's expression told that the Dulsinian had not guessed awry.

Utha winced as she felt her bowels flare again. An invisible fire coursed through them: a poultice applied in the most delicate of regions would help to quench it, but she could hardly worry about that now.

'Dammit!' she cursed, her ailment lending venom to her mounting anger. 'This alliance of barons is falling apart before we've even brokered it. Chances are Lord Hengist won't budge either – he's got two enemies on his doorstep now, why would he bother sending men to help us?'

'In which case our suit here is cold,' said Ruttgur bluntly. 'With all due respect, Your Highness, but we must request leave to depart.'

'Where would you have us go?' demanded Agravine. Utha could sense a rivalrous tension between the two, but that was typical of young bachelors.

'Back home, where we belong,' answered Ruttgur stubbornly.

Agravine shook his head impatiently. 'We've scarcely a home left to go back to,' he said. 'For all we know Hengist has completed the conquest of Dulsinor. We're better off chancing the fortunes of war down here.'

'That is a disloyal remark to make!' cried Ruttgur. 'Sir Urist sent us down south to save Dulsinor, not abandon it in service to another barony – with all due respect, ma'am,' he added, nodding towards the Princess Consort.

Agravine was about to reply, but Utha waved them all to

silence. 'Please, noblemen, it's really no use bickering amongst ourselves,' she said, 'we're in a parlous enough state as it is. Sir Ruttgur and Sir Agravine, rest assured that if you lend your services to us, we will put pressure on Lord Storne to relinquish his grip on Dulsinor.'

'And how do you propose to do that, ma'am?' asked Ruttgur pointedly. Perhaps he wasn't as simple as she'd taken him for – her son and advisers were looking at her keenly now, expecting an answer.

Her own audacity surprised her.

'I'll make Hengist an offer he can't refuse,' she said. 'If he agrees to desist from his invasion of Dulsinor, he can marry my daughter Lana. We've enough coin to dowry her very well, and Stornelund would benefit from such a prestigious union. No, it'll work,' she persisted, ignoring Franz, who was gaping at her now. 'It'll free up Dulinsor to send whatever men it can to help us defeat the Pangonians, whilst leaving the Stornelendings to choose between helping us too, or the eastern baronies against the Thalamians – or both, if that's what they decide.'

'What's to stop the Dulsinians attacking Stornelund once they leave their territory?' asked Franz. 'It's what I'd do in their position.' The faces of Agravine and Ruttgur evinced the strength of his argument: revenge had spurred many a conflict before. 'I hardly think Hengist will agree to such terms under the present circumstances.'

'Circumstances in which not one but two foreign realms are invading our country,' shot back Utha. 'Don't be so sure, my dear boy – Hengist may be a drunken fool, but his steward and marshal aren't. Albercelscus and Adso will recognise the virtue of such a plan, as will the Dulsinians' – she turned a beady eye on her guests – 'because these emissaries are going to return home and vouch for the plan as being the non-negotiable terms for our aid. Once that aid has secured the truce that allows them to return home safely.'

Agravine and Ruttgur exchanged awkward looks. Utha allowed herself a moment of triumph. She had them, and they knew it. The Princess Consort hadn't been long on her husband's throne, but politicking came naturally to her. Small wonder, she reflected: in a man's world of sword and thew, intrigue was a woman's most potent weapon.

'It sounds like a tenuous plan at best,' hedged Agravine at last. 'But in the absence of a better one, I don't really see an alternative. If Hengist hasn't taken Graukolos yet, he might just prefer the idea of a fresh marriage alliance that allows him to repel a foreign invader.'

'If it gives us a chance of saving Urist's life, and any other Dulsinians, I would try it,' added Ruttgur. 'Though making a truce with Stornelund sickens my very soul.'

'You're a nice boy,' Utha told him kindly. 'Very sincere. Unfortunately we're at war, and can't afford such virtues. Now, if you'll all excuse me – I've medicine to take back at the castle.'

Leaning on her mahogany cane, she turned and began hobbling back towards the fortress, motioning for her ladies-in-waiting to accompany her. A long and difficult road up the side of the cliffs beckoned to her with cruel fingers of rock and stone, but sitting a horse in her condition was unthinkable.

Her son caught up with her. 'Mother, are you wise?' he hissed. 'You'd marry my sister off to that... you know Hengist's last bride disappeared, don't you?'

'Yes dear,' replied Utha affably. 'I also know that a head-strong and beautiful girl like Adhelina of Dulsinor wasn't likely to play along with political marriages, Luviah bless her. A pity she remains unaccounted for...' She was about to say something else, then thought better of it. Best for now to concentrate on what was, not what might have been. Instead she added: 'My daughter, with the best will in the world, is neither beautiful nor strong-minded. That makes her a perfect bartering piece.'

'Mother, that is low,' said Franz.

'My dear boy, that is politics,' said Utha, smiling wanly. 'And as I said, we are at war – we've no leisure to consider niceties. You stick to training and tactics, leave the politicking to me. Now get back to those quintains where you're needed.'

She left him spluttering in her wake, hobbling back towards the castle she hoped to defend from foreign invasion.

CHAPTER 12
A SUDDEN DEATH

Princess Hjala steadied herself against the crooked paddock fence, trying to take in the ill news whilst fathoming what it meant.

'But... when? How?' she gasped.

Sir Manfry's face was set grim as he replied: 'They say Lord Ulnor died in his sleep two nights ago. It was a peaceful passing, most like his heart gave out. He was very old, after all.'

'You really think it was... natural causes?'

Manfry shrugged. 'Can't think why anyone would assassinate him, Your Highness,' he said. 'His Lordship was always held in high regard at court. Sounds like the most dashed coincidence if you ask me.'

Hjala reflected on that. Manfry was an ingenuous soul, but he was probably right: no one besides the Royal Seneschal's henchmen had known of their plan to do away with Lorthar. And sworn swords of House Canwolde were likely to be loyal.

She pushed herself away from the fenced enclosure, where she'd just finished feeding her horse. 'Let's go inside,' she said. 'I need to contemplate this over a stoup of wine, and it please you, Sir Manfry. We should tell my brother and aunt, too.'

'Princess Walsa and Prince Thorsvald have been informed as well,' said Manfry, falling in beside her as they walked back to his humble wooden hall. He looked nervous, and wasn't hiding it this time.

Her brother and aunt were gathered around Manfry's rickety table, drinking his vinegary wine. Hjala suppressed an inward sigh. Being a royal fugitive from royal justice had long lost its novelty.

'So now what do we do?' cried Thorsvald, raising his arms and nearly spilling the contents of his goblet. 'We can't very well... remove Lorthar with our chief contact at court dead.'

'No we can't,' said Hjala decisively. Though she secretly wondered how successful their abortive plan would have been in any case: two weeks had passed since their clandestine meeting with Ulnor, and he'd apparently made little progress. She'd heard that in the heathen Sassanian lands, assassins were experts at their craft and relatively easy to find. Here a footpad with a dagger in his belt and a murderous glint in his eye was about the best you could hope for. Poisons weren't unheard of by any means in the Free Kingdoms, but rumour had it the Arch Perfect had taken to using a food taster. They had even considered trying to bribe Lorthar's personal bodyguards to do the thing, but so far that idea had come to nothing. A high-ranking Temple priest could afford to pay his freeswords well.

'It was hardly going to plan as things stood,' said Walsa, giving voice to her niece's despondent thoughts. 'A fine trio of plotters we make. At this rate, they'll have marched on Thraxia by the time we even think of how to get near Lorthar.'

'You're bally well right about that,' supplied Manfry, helping himself to wine. 'I bumped into my neighbour when I was out hunting yesterday. Sir Jarvis says they've begun mustering near Vandheim – the Royal Fleet under Lord Aesgir plans to reconnoitre there and ferry an invasion army north and west. His Majesty has opted for a coastal attack, while the Thraxians are busy rebuilding their kingdom.'

'So that rumour proved true then?' asked Hjala. Word of Abrexta's removal had reached Strongholm recently, borne into port on the spring tides. She supposed that was cause for celebration – it meant Horskram's mission was succeeding. But it was hard to celebrate when your own kingdom was being spat from the cooking pot into the hearth.

'Every merchantman from Thraxia to dock in the past tenday has confirmed as much,' said Manfry. 'At least my uncle seems to be having some luck.'

'If only we were as good as Master Horskram at getting things done,' sighed Walsa, allowing her passion for the monk to get the better of her. 'It won't be long before my idiot nephew sends half the able-bodied fighting men in Northalde out of the country. Then we'll be ripe for a North-land invasion.'

'Tell us something we don't know, aunt,' sighed Hjala, draining her cup.

'What about Lord Toric of Runstadt?' queried Walsa after a few moments of brooding silence. 'He was friendly to our cause ere now – and he commands the White Valravyn, sworn to protect the Dominions. Surely he'll see sense in aiding us again, once we tell him of the Northland fleet Thorsvald's men witnessed.'

'Lord Toric has had his hands full completing the pacification of the south,' said Thorsvald, shaking his head. 'As soon as he has new knights and nobles secure in the secessionist provinces, he'll be called to join the muster. The White Valrayvn must be loyal to the realm, always – and whoever rules it.'

'He's right,' said Hjala, 'we can't-'

She was interrupted by the sound of horses approaching outside. No few of them at that. Hjala already knew who it was when the familiar voice called for them to come out.

'Lord Toric, we were just talking about you,' she deadpanned as the four of them emerged from the hall. The High Commander of the White Valravyn sat astride his Farovian, dressed in full panoply of war, the ten knights with him likewise caparisoned.

'Good morning, Your Highness,' he said, his granite face betraying no emotion. 'It is good to see you in fair health. I only wish we could be meeting again under different circumstances.'

'I shall not be one to disagree with you there, High Commander,' she replied. The clouds had begun to drizzle a light rain. She supposed that was appropriate to their sudden change of fortunes.

'Who betrayed us?' asked Thorsvald. 'You owe a prince of the blood royal that much at least.' Her brother stood stoical and firm in the grey light, though Hjala could see the pain behind his eyes. Even in just cause, being held a traitor must be agonising for the loyal prince.

Lord Toric appeared to consider a moment, then he answered: 'Three knights in service to Lord Ulnor. Upon the late seneschal's death they felt their vow of secrecy no longer held, and could not betray the King a moment longer.'

Walsa barked a brittle bark of derisive laughter at that, but Hjala only smiled. *So those sworn swords of House Canwolde weren't so loyal after all,* she thought. *I'm sure my brother Wolfram will happily take them into his personal retinue for their service to the Crown.*

'Well you'd best be getting on with it then,' said Lady Walsa, the contempt not leaving her voice. 'I don't suppose we'll get a trial?'

Toric's face remained expressionless as he said: 'Your Royal Highnesses will be treated with all due courtesies that befit your station.'

'And what of Sir Manfry?' interjected Hjala. 'He has helped us out of the goodness of his heart, believing the realm's interests best served by doing so. I trust he will be treated kindly as well.'

Toric acknowledged the vassal with a curt nod. 'As a member of the nobility, Sir Manfry will be entitled to answer for any accusations levelled against him. I believe the law is quite specific on that point.'

She threw Manfry a glance that she hoped was reassuring. Toric's words proffered but cold comfort, but they would have to do for now.

'Well then,' said Walsa, 'we'd best have our horses saddled – it looks as though we're all going back to Strongholm.'

And perhaps that is for the best, reflected Hjala as Manfry called for his squire. *Get us close to Lorthar and Wolfram and the rest of the court, and we might be able to influence things. Even if we are going there as prisoners.*

It was a brave and resourceful way of looking at things, yet for all that Hjala's mood lightened no more than the gloomy skies above.

AN AUDIENCE WITH DRUIDS

At the summit of Malhavern's Point, the wind had a raw elemental savagery. The rain had hardened during their long journey up through the tunnels and grottos of Skelnaervon; now it lashed about them with a supernatural frenzy, one that made Torgun wonder if they hadn't sailed to the Other Side. Lashed *about* them, yet did not touch them. The half dozen monoliths of Aurgelmir's Teeth cradled the vast basin of rock on to which they had emerged; this close the knight could see the sorcerous symbols etched into those mighty stones in more detail than he cared for. The wind and rain did not so much as venture a gust or drop beyond them.

'Our command of Thaumaturgy and Transformation has dwindled since the Old Time, but the Moon Goddess permits nothing to dampen our revels during the Festival of Spring's Awakening!' beamed Morcant. The mage looked genuinely happy to be home. Torgun could hardly fathom why: his adventures had brought him far and wide, but next to the Warlock's Crown and the Draugmoors, this was the most godforsaken place he had ever seen.

And yet its inhabitants seemed to think otherwise. The magical shield took on the appearance of a vast dome of water as the abjured rain sloughed off it in cascading sheets; floating lanterns of translucent bone bathed it in a rich orange glow.

'Aethi have been bound to yon lanterns,' explained Morcant, when he caught the knight staring at them. 'The air spirits carry them to wherever they are needed.'

Torgun clutched the relic about his neck. His newfound piety had not left him. 'I suppose you have Saraphi bound to them as well,' he muttered. 'To keep them burning.'

Morcant looked genuinely shocked at that. 'Why no!' he exclaimed. 'On holy days that celebrate the earth's awakening, use of fire magic is a blasphemy. For fire destroys what nature has wrought.'

Torgun shook his head. 'I won't pretend to understand your depraved faith,' was all he said to that.

The basin that crowned the summit of Malhavern's Point eddied downwards in sloping ripples of rock towards a massive bonfire at its epicentre. Hundreds of Westerlings were crammed on to its shelves: many of them went skyclad, cavorting naked and unashamed to frantic pipes and frenetic drums. Like the warriors who had escorted them, many had strange sigils tattooed across their bodies and bound their hair with bones, though some wore it long and unfettered. Younger men and women coupled openly, rutting frenziedly on bizarre blankets fashioned of moss and sedge.

'Many a babe will be kindled into life this lunar month,' said Morcant, raising his voice to be heard above the din. 'For only at Spring's Awakening does Kaia acknowledge her brother the Sun, whom we do not name. Oh yes, many an offering will the Queen of Paramours receive!' The warlock's vulpine grin as he stared at the rutting couples was matched for intensity by the expression of revulsion smeared across Joram's face. 'Of all the places my calling has brought me to, this must surely rank among the foullest,' he spat.

Sir Torgun proffered him St Argo's rood. 'Perhaps the relic of your Order's founder might comfort you?' he suggested, but the adept shook his head. 'Only swift flight from this pagan bourne of filth and wretchedness shall do that,' he declared. 'Morcant! Where is this blasted All-Meet you spoke of? Where is the Druiding Council?'

The mage pointed up to the highest lip of rock over-looking the basin. Several of their guides had remained to guard them, whilst the rest made their way up towards the summit. Other warriors and lesser druids clustered about the shelves, peering at the new arrivals with mistrustful eyes. Suspicion ran deep among the Westerling people: all of them except Morcant had been blindfolded on the journey up through the caves of Skelnaervon, whence queer sounds had come and gone. Much as he'd resented being blindfolded, Sir Torgun wasn't sure he cared to learn their origins.

These people guard their secrets carefully, he thought. *And yet they have been tricked ere now, by Andragorix and other renegades.*

'The Druiding Council will convene shortly,' said Morcant. 'As will the Marcher Lords. A great honour is an emergency All-Meet, so think not my kinsmen take your visit lightly!' The weaselly wizard looked troubled now. Torgun guessed he would have plenty of explaining to do.

'I don't suppose there's any chance of them feeding us?' asked Wrackwulf, eyeing the roasting joints of mutton being expertly turned on long sticks over the bonfire by scrawny youths. 'That was a long march up here, and I'm rightly famished.'

Morcant twined his fingers awkwardly. 'Would that we could, but rarely do we have the luxury of meat,' said the warlock. 'For our winters are harsh, our command of the seasons long faded-'

'Spare me the tales of hardship and long lost bounty,' sighed Wrackwulf. 'I've a feeling we're going to hear plenty of that from our hosts. I was just hungry is all.'

'Look, oi thinks they're a' coming,' said Garhan, pointing with a finger that trembled. A group of men and women some thirty strong was making its way down towards them via stony rivulets running through the rock, rough hewn by the elements over long centuries. As they passed by, the islanders ceased their cavorting. Even the couples somehow knew to break off their lusty embraces.

Garhan's fingers strayed to the hilt of his knife, but Torgun caught him by the wrist. 'We swore an oath,' he reminded the pirate. 'And these paganers overmatch us. Keep your hands where they can see them.'

Garhan scowled at that, but acquiesced. 'Oi agree with the monk,' he growled. 'The sooner we're off this rock, the better oi'll loike it.' His two surviving crewmen looked terrified. Gathrod had already proved himself an impulsive sort – Torgun hoped his captain would keep him in line this time. It didn't take a farseer to realise that the Westerlings would kill them all out of hand if they felt so minded.

By the time the welcoming party had reached the bottom of the basin, everyone had stopped what they were doing and fallen silent. Only crackling flames, spattering rain and keening wind could be heard. Hundreds of pairs of dark eyes were now fixed on the outlanders.

Their guard fanned out, nudging them with spear butts towards a space that had been cleared before the bonfire. A great circle had been chalked out on it. Tall candles of a luminous green substance that resembled neither wax nor tallow were laid about its perimeter at regular intervals. The circle itself was divided into four quarters, each one carved with a single hieratic symbol of the accursed sorcerous script.

'The Four Airts,' breathed Morcant. 'One for each of the winds and elements – North for earth, South for fire, West for water, East for air! The last three rage about us – upon the first shall we be judged.'

As if on cue, the guards nudged them into the northern quarter of the circle. The welcoming party formed a ring around the seven new arrivals. Looking beyond them, Torgun could see the rest of the Islanders had done likewise, as if sitting in an auditorium fashioned by nature herself. Several of the magic lanterns had floated towards the centre, intensifying the light as they bobbed up and down above their heads.

Sir Torgun returned his gaze to the foremost islanders. Two thirds appeared to be Marcher Lords and their retinues of warriors, dressed in richly embroidered sashes and carrying weapons of similar quality to their armed escort. The nine members of the Druiding Council made for an even more outlandish sight. The archdruids and high priest-esses put him in mind of the Earth Witch, wearing a plethora of amulets and clad in garments fashioned of leaves that seemed to rustle of their own accord. The knight tensed at the reminder of his unavenged comrades-in-arms, and had to stop himself reaching for his own blade.

Joram and Garhan aren't the only ones who'll be right glad to be gone from this place.

But it was the central figure who really caught his eye. Dressed in earth-coloured robes that left his arms bare, and crowned in a wreath of mistletoe, he carried a wooden staff carved to resemble a ram's head and a gently curving stick about the length of a forearm painted with the colours of the rainbow. A corpulent whale of a man, he sported a bald shiny pate, flabby jowls, and eyes limned with kohl that accentuated his androgynous nature. The Grand High Druid's sexless appearance befuddled him at first – then with a shock, he recalled Morcant's tale-telling in the Fernwood.

The wizard spoke true – they really do castrate their religious leaders. That thought made Torgun shudder more than all the witches and golems and draugar in the Known World.

The Grand High Druid raised the wand. His fingernails were varnished black as night. As he traced a hieratic symbol in the air, his raiment responded with a peculiar clacking sound – it was only then that Torgun realised it was fashioned from an overlapping quilt of what appeared to be pieces of tree bark. Even more disturbingly, sentient animal eyes were dotted all over the curious mantle. The druid did not utter a syllable, but his pudgy brow furrowed momentarily in concentration. The air about the magic circle suddenly shimmered, a light dusting of lucent cobwebs ghosting an invisible barrier that suddenly sprang up around them.

No chance of escape then. Not that Torgun minded over much – escape was for cowards – but he hoped the timorous pirates would keep their wits about them. *Perhaps it's a shield to protect us in case they don't,* he reflected. He could only hope so – Gathrod was already fingering the two knives he wore at his belt, casting about him shiftily. Torgun caught his eyes and motioned for him to be still.

After a pregnant pause, the Grand High Druid spoke in a high-pitched voice. It seemed to knife through the rocky levels about them. Though he addressed Morcant, who had abased himself, his words were clearly intended for the All-Meet. The mage rose at his bidding, tugging nervously on his braids as he replied in the Westerling tongue. Torgun twitched, more than a little perturbed himself. He hated to show fear, but sorcery always unnerved him. Now here he was, positively drenched in the stuff. Joram's eyes had narrowed: Torgun guessed the monk knew enough of their language to follow the exchange. Some of the archdruids and high priestesses were joining in now, punctuating the interrogation with comments of their own. The Marcher Lords said little but exchanged dark looks, some shaking their heads and scowling. One even spat on the ground, just outside the circle.

'A translation wouldn't go amiss,' hissed Wrackwulf, nudging Joram, but the monk just shook his head and returned his concentration to the islanders, as they continued to trade words in their lilting tongue. Before long he was butting in, ignoring the stony faces of the marchers as he addressed them in their tongue. Their anger welled up as the rain outside became fiercer still, the elements seeming to mock the mortal choler they presided over.

Soon everyone was shouting, catcalls and hisses filtering down from the rest of the All-Meet for good measure. Some of the marchers were even arguing with each other, Torgun noticed: a short rotund fellow with fiery whiskers and beard dressed in a sash of interlocking black and white moon patterns was squaring up to another lord, this one with elongated arms and bow legs dressed in a sash of horizontal zig-zagged lines of yellow, blue and red. They made a good show of shaking their fists in each other's faces, as they spat curses at one another. The Northlending knight wondered what they were arguing about, and if it even pertained to them.

Lords are much the same wherever you go, he reflected wryly. *Thank Palom 'twas my brother Toros who inherited Vandheim, and not I.*

Presently the Grand Druid raised his staff for silence. It

descended with a swiftness that under the present circumstances could only be described as eerie. He flicked his wand again, and Torgun sensed the invisible barrier about them dissolve. A short, agile-looking young woman sporting indigo four-pointed stars interlocked with green diamonds on her sash motioned to their honour guard, who closed around them again.

'Taken down to Kell we will be,' said Morcant. 'The Druiding Council aren't pleased, away for far too long I was! And the Marcher Lords like not your presence here.'

'Now tell us something we don't know,' growled Wrackwulf. 'Any chance of some food in your fine capital?'

But Morcant simply ignored him. Their escort produced blindfolds again. All about them the Westerlings were returning to their sybaritic rites, the music striking up once more as nubile figures resumed their ritual rutting. The lords and druids had fallen back to their bickering.

'Where exactly in Kell are we being taken?' demanded Torgun. 'What is our status – are we emissaries or captives?'

'Both,' replied Joram bluntly. 'They haven't yet decided what to do with us. I've explained why we're here and asked to inspect their defences, but they are chary of letting outsiders see where the fragment is kept.'

Hardly surprising, thought Torgun. *Even I could have fathomed as much. Joram, what are you playing at?*

Garhan's sinewy face was a mask of confusion. 'Fragment? What's this abowt a fragment? What in the Salt King's seas are ye talkin' abowt?'

'You aren't being paid to ask questions,' snarled Joram as a warrior blindfolded him. 'Now be silent, and let me think!'

Torgun was about to say something when another warrior blindfolded him, too. Then he was being nudged by a spear butt, back towards the rocky stairwell from where they had emerged. The sound of skirling drums and whooping clansfolk crammed his suddenly sharpened ears. He hoped it wasn't the last music he would ever hear.

CHAPTER 14
SKULDUGGERY IN THE SOUTH

'... And next let us honour St Brother Sir Orfeus, fourth paladinus of our Order, who took upon himself the emanation of the Seraph Virtus, avatar of fortitude, that he might better resist the Sassanian infidels in their efforts to overthrow Reus' kingdom on earth...'

Adelko stifled a yawn as Grand Master Tobin droned on. This was the third morning in a row he'd had to listen to the same litany. The oblong chapel was chilly; the few meagre windows in its clerestory allowed for little sunlight to penetrate. Lining the walls below these, seven statues of the warrior saints who had founded the Bethler Order stared sightlessly at the two-hundred strong garrison kneeling on the cold stone floor, pitted whitestone hands clasped in prayers of their own.

'... and let us give thanks to St Brother Sir Armand, fifth paladinus of our Order, imbued with Logos, archangel of prosperity, that he might harness wealth in the eternal fight against the heathens that oppose us...'

The journeyman almost snorted out loud at that one. Armand had invented a canny concept known as *banking*, an obscure discipline that apparently allowed the Bethlers to conjure money out of thin air. Adelko still didn't understand quite how this was supposed to work, but the Order was undeniably rich: it was said that even a king or sultan might envy its wealth.

Gold over god, he thought again ruefully. *This lot really have a fascinating interpretation of the Creed.*

Logos was also held to be the avatar of tolerance, though Adelko had seen little evidence the Bethlers revered him in that aspect. What little conversation he'd heard among the brethren was limited to enthusiastic exchanges about the chance to spill Sha'abatian blood in the coming crusade.

'... and sixth, let us not forget St Brother Sir Hugo, whose embodiment of Euphrosakritos reminds us all to drink deeply of the rye and barley beer bequeathed us by the archangel, in reward for our endless labours...'

Adelko exchanged a wry glance with Horskram, kneeling beside him. A brief wrinkling of the nose told him all he needed to know of his mentor's thoughts. True, the seraph of merry-making bade men enjoy the fruits of their labour on celebration days... but the Bethlers seemed to believe every day was a celebration day. They might shun women and be strict about what they ate, but they certainly didn't stint on the ale.

Perhaps that's what sustains them when they can't drink the blood of their enemies, he reflected grimly.

Adelko let his mind drift off as Tobin finished his pane-gyric, trying to ignore his rumbling stomach. At least they'd get a chance to break their fast soon: unleavened bread, unseasoned pork and watered wine made for plain enough fare, but it was better than nothing.

That, and more prayers, were about the only certainty the day would bring. The Grand Master had kept Horskram at arm's length since receiving them, leaving the two monks none the wiser as to whether he would help them reach Abdel Sha'arza. Adelko had spent much of the past two days in the Bethler library: maps of the region suggested the Watchtower of Leviathan lay about halfway down the Abydos ranges, many days' ride south and east across leagues of dangerous Nazharyan territory. He'd pored over other tomes detailing the sultanate's military forces: *amluqs*, elite slave soldiers trained from birth to kill in service to the Sultan and his satraps; *fariz*, mounted warriors akin to Urovian knights; and farther south, where the desert tribes held sway, the *sarakim* warrior caste patrolled the dunes. With their horn bows they could hit a target from horseback at full gallop a hundred yards away.

What chance do we stand against that lot without an armed escort? Adelko wondered, as they exited the chapel and made their way to the refectory. This was another converted palatial manor in the Sassanian style, consisting of an enclosed garden cloistered by four spacious vestibules, with filigreed archways that opened on to its lush orange trees and ornate blue porcelain fountains. The hundred resident knights sat before trestle tables in one of the vestibules; the hundred lay serjeants were seated opposite on the other side of the garden; Adelko and Horskram headed towards the third vestibule, where a smaller table was reserved for Tobin, his captains, and honoured guests.

So honoured the Grand Master barely speaks a word to us, thought Adelko disconsolately, as he took his place beside Horskram. At least their surroundings were luxurious – he'd already seen enough of Sassanian civilisation to realise it put his own to shame in many respects. The latticed light that filtered in through the abstract designs of the purple tamarind screen set into the wall behind them created a soothing effect; likewise the bubbling fountains somehow contrived to offset the sweltering heat already rising from the streets outside.

Lay serjeants served them their repast on pewter trenchers, and all thoughts of luxury vanished from Adelko's mind.

'Where is our meat, Master Horskram?' he whispered in dismay. Bread and wine made for a pitiful sight on their own.

The adept smiled wryly. 'Bethlers only partake of meat three times a week, holding it bad for both morals and constitution to over-indulge. Surely you had not failed to notice how trim our pious hosts are?'

Gazing about him, Adelko glumly acknowledged the truth of that. He'd also read that many Urovians sickened and died a few years after coming to the Blessed Realm; some loremasters held that their gluttonous northern diet did not help. The Bethlers were certainly among the most well-made fighting men he had yet encountered – there was a mean leanness to them that even the White Valrayvn could not have boasted. He wondered what his erstwhile comrades would make of such knights, who did indeed seem almost like monks at times.

'At least they haven't forgotten about the wine,' sighed the journeyman, making himself a miserable sop using a hunk of chewy barley bread.

'Be of some cheer, master monk – a temperate diet makes for a stronger soldier, as the Redeemer sayeth.'

Adelko glanced over quizzically at the speaker, sat a few places up from him on the other side of the polished cedar table. The knight looked unusually jovial for one of his kind, and yet he was unmistakeably a warrior-monk of the Order. His pate was shaven like the others, but he sported florid moustachios and a trim goatee that set him apart.

He smiled affably as he caught the journeyman staring. 'Nothing in the Rules of the Order says we can't adorn our faces with hair – so long as we shave our locks up top!'

'But... you're speaking to us,' Adelko dared to observe. 'I don't think the rest of your brethren have said that many words to us since we got here.'

Horskram flicked a sharp glance at Adelko, but the Bethler waved his misgivings away casually. 'No, he's quite right,' he said. 'We aren't used to interacting with outsiders, and many of the brethren are... a tad shy.' The continued silence of the other commanders seated near them bore silent witness to the truth of that. They didn't even glance up from their trenchers, or indicate that they had noticed their brother speak.

'Brother Sir Balian, at your service,' continued the Bethler commander. 'It is a privilege to have Argolian friars as guests.'

Faces that suddenly soured suggested not all his brother knights felt the same. From his place at the head of the table, Grand Master Tobin fixed Balian with a stern glare. 'I will be the judge of that,' he barked curtly.

'I do hope so,' interjected Horskram dryly. 'I had hoped to hear your opinions on us sooner rather than later.'

Tobin's bust of a face did not shift a granule as he replied: 'As it happens, I have a forthcoming crusade to keep my thoughts and prayers occupied. But I had thought to give you the audience you crave, this afternoon and it please you.'

'It most certainly does,' confirmed Horskram. 'The Most Learned Argolian Order salutes the Most Holy Order of the Bethel for its munificence in this matter.'

If Tobin perceived his sarcasm, he gave no indication of it. 'Very well,' he said peremptorily. 'Brother Sir Balian – seeing as you are so keen on befriending our guests, you might as well show them how we drill our knights and serjeants. Perhaps they can learn something about how we channel Stygnos' fortitude in the fight against the Fallen One and his Sha'abatian agents.'

Balian nodded. 'It shall be both an honour and a pleasure,' he said, rising and beckoning for the monks to accompany him. The knights and serjeants were already rising from their own places.

'Don't you worry about His Eminence,' said Balian as he ushered them back out into the sun-soaked courtyard. Still early morning, it was already hot. 'Just preoccupied with the holy war, is all – I'm sure he'll lend ears to your business today.'

'Why are you so... cheerful?' Adelko piped up again. 'If you don't mind my saying so, you're not half so taciturn as the rest of your brethren.'

'Pray forgive my colleague,' said Horskram as Balian steered them towards the barracks. 'He has a persistent habit of opening his mouth to free thoughts best left fettered.'

Balian laughed at that. 'No, it's quite all right,' he said. 'I am rather more jovial than the other brothers, it's true! But does not Euphrosakritos tell us to make merry, even as we strive towards Palom's perfection?'

Adelko thought back to Tobin's sermon. 'So I take it St Hugo is your favourite of the seven founders then?'

Balian just chuckled again. 'A good Bethler shouldn't have favourites, but hold all seven Paladini in equal reverence,' he said, taking them into the barracks. Its walls were lined with hauberks, helms, shields, swords and other weapons and pieces of armour. 'But Brother Sir Hugo does hold a special place in my heart, 'tis true!'

'He was also nephew to Sir Lancelyn of the Pale Mountain,' Horskram pointed out. 'St Hugo came from a high house and an honourable. The Bethler Order drew its first adherents from among the finest of Pangonia's surviving chivalry, after the Battle of Avalongne brought the reign of Vasirius low. If one must venerate killers, I can think of worse ones, I suppose.'

Balian decided to ignore the last remark, pointed as it was. 'You certainly know your history, but then I'd expect nothing less from an Argolian!' A lay serjeant stepped over to help him with his armour. The barracks were filling up with other men doing the same. The persisting silence felt odd to Adelko; the warriors he knew were a boisterous lot on the whole.

'Why didn't you join our brotherhood?' asked Balian as he put his gambeson on. 'You were accounted as valiant a knight as any in your day, and your piety speaks for itself. We could have used a man like you.'

'The Unseen guided me elsewhere,' replied Horskram laconically, though Adelko didn't need his sixth sense to see the subject pained him.

'Fair enough,' said Balian as the serjeant slipped a mail shirt over him. 'But you seem to have a healthy respect for our Order.'

'I did not say that,' replied Horskram bluntly. 'I admire your founders for their personal virtues, but have learned to question the validity of war waged in Palom's name.'

Balian's face darkened as the serjeant laced up the byrnie. *Now whose thoughts are unfettered,* thought Adelko wryly.

The Bethler's manner stiffened somewhat. 'All right, give me a few minutes to finish with my harness,' he muttered as the serjeant reached for a white surcoat of plates to go over his mail. 'Then I'll show you what those heathen Sassanians can expect to get from us this summer! Rest assured, wars can be holy, master monk. The Pilgrim Kingdoms are a light, in a dark vale of iniquity, and by our blood and toil do we defend them.'

'Perhaps,' was all Horskram said to that. 'Adelko, come along! We'll await the commander without as he wishes.'

Adelko flicked an apologetic look Balian's way before

following his mentor back outside. But he kept his feelings to himself. The last thing he wanted now was to provoke another sermon on befriending warrior types. It was fairly clear Horskram's old injunction applied to warrior-monks, too.

Adelko absently watched the knights drilling under a hardening sun. The Bethlers were said to be the deadliest swordsmen throughout Urovia and Sassania; he had seen little yet to cast doubt on the veracity of such claims. The lay serjeants were also practising in earnest, wielding sword and mace to devastating effect.

'This is but a rump of the Order, stationed here to oversee their holdings in the heart of the Blessed Realm,' commented Horskram. 'Expect to see ten times these numbers marshalled on the borders of the Pilgrim Kingdoms by high summer. The Bethlers intend to spearhead the first attack against the Nazharyans, though by then they may well be mounting a defence instead.'

Adelko raised an eyebrow, trying to ignore the sweltering heat. It wasn't even noon, and already he was sweating. He cursed his woollen journeyman's habit, so recently a prized acquisition.

'What do you mean by that, Master Horskram?'

'More news has come out of the south,' said the adept. 'Muqmurlish tek Nazar has succeeded in uniting the southern desert tribes. The Sultan can now add a highly motivated horde of *sarakim* to his growing war tally. Not in a hundred years has the sultanate of Nazharya been so strongly ruled. This new crusade will be met with stiff resistance.'

Adelko felt his agitated thoughts swirling with renewed vigour. 'I suppose that means our journey won't be any the easier,' he sighed.

'No indeed,' said Horskram, 'which is why I must persuade-' He was interrupted by Sir Balian approaching them. He had just been overseeing a cluster of serjeants, and carried his greatsword casually over one shoulder. He'd sparred earlier himself, but barely seemed to have worked up a sweat despite the heat.

'I've an idea,' he said, drawing level with the monks. 'After this, I'm due to take some of the laymen on patrol. Why don't you come with us? Give you a chance to see how the Bethlers discharge their other duties. We aren't all about slaughtering heathens and lending money, you know – we keep the peace in Ushalayim, too.'

Horskram looked as if he was about to demur, but Balian cut him off. 'Oh, don't worry – my shift only runs till an hour after sun's zenith. I'll see you back in time to have your audience with Tobin.'

Horskram still looked reluctant. Balian leaned in and winked conspiratorially. 'His Eminence takes a great interest in those who show an interest in our Order.'

The adept pursed his lips and mulled the warrior-monk's words. 'All right,' he said. 'But you'd best put in a good word for us!'

Balian grinned and clapped him on the shoulder. 'Never fear, Brother Horskram,' he said. 'Logos is already doing that for you! For a godly man is a fortunate man, as the Redeemer sayeth.'

Horskram rolled his eyes as Balian strode off to bark some final orders at the serjeants. Adelko held his peace again. Right now, getting out of the fortress monastery and exploring the city it guarded sounded like an excellent idea.

The Bethlers were nothing if not disciplined. Within half an hour Adelko and Horskram found themselves riding next to Balian through winding streets between sun-drenched adobe tenement buildings. The area he had chosen to patrol was less prosperous, and put Adelko in mind of the bustling Mercadian Quarter. Once again the journeyman let awnings, bricks and flesh of differing hues swallow him up. The heat rose steadily, dust clogging his nostrils and clinging stubbornly to the back of his throat, making him hack and splutter like a greybeard. Half a dozen serjeants flanked them on foot, affecting a nonchalant stroll in loose formation, but Adelko's sixth sense told him the men were tense and alert.

'We recruit them from respectable burgess families,' Balian explained. 'Descendants of commoners who forsook the plough long ago to fight in the First Pilgrim War. They were rewarded for their valour and piety with plots of land and good lodgings in the Blessed Realm. So you see, the crusades are good for the common folk too.'

'As long as they don't happen to be Sassanian,' Adelko dared to point out.

'Actually, you'd be surprised,' said Balian. 'It's true that heathens are... discouraged from living in certain parts of the city, but by and large we don't tax or tithe them any worse than the satraps who ruled before us. In some parts of the Pilgrim Kingdoms, they even fare better under our rule!'

'And in others a lot worse,' put in Horskram. 'I hear the Sha'abatian subjects of Keraka are oppressed as cruelly as ever.'

Balian wore a troubled mien now. 'Aye 'tis true, the House of Agramonde can be somewhat over-zealous in its persecution of the infidels,' he allowed.

'And that, I believe, is the ruling family from which your own Grand Master hails,' said Horskram.

'It has ever been tradition among the scions of Agramonde to send their younger sons into the Bethel,' was all Balian said to that.

'What about you?' broke in Adelko, trying to lighten the tone. 'Where do you come from?'

Balian brightened up visibly. 'I was born and raised here,' he beamed. 'A true subject of Our Holy Kingdom! My uncle is the Ruling Prince of the House of Jeandarme – perhaps you have heard of us? We own the finest vineyards in Ushalayim.'

'You also control a healthy share of the kingdom's coastal trade,' said Horskram. 'That's quite a life of leisure you've forsaken, Brother Sir Balian.'

The Bethler looked genuinely shocked at that remark. 'Brother Horskram,' he replied testily, 'I may indulge in levity, but I can assure you my loyalty to the King of Heaven is as stalwart as yours. Leisure does not interest me.'

Horskram was about to reply when they were distracted by a commotion. Three of the serjeants were already moving through a crowded bazaar towards the noise, roughly elbowing natives aside and brandishing short spears and swords. The parting servants and traders revealed two more Sassanians, dressed in ragged homespun clothes, grappling on the ground. A glint of metal indicated at least one was armed.

The crowd were congealing about the intervening serjeants again. Adelko craned his neck as he tried to peer over them from the saddle. Sir Balian drew his sword just as the journeyman's sixth sense flared.

'This doesn't feel right,' muttered the knight.

'On that I think we can all agree,' said Horskram, unslinging his quarterstaff.

It happened quite suddenly. The crowd parted just as a scream pierced the heavy air. The two brawlers had risen to their feet. One of them held a bloodstained knife. A serjeant was staggering back, clutching at his bleeding groin where a treacherous blow had caught him below the byrnie. His two companions moved to engage the footpads, now both armed.

'They were never fighting each other,' cried Balian. 'This is a tr-'

A shrill cry tore another rent through the crowd's panicky hubbub. The words were spoken in thickly accented Panglian.

'Death to all *jhufa'ar*! The One-Eyed Sultan is coming! Death to all *jhufa'ar*!'

Adelko recognised the Sassanic word for 'infidel' as a

group of swart men about a dozen strong surged towards the rest of the serjeants from the other side of the bazaar. These were dressed in ragged clothes and carried knives like their comrades, but wore crude wooden masks with a lurid red eye daubed on them. Another serjeant went down, his neck spurting crimson.

Cursing in a manner that suited a warrior more than a monk, Balian spurred his charger towards the masked attackers, scattering Sassanian and Urovian alike. Adelko drew his quarterstaff but hesitated, unsure of what to do next.

Horskram clearly had ideas of his own.

'Let's dismount and help them,' he said, a cunning glint entering his eye. 'That way Tobin is more likely to do the same for us!'

Another fine plan, thought Adelko as he swiftly dismounted on legs that had become pleasingly strong and agile. *At least I'll get a chance to practise everything Edemus taught me.*

People were milling about pell-mell now. The partisans had chosen their war-cry well – everyone within earshot, Sassanian and Urovian, would understand their intentions. Adelko jostled past a frantic porter, knocking a basket of fruit from his head as he engaged a partisan.

There was a feral look of hatred in the eyes behind the mask as the partisan lunged at him... in the blinking of an eye Adelko pivoted on one leg, bringing his staff around in a swooshing motion that knocked the man's legs out from under him. He almost sensed where the attacks were coming from in advance: turning and ducking a blow from another partisan who had come up behind him, he brought himself up in a U-shape as Edemus had taught him, pitching himself to his assailant's left. A split second later, the young monk's quarterstaff found the partisan's temple.

Pull a head blow, Edemus had always taught him. *By all means knock a man unconscious in self-defence, but kill him and you'll have one foot in Purgatory.*

Adelko hoped he'd mastered that part of his combat tutor's lessons, as the Sassanian fell to the ground like a sack of oatmeal. The other partisan had managed to scramble to his feet after slipping on spilled fruit; Adelko went to incapacitate him before he could rearm, but a couple of shrieking servant women barged past him... The partisan took advantage of the distraction to dart off down a nearby alleyway.

And then, just as suddenly as it had begun, the fight was over. Several more partisans lay dead or dying in the street, their bleeding forms revealed by the rapidly thinning crowd. Another couple of serjeants had been injured but remained standing. Balian dismounted, not bothering to clean his bloodied sword before sheathing it.

Horskram stepped back from a partisan whose fingers he had just shattered, as Balian strode over and yanked the groaning man to his feet.

'You'll speak and tell us who sent you,' he snarled in Sassanic, wrenching the mask off the man's face.

No, not a man – a boy. Adelko's jaw dropped. The frightened youth that stared at them was younger than he was.

'But I know you,' Balian hissed. 'You are Umqar, the

weaver's son. By all the archangels lad, who put you up to this?'

The boy named Umqar managed a look of defiance, though he was plainly terrified.

'The One-Eyed Sultan foretold in scripture is coming,' he stammered in a reedy voice. 'We but do Ashanti's bidding.'

Balian's face darkened. 'Umqar tek Umqar,' he declaimed, flinging the boy back to the ground. 'You have been found guilty of high treason and sacrilege, for striking against lawful agents of the Crown and Temple. The sentence is death.' Nodding at two uninjured serjeants, who came and held the boy face down in the dirt, he stepped back and unsheathed his greatsword again.

'But he's so young,' blurted Adelko. 'Sassanian or not, you can't just execute him!' But he had seen enough of conflict to know the lie even as he spoke it.

'Stay your hand,' said Horskram as Balian raised the greatsword. 'At least keep him alive for further interrogation – he may know more about this insurrection.'

The youth was weeping and trembling now, not daring to look up at his executioner. Adelko could see the troubled look in the Bethler's eyes. He could sense his anguish too, feel it pouring off his psyche in painful waves; Balian had been on friendly terms with the lad and his family. He stood poised to deliver the death stroke, sweat beading on his tanned forehead. The two serjeants looked at him askance.

'Reus dammit!' the knight cried, putting up his blade. 'All right, take him and bind him. We'll have him back for questioning, see if we can't learn any more.'

The two serjeants exchanged brief glances before hauling Umqar to his feet and binding him with manacles. They were well disciplined indeed, obeying orders without question.

Balian stalked over to where the rest of his men were crowding around their fallen comrade. They shook their heads grimly and scowled. The soldier had bled out.

'Reus dammit!' snarled Balian again. 'That's two good men I've lost, and two more that need chirurgery. These infidel scum have grown bold – news of Muqmurlish's muster has given courage to their faint heathen hearts.'

So much for keeping the peace, thought Adelko wryly. But he found little joy in his humour.

'And don't think you've spared that misguided wretch anything,' he snapped at Horskram. 'A trip to the torturer followed by impaling at dawn is all you've earned him. My way would have been quicker and cleaner.'

Horskram sighed wearily. 'In the heat of the moment, I'd forgotten your Grand Master's reputation for cruelty to Sassanians,' he said glumly. 'At least it won't be you that has to do it... I gather you were somewhat friendly with the lad.'

'Palom's wounds!' cried Balian. 'We try to dispense even-handed justice to Sha'abatian and Palomedian alike, and this is the thanks we get for it.' He looked deeply embittered now.

'Even-handed justice under Pangonian law,' Horskram reminded him. 'Urovians here will always be resented as an occupying power, no matter how justly you treat or lightly you tax your Sassanian subjects.'

Balian scowled. 'Enough of this prating cant – we've to

return to headquarters immediately. Grand Master Tobin will want to hear of this right away.' All his good humour seemed to have vanished.

'What was that they kept saying?' Adelko queried as they remounted. 'About the 'one-eyed sultan'?'

'It's an old prophecy from scripture,' supplied Horskram. 'We have it in our *Holy Book* too – something about a one-eyed general who fights a great war to end all wars. It's been invoked by priests and farseers down through the ages – warriors are more likely than most to lose an eye, so there's rarely a shortage of candidates.'

'And let me guess,' said Adelko, as they began their journey back to headquarters, 'the Sultan of Nazharya lost an eye in battle.'

'The very battle that brought his coup to a successful conclusion two years ago,' finished Horskram.

Tobin stood stock still upon the ramparts overlooking the city as Balian gave his report. His face did not betray a flicker of emotion.

'I trust the men are being treated for their injuries, their comrades buried in the cemetery,' he said coldly when Balian was done. 'Notify their families and have the almoner give them their due. As for that heathen dog, instruct the gaolers to keep him behind bars for now. I want to preside over his torture personally, for the satisfaction it brings me to do the Redeemer's work.'

'The Redeemer condemned torture, even in times of

war,' Horskram reminded him. Adelko could sense his rising rage like an iron being heated over a fire.

Tobin turned to stare flatly at the monk. 'He also said 'the flail must not be spared 'gainst the devils of iniquity'. Yon tawny rug-rat is clearly doing the Fallen One's work, and shall receive just punishment.'

'Palom was speaking in metaphor, Your Eminence,' Horskram protested. 'He meant that we must not cease from spiritual fight against-'

Tobin raised a calloused hand in that peremptory way Adelko had already learned to despise. 'I shall be the judge of how scripture is interpreted, here in the holy city Reus has ordained me to protect. Now, you I believe have a petition that needs answering. This I shall do, as promised. Brother Sir Balian, you are dismissed. Go and see to my orders.'

The commander nodded and hastened down the stairs to the courtyard below.

'I have prayed to the Seven Seraphim for guidance on the matter of your mission,' said Tobin, clasping his arms behind his back as he resumed staring at the minarets and domes of Ushalayim.

'... and?' asked Horskram presently. The warrior-monk's desultory pauses were almost as maddening as his sententious bigotry.

'And I find your cause wanting.' The Grand Master turned his piercing scrutiny on Horskram, and Adelko could sense an awful battle of wills taking place between them. The journeyman clenched his fists nervously at his sides as Tobin went on. 'As you can see, my hands are full keeping these Sha'abatian devilspawn in check – would that I could do here as my kinfolk have done in Keraka! But nay, the King in Ushalayim is a gracious but misguided man, and insists on a false doctrine of tolerance. And that is to say nothing of the pending crusade, which as I'm sure you'll appreciate far outranks your mission in Reus' eyes.'

Horskram managed the thinnest of smiles. 'But of course, Your Eminence,' he said in a brittle voice.

'However, I do have the utmost respect for your leader, Hannequin, and as such here is what I am prepared to do. On the other side of the Utna'aruf ranges, just beyond the southern borders of our kingdom, lies the trading outpost of Sha'iza'ar. Doubtless you will recall it from your travails here, when you took the Wheel in your youth?'

'I recall it well from my 'travails' here,' replied Horskram. Adelko could feel his mentor's rage practically smoking now.

'Good,' said Tobin. 'It is still a place of caravanserai and traders, as such you should be able to commission *taziqs* to protect you. Tomorrow morning, at first light, I shall send two knights to escort you there. And for the sake of your esteemed Grand Master, my Order shall match whatever coin he has furnished you for your enterprise. That should enable you to hire a decent number of swords.'

'Sassanian freeswords?' said Horskram. 'That is what you offer us? And how do I know they won't turn us in to the nearest satrap once we're a few leagues deep into Nazharyan territory?'

'You don't,' replied the Grand Master bluntly. 'That is precisely why the Order doesn't employ *taziqs* – that and the foulness of the very idea of using heathen mercenaries to fight Palom's war.' He made the sign of the Creed in militaristic fashion again, before turning back to stare out across the battlements.

Horskram was about to say something but the Grand Master cut him off. 'Your audience is at an end. I suggest you spend the rest of the day fasting before sunset prayers.'

Tobin spoke no further word but remained where he was, gazing across the city, hands clasped behind his back. A statue might have shown more emotion.

'A black day this is for our Order,' said Balian, taking another slurp of rye beer.

'A black day for us all,' muttered Horskram, following suit.

Adelko frowned into his own stoup. At least there was some pleasure to be had breaking with Tobin's parting suggestion – drinking seemed preferable to praying right now. Not the most pious of notions, but Balian himself had suggested a flagon or two to take the sting out of the day. He gazed around the capacious scullery, where serving lads scurried to and fro preparing the evening meal. It reminded him of the monastery at Rima, and Ulfang, so many moons ago.

'I am sorry your suit here has waned,' said the warrior-monk. 'I shall escort you to Sha'iza'ar tomorrow myself.'

'I shouldn't worry,' sighed Horskram. 'Doubtless your Grand Master will not see fit to spare a commander on the likes of us. We may not agree on everything, Brother Sir Balian, but you are an honourable man. Attend to your duties as your conscience dictates.'

Balian frowned as he refilled their flagons from a pewter jug on the table. Adelko could sense he was still deeply troubled.

'I don't think Brother Sir Balian wants to attend to his duties just now,' he faltered. As a journeyman, he should be free to speak his mind more often – whatever Horskram had to say about it.

Balian eyed him keenly over the rim of his stoup. 'You are indeed shrewd for one of such young years,' he said. 'And you're right – I've no wish to preside over Umqar's... interrogation.

Or his execution, Adelko thought grimly.

'All right,' said Horskram. 'I can't say I blame you for that. Accompany us tomorrow if you will then. But tell me, is there no chance of saving the Sassanian youth?'

Balian shook his head sadly. 'Grand Master Tobin will not hear of it. His Eminence means well, though like most Kerakans he can be overly zealous at times.'

Overly cruel and fanatical, more like. But this time Adelko kept his thoughts to himself.

Inside the dank dungeon it was stiflingly hot. The boy Umqar screamed and squirmed against his manacles as the torturer took off a third toe. As he threw the severed digit into the fire, Grand Master Tobin looked on with hard eyes devoid of emotion. In his flat voice he gave the torturer his next order. The beefy bearded Urovian put down the pincers and took up a strange-looking implement. Fashioned of iron, it looked as though it might have been made to crack a nut. Umqar screamed even more loudly as the sweating torturer tore off his loincloth, before fastening the contraption about him...

Adelko sat bolt upright on the divan. He was bathed in sweat. Not the cold sweat of demonfear, but the hot perspiration that comes with knowing that human evil is being done under one's roof.

Moonlight was streaming in through the archways leading onto the verandah, barely obfuscated by transparent silk curtains. Horskram was snoring softly on the divan next to him.

The journeyman was too long in the tooth by now to deceive himself. That had been no nightmare.

How much more suffering do I have to witness, in person or in visions? he asked himself futilely as he put his bare feet on the tiled floor. Umqar hadn't been blameless, but he didn't deserve this. And why should the Pangonians hold Ushalayim anyway? So far he'd seen little of Palom's work being done in this holiest of cities. Adelko glanced at his mentor again. He felt another sudden rush of emotion, the ones he was getting more often nowadays. How did Horskram sleep the sleep of the innocent like that? It angered him.

And that was when he made up his mind to act. The impulsiveness that had been growing in him of late took a firm hold. He would not stand by and do nothing.

Let Horskram make his own decisions; I'm going to bloody well follow my conscience.

Getting up, Adelko scrabbled around for his quarterstaff and boots. Balian seemed a decent enough man at heart, surely he could be persuaded to do the right thing? They would go to the dungeons together, put a stop to this madness once and for all. Reus Himself had just gifted him with a vision, and that meant –

His sixth sense flared not a moment too soon. Bringing up his staff in a movement that was virtually automatic, Adelko registered a screeching whine as a metal object careened off its iron-shod shaft and buried itself in the wall. A second one ripped through the curtain; Adelko brought his quarterstaff back across his chest, sending it hurtling into the ivoried partition screen. Horskram, ever a light sleeper, stirred and awoke just as four shadowy figures burst through the torn curtains. They were clad from head to toe in black, and each wore a bandolier of throwing spikes. Long curved knives glinted in the moonlight as the assassins raised them and fanned out, penning in the two monks. Horskram gasped and grabbed up his quarterstaff just as they lunged.

Their movements were swift and deadly. Were it not for Edemus, Adelko would have been dead inside the minute. As it was, he barely managed to fend off his two assailants, struggling to get in a riposte. His blow glanced off the assassin's forearm with a muffled ring as he parried Adelko's attack deftly.

Concealed vambraces – a neat trick.

The assassins came at him low and high at once, orchestrating their movements perfectly, and Adelko had to rely on his heightened sixth sense just to keep up and preserve his life. He shot a glance Horskram's way. The adept was hard pressed too; he was getting in more attacks of his own, but the assassins skilfully parried with their iron sleeves.

'Why doesn't somebody help us?' cried Adelko, dodging another silvery arc as an assassin slashed at his midriff.

'We're stuck in the guest wing away from the barracks,' Horskram yelled back. 'No one can hear us!'

The next strike was close enough that Adelko felt the blade whistle past his cheek. At that moment his sixth sense flared again. Something about that knife...

'They're using poisoned weapons!' he cried as the realisation dawned on him.

'Of course they are!' snarled Horskram. 'They're assassins, not chivalrous knights!' This time the adept managed a disengage counter-attack that caught an assassin in the ribs. He grunted and did a backflip somersault, landing a few yards away. Horskram took advantage of this to press his other foeman, but the assassin repeated the same manoeuvre as his comrade. In the blinking of an eye, the two killers hurled throwing spikes at Horskram, which he barely managed to parry in quick succession. One struck a torch stanchion, another shrieked off into the night as Horskram sent it flying across the verandah. Without pause the assassins renewed the attack again at close range, Horskram's advantage nullified.

Adelko was only peripherally aware of this as he struggled to hedge his way around his attackers. They anticipated and kept him tightly pinned against the divan. The fight raged on. Adelko fought valiantly, but not even with Edemus' training could he hope to best two such deadly opponents at once.

Not for the first time, he saw his young life flash before his eyes...

The door to their chamber burst open and in rushed Balian. Lightly armoured and clutching only a dagger, he raced towards the fray. One of the assassins menacing Adelko turned to face him, flicking another spike lightning-fast. It glanced off his byrnie and the knight tore into his opponent.

Adelko forced himself to focus on the remaining assassin. He felt confident he could best him in a one-on-one fight. They circled each other warily, both looking for an opening... Adelko felt something jolt his psyche. Surely not – his antagonist was trying to *neutralise* his sixth sense. How was that even possible?

The journeyman rapidly cleared his mind as the assassin lunged again. This time their exchange felt different – as though the blows resonated on a different plane from the mortal one they fought on. Adelko circled again rapidly, dividing his concentration between fending off the psychic assault and trying for the upper hand in their clash of arms.

A scream behind him told that one combatant had fallen. Adelko did not concern himself with who, as he launched an all-out offensive. He'd never fought like this before, not even when he'd sparred with Arik, and felt his battle choler almost rob him of self-possession. This time there was more control in the fury somehow. Adelko almost fancied he had absorbed the assassin's mystic assault and turned it against him.

Perhaps he had. The assassin's eyes widened behind his mask as Adelko pressed him back with a rapid flurry of blows; his last strike caught the man's dagger hand, sending the weapon skittering out of reach. The assassin back-flipped towards the verandah, exiting through an archway with the speed of a panther.

Balian and Horskram were engaging the two remaining assassins. Seeing the tide turning, they somersaulted back towards the verandah too. As the last one came up, he hurled what looked like a handful of orange powder to the floor. An explosion of light momentarily blinded them. When their eyes cleared, the three assassins were gone from the chamber.

Adelko lurched towards the fourth, who was lying on the ground with blood pouring from his side where Balian had stabbed him. A strange choking sound came from behind his mask. Tearing this off, Adelko cried out in horror as a torrent of blood poured from the swart man's mouth, along with a thick piece of flesh. With revulsion, he realised the assassin had bitten off his own tongue.

Following Horskram and Balian out onto the verandah, Adelko saw a thin cord of waxed wire attached to what looked like a miniature grapnel buried in the terrace balustrade. This stretched across the gap between the guest wing and perimeter wall: the three assassins were dancing along this with a speed and agility that could only be described as breathtaking. Soldiers on the battlements were racing towards the point where the cord met the walkway, Balian having raised the hue and cry.

But they were too late: reaching the other side, the black-clad men pitched themselves over the side of the wall, and were gone into the night.

'Shadowmen,' breathed Balian. 'Sent to kill you in your sleep, by the looks of things. You've made some powerful enemies, Brother Horskram.'

'Tell us something we don't know,' replied the adept sardonically.

'Shadowmen?' Adelko queried. 'I certainly don't know what *they* are.'

'Adept devotees of the Order of the Silver Shadow,' said Horskram. 'Unorthodox adherents of the Faith, who serve the Old Master of Time's Arrow. Usually they target Orthodox priests and satraps – they've even been known to make common cause with crusaders from time to time. Another puzzle for us to solve.' Turning to Balian, he added: 'We owe our lives to your timely intervention.'

'Ordinarily, I would have been asleep in the barracks,' said Balian, and a look of sorrow crossed his face. 'But Grand Master Tobin insisted I was present at the interrogation. I left the dungeons to... to get some air. I saw something metallic flying out of your window, so I came to investigate. At least some good has come of this frightful business with Umqar.'

I doubt he'll see it that way, thought Adelko sadly. But the poor wretch's fate had saved them in more than one way: Adelko felt sure he would not have awoken if not for the frightful vision bequeathed him by the Unseen.

Presently Tobin arrived at their room, a party of serjeants in tow. A search had been ordered of the streets outside the fortress, but of their would-be assassins there was no sign.

Tobin's face was half lost in the shadows cast by an oil lamp Balian had lit. He listened wordlessly as the commander gave an account of the night's unexpected events.

'I am deeply sorry,' he said after Balian was done. His tone gave little indication that he was.

'Indeed, a breach of Bethel security is most unfortunate,' said Horskram diplomatically. 'However, it is obvious that we were the intended targets. As such, I think the sooner we are on our way-'

'That is not what I meant,' said the Grand Master, turning his cold eyes on Horskram. 'What I meant is that I am sorry I did not see it sooner.'

The adept frowned. Adelko could sense his consternation. 'There really is no point in crying over blood already spilled,' said Horskram. 'Doubtless you will wish to increase security after we leave, but right now-'

'Still you do not grasp my meaning,' said Tobin. 'Or rather, you grasp it all too well, and think to continue your dastardly dissimulation. But a true servant of Palom's will is not so easily deceived!'

Horskram gaped. 'What in the Known World are you talking about, Tobin?' he demanded, dropping all pretence of protocol.

'You arrive here from across the sea, bearing letter of introduction written in weasel words. You declare yourselves true servants of Reus, yet seek audience with a thrice-cursed demonologist. You try to inveigle me into sending good knights with you, on the eve of the most important war they will ever fight. And now, you bring upon this holy house heathen Shadowmen, who never dared cross Bethler soil till now.' He pointed implacably at Horskram. 'Horskram of Vilno, I name thee accessory to the Fallen One. Guards! Seize the monks – bind them in links of cold iron, and take them to the dungeons.'

Without a second's pause the lay serjeants closed around the two friars, swords in hand and fell looks in their eyes.

'Your Eminence,' spluttered Balian, 'you must surely be in error. These Argolians are good men-'

'SILENCE!' boomed Tobin. 'You've already shown the weakness of your stomach once tonight – don't force me to strip you of your tabard.'

Balian's eyes sank to the carpeted floor. 'Apologies, Grand Master,' he mumbled.

'What mummer's foolery is this?' demanded Horskram. 'Have you lost your wits, Tobin?'

'That is *Grand Master* Tobin to you, traitor,' said Tobin. 'And I'll not bandy words with men who ally themselves to Abaddon's cause. Guards, disarm the apostates and bind them! Kill them if they dare resist.'

Adelko struggled to calm his rattling heart. 'Horskram, there's but half a dozen of them,' he began, but the adept cut him off. 'Nay, Adelko, the whole bloody fortress is on high alert now – we'd never get out! We've no choice but to see how this madness plays out.' Reluctantly, he proffered his quarterstaff to a serjeant. With heavy heart, Adelko did likewise.

'You won't get away with this,' said Horskram as the soldiers bound them in manacles. 'I have powerful friends, too.'

The Grand Master's voice did not waver as he replied: 'Oh, I don't think your powerful friends will be coming to your aid, not here in the heart of hallowed sanctuary.'

'You have no idea what your fanaticism will cost mortalkind,' said Horskram as the soldiers bustled them out of the room. The adept sounded almost desperate now. 'The whole world shall suffer if you do not let us go unmolested.'

'The world suffers precisely because of varlets such as thou,' replied the Grand Master with the same old certitude. 'It falls to loyal servants of the Almighty to root you out and expunge you from this earth.'

'But we've done nothing wrong!' cried Adelko. 'You've no evidence!'

'On the contrary, I have the evidence that my faith in the Unseen places before me,' retorted Tobin, with warped logic. 'I shall pray to Palom for guidance on how best to dispose of you. The stake, the spike, or the sword? 'Tis a conundrum devoutly to be pondered.'

The Grand Master loomed large on the landing as the soldiers forced them down the stairs. Silhouetted against the torchlight, he looked more like the Angel of Death than a holy warrior.

But even Azrael would have been appalled at such malice.

CHAPTER 15
OF CARDS AND CONUNDRUMS

The last remaining merchant threw his cards down on the low table in disgust. Hettie did her best to conceal a smirk. That was thrice in a row she'd beaten the four Mercadians. Daintily pulling the gleaming pile of coins across the table towards her, she did a mental count. The Mercadians had only just arrived in Ushalayim and were playing with the cruzados of their native country – larger than most gold pieces, each one would fetch a good thirty silvers.

These fools do so love to play for high stakes, she thought triumphantly. *But they can't accept a woman plays better than they do – I hope those Mercadian trading privileges still hold good, for their sakes.*

One of the merchants, a stocky fellow wearing a fustian outfit that Hettie thought too showy for one of his class, had other ideas about how to recoup sunk costs.

'I think this is not possible,' he said in thickly accented Panglian, his black eyes turning venomous as he laid a hand none too subtly on the hilt of his dagger. 'To win so many times. I think the lady cheats.'

'And I think,' said Anupe, stepping up behind him and resting a hand on his shoulder, 'that you should not be making... false accusations, yes?' Her other hand on was on the hilt of her dirk, her hood pulled over her head tightly to give her a sinister look.

Luckily for him, the merchant wasn't a stupid man. 'Pray accept my apologies,' he said hastily as he rose to his feet. 'I think I will seek entertainment elsewhere.'

The other Mercadians plainly thought this a good idea too, and left hurriedly with their fellow.

Hettie grinned as Anupe took the merchant's seat.

'As always, you've done your part admirably,' she told the Harijan. 'You'll get your cut of my winnings, as agreed – just as soon I've taken this latest haul to the moneychangers.'

Anupe made a casual gesture of acknowledgement. 'In good time,' she said. 'Right now, you can get us a pitcher of wine – so long since I was in proper heat, and guarding you is thirsty work!'

Hettie roved the busy yard with her eyes, looking for a serving wench and humming cheerfully to herself. The place was always bustling with guests, who took advantage of the air circulating through cunningly wrought vents in the walls, and the ornamental trees that provided some respite from the sun. Her time in the *Hallowed Sojourn* had been a contented one so far, as Hettie rested and ate the stinking ship's hold and its wormy biscuit out of memory. She was still short of the tidy sum the watch had fleeced from her in Panya, but a large hostelry that catered to affluent guests promised plenty more gulls.

It catered to its fair share of poorer ones, too. Hettie had kept a healthy distance from the shabby pilgrims staying in the common room that adjoined the yard. For the most part, they seemed content to cleave to one another's company, singing holy songs in loud voices that irritated the less pious guests (including her) no end.

'So where is your mistress?' asked Anupe, after Hettie had collared a serving wench and given her their order.

'I wish you wouldn't keep calling her that,' she snapped. 'As far as I'm concerned, my terms of service expired the minute we left Urovia.'

She felt sure the Harijan was smiling underneath her hood. 'It sounds as though your terms of friendship expired, too.'

'Oh, give your foreign mouth a rest,' said Hettie, angrily sweeping away her coin and cards. She found herself thinking of Vaskrian, as she tended to when she was at her most irate. Recollection of his hot kisses and lusty embraces had Hettie's mind going to places she really didn't want to visit. Of course, the feckless squire would be off doing whatever the hell he liked – but then that's how it was for men. Really, a woman's life was intolerable: she could agree with Anupe on that much at least.

'Why don't you take me with you?' she asked suddenly. 'When you go back to your Harijan Isles. You're always going on about how wonderful it is for women there.'

'I did not say wonderful,' corrected Anupe, raising a

finger. 'Merely that women do not suffer men and their delusions. That does not mean that we do not suffer.'

Hettie pondered that as the Harijan added: 'In any case, you would not be welcome there. And, sadly, neither would I.'

Hettie was about to press her on this when the sound of a flute drifted across the leafy yard. The sun was descending towards its nocturnal destination; the soft notes trilled mellifluously through the cooling air, seemingly borne on distending beams of coppery light.

'That's the second evening running I've heard that sound,' muttered Hettie.

'Perhaps your mistress – sorry, your companion – has taken up the flute.'

'I doubt it,' said Hettie. 'She sings and plays worse than she dances.' Where Adhelina was these days was her business. The pair of them had scarcely spoken since arriving in Ushalayim, pointedly getting separate rooms, with one for Anupe in between them. The hostel keeper Amalric had said little to them, but clearly respected his old friend Horskram enough to give them accommodation on the upper level without question.

Looking around the gaggle of patrons for the source of the sound, Hettie found it: a wizened-looking elder with the tawny complexion of a Sassanian, wearing a homespun robe of bleached cotton. His white hair was cropped in a tonsure that tapered inwards to form a bizarre-looking topknot. Even with his lips placed to the flute, it was possible to see he had gentle features. Long, dextrous fingers glided across its wooden form as he played effortlessly.

Around his neck he wore a simple wooden amulet carved to resemble a coiled serpent. His feet were bare and leathern-soled, from many years of travelling unshod.

'That is a mystic of the Sufieli Sect,' said Anupe. 'We have heard of them even in my land, for they travel the Sha'abatian realms widely. He plays the *Song of Ashanti's Calling* – it is time for sunset prayers here in the Sassanian world.'

'A wonder he's tolerated in a place like this,' observed Hettie. Though she couldn't deny the mystic's tune was more pleasant to the ear than the raucous pilgrims. Thankfully most of those were away in the Temple Quarter, observing their own religious rites. Hettie had little time for faith of any kind, though she could not deny the old man's playing soothed her soul. Out of the corner of her eye, she noticed Adhelina had descended the sandalwood stairs from the upper storey, and now stood looking at the mystic as though entranced.

If he keeps her quiet a bit longer that will do nicely. But she felt the ignobleness of the thought immediately; it was almost as though profane rivalries were unworthy of such a sacred presence. Without knowing exactly why, Hettie got up and went to stand next to Adhelina. Several pilgrims returning from the Holy Sepulchre had stopped to listen too, and even one or two merchants now joined the growing crowd.

Presently the old man stopped. This close Hettie could see he had a closely cropped beard too; its white stubble seemed to catch the dying light and hold it. His old brown face was crinkled with age, but looked peaceful not weary. With a soft smile, he tucked the flute away in his homespun.

The merchants and pilgrims were wandering off, as though recovering from an enchantment. 'Wonder they let 'is sort in 'ere,' commented one of the rougher pilgrims as he left. Hettie supposed even the music of a mystic could only keep gut prejudice at bay for so long.

'You play beautifully,' said Adhelina, addressing him in faltering Sassanic.

The old man smiled more widely, and simply pointed a single thin finger towards the heavens.

'It is not I who makes the music,' he replied in fluent Panglian. 'I am but the conduit.'

'You're a mystic, my bodyguard tells me,' said Hettie. 'What does that entail exactly?' She didn't normally like to pry, but something about this old man made her curious.

The mystic gazed at her impassively. 'The Sect of Suf, whom we call the 'little prophet', is an ancient one. Centuries have passed since the blessed line of Enlightened Sultans failed. Some in our world believe that line never truly died, though that is not for us Sufielis to say. Our work is simply to live and teach the ways of the First Prophet wherever we can, just as Abu'cuchaza'ar Kardin and his heirs did. This was what the savant Suf taught his first disciples, many years past.'

'I see,' said Hettie. All these foreign names were impossible to keep up with; now she regretted asking questions.

As ever, Adhelina was much keener to talk about strange things. 'I've heard of Suf, they say he was one of the most enlightened men of the Faith, not unlike St Argo in our lands,' she said. 'As for Abu'cuchaza'ar, I've read he was the first of the Enlightened Sultans. He founded the ruling house of Kardin when he took on the First Prophet as his vizier. It's said he was the first of his kind to do so... I don't know much else, except that the Almighty rewarded him with great powers for his faith.'

The old mystic nodded approvingly. 'The *jhufa'ar* lady is most well informed. But then the Second Sight is never bestowed on the ignorant.'

Adhelina's jaw dropped. 'How do you...?'

The mystic merely smiled and raised his delicate finger to the heavens again.

'I suppose there had to be a reason why I was drawn to your music,' she said in a low voice. Hettie glanced around nervously, but none of the other patrons were paying them much attention. Anupe was getting stuck into the jug of wine, oblivious to their conversation. Presumably their bodyguard didn't think her duties extended to protecting them from old mystics.

'Ashanti has ordained that our paths intertwine,' the mystic confirmed. 'But right now there is something else you must see to. Something' – he fixed Adhelina with inscrutable eyes of darkest brown – 'that you have foreseen. This was what you were coming downstairs to speak of.'

Adhelina flicked a glance Hettie's way to indicate the old man was right. 'Do business as the Father of All wills it,' he went on, 'and when that is done, we shall meet again. There is something I can help you with, but it is not this.'

So saying, he shut his eyes and appeared to fall into a deep meditation.

'All right,' sighed Hettie, turning to her estranged friend. 'I suppose you've got something to tell us.'

Anupe's black eyebrows made a V shape as she pondered Adhelina's story. With just the pale orange light of oil lamps to see off the balmy evening, she had felt secure enough to pull back her hood a little. Women were seldom admitted to the *Sojourn* – a warrior-woman would be a step too far.

The three of them were huddled around their table, sipping pink Kallandhari wine from painted ceramic cups as they considered what to do.

'Meaning no disrespect to your new gift,' said the Harijan, 'but your vision does not sound so specific. You dream of two monks being broken on a wheel, and a serpent coiling around a tower. This does not tell us much.'

'Night after night since we got here,' insisted Adhelina. 'Oh, I know this gift is unpredictable, Iveline's governess told me as much in Rima, but clearly the sight is trying to warn me – Horskram and Adelko are in danger!'

'But what do we do about it even if that's true?' said Hettie.

Adhelina cursed inwardly. They weren't on good terms, but she had to admit Hettie was as practical as ever. If the friars really were being detained in the Bethler headquarters, a place that suffered no women to enter its doors, getting access to them would be more than difficult.

'We'll just have to settle for sending a messenger,' she sighed. 'I can ask Sir Amalric for some parchment, I'll scribble a note to Horskram and we can get a porter to take it.'

'And you plan to mention in this note that the gods have

given you a special gift?' asked Anupe. 'Why don't we send the mystic with the message? Extra dramatic effect, yes? Perhaps Horskram will take us more seriously then.'

Adhelina cursed again, out loud this time. The freesword's sarcasm wasn't helping, but she had a point. The old monk would never believe them.

'Perhaps if I make mention of some of the visions I've seen...' she stuttered.

'Of things that have either happened already, or haven't happened yet,' said Hettie. 'Yes, I'm sure Master Horskram will readily believe you then.'

'Well, do you have any sage ideas?' she snapped.

'Ladies...' said Anupe, admonishing them as she refilled her cup. 'I think this Sassanian wine is stronger than it tastes, yes? Quiet a minute, please. Let Anupe do some thinking.'

'Message for Lady Helene!'

The serving boy's shrill voice startled them. Rising from her place, Adhelina walked over to the common room entrance, where a slight lad of about twelve summers stood proffering a sealed parchment. She brought it back to the table and they examined it in the lamp light. The red wax bore a wheel-and-crossed-swords motif.

'Bethler seal,' muttered Adhelina. 'It looks as though Horskram may have anticipated us.'

She tore it open and read the contents, chewing her lip fretfully as she did.

'Well?' said Anupe.

'Well,' said Adhelina. 'It looks as though my gift is getting more precise. Horskram and Adelko are being held in the Bethler dungeons, pending execution.'

'WHAT?' Hettie gasped.

'On what charges?' asked Anupe.

Adhelina scanned the letter again. 'This is from one Brother Sir Balian, a commander in the Order. Charges of witchcraft and demonolatry, he says. Doesn't believe them himself, that's why he's sending us the letter. Says he managed to get an audience with the monks in the prison cells, and Horskram told him to contact us.'

'He must really be desperate to ask us for help,' said Anupe dryly.

'No,' mused Adhelina. 'It makes sense. He's just been betrayed by someone he thought he could trust in Usha-layim. Who else would he turn to?'

'But what can we do?' said Hettie.

'The letter says we need to seek an audience with Sir Amalric, privately. He's influential in the city – Horskram seems to think he might know people who can help.'

'He's going to love his female guests even more,' said Hettie. 'Don't be surprised if the room rate goes up.'

Sir Amalric had clearly been a fighting man many years ago, but those years had not been kind. His midriff and chest had traded places, one growing a paunch while the other retreated into itself. His thick arms still hinted at hands that had been taught to make war, though now those hands gripped nothing more offensive than a gnarled old walking staff.

His private suite of chambers overlooked the yard, on the other side of the common room. Silks and tapestries decorated his parlour room, which was festooned with richly embroidered divans and cushions: clearly Horskram's old friend had done well for himself.

Perhaps that was why he looked so crestfallen now. If he got involved with what they were proposing, he stood to lose everything.

'Confound it,' he muttered, looking scarcely appetised by the silver dishes of spiced meats, deep-fried aubergines and seasoned breads he had been enjoying. 'Horskram was always one for getting himself into trouble – I haven't forgotten the time when he charged a platoon of *sarakim* archers single-handed. The rest of the chaps and I had to stop him being turned into an iron pin cushion by their blasted bodkin arrows!'

'I'm sure you could tell us many a tale of Horskram's heroics on crusade,' Adhelina said diplomatically. 'But what is of the essence now is – why would the Grand Master of the Bethlers level such accusations at him?'

'I've no bloody idea,' said Amalric, tugging at his grey beard fretfully. 'All I know is that Grand Master Tobin has a reputation for excessive violence and fanaticism. Before he took up his post here in Ushalayim, it's said he put an entire town to the sword in Keraka for harbouring Sassanian dissidents. The man is clearly operating out of all measure. Some say his promotion has gone to his head and he's even worse now.'

'Well by the sounds of it, our friends are shortly to lose theirs if we don't do something,' put in Anupe.

'Horskram intimated you are influential,' pressed Adhelina. 'Surely you can intervene?'

Amalric looked pained as he shook his head. His eyes found his supper as he said: 'Would that I could! I put my life on the line for Horskram's many a time in our youth, and he did the same for me. But Tobin is as powerful a man as any in the Pilgrim Kingdoms.' At last his eyes found hers. 'Understand, I've a wife and three children to consider – and their children, too! I can't risk crossing the Bethlers.'

'We can't just stand by and do nothing!' protested Adhelina. She was racking her brains for something, one of her clever plans, but out here she felt completely alien. She didn't know anyone. What was the use in having special powers if you couldn't act on them?

'Can't we petition the King in Ushalayim? He's said to be a just man.'

'Rexus is just as invested in the coming crusade as Tobin,' said Amalric, shaking his head. 'He'll not want to cross such a vital ally.'

'So political persuasion is out then,' said Adhelina. 'In that case, there's only one thing for it – we're going to have to organise a rescue mission.'

Amalric's eyes bulged. 'Are you mad? You're talking about a gaol-break! The very idea is treasonous.'

'Yes, I could tell you plenty about betrayal,' said Adhelina bitterly. Amalric looked at her quizzically. She hadn't told him her true identity, and so far he hadn't asked too many questions.

'Nothing,' she said quickly. Then she leaned forward against the desk. 'Sir Amalric, this is your friend and comrade-in-arms. We can't just leave him to be killed out of hand by a ruthless fanatic! And his second hasn't even seen sixteen summers.'

'All right, dammit,' said Amalric, turning from her scorching gaze. 'Let me ponder this a while.' He stared absently at a silken tapestry, covered in abstract floral motifs. 'Wait,' he said presently, tugging at his beard thoughtfully. 'I do know someone who might be able to help.'

'Somebody influential?' asked Adhelina, her hopes rising.

'Yes, but not in the kind of circles you are thinking of. Hari Yassin controls most of the waterfront smuggling in the Mercadian Quarter – if anyone knows how to spring Horskram and his young apprentice, it'll be him.' The old knight reached for his goblet and took a hearty swallow of pink wine. He was clearly nervous.

'I know you risk much by aiding us,' said Adhelina, smiling kindly. 'You are a gracious host and a loyal friend.'

'Spare me the charm, young woman,' said Amalric. 'I'm too old for such flattery. But no, you're right, we can't just stand by and do nothing while Tobin torments our friends on a madcap whim. Yassin knows how to cover his tracks well, so hopefully he'll be able to handle this as discreetly as possible.'

'And you know this Yassin how?' Anupe could not resist asking.

Amalric scowled. 'He controls a lot of pilgrim shipping,

that's the front for his smuggling operation. He steers many pilgrims towards the *Sojourn* and in return I... make certain investments on his behalf.'

'I see,' replied the Harijan. Adhelina felt sure she was smiling under her hood.

'I don't much care what your dealings with him are,' said the damsel. 'I just want to see our friends safe.'

'Reus willing and you will, though this is a dangerous business and no mistake,' said Amalric. He reached into a drawer. 'Give me a few minutes, I'll write a letter of introduction to Yassin. I'll put in a word for you to get you past his henchmen, but after that you're on your own – you'll have to fix up whatever kind of story it takes to persuade him to help you. You take it to his harbourside offices first thing tomorrow morning. One of my boys will show you the way.'

The three of them left the parlour a while later, satisfied if not exactly triumphant. Together they had hastily concocted a cover story to entice Yassin, though Adhelina wasn't sure their pooled ingenuity would be enough to fool one of the Ushalayan underworld's chief operators.

'It is the best we can do given such short space of time,' said Anupe when they'd run through it one last time. 'If you please, I will take one more stoup of wine before bed. If anything else occurs to me, I will let you know.'

Adhelina nodded absently and bade Anupe goodnight. Hettie made a point of descending back into the yard with the Harijan, instead of accompanying Adhelina back to their rooms. Clearly their friendship was badly damaged, but she couldn't worry about that now.

She felt a strong sense of foreboding as she made her

way around the open-air gallery towards her room. From the velvet canopy of the night skies, diamond-hard stars seemed to stare at her broodingly.

What unsettling dreams would the second sight bring her tonight, she wondered.

CHAPTER 16
IN THE MAD KING'S HALL

'**W**ell, well, what am I to do with you?' King Wolfram lolled on the Pine Throne, gazing at his siblings with a single eye glazed by madness. 'I've longed for this moment, but now I have you captive, I'm at a loss as to how to punish you for your base betrayal.'

'We didn't betray you, brother, we sought to protect you,' said Princess Hjala. 'If only you could believe that.'

'And why should His Majesty believe a word that comes out of your mouth?' interjected Lorthar, his refined lips curled in sneer that told of equally refined cruelty. 'After you schemed and machinated against the rightful heir?'

'Scheming? You dare accuse us of that?' Walsa practically spat the words out onto the throneroom floor. 'Look at you, in all your pomp and finery – still a fraud and a popinjay! Be silent before the blood royal. You may have toadied your way into a king's court, but know your betters!'

'You will NOT address my most trusted adviser thus!' boomed Wolfram, growing enraged far too swiftly. 'It is YOU who will be silent, treacherous aunt!' Walsa made a disgusted noise from the back of her throat, but even she knew better than to gainsay him in this wood mood.

Wolfram was dressed in gilded mail and a rich surcoat emblazoned with the double unicorn insignia of House Ingwin, a more martial, spikier crown than her father had worn adorning his brows. This one had a wheel motif embossed on its electrum surface. But it was the bejewelled eye patch that inspired the most contempt in her. Another of Lorthar's ridiculous ideas, no doubt.

Heralding the Half Blind King foretold in his precious scripture, Hjala thought with bitter irony.

'So out with it, brother,' said Thorsvald. 'We are here, returned to Strongholm, and in your power. Tell us our fate and be done with it.' It was the first time during the audience he had spoken. His voice was measured, his face calm though also streaked with tear tracks. Wolfram had kept the trio under palace arrest in their old rooms for a day before summoning them to appear before him.

Their father would have done it discreetly. A private audience, in a more secluded wing of the palace. Not Wolfram. He'd insisted on dragging them all into the throneroom, under heavy guard by chequered-cloaked soldiers of the White Valravyn, with half the court nobility gaping on. He hadn't even sent the craftsmen away – weavers who had been commissioned to depict Freidheim's last great victory on the mighty tapestry running the length of the throneroom wall. They weren't doing much weaving right now.

I hope this pleases you, brother – you always were one for grand spectacles.

'In truth, I haven't yet decided what to do with you,' replied the King, a discordant note of smugness entering his voice.

Father would never have been smug on an occasion like this – never.

'My late adviser Lord Ulnor counselled a fair trial,' he went on, 'but he was old and infirm of mind. Lorthar, as my newly appointed Royal Seneschal, what say you on this matter?'

Some of the court officials looked distinctly uneasy. Hjala knew why – appointing the head of the Temple to secular high office was unheard of. It went against all the customs of the realm that formulated its unwritten constitution.

Oh Wolfram, you're naught but a dancing bear on this man's string – and you don't even realise it.

Lorthar drew himself up pompously as he declaimed: 'Ordinarily, the Almighty injuncts us to be clement when dispensing justice,' he said. 'But given the odious nature of their crimes, I believe your kinfolk should be treated more harshly. Blood royal cannot be spilled – but sequestered they might be, in the Prison Tower, where they can do no more harm.'

Hjala gasped. 'You'd lock us away in the dungeons? Lorthar, even by your standards that is truly despicable. Wolfram, how dare you let a lesser noble speak thus of us!'

'That's KING Wolfram to you, sister!' raged her brother.

'Then in Virtus' name, act like one!' shrieked Hjala. She

felt a tide of desperation threatening to overwhelm her. The watery ghosts of her drowned children flickered before her mind's eye, and she wondered if she wouldn't be joining them presently.

'You have the power to dispense justice, *real* justice,' she said, hoping she didn't sound like she was begging. 'Keep us under arrest in the palace if you must, but don't put us to this ignominy! We may not have shared your interest, but we acted in defence of the realm!'

Wolfram's rage turned icy, and Hjala knew immediately she'd said the wrong thing.

'You mean to say the defence of the realm is not in my interest?' he said, half rising out of the throne. There was real menace in his voice now, not just anger. Hjala fumbled for better words.

'Of course it is, Your Majesty. What I meant to say was-'

And then it came. No ordinary clarion call, but a sound that had not been heard in the Strang Estuary for a hundred years, not even when the Young Pretender Krulheim had sailed his rebel fleet out of Urring to contend with Freidheim for mastery of the Wyvern Sea. And yet all who heard the sound knew what it was, and what it portended. Long and deep the slow notes sounded, each one seeming to thicken the very air. The horn that made them had been carved from the gargantuan tusks of Gargax, the woolly mammoth slain by Søren, before he had set out with the First Reavers to help found the kingdom whose fate they now debated.

'The Horn of War's Thundering,' said Thorsvald, awe

and reverence in his voice. 'That means the city is under attack by sea.'

'The Northlanders have come at last,' said Hjala.

Walsa turned to look pointedly out of the sash windows that abutted on to the harbour. 'Where are your warships, Wolfram?' she asked. 'Awaiting their mighty one-eyed king in Vandheim, leagues north of here with half the North-lending army, if what I've been hearing is right.'

But her nephew simply stood where he was, a perplexed look on his face.

Some of the courtiers were pressing up against the windows as the horn continued to sound, searching for a glimpse of the deadly fleet spotted by sentries in the coastal fortresses that ringed the estuary. It was a typically grey spring day, so they wouldn't be able to see it yet. Hjala had no doubt there would be a general panic when they did and realised how defenceless they were – Lord Aesgir had been despatched with the entire royal fleet more than a tenday ago.

'Well don't just stand there gaping,' snapped Walsa. 'Do something, you're the bloody King.'

'We have to mount a defence of the city,' said Thorsvald quickly. 'If they're Northlanders they'll be hardy and numer-ous, but they won't have mastered siegecraft. We need to get as many men on the walls as we can, prepare to receive assault.'

'His Highness has the right of it,' put in Lord Toric, getting a nod of assent from Lord Visigard. The two senior ravens had remained stoical throughout the proceeding;

now here at least was a problem they knew how to deal with. Or try to, at least.

'All right, Ezekiel dammit!' shouted the King, recovering his composure. 'Visigard and Toric, see it done. In the meantime, take the prisoners and-'

Hjala could almost have thanked Ma'alfeccnu'ur for what happened next. Never was the dark angel of pestilence and affliction more welcome than now. Wolfram's eyes rolled back into his head as the now familiar fit took him.

'His Majesty has been bequeathed a vision by the Almighty, to help us in our darkest hour!' cried Lorthar, stepping forward to catch him before he fell. Wolfram was too heavy in his armour for a feeble man like the Arch Perfect to support alone, and several ravens dashed over to help him. 'Get the King to his chambers,' cried Lorthar. 'I shall preside over him while he has his vision.'

The soldiers scurried to obey and Lorthar and Visigard hurried out of the throneroom with the King. Shouts were going up from some of the courtiers now: presumably they'd had their first sighting of the invasion fleet.

The erstwhile captives were all but forgotten in the commotion.

'Lord Toric, get us up on those walls where we can be of some use,' she said.

The bald commander of the White Valravyn stared at her. 'But His Majesty-'

'-collapsed before he could issue an order concerning us.' She held his stolid gaze. 'In heaven's name man, you know the difference between right and wrong. Just for once in your life, see sense and break with protocol. The people have been half abandoned to barbarian invaders thanks to Lorthar and Wolfram – they will need strong leadership in the coming days.'

Toric paused as if making up his mind. The shouts at the windows became more frantic. Knights were calling for their squires as they left the throneroom. Ladies were already talking of chirurgery and setting up hospices for the injured.

He nodded. 'All right, the three of you come with me.'

'And don't forget about Sir Manfry,' put in Walsa. 'He's a decent man, and we'll need every sword arm we can get by the looks of things.'

Toric sighed impatiently. Beckoning to a soldier, he issued an order. 'Sir Manfry of Vilno is being held in the knights' barracks. Release him for service and escort him to the armoury.' The soldier nodded and strode off.

Hjala smiled graciously. 'Thank you, Lord Toric,' she said. 'You are a wise commander.'

'Let's hope so,' he growled as the rest of them made for the double doors. 'Something tells me we'll need every quality we can muster.'

From her place at the prow of *Valhalla's Serpent*, Magnhilda gazed at the proud grey walls of the city she had come to conquer. All about her longships swarmed – even with her forces divided at Ragnar's behest, she commanded five thousand fighting men. If what her half-brother had said was true, the Northlendings would have far fewer trained swords than that with which to defend their precious capital.

'It is a fair sight,' thundered Canute behind her, the fingerbones in his braids clacking in the wind. 'A worthy gem to be plucked!'

She spared him a wry glance. 'I'm not sure one plucks gems, Canute, but I've more faith in your battle strength than your battle speeches!'

The Mountainside cracked an ugly grin that prompted a landslide across his gargantuan face. The bracing sea voyage across the Valhalla and into the Wyvern seemed to have revived his spirits since his humbling at Ragnar's hands. In place of his ruined poleaxe, he carried two stout battleaxes. Canute wielded them as though they were hatchets: Magnhilda did not envy his coming opponents.

She felt a strange power surging through her own axes: but then Hjalmbitr and Lindbrotna had been forged by sorcerer-bladesmiths in Søren's day, when the Unseen had whispered a little more loudly in the ears of mortalkind. Ragnar said even those times paled into insignificance next to the thousand-year era of the Wytch Kings, but she didn't care for such topics. Her half-brother spent altogether too much energy dwelling on that eldritch era for her liking. And yet it was that same eldritch power he sought to tap now, supposedly to her benefit. As her fleet closed in on the Strang Estuary, she put aside troubled thoughts, trusting to the gods to smile on her venture.

The low rumbling sound of a distant horn seemed to push the waves back towards them. The Shield Queen felt an atavistic stirring in her soul: no lover of sea and slaughter could hear the horn that Søren had made without being moved by it. Overhead, a wan shaft of sunlight pierced the thick layers of cloud. Magnhilda chose to interpret that as a good omen.

'Fyr shows us his favour!' she cried, so the men and women in the nearest boats could hear too. 'Let's plough furrows of battle sweat through the sail road, and bring storm of axes to yon Northlending walls! The northern peoples shall be reunited beneath the blood ember!'

Rousing cheers from the two ships flanking the *Serpent* showed what her warriors thought of that. Gradually the cheering was taken up by the next ones in line – until a hundred warships resonated with the joy of Tyrnor. Magnhilda felt her heart soar as the sun routed the clouds and Strongholm loomed closer, its walls silvered by Fyr's hardening beams.

Let the sun god shine howsoever brightly he might – soon the mainlanders would feel naught but crimson weather of weapons.

The sun had never felt so unwelcome to Hjala. From the windswept palace battlements, she gazed at the awful sight revealed by its waxing rays. Dozens of ships smeared the horizon, cutting the returning blue skies aggressively with their square sails.

It's every bit as bad as Thorsvald's men reported, she thought as she turned to address her brother.

'How many would you say?' she asked.

The erstwhile Sealord chewed his bearded lower lip, red hair flying in the rising wind. 'More than enough to give us trouble, but possibly less than Vaska reported,' he said. 'Where could the others have got to, I wonder?'

Hjala's eyes bulged. 'You mean there will be more?'

'Mayhaps. We can't worry about that now.'

Men were scurrying to and fro on the walkways; some loading crossbows, others preparing hand weapons if it came to that. Down below on the wharf, companies were hauling catapults into place. Panicky sailors were already casting off, trying to get their useless cogs and sloops out of the way.

Thorsvald remained staring out to sea as Toric and his serjeants barked orders in the background. He wore a perplexed expression on his face.

'What is it?' asked Hjala.

'Something isn't right. Northland longships are fast – but not this fast.'

Her heart sank as she remembered accounts of the Sea Wizard and his elemental sorcery during the last war.

'They're using witchcraft to speed up their fleet,' she said.

'That isn't all they're doing,' said Thorsvald, grasping her sleeve. 'Look!'

The fleet was splitting in two now, reforming into what looked like some kind of elaborate pincer manoeuvre.

'They're too smart for a frontal attack,' growled Thorsvald. 'They mean to outflank us and beach instead. They're going to bypass our coastal forts and come at us by land. They're too quick, Reus dammit – they'll be on us before we know it.'

He was all too right. An ordinary fleet could have been anticipated: catapults realigned, fortress garrisons deployed. But this was no ordinary fleet. Even Hjala could see the longships were moving at twice their ordinary rate of knots. Many of them were huge too, vaster than any Northland warship she'd heard tell of.

The hue and cry had gone up in the lower city; word had spread from the citadel, and now the common townsfolk would be preparing for attack as best they could.

Visigard emerged onto the battlements just then, barking orders. He strode up the walkway towards them.

'Lord Toric tells me you're needed in time of war, and he's High Marshal so it's his word over mine,' said the whiskered knight. 'But just remember I'm in charge of this city's security – I'll be keeping a close eye on you, Your Highness.'

Hjala and Thorsvald exchanged wry glances. Visigard always did things by letter of the law – this situation must truly have him torn in two.

'Rest assured, we're all on the same side,' said Thorsvald, laying a brawny hand on Visigard's mailed shoulder. 'Escort me to the armoury your bloody self if you have to – but I'm arming, like it or not!'

The jowly raven nodded curtly and motioned for the prince to go ahead. 'I'll trust you both to get to safety,' he said to Hjala and Walsa as he left in Thorsvald's wake. 'The battlements are no place for women in wartime.'

'I do hope he makes himself useful,' said Walsa acidly,

her eyes throwing invisible daggers at Visigard's retreating back.

'Speaking of which, it's time we did the same,' said Hjala.

Walsa frowned at her. 'I hope you're not thinking of putting on armour yourself, like one of those silly stories in the lays.'

'No, I'm not,' replied Hjala sharply. 'But as I said to Toric just now, the people are going to need strong leadership. They aren't about to get that from either of my brothers, under present circumstances.' She gazed across the palace grounds to where the walls on the other side overlooked the citadel.

'We need to get over there,' she said firmly.

'And do what?' inquired her aunt.

'What our kind does best – run things properly while vain men seek glory. My guess is there won't be more than a thousand fighting men garrisoned in the city. We need to inspire courage in our people.'

'Get that battering ram over to the gates!' shrieked Magn-hilda. She stood at the centre of a vortex of steel and flesh, as men surged about the walls of Strongholm, smothering the bright green fields with the cruel iron hues of war.

Weather of weapons indeed. The clutch of men led by Canute marched off, hefting the battering ram they had hastily constructed, another clutch of shieldmen bearing targets to protect them against archers.

'Vilm, how are those palisades coming along?' The

Thegn of Kvenlund had only just hied up to her. He looked flustered as he answered. 'They'll be ready soon, Your Majesty.'

'How soon is soon?' barked Magnhilda. Her *leidangs* weren't used to siege warfare, nor were they used to planning stands against mounted troops. But ditches had to be dug and fences raised – the Northlendings might be short of men, but that wouldn't stop them sending what knights were left in the Dominions to harry the invaders.

'By nightfall,' said Vilm, his corn-yellow beard streaked with blood. The killings had already begun – a few stragglers had been hewn down before they could reach the safety of the city.

Magnhilda raised her eyes to the horizon, where ridges cradling the plains rose to meet the westering sun.

'Not quick enough,' she said. 'That's two hours away at least. I want it done in one!'

Vilm nodded and loped off to redouble the men's efforts, the harried look still plastered to his face.

Archers on the gatehouse turrets and surrounding walls were firing at Canute's contingent now. But Ragnar had been right – they were thinly stretched across the walls, as were the men-at-arms who would protect them at close quarters. King Wolfram really had half emptied his realm on some foolish war abroad.

Bjorg was next to report. The Thegn of Jótland powered up the hillock from where Magnhilda had chosen to preside over the siege of Strongholm. The tattoos on his ugly face seemed to writhe as he grinned wolfishly. 'We've got laddermen approaching from the north side,' he said. 'They have archers over there too, but we've enough shieldmen to protect us.'

'Good,' she said. 'Let the Northlendings worry about our ladders for now, we'll hold the grappling hooks until later.'

This had been a well-rehearsed plan. Men carrying ladders and battering rams could move in tight formation, allowing shieldmen to protect them more effectively from arrows; individual raiders using ropes and grapnels were less easily defended. Better to get the first sallies up on the walls to despatch the archers, before sending the grapnelmen to aid them against the soldiers.

It was a plan she hoped would work.

Bjorg must have caught her anxious look. 'Are you sure we should be doing this, so close to sunset?'

'Quite sure,' she said firmly. 'Northlanders have ever thrived off the fear we instil in our enemies. Let us attack them now, and bring the wrath of Tyrnor upon yon mainlanders while they are still recovering their wits.'

Bjorg nodded and she sent him on his way, just as Valkyria came striding up the hillock.

'Your berserkers stand ready to attack, my Shield Queen,' she said. The warrior-priestess was daubed in war paint that made her look even fiercer than usual. Clearly she ached to be in the fray, but her sometime lover and loyal bodyguard would have to wait a little longer.

'And they shall taste the battle sweat of their enemies before long,' Magnhilda reassured her with a smile. 'Just a little patience, Valkyria! We'll soften them up today, then tomorrow we'll-'

She turned as she heard the tumult of axes harden

behind her. Some of Vilm's men had raised the alarm; beyond the unfinished palisade they were constructing, she could see it approaching from the south. A company of armoured knights, closing on them at a gallop.

'Crossbows up there on the double!' bellowed Magnhilda. Valkyria repeated the command, which was taken up by another warrior, and another still – until the crossbowmen were scrambling towards gaps in the palisade wall. Soon its inchoate wooden flank bristled with dozens of bolts, as the Northlanders beckoned the thundering knights closer with wood and steel.

Magnhilda waited for the riders to come a little closer; there wouldn't be time to get in a good shot at close range and reload for another volley, so the first would have to count. Now she could see the variegated standards streaming above the charging knights – she guessed these would be smallholders, lesser vassals who held land in the area immediately about the city. Wyverns and stags and other stylised beasts cavorted on the winds as the knights drew closer...

'Loose!' she cried.

'LOOSE!' repeated Valkyria. The single word was echoed down the chain of command. From her high vantage point Magnhilda allowed herself a smile as she watched knights go down. There couldn't have been more than fifty to begin with – but she'd heard what trained cavalry had done to Hardrada's mighty seacarls.

'Now for the next part of the plan we discussed,' she said to Valkyria, hoping Vilm's men would remember. Valkyria nodded and turned, crying down the line again.

'SPEARS!'

Where a rash of quarrels had bristled from the walls, there now appeared a thicker pelt of broadhead spikes on poles, each one longer than a man. The surviving knights closed on the Northlanders, but the partly finished palisade made it difficult for a full frontal charge to be effective. Some of the knights had the sense to ride around the gaps, but Magnhilda had anticipated that too: her *leidangs* were forming into tight-knit companies at right angles to one another.

The charge was dissipated before it could reach its climax. Some of the bolder knights managed to break past the Northland defence and hew down warriors here and there, but for the most part the others were driven back by the spears. More than a few were driven from the saddle, where shieldmen quickly stepped in to finish them off with axes and swords.

About half the company remained ahorse when the Northlendings sounded a retreat.

Magnhilda grinned as she watched them flee the field. 'That's given them a message to take back to their lords! We should have bought enough time to see out the day – tell Vilm to get that palisade finished.'

'There will be a lot more than fifty knights next time,' said Valkyria. 'I hope you'll allow my berserkers to taste blood.'

'You'll drink your share,' said Magnhilda, stroking Valkyria's scarred cheek fondly. 'But we need to be prepared – my half-brother says many Northlendings have ridden to the muster in Vandheim, but I would be sure of that with my own eyes.'

She could feel Valkyria practically reading her thoughts, as the berserker stared at her with savage eyes in the fading light.

In other words, I no longer trust Ragnar implicitly. But how can one be expected to trust a demonolator?

'But we can't fight! We're just ordinary craftsmen.' The lead guildsman's face was anxious in the torchlight. Hjala sighed inwardly as she raked the central square's inhabitants and saw that anxiety replicated a hundredfold.

She fixed the master armourer with an imperious glare. 'You've thews to match any soldier up on yon walls,' the princess told him, trying to sound inspiring. 'Aye, and I see many strong, well-fed men gathered here this e'en! 'Tis only want of courage that stops you taking up arms to stand shoulder to shoulder with your comrades.'

Discontented mutterings showed the assembled freemen weren't too impressed with that rhetorical flourish. Hjala felt like screaming in frustration. She wished she'd inherited her father's talent for rousing speeches. Freidheim would have made warriors out of this lot just by glaring at them.

'I think you've just called them all cowards,' whispered her Aunt Walsa, from where she stood behind Hjala on the stockade she'd had erected at the edge of the square. Up and around them shouts broke the incipient night: her brother and Toric and Visigard were busy posting watches and supervising victualling, in anticipation of the coming siege.

'Yes, I bloody well realise that!' she hissed. 'Why don't you try speaking to them?'

'Oh, I wouldn't say anything different,' muttered the old harridan. 'As far as I'm concerned, they *are* all damned cowards. They get to ply a thriving trade for decades, thanks to the security this city affords them – the guildsmen weren't even touched by the last war. Now it finally comes knocking on their gates, they won't take up so much as a stave to defend their livelihoods.'

The assembled craftsmen had fallen to bickering amongst themselves. A herald called for order, but struggled to get it. Hjala could tell some of the younger men *did* want to fight – a city of twenty thousand should easily furnish hundreds of able-bodied men to bolster the trained ranks they had on the walls. That might just be enough to hold off the marauding Northlanders, give the rest of the King's men a chance to arrive at the capital and relieve the siege...

A messenger interrupted her reverie. He briefed Walsa, who nodded and sent him on his way with a curt order.

'What news from Thorsvald?' asked Hjala.

Walsa frowned, looking unusually perturbed. 'He says the Ice Thegns have blockaded the Strang, so Aesgir will be stiffly met if he tries to mount a relief expedition by sea.'

Hjala nodded, not in the least surprised. The enemy had more than enough longships to do such a thing.

'What about the rest of the defence?'

'All going according to plan,' said Walsa ironically. 'We've five hundred men of the King's Watch plus another three hundred of Visigard's ravens. Besides that, we've a few dozen knights who just happened to be within the city walls.'

Hjala bit her lip. 'Less than a thousand then, as feared. How are they faring?'

'Thorsvald is supervising the citadel defences, so they can't break in past the harbour. Visigard has his hands full seeing off laddermen, they're fighting on the walls on the north side of the city. They've also deployed grapnelmen to support them. There's another company of Northlanders trying to batter down our gates. Toric's doing a good job of holding them off so far, but they seem set on trying through the night and aren't afraid to lose men.'

'Ezekiel's wounds, we need more men up there on the walls with them – they'll be overwhelmed otherwise!' cried Hjala.

'I think that's the gist of it, dear,' breathed Walsa.

The herald had just about managed to silence the baying crowd. Hundreds of city freemen had thronged the main square to debate the siege. Many were calling for their King, but of Wolfram there had been no word.

The King would not be there to lead the common folk. It fell to his sister to try.

Taking a deep breath, Hjala stepped forward to address the men of Strongholm again, and prayed to her father's ghost for inspiration.

CHAPTER 17
AN INVASION GLIMPSED
FROM AFAR

I von de Vichy spoke a word of power, and the tapestry in his dressing chamber began to change. The threads that had been woven painstakingly to depict knights tilting on a plain seemed to shift and come apart in the soft candlelight; the warlock visualised the abstract symbols of a craftsman's tool, a caterpillar and a butterfly in quick succession, as he transformed the tapestry into a thing of flowing light. Then he incanted a clairvoyance spell, channelling his powers of divination through the scrying tool and tapping the violet candles he had artificed for supplementary power. The incantation was simple enough, but his elan was already taxed as it was, and saving it wherever he could helped.

The candles guttered momentarily, and when they flared up again Ivon was gazing at a real-life spectacle of war.

A column of soldiers hundreds strong marched across fields studded with burning villages and gutted manors; mounted knights rode to and fro, hewing down fleeing footsoldiers. Many war standards cut the smoking skies, their escutcheons clearly visible against a strong sunset.

As he settled more comfortably in his ebony chair and took a sip of Armandy red, Ivon scoured his conjured vision for the standard he was looking for. The vintage was laced with Tyrnor's Foil: he shivered at its potency, but he would need a little artificial energy tonight.

Soon he found it. A hippogriff rampant in gold on a sable field, the coat of arms belonging to the House of Guye. Next to it flapped a white manticore prowling on a vert background, the arms of House Chorlangue.

Ivon smiled fondly. Aravin and Kaye, thick as thieves always, his two chief understudies. No pawns these, but full-blown knights in the great game of Jedrez he was playing. Gently pushing aside his sentiments, he focused his elan, bringing himself in closer. Pavilions were dotted about the standards, along with grazing horses and other tools of warfare. Many more tents were being hastily erected by squires: another day's slaughter done, the Royal Army was making camp for the night.

It didn't take him long to find Lord Kaye. He was standing next to a bonfire, presiding over what Ivon took to be a torture session. A Vorstlending soldier's mouth opened in a silent scream, as Pangonian footsoldiers held his bare feet in the fire. Kaye stood straight as a sapling, his face expressionless as he methodically asked questions.

Nudging his elan a little further into the interstice, Ivon tapped the scrying tool he had given Kaye and began to sense rather than hear some of the margrave's words:

... have they laid ambushes?

... how well provisioned are their forts?

... how many are their garrison?

Ivon hung back, idly scanning the other knights and nobles while he waited for Kaye to finish his work. Aravin was there of course, looking bored; young Clovis, Margrave of Narbo, gazed intently at the writhing soldier, a cruel light in his mean eyes.

Got a taste for blood that one, reflected Ivon. *He'll make a very useful idiot indeed. More useful than his fat, good-for-nothing-but-sacrifice brother Rodger.* Memories of that service to the Fallen One were still pleasant: how he'd loved the taste of Rodger's entrails – and the power offering his soul up to Abaddon had brought him.

Returning his attention to the vision before him, Ivon noted that not all the lords looked pleased. Aeron de Leon, Margrave of Gorleon, foremost among the Occitanian barons, had an ugly scowl stamped across his blunt features. Annoying man, always prating on about his precious honour.

Your precious honour hasn't stopped you scheming with me, to overthrow Carolus once this invasion is done. But then you do so hate the King for promoting your bastard brother Alaric to Sea Marshal, don't you?

The Great Western Ocean was said to run in the veins of the scions of House Vantery – the King's appointment of Lord Aeron's illegitimate younger sibling had irked the proud lord no end. But then that was the purpose of the Purple Garter, Ivon reflected – it was a handy way of checking powerful nobles. So much for all the legends of Vasirius and the Crescent Table.

The interrogation done, the Pangonian soldiers yanked the captive out of the fire and cut his throat. Another reality of war: only knights and lords were worth anything in ransom money. As they dragged the twitching soon-to-be corpse of the soldier away and the nobles dispersed to see about their supper, Ivon homed in on Lord Kaye. Picturing an ear and a mouth and a swift bird, he muttered a few more words and stroked the white amulet he wore. Kaye blinked as he felt his sympathetic tool respond. The Margrave of Quillon had proved a decent apprentice: Ivon had taught him the rudiments of Scrying and artifice. By far the most intelligent of his servitors, he would reap the reward for his talents, when the Headstone was reunited.

Ivon watched as Kaye excused himself and stalked over towards his own pavilion. Two liveried squires opened the flaps, sealing them behind him as he entered. The interior was already lit by hanging oil lamps, not braziers: Kaye had refined tastes. Another thing he'd learned from his master. Ivon flicked a glance at his own lights to check they were still burning brightly. Drawing on their power, he spoke with his mind. Reading thoughts was more difficult than simply communicating through a pool or mirror, but a lot safer. He couldn't very well have his chief disciple caught practising sorcery on campaign, now could he?

How speeds the invasion of Westenlund, my sweet margrave? Looks to be going swimmingly well, from what I can see.

Kaye self-consciously raised a white-gemmed silver ring to his lips and whispered into it. He wasn't powerful enough to speak in minds as Ivon did, so he had to settle for using a surreptitious scrying tool. But at least this way he could always claim just to be thinking out loud – no one would suspect more than an agitated warlord on the campaign trail if they overheard him muttering.

'It goes according to plan. The Purple Garter are leading the vanguard north towards Westerburg. We are bringing up the rear as you can see, and ensuring their southern fiefs are rendered impotent. The border castles Altkass, Vizvant and Howfaste are holding out as we expected, but we can spare the men to keep them pinned under siege. We've got the Vorstlendings on the back foot – there will be no relief army when Sir Hugon invests the city and its castle.'

Excellent. And the Royal Marshal and Captain of the Garter has sent word of his own exploits, I take it?

'Last we heard, the vanguard is a couple of days' march from Westerburg.'

Good. So you've secured enough territory to use messengers safely. That will save me having to waste valuable elan spying on Hugon myself.

For the first time, Kaye looked a little perturbed. 'You are feeling strained?' the Margrave of Quillon asked.

Ivon allowed a slight frown as he took another sip of drugged wine. *My studies tax me is all, and it is a quite a while since we held our last service.* A stab of pain transfixed him as he recalled burying Wolmar in a shallow grave not far from where he had summoned Molaach, temporarily manifesting the mighty Second Tier demon through the hapless slip of the girl he'd violated and sacrificed. He still wasn't quite over the loss of his former lover yet – in spite of his stubborn resistance to his call to power, Ivon had been genuinely fond of the wild rough Northlending.

'And are we close? To getting it all, I mean?' Kaye looked nervous just alluding to the Headstone.

Now, now – you worry about your duties, and I'll worry about mine. He couldn't tell even his closest disciples everything. The art of power lay in dissimulation, always.

'As you command,' replied Kaye. 'Just tell me one thing – how speeds our glorious king?' The contempt in his voice was palpable, even over a foggy connection.

His Majesty is making good speed. He should arrive just in time to preside over the final siege, when all the dirty work has been done.

Kaye's upper lip curled in a sneer. 'He isn't much better than Rodger was. The sooner our plans come to fruition, the better.'

And speaking of which, I saw the late margrave's young heir Clovis just now. How is he faring?

Kaye actually looked a little horrified. 'I thought I'd seen cruelty on the battlefield. He fights like a lion and just as mercilessly. We've already lost a few ransoms because he refuses to spare fallen foes, even noble ones. And I practically had to force him not to get directly involved in the interrogation just now.'

That didn't surprise Ivon too much. A lot of his allies and thralls enjoyed inflicting pain. They always told themselves it was for one higher purpose or another, but Ivon knew better. Zolthoth's arm was long: the archdemon of cruelty had always had a firm grip on men's hearts.

Keep an eye on him. Useful idiots are precisely that. We can dispose of him after the thing is done if he proves... intractable.

'By your command. Anything else?'

No, just tell me when His Majesty turns up. And keep me abreast of how Hugon speeds in the north.

'I will.' Kaye indulged a sly smirk. 'No doubt they will both be missing their ravishing queen.'

Ivon smirked back as he made a beckoning motion behind him.

No doubt. Abaddon's speed, Kaye.

He murmured the closing words and the tapestry resumed its normal form. A naked and beautiful woman moved over softly to stand behind him. Reaching for his wine cup with one hand, he let the other run over her flat tanned midriff, before slowly making his way down to the clump of hair beneath it.

'The war in Westenlund goes well?' Isolte's voice was husky, sultry as a summer night. Ivon gazed up at her lustrous eyes, framed by her long lush tresses. She almost took his mind off Wolmar. Almost.

'It'll be a war in the whole of Vorstlund before long, my sweet,' he beamed up at her. Gently, he slid his hand between her thighs as he drained his cup. He felt the drugged wine pumping through his body, giving spurs to the hot lust that coursed through his loins.

'My people have invaded the eastern marches,' confirmed the Queen, her own voice growing thick with desire. 'And when Vorstlund falls...'

'... we march further north, and consolidate with Ragnar and the Northlanders,' Ivon finished for her. 'Once the Free Kingdoms are no longer that, we will have our empire.' He worked dextrous fingers inside her cleft, which was already dewy. She stroked his shoulders with her own long, delicate fingers. On impulse, he took one in his mouth and began sucking it.

'But what of the rest of the Known World?' she asked. 'The Sassanian Sultanates will go to war against the Pilgrim Kingdoms soon, and what of the Empire and the Eastlands beyond?'

Ivon took her finger from his mouth and gently shushed the Queen, bringing her down on her knees. It pleased him to have such a powerful lady for a plaything, though he sensed that Isolte knew very well the game she was playing. Like one of his raptors on the hawking field, she consented to be bound, knowing what fruits that bondage would bring her. He could only admire the native Thalamian's pragmatic intelligence, born of an ancient race that had ruled the world in the wake of the Elder Wizards.

'Don't worry, my sweet,' he whispered softly in her ear. 'The master we both serve has thought of everything. Not even I could hope to match his ken.'

The Queen gazed at him with dark, brooding eyes. Though he had her enthralled, it was still difficult to fathom her subtle thoughts.

'I hope you are right about this master, whoever he is,' she said. Then the smile returned to her face, and she unlaced the drawstrings of Ivon's hose and obeyed his simple command.

As Isolte bent to pleasure him, Ivon leaned back in his chair and thought of Wolmar.

CHAPTER 18
OF UNANSWERED QUESTIONS

Through the crooked window of the crumbling sentry tower, Torgun gazed at the scarred hinterlands of Skulla, huddling resentfully under rain-washed skies. From the highest point of the curtain wall overlooking Kell, one could look north and see the broken leagues stretch for miles towards an uncaring firmament.

This is truly a desolate land, he reflected. *No wonder its people turned to sorcery to survive.*

But beyond the bleak wilderness vista there was something else, something more ruinous to the *soul*. The knight felt more grateful than ever for the relic slung about his neck.

'Feel it you can, even after all these millennia!' breathed Morcant beside him. 'The Valley of the Barrow Kings lies beyond yonder ridges. There the Draug Princes wait in torpor, for the Hour Of All's Ending.'

Torgun shuddered. He didn't care for the warlock's blasphemous prophesying. Memories of the undead warlords he'd encountered in Vorstlund still groped with inky fingers at the back of his mind.

'And that was where it was broken,' he murmured. They had travelled hundreds of miles, now finally they stood on the threshold of the place where all their troubles had begun.

'Aye, Morwena and Søren's tales did intertwine here,' said Morcant. 'Her watchtower was once visible from this point, though nowadays but ash-choked ruins remain.' The mage almost sounded wistful. But then he was a sorcerous type.

'Is that where the druids keep the fragment?' They had been held in a wing of the ruined fortress overlooking Kell for a couple of days. Islanders had come to feed them, but no one important had sent or spoken word to them since the All-Meet. That was enough to make a man inquisitive.

'Certainly not!' exclaimed the warlock. 'A fine place to guard such cursed relic that would be. Though other eldritch things lie below the levelled ruins...' Morcant's voice trailed off, as he gazed with pale eyes at the cheerless ridges. 'But formidable the druiding guardians are... tell you more I would, but I'm bound by wizard's pact you see.'

Torgun sighed. 'I suspected you might say as much. But then if Master Joram can't get it out of you, I don't suppose any of us can.'

'Well if you can't get it out of him, I don't see how any of us can,' said Wrackwulf, chewing greedily on a leg of mutton. It was the first time since they had arrived that the islanders had given them any meat. 'I'm a trained killer, not a torturer.'

Joram eyed him sourly over a cup of no less sour ale. The Westerling folk would certainly not be getting lavish praise for their hospitality. 'And I suppose you mean to say that I, a man of the cloth, am such?'

'You seemed to be making a good fist of it – quite literally – when we first met you and the pasty-faced mage.' With a contented sigh, Wrackwulf dropped the ravaged thighbone on his wooden platter and took up his own ale. The chamber they were being kept in was cramped and none too warm. The fire that burned meanly in the corner did little to change that (Morcant had muttered some nonsense about not using fire magick during spring).

'At any rate, we'd best be finding out something soon – or I'll be breaking my troth!' His eyes moved meaningfully to where his double-headed axe leaned against a stool. She looked lonely and forlorn, but then she hadn't tasted blood in a while.

'Just muster some patience, sir knight,' growled Joram. 'As like as not, yon savages are taking their sweet time debating what to do with us.'

Wrackwulf nearly spluttered up the last of his ale. 'You mean that all-men thing is still going on? But we've been here nigh three days! And I thought you told them plainly enough what brings us here.'

'I did, and you may have noticed how pleased they were to hear it,' said Joram with rare irony. 'But the islanders believe in giving all their notables a say in matters of policy. That means hundreds of warriors and druids will have an opinion on our mission that needs to be heard and weighed.'

Wrackwulf groaned inwardly. 'We could be here forever. What about Morcant? He may not want to tell us everything he knows, but surely he can put in a word for us, speed things up a bit? I thought he had influence here.'

'Have you seen him called back up to the Teeth?' asked Joram pointedly. 'I don't think our friend's standing here is quite what he led us to believe.'

'It's true,' said Morcant, lowering his eyes in response to Torgun's question. 'My reputation among my folk is not... quite what it was.'

The knight almost felt guilty for asking. Prying into a man's private affairs was bad form – but his adventures had brought him to outlandish places, and sometimes that called for outlandish behaviour. And it was obvious Morcant wasn't proving nearly as helpful as he'd claimed he would be.

'You would have said anything to save your skin when first we met you,' said Torgun, not unkindly. 'A man can hardly be faulted for trying to spare himself the rod.' He laid a huge but gentle hand on the warlock's round shoulder. 'Just tell me what you can – the more we know, the better for our mission.'

Morcant turned back to gaze at the forbidding horizon. 'On our journey here, recall you may I spoke of Magwych Fada-Radharc,' he said. 'The most powerful of the druids during the last years of the Old Time he was, so gifted that some even claimed his understanding of sorcery rivalled his ancestors, them that first learned at the feet of the Moon Goddess! But planted a seed in his mind did that yearning for knowledge, and he sought powers he should not have. For Morwena was not the first to delve into the secrets of the Watchtower of the Valley of the Barrow Kings.'

The mage paused, watching the rain wash the silvery flint stones of the keep wall beneath them.

'Go on,' Torgun prompted him. 'You mean to say this Magwych took up residence in yon cursed tower, as Morwena did after him.'

Morcant favoured the knight with a wan smile. There was a sadness in his voice now. 'Oh no, for Radharc, despite his faults, was wise enough not to do that. But curious still enough to explore the ruins he was! Even in those days, badly damaged the tower was, thanks to the Curse of the Gods before the Great Darkness.'

'You speak of the Breaking of the World,' said Torgun softly. 'In our faith, we call it the Wrath of the Unseen.'

Morcant nodded. 'Well versed you are in such matters, for a man of the sword.'

'I've had to be of late,' replied Torgun grimly.

Morcant nodded sagely and went on with his story. 'Rad-harc ventured below the surviving levels of the Watchtower, and enough he saw inscribed on its eldritch walls to corrupt that seed in his mind. He returned a few nights later, so the *Westerling Chronicle* tells, but never quite the same was he thereafter. Stopped short of delving down the Left Hand Path he did, but he coveted power nonetheless – not for himself directly, but for the synod of druids and priestesses he ruled. Managed he did to unite the Marcher Lords of Skulla behind him, but those of Kaluryn stood against him. And thus began the Wars of Kith and Kin, that destroyed the Westerling Kingdoms of the Old Time.'

'And what has all this to do with you?'

Morcant's eyes did not leave the gloomy skies as he answered. 'I too became... curious.'

Torgun started as the realisation hit him. Stepping back from the mage, he reached a hand for his sword-hilt and another for the circifix about his neck.

Morcant chuckled humourlessly. 'Never fear, pious knight!' he said bitterly. 'I turned back as soon as I crested yonder ridges and saw ghostly daemons rise from the valley floor. Young I was, but not so young I couldn't recognise a folly in time to save my soul!'

Torgun frowned, releasing his grip on the sword but not the circifix. 'So what ails thee then? You said yourself you turned back before you could commit yourself to madness.'

'Ah, but necessarily strict the laws of my people are,' sighed the warlock. 'And judged I was, upon my return here. Not enough to warrant death had my transgression been, but enough to warrant exile.'

Torgun nodded as the last piece of the puzzle fell into place. 'And that's why they sent you on your mission to the mainland. It wasn't a duty, it was a punishment.'

'Not just a fair face and a strong right arm are you,' said Morcant, favouring the knight with a sardonic grin.

'And you are not quite what you purported to be,' replied Torgun, frowning.

'And what about you?' asked Wrackwulf, glaring suddenly at the dour monk. 'I'm not so convinced we know the whole of your story either.'

Joram paused at his ale. He eyed the freelancer coldly over the rim of his cup. 'And what mean you by that exactly?' The very air suddenly seemed to have taken on a more frigid quality. Outside, the rain continued to run down the translucent panes of bone and cartilage that covered the windows.

Wrackwulf leaned back on his stool against the spiny wall, ignoring the discomfort as he affected an air of nonchalance. 'You just don't seem like a typical Argolian to me, is all,' he said. 'One minute you want to execute Morcant for witchcraft, then you're happy to let him live and tag along with us to this wind-ravaged rock he calls home.' Wrackwulf leaned forwards again. 'I may not know much about wizardry, master monk – but I know comrades-in-arms when I see them. You and yon wizard have grown passing cosy of late, it seems to me.'

Joram put down his unfinished ale. 'I am but following orders,' he said icily. 'As Grand Master Hannequin commands, so I obey. You yourselves delivered the letter instructing me to help you in your accursed mission – by any means necessary. The warlock is an odious ally, but an ally nonetheless. Without him we might never have gotten this far, much as it pains me to admit it. And so, here we are.'

'Yes,' said Wrackwulf, wishing there were more ale. 'Here we are, thanks to you and your unlikely ally. Still, it's very curious to find oneself with an Argolian trapped in a den of sorcerers. I would have hoped your orders were a bit more specific about what to do now we're here.'

Joram's face was neutral as he picked up his ale again. 'I'm thinking on it,' was all he said before draining his cup.

'Think on it,' insisted Torgun. 'There must be something you can do! Surely your years in service will have redeemed you in the eyes of your people? You helped us defeat Abrexta, and did you not say she was understudy to Yathaga, the very same witch banished from these shores?'

'Aye, Yathaga it was,' confirmed Morcant. 'She fled execution after looking upon the same runestones in the Watchtower's dungeons as Radharc. From there she learned her necromantic arts, but not powerful enough was she to master the eldritch fortress, as Morwena had been. You have a point about my part in Abrexta's defeat, but gone I was a long time, and scrying home has been difficult in recent years... many a year I had to serve her, as part of my subterfuge. Many days discussing my trustworthiness the Druiding Council will be.'

Torgun threw up his arms in exasperation. 'You and your blasted sorcerous ways!' he cried, for once losing his patience and his manners. 'Why don't you just have a king to make difficult decisions, as we do?'

'No wise king would make a difficult decision without consulting advisers at length,' Morcant reminded him, shaking his head wearily. 'Wait we must.'

'Well, it looks like we're stuck waiting in this rathole until you think us up a bright idea,' sighed Wrackwulf. 'Pity those savages didn't leave us more ale.'

In truth, rancid beer was the last thing on his mind. He was just trying to convince Joram he had given up on his inquiry. But from what Wrackwulf knew of Argolians and their ability to sense thoughts, there wasn't much chance of that. Had he been foolish to confront the monk just now? Perhaps – but being cooped up like a ransom prisoner didn't do wonders for a knight's patience. He had to do something if he couldn't fight. And besides that, he was quite sure the surly monk was hiding something. He just couldn't put his finger on it...

Joram got up abruptly and strode over to the rusted iron-bound door, banging on it with his empty cup. Silence greeted him and he struck again, the tinny report ringing uncomfortably in Wrackwulf's ears.

'What are you doing?' asked the freelancer.

'What does it look like?' replied Joram. 'Alerting our gracious hosts. I've done my thinking.'

Wrackwulf shrugged helplessly. 'I thought you'd already told them why we're here – what more is there to say?'

A shuffling sound told of the arrival of a guard. Joram leaned against the barred door window, speaking urgently in the lilting island tongue. After a while the islander shuffled off again, having barely spoken a word himself.

'You said they'll take forever to decide whether to let us inspect their precious fragment,' said Wrackwulf. 'What more could you possibly say to change their minds if they decide not to?'

The monk's reply surprised him.

'Nothing. I've changed *my* mind – we've warned the Westerlings somebody is halfway to reuniting the Headstone, and Morcant and I have told yon druids everything we know about the matter. So the core part of our mission is done. If they aren't willing to let us help them any further, there is little point lingering here. There's trouble aplenty brewing on the mainland, we're all needed there. I've put in a request that the islanders allow us safe conduct home immediately.'

Wrackwulf raised a bushy eyebrow. 'I won't say I'm not pleased to hear that, but don't you think Sir Torgun will want to have a say in this?'

Joram sneered dismissively.

'That knight was never the true leader of this expedition, as Hannequin made clear to me in his letter. This is Argolian business, and Argolians shall conduct it.'

Showing your true colours at last, eh? But some instinct told Wrackwulf to keep that thought to himself.

'Sir Torgun and Morcant are taking some air up on the ramparts,' was what he chose to say. 'Given the fine weather, I imagine they'll be back soon enough.'

'That's right, they will be,' said Joram. 'I told the guard to bring them both back here. I'll tell them of the change to our mission directly. I've still got Hannequin's letter as proof of my authority, if it's needed.'

And you know full well neither of us can read.

'What about the warlock?' asked Wrackwulf, trying to

stall for time while he thought of some other tack to take. 'I thought you wanted to take him back to Thraxia to stand trial for his crimes.'

Joram favoured Wrackwulf with a crooked smile that looked altogether too cunning for his liking. 'This is war, sir knight. No petty war the like of which you've ever known, but a war for the world – nay, both worlds! Sacrifices must be made, pawns traded. Morcant's usefulness is at an end – by the sounds of it, the islanders may well punish him according to their own laws anyway.'

The adept said no more, but took to pacing the cramped cell impatiently while they waited for the others to arrive. Wrackwulf sat back to ponder his words. Everything Joram said seemed to make sense: the first part of their mission was done, and the suspicious islanders didn't seem likely to let them anywhere near the fragment. War on the mainland was clearly afoot – perhaps the biggest the Free Kingdoms had known in centuries. Better to return there with all due speed, where they could be of service.

So why do I feel like a pawn in a game of Jedrez myself?

The rain that rolled in rivulets down the windowpanes had no answer to that question.

CHAPTER 19
TO CATCH A THIEF

Hari Yassin leaned back in his chair and feigned nonchalance.

'Come, come, Suli, you should know better than to ask me that!' he said, painting a winning smile across his swart handsome features. That smile had won him into many a man's money purse and harem. 'What fool merchant keeps his coin by the waterfront, where any thief can take it?' he added. 'I'll have the rest of what I owe sent over to your offices at first light tomorrow, upon Sha'abat's Passing I swear it!'

Suli's half-scarred face was ugly in the morning sunlight that streamed through the latticed windows of Hari's office chamber. 'Don't bandy the Prophet's name my way, Yassin!' he spat. 'You're no merchant, but a lying thief yourself – as everybody in the Quarter knows. Ten crates of vintage Aquitanian red wine I passed your way – and a hundred gold bezantis was the amount we agreed for it! I should have known better than to trust a scoundrel like you.' His tone became menacing as he leaned across the table. 'You know very well who I'm in business with – and trust me, you don't want me to get *him* involved.'

From where he stood leaning against the door jamb, Kemal moved his hand to the hilt of his dagger, but Hari motioned his burly henchman to stop with a flicker of an eyebrow. It was already becoming clear how this would have to be handled.

'And as I've already told you,' Hari went on, surreptitiously moving his right hand underneath the table, 'I have nothing but the utmost respect for Haider Jortmund, and the influence he commands. That is why I choose to be honest. A scoundrel would lie to your face, but no! I give you only the truth, Suli. A few days more to raise the monies will it take.'

Reaching slowly forwards whilst he talked, he found the trigger of the hand crossbow bolted to the table's underside. Still smiling, he added: 'I have nothing but respect for our Urovian brothers in trade, whom you serve so loyally.'

That got Suli's blood up and no mistake. As a full-blooded Sassanian, he hated being reminded that he enforced for a Vorstlending *jhufa'ar* – especially by a half-breed *al'Hajin* like Hari. But angry was just where Yassin wanted Suli. Angry, and distracted. So that he wouldn't notice as Hari tightened his finger on the trigger –

A shocked expression contorted Suli's face. Looking down at the dart buried in his midriff, he looked up again, anger returning redoubled to his features.

Anger, and fear.

'Do not trouble yourself, my good Suli!' exclaimed Hari,

rising from the table and walking around it to stand over the enforcer. Kemal had drawn his knife to cut Suli's throat, but Hari shook his head. 'The venom of the desert scorpion is not lethal when combined with certain herbs I know of. This agent merely paralyses temporarily – whilst opening the mind to a certain... suggestion.'

Yassin perched himself on the edge of the table, just above where Suli sat rigidly as though suddenly bolted to his chair. Some of his muscles twitched, but he was otherwise motionless. That was good – one in a hundred victims did die from the Stinging Kiss, but if Suli was one of those, he would be convulsing by now and the whites of his eyes would be turning blue.

Adjusting his scarlet silk neckerchief, Hari continued in the same affable tone: 'Now, here is what you will tell Haider. After much negotiation on our part, you have decided to give me the benefit of the doubt, and permit me another seven days to come up with the money. You are doing this because of the obvious respect I have for Jortmund and his smuggling concern, in anticipation of much fruitful future business between our organisations.'

Reaching down, he plucked the dart from Suli's belly and tucked it into one of his many inner jerkin pockets, after first carefully wiping it. 'In thirty heartbeats the paralysis will wear off, at which point you will get up and leave my offices. You will remember absolutely nothing of this encounter, besides what I have just told you.'

Kemal's bearded face was dubious as they watched Suli leave, wearing a bewildered expression. 'That was a risky tactic to say the least,' commented the bruiser, folding his arms disapprovingly.

Yassin sighed as he shut the door firmly behind Suli. 'There was no help for it, Kemal. I'm up to my ears in debt to the Bethlers, and you know I can't afford to cross them. Haider will get his damned money, but I need to work out how to pay Tobin his due first, and I don't have time to sit here arguing with that idiot all day. Who do the Shirt Tails think they are anyway? They climb into bed with the Temple, and suddenly they think they run the Mercadian Quarter.'

'They are one of the most powerful gangs on the water-front,' Kemal reminded him.

'Not as powerful as the Knights Bethler,' Hari reminded him in turn.

'It doesn't help matters that we ended up losing money on that fake piracy venture last summer,' muttered Kemal. 'I still can't believe we didn't see that one coming!' He shook his head ruefully and took a pinch of sherbet from the silver bowl on the table, washing it down with a rhyton of fruit juice. The man's sweet tooth could be over-matched by his taste for blood, if called for. 'Hamidul did the ledgers again this morning – we're still nowhere close to recovering from that loss.'

Hari pinched the bridge of his nose. So early, and he already had one of his headaches. A meditation trance would get rid of it, but he scarcely had time for that today. Putting his winning smile back on, he clapped Kemal's broad shoulder. 'Look at the Prophet's blessing,' he said. 'At least we paid back Abnaz the Knifer and Usman Three Times for putting us up to that fraud.'

Kemal grinned darkly. 'I still take pleasure in the memory,' he said through teeth that were black and snaggled. 'Usman died living up to his name, all right – the wretch screamed thrice when I opened up his belly before sending him to the bottom of the harbour!'

Yassin wagged a finger in his face. 'You'd better have remembered to put rocks in that belly, like I told you! I don't want either of those jokers turning up on the wharf. We've enough on our platters as it is.'

'Don't worry,' said Kemal, the grin not leaving his face. 'Abnaz and Usman dance with the Seakindred. You won't be seeing either of them again, not in this life.'

The same might be said of us in a month, if I can't think of a way out of this fix. Hari kept his unsettling thoughts to himself as he told Kemal to fetch Hamidul. He might as well know exactly how badly short they were, before he decided his next move.

Anupe kept her hand rested lightly on the hilt of her falchion as she escorted the damsels down to the docks. Already the Mercadian Quarter was a riot of activity, as Sassanian traders jostled each other for stall space. The lighter-skinned burgesses had plots of their own removed from the native areas: they might live cheek by jowl, but commerce was carefully segregated. They spotted the

Merchant Courthouse, from where the Mercadian princes oversaw their slice of the Porcupine's bounty. A domed colonnaded edifice built of sandstone, it was clearly of Urovian origin but had adopted some of the Sassanian abstract motifs in its light frieze work.

They mingle and influence each other, yet they insist on setting themselves apart at the same time, mused Anupe. *What a strange country is this.*

'Amalric said this Yassin's quarters are just between yon courthouse and the waterfront,' she observed. 'Do you know for sure that this is what you want to do?'

'I don't think we've much choice,' said Adhelina behind her shawl. Many native women went about veiled; the one-time heiress had decided this a handy custom to adopt. 'We can hardly abandon Horskram and Adelko to torment. Besides, this is what my vision said would happen. It's why we're here.'

'Then we'd better keep our minds focused on the practicalities, hadn't we?' put in Hettie, scowling as a fat porter carrying peaches barged past her none too politely. 'This Yassin won't be easy to deceive, if he's such a rogue himself.'

'We've rehearsed the story a dozen times,' said Adhelina as they pushed their way through the expansive square that surrounded the Courthouse. Every spare inch of its smooth triangular flagstones was covered with shrieking traders and haggling shoppers. 'We've lied our way out of trouble many a time before now. If everyone keeps to their part, we can do it again.'

Set a thief to catch a thief, thought Anupe wryly. *We'll see how that plays out.*

'But Hari, they are quite insistent! Three ladies without, two of them obviously high born, and they will not leave until they see you.' Umar's youthful face wore the same perplexed look as it always did when something unexpected happened.

Sitting back from the ledgers he had been scrutinising with Hamidul, Hari sighed exasperatedly. Today of all days. But something had his curiosity piqued. It wasn't every day you had two *jhufa'ar* noblewomen and a female *taziq* turn up on your doorstep. What's more, nobles usually had money – and that he needed badly. Hamidul's stolid account of their finances had not made his problems look any the less pressing. Grand Master Tobin simply knew too much of his clandestine affairs to be dismissed: the man could crush him, if he was so minded. And Tobin expected to be paid regularly, just as any other crime lord did.

'All right, Umar,' he said, pouring rhytons of sweet cherry juice for himself and Hamidul. 'Better let them in, then.'

He had time enough to sip his juice and exchange bemused looks with Hamidul before Umar returned, ushering in the three visitors. In behind them walked Kemal, as he always did when strangers were present in front of the boss. Security could never be taken for granted in the Porcupine.

The lady in the middle removed her veil as Umar shut the door and left them.

Yassin had to stop himself taking a breath. The *jhufa'ar*

woman was undeniably a beauty. Her hair shone like beaten gold in the light, tinged with a russet hue that had him thinking of rubies. Her pale heart-shaped face was sad and winsome; her emerald eyes spoke of one who had seen too much suffering in a young and pampered life.

Intriguing, to say the least.

'Pray be seated,' he said, quickly collecting himself and proffering her Hamidul's chair. His wiry lieutenant vacated obligingly. Like Hari himself, he was *al'Hajin*, fathered by a visiting Urovian noble on a Sassanian pleasure girl. Hamidul's tawny complexion was a little paler than the norm, though his weaselly face could have belonged to a thief of any land.

The damsel obliged, seating herself directly opposite Hari. Her movements were confident, strong rather than graceful.

This one has seen far too many adventures for my liking. Perhaps best not to try and seduce her. Not until I find out more, anyway.

'Hari Yassin of Ushalayim is at your service,' he said politely. 'What, may I ask, brings you here?'

'Sir Amalric of Bodain recommended said service,' replied the lady. 'He suggested you might have the... skills I require.'

Hari flicked a glance Hamidul's way. The weaselly thief just smirked. 'And what skills might those be, I wonder?' he said, returning his gaze to the *jhufa'ar*. 'More to the point, who might you be? Your Panglian is excellent, though accented – you have a look of the northerly Palomedian kingdoms about you.'

The visitor was unsmiling as she replied: 'You are of course a worldly man, and will be the best judge of the accuracy of your own guess. As for my name, that is something I would prefer not to disclose, for now.'

Hari said nothing by way of response to that.

A foreign noblewoman with a bodyguard and something to hide – this gets more interesting by the second.

'Go on,' he said, motioning for Hamidul to pour rhytons of juice for the guests.

'You are correct about my provenance,' said the mysterious woman. 'I am in fact a noble living in exile, for my rightful inheritance has been usurped. I would fain have my revenge, and my lands back – but for that I need an army. And an army requires money.' She paused to take a sip of juice.

'This is a long way to come for such a purpose,' Hari pointed out.

'The traitor who slew my father and took my lands is a powerful man,' replied the lady. The hatred in her voice sounded genuine enough. 'His arm is long, and women are no more respected in my country than they are in yours.'

'My lady, I can assure you that here in Sassania we treat women-'

She waved a hand dismissively. 'Spare me. The only way for a woman, even a noblewoman such as myself, to gain power is to take it – by force of arms.' She slammed a fist down on the table, making Hamidul start. 'And I will! Which brings me to why we are here. Before I was turned out of my ancestral home, I cultivated much reading in matters recondite and hermetic. I learned many of the legends of our world and yours. I take it, Hari Yassin, that you are familiar with the legendary Tombs of the Warlock Princes of Kishai?'

Hari smiled. 'Only as legends. That line of kings died out centuries before even the Thalamians came to these shores. The Kishan Empire is an ancient one and long lost.'

'Not quite,' replied the lady crisply. 'The Shemite tribes that founded it did not die out, as very well you know.'

Hari nodded. He himself had spent time among their descendants, the Halamites, in the deserts of southern Nazharya, after fleeing his old mentors. They were a pastoral folk, ancient and proud, wise and strong, but a shadow of their former selves.

'The lady is indeed most well informed,' he conceded. 'But not even the hardy Halamites would choose to go near the hecatomb cities of their Shemite ancestors. For as you must know, the warrior-princes of Kishai were also great sorcerers. They did not leave their tombs unguarded.'

'No indeed,' said the lady. 'Which is why, upon discovering the exact location of those tombs, I decided to commission the services of two Argolians. To deal with sorcerous traps and suchlike.'

'Wait, wait, just a minute,' interjected Hari. 'Tell me if I have this correctly. You have discovered the precise location of the legendary Kishan Tombs, and intend to ransack them for their fabled treasures – which you will then use to hire a mercenary army so you can take back your lands up north?'

For the first time, the *jhufa'ar* lady permitted herself a slight smile. 'That, indeed, is the sum of it.'

'I see,' said Hari. 'And to help you do this, you have

enlisted the aid of two mystic monks, whom you have somehow interested enough in worldly gain to go along with you?'

He exchanged another look with Hamidul, whose smile matched his own. Even dour Kemal was grinning openly now.

'A most likely tale, I am sure,' said Hari, stifling his laughter. 'From what I know of the monks of St Argo, they care more for spirits than sapphires.' It was an old saying in those parts, used in reference to the ascetic Sufielis, but it seemed appropriate enough in this instance.

Clearly the *jhufa'ar* felt otherwise. 'And if you knew more about the monks of St Argo, you would also know that the Order needs money to prosecute its age-old struggle against the Other Side.'

Hari steepled his graceful fingers as he pondered that. She probably had a point, he decided. From what he knew, the Argolian monks were somewhat more worldly than Sufieli mystics, who shunned material luxuries altogether and congregated in simple rude *rabats* that were scarcely more decent than hovels. Perhaps she had convinced two such monks to go along with her mad plan after all...

'And so what brings you here?' Hari had an inkling as to that, but it was best to remain cautious. He had no idea how much Amalric had told the damsels of his enterprises.

'The sorcerous denizens we have covered, thanks to our monastic allies,' said the woman. 'The more conventional traps we do not... as yet. I've heard you have some experi-ence as a tomb robber.'

Hamidul and Kemal exchanged nervous glances, but

Hari only laughed. 'Sir Amalric of Bodain has been telling many tales, I see! I wonder what you have done to make him so candid with other people's truths?'

'One of the monks I have commissioned is on friendly terms with Sir Amalric,' replied the damsel, ignoring the witticism. 'Which is why he would fain have your help in one other matter.'

Yassin raised an eyebrow. 'You aren't done telling stories? Please go on.'

The mysterious damsel obliged. A few minutes later, and smirks had become guffaws.

'Oh, this really is most superb,' gasped Yassin in between breaths. 'You mean to tell me your monk friends were foolish enough to ask Grand Master Tobin for aid, and he has mistaken them for apostates and sorcerers!? I beg you a thousand pardons, my lady – but this is too much! And now you want me to break the monks out of gaol – as part of my services on this quest of yours...!'

Kemal and Hamidul were laughing loudly now. Yassin joined in with their mirth freely. But as always, behind the laughter there was a grimmer interest. How much had Amalric told this foreigner of his business? The mysterious lady just pursed her lips, giving no signs of being irate, though her handmaiden huffed and glared. The rough-looking outlander simply kept one eye on Kemal, and one hand on her falchion.

'Do you have any idea how powerful a man Tobin is?' asked Hari, suddenly becoming serious. 'Why on earth should I want to risk crossing him?'

'If you are as good as they say you are, you won't,' replied the damsel. 'Because he won't know it was you that sprung our comrades. Besides that, I hear you're already in trouble with the Bethlers anyway. Another thing I hear is that a tidy sum of money could help relieve that trouble.'

That remark put an end to all mirth. Hari cursed inwardly. Amalric really had been liberal with other people's truths. This old monk and he must be very good friends indeed.

'I understand that, by virtue of his occupation, Sir Amalric is a knowledgeable man about the doings of this city,' the damsel went on coolly, 'and that because of this knowledge he is considered very influential. But Sir Amalric used to be a knight as well, a crusader no less – as did his colleague, who now languishes unjustly in a Bethler prison. Such ties are not easily broken.'

She was practically reading his thoughts now. The more psychic aspects of his old profession had never come easily to him, but Hari had an uncomfortable feeling there was more to this foreign damsel than beauty, book-learning and a smooth tongue.

'So Amalric has spared nothing in informing you of my situation,' replied the smuggler. 'Very well – you are offering to take me out of a present difficulty, but to do that I must put myself into many dangers. A gaol-break that risks creating a powerful enemy, a dangerous journey through hostile country, not to mention the tombs themselves... I don't think so, my lady, thanking you most cordially for the offer. I'll take my chances as they stand.'

Adhelina leaned forwards. 'The treasures of the Kishan Tombs are nothing short of fabulous,' she reminded him.

'All the tales agree on this. You would of course be rewarded with an equal share for your efforts. Such a share would make you rich beyond the dreams of avarice.' She spread her arms wide. 'All of this would seem as but a child's game, compared to what business you could command with such treasure to invest.' A cunning light entered her eyes. 'And I'm sure a man of your expertise would know how to fence stolen booty. Once again, your colleagues in this venture would be happy to reward you further out of their own shares – I for one shall be needing portable wealth when this thing is done.'

Hari held her gaze. He could normally spot a lie as quickly as he could spin one, but this woman was inscrutable.

He couldn't deny the offer piqued his curiosity and tempted his greed. He had murdered, intrigued and stolen his way to a respectable position in the Porcupine's under-world – but he missed the dust of myriad countries on his boots, the initial thrill as a tomb's first defences were broken past... And the Kishan Tombs were the biggest prize of all. If he pulled this off, his name would be more than respected, more than feared.

It would become a legend.

Feigning indifference, he folded his arms across his chest.

'If I took an interest in your venture, this would necessitate weeks of my time. How are my colleagues here supposed to fend off our creditors in the meantime?'

The mysterious damsel smiled. 'Sir Amalric of Bodain has agreed to put in a word with the Bethlers. The story he uses will be that he does not wish to see his own business interests with your outfit jeopardised – you steer many a pilgrim to the *Sojourn* when they embark, and he would be understandably loath to lose that business if your replacement decided not to continue the arrangement. Sir Amalric is not the richest man in Ushalayim, but he is highly thought of, as you know – the worthy knight is confident he can grant you a stay of execution, figuratively speaking.'

No, that is quite literally what will happen to me if I can't pay Tobin his money.

'And, just one question more that bothers me,' said Hari. 'What, if you don't mind my asking, are you contributing to this expedition?'

The lady smiled. 'Detailed knowledge of the tombs, their whereabouts and their traps – without that knowledge, this venture comes unstuck. I trust you will not insult my intelligence by asking me where I keep such knowledge, or how I came by it.' As if for emphasis, the foreign freesword tightened her grip on the falchion.

This could all be a confidence trick – no way I can verify the truth of what she says. But then why go to all this trouble if there is no treasure hunt?

Try as he might, Hari couldn't see the angle. They needed his labour up front, but no coin was being asked of him.

That meant this woman might even be telling the truth.

Kemal and Hamidul were looking at him sidelong. Hari could virtually sense the mingled feelings behind their eyes – trepidation, lust for gold, perhaps even excitement. The lady had certainly spoken true about one thing – the Princes of Kishai had been fabulously wealthy. Their maritime trading empire had once straddled the entire northern and western rims of the Great Inland Sea. Some even said their bravest heroes had plundered the cursed Forbidden City of the Varyans at its centre. Doubtless the sorceries they had acquired from the legacy of the Elder Wizards had been formidable.

The ultimate adventure was being dangled in front of him – dizzyingly high in both risk and reward. The silence drew out painfully as five pairs of eyes continued to stare at him.

Presently Yassin slapped his hands on the desk and beamed at all of them. 'Well now,' he said. 'I believe we have a gaol break to plan.'

From behind her mask of dissimulation, Adhelina breathed an elongated inward sigh. She had felt the smuggler scrutinising her minutely, and it had taken all her practice at the art of deception to keep him fooled. Beyond that, she'd even fancied the second sight's inverted powers were needed; at times it had almost felt as though the waterfront rogue were probing her in the way an Argolian might.

Of course there was no map, no treasure, no tombs – all she knew about the latter was that they were conveniently believed by most to be located in the foothills of the Abydos Ranges, not far from the Watchtower of Leviathan. Yassin was affable and charming enough, but Adhelina did not doubt he would pass a knife across her throat if he learned she had tricked him.

As she commenced telling Yassin what little she knew of Horskram and Adelko's capture, Adhelina hoped it wouldn't come to that.

CHAPTER 20
A FRAGILE COALITION

Princess Utha's eyes became bodkin heads as she saw Lord Hengist sweep into the Chamber of Council. At the centre of its circular precinct was a life-sized Jedrez board of obsidian and marble, set flush into the limestone floor. The Herzog of Stornelund swept across it toward his allotted place, flanked by his marshal Adso and steward Albercelsus.

Finally you grace us with your presence, Hengist. Now perhaps we can make some progress, and come to a real agreement. Preferably before half of Vorstlund falls to foreign lances.

The wind shrieked about them ominously, as if presaging the coming slaughter, whistling about pillars and billowing the standards depicting the coats of arms of the Nine Great Lords of Vorstlund.

Another four of those lords entered behind Hengist, bringing retinues of their own.

Eadgar the Dandy lived up to his name, dressed head to toe in the grey and black chequers of the House of Dreylock.

Doubtless Eadgar thought it a fitting show of patriotism; Utha thought it made him look like a jumped-up harlequin. But he commanded the best navy in the realm – the Dreylunders had learned much from their Cobian neighbours. And that made Eadgar a potentially crucial ally.

Next was Aethelfrith, Eorl of Upper Thulia. The ageing baron had to be supported by two stout squires – he'd lost the use of his legs on campaign against the late Lord Wilhelm of Dulsinor, and the winding stairs leading to the Chamber of Council would not accommodate his palanquin. The two squires sat him down on a folding chair and he looked around, darting an approving glance Hengist's way.

He was always a hated rival, but you pretend to like him well enough since he had Wilhelm treacherously killed last year, Utha thought. She'd never liked Aethelfrith, but she needed his knights and soldiers.

Third came Bjornwulf Firmhands. Probably the most powerful baron after Prince Leopold, the Herzog of Lower Thulia looked every inch the man in control: strong and stocky, well-dressed without being gaudy, his keen grey eyes seemed to take in every detail of the room. His eyes lingered longest on Hengist, she noted.

Sizing up your closest rivals already, thought Utha. But this was a man she could not afford to cross. With his forces undepleted by any recent wars, Bjornwulf would have the most able men to field.

The last lord to enter could not have been more different. Gunthor of the Kennels was so called because he loved his hunting dogs more than anything else. He presided over the poorest of the great baronies, Hyrlund. Despite that dubious status, he seemed oddly serene. But then a land-locked province tucked away in the hinterlands of the realm attracted few attempts at conquest, Utha noted.

I wonder what you make of this situation from your scrub-land holdfast, Gunthor, she thought as she eyed the spry middle-aged lord taking his place lightly to one side of the Jedrez board. *But even your help would be most welcome to us.*

Next to her, Franz cleared his throat. 'By the power vested in me, I hereby convene the thirty-fourth Council of the Nine, convoked in direst emergency-'

Gunthor made a point of clearing his throat loudly. 'I don't see nine lords here,' he said in his syrupy voice. A few snickers showed what the other barons thought of that, though Bjornwulf scowled, contempt for the eccentric lord stamped across his blunt, clean-shorn face.

Patiently, Franz went on: 'As you'll be aware, Lord Gunthor, the very invasion that prompts us to be here means that the lords of Aslund and Ostveld are unable to attend-'

'And what of Dulsinor?' inquired Hengist bluntly, cutting him off. 'Oh yes, they don't have a lord any more do they?'

Utha eyed the Herzog darkly, firing invisible bodkin arrows at his awkward frame. His face was flushed from too much wine, as usual. His drooping moustachios practically dripped with the stuff, and his outsized bald pate shone with a liquor-induced sheen of sweat.

'I think you know that all too well, Lord Hengist,' she said, her voice still affable. 'Seeing as it was you that took it upon himself to wipe out Dulsinor's lord and half his house, including his marshal and steward, while scaring off his only surviving heir into who knows what kind of hiding.' Using the same pleasant tone she always did when knifing a man with hard words, she added: 'I also know that despite all your efforts, you have failed to capture Graukolos after nearly a year at siege, and that brings you here to accept our offer of alliance.'

Hengist shot her a look that could have killed. He was about to say something, but Albercelsus gave a slight shake of the head, while Adso laid a brawny hand on his arm that was gentle but firm.

Still haven't lost your passion for the wine and your own self-regard, have you Hengist? Oh, but I know who's really in charge of Stornelund – Dulsinor isn't the only barony lacking an able lord.

'We have considered the terms and do indeed find them amenable,' said Albercelsus, as if reading her thoughts. The scrawny seneschal was bereft of one arm, after the initial attack launched against the Markwards the previous year had left him in need of an amputation. The official story was that one of Wilhelm's bodyguards had dealt the blow, though some of the more outlandish rumours had it that an outraged serving wench had stabbed the waxy-faced steward with a meat prong. Utha didn't honestly know which account to believe, but she knew which one she'd like to.

Beside her, she felt Franz stiffen at the confirmation of her daughter's betrothal plans. Lana was hardly woman enough to protest the unpleasant match, but that didn't mean her brother didn't feel strongly about it on her behalf.

'And I take it you have seen fit to invite the rest of us here, so we too can discuss this marriage plan?' put in Bjornwulf. 'I like news of this alliance no better than that which was proposed between Stornelund and Dulsinor.'

'Because you feel it pertains not well to your power, which you like well enough,' said Utha, still smiling. 'But know this, Lord Bjornwulf – the Pangonians are on our very doorstep, the Aslunders and Ostvelders struggle to hold off the Thalamians even as we parlay. If we don't agree on a plan of unity this very day, no one in this room will have any power for much longer.'

She let those words hang in the windswept chamber for a few seconds.

'All right,' said Bjornwulf gruffly. 'I suppose I can see the sense in it. Though my son-'

'-at twelve summers, is still too young by the laws of the land to marry,' Utha finished for him. 'You know that as well as I do, and besides, tactically such alliance would serve us nothing. You know that full well too, Lord Bjornwulf.'

The Herzog of Lower Thulia was nothing if not pragmatic. Suppressing a sigh of irritation at not getting his own way for once, he motioned for her to continue.

'Lana marries Hengist, uniting the Houses of Drüler and Lanrak, in return for which we dowry the Lanraks with a king's ransom, and His Grace swears a treaty here and now to stop invading Dulsinor. Once that's secured in writing before all these nobles here gathered, the Dulsinians will come to our aid. That in turn frees up the House of Lanrak to help the Ostveldings and Aslunders repel the Thalamians.'

'The rest of us can make common cause as we see fittest,' added Franz. 'Right now, Thalamy and Pangonia hold all Vorstlending land directly north of the Orne ranges, and the former are pushing up into Ostveld, too.' He shot a meaningful look at Adso. 'Meaning if they're unchecked, you could have a Thalamian army on your doorstep before the summer is out.'

'It's a sensible plan, all told,' acknowledged Adso. 'And if we can't annex Dulsinor, at least we can be compensated for our trouble with this dowry arrangement.' Tall and well-made and intelligent, the broad-shouldered knight shared only his liege's ruthlessness. A more competent marshal could not be found in the realm, now that poor Urist had met his end in one last gambit against the occupying Stornelendings. For that reason alone, Utha had seen fit to ensure representatives of the decimated House of Markward weren't present. The last thing she needed was a council of state descending into duels of honour.

'I too would urge that we follow this strategy,' added Albercelsus, awkwardly tugging at his truncated brocade sleeve. 'The defence of the realm demands it.'

Not to mention your ambition. You'll hold to this new treaty as long as the external threat remains, and not much longer.

But Utha had already begun making plans on that.

'But what of the Treaty of Lorvost?' Eadgar protested, stroking his tapering goatee thoughtfully. 'It's held the balance of power in the realm for two hundred years.'

'And will continue to do so,' Utha reassured him. 'The

marriage alliance we have taken the liberty of drawing up specifically precludes uniting our two baronies under any single ruler. All that will happen is Dulsinor will become a vassal state of Westenlund, under its protection, until the question of succession can be addressed properly. Needless to say, the lineages of Stornelund and Westenlund shall remain distinct – my son Franz will inherit the principality in his own right. The marriage is simply an expediency, to bring all civil war to a close. It's one the House of Drüler is happy to fund.'

In other words, we're bribing you idiots to stop killing each other for long enough to prevent the entire realm being conquered by foreign invaders. Heavens, noblemen, recognise a boon when it's placed in front of you!

Fortunately, the gathered lords and high officers were not entirely bereft of common sense. It took an inevitable hour or two of the usual internecine bickering, but eventually they had an agreement.

'Excellent,' said Utha, clapping her hands. 'Now we can proceed to war planning. My lord Eadgar – how soon can you send your navy to attack the blockade of Westerburg?'

The Eorl of Dreylund switched from his goatee to pluck at the long brown mustachios flanking it. Were it not for his bulbous pointy nose, he could almost have been handsome – perhaps that near miss at comeliness informed his sartorial flamboyance. But what counted to Utha was that Eadgar was a skilled mariner, along with many of his folk and most of his house.

'I'll be back with sails aplenty within the next moon,' he said. 'I trust I'll be well recompensed for this.'

You'll be recompensed by not losing your own holding once they overrun ours, you great fool.

'Of course.' Utha smiled at him.

'I scarcely see how I can help,' piped up Lord Gunthor. 'I've barely two hundred knights.'

'Aye, but you've a hundred times that number in fierce hounds,' said Bjornwulf, getting a laugh. To his credit, Gunthor had the grace to join in with the rest of them.

'Just contribute what you can, Lord Gunthor,' Utha told him kindly. 'Remember, it's your lands next if Westenlund falls.'

Gunthor frowned. 'We're hardly a rich barony,' he said, growing melancholy for the first time. His clothes were the colour of mud and scarcely more glamorous – the highest noble of Hyrlund dressed modestly even by Vorstlending standards. 'I can't see why these foreigners would care to invade us. Nobody else ever seems to bother.'

'This invasion is being led by Sir Hugon of the Purple Garter,' Utha reminded him. 'That man craves glory for its own sake, and little else from what I know of him. He won't stop at your rugged hill-lands just because they're poor, believe me – some even think the Pangonians plan to push farther north after they're done with Vorstlund.'

That was a sobering thought. Not even King Vasirius had been so ambitious, and most of the greatest Pangonian conquests since his time had taken place south, across the Sundering Sea, not deeper into Urovian territory.

And Carolus, you seemed such a cautious monarch when first you took the throne – who put you up to all of this, I wonder?

'Her Highness has the right of it,' declaimed Adso,

presuming to speak for Hengist, who looked distinctly bored now the talk of marriage dowries was over. 'These southern devils mean business, and we need to show them what Vorstlendings are really made of! Let's unite and send them packing!'

Utha smiled as the high lords about her took up the cheer. *Oh we're going to unite all right, Adso – but not in the way that you reckon.*

Later that day Princess Utha was in her bedchamber, gratefully slurping down the bitter brew her handmaiden had prepared. A wave of relief coursed through her as she felt the tendril of fire lacing through her bowels gutter. It wouldn't last as long as a poultice, but she was damned if she'd spend the rest of the day sitting on a sticky salve. Not this day, at any rate. The evening air was crisp and cool outside her window; the winds had died down and it felt more like late spring again.

A knock at her door. She'd bade her serving maids leave, wanting time to be alone. So far her preliminary inquiries had not borne fruit – but nor had they caused her to give up on the next part of her plan.

'It opens, I believe,' she said in her soft, kind voice.

She smiled at her son as he entered. He glanced towards the bed, from where a groaning sound told of her long-suffering husband.

'Your father's no better, I'm afraid. We've had to send to the monastery for another Marionite.'

Franz stepped softly so as not to disturb his ailing sire, taking a chair opposite his mother.

'The war plan is as ready as it can be,' he began. 'Lords-'

Utha raised a hand. 'As I told you before, my dear, I'll leave battle tactics and strategy to you. It's what you're good at. I wanted to talk to you about another matter.'

Franz arched a blond eyebrow. 'More politics, mother?'

She smiled. 'I'm afraid so. That is what your old mother is good at.'

Franz snorted. He was such a traditionalist, the idea of a woman scheming all the time didn't sit well with him. But he would just have to abide it a bit longer.

'Franz, you know this alliance will never last,' she said. 'At best, it's a binding rag to stymie a wound. This realm is grievous injured, and more drastic measures will be needed to heal it.'

Franz arched a second eyebrow. 'But we haven't been a proper realm since the War of the Four Kings,' he said. 'All we can ever be is a military alliance in times of emergency, such as now.'

'And that will work... for a time. But I'm quite certain Hengist and his coterie won't keep to their part of the bargain, new treaty be hanged – not as long as the question of the Dulsinian succession remains open. And the Lanraks aren't the only ones who'll be hungry for Graukolos and her lands. Aethelfrith the Crippled said barely a word all afternoon, but his lands abut on to Dulsinor's, and he has an old grudge to nurse against the Markwards. He'll be playing the long hunt, mark my words. Then there's Lord Bjornwulf... he hates Aethelfrith, always has – he won't sit by and let

Dulsinor pass into his rival's hands.' She sighed wearily. 'And that's just the half of it. No, there are far too many reasons for that lot to go back to fighting one another, and that's why we need strong unity.' She held his gaze. 'True unity.'

Franz nodded. Her beloved son was an idealist, but he wasn't stupid either.

'Go on, mother.'

'Soon your father will pass. Then you are Prince of Westenlund, or whatever's left of it. I'd see you become more, if possible. I'd see you become King of Vorstlund – now is the time to push for it. Your ancestor King Aelle was the last person to hold that title, so there's precedent.'

'But mother, the rest of the lords – you just said yourself how fractious they are! They'll never agree to it.'

'They will, if it's a flat choice between that and seeing Vorstlund under a foreign yoke. And if we can secure for ourselves the very alliance the Lanraks sought in the first place... I've been making inquiries. No one has had sighting of the heiress of Dulsinor on these shores in months, but several sources in the city agree that someone looking very much like her took a ship heading south last summer. Franz, she's alive – somewhere. Adhelina of Dulsinor was as intelligent and headstrong a noblewoman as any I've ever met, and if anything the years will only have sharpened her acuity since I saw her last. I think she's managed to evade the Pangonians, too – by my reckoning, if she was being held for ransom there, we'd have heard of it by now.'

Franz's brow was creasing as he tried to keep up with his

mother. He didn't have her Jedrez mind for intriguing yet – but she'd teach that into him, given enough time.

'My dear boy, there are only so many places a girl on the run of that kind of standing can go to without being caught. My guess is the Lady Adhelina isn't even in Pangonia any more. I'd say that leaves her most likely to go to the Empire, or the Pilgrim Kingdoms – somewhere remote enough that the nobles can't get at her, but where she'd be able to fit in well enough to go unremarked.'

Franz breathed out slowly. 'Mother, that's a bit far-fetched.'

'Perhaps, but what does it cost us to try? Once Eadgar breaks the blockade, I'm going to send emissaries south to try and find her.'

'And what then? Even if they do succeed in such a task? What will you have them say to her?'

Utha couldn't resist smiling as she answered her son's question. 'I'll have them make her an offer she can't refuse. To return home, marry my son, and become the Queen of Vorstlund.'

CHAPTER 21
A GAOL-BREAK BY NIGHT

The night sky was as black as Hari's costume. He hadn't worn it in an age; already he could feel his pulse quickening. He forced himself to find his inner quietude, channelling the lightness of air as he remembered what his old masters had taught him. A few stealthy foot-falls had him within a stone's throw of the fortress bailey.

It was heavily guarded, but then that was to be expected just two days after a breach of security. The first line of defence consisted of pairs of Bethler serjeants, positioned at regular intervals around the walls beneath hanging braziers.

The first line of defence is usually the weakest, thought Hari as he recalled his training. Slipping from the shadow of the town house he was crouching in, he channelled the essence of water and air as he dashed silently towards the perimeter. Scooping up a pebble in one fluent motion without breaking his stride, he hurled the stone into the brazier, directly behind the guards he had chosen. Both turned as one, only to see the flames guttering, before turning back to stare out into the night. Hari knew both guards would be blinded by the fire's after-glare for just a second, but that was all he needed. He slipped past them in the blinking of an eye and leapt up to grasp the wall, agile fingers expertly finding gaps between the stones as he began scaling it rapidly.

The second line of defence would be tougher. From where Kemal had stopped the covered wayn on the Street of Sentinels, Hari had seen the doubled night watch sketched against the black skies, as they patrolled the ramparts. Unlike the guards below, these would not be stationary, though Yassin had allowed for that, timing his sprint towards the wall to permit the largest possible gap between patrols. Counting off seconds as he scaled the wall, he allowed himself a burst of satisfaction as he registered being out by just a single second in his estimate. Like a shadow in motion, he slunk over the crenelations and on to the ramparts.

He'd picked the corner closest to the north-west turret. Along the northerly wall he saw a pair of serjeants moving steadily towards him. Yassin froze, crouching as he pushed his slender frame against the wall and channelled earth, willing himself to be one with the stones behind him. Hari knew that masters of his age-old craft could really conjure the illusion of invisibility, some said by tricking men's minds in much the way an enchanter would. But Hari was no master of the Way of the Shadow, just a likeable rogue who'd had better training than most. That would have to do: he was just beyond the ambit of the nearest torch, he hoped his subterfuge would be enough.

Yassin held his breath for a dozen seconds as the soldiers drew level with him. Laymen who served the Order he was infiltrating, they lacked the acuity of their superior brethren but would still be alert. Sure enough, no idle banter went back and forth between the men. Hari felt his heart pounding in his ears as he continued to channel earth, and count.

Thirteen... fourteen... fifteen...

On the count of sixteen, he detached himself from the wall and crept behind the two sentries as they entered the turret before moving directly on to turn the corner it straddled. Leaving them to continue their patrol, Hari descended the spiral stairs nimbly, two steps at a time. He passed another guardhouse midway down the turret, but these sentries were off-duty. Given the Bethlers' strict regime, they wouldn't be dicing like the usual guardsmen, but they weren't paying attention either and Hari had little trouble getting past them.

Reaching the bottom of the turret, he risked a quick glance out of the exit. The courtyard was quiet, the temple and refectory and guest quarters looming shadows to punctuate its sparse inky canvas. It was well after dark: most of the warrior-monks would be meditating in the barracks, praying on their swords as only their kind could. A flicker of light from the library building told Hari that some were studying.

But what really interested Yassin was the place Tobin had shown him, when the Grand Master had treated him to a little tour of the Bethler headquarters a few years ago.

The entrance to the dungeons was just as forbidding as

it had looked when he'd first set eyes on it. A ghastly black hole at the base of the keep, from which few were lucky enough to emerge alive and whole. He had been one of those, but the Grand Master had wanted to instil fear in him so he could use him. Tobin had remained chillingly calm throughout as he showed Yassin the instruments of torture that awaited him, should he ever cross the Order.

Thank you for showing me around the place, Tobin.

The Grand Master had always taken him for an ordinary thief: a tomb robber-turned-smuggler, a gang leader and nothing more. How wrong he was. Hari Yassin's better-than-average training included perfect recall, and it was a gift he was glad to put to use now. Tobin was a master in the use of fear: turning that same weapon against the Grand Master to defy another of his wanton acts of cruelty was no small pleasure.

Even if there is no damned Kishan treasure, doing this for its own sake alone might just be worth my while.

Slinking away from the exit and turning to another door within the turret's ground chamber, he silently thanked his gift of recall despite the stench that greeted him as he opened it. Smiling ruefully behind his mask, Hari stepped into the garderobe and bolted the door behind him.

'See, sometimes wot Tobin likes ter do is 'e skins 'em alive, one strip at a time.'

The gaoler shifted his feet on the table, as he peeled an orange with a knife to demonstrate his meaning. His leering fellow shook his head, displaying a handful of remaining teeth, all of them rotten. Clearly these men had availed themselves of Sassania's rich diet, but not its customs of personal hygiene. 'Naw, Gretch, ye've got it all wrong,' he said, sucking on a sugar cane. 'These 'ere are *witches*, they said. Gran' Master won't waste time torturin' 'em, 'e'll just burn 'em at the stake come mornin'. You'll see.'

Horskram scowled at the men, letting recollections of his last torture session at Cyprian's hands drop away before such thoughts unmanned him. He was in no mood for the gallows humour of unwashed riffraff, especially not at his expense. Their duty serjeant had stepped out to use the privy, giving the menials free rein to indulge their gruesome fantasies. He and Adelko were crammed into a mean little cell, about half the size of the one they had shared at Staerkvit; last night they had taken turns to sleep on the single bench they both now sat on.

The adept hadn't given up hope of rescue. Tobin would, as like as not, leave the pair of them to suffer captivity for a few days, in slow agonising anticipation of the tortures he would inflict on them in the name of the Almighty. Such cruelties of the mind went hand in hand with cruelties of the body – his ordeal at the hands of Cyprian had taught him that much first-hand. Even before the Purge, it was a mindset Horskram knew all too well: the Pilgrim Kingdoms furnished far too many men of Tobin's stamp. One of many reasons why he had forsaken the crusades.

Blessed Realm, I've missed you not. One day, I hope the Almighty sees fit to put you in more deserving hands.

He spared a glance at Adelko. The journeyman was

meditating, trying to maintain his serenity, but even so Horskram could tell the lad was taking this badly. Their conditions were worse than when the Valravyn had held them captive and their prospects of survival a lot lower, even if Balian had succeeded in getting word to Amalric.

Horskram's sixth sense told him the Bethler could be trusted to do that much. What it didn't tell him was what Amalric could do about their situation. He was influential, but Tobin was one of the most powerful men in the kingdom. And evidently mad, as well.

Come on Amalric, pull some strings, Reus damn you – it's our heads if you don't.

The sound of the door opening alerted the slovenly gaolers. The first whipped his feet off the table, thrusting the half-eaten orange into the pockets of his grimy hose. The second discarded the used sugar cane. The lay serjeant who entered was different from the one who had left. Horskram presumed him to be the relief watch.

He felt the blood drain from his cheeks when the serjeant disabused him of that notion.

'Open the cell door,' he said gruffly, motioning towards the barred gate of blackened iron that held the monks captive. 'These two are to be executed immediately. Grand Master Tobin's orders.'

The gaolers exchanged surprised looks. 'Thought 'is Eminence wouldov waited fer tomorrer,' said the first.

'You thought wrong,' replied the serjeant, unsmiling. 'His Eminence feels they can't be kept alive safely a moment longer – even shackled in links of cold iron, a witch is always dangerous. We're to burn them in the courtyard.'

'I said it would be a burnin'!' cried the second gaoler triumphantly. 'Shoulduv bet ye, Gretch!'

The serjeant shot him a dark glance. 'I think you two have had enough sport for one night, betting and japing and eating when you're supposed to be on duty. You can clean out their cell while the execution takes place – looks like they've managed to fill yon chamber pot, for all that we've starved them this past day.'

The gaolers looked crestfallen at being deprived of further entertainment, but did as they were told. The first unlocked the door while the second shuffled in. They were armed with naught but cudgels, but shackled hand and foot and deprived of quarterstaves there was little the monks could do.

Adelko's face was ashen as he registered what was happening to them. The lad's fortitude did him credit, but he was obviously terrified.

'Take strength in Stygnos and Virtus, lad,' breathed Horskram softly, fighting back his own fear. 'It'll be over shortly.' To the Bethler serjeant he said: 'Tobin won't get away with this. When Hannequin hears of our summary execution, there'll be hell to pay.'

The serjeant sneered. 'I suppose you'd know all about hell, being witches. As for Hannequin, tell me this – how many companies of men has your Grand Master?'

Horskram was about to retort when his sixth sense told him something strange. Flashing a glance Adelko's way he fathomed the journeyman had picked up on it, too. The lad's face no longer looked quite so pale.

An impostor, thought Horskram as the gaoler nudged him over to the serjeant. *But sent by whom?*

Hari Yassin kept his breathing calm as he escorted the two friars out of the gaol. He'd been able to lighten his skin tone in advance of his mission, and perfecting local accents had been a trick he'd learned even before he left Ushalayim to embark on his training, but packing a convincing disguise that wasn't too bulky had been awkward. He'd had to settle for a white kirtle and tabard in the end, hoping the gaolers would be too simple to notice his lack of armour and weapons. A dagger in the belt was the most he could opt for under the circumstances.

Fortunately, the pair of scoundrels seemed too busy pining for their missed spectacle to realise anything was amiss.

'Your friend sent me,' he hissed at the monks, as he shoved them up the stairs towards the courtyard. 'Just play along with everything I say and do, and we'll all get out of here in one piece.'

'How exactly do you plan on doing that?' growled the older monk as Yassin ushered them through the exit.

'Wait and see!' The damsels had warned him this Horskram could be implacable and irascible.

They were halfway to the gatehouse when someone called out from across the courtyard. Hari cursed inwardly as a youthful-looking knight approached him. He moved briskly and seemed unusually agitated.

'What in the Almighty's name do you think you're playing at?' he demanded. Hari felt his heart rise into his mouth, but then he registered the knight's nose wrinkling in disgust. 'The privy in the north-east tower is still blocked.'

'I'm sorry, sire,' Hari mumbled. Relief put welcome wings to his anxiety as he realised the knight had taken him for the duty serjeant. Here in the middle of the courtyard, there were no torches or braziers nearby, perfecting his disguise.

'Need I remind you that it's your job to see to such things while on night watch?'

'I'm sorry, sire, but I've been given fresh duties,' replied Hari, thinking fast. 'I was escorting these prisoners to the gatehouse, on orders of Brother Sir Balian.' Before the warrior-monk could mull that he improvised, adding: 'But now the cells are empty, yon menials on gaol duty are at a loose end for the rest of their shift. I'm sure they'd be happy to help.'

'Yes, I daresay they would,' snarled the knight sarcastically. 'In the meantime, I'll just have to use the upstairs latrine, I suppose. See it done once you've escorted the prisoners.'

Without another word the Bethler strode off, his mind clearly on his bowels more than anything else.

'Young recruit,' muttered Horskram quietly. 'Lucky for us, else his sixth sense might have detected us.'

'I suppose praying to Ashanti for wisdom only gets you so far,' grinned the rogue. 'Now look lively, my fair friars! Like as not, our friend will be bumping into the real duty serjeant on his way to the upper privy. We're nearly out of here, just one more obstacle to go!'

The gatehouse looked dark and forbidding as it loomed above them. It was crawling with serjeants led by a doughty-looking knight. Stepping forwards to address the latter, Hari channelled air, feeling light of heart as an innocent babe. He hoped that would be enough to deter whatever extra senses the warrior-monks had.

This Bethler was in early middle age, and clearly no new recruit.

'Well?' he asked curtly, eyeing the shackled monks suspiciously.

'Orders of Brother Sir Balian, sire,' said Hari. 'These here Argolians are to be taken to the King's palace. His Holy Majesty wishes to interrogate the prisoners himself.'

The Bethler raised an eyebrow. 'In the middle of the night? Who sanctioned this? Last I heard, Grand Master Tobin planned to execute these as witches after dawn prayers tomorrow.'

'Last-minute reprieve, sire,' replied Hari. 'King Rexus heard of their plight and is reluctant to have Argolians executed on his soil without further investigation into their guilt or innocence. His Holy Majesty is insisting the monks be brought to the palace dungeons right away.'

Hari could not even pray his ruse would work; he was too busy channelling air. This final deception had been hastily sketched out at Amalric's office. If there was one thing anyone might believe, it was that Ushalayan politics could turn messy at the drop of a knife.

'Can't say I'm overly surprised at that,' growled the knight. 'Killing Sha'abatians without proper trial is one thing, but Palomedian monks? Step too far, meaning no disrespect to His Eminence's judgement. All right, soldier – just wait here while I send word to Balian for confirmation. Can't be too careful nowadays, with assassins on the loose and whatnot.'

Hari's heart sank like a lodestone in a deep pool. And they had been so close...

'You won't be hearing anything out of him tonight, sire,' said Hari, trying one last desperate gambit. 'Been taken ill with food poisoning.' He took an inward breath, and took another risk. 'If you like, send word to the Grand Master. I've no doubt the order came from him originally.'

For a second that felt considerably longer, the Bethler held him in his grey-blue eyes. A battle of wills seemed to happen between the two of them.

Then the knight turned, motioning for the serjeants to open the gates. 'Can't see the merit in it, bothering the Grand Master at this time of night – you know how he hates to be disturbed from his nocturnal devotions. Be careful, mind! There are partisans crawling the streets like vermin. Blasted heathens doing the Fallen One's work for him.'

'Right you are, sire. I'll be very careful.'

More than you could possibly know.

Yassin half expected to hear another cry, or even feel a quarrel in his back, as he escorted the monks out of the fortress and back towards the town house he had used for cover. But none came. Rounding the corner, he found Kemal waiting for him with the cart and horses. Bundling the friars under a tarpaulin into the back of the wayn, he bade them hide in the straw beneath. Scanning the deserted streets quickly, Hari stripped off the mantle and kirtle and shoved them under the straw. He was down to his underhose and tunic, but the night wasn't cold.

Jumping up beside Kemal, he nudged his henchman. He flicked the reins and the horses started off down the street. Hari was already wiping make-up off his face, peeling away the false beard and pate he had used to disguise himself. He'd just look like one more raggedy nightsoilman about his work if any sleepless townsman chanced to glance at him in the darkened street.

Leaning back against the cart, Hari cast a grateful glance at the star-seamed skies and whispered a quick prayer to Ashanti.

Mission accomplished, he thought gladly as they rumbled on their way to the *Hallowed Sojourn.*

CHAPTER 22
A FAREWELL TO THE CITY

Hettie picked at the abundant repast Amalric had placed before them on the skirting table: skewers of spiced meats and roasted peppers, wafer-thin baked breads, tomato chutneys, chickpea purees seasoned with herbs, olive oil, dates, plums, raisins, sherbet and sugared sweets... She appreciated the effort the master of the *Sojourn* had gone to put them at ease, but scarcely had an appetite.

What she did appreciate was the rich dark liquid flavoured with sugar cane that Amalric kept serving up in tiny ceramic cups. It tasted delicious and lifted her off her feet like one of Adhelina's potions. Though it must be nearing the Wytching Hour, she scarcely felt tired. Adhelina had clearly drunk far too much of it. Would she ever cease her pacing of Amalric's parlour?

The old knight must have been thinking the same thing, for suddenly he said: 'My lady, I would be more than grateful if you'd ease your frantic footsteps. That carpet cost me many bezantis to import from Kallandhar, and I'm quite sure you're wearing a hole in it. Sit down and eat, for heaven's sake.'

'I'm sorry,' she replied glumly, taking a seat and eating perfunctorily from her bowl of stew. It was lamb cooked up in a thick spicy sauce, so hot you needed to swallow a bland white creamy substance called *yoghurt* just to get over it. Hettie wondered if all this rich food and drink was good for the nerves. No wonder they were always warring in the Pilgrim Kingdoms, if this was their regular diet.

'You can hardly fault us for being nervous,' she said. 'Sitting around here waiting for our friends to arrive...' *Or not.*

'Yes well, it isn't your livelihood and neck on the line if this thing fails,' snapped Amalric, reaching for a silver ewer and pouring himself some purple Muradi wine.

'I wouldn't mind some of that,' said Adhelina. 'This...' – she motioned to her cup, still half full of the dark sugared liquid – 'what do you call it again?'

'Coffee,' supplied Amalric.

'... coffee isn't doing my nerves any good.'

No wonder, seeing as you guzzled a gallon of it. But Hettie wasn't slow to take up Amalric's offer of a goblet herself.

'Thanks be to Kaia!' exclaimed Adhelina, gulping down the vintage. 'This is much more like it. That brown stuff is stronger than all my teas put together.'

'Coffee enlivens the wits, they say, and you'll be needing those about you by the looks of things,' said Amalric. 'You've a journey ahead of you tonight.'

Adhelina waved a hand dismissively. 'We've done this sort of thing before,' she said. 'We know how to look after ourselves.'

Amalric frowned into his cup. 'Evidently.'

There came a knock at the parlour door.

'Who is it at this time of the night?' bellowed Amalric. He had to keep up the act, Hettie supposed.

'One of the guests wants ter see yer,' came the timorous voice of one of Amalric's serving boys.

Amalric exchanged furtive glances with the damsels. Fingering the damasked silver poniard at his belt, he got up and edged his girth around the ornate table he had been eating at. Walking over to the door, he flung it open. The boy was standing in the hallway. Behind him was a figure Hettie recognised immediately. The old flautist they had met in the yard had the same placid expression on his face, and gave no indication that he remembered them.

'What in Palom's name do you want with me at this ungodly hour, Tipu?' demanded Amalric. His voice was gruff but not entirely devoid of kindness; Hettie guessed the wandering mystic was a regular at the *Sojourn*.

'Always it is a pleasure to speak with the master of the house,' said Tipu cordially. He glanced over the old knight's shoulder. 'Though it is not you with whom I wish to break words.'

Amalric's gaze hardened suspiciously, but Adhelina called out. 'No it's all right,' she said. 'We know this man. Please let him in.'

Shaking his head in perplexity Amalric sent the boy away, shutting the door after the mystic had entered.

'I won't offer you board or wine as I know how ascetic you mystics are,' he said. 'I hope you won't mind my asking what you want with my distinguished guests.'

'Your plan speeds well,' said Tipu. 'The one who calls himself Hari Yassin is on his way back here with your friends.'

Hettie could only smile as Amalric's jaw dropped. She wasn't in the least bit surprised to hear such a revelation coming from the mystic. She'd seen and heard stranger things on her adventures.

Adhelina was smiling, too. '"You shall know a Sufieli by the quiet potency he wields",' she quoted.

The mystic nodded approvingly. 'You know our ways well,' he said.

Adhelina's smile broadened. 'Sir Guillaume of Tyros's *Histories and Peoples of the Pilgrim Kingdoms* proved most informative.'

'Learning is Ashanti's gift to the wise,' said Tipu, seating himself cross-legged on the carpet. 'Now it is time you learned something of me. When first we met, I said our paths should intertwine. That was true, and so it has proven. But our paths are fated to cross but briefly, for I am here to set you on a different course.'

Adhelina blinked. That she hadn't expected.

The mystic went on. 'Soon, Hari Yassin will arrive with the monks he has freed at your behest. I know a little of the story you wove to persuade him to help you. For this to be believable, you must remain here. No woman of high birth would risk her life on a foreign adventure in enemy territory.'

Adhelina protested. 'But I've told him I'm the one putting this whole venture together...'

'A woman of power must lead from the centre, not the

front,' said Tipu, shaking his head. 'You have presented yourself as such. For the deception to keep Yassin fooled, it must hold up to scrutiny.'

'Much as I hate to get involved any more in this frightful business, I think Tipu is right,' said Amalric. 'Any mission behind Sassanian lines is dangerous. If it's an Argolian mission, doubly so.'

'But I've intimated to Yassin that I have the maps, the knowledge, everything about the tombs...'

'... which you have entrusted to your swordswoman friend here,' Tipu finished. 'A stronger guardian of such important knowledge in any case.'

Anupe raised an eyebrow from where she had been sitting quietly in the corner, sipping Muradi wine and nibbling at Amalric's delicious sweetmeats. 'I am not going anywhere,' she said. 'Ushalayim has prospects for a woman of my talents.'

'The Sassanian hinterlands even more,' smiled Tipu. 'A lot of work in the Sultan's army nowadays for a freesword like you.'

Hettie stared at Tipu. For a mystic he was certainly quite cunning.

'We're going with Horskram,' persisted Adhelina stubbornly. 'That's what my visions have been telling me-'

'I see,' said Tipu. 'Then tell me, what do you make of the vision you had last night of your homeland? The one where you lead men and break sieges, uniting those behind you as you drive your enemies back?'

Now it was Adhelina's turn to gawp. 'I... hadn't had time

to consider it,' she said. 'In truth I'd simply thought it a hopeful dream, born of a hopeless spirit.'

Tipu smiled sadly. 'So bereft of faith your trials and tribulations have left you,' he said. 'And yet you concocted a story for Yassin similar to this very vision that was bequeathed you. Most peculiar, I would say.'

'It's true I did embellish our cover story quite a bit,' Adhelina allowed. 'But I had to, for just the reason you said – to make it sound convincing.'

Tipu remained smiling. 'And what if I were to tell you that a false story might prove true, from a certain point of view? Or as the Prophet sayeth, truth is a river with many tributaries.'

'Just a second,' interrupted Hettie, pushing her wine away so she could think clearly. 'You're trying to tell us that thanks to some shared visions the pair of you have been having, the Unseen have decided that it's our destiny to go back home to Vorstlund after all? Then why come here in the first place?!'

Tipu smiled. 'Your answer will be walking in through the door any minute now,' he said. 'Without your help, the goodly friars would most certainly have been doomed to execution. In saving them, you have saved their quest. Now your purpose here is accomplished, it is time for you to accomplish your next task. And that lies in the northlands, whence you came.'

Hettie had to laugh. 'Well, the Unseen move in myste-rious ways,' she trilled, reaching for the wine goblet again.

'Their ways are not mysterious to those who have eyes to

see,' said Tipu. Hettie thought he sounded rather smug now, but she let it go.

'At any rate, I shan't complain,' she said, draining her cup. 'It's high time we went home, if you ask me.'

'But that's not possible,' said Adhelina. 'Lord Hengist, the Pangonian King, even the Mercadians, they're all looking for me...'

'As are others who would not do you harm,' interjected the mystic. 'You must be patient, and bide your time here. Before very long men will come for you, from your country. Stay well protected, but easy to find. You are resourceful and know how to do this. It is what your adventures have prepared you for.' He fixed her with his deep brown eyes. 'At first they will seek to use you, as all men of power do. But in time, if you are wise and cultivate your gift, the serpent will turn in their hands and bite them. Your people shall look to you for succour, and you shall be a shield to them. That is your destiny, Adhelina of Dulsinor.'

Amalric did a double take as he caught the name. But any protest he might have had was silenced by another banging on the door.

'The draymen have arrived early.' The agreed code message they had given the boy. Draymen usually delivered ale and wine in the early hours, so it would seem innocuous enough.

Amalric got up and opened the door again. The boy was standing in the passage, with Hari Yassin behind him.

The trickster grinned. 'I have a delivery for you,' he said.

～

Adelko rubbed his wrists and ankles. It hadn't taken the rogue called Yassin long to pick the crude locks binding their manacles, but he hadn't appreciated having to wear them like a witch in the first place. Nor had he appreciated being divested of quarterstaff, prayer book, circifix and holy water, not to mention all the ready money he and Horskram had brought with them.

They had exchanged a grimy prison cell for a dank cellar, but Adelko wasn't complaining. Fortune had turned their way strangely. Now they had two local men to help them. Men with uncommon skills and powers at their disposal, by the looks of things. And he'd gathered Anupe might be coming with them, too.

'We'll just have to see about picking up more supplies when we get to Sha'iza'ar,' said Horskram.

'With what coin, Master Horskram?'

'With the coin Sir Amalric is most kindly going to lend me,' replied his mentor.

'Oh, that coin,' said Adelko, half smiling.

The cellar door opened and Amalric walked down a short flight of stone steps towards where they sat on a couple of stools. Adelko gazed at the barrels lining the cellar, longing for a drink of their contents. Their gaolers had given them scarcely more than a few sips of stagnant water.

'Horskram of Vilno,' said Amalric, 'I can't say I'm pleased to see you under these circumstances.'

Horskram stood and embraced his old fellow crusader. 'I can only say I am, for my part,' he replied. 'A thousand blessings on you, Sir Amalric. You have saved our lives, and many more besides.'

Amalric pulled away from his embrace. 'Don't give me all the credit,' he said brusquely. 'Your lady friends must be very persuasive.' Lowering his voice, he added: 'Whatever tale she's told Yassin, best to go along with it. She scrawled down the salient details, so you can learn your part in the cover story.' The old knight pulled a scrap of parchment from his silken gown and pressed it into Horskram's hand.

The old monk frowned. 'I did not intend for Her Ladyship to get so heavily involved in the ploy to rescue us.'

Amalric snorted with laughter at that. 'You surely didn't think I was going to risk everything I own – including my life – to save you all by myself, did you? Spare Helene, or whatever she's really called, a prayer when you give thanks to the Unseen for your delivery.' Horskram seemed about to ask further questions but Amalric turned on his heel, beckoning for them to follow. 'Come, we haven't much time before the Bethlers discover you're missing, and I want the pair of you long gone from my hostelry by then. I've prepared swift horses – they cost me a pretty penny, but I'll just have to trust you to pay me back the money when you can.'

Horskram winced. 'Speaking of money, Sir Amalric...'

It was still dark when the five companions left the courtyard of the *Sojourn*. Adhelina and Hettie stood beside Amalric in his parlour, watching them go from one of its many windows.

'I hope they aren't intercepted,' she said.

'Traders' Gate is still open at this time of night,' said Amalric. 'The Sassanian caravan routes never sleep – some merchants even employ savants of the Sect of Light and Fire so they can travel more easily at night.'

'It won't stay open much longer once the Bethlers find out they're missing.'

As if to mark her words, a clarion call sounded from the direction of the Bethler headquarters.

'In the nick of time,' said Amalric. 'Well, that's our part in it done. If you don't mind, I'll thank the two of you to pay up and leave at first light tomorrow. The less contact we have, the better.'

The better for you, she thought. But she could hardly fault the old knight for trying to preserve his hide. She watched the five figures turn up the winding Street of Caravanserai. She suddenly felt naked without Anupe.

Next to her Hettie sighed. 'I suppose it's just us again, milady.'

Adhelina caught her last word, then shot Hettie a sidelong glance. 'Milady,' she murmured. 'You haven't called me that in a long while.'

Hettie smiled a small smile. 'It's been a long while since it's felt appropriate,' she said. 'But now by the looks of things we're going home, to claim what's ours. Well at some point in the near future we are, anyway.'

Adhelina took a deep breath of cool night air, reflecting on that. Something deep inside her said the mystic Tipu could be trusted, though she also knew that no prediction could ever be exact.

But still, she liked the way Hettie had put it.

'Yes, Hettie,' she said, reaching out to pat her arm. 'We're going home, to claim what's ours.'

PART II

CHAPTER 1
A DECISION REACHED

Far below the cave mouth, the lights of Kell twinkled against the vaporous evening. Fog rolled in off the surging seas, as the ghostly mariners began their eldritch whining for another night. Ariadha ap Madrix pulled her sash more tightly about her lithe frame, hugging its indigo stars and green diamonds closer as the wind rose steadily.

She loved it up here, always had done. A forlorn and frightening landscape this might be to outsiders, but to the Marcher Lady of Clan Nuallán it was home. She inhaled sharply, fancying she could taste a salty tang in the crisp sharp air even up here, hundreds of hands above the coastline.

Reluctantly she turned to face the cave interior, to see how the others were faring in their deliberations. Three days it had gone on. As the moon slowly birthed herself again, the lords and druids had repaired into the bowels of Skelnaervon to continue debating. Connaer ap Morgaan was arguing with Epidorix ap Olwyn, but that was typical of the two: the Marcher Lords of Clans Paelyn and Arawn always came to grief whenever there was an All-Meet.

'Have they bothered addressing the matter at hand, or are they still just bickering over their border dispute?' she asked the slight girl loitering at the back of the circle of lords, warriors, priestesses and druids. She was fond of Lyna ap Fadwyn; though she had seen only thirteen springs, the Marcher Lady of Clan Draghain was measured beyond her years.

'No, and not likely will they,' piped Lyna in her alto voice. 'Connaer has added two more ears to his necklace since last we gathered. One of them belonged to Epidorix's nephew, and but fifteen the lad was when Connaer slew him.'

Ariadha had no sympathy for the quarrelling lords. 'That's what they get for not resolving their land dispute moons ago,' she said. 'It's us who belong to the land, not the other way around. Just custodians we are, Lyna.'

'Try telling that to proud men,' smirked Lyna.

The Druiding Council sat in chairs fashioned of roots that shifted to accommodate them, vestiges like Ys's crystal throne of the fabled Old Time. So were the seams of luminescent quicksilver that lit up the cavern at night-time: in ages past, sorcerer-smiths had used the magic metal of Skelnaervon to fashion limbs that moved, but few nowadays could master such craft. The last to learn it had fled the islands with a death-geas on his head for demonolatry, Ariadha reflected. One more piece of good news that Morcant had brung – Andragorix the renegade was dead.

Ys was banging his staff down loudly now. The Grand

High Druid had clearly had enough of the Marcher Lords and their antics, too.

'Silent you'll be now!' he bellowed, his fruity voice surprisingly strong. 'Not here to discuss your fool land wars are we, Connaer and Epidorix. Step back to your places, and let wiser tongues speak.'

The high priestesses and archdruids sitting in a semi-circle behind Ys all murmured their assent. Somewhat abashed, the two lords stepped back and emptied the space so someone else could speak.

'I'd say something, if it please the All-Meet,' said Ariadha, stepping forwards.

'Please us it does,' chorused the convocation.

'But short time ago, guards brought me word from Kell – the mainland monk now says he wishes to withdraw his request to inspect our defences. Safe conduct home for him and his companions is all he now asks.'

The All-Meet shared a baffled silence at that. The monk's insistence that their share of Morwena's Doom might no longer be safe had unsettled the lords and druids deeply; his subsequent request – which sounded more like a demand coming from the arrogant mainlander – that he be allowed to assess their defences had provoked outrage. Who was this foreign unbeliever, to cast aspersions on their sacred guardianship? A man who had devoted his life to hunting down their kind, no less, compelling one of their own to bring them here on pain of death.

Ariadha had to hand it to the Argolian – he wasn't a weakling, this one. He had *roots*, as they liked to say on the islands. But now this oaken man was retracting his demand

– surely such a person would not be dissuaded by mere intransigence? Something was afoot.

The silence had given way to murmurings, as the warriors and druids fell to debating the matter among themselves. Finally Ys spoke again, his loud voice cutting across the returning hubbub: 'Odd that this Joram should change course so, given strong winds of mind that drove him to us. What prompted you to guard this news, Ariadha ap Madrix, like precious nugget concealed beneath hollow earth?'

Ariadha smiled wryly. 'Scarcely could I birth single word in past half hour, for yon lords' talk of travails over land.'

Laughter greeted that. Some of the lesser druids and priestesses even joined in the warriors' mirth, though the Druiding Council remained unsmiling. Epidorix's bulbous nose flushed as red as his whiskers, as was always the case when he was abashed; dark-haired greying Connaer, more of a patrician warrior than his rival despite his older years, drew himself up on his bow legs and glared about the All-Meet.

'For another audience does Joram of Kilucan now plead,' went on Ariadha. 'That he may petition us in person.'

Ys nodded, the eyes in his overlapping coat of bark blinking in the turquoise light from his crystal throne. 'High time it is we undammed that river,' said the Grand High Druid. 'In light of words broken betwixt us these past days, shall we examine their story again?'

It was a question, not a decree. Ariadha breathed a sigh of relief as his eight fellow Aspirants and the rest of the All-

Meet gave its assent. These things had been known to run for weeks on occasion.

'Not over yet is it,' said Lyna, noting Ariadha's relieved expression as she rejoined the convocation. 'No real decision have we reached.' Her button nose twitched as she looked up at Ariadha with round black eyes under her boyish mop of ginger hair. Even for her age, Lyna was very small, barely level with Ariadha's shoulder.

'Disorderly government that's fair and free do I prefer to swift-serving tyranny,' was what Ariadha said to that. Clan Nuallán traced its ancestry back to Caedmon the Far-Sighted and beyond: its scions had ever been wary of concentrating too much power into too few hands.

Caedmon, the same chieftain who had decreed that the broken Headstone be scattered to the four corners of the world, seven hundred years ago.

It worked for a time, she thought. *But now someone seeks to do as Morwena once did. And we haven't even decided what in Kaia's name to do about it. We ought to make common cause with our fellow guardians, but then again why should we trust the mainlanders?* That was not the least of questions that had divided the convocation.

Menials came to serve them platters of boar meat, with ale in hollowed-out tusks, while the All-Meet awaited the detainees. As she quaffed from her horn, Ariadha reflected that perhaps one reason why the lords rambled on about unrelated matters was because none of them wanted to confront the age-old threat that had resurfaced.

She looked over at Ys, who did not partake of any food or drink. His shiny eunuch's face was stolid, but his eyes were heavy-lidded from lack of sleep; she knew the Grand High Druid well enough to realise how perturbed he must be. The Druiding Council had long fathomed a deep disturbance in the Veil, but Ariadha suspected the Nine Aspirants had hoped things would not develop so far in their lifetimes. That Morcant had taken so long to return with any news had made the All-Meet even more skittish, though Ariadha supposed he could not be blamed for the disturbance in the Veil that jammed his attempts to scry home.

Someone is going to every effort to cover their tracks. Somebody with more powerful command of sorcery than any seen on this side of the Veil in a dozen lifetimes.

Presently guards returned with Morcant and three of his companions, the monk Joram and two knights. Ariadha had kept the sailors in separate quarters – better if they knew as little about their reason for being here as possible. Besides, she wanted to keep Morcant and his unlikely Palomedian ally under close scrutiny. Though she was no druid, it seemed to Ariadha that there was a strange symbiosis between the pair, one that was altogether unwholesome.

'Long have we deliberated on your request, now we hear you have another.' It was fair-faced Ianna who spoke, incipient crow's feet around her sultry eyes and tassels of grey in her raven locks betraying her true age. Most powerful of the high priestesses, she presumed to speak up first. Her witcheries were great by the dwindled standards of the Latter Time, though in truth Ariadha had never liked the haughty matriarch.

'We do indeed,' said the monk in thickly accented Gnáthtéanga. 'If our suit troubles you so much that you can't reach a decision, we would ask that you free us and our crew, so we can return home across the seas. Preferably unmolested by your demon sorceries this time.'

Ianna's full elegant lips curled in a scowl, as other druids and warriors voiced their displeasure. 'What sacrilege is this you offer? No demon sorceries did we employ, just the usual Thaumaturgy to deter visitors. But no, you seek to provoke us into rash decision. Not so swiftly or recklessly will the winds of our judgement blow!'

'I don't see much risk of that,' replied Joram smugly. 'The winds of judgement on these isles seem more like a gentle breeze to me. Swift is not a word I would use to describe your counsel-taking.'

'We judge matters of import in our own time,' retorted Ianna, the scowl not leaving her face.

'You sue for access to our direst secret, now suddenly your desire melts away like winter frost before first touch of spring,' said one of the archdruids, leaning forward in his chair. Tall and athletic, Fanwyn had not lost any of the vigour of youth, though he was close on fifty winters and near bald. As most powerful of the male aspirants, he arrogated much the same liberties as Ianna. 'Ianna speaks the Moon Goddess's truth,' he went on. 'This sudden change of course casts a shadow of suspicion upon the field of this discussion.'

The two exchanged self-satisfied smirks. Ariadha knew that the pair had been lovers, before their ascension to druiding adepthood compelled them to take vows of celibacy. But they remained thick as thieves nonetheless. Ariadha didn't care much for Fanwyn either.

'Rather than argue over what prompts the monk to change course, perhaps we should decide whether to grant him his original request,' said Ariadha, ignoring protocol to speak again from the fringes of the circle. 'After all, isn't that what we've been debating these past three days?' Much as she didn't trust mainlanders, she was beginning to suspect that spurning the monk's offer of help might not be the wisest course of action. Whoever wanted to reunite the Headstone had already succeeded in obtaining two of the four fragments.

The All-Meet had fallen to muttering yet again.

Joram sneered. 'Three days!' he exclaimed, echoing Ariadha's last words as he rounded on the convocation. 'Why not debate another three weeks, just to be really sure? I hadn't realised your pagan society was so timid when it came to taking action. Perhaps I shouldn't be surprised.'

Angry growls from many of the warriors greeted that statement. The lesser druids and priestesses, though usually slower to anger, looked none too pleased either. Ariadha felt herself tensing. *He strikes at the heart of the matter,* she thought. *We ramble on and argue, and no action is taken. A wonder Caedmon ever succeeded in scattering the Headstone fragments in the first place.*

'Forgive me if my candour riles you,' said Joram, not sounding like he cared a corn stalk for forgiveness. 'But we arrive on your shores bearing news of the worst sorcerous catastrophe of our era, and how do you address the matter? With endless discussion!' The monk was scoffing openly now.

Ys glared at him coldly. 'Our ways are not the ways of the

mainland,' he said. 'Here on the islands, we debate matters of state thoroughly. No one rules by decree.'

Joram scoffed again. 'Ah, like the Thalamian Electors of old! Mightily impressed are we by your enlightened self-governance! Now if you're done impressing us – get a move on and MAKE A DAMNED DECISION!'

'Right he is,' said Morcant, his voice tremulous. 'Pains me to agree with a mainland priest it does, but right he is! Long enough it took to bring you this warning, no more time to spare have we.'

Ianna cast him an imperious stare. 'If time is short as winter's sun, whose fault is that?'

'Those are unjust remarks, Aspirant Ianna,' admonished Ariadha. 'Morcant bore his punishment geas without complaint, and has fulfilled its terms faithfully. Long and hard did he work to infiltrate this conspiracy of wizards, and even if he didn't uncover its ringleader, he helped defeat Yathaga's chief understudy.'

'You've had your say, Ariadha ap Madrix,' replied Ianna coldly. 'And matters of witchery are for druidkind to discuss.'

Matters of witchery that revolve around an artefact kept on my lands, she thought bitterly. But she knew better than to voice that opinion in front of the mainlanders.

'I would not seek to gainsay the Druiding Council in any such matters,' she replied diplomatically. 'Merely to point out that Initiate Morcant has served us well.'

'Perhaps we should elevate him to full druidhood,' sneered Fanwyn.

'Perhaps you should!' cried Ariadha, ignoring his

sarcasm. 'Morcant may once have been foolish, but he has done more to serve our cause than anyone here.'

'And what is our cause exactly?' demanded Connaer, his salt-and-pepper eyebrows knitting in consternation. 'For seven hundred years, we have borne our share of Morwena's Doom – what more is there for us to do? If the mainlanders have failed in their part, what business is that of ours? So long as we keep our fragment well guarded, the realms of mortalkind need not fear.'

A loud chorus of throats showed that many of the dignitaries agreed with the brash lord. Distrust of the mainland ran deep among island folk.

'We can't just turn our backs!' cried Ariadha, ignoring Ianna's admonition. 'My ancestor Caedmon would never have advocated such complacency.'

'Knew him personally, did you?' grunted Connaer, getting laughs from his warriors.

'Have you forgotten why we're called the Marcher Lords?' Ariadha shot back. 'Because we guard the fringes of the world.' She pointed out west, where the seas raged for leagues without number. 'At the end of the Great Western Ocean lies naught but the Veil, and beyond that – you know what dwells there! Our mission it was, entrusted to us by Kaia thousands of years ago, to protect that divide.'

Connaer laughed derisively. 'Are you a druid yourself, now? I say 'tis for the Aspirants to decide on such matters, not us.' The lowly title archdruids and high priestesses took was misleading; aspirants in the eyes of the Moon Goddess, they were nonetheless the foremost religious authorities in the land.

All eyes turned to Ys and his brethren.

At least now we are getting somewhere, thought Ariadha. *Let somebody assume command, and make a decision as the monk urges.*

The Grand High Druid was deep in thought, the light within the throne pulsing softly, giving him an ethereal look as the eyes in his mantle blinked and rolled. Then he spoke.

'Ariadha ap Madrix speaks the Moon Goddess's truth – our age-old share of the burden this was, entrusted to us by the Unseen. This monk may not be of our faith, but collaborated he has with one of our own to defeat the traitress witch Abrexta the Prescient. Guarded a share of Morwena's Doom for centuries did the Order he represents – if he wishes to see how we protect ours, I say owe him that much we do. And perhaps we can learn from the mainlanders' mistakes.'

That provoked another rash of protests.

'Sacrilege that is!' cried Epidorix. 'To let unbelievers look upon such a thing – no good will come of it, I say!'

Ariadha exchanged another wry glance with Lyna. Clan Arawn were also noted for their piety: like most marchers on the northerly isle of Skulla, Epidorix seemed able to muster passion for matters both temporal and spiritual at will. His rival Connaer by contrast was now beginning to look bored – as a lord of southerly Kaluryn, he was less interested in eldritch things; Ariadha knew he would be happy as soon as the unwelcome strangers were off the islands. Out of the corner of her eye, she caught Diarmuid ap Morraugh, Marcher Lord of Clan MacRoth, shaking his head. That wiped the smile off her face. She'd always respected Diarmuid, who ruled the bridging isles of Blenau modestly and shrewdly. A small, quiet man, he had studied the druiding rites in his youth, and knew more than most lay marchers about such matters. Diarmuid obviously didn't think it a good idea to share secrets with outsiders, and that gave her pause.

The Druiding Council had fallen to arguing amongst themselves, mirroring the fractiousness of the entire convocation. Ianna and Fanwyn were against letting the outsiders view the fragment, taking about half the council with them. The rest of the aspirants appeared to be of Ys's mind. Ariadha caught Joram and Morcant exchanging shrugs, whilst the two mainland warriors simply looked aghast at the disorder unfolding about them.

After a while Ys banged down his staff again for silence. When he didn't get it, he mouthed a word of magic and the throne pulsed brilliantly once, twice. When her dazzled eyes cleared, Ariadha looked upon a silent cave.

'See you can how divided we are,' said the Grand High Druid, addressing Joram directly. 'The convocation knows not what to do with your request. When Caedmon the Far Sighted sent Orbegan and Jedda and Corann and Cael to the Four Winds with your shares of the burden, it was not intended that you should return to us in failure.'

'The Far Sighted didn't see that coming,' quipped Connaer, to more laughter from his men. He was well in his cups by now.

Ys glared at him and went on. 'Put it to a vote of the Nine we will – if the rest of the Convocation of Kaia agrees.'

Joram rolled his eyes, then briefly translated for his two

companions. The knights stared at the monk in exasperation. Fortunately for them, the islanders were getting just as weary of the interminable debate. As one, the All-Meet voiced its assent. The vote went as Ariadha expected it to – in the end Ys tipped the balance, taking two archdruids and two high priestesses with him. Fanwyn and Ianna took one more apiece, but at four votes they fell short of a majority.

'So it is,' declaimed Ys, rising from the throne, which pulsed once more and went dark. The eyes in his mantle looked positively sleepy. 'Ariadha ap Madrix, at first flush of dawn shall you escort these mainlanders to the Place of Doom's Keeping. Morcant shall go with you, plus ordained druids and priestesses I will send.'

'It shall be as the Convocation has willed,' replied Ariadha stoutly, though in truth she felt afraid. Save by occasional members of her own clan, the Guardians had not been disturbed in an age; how would they react to mortal trespass after so many decades? And before they even reached them, an arduous trek awaited to the hinterlands beyond her ancestral home in Penhalain Vale – and that would not be without its own dangers.

'Rather you than me,' deadpanned Lyna, catching the expression on her face.

Servants began passing among them again, with more meat and ale. Ariadha had little appetite for either. She watched as Morcant and Joram left together with the knights. There was little love lost between the unlikely pair, that was obvious: but she could still sense the connection between them. And if a lay marcher like her could sense it, presumably everyone else could as well.

'A Palomedian monk and one of our under-druids making common cause,' she murmured. 'Strange and unsettling times these are, Lyna.'

'Yet still you think it right the monk looks upon what no outsider has?' The question was pointed: Lyna was indeed wise for her years.

Ariadha frowned. 'Right now, Lyna, I don't know what to think,' she said.

CHAPTER 2
TO THE CITY OF CARAVANSERAI

Squinting against the hardening ball of heat to his right, Hari Yassin gazed across the lands they had spent the night traversing. The highway stretched away to the north, before bending sharply west back towards the Holy City: they had kept to the safety of the road until past the Wytching Hour, before breaking off it to ride under moonlight. The chances of being attacked by demonic ifrits would be slim with two Argolians and a Sufieli along, though Yassin felt uncomfortable all the same.

The sun had begun to rise as the five of them crested a series of brown-red ridges that cradled a broad expanse of lush plains in its crooked arms. Out here, the Blessed Realm finally started to live up to its name: healthy-looking peasants tilled fields of sugar cane and coffee beans, though these were mostly pureblood Urovian stock. Well-kept manors of elegant Sassanian design dotted the pastures, studded with wells, orchards, vineyards, beehives, and enclosures for yaks, camels, cows and sheep.

Hari Yassin's eyes were not on the bounties of his native soil, however. Of far more interest was the group of riders growing against the flat horizon as it moved towards them. Less than a day out of Ushalayim, and it was obvious they were being pursued: the riders had taken advantage of the dawning light to break clear of the highway and cut across country towards them.

Only Bethlers could follow our psychic spoor like that, he thought. *Tobin has sent warrior-monks to chase us down. He really wants this lot dead.*

Riding down from the ridges towards his new companions, he said: 'Hard to be sure at this range, but I count at least six horsemen. Bethler knights, judging by the white tabards and their uncanny ability to track us. They're riding hard, so best if we do the same! It's three days swift riding before we reach the safety of the borderlands.'

Horskram laughed. 'Safety for you, perhaps.'

Hari grinned at him. 'You forget I am *al'Hajin*. Sassanians may not take kindly to a mongrel like me either.'

'Acknowledged,' said the monk, spurring his lathered courser into a reluctant trot. 'Still, I'll take my chances with Sassanian *fariz* over Bethler knights.'

'You must have offended the Grand Master considerably, for him to go to all this trouble,' said Yassin, urging his own tired steed behind Horskram's. 'Perhaps he wants the treasure for himself.'

'That would hardly surprise me,' said the adept over his shoulder. 'You know what they say about Bethlers and gold.'

～

Not this again, thought Adelko wearily as they spurred their horses between clustered groves of lemon trees. *Another game of cat and mouse – with us playing the mice.*

How many more times would their adventures lead to being pursued by deadly enemies, he wondered. At least now he could see what all the fuss over the Pilgrim Kingdoms was about – every league they covered seemed to throw up new treasures of the soil. But that soil would turn foreign a hundred miles inland; once they reached Sha'iza'ar they would be on the northern fringes of the Nazharyan sultanate. And that would bring hardships and dangers all of its own.

As he pushed his tired horse from the groves and into serried fields of rye and barley, Adelko found himself envying the peasants their simple toil. Perhaps shoeing horses in Narvik wouldn't have been so bad, after all.

Presently they were forced to stop and rest their exhausted mounts, watering them at a stream. Horskram slid off his, feeling every one of his sixty-two winters. Tired as he was, he could not afford to stop thinking.

You send half a dozen of your precious knights to pursue us into enemy territory – this is no mad whim, Tobin. The question is, why do you really want us dead?

'He has to be involved somehow,' muttered the adept, taking a swig from his waterskin. Admittedly, a fanatical warrior-priest seemed an unlikely candidate for being part of a conspiracy to reunite the Headstone. But after everything Horskram had learned in the past year, nothing seemed impossible.

Adelko's ears pricked up as he caught the remark. 'I must say I never did trust Tobin either, Master Horskram,' he said. 'I think he's corruptible enough to covet that kind of power. And a man like him would use any justification to get it.'

Horskram nodded, keeping his voice low so the others wouldn't hear. Their three companions were sprawled gratefully by the bank of the stream. Anupe rose wearily to break out rations.

'I am now convinced that Bethlers were involved in the abortive attempt on our lives in Vorstlund,' said the adept, 'but given that Brother Sir Guthrum intervened to save us from those freeswords at the inn on the road to Regensburg, not all the Order can have been corrupted.'

Adelko frowned, taking a grateful slug from his own skin before dashing some water across his face. 'But you said yourself, you suspect Prior Johann of hiring the freeswords using the local Bethler preceptory in Vorstlund as an intermediary.'

'But the commander there could himself have been duped by Johann,' mused Horskram. He sighed wearily. 'So far have we come, Adelko, yet so many of our hypotheses remain just that.'

'Still you're probably right, about not all Bethlers being corrupted,' said Adelko. 'Brother Sir Balian helped us against Tobin, so not all of them can have been turned.'

That seemed cold comfort to Horskram. 'Things aren't looking good for our cause,' he said seriously. 'Our elusive mastermind's list of allies grows ever more long and illustrious. As well as possibly corrupting senior members of the Knights Bethler, it looks as though they've done the same with high-ranking nobles at the Pangonian court.'

That last statement caught Adelko's attention. 'Meaning?'

'Before we left, the Lady Adhelina told me she had learned that Ivon, Margrave of Vichy, is involved somehow. She even seemed to think he might be the very ringleader we've been after, though that doesn't seem likely to me.'

Adelko raised an eyebrow. At least he was learning to stop his frightful gawping (most unbefitting a journeyman of the Order). 'And how exactly did her ladyship come by that kind of information?' he asked sceptically.

Horskram shrugged. He shared that scepticism, truth be told. Adhelina was resourceful, and had spent a few months at the Riman court; men could be loose-tongued around a beautiful woman when in their cups, but still...

'She wouldn't tell me how. I would have pressed her on the matter, but we scarcely had time. Frankly I'm not sure she was entirely convinced of its veracity herself – otherwise I expect she would have mentioned it before. Yet if there is some truth to it, that means this conspiracy is more widespread than we could have imagined – it isn't just rogue sorcerers like Andragorix and Abrexta manipulating warlords into going along with their schemes, warlords themselves are party to it. And that's to say nothing of our own Order's involvement, assuming Johann is guilty. This has been planned for years, perhaps even decades.'

Adelko nodded, gazing back towards the tree-lined horizon. 'It's as much as we suspected, Master Horskram,' he said. 'I just wish we had our quarterstaves. Perhaps then we could persuade our pursuers to enlighten us further. I can't stand all this fleeing.'

Horskram sized him up over another swig of water. No longer the novice, indeed – the journeyman stood strong and stout, defiance in his gaze and steel in his voice.

'Steady on, lad,' grinned the older monk. 'Edemus may have made a fighter of you, but you're not ready to take on half a dozen Bethlers just yet!'

Adelko managed a rueful half-smile. 'I suppose not, Master Horskram. But at this rate, I don't see how we'll have much choice. Their chargers are as swift as our coursers, and twice as strong. They'll catch up with us soon enough.'

Horskram said nothing to that as they reached into their saddlebags for provisions. With all his thinking about who was behind what, he'd hardly spared a thought for their more immediate danger. They ate a few snatched mouthfuls in pensive silence. After that Horskram walked over to the others and told them to get back in the saddle. Resting time was over.

Anupe could feel her courser tiring beneath her. It was a fine blood-bay Valacian gelding she had brought with her all the way from Rima, but not even such a horse could be pushed this much with so little rest. She was not surprised when Horskram called a halt. They had left the fields behind and entered some hilly grasslands; at least they should be able to get a view of their pursuers.

Hari Yassin scampered up the highest nearby hill to put his sharp eyes to use again. He drew his scimitar, grimly shaking his head. Anupe was about to do likewise when suddenly he cried: 'Wait! Come and see this!'

The four of them went up the hill and stood next to him. Following his outstretched finger, the Harijan could see the outlines of six horsemen, veering off towards a fortress on the outskirts of the hills overlooking the plains they had just crossed.

'They mean to commandeer fresh steeds,' said Horskram. 'Unsurprising. They've ridden night and day themselves. Kallandhari chargers are fine warhorses, but lack stamina over long distances.'

'That should buy us some time to get ahead of them, shouldn't it?' said Adelko.

The older monk shook his head. 'Our nags are as weary as overworked cart horses. They can't go on without proper rest. We'll just have to make a stand here.'

'Are you mad?' said Hari. 'They'll cut us down like sugar cane.'

'That they will,' said Horskram. 'But not if they can't find us.'

'They are following our psychic spoor, are they not?' said Hari. 'We can't hide from them.'

'That's right,' replied Horskram, shooting him a piercing glance. 'You know much of the ways of the Bethlers.'

'I have learned much about the Order in my dealings with it.' There was something a little too defensive in the way Hari said this, to Anupe's mind. Horskram himself scarcely looked convinced by the rascal's statement, but let it go. He had other things on his mind. 'If we pool our elan, Adelko and Tipu and I might be able to disrupt our spoor enough to throw them off the scent, as it were.'

Tipu had said not a word during the journey, but now broke his silence. 'We might be able to confuse our pursuers, indeed, but it's risky. We will need to be stationary to pool our elan as you suggest.' Despite the danger he'd just described, Tipu looked as serene as if he were on a pleasure jaunt. Anupe could swear the mystic had always known they would take this course of action.

'It is a risk, but we have a chance at least,' said Horskram. 'The Bethlers' penchant for blood-letting means their psychic acuity is limited.'

Hari shrugged, motioning towards their panting steeds. 'It's a risk worth taking, surely? Unless they have a tracker with them, I doubt they will be able to follow our hoof prints cross country.'

'It sounds like the best idea under the circumstances to me, Master Horskram,' said Adelko, eyeing their exhausted steeds dubiously.

Horskram nodded. 'Very well.'

Tipu squatted down on the summit of the hillock and produced his flute. Smiling broadly, he said: 'If the good friars would be so kind as to provide the words, I will be happy to contribute the music...'

The resulting sound was strange to Anupe's ears. Strange, yet also beautiful. The music of her people tended to be more percussive, but the intertwining melodies of the monks' sonorous chanting and the mystic's sublime fluting reached something within her she had thought long buried.

She thought of Kyra and all the other loves and losses in her life, as the sacred music caught the sultry afternoon air, motes of dust seeming to swirl about and dance in the warm breeze...

Her trance was interrupted by Hari. His hand was on her shoulder. He looked to have awoken from a state of deep meditation himself, and there were tears in the corners of his eyes.

'It's done,' he said, his voice cracking. 'We should eat and rest, for dusk will soon be on us. Now it is for Ashanti to decide if we have done enough to save our skins.'

Blinking and looking around, Anupe saw it had become much darker. She could barely see the fortress now, a spidery silhouette sketched against a dimming horizon. Glancing over, she saw the three holy men sitting in a triangle, their hands joined. None of them spoke, but she fancied there was a distinct aura of peace about the trio.

If only men were always thus, she thought wistfully. *They would be so much easier to control.*

As the dawn gave birth to an ochre landscape, Adelko rubbed his cramping muscles and went to wake his sleeping companions. He had drawn the last watch; nothing had disturbed the grove of olive trees they'd chosen to bed down in for the night. This crowned a hummock that allowed a vantage point across the brightening hills, but the green knolls that sprouted to life beneath the sun's golden caress were pleasantly free of dangers.

Anupe, practical as ever, set about preparing them a simple breakfast from the supplies Amalric's servants had packed in their saddlebags. 'Here,' she said, tossing him a round pock-marked fruit that was a similar colour to the sun. 'I'll wager you have not tried this delicacy of the south yet.'

'What is it?' Adelko scrutinised it in the light. It reminded him a bit of the lemons Sholto had used to make his scrumpy, back in Ulfang.

'In your tongue, you simply call it an *orange*,' said the Harijan, pouring some yak's milk into a bowl of oatmeal and raisins. Adelko hadn't explored nearly enough Sassanian food for his liking: he'd gazed longingly at some of the unfinished platters in the courtyard of the *Sojourn*, but there had scarce been time for sampling the local cuisine.

Taking a bite, he registered the tough chewy skin as an acrid taste shot into his mouth. 'But that's revolting!' he complained, spitting out fragments.

Anupe threw her head back and roared with laughter. 'You are supposed to peel it first!' she cried. 'They didn't teach you that in your books, hey?'

Feeling suddenly abashed, Adelko gazed at the fruit where he had bitten into it. Below the outer layer of skin, soft succulent fruit brimmed with juice. Flicking her a wry glance, he began to peel it. 'Thanks for telling me,' he muttered sarcastically. He didn't like being made a fool of.

The Harijan was staring at him keenly now. 'Your temperament is different since I know you,' she observed. 'You are – how do you say it? – quicker to anger now.'

The journeyman frowned. He had learned to master his

new intensities of emotion better since his duel with Arik, but it was still difficult at times. He suddenly wondered how his friends were getting on back in Pangonia, his old rival and gentle Hargus. Adelko hoped they learned something, by now it was obvious Johann couldn't be the only monk involved in this great conspiracy of wizards. Horskram had definitely been right about one thing: their enemies seemed to multiply from the shadows.

'Break your fasts swiftly,' said Horskram grumpily. 'Something tells me our Bethler chums won't give up the chase so easily. They know we are headed to Sha'iza'ar, so we aren't out of danger yet.'

Yassin sighed. 'There's a brook on the other side of the hummock,' he said. 'We should bathe before we set out again.'

Tipu seemed to agree. 'Yes, it would be most fitting. For a clean body better houses a pure spirit, as the Prophet sayeth.'

Horskram rolled his eyes. 'Heavens, gentlemen, we don't have time for your southern niceties,' he snapped. 'Eat, empty your bowels if you must, then get back in the saddle. The Unseen will take care of our souls, Reus willing.' Putting aside his empty bowl, he stalked off to follow his own advice.

Adelko glanced at the two Sassanians apologetically. Yassin was shaking his head, but Tipu just sighed wistfully.

'Northern mystics are a strange breed,' said Tipu. 'But Ashanti wills Himself in many ways.'

With a smile, the mystic got to his feet and gathered up some grubby utensils. 'I'll clean these much at least.'

The day was long and hot, but they made steady progress. The hill lands levelled out again into plains dotted with fields of crops, some of which Adelko did not recognise. The yeomanry in these parts were of mixed stock, native and Urovian.

'They permit *al'Hajin* such as I and native Nazharyans to work the fields as cottars,' said Yassin when they stopped to eat and water their horses. 'But to own lands and bondsmen, one must be of Urovian burgess stock.'

'That hardly seems fair,' observed Adelko, feeling hot anger rising as if in mockery of the fierce sun. 'The Nazharyans were here first, after all.'

Yassin merely laughed at that. 'I am sure the inhabitants of your country feel the same. For were the northern kingdoms you hail from not conquered centuries ago, by enemy tribes?'

Adelko reflected on that. What Yassin said was true enough, he supposed. In the time of Søren, the Ice Thegns had wrested Northalde from the old Westerling clans. Seven kingdoms had once dotted the peninsula he called home; by the time the First Reavers were done but four had remained, to the west of the Hyrkrainians. He saw once again a chain of iniquity, each link a cycle of oppression and suffering, tightening about the circumference of the earth. He was suddenly back in the Earth Witch's girdle, looking on visions of the Universe, while angels and demons alike turned their backs on the world they had once sought to shape and rule.

Hari turned back to his meal, but Tipu laid a gentle hand on the young monk's thigh. 'Ashanti shows us the picture but one brush stroke at a time,' he smiled. 'Have patience, Adelko, and in time you will see it in its entirety.'

'And will I like what I see, Tipu?' he asked pointedly. The old mystic just smiled and resumed eating.

Before long Horskram bade them all get up again. Adelko was happy to comply. The last thing he felt like doing now was sitting around and ruminating.

The wilderness was strewn with broken bodies. The stink of blood was in Sir Horskram's nostrils as he hefted his sword. It too was painted red with the horrid hue of war. He felt his gorge rise as he gazed upon the Sassanian infidels they had just put to the sword. They'd fought well and bravely before surrendering: by the Code of Chivalry such *fariz* should have been spared and held for ransom.

But his commander, Sir Rothgar, was having none of it. The battle-scarred veteran of Vorstlund motioned towards the township with his warhammer. The brains of the *fariz* he had just executed still sloughed off it. 'No rules of honour apply to such Sha'abatian scum,' he spat. 'Our war against the heathens must be total and unrelenting.'

Beside him, Sir Angrim's butcher's face cracked a vulpine grin. He motioned towards the village. 'Now for their women and children,' he said. 'Let's make sure they don't live to breed more verminous infidels.'

Sir Horskram steeled himself. He'd joined Rothgar's

group of two-score knights, a motley sortie of freeriders attached to the wider pilgrim war, where most crusaders not in direct service to the great Pangonian or Thalamian warlords usually ended up. He realised now what a mistake that had been. His soul was tainted forever, with blood no water could ever wash off.

'Killing surrendered men in arms is bad enough,' protested the young knight. 'But I draw the line at civilians.' As if for emphasis, he ran his blade through the sere turf. 'This goes against everything taught by Palomedes, whose very cause we prosecute.'

Angrim sneered at that. 'Holy Horskram and his book learning,' he said mockingly. 'You spent far too much time at your precious letters – it's left your stomach too weak for fighting!'

Horskram pointed his bloodied blade at Angrim. 'Try me,' he said, hoping fervently the hefty knight would oblige and give him satisfaction. 'I believe I have fought as well as you these past few weeks.'

But Rothgar interjected. 'Come!' he said, clapping Angrim on his mailed shoulder. 'Leave this prating fool to his tender conscience. We've real crusading to do.'

Rothgar barked a command, and the rest of the freeriders followed him and Angrim as they remounted and nudged their chargers towards the doomed village. Horskram could see its panicked occupants fleeing already, but on foot they would not get far. Remounting his own destrier, Sir Horskram turned his back on the village, and the entire crusade. He wished he could ride faster as the first screams of the Sassanian peasants reached his ears...

Horskram jerked upright. The pallid moon glared down at him unsympathetically. He was soaked in sweat. The old monk hadn't dreamed of that part of his life in a while, but he knew all too well why he just had.

Not far now, he thought grimly. *A few more days, and I'll be back there, where my education in the ways of mortalkind truly began.*

Not for the first time, sorrow coursed through him like poison, transfixing his heart. He had repented that deed a thousand times, in both prayer and service, and yet it had never left him. He had to hope that would be his only penance; that he would not be condemned to everlasting torment on the Other Side when his time came.

And that time was not far off – the old monk knew that with a hollow certainty. When and how would not be of his choosing, but Azrael would come for him, as surely as he had for every other soul flesh had ever clothed. When the Angel of Death did smile on him, Horskram hoped it wouldn't be to put him in an iron galley and send him to the island of Gehenna to join the Fallen One.

After all the years I spent fighting him, it's doubtful Abaddon would make me feel welcome, he thought ruefully. *Assuming the Archfiend hasn't taken up residence in the mortal vale by then.*

That thought did not comfort him in the slightest.

Getting up, the adept went over to tap Anupe on the shoulder. The alert Harijan, standing stock still with her back to him, spoke before he touched her. 'You are up early,' she said, without taking her eyes off the night-smothered landscape. 'I am still on watch for another hour.'

'Might as well get some rest now,' he said. 'There is no more sleep in me tonight.' He felt a little awkward. Things had seldom been easy between him and the paganer, but he couldn't deny she was bound up in his Wyrd. That made her a crucial ally, like it or not.

'Go on,' he urged. 'You've more than earned it.'

Anupe shrugged and complied, sheathing her falchion as she sought her pallet.

Bizarre allies and uncertain enemies, he thought wearily as he settled into his watch. *This damned puzzle never seems to get any easier.*

Dawn came upon them slowly, and Horskram watched the Utna'aruf ranges coalesce into life, seeming to bleed from the wakening skies down into the flat plains in vivid colours of orange and purple. In the foothills on the other side of those low-lying crags lay Sha'iza'ar – one more day in the saddle would bring them there.

Hari was the first to awake. He seemed to rise effortlessly at the sun's first touch – there was clearly more to him that just a waterfront rogue, though Horskram had little energy to ponder his origins.

'We should reach the city of caravanserai by sunset,' said Yassin. 'The highway lies about two leagues to the west. Shall we risk it?'

Horskram nodded. 'We may as well,' he replied.

'Chances are the Bethlers will have used it to ride ahead, and will be waiting to apprehend us at Sha'iza'ar. They aren't exactly subtle types, I doubt they'll bother with subterfuge.'

Yassin squinted at the ranges. 'You know, we could just skip it,' he said. 'Make our way directly across the border. There are many trails that lead through the Utna'arufs.'

But Horskram shook his head. 'We need proper supplies if we're to survive the journey across Nazharya. Bodyguards too – Adelko and I are unarmed, and yon mystic will shed no blood, not even in self-defence.'

Hari nodded. 'Sha'iza'ar it is then,' he said, before sauntering off to prepare breakfast.

Hardened as he was by Edemus's training, Adelko was beginning to feel saddle sore by the time they crossed the Utna'arufs. Months of study at the monastery followed by weeks amidships meant he'd had little time for riding, and his rear felt chafed and raw.

At least here was a sight to take one's mind off a sore backside – the city of caravanserai sprawled at the foot of the hills, straddling the highway. He counted more than a hundred caravan trains drawn up in circles, some numbering as many as twenty camels. In the fading light Adelko scrutinised the strange hump-backed beasts, thinking the Almighty's diverse creation a great wonder. Most of the caravan trains were enclosed by large open courtyards, lined with stalls and crammed with people. The setting sun caught the orangewood of the caravans and sandstone of the enclosures, making the city seem almost as spectacular as Ushalayim, in its own humble way.

As usual, Horskram was quick to disabuse him of any romantic notions. 'Don't be fooled by its exotic appearance,' growled the adept. 'Yon city is replete with rogues of even worse character than Yassin here. Sha'iza'ar attracts ne'er-do-wells from both sides of the border, and the wilderness it sits in has been a restive no-man's land since the First Pilgrim War.'

'I assure you, I am a man of fine upstanding character,' beamed Hari, though even he didn't seem to believe that.

'At least we should not have to spend your precious coin on lodgings for the night,' said Tipu. 'Many of these vagabonds will be only too glad to shelter a holy man, to claw back some *karma* for their souls.'

'Karma?' queried Adelko. That Sassanic word Johann hadn't taught him.

'Put succinctly, as ye spend so shall ye acquire,' supplied Horskram. 'Merchants, they're no different anywhere you go – always trying to buy back their greedy souls.'

Tipu only smiled sadly, while Yassin guffawed.

'What's that, over there?' asked Adelko. It had just caught his eye – a large sunken circular stockade made of wood, roofed with an awning of quilted camel hides.

Horskram's lip curled. 'A Sassanian fighting pit,' he said. 'If you think Urovian tourneys are a gruesome spectacle, try gladiatorial combats.'

'They were banned by Abu'cuchaza'ar Kardin, first of the Enlightened Sultans,' put in Tipu, 'at the Prophet's urging. But that dynasty was destroyed at the Battle of Kurashan Heights, and when lesser men took power the custom gradually resurfaced. The pit you see was commissioned by the Sultan Uzman tek Jahal a hundred years ago, and has stood ever since.' He sighed gently. 'I am afraid it has become part of the enterprise of Sha'iza'ar – many monies are wagered in the pit by the wealthy merchants who come here.'

'To be fair, there aren't many other cultural amusements in a place like this,' observed Hari. Tipu looked at him disapprovingly, while Horskram fixed him with one of his milk-curdling stares. The thief shrugged, and held his peace.

Warily they made their way down towards the caravan city. Adelko half expected to see a host of warrior-monks launch themselves from the rocks that tumbled about them, etiolated in the fading light. But none appeared. He was just beginning to relax when Yassin pointed. 'There,' he said. In one of the central enclosures, Adelko could just about make out six burly men clad in white tabards. They weren't mounted, but the reddening sun revealed the telltale glint of mail.

'The Bethlers don't have strict jurisdiction here,' said Horskram as they reined in their horses, 'but that won't stop them throwing their weight around to convince the merchants not to do any business with us. Every trader has need of borrowed money occasionally, and the Bethel is the chief banker in this region.'

'Once they've done that, all they have to do is retreat to the outskirts of the city and wait for us,' said Yassin. 'No business dealings, no *taziqs* – no freeswords, no protection. Clever enough.'

'Except your knight friends have not reckoned on one factor,' put in Tipu. 'The words of a Sufieli mystic should carry more weight in these parts. I can help.'

Horskram snorted. 'With all due respect, farseer,' he said, 'I hardly see how yon merchants will place their cankered souls above the chink of coin.'

Tipu sighed again. 'So much we have wandered, you and I,' he said, 'and yet I fear your experience of the world has but hardened your heart. Not all men are wicked, Horskram of Vilno. Some of these merchants are god-fearing men, believe it or not – and they have no love for the arrogant *jhufa'ar* who have invaded their land. I know some of these fellows well – I believe I can get them to help us.'

Was that a grudging look of respect in Horskram's hard eyes? 'Very well,' he said, 'for truly the Sufielis are our closest counterparts in the Sha'abatian world. I have had dealings with your sect in the past, and will defer to your wisdom in this case.'

Adelko's mouth nearly dropped. *Did I just see Master Horskram defer to someone? And a man of the Faith, no less.*

'I hardly see what other course of action is open to us,' Hari pointed out dryly.

'Whatever action we take, let us take it fast,' said Anupe, nodding towards the crimson disc half buried on the horizon.

'Yes, let us go down,' said Tipu confidently. 'Best if I lead the way.'

Anupe kept her hand on the hilt of her falchion as Tipu led them through the labyrinth of adobe corridors that connected the caravenserai. Loitering freeswords stared surlily as they passed. Some even had the temerity to hiss. She kept her hood up – from what she knew, men in these parts had even less respect for women than their Urovian antagonists.

Link boys were lighting the central enclosure when they entered it. The Bethlers had not left. With them were some twenty merchants, most of these dressed in beige robes and cloaks suitable for travelling. About twice that number of *taziqs* were assembled there too, hands not far from their scimitars. Some of the merchants also had weapons at their belts, long curved knives in jewelled scabbards for the most part. Dotted about the throng was the odd Zarumani priest dressed in orange robes – scions of the Sect of Light and Fire. They carried knives too, only these were modestly sheathed. Anupe did not doubt the quality of the steel within, however.

Good – that should keep our holy warriors in check, for now at least. But her hand did not leave the hilt of her sword.

She felt her caution vindicated when she noticed one of the Zarumani priests staring at them intently. Anupe knew only a little of the reclusive sect, said to worship a conjoined entity of the sun goddess and the god of fire. Their lair was in the Abydos ranges, whither they were bound; they seldom ventured forth but were occasionally known to hire out their services to merchant caravans.

The Zarumani's eyes did not leave them as they approached the merchants. His swarthy pate was shorn of all locks after the manner of his sect; his blank face was likewise devoid of emotion. The priest made no hostile move towards them, but Anupe did not care for his look. She glanced sidelong at Horskram, but his attention was elsewhere.

The knights turned as one to face them. Horskram recognised the oldest immediately, though it had been decades since he had last seen him. The old monk threw up his head and laughed bitterly as they squared off against the Bethlers.

I should know after all this time how to spot a vision of the future in a dream of times past.

The knight he'd recognised smiled darkly. He clearly remembered Horskram, too.

'Horskram of Vilno,' he sneered. 'How nice to meet again, after all these years.'

'Sir Rothgar,' replied the adept, putting aside his feigned mirth in a flash, 'or should I say *Brother* Sir Rothgar, how unfortunate we did not meet in Ushalayim.'

'I had a prolonged spell in the infirmary,' replied Rothgar, close on seventy winters by now. 'Age has not been kind.'

'Oh I'd say it has been rather too kind, in your case,' replied Horskram. 'No small wonder the Angel of Death didn't send you packing to Gehenna years since. Yet here you are, alive – and a member of the Order! Goes to show they'll take anyone these days.'

Rothgar's face darkened. It was pinched, like a dried-up raisin, with tasselled wisps of white clinging stubbornly to his tanned chin. The once burly warlord had been steadily attenuated by the passing of the years. Though not nearly enough for Horskram's liking.

'I served well and loyally in the Blessed Realm for years, which is more than can be said of you, recreant,' Rothgar spat. 'When Grand Master Tobin informed me of your escape, I volunteered to lead the mission to bring you to justice. This reckoning has been a long time in the coming, apostate and demonolator.'

One of the merchants cleared his throat loudly. He was tall and well-made, and could have been a warrior himself. A scimitar was girded at his side, and like the *taziqs* that guarded him he wore boiled leather armour studded with nuggets of iron.

'As much as it pleases us to see such pleasant reunion, I should remind the noble *effendis* that they stand on no-man's land,' said the merchant. Judging by his dialect of Sassanic, he hailed from the hinterlands of Nazharya, close to the Ghorabi desert. 'These are serious accusations, Tipu,' he went on. 'Ashanti knowest, the Seven Seraphim shield the Sufieli with their blessed shadows – but what are you doing in such company?' The burly merchant arched an eyebrow and looked askance at Tipu, but Horskram sensed relations between the two were usually warm.

Tipu bowed low. 'A thousand blessings of the Prophet on you, Abdul tek Nu'ur, merchant satrap of Harahindi!' He laughed, a glad sound, curiously light for such a tense situation. 'I can assure you, Your Prominence, these are no devil-worshippers, but holy men themselves.'

'He lies!' snarled Rothgar, speaking in heavily accented Sassanic. 'Or else this vagabond mystic knows nothing of the Argolians, if that's what he really believes!'

Impressive, you managed to stay out here long enough to bother learning the language. Perhaps you even found time to get your letters, when you weren't busy butchering the local women and children. How salutary the Bethler Order has been for you, Rothgar.

Horskram felt an old blood rage welling up inside him, one he quelled with difficulty. Swallowing back a hatred that tasted worse than any bile, he forced himself to concentrate.

Abdul's face had a graver cast to it now. 'Have a care, warrior-priest,' he admonished Rothgar. 'Remember that you stand on no-man's land. We will not tolerate disrespect for our holy men.'

'And the Order will tolerate no disrespect from a merchant prince,' said Rothgar. 'Remind me, how much coin does your house owe the Bethel?' The pointed remark was blunted by Rothgar suddenly being seized by a wracking cough. In the torchlight, Horskram could see his face glistened with sweat. Whatever fever ailed him had not yet broken.

Abdul was muttering to his cohorts now, who eyed the newcomers sidelong and shook their heads and frowned. Many of the Zarumanis looked angry, perhaps expecting to be insulted next, while the *taziqs* eyed them all murderously.

They'll kill us all if we're not careful. Tipu, tread warily.

He sensed the mystic was thinking along much the same lines. After praying together, the three of them had become attuned; such inter-religious communions had been known in the past, yet another reason why Argolians were reviled by mainstream clerics of the Creed.

Unfortunately, the same can be said of how some Orthodox Sha'abatians feel about Sufielis. Tipu's sect was more respected in Nazharya than the Unorthodox Faith, but it wasn't universally loved: Horskram caught more than one murderous look aimed at the slight mystic.

Unabashed, Tipu went on: 'These monks and their bodyguards must be allowed to pass unmolested. Think not of gold or bloodfeud, I implore you all – the pestilence of Ma'alfeccnu'ur shall be visited upon he who hinders them, this much I have seen!' The mystic made the sign of the Faith, touching his forehead and glancing heavenward in symbolic marking of Sha'abat's ascension. Many of the merchants followed suit, and no few of the *taziqs* either.

They pay lip service well enough, thought Horskram. But he kept his cynicism to himself; the mystic appeared to be making headway. Some of the murderous looks had dropped, and some of the merchants appeared to be siding with Tipu, though Abdul looked none too pleased at the prospect of angering his creditors.

The Bethlers were conferring amongst themselves too, and appeared to have reached a decision. 'Very well,' cried Rothgar in his rasping voice. He managed to make the guttural Sassanic tongue sound even harsher. 'If you will not see your own interest in giving up these demonolators, I have no choice but to invoke no-man's law. Let this dispute be put to the pit.'

Abdul's bushy eyebrows tapered across penetrating black eyes as he registered the Bethler knight's words.

'You would prosecute this quarrel under our laws, *effendi*?'

Rothgar scowled. 'I won't pretend to like the idea, but if you will not agree to give the monks up or let us pursue them into no-man's land, I can't see a better alternative.'

'What's he's talking about, Master Horskram?' hissed Adelko.

Horskram felt his heart sinking. He'd known it might come to this.

'Any disputes that cannot be resolved in Sha'iza'ar by open counsel of its leading merchants are referred to the fighting pits,' said Horskram. 'Champions are selected to fight it out on behalf of plaintiff and defendant, or they fight it out themselves. Much like our own duel of justice.'

'This is an ungodly way to seek Ashanti's justice,' protested Tipu. 'The Father of All does not bless such conflicts.'

But the nodding merchants and grinning *taziqs* told Horskram that the tide had turned. Even the Zarumanis looked approving. Tipu might be respected, but that wouldn't overturn their love of spectacle or the convenience of summary justice by the sword.

The old monk sighed wearily. 'Our thanks for your intervention, Tipu,' he muttered, 'at least we will not be handed over to yon scoundrels out of hand.'

'We aren't out of the lion's maw just yet,' said Hari. 'One

of us must fight to the death and win if we're to escape.' From the way he said it, the rogue had clearly already decided that person wouldn't be him.

Horskram looked back towards Rothgar and the other knights, who were smiling now. Rothgar himself was infirm and would not volunteer. But the five men he commanded were all tall and strong, elite swordsmen who some said could use the sixth sense to fight even better. Abdul was announcing a pit fight above the hubbub of excited chatter, which thickened into a roar of approval as he made the formal declaration. The customary period of three days would be allowed to make preparations, then blood would be spilled in the arena to decide the matter.

'At least they will harbour us for now and treat us well,' said Yassin. 'Those who seek the justice of the pits are as honoured guests.'

'That'll be small consolation if we lose,' said Adelko. The bold journeyman didn't look quite so bold now.

Servitors came to usher them towards where sequinned rugs had been set up in a corner, proffering food and drink and rest: Sassanian hospitality, once granted, was legendary. But that was small comfort for Horskram as he pondered their latest dilemma. Adelko was yet too green to take on a Bethler knight, and for all their skill Yassin and Anupe would be no match for a warrior-monk in a straight fight. Tipu was a sworn pacifist...

As they sat down and servants brought them rhytons of fruit juice and dishes of spiced meats and salted peppers, Horskram accepted with grim certainty the obvious solution. Only a hierophant could muster the elan needed to triumph over a Bethler in single combat.

A great darkness came over him then, though it was still twilight. He would have to take up the sword again – the laws of Sha'iza'ar stipulated a fight to the death. But use the powers the Unseen had gifted him to take another life, and his soul would be forfeit.

As succulent food turned to ashes in his mouth, Horskram raised his eyes to heavens he would never see, and resigned himself to his fate.

CHAPTER 3
A MARCH OF MISERY

Wrackwulf eyed his companions sullenly. They made for a motley and shabby band, mounted on garrons and dressed in bearskins, despite it being nearly summer on the mainland. The two aspirants from the council Ys had sent with them spoke quietly among themselves, ignoring the rest of them. Fanwyn and Ianna evidently had some shared history, not that they were sharing it with anyone else. It turned out islanders could be just as haughty as mainlanders, but that didn't surprise Wrackwulf much. People were the same underneath wherever you went, try as they might to assert their differences.

The female marcher who would escort them across the northern wildernesses of Skulla to where the mysterious fragment was kept was even worse. In all his years, Wrackwulf had never seen so ferocious-looking a woman. She made Anupe look civilised. Her copper-coloured hair was completely shorn on one side of her head; as if to compensate, the surviving side was braided so that it sprouted manically in all directions. Her septum was pierced with a silver nose-ring, and an orange streak of lightning was tattooed down one cheek. Her eyes were as green as a wildwood, and scarcely more tame. She scorned to wear armour over her hotchpotch sash, but carried a great spear across her back, its painted haft covered in queer raised inscriptions that Wrackwulf didn't care to inspect too closely.

She had barely spoken to anybody all day since they'd left Kell at break of dawn, just a few muttered words to her personal retinue. Wrackwulf didn't know if she spoke any languages but her own, but Ariadha ap Madrix clearly knew more about the thing they sought than he did. The Argolians had not exactly been forthcoming with details when they had commissioned him in Rima.

Oh aye, a chance to save the bloody world and earn a tidy profit while I'm about it – doing well whilst doing good, that's what you told me, Master Horskram. Pull the other hoof, why don't you?

What in the Known World had possessed him to take the crafty monk up on his offer?*You might as well have thrown me in a boat with a bag of gold, and shoved me off into the Great Western Ocean.*

The freelancer shook his head and spat to the side of the crooked hill path they were following. He could almost swear the bedraggled soil bubbled resentfully as it received his spittle. This land was cursed. He'd only been out in it for a couple of days, but already he knew that much. The skies were grey. The rocky hills they travelled through were grey. The mean drizzle that came and went with irritating regularity was grey. Even the cottars working the pathetic little plots of land scrunched between the hills were dressed in grey.

'Be of some cheer, friend,' Morcant had told him when he'd voiced his displeasure. 'Soon it will be over, whatever we decide to do. Then free you will be to return home!'

And that I'll do gladly, he thought. *I'll swyve half the wenches in Ongist when I get back to my strongbox full of coin at the palace. Might even take service at the Thraxian King's court for a while.*

Wrackwulf never thought he'd hear himself say it, but he was sick of wandering. It would be nice to settle down somewhere comfortable. As far as he could recall, he was some way past his thirty-fifth winter. He should think about retiring from errantry and freelancing, leave it to the younger bucks.

I'm too old for all this nonsense. What on earth does Joram think he's doing anyway? One minute he says we should abandon our suit and go home, now here we are riding after it.

He had to hand it to the burly adept, he was clearly a shrewd negotiator as well as a heavy bruiser. But that shrewdness made Wrackwulf even more uneasy. The freelancer could not shake the feeling that Joram had known the outcome of their suit all along. *What else does he know, I wonder? There's more to that monk than he lets on. A lot more.*

He nudged his pony forwards and tapped Morcant roughly on the shoulder. 'Ask our gracious guide how far away this keeping place is,' he said. 'I want to know how long I have to spend being bored out of my skull.'

Morcant favoured him with a crooked-toothed grin. 'The Place of Doom's Keeping is more than two hundred miles north of here, so we've a few days in the saddle! But bored you won't be – to reach it we must brave the custodians of the ancient city of Taras Cerawn, for that is the only route through the Farfahailan ranges that lie north of here. Few have set foot there since the Old Time, little I know of what awaits us there. 'Tis rumoured the custodians are half-man, half-faerie, from the days when our high kings took Fays to wife – more of the Other Side than this world. But before we even get there, we have to skirt the Valley of the Barrow Kings, where Morwena's doom was broken by the hero you call Søren. Like the Draug-moors you told me of, only much worse – not for nothing did I turn in my tracks when I looked upon that cursed vale!'

'Wonderful,' said Wrackwulf. 'So I won't be bored then, as you say. Just petrified.'

Bloody adventuring. More trouble than it's worth. Should have stuck to blasted tourneying and skirmishing. 'You say these custodians we have to pass are faeriekind – but what about the Guardians themselves? You've told me even less of them.'

Morcant's smile dimmed. 'Not hostile are they – just as long as you treat them with respect,' was all he said to that.

'What are they, exactly?'

Morcant scratched his head, as if struggling to explain. 'Think of the Guardians as nature spirits, bound up in plant form – we have used them as allies for many centuries.'

That assurance scarcely pleased Wrackwulf. 'Now I've heard it all – I'm supposed to show respect to a damned bush? We really are at the bloody edge of the world, aren't we! What kind of land is this to call home?'

Morcant's angular smile returned. 'Home,' he said simply, and shrugged.

Ariadha glanced resentfully at Ianna and Fanwyn as they pushed their garrons onward through the flinty hills, following the winding path that took them through the lands north of Kell. Another two days of riding would bring them to the Bruach river: cross that, and they would be on lands ruled by Clan Nuallán, not far from her ancestral seat in the Vale of Penhalain. She needed members of the Druiding Council to treat with the custodians of Taras Cerawn and so pass through the impregnable mountains, but only a direct descendant of Caedmon's could gain entry to the city – it was the outer line of defence laid down by her ancestor and the druids hundreds of years ago, to ensure no single person acting alone could gain access to the Place of Doom's Keeping.

Ariadha still didn't like having the haughty druids along on the expedition, but at least her word would carry the same weight as theirs on lands entrusted to her family.

Unfortunately, so would the rest of her clan's. She knew her Uncle Owyn would be the most vociferous in his protests, but then what choice had she really had? Connaer might joke that Caedmon the Far-Sighted hadn't seen this coming, but as a scion of the clan he founded, Ariadha knew better.

Caedmon's deathbed prophecy had been a closely

guarded secret, his words passed down to all inheritors of his title, and the responsibilities that came with it.

It came upon me not long after the Battle of Cullingan Fields, on the mainland. We'd just put down the Mad King Cadwyn, whom our mainland cousins called the False Friend. And he it was that betrayed Corann unto his death, leaving the fragment he should have guarded at Roarkil while he prosecuted his war of conquest to unite the Four Old Kingdoms, our one-time friends and allies. Ah, I should have brought the cursed thing back with me after I slew Cadwyn, but I could not bear the thought of two burdens lying upon our little island nation... So I presided over the Settlement of Thronduil, which brought Lochlaine to the throne as the First True King of Thraxia, and as my part in that I led the remnants of my men back across the Tyrnian Straits, vowing that would be the last time islanders had any involvement in the doings of mainlanders. Our responsibility I had held it, that we helped undo the wrongs brought to our cousins by the fragment, but their duty now I judged it to guard the stone.

But as our galleases struck for home, and I caught sight of the Druiding Stones above Malhavern's Point, a vision came to me from the clouds, and though it were plain day I knew it for The Mistress of the Tides herself. And she said unto me: 'Not well have you done, Caedmon, so far-sighted in many things, yet so blind in this one. For you know 'twas the stone that brought Cadwyn to madness in the first place, corrupting his soul and causing him to lust after power beyond all measure. Our mainland cousins have grown weak of mind and frail of heart, the wisdom that guided them during the Middle Time long faded with the grandeur of Anarlion. In time there will come another, from a people even less wise: and he shall seek to reunite what must not be reunited, and the descendants of your Thraxian kindred will be powerless to stop him...'

I knew then that I had judged in error, for the Moon Goddess does not lie. But by then we were almost home, and I was weary and sick of war and foreign adventure. So it will fall to my descendants to set aright the ill I have done, in times far flung from these...

Those had been the Marcher Lord's dying last words, recorded faithfully by an amanuensis before he expired. Since then, the scrap of vellum on which they were written had been kept in a chest in the attic of Nuallán's ancestral keep, and shown only by its incumbent lord to the heir apparent when the time was deemed right. Ariadha's father Madrix had shown it to his only daughter, after her brother died of the ague seven years ago.

But she still wasn't entirely convinced this was the best way of fulfilling Caedmon's death-wish. They could not turn their backs on the mainlanders' problems any longer, of that she was certain, but she didn't trust the surly monk who had brought them news of the fragment thefts. Turning in the saddle, she positively glared at Joram. Look hard enough, and you could see the Westerling ancestry in him: the broad features, the thick red hair, the stocky frame. And he spoke their tongue well, despite his strong accent. But he was a devotee of the Creed. That same Creed that had all but wiped out the so-called old faith on the mainland. Joram was a man who persecuted witches without discrimination; the Argolian conflation of the right and left hand paths was sacrilegious in the eyes of any true-believing islander.

And besides all that, she didn't like him. Strong-willed

and clever as he was, the monk had a smug haughtiness about him. Behind that, she had begun to sense an anger and a lust for violence that made him even less trustworthy.

Unlikely allies and strange times indeed, she thought again.

Torgun stared about him as they made their way deeper into the craggy hinterlands, though he scarcely had eyes for the bleak terrain his Wyrd had brought him to.

Truth to tell, his head ached from too much thinking. He actually found himself wishing his old love rival Braxus were here – the two had never seen eye to eye, but the Thraxian had always seemed more at ease dealing with eldritch matters and creatures of the Other Side. But Braxus was a lord of men now, and his responsibilities lay much closer to home. Though Torgun didn't envy him those duties, he did envy their straightforwardness at least.

He wasn't the smartest of men. Never had been. It wasn't his duty to be clever – that was for the loremasters and princes and perfects. But even he could see that something wasn't right about this mission. The more he saw of Joram, the less he trusted him. Horskram he hadn't liked much either – honourable as their calling was, the Argolians did little to endear themselves to ordinary mortals. But where Horskram had at least been candid in his irascibility, there was something sly and underhand about the way Joram conducted himself.

He pretends to have no interest in coming here in the first place, but the closer to the fragment he gets, the more determined he becomes to see it. Claims to have given up the struggle to do that, and sues for free pardon to go... only to convince the druids to take us to it after all. Professes to despise Morcant and all his kind, but isn't above using him to get what he wants. What kind of man are you really, Joram?

His older brother Toros had always been the smart one. The Jarl of Vandheim was a good Jedrez player, adept at thinking more than one move ahead. Toros said that was what it took to be a ruler, more than being able to sit a horse in a tourney or win at swordplay. Torgun hadn't doubted his sibling, and had no reason to doubt his words now as he recalled them: *Sometimes a prince will get what he wants by feigning indifference to it, brother – show timorous men the opposite of what they fear you are up to, and chances are they'll believe it. Because timorous men are always afraid they have missed something. That lack of self-courage is a weakness worth exploiting to get what you want.*

He'd been just fifteen when his older brother told him that. At the time, Torgun had been a squire two years from knighthood, Toros a knight six years from lordship. *Typical Toros,* he'd thought at the time, *always the cynic.*

But those cynical words seemed to be making more and more sense. The Westerling islanders were timorous to a fault: Torgun didn't need an Argolian's mystical powers to scent the fear in them. None had wanted this burden to fall upon them in their lifetimes, but fall it had. And that had made them into the kind of fearful folk a man like his brother would exploit to achieve his goals.

A man like his brother Lord Toros of Vandheim – or Brother Joram of the Argolian Order.

Torgun continued to mull things over as their guides showed them into a little dell, ringed with a handful of sick-looking rowan trees where they would take the afternoon meal. While they were eating in cheerless silence, he looked at Wrackwulf. He liked the freelancer: though a minor noble bereft of land and lord, he was honest and brave – if a little crude and coarse. But more than that, he had something of Braxus's cleverness. And that was what Torgun needed right now.

Making up his mind, the Northlending stepped over to Wrackwulf and put a hand lightly on his shoulder as they were all rising to take the saddle again.

'What ails thee, Sir Torgun?' he asked, seeing the intent look in his fellow knight's eyes.

'I despise subterfuge as any true knight should,' said Torgun, 'but I'd appreciate it if you didn't make this too obvious.'

Wrackwulf's eyebrows furrowed as Torgun stepped over to his garron, checking her saddle girth was on tightly. Riding a mare was a lowly thing for any knight to do, but they were in barbarian lands, and mainland customs were strange to these folk. He couldn't worry about that right now, though.

Without taking his eyes off Morcant and the rest of the islanders, Torgun mounted up and said in a soft low voice, so only Wrackwulf could hear: 'We need to talk. About Master Joram.'

~

Deep thunder rolled across the valley floor, as they struggled to hoist up their tents against the incoming deluge. Night would not be far behind the mustering storm.

Another fine evening in the armpit of the world, thought Wrackwulf reproachfully. *There's nary even a hamlet in these parts to beg shelter from – were these really a great people once?*

'Oh yes,' Morcant reassured him a short while later, as they huddled inside the porch of their tent for shelter. 'These isles were host to great kingdoms once, long ago, when the city states of Thalamy were young, and the yellow-robed devil-priests of Sendhé were only just relearning their eldritch craft after the World's Breaking.'

Wrackwulf wouldn't ordinarily choose a sorcerer to bed down next to, but after his afternoon's confabulation with Torgun, he was determined to get what he could out of the weaselly mage. Even if it did mean listening to his bizarre stories.

'The First Kingdoms of Dûn Barad and Azûl Thân, to the west and east of here, were surpassed in splendour only by Arat Ingor, on whose very lands we sit now,' Morcant went on. 'The Kingdom of Mountain's Summit it means in our tongue, and Marchers and Druidings alike ruled from their ancient seat in Taras Cerawn, the High City of the Moon.' His voice softened, and a gentle sadness came over him as the skies above them wept freely. 'It was a grander age than any we have ever known since, or will – in the days between the Two Darknesses, when the gifts of Kaia were fresh and wisely used by our ancestors. Tíran, the Torch of the Skies, blessed our pastures at his sister's behest, no mean farmsteads did we scratch rough living from then –

the barren hills you see now bloomed all year round, and even greybeards forgot winter's bitter taste.'

Morcant fell silent, gazing at the hard heavy droplets that spattered against the tent porch. The barren valley they had chosen to bed down in could not have seemed further away from the halcyon realm the wizard's words conjured up. Wrackwulf grunted as if unconvinced, fishing around in his bag for the last of the mead they had brought with them from the mainland. 'You speak almost as if you were there,' he said, uncorking the bottle.

'Sometimes, the Unseen reward me for my studies, and when I have chanced to look into my scrying tool I have caught a glimpse of those far-gone times. Hundreds of years, aye and tens of hundreds besides, have elapsed since the Old Time, but exist it did.'

Wrackwulf proffered the bottle, but Morcant shook his head, staring absently at the gushing heavens, seemingly content with his arcane reminiscences.

Wrackwulf took a swig of the souring mead. Now was the time to press, he decided.

'You've such a grand tradition, yet your people are all but ignored by mainlanders. Strange indeed that you should find yourself making common cause with us, not to mention an Argolian witchfinder.' He let the words hang in the wet air between them, hoping Morcant would bite. Just below them on the valley slope lay Joram's tent, which he shared with Torgun. He wondered what kind of exchange the two would be having now. Both knights had agreed to try and learn more, to see if their shared suspicions were justified, but intrigue didn't come naturally to either of them.

Finally Morcant spoke. 'Not as other Argolians is he – different is Joram, somehow.'

The wizard's candour was revealing. Perhaps the two weren't conspiring, after all.

'What do you mean by that?' asked Wrackwulf, feigning ignorance.

Morcant continued to stare at the rain, which had hardened into a thick sheet now, as he answered. 'When I tap the powers of the Other Side, sense him I can.'

Wrackwulf raised an eyebrow. 'How do you mean? Countering your sorceries?'

The wizard shook his head. 'At first that was what I thought. But when we were in the Palace of Bending Branches at Ongist, felt him I did... *aiding* me somehow. That fay-trapped corridor would have overcome us all, but I found the strength... *we* found the strength. Just a trick of the mind I thought it at first, but when Abrexta and her bodyguards we confronted, again I felt him do it – bolstering my magick.' He turned to Wrackwulf suddenly, his eyes intense in the first fork of lightning that split the valley into a chiaroscuro of black and white. 'Not that powerful a Thaumaturgist am I! Yet all those men I destroyed, with but a single throw of flame!'

Wrackwulf felt his eyes grow wide. 'What are you saying? That Joram is a sorcerer?'

'They're all sorcerers, if you ask us pagans,' said Morcant, growing exasperated. 'That's what we've been trying to tell you mainlanders all along! Gods and angels, spirits and demons, they're not so very different as you like to think! And if you haven't realised that yet, Joram certainly has.'

Wrackwulf had no time to ponder that statement, for just then a cracking peal of thunder came hard on the heels of another blue-white fork of lightning. The clouds seemed to rear up monstrously in its light, looking like great winged devils themselves, fashioned of wreaths of smoke. Beyond that, howling sounds could now be heard, coming from all directions. Just above and behind them on the valley slope, the Westerlings were out of their tents, yelling at one another in their own tongue.

'What the hell's going on?' cried Wrackwulf, suddenly afraid.

'The Animal Kings are paying us a visit,' said Morcant. 'Something has them stirred up – leave us well alone they do normally, as long as we don't disturb them.'

'What kings?' demanded Wrackwulf, but Morcant had sprung out of the porch and was making his way up the wet slope to join the others.

With a curse, Wrackwulf grabbed up his axe and struggled after the mage. He wasn't wearing full armour, but it was an awkward climb through sodden turf and loose scree, and it took him a while to catch up with Morcant. When he did, he saw that the islanders were gazing across the valley. Trails of pinpricks told of many lanterns, converging towards their camping place. Torgun and Joram had also struggled up the slope to join them. Ianna and Fanwyn began muttering to each other frantically, while Ariadha stood staring ahead, her face pale in the light of her own lantern. Morcant addressed her hurriedly, and she nodded.

Gripping the haft of his axe more tightly, Wrackwulf

edged towards Torgun. The Northlending had his sword drawn.

'Any idea what this is about?' he growled.

Torgun shook his head. 'No idea. Joram seems at a loss, too.'

'Speaking of which... did you get anything out of him?'

Torgun's face looked even paler than Ariadha's as the flickering skies continued to go to war. 'Nothing. He proved evasive, but I'll be damned if he isn't hiding something.'

'Morcant seems to feel much the same. Says the monk has been interfering with his magick, to make it more powerful.'

Torgun glanced sidelong at the freelancer. The lamps were getting closer, moving steadily up the hillside. There had to be dozens of them. 'More powerful!? That doesn't sound like an Argolian at work to me.'

'Aye, more like a sorcerer, I told him. Only here's the thing – for Morcant and the rest of these paganers, there's no difference.'

'Many on the mainland hold to such a view,' put in Torgun. 'The perfecthood for one thing-'

'Yes, yes, spare me the theological debate,' said Wrackwulf. 'There's more to it than that. Morcant's *afraid* of him – deadly afraid. I can see it in his eyes when he speaks of him.'

Torgun frowned. 'The monk almost killed him in Thraxia.'

'No it's more than that, I'm telling you,' insisted Wrackwulf. 'We need to find out more, learn what kind of powers-'

But there was no more time for subterfuge. The lantern bearers had drawn close enough to be seen now, and even with silhouettes to go by, Wrackwulf could see that they were definitely not human. Their naked torsos were covered head to toe in thick animal fur; their arms were too long for their bodies, their feet splayed; their nails looked more like claws. The heads were those of assorted animals – bulls, stags, deer and boar gazed at them with eyes that were queerly intelligent.

'The Animal Kings have come!' cried Morcant. 'Stay your hands, sir knights! Make no foolish movement, if make any other you would in this life.'

The hundred-strong throng of hybrid creatures had moved to within a few swords' length away from them. Besides a lantern each one clutched a wicked-looking sickle, its blade the size of a short sword. The creatures were of a height with Torgun, their muscles huge and powerful beneath their furry hides.

One of them stepped forwards. Slightly bigger than the rest, its great aurochs maw opened as it started bellowing, a series of cries that almost drowned out the raging thunder.

As one, Ianna, Fanwyn and Morcant responded. Wrackwulf had heard the mage use the sorcerer's speech like that once before, when he'd summoned his familiar Scratcher.

'Ye Almighty,' he breathed. 'They're talking to each other.'

The strange conversation went on a short time. Then Ianna spoke, in Thrax this time: 'The Animal Kings have come from Vale of Shadow's Lingering,' she said, her voice tight. 'They say there is something there for one of us.'

'What the hell is that?' asked Wrackwulf. He had a sinking feeling he knew the answer.

'The Valley of the Barrow Kings,' confirmed Morcant, 'where Morwena's Doom was broken and the Watchtower once stood, where draug lords lie in wait for the Second Calling.'

'I thought we're only meant to skirt that place,' said Wrackwulf. 'Isn't that supposed to be where all the trouble started?'

Ianna only laughed at that. 'The trouble started a long time ago,' she told him. 'And far away from here. But have no fear, it is not you the Animal Kings seek.'

'Well that's a blasted relief,' said the freelancer sarcastically. 'Which of you Westerlings is it they want, then?'

'None of us,' replied Ianna. 'It's him they want,' she added, pointing at Sir Torgun.

CHAPTER 4
THE JUSTICE OF THE PITS

The hilt felt strange in Horskram's hand as he tested the sword's balance. The blade was broad and straight, of Urovian design; probably the merchant had obtained it in the Pilgrim Kingdoms. He lunged and slashed, tried a few old moves. It felt all wrong. Decades had passed since he'd wielded a sword, he was used to fighting two-handed with the quarterstaff. A greatsword would suit him better – besides, that's what Brother Sir Danton would be fighting with.

'You don't have anything larger?' he double checked with the brightly garbed trader. The wizened man shook his head forlornly, as though he had just been asked if a sick man still lived. 'A thousand curses, *effendi*, but no,' he confirmed. 'Such workmanship is hard bought, and times have not been so fortunate to Yazir, merchant of Imanabad!' The arms trader grimaced as he gestured towards the pitiful array of weapons on his stall. 'Waylaid I was, by *sarakim* in the Ghorabi, on my way back from the desert city of Tesh, and the rogues stole all my wares! In fact, my tale in its hardship and misfortune is comparable to that of the Houri and the Ninety-nine Bandits...'

Horskram waved him to silence. The further south you went in Nazharya, the more folk loved to tell tall tales that went on forever. Yazir was no exception.

'A standard arming sword will have to do,' he told the trader, going through a few more practice moves. Under his breath he muttered, 'What difference does it make how I speed myself unto shores of Gehenna?'

The Bethlers had announced their champion the following morning. Brother Sir Danton was lithe and athletic, as agile as he was strong, with fifteen years in the Order behind him: Horskram was in no doubt about the man's prowess: even channelling the powers of a hierophant, victory was far from certain.

What was certain was that he would taste hellfire if he won. But the sacrifice had to be made.

Hari Yassin sidled over just as Horskram finished haggling with Yazir for the sword.

'Thirty-five silvers, and I'd better get a scabbard with that,' Horskram told him sternly.

Yazir grinned. 'But of course, *effendi!* For a good friend like you, this I will do.'

'What do you want?' Horskram inquired darkly of Hari as he belted the sword on.

Hari jerked his thumb towards the outskirts of Sha'iza'ar. 'It's nearly noon. The first bloodlettings will be happening.

As honoured guests, we're permitted free space in the stalls. I'd suggest we take advantage, so you can observe the ground you'll be fighting on.'

Horskram didn't pretend to like the idea, but he could see Hari had a point.

'Agreed,' he said sullenly. 'Where are the others?'

'Tipu won't look on such a spectacle. He's still with Abdul and the other senior merchants. In truth, I think he still believes he can convince them to let us go without fighting.'

Horskram shook his head. 'Tipu is a good and ingenuous soul, but I doubt he'll succeed. Rothgar has too much of a hold over Abdul's purse strings. What of Anupe and Adelko?'

Yassin grinned. 'They are warming our places for us, I believe.'

Adelko felt a mixture of trepidation and excitement as he watched the sunken arena fill up with people. They weren't just merchants, but drovers, ostlers, husbandmen, crafts-men, artisans and, of course, mercenaries. Not all the crowd were native Nazharyans either: there was the odd pale face that told of an Urovian here and there, along with curly-haired Muradis and tall Kallandharis. One or two men had ebony skins, and looked very different indeed. And yet, Adelko could have sworn he'd seen such folk before, somewhere...

'Most like they come from the Arid Kingdoms,' said Anupe when he asked. 'The great mercantile realms beyond the Zhosa desert to the south of Sendhé. Naturally the Southrons shun that cursed realm, but some of their merchants take ship up the Malabar Coast to do trade with the Sassanians.'

Adelko had to marvel. He began to think that of all species on the earth, perhaps mortalkind was the most diverse. Such a pity mortalkind insisted on killing one another for the sake of those differences, though he supposed Horskram would consider him naïve for uttering such a statement. He still couldn't work out where he'd seen Southrons before though, he didn't recall seeing any in Ushalayim.

But there were other things to occupy his mind. Horskram had been of even darker mien than usual since the gladiatorial contest had been declared yesterday. Adelko knew why. The iron galleys of Gehenna awaited him on the Other Side, unless of course he lost – in which case they were probably all dead. But then at least Horskram might be admitted to the Heavenly Halls. How did that make sense?

Question everything.

Scripture was believed to be the sayings of prophets and saints – angels sent to earth in mortal form to guide their own kind to better ways, or mortals gifted by the Unseen for the same purpose, depending on how you looked at it. But words could be misinterpreted – Tobin was a prime example of that. What was the point in gifting men with wise counsel if they were too unwise to interpret it correctly?

Perhaps it was better to question nothing, Adelko reflected gloomily, to be a fool and wander through life in blissful ignorance.

Anupe only laughed when he mentioned this. 'I'm sure these fools would agree with you – if only they were clever enough to realise they were fools in the first place.'

Adelko shot her a wry glance. He was learning to appreciate the Harijan's warped humour.

The fools were clearly happy in some fashion: bright dots of gold caught the sun as wagers were made. The hubbub was almost deafening – there had to be several hundred of them crammed into the arena, which was fashioned of barked logs and had two entrances connecting to underground tunnels. The arena floor had been covered with sand, which seemed to glow in the light. To better soak up the blood, Hari had told him. As honoured guests, they were in the fenced enclosure reserved for Abdul and the other wealthiest merchants. It had the advantage of being closest to the pit.

Presently Horskram and Hari joined them. The wealthy merchants and their *taziq* bodyguards made way for them, a mingled look of awe and curiosity on their faces as they registered the unlikely future combatant. Horskram had explained that most pit fighters were slaves, owned like chattel by their masters: but when a free man chose the justice of the pits, he was paradoxically held in high esteem for his bravery.

Not to mention entertainment value, Adelko thought grimly.

He glanced sidelong at his stony-faced mentor, as a bare-chested master of ceremonies winded a huge horn chased in brass. The metal was appropriate – the City of Burning Brass was where Horskram was headed if he killed Sir Danton tomorrow.

Adelko refused to let that happen, but hadn't had one of his bright ideas yet.

The hubbub silenced as the portcullises guarding the entrances were raised. Five men were led out of the first tunnel by a clutch of *taziq* guardsmen. Around the perimeters of the arena, high on the stockade, archers were stationed – arming trained slaves in public could be a dangerous business, and it was best to take no risks. The horn sounded again, and men emerged from the second entranceway, bearing weapons and armour.

'It's the first fight of the day, so the ceremonial arming is done in full view,' explained Hari. 'It's all part of the spectacle.'

Adelko could see at first glance that the weapons had been made with deliberate cruelty in mind: the gauntlets strapped to the right hand of each fighter had a short stabbing blade emerging from where the knuckles should have been; one side of this was serrated, which would make stitching up a wound more difficult. The other glove had a buckler attached to it, but a wicked spike shaped like a talon protruded from the boss piece. The armour was simply ridiculous. Seemingly quite arbitrary in its design, made more for show than actual thought of protection, it consisted of a pauldron here, a vambrace there. Torso, groin and legs were left completely undefended.

But it was the helms that had Adelko gasping.

'They're covered!' he exclaimed. 'The visors are covered – how are they supposed to see?'

'They aren't,' said Horskram, his lip curling in disgust. 'That is why I told you pit fights are even worse than tourneys. At least with duels of honour, knights fight on their own terms, under conditions conducive to their survival. But these are slave warriors, mostly *amluqs* who became the property of another after their former masters were slain in battle. It is not uncommon for excess *amluqs* to end up in the fighting pits of Sassania.'

A sudden thought occurred to Adelko. 'The Thalamians had fighting pits didn't they, Master Horskram?'

The adept nodded as the armourers trundled back out of the arena, their carts empty. 'The custom is thought to have been invented by the Assurians. The Thalamians took a liking to it after they conquered these lands, and adopted it.'

The major-domo was calling for silence now, declaiming the coming event in a stentorian voice as four of the gladiators were led back to the edge of the arena, arranged at points of the compass. The fifth was turned slowly a few times, then left standing at the centre of the pit.

The crowd took a while to quiet, as last-minute bets were placed and boy vendors came around with rhytons of fruit juice and wine, and sweetmeats skewered on sticks. Adelko caught one figure who stood out from the crowd – an orange-robed priest of Zaruman, a false prophet said to have been visited by Mithras, a twin avatar representing the archangels Solus and Nurë.

What's a Zarumani doing at a pit fight? he wondered. The strange priest seemed to have eyes for them as much as the arena: perhaps the Sassanian was asking himself the same question about them.

The major-domo called once more for silence, and finally got it. It hung heavy in the thickening sultry air, then he blew his horn again.

Slowly, the five blind warriors began to stalk the arena.

A short, squat Muradi was the first to go. The man screamed as a tall, lean Southron from the Arid Kingdoms flanked him, puncturing his armpit with the spike on his buckler before rending his thigh with the jagged edge of his blade. Blood welled in pools on the sands as the Muradi went down; the two rolled and grappled awkwardly as the copper-skinned Southron toppled clumsily on to his opponent, before getting the best of him and stabbing him repeatedly in the chest.

The howling crowd gave vent to its mounting bloodlust, which would not be sated until three more men lay dead. Adelko could even make out a few womenfolk, wives of merchants and traders, tearing at their headscarves as the excitement took them. That spectacle sickened him almost as much as the fight itself.

'You were right, Master Horskram,' he said. 'This isn't ritual combat, it's ritual slaughter.'

The other three combatants had heard the clash and two of them were edging towards it, while the third hung back. The Southron got to his feet unsteadily, before lowering himself into a crouch. Adelko could practically feel the gladiator's ears straining as he struggled to anticipate the next attack.

He sized up the other three combatants. Two were obviously of local provenance, probably *amluqs* or captured *sarakim* from the southern desert lands. But the last was obviously Urovian – though tanned from years in the hot south, his skin was too pale for a Sassanian. But something else about him held the young monk's attention... there was a calmness to his poise, as though his circumstances didn't trouble him over much. For some reason, Adelko felt his sixth sense tingle.

The two Nazharyans were straying closer to one another now. The Southron had kept his cool, wisely judging that his blinded assailants would be unlikely to find him now he'd stopped fighting and making a noise. The major-domo was calling for silence again from the crowd. 'Quiet please! As a courtesy to those about to die, do not call out during combat,' he cried. The banality of the words seemed to carry the nightmarish aspect of the scene to a new level.

The crowd was shushing itself as the two Nazharyans inched ever closer to one another, as though drawn together by an invisible chain that contracted. One was aware of his opponent just a shade more quickly; stepping forwards he risked a swipe of his blade, but some desperate instinct saved the other and he brought his shield up to parry. The two traded blows and blocks unsteadily for an agonizing half minute. The dark-skinned Southron circled warily around where he thought the fight was, and from the corner of his eye Adelko saw the Urovian start to move steadily towards the centre of the arena. Archers on the stockade relaxed their bent bows: Adelko guessed cowardice in the pits was rewarded with swift execution.

The Nazharyans had stepped back to get some respite. Adelko could practically feel the fear pouring off of them. The Southron chose that moment to attack, stepping in towards them and swiping wildly with sword and shield. His instincts must have been good: he caught a Nazharyan a glancing blow across his helm, forcing him to engage him. The second Nazharyan lunged back in and a three-way fight took place. Not even the major-domo could silence the roaring of the crowd now.

That should have stopped the Urovian in his tracks, but even bereft of hearing thanks to the din of the crowd, he continued to move unerringly towards the fight.

A Nazharyan recoiled with a scream, his left arm spurting blood where a serrated blade had torn veins asunder. His courage broken, he staggered backwards out of the fray... before he could take half a dozen steps the archers peppered him with arrows. The other Nazharyan clashed with the Southron just as the Urovian reached them both. The three of them traded blows, but there was something about the northerner... he almost moved as though uninhibited, despite being as blind as the others.

The second Nazharyan fell with a groan, the Southron's shield spike rammed deep inside his gut. The dark-skinned warrior wrenched it free and turned, somehow blocking the Urovian's next attack. The two grappled for a while: the Southron towered over the Urovian, yet he seemed equal to the task, and gradually he pushed his antagonist back... the Southron caught his heel on the dying Nazharyan and toppled backwards. He dragged the Urovian down with him, but the northman somehow managed to pull his spiked buckler across his torso. Then the Urovian began to lean heavily on his opponent, pushing the spike down, down, closer towards the Southron's chest. The Southron thrashed around desperately, but the Urovian had him pinned, using his legs to trap his arms whilst placing the rest of his body weight directly above the shield.

It was a slow, drawn-out death, and Adelko had to look away as the Urovian buried the shield spike in the Southron's heart inch by inch.

When it was over the crowd gave vent to a blood-curdling roar. Some even threw gold coins into the pit, to signify their approval of the Urovian's performance. The surviving gladiator simply stood, arms at his sides, his mouth a flat line beneath his helmet. Adelko could sense the sorrow in him.

But he could also sense there was more to this man than a gladiator. And what was an Urovian doing in a Sassanian slave pit?

Horskram merely shrugged when Adelko asked him. 'Might be a prisoner of war that couldn't afford to pay his ransom.' Clearly Horskram's mind was on other matters, for he quickly added: 'It's been an age since I fought on sandy terrain, so I'll have to watch my footing. But at least they won't be blindfolding me like yon poor wretches.'

The plan came to Adelko moments before it exited his mouth. 'Except you won't be fighting in the pits tomorrow, Master Horskram.' Three pairs of quizzical eyes turned to him. Adelko nodded down towards the pit, where guards were leading the champion away. 'He will.'

'No, absolutely not!' Horskram's face was flushed and angry in the late afternoon light.

'But, Master Horskram, you just admitted yourself that the laws of no-man's land don't forbid it. We're entitled to choose a champion to fight on our behalf.'

'That man is a *slave*, Adelko,' he pointed out. 'To have him fight for us, we would need to buy him from his current owner. I will not become a slave owner just so I can save my soul.' The adept took up his rhyton and drained it of wine. They were reposing in one of the caravanserai's common rooms. Enthused spectators had converted their bloodlust into lust for drink – and lust for other more venal sins, judging by the shrieking of harlots to be heard from the enclosed courtyard out back.

Adelko threw his arms up in exasperation. His mannerisms were becoming more like his mentor's every day. 'Slave, serf – what's the difference?' he demanded. 'In Urovia the lords work their peasantry into early graves every year – half of them are bonded to the land they till and sow. Just because we don't call them slaves, doesn't mean they aren't. That means you've lived off slavery every day of your life, one way or the other.'

'Ah, more of your moral equivalence, is it?' shot back Horskram. 'I'll thank you to keep your sententious notions to yourself – this is completely different from being a bondsman, and you know it.'

Adelko lost his cool then. 'What I do know is this – if you fight Brother Sir Danton tomorrow, win or lose you're finished! And I won't stand by helplessly and let that happen!'

Anupe and Yassin exchanged surprised glances. They hadn't expected this kind of emotion from him.

'Perhaps he has a point,' ventured Hari. 'You are valiant, master monk, but with respect this Danton is at least twenty years your junior. And much more accustomed to fighting to the death, by the looks of it.'

'I agree,' put in Anupe. 'We should make inquiries at least, find out what this owner would charge. Perhaps he would agree to lend us his slave – that way you are not actually becoming a slave owner yourself.'

Horskram looked genuinely conflicted now. 'Aye, I wouldn't,' he allowed. 'But I'd still be profiting by another man's enslavement. That'll see me in Gehenna as surely as killing. No, it's settled – tomorrow I fight Danton.' Reaching for the ewer, he poured himself another rhyton of wine. 'One more cup, then prayers and sleep. I'll be needing my wits about me.'

Haroun tek Haroun was so fat it took more than a dozen large cushions to support him. That didn't stop him availing himself of a low table crammed with glazed saffron-coated chicken legs, skewers of spiced lamb and red onions, vine leaves stuffed with jasmine-scented rice and salted aubergines replete with minced meat cooked in a rich tomato sauce.

Adelko felt his mouth watering as he took advantage of the merchant's hospitality. A veiled slave girl poured them rhytons of sweet white Kallandhari wine. So far this was the only part of his latest task he was enjoying: if Horskram caught wind of this, he'd visit fires of Gehenna on him personally. There'd be no need for the iron galleys of Azhoanarn to take him there.

'So tell me,' said Haroun, sucking the meat out of an aubergine in one go. 'How may Haroun be of service to you? The hour grows late, and I must away to sunset prayers soon.'

The gimlet greedy eyes that glittered beneath his jewelled turban told of a man who loved wealth well enough to forgo devotions.

As they had agreed, Yassin opened negotiations.

'The archangel Cyrius shines down upon Haroun tek Haroun a hundred times each day,' said the rogue, inclining his head deferentially. 'Amwal has justly bestowed the blessing of prosperity on him, granting lifelong success in all his dealings.'

Haroun flicked greasy fingers dismissively. 'Yes, yes, you flatter well, *al'Hajin*. Now tell me why you are here.'

'We watched your pit fighter this afternoon,' said Yassin. 'As you may know, we have recently sought the justice of the pits. We would hire your gladiator's services, for a handsome fee of course.'

Haroun chuckled at that, beckoning to the slave girl for a finger bowl of rose-petalled water. 'The Pangonian is my best fighter,' he said, rinsing his hands. 'His services do not come cheaply. Especially not when you are asking me to put him up against a holy *fariz* of the Bethler Order. Such a clash carries considerable risk, you understand.'

'Of course we understand the risk involved,' Hari confirmed. 'And are willing to pay accordingly...'

Haroun bargained harder than a mail gauntlet, and not all Yassin's guile could get him below the sum of fifty gold riyaads.

'And that will be another fifty as collateral should my slave lose the fight,' Haroun reminded them. 'This you will get back in the event he survives and is able to continue to serve me as a gladiator.' The fat merchant clapped his hands, and an old slave missing half a foot limped into the room bearing parchment, ink and quill.

'I shall draw up the contract between us,' he said. 'Come back at first light tomorrow with the money and we will sign the agreement then.'

Hari rose and bowed courteously. 'Haroun tek Haroun, you have the wisdom of the Prophet and the munificence of Zendigi – may their peace always be upon thee!'

Adelko followed him out awkwardly, bidding a silent farewell to Haroun's delicious viands.

'How are we going to get a hundred gold pieces by tomorrow?' he asked as they made their way back towards the caravan where the others would be waiting for them.

'Ashanti only knows,' replied Yassin, 'for that fat camel is as greedy as Sha'amiel himself. I hope Sir Amalric was generous with his coin.'

Any doubts as to their ability to finance the deal with

Haroun were soon rendered moot by Horskram, who stubbornly persisted in embracing his plight.

'A thousand times, no!' he cried, after they had explained their gambit. 'I will not be party to this.'

Adelko was about to protest, but Yassin laid a hand on his sleeve. 'And what if we freed the slave? Would that still trouble your conscience?'

Horskram laughed. 'I've barely enough borrowed coin to hire him, let alone buy him. Yon merchant would ask ten times the sum you've just agreed for a valuable slave like that.'

Hari smiled thinly in the waning light. 'Who said anything about buying?'

Dawn light was spilling into Haroun's luxuriously appointed caravan through open shutters. The merchant was up and scrutinising his ledgers, though Hari noticed the slave girl that lounged on the divan was more scantily clad than last time.

I'll bet you got your money's worth from her last night, you lucre-sucking pig, thought Hari. *My mother and her harem sisters spent years pleasuring oafs like you.*

That only made what he was about to do all the more appealing.

'You have my money?' asked Haroun absently, not bothering to look up from the ledgers.

'A hundred riyaads, as agreed,' replied Hari, setting a chinking purse down before the merchant. He'd had to rob a few of the less well-guarded caravans the previous night to make up the difference. Not that he minded the extra work – he'd already agreed an enlarged share of treasure from the Kishan Tombs, for saving their necks before the adventure had even begun. The monk had agreed reluctantly to their plan, though the sun had disappeared beyond the horizon by the time they managed to persuade him. Really the Argolian was as stubborn as a camel at times, how on earth did the others put up with him?

The chink of coin soon got Haroun's attention. Counting the pieces, he smiled and reached for the contract. Yassin passed it over to Adelko. 'He will sign, and I will bear witness,' said the trickster.

'You are familiar with Nazharyan law then,' observed Haroun. 'Very good, he and I will sign it.'

Of course I'm familiar with the Sultan's law, you cretin. I'm al'Hajin, *not a* jhufa'ar *straight off a pilgrim ship.*

'Of course, we'll want to inspect the slave,' said Yassin when the contract was signed. 'Perhaps brief him on what to expect.'

Haroun waved a fat-fingered hand impatiently. 'Of course, of course. Your trial does not begin until noon, you have plenty of time.'

The pit cells reeked of sweat and urine. Adelko guessed the gladiators were not kept particularly well. He'd read that Thalamian potentates once housed them in villas and feted them like kings, though that clearly didn't apply here and now. Haroun escorted the five of them along a corridor lined with stout teak doors, stopping at the last one. He motioned for his *taziq* bodyguards to open the door.

Entering they saw an athletic-looking man lying on a straw pallet. His face, covered with an unkempt beard of many months' growth, was turned to the wall, and he muttered what sounded like a prayer over and over again.

Adelko caught a few words. The Psalm of Redemption's Beseeching. He felt his sixth sense tingle again.

Haroun cleared his throat loudly. 'Up, Pangonian,' he said. 'Time to meet your latest employers.'

The Pangonian turned to regard them. His eyelids were black and hooded as if from many nights' lack of sleep; beneath them blue-grey irises caught the wan torchlight. There was a desperately lost look in those eyes, like a drowning mariner caught up in strong waves who has forsaken all hope of life.

The Pangonian said nothing. One of the *taziqs* stepped forward to grab him roughly, but the slave shrugged him off, sitting up on his pallet. Adelko could see his muscular torso was criss-crossed with scars old and new; his dirty black hair fell in unruly tides down his back. Though no taller than most of his countrymen, the Pangonian's frame exuded power and strength. Knotted cords of sinew rippled beneath the zigzagging scars, the shoulders were rounded out and hard like pauldrons of steel, the calloused fingers dextrous yet strong. He could not have been older than forty, but to Adelko it seemed as though this man had made war for a hundred years and more. His sixth sense flared up a notch.

'You are to fight this afternoon,' Haroun went on. 'A

knight Bethler seeks the justice of the pits. You are to fight him on behalf of these people.' He indicated Horskram and his band.

The gladiator's response surprised them. Throwing back his head, he roared with laughter. A long, drawn-out mocking sound, it almost felt as unpleasant as watching his last opponent's drawn-out death. Haroun scowled at the impudence. The *taziq* moved to cuff him, gaping as the gladiator caught his wrist. He had not even stopped laughing. The second mercenary stepped in, menacing him with a spear, and the Pangonian let go. Adelko sensed the fear in both *taziqs*.

Finally the Pangonian spoke. 'Have a care, Haroun,' he said in fluent Sassanic. 'You don't want to mess me up before my big fight.'

Haroun flicked his hand again, and the *taziqs* stepped back to flank him. 'You are a most unruly slave!' he chided. 'Do I not reward you well when you fight, with bread and meat and strong wine? I even offer you harem privilege, but this you will not take.'

That caught Horskram's attention. 'A gladiator refusing brothel rights? That is odd.'

Haroun shrugged. 'In truth, we know not who he truly is. Sold to me he was, by a slaver out of Tesh. Said he'd come by him near the border with the Pilgrim Kingdoms, that he was a deserter or some kind of coward punished with slavery.'

The Pangonian sneered at that. 'I am no coward,' he spat. 'And prove that every week in the pits.' All at once, the fight seemed suddenly to go out of him. 'But have it as you will, it makes no odds to me.'

Horskram scrutinised him. 'You speak the local tongue well for a Pangonian freesword,' he observed.

The gladiator shrugged. 'Thought I might as well learn the language of the people I came here to kill.'

Haroun sounded almost apologetic now. 'I can assure you, his skill at arms is unsurpassed. Only last week, I put him up against three Halpnese spear-casters, and he slew them all single-handedly. Before that he defeated Tyro of Argossia *and* his lioness! And, about a month before that, he fought the Harijan Twins and...' His voice trailed off as he caught Anupe glaring at him. Haroun cleared his throat nervously. 'I was going to say, he bested them fairly and refused to kill either one! Knows how to please the crowd, this one – he may lack manners, but he's the best fighter I've ever had.'

'I don't doubt it,' said Horskram, sizing him up. Addressing the Pangonian, he said: 'You'll know how well these Bethlers fight. In a few hours you'll go up against one of their best swordsmen. He'll be using a greatsword and clad in-'

'I know how the Knights Bethler fight,' said the Pangonian, sounding bored now. Hauling himself up, he added: 'Just get me to the armoury. I'll tell you what weapons I require.'

They watched Brother Sir Danton limber up in the sun. Beneath his white surcoat of plates he wore a mail byrnie; vambraces and greaves completed his armour, though he went bare-headed, his bald pate shining. Two scars criss-crossed his otherwise handsome face. He had an air of studied composure about him as he went through his moves, ignoring the cooing crowd that seemed to expand across the arena's stockades by the second. His two-handed sword made great swishing arcs, flashing as it caught the sun in brilliant rills of light...

On the other side of the pit stood the Pangonian. Their slave champion, the man who would determine whether they lived or died. He had chosen a quite different array of weaponry, though Haroun's stock was predominantly Sassanian anyway. Anupe had nodded approvingly as she watched him pick a falchion, complementing this with a broad target shield of burnished brass, and a studded corselet of boiled leather. Two pauldrons of crude bronze and a stylized winged helm of the same metal completed the array.

'He certainly likes to make a show of it,' commented Hari, from his seat next to Adelko. 'I didn't think winged helmets existed until I saw my first pit fight. Even down here, they are rare!'

The thing gave the Pangonian the look of a raptor. Only his lower jaw was visible. Adelko supposed that might be menacing to some opponents, but Danton was unlikely to be cowed by such a tactic. Almost lazily, the Pangonian began a few warm-up exercises of his own. Some members of the crowd booed as they caught him slowly, almost drunkenly, taking swipes with the falchion. Clearly they hadn't seen him fight yesterday.

The major-domo called for silence and declaimed the event, drawing on different protocol this time.

'*Effendis*, and most exalted harem consorts! Today we have no ordinary pit fight, but a justice fight, witnessed by the Unseen to determine guilt or innocence! Our plaintiffs accuse the defendants of black witchery and blood magic, charges which they most strenuously deny! Now two champions will fight to determine who has the right of this matter – for the plaintiffs, step forward, Brother Sir Danton of Siraka!'

The tall knight swept forwards to the centre of the arena, bowing curtly and skewering his sword in the sand. On the other side of the pit stockade, Rothgar and the other Bethlers smirked and applauded, confident of success.

'And for the defendants, step forward the Pangonian Punisher, the Worst Man of the Pits, Haroun's Harbinger of Doom!'

The crowd roared its approval. Clearly most of them *had* seen him fight.

Adelko felt his spirits rise, before remembering that they were watching a fight to the death. The gladiator advanced to the centre of the pit, and squared off against his opponent. Once again Adelko was struck by the sense of calmness emanating from him. It put him in mind of Sir Torgun, who never got rattled during a fight no matter the danger or the odds.

The major-domo called for silence, then gave the command to fight.

Adelko had half expected the Pangonian to repeat his

previous opening tactic, and simply stay still and wait for the fight to come to him.

He didn't. The man moved like lightning as he flanked Danton, before stepping in and thrusting at his side. Danton reacted quickly, half circling and taking a single step backwards as he brought his blade around to parry and riposte. The two traded blows and blocks like that for a minute. Both men were breathtaking in the skill they commanded. Danton had the benefit of better range thanks to his longer blade, but the Pangonian was able to riposte more effectively because of his shield.

Presently the two men backed off and began circling each other. The crowd should have been baying by now, but they weren't: even the bloodthirsty citizens of Sha'iaz'ar were silenced by the exceptional contest they now witnessed. Out of the corner of his eye, Adelko saw the Zarumani priest again, but he was too caught up in the fight to pay him any heed now.

Once again, it was the Pangonian who took the initiative. Darting in, he ducked under Danton's questing blade and slashed at both his legs in quick succession. Danton leapt back from the first swipe while his greave took the second with a resounding whine. An overhead strike would have been the obvious counter attack, but Danton wasn't obvious: instead he stepped around the gladiator nimbly, forcing him to swing around with him. Abruptly the knight changed tack, spinning around to his left and bringing his huge blade in a sweeping inside-out arc towards the Pangonian's head. The latter seemed to sense the move at the last moment, and swerved back out of range, his helm ringing as the sword point caught it a glancing blow.

And then something peculiar seemed to happen. Adelko felt it at once: from then on it appeared as though the fight was choreographed, as though both swordsmen were dancing together rather than trying to kill each other. He watched transfixed as sinewed limbs and silvery blades blurred together in a canvas of motion that was both elegant and deadly; the stunned silence seem to grow about his companions and the wider crowd, enveloping them hypnotically...

And suddenly the show was over. It took Adelko a few seconds to register what had happened. The Pangonian had suddenly flung his shield up. Not to ward off an incoming blow – its polished brass surface caught the sun's glare, reflecting stabbing rays of blinding light into Danton's face. His cry of consternation quickly turned to one of pain and fear as the gladiator slipped his blade past his befuddled guard, the razor-sharp point slicing effortlessly through his throat.

The crowd gasped as the knight slumped to his knees. Rothgar and his brethren were on their feet, crying foul and pointing in outrage. But the Pangonian had no ears for them, and neither did the major-domo.

By one supreme last effort of will, Danton raised his sword in both hands. Blood was gushing from his larynx, and it was a futile though defiant gesture. The Pangonian stepped back out of range and surveyed his dying opponent impassively. Adelko could still sense the lingering sadness in him.

With a final gurgling cry, Danton let go of the sword and pitched over into the growing pool of his own blood. Only then did the crowd recover its wits, turning wild at the spectacle, tearing at turbans and headscarves and kaftans, some dancing in the aisles. It certainly had the effect of drowning out Rothgar's screams of protest.

The object of their adulation stuck his falchion in the sands before tossing the shield away. Sinking to his knees himself, he bent over double, pressing his face into the arena floor.

Adelko could have sworn he was weeping.

CHAPTER 5
A DESTINY REVEALED

Torgun did not react as Ianna pointed him out. The grotesque animal-men turned as one and regarded him with their sentient eyes. Then the aurochs-headed leader raised its sickle and used it to beckon to him.

The knight drew himself up. 'What is the meaning of this?' he asked. He caught Joram sidelong gazing at him, his face looking ghast and grim in a flash of lightning.

Fanwyn spoke, addressing him in stilted Decorlangue. 'Animal Kings have guarded Valley of Barrow Kings for centuries, kept draugar in mounds where they belong. But foretold long time ago great power would return, to stir draugar from barrows, defeat Animal Kings' magic. Kept something have they, to give to chosen one in same dark hour.'

'Smells like a trap to me,' growled Wrackwulf. 'I think we'll pass on their hospitality.'

Ianna laughed. 'Venturers into Arat Ingor do not refuse Animal Kings. Not even we do this. You must do as they say.'

'Though why they want outlander like you, our best guess cannot tell,' added Fanwyn.

'I second that sentiment,' said Torgun. 'I'm just a knight errant of Northalde, what is all this nonsense about chosen ones?' He felt as though he'd just walked into a lay.

Then he realised in a flash of insight just how wrong he was.

He hadn't just walked into a lay: he'd walked into one the minute his King had sent him off with Horskram. He thought of his clever brother Toros again, reading aloud from a tome in their father's small library at Vandheim. It had been some anthology of poesy from the Golden Age – Torgun hadn't had much interest at the time – but one line had stayed with him. It came back to him now, seemingly borne on another flash of lightning.

No honest man thinks himself a hero/Until his deeds seem more of quill than sword.

And then he knew. No chance had brought him to this bleak shore at the edge of the world. Duty had bound him in its unwritten iron law, compelling him down a path that led to high events and final conclusions. Perhaps for the first time in his life, he knew true dread. It was as if, for one instant, the flaring skies lit up his future, and he saw everything that would become of him. The rolling thunder tolled across the night like a death knell.

Steeling himself, Sir Torgun embraced the fear, making a friend of it as best he could. Now was not the time to be unmanned.

'Tell the Animal Kings I shall go with them,' he said.

Sir Torgun was grateful for the Circifix of St Argo, for an increasing aura of palpable evil shrouded itself about him as the animal-men led him through winding trails deeper into the craggy foothills of the Farfahalains. His beastly guides did not speak. But if they reeked of sweaty animals, at least they lacked the preternatural stench of the Wadwos. By now he was learning to discern different types of magic, to some degree: the sorcery that had fashioned these monsters seemed less unwholesome than that which had bound the Woses in their lumpen forms.

The moorlands rose steadily for an hour or two, and Torgun found himself clutching the relic about his neck, muttering what scattered few prayers he knew. The knight tried to picture the fingerbone of St Argo, resting within the silver rood about his neck, and drew some strength from that. The frightful vision the Unseen had bequeathed him back in the valley had receded somewhat; but Torgun knew deep in his heart it would never vanish completely, not until its entire prognostication had been played out for good or ill.

Presently the path they followed crested a pass, only this was topped with a gigantic dolmen that seemed to function as some kind of gateway. As they drew closer, Torgun could see markings on its three great stones, which were each thrice the size of a man. The Animal Kings did not pause, but continued to march two abreast through the archway; as he passed under it, he recognised the eerie glyphs used by wizards carved into the dolmen stones. An uncomfortable tingling sensation that passed through his body only confirmed this; it could have been the lightning, but he fancied the relic he wore flared resentfully.

He emerged onto a flat outcropping of blackened rock that overlooked their destination. Torgun's first sighting of the Valley of the Barrow Kings was a fearful one. It was vast, far bigger than the draug lair he'd looked upon in Vorstlund. Torgun felt his hackles rise as he turned his head from side to side, his eyes sweeping the cursed vale, a huge ugly scar that cut the cruel crags about it. Both sides were studded with burial mounds covered in eldritch markings; they looked just like the ones he'd seen on the Draugmoors, only here there were too many to count. But it was the stinking black crater, ringed with charred lumps of what could almost have been volcanic rock, that petrified the knight. From here, he could sense, the evil that polluted the vale flowed. Torgun guessed that this must be the remnants of the Watchtower built by the Elder Wizards that Horskram had spoken of, ruined for a second time when Søren slew its last mistress.

The Animal Kings gathered around him, holding their lamps aloft. Their moves were curiously synchronised. Together they began a bellowing chant, and even the cracking thunder seemed to recede a little as if cowed. The lightning flared once, twice, turning the valley into a terrible ghostscape of white and black. A third time it sundered the skies, and that was when Torgun saw it: a figure making its way, seemingly out of the depths of the crater, steadily towards them. The thick rains seemed to attenuate a little as the figure approached, ambling up the side of the valley to where they stood waiting. Torgun fancied there was something almost casual in its manner, and that only increased his trepidation. He clutched the relic more tightly.

The Animal Kings did not cease their chanting, but continued to shake the rocks about them as the figure drew ever closer. Peering at it, Torgun saw it was unnaturally tall and gangly, swaddled in a voluminous woollen robe the colour of mud. At last it reached them, stepping up onto the shelf of rock and pausing to allow the Animal Kings to step aside. Reaching up it pulled back its hood, and Torgun gasped as he looked upon a smooth ovular face devoid of any features – bereft of eyes, lips, or nose, the apparition would have made a Wadwo seem human.

'What art thou?' The words spilled from lips made nerveless by mingled fear and astonishment.

He was just thinking how ridiculous it was to ask a creature with no mouth a question, when he heard the reply inside his mind, resonating perfectly in his native tongue.

This is not a question that requires answering. Rather, the question is – what art thou?

Sir Torgun caught his breath as he recalled the vision he'd had that night. But even then, his natural modesty got the better of him.

'I... but serve as any knight should.'

Your humility does you credit. But the time for false modesty grows old. Soon champions must step forward, and do as the Unseen command. No one outruns their Wyrd.

The apparition stepped forward. Torgun thought he could see raindrops passing through it, yet the figure appeared corporeal enough when it reached into its robes and pulled out a glinting shard. It proffered the piece of metal.

Gazing upon it, Torgun blinked. It shone with a brilliance that was almost liquid in the lamplight, putting him in mind of the quicksilver running through the druids' cavern at Skelnaervon, and some of the finer weapons he'd seen the Marcher Lords clutching. But there was something beyond that too, a resonating puissance he had never seen in any metal before, not even the best Staerkvit steel.

This you have earned, by dint of your valour and prowess. Take it, and when you return home, smelt it into your blade. Then you shall wield the power of your great ancestor's sword, when the serpents of the earth rise up again to terrorise mortal men and women.

Torgun did not even think to question the impulse that compelled him to obey. The shard felt light yet strong in his gauntleted hand; he almost fancied the rood about his neck flared again, only this time in approval.

Looking up, he wasn't entirely surprised to see the mysterious figure had vanished. The Animal Kings closed about him, facing back the way they had come and pointing ahead of them with their sickles. Sir Torgun needed no further encouragement. Turning, he left the Valley of the Barrow Kings behind.

Sunrise was about an hour away by the time he rejoined his companions. The Animal Kings had disappeared as soon as they reached the outskirts of the valley where they were encamped; he did not expect to see them again. He could only pray their age-old magick would be enough to keep the barrows he had seen closed for a little while longer.

Pulling out the shard of metal, he studied it again. It was hard to be sure in the weak pre-dawn light, but it did indeed look as though it might have come off the edge of a blade. But who was this great ancestor the apparition had spoken of?

Approaching the camp, he found the female marcher on final watch. She glared at him as he appeared, and pulling her tent flap up, she disappeared inside. Torgun didn't mind over much: some time alone was just what he needed. Sitting down on a rock, he began to ponder the riddle. He might not be as smart as Toros, but he'd always listened to his older brother – even if his stories hadn't interested him much at the time. As the heir, his brother had understandably been proud of the House of Hamlyn and its noble lineage. Their father Torrin had been the sixteenth Jarl of Vandheim, having inherited the title when his older brother Thorne took holy orders. Before that it had been his grandfather Jord, who died before Torgun was born.

The young knight turned the fragment over and over in his hands, as he recalled Toros and his obsessive reading aloud from the book of Hamlyn's genealogy. Their great-grandfather had also been called Toros, he'd been killed by the Red Plague; his great-uncle Vordegil had been killed in a joust at the first Linden Tourney, to celebrate that mighty castle's building; his father Torrin had died in a hunting accident; his father Oran had perished of the Bleeding Bowel Sickness...

Torgun sighed with exasperation. The scions of his family had ever been loyal to the crown and stalwart in service. But could any of them truly be said to be great men, the kind an apparition might invoke in some far-off land? It didn't make sense. Holding up the shard to the gradually thickening light, he racked his brains. No, he needed to go further back – the apparition and animal-folk had the air of having waited many centuries for this. According to his brother, their ancestor Oran had died some two hundred years ago, that wouldn't seem so long to such beings.

Further back he delved. Three hundred and fifty years ago, twins had been born to Kolbjorn, fourth Jarl of Vandheim. Agmund and Sigmund had been great warriors of renown – the brothers had ruled one after the other, Sigmund dying during the War Of No King that had put Beortwulf I on the throne and established the royal house of Caarl. Agmund had taken his place as Jarl, finishing the fight to unseat the old house of Jorvik, but the troubadours told how he never got over his beloved brother's death, and in the end the Melancholy Sickness had taken him. Tragic and heroic both brothers had been, but what could they have to do with a sword fragment located on the Island Realms, hundreds of miles away from Vandheim? Still it didn't make sense.

What about the founder of their house? Karlang the Loyal had been the first Jarl of Vandheim, earning its rich demesnes after helping to topple King Danveld the Blood-Shamed, who murdered his nephew so he could inherit the throne of the fledgling Kingdom of Northalde. That had been close on five hundred years ago; Karlang had surely been a noble man and a just. But a great hero? And nothing in the accounts of his rule mentioned anything about a sword.

The more Torgun pondered it, the more he realised that his ancestors had secured much of their status by simple loyalty to the crown – and justice when the crown had proved wanting, as in Danveld's time. That humbled him all the more – why should he be any different? – but it didn't solve the riddle.

'Sir Torgun, you are back. Right pleasing it is to see you safe again.'

Morcant had emerged from his tent. Torgun had been so lost in his reverie he'd barely noticed. He noticed now as the wizard crouched behind a rock and began relieving himself.

He never goes privately – these islanders are coarse to the very marrow. But Torgun kept his sentiments to himself.

'So, our animal friends had something to show you, heh?' inquired the warlock without getting up.

'This.' Torgun didn't see much point in hiding it. From what Wrackwulf had told him, the warlock was just as uneasy about Joram as they were. He decided to take a risk and trust him.

Morcant finished and wiped himself with a handful of moss, pulling down his grubby robes and sidling over.

His casual manner evaporated as he saw what the knight was holding.

'That can't be,' he gawped. 'Who gave you this?'

Torgun described the apparition as best he could.

'Twas a spirit keeper that visited thee,' said Morcant, awe in his tone.

'Spirit keeper?'

'What people of your faith would call an un-angel, neither of heaven nor hell. Set by the Unseen to guard something, until its rightful heir should come to claim it.'

'I am no heir, but a second son,' said Torgun stubbornly. Bequeathment had always unsettled him; a man should earn his entitlement.

'And do not your own scriptures say 'the second son shall inherit the earth', when the Hour of All's Ending draws near?'

'I've no idea what the scriptures say,' replied Torgun bluntly. Apocalyptic talk unnerved him more than bequeathment. 'Are you going to tell me whom this sword fragment belonged to, or not?'

Morcant smiled. 'The shard you hold is from Orm-Killerin, the blade that Søren used to slay Morwena... and a great many other foes besides. That blade she fashioned for him, from the great silver axe wielded by the giant Arthrax, whom he slew in service to her.'

Torgun paused to reflect on that as the sun poked its lemon-yellow head above the ranges. It looked to be a clear day on the islands, for once.

'Yes, I remember Horskram telling us the tale,' he said. 'When the ancient threat we faced became apparent. I had not heard anything about a shard though.'

Morcant nodded enthusiastically. 'A less well-known part of the legend that is,' he explained. 'When Søren used Orm-Killerin to punch past Morwena's magic shield, a sliver of it broke off. In his grief and anger Søren never noticed, departing the Watchtower after it burned to the ground and setting sail in Jürmengaard for the Veil at the World's Edge. But a keeper was sent from the Other Side, through a rent in the Veil caused by the dreadful sorcery of the valley you have just visited. The broken Headstone it would not or could not keep, for probably even immortals fear being corrupted by such an eldritch thing. But the sliver you hold it took, knowing that in time the power of Orm-Killerin would be needed again. So the legend goes, only a descendant of that mighty hero – himself a demi-god – could wield it. And by the looks of things, that descendant, sir knight, is you.'

Morcant was still smiling his sly smile. Torgun had never liked it much, and he liked it even less now.

'I am no pagan reaver's descendant,' he protested, rising in his indignity.

'Oh, but you are,' countered Morcant. 'I've read enough of your people's history to know that as well as you. Your ancestors came from the Frozen Wastes, driving mine from the eastern watches of the mainland. Three Westerling kingdoms fell, and three were erected in their place by the Northlanders. In time those nations became Northalde, the very land you call home.'

Torgun closed his gauntleted fist around the metal. It stung him suddenly. Opening his hand he saw it had punctured the mail, opening a small cut in his palm.

'Still so sharp and strong, after all this time,' he murmured.

'Orm-Killerin was used by Søren to slay Hydrae, Mother of Dragons, who dwelt in captivity on the Forbidden Isle of Varya. It was said to have powers far beyond any ordinary blade, and most magic ones at that. No mean heirloom is that you hold, Sir Torgun of Vandheim.'

Torgun thought back. Karlang, the founder of his house, had been a mighty warrior himself; his own ancestry was shrouded in legend. He had to admit, Morcant probably had the right of it – most noble families in Northalde did trace their ancestry back to the First Reavers. It wasn't something many liked to admit freely – high houses tended to enjoy the myth that they held their lands and titles by right, not conquest. But being descended from Søren, a man who some said was the son of Sjórkunan, the un-angel of the seas? And yet he had been among the First Reavers, helping to conquer the three old kingdoms Morcant had spoken of, before heading further west to his fateful rendezvous with Morwena.

Descended from a demi-god: the thought made the knight shiver. A year ago, he would have dismissed the idea as pure superstitious nonsense. Nowadays, he found himself of a different cast of mind where such things were concerned.

The others were emerging from their tents, stretching and blinking themselves into wakefulness. Spotting Torgun, Joram and Wrackwulf walked over.

'So they didn't turn you into a suckling pig,' quipped Wrackwulf. Joram eyed the shining sliver in his hand keenly.

'What is that?' he asked.

Torgun looked at him, suddenly feeling very remote.

'Unfinished family business,' he replied, closing his fist gently about the shard.

CHAPTER 6
THE MAN WHO WOULD BE KING

Through the polished steel buckler hanging on the wall of the hunting lodge, Ivon looked upon Franz and his mother the Princess Consort, and wondered what they were talking about. The pair had been holding more private meetings in the solar at Westerburg Point lately: Ivon had tried to get a spy in there, so far without success.

The Crown Prince had proved most resourceful. Given less than two months, he had whipped the ragtag remnants of his realm into passable shape, and every castle within a fifty-mile radius of Westerburg was prepared in anticipation of a protracted siege. On top of that, the lords of Dreylund and Lower Thulia had sent hundreds of knights and men-at-arms to bolster their garrisons; those of Upper Thulia and Hyrlund were not far behind. That meant the Westenlunders would give Sir Hugon, Lord Kaye and Lord Aravin and the rest of the invading margraves a run for their coin: both Pangonian armies were moving forwards in a circling movement, but even an invasion force fifteen thousand strong would have pause before half a dozen castles garrisoned to the rafters with stout swords. It promised to be a long and bloody summer of campaigning.

Shifting his focus to the ancient bronze mirror on another wall, Ivon saw that the Thalamians had been similarly stopped in their tracks. The Stornelendings and Dulsinians had ceased slaughtering each other long enough to make common cause, and come riding to the aid of Ostveld and Aslund; likewise the two Thulias had sent men of their own to help their neighbours.

Clever pair: mother and son have practically reunited the kingdom, he thought grudgingly as he flicked his gaze back to mother and son exchanging words, ones he wished he could hear. *If only I was attuned to one of you as I am to Kaye; I'd fain know what you are plotting.*

A small party of knights and their squires leaving Westerburg via a postern gate seven nights ago had not escaped Ivon's notice: the last he'd seen, they had taken advantage of the distraction caused by Dreylund's relief fleet of warships to sneak past the Pangonian naval blockade on a ship heading south, but even with his Scrying it was impossible to keep eyes on everybody at once.

What are you up to, little birds? To whom are you flying, and why?

It was a question that would just have to wait. There was plenty closer to home to preoccupy him. A rare moment of nerves ghosted Ivon's psyche, as the enormity of the task his teacher had entrusted him with loomed large in his mind.

Letting both scrying tools go dark, the warlock stood and poured himself a cup of wine. Outside the sun was shining brightly: another summer was almost upon Rima and the lands about. His powers remained depleted, but another black mass was out of the question now – soon the Master would be ready, to take many of the faithful that Ivon had gathered at the appointed hour. As chief disciple, it would fall to him to remain here, supplanting Carolus when the time was right and tightening his grip on Pangonia. The King had ridden off to join the war four days ago – he wouldn't get to preside over the easy conquest he had hoped for.

Who knows, Carolus, you might even have to wield a sword – even if it's just for show, to 'inspire' your men.

Ivon glanced at the ornately carved wooden cot where he and Wolmar had spent cosy nights the previous year, lustily tumbling beneath the deerskin quilts. That time already seemed an age away. The mage steeled himself, pushed the recollections from his mind. The Master did not tolerate idle pleasures in his most exalted disciples; Ivon had only justified his passion for Wolmar by arguing that the princeling would make a useful lieutenant. That gambit had backfired badly: the Northlending had gone on to defy them, causing ructions in the Rent Between Worlds that had alerted the Argolian Order to their activities. They had enough men within its ranks for that not to be a catastrophe, but even so... The monk Horskram was too doggedly persistent by far. Ivon had wanted to move against him right away, but the Master had called for patience and told him to let the matter drop. And then there was the mysterious Vorstlending damsel he'd cornered at court. Ivon sensed there was more to her than met the eye. She had slipped through his fingers... only to reappear on a pilgrim ship bound for Ushalayim.

Ivon took another sip of Armandy wine, scarcely appreciating its bouquet. The great game of Jedrez was growing ever more complex.

Putting the goblet down, he invoked the power of wizards once again, this time focusing his attention on the bronze mirror. Before long Ragnar's icy features materialised before him. The northland warlock looked worse than Ivon felt; drained and haggard, with a beard that seemed to hang off pinched features in fragile-looking icicles.

'My dear Ragnar, how do things fare in the Frozen Wastes? Well, I trust.'

Ragnar snorted. 'Spare me your southern charm, Ivon de Vichy, I'm in no mood for it.'

Ivon scowled. All pretence at protocol had long been dropped between them. The Master had entrusted the Northlander with a daunting task, and his vanity had ballooned along with his powers. But for all that, Ivon wasn't sure he envied the elementalist his duties; before the Great World Serpent even greater demons might quail.

'I won't take up your precious time for too long in that case,' said Ivon venomously. 'But you can expect plenty more of it to elapse before Pangonia and Thalamy march on Northalde and Thraxia – these Vorstlendings are putting up stiffer resistance than expected.'

Ragnar nodded. He seemed distracted, absent. 'We shall need plenty of time to be about our own work. The Northlendings are resisting, too – they are marching two armies from north and south to relieve the siege of their capital.'

Ivon tried not to feel smug about that. 'Your sister has long prepared her invasion fleet,' he said. 'You should over-match them.'

Ragnar's face betrayed not a flicker of emotion as he said: 'The match will be closer than you think. Half our forces are ravaging the coastlands.'

That caught Ivon off guard. 'Why are you splitting the fleet? I thought the idea was to cut off the serpent at its head?'

'You leave me to worry about serpents,' Ragnar said ominously. 'Slaves I require, for my work here.'

Ivon smirked to hide his trepidation. He could feel the Sea Wizard was turning into a closer rival by the day. 'Of course,' he sneered. 'Feed the serpent and bind her toad-thing worshippers to our cause.'

Ragnar's face remained unsmiling as he replied: 'Bind the Tritons, yes. And other far more powerful things.'

The smirk dropped from Ivon's face. 'You clearly have your work cut out for you up there,' he hissed. 'I do hope your sibling is up to the conquest of Northalde.'

'My sister is good at what she knows. War and conquest are what she knows. I have my hedge servants, just as you have yours. Expect to see Northalde capitulate by the time your armies reach its borders. Assuming they do.'

'I shall look forward to that, brother,' said Ivon, seething inwardly. The ephemeral language of sorcery had never sounded so curt on his lips as he mouthed the complex vowels that closed the scrying spell.

Ragnar knows far too much that I don't, he thought resentfully. The elementalist's lair up in Narborg had grown difficult to penetrate of late. The walls of the Serpent's Maw were said to be inscribed with hieroglyphs endued with mighty powers by the Elder Wizards, just as were the vaults beneath the levelled Watchtower in the Westerling Isles. Andragorix had benefited from looking upon such too, during his time at Kell. The margrave inwardly cursed the fate that dictated he remain here, so close to the Argolians. He'd had to make do with second-hand copies of tomes and scrolls, although to be fair his teacher had greatly expanded his stock of knowledge during their long association.

But then the Master had come by a Grimoire, an original text written by the Priest-Sorcerers of Varya. Such power could not be disputed, and yet Ivon had not tasted nearly enough of it for his liking.

Taste a little power, and you want a lot of it. Taste a lot, and you want all of it. Words of the Thalamian founding emperor Vaxus the Great. *Keep your allies close – so close they can never become enemies.* More Vaxus, who had known well the virtue of keeping watchful eye on ambitious underlings, as he consolidated the ancient city states into a single polity that would conquer much of the Known World.

Unfortunately, the Master also knew the bygone warlord's writings all too well. He was too clever by half, and yet in his own way he was fair: Ivon was confident he would be richly rewarded in body and mind for his service. That, and sheer awe, were enough to stay his hand.

For now, at least.

A flickering of red distracted him from his thoughts. His

alarum amulet was blinking from where it hung on a chair. That meant Cyprian was ready. Mouthing another set of interlocking syllables, he pictured a carrier pigeon, a scroll and a ray of sunlight. A beam sprang from the alarum, striking the mirror and revealing the docks of Montrevellyn in a sunburst explosion. Half a dozen vast crusader ships stood ready to weigh anchor: a flock of thurifers were on the wharf, swinging censers of incense that cast tendrils of smoke through the air. At their head stood the Supreme Perfect, holding aloft a circifix staff of ebony and gold as he intoned a prayer. Before him kneeled the five margraves of Lower Vallia, foremost among them Lord Uthor of Aquitania; each was clad in full harness of war, heads bowed and hands clasped in prayer.

Ivon smiled nastily. *You'll do Abaddon's work for us nicely, you pious dolts.*

The warlock knew he wasn't wrong. More than a thousand knights, men-at-arms and crossbowmen were crammed into each of the warships; Isolte had assured him a like number would be setting sail from Thalamy. Mercadia too would be sending galleases, with soldiers and sappers and other engineers. The total crusading expedition was said to number close on twenty thousand fighting men.

Five of the ships bore the standards of the high houses of Lower Vallia on their foresails. Ivon counted them off, one by one: the *gules* griffin of Thringia on an azure field; the crossed *argent* poignards on *purpure* of Vania; the *vair* grey and green of Tristia overlaid with a *vert* kingfisher; the leopard couchant on sable of Troye; the lion rampant in *or* on ermine of Aquitania, mightiest of the southern margravates. These were purely for the purposes of distinction, the mainsails of each ship being given over to the simple crusading red-wheel-on-white-field motif. The sixth ship sailed entirely under white, and was bereft of heraldry – Valacia's forces had been commandeered by the Knights Bethler when its foremost scion Azelin joined the Order fifteen years ago.

Cyprian finished his prayer, and as one the five lords rose. Brother Sir Godfrey, Master of the Bethler Preceptory at Rima, stepped up to take his place alongside them. The pinch-faced old worthy would command the forces of Valacia. Ivon knew what the erstwhile lord Azelin's younger brother Sir Hugon would make of that – but Hugon had been bought off, with the glory he so lusted after. Let him indulge his appetite for war in the conquest of Vorstlund. He'd be easy enough to manipulate after that, thanks to Isolte.

The Queen herself had remained in Rima. Carolus had left Sir Odo his royal steward in charge in his absence, though with Isolte keeping an eye on him, Ivon wasn't too concerned about that.

What did concern him was the power vacuum that would be triggered by the Departure – when the Master took his closest brethren with him, a swathe of the realm's most influential courtiers and perfects would rise up in their wake with Ivon at their head, and Rima would know anarchy. But by then the King would be dead in Vorstlund, and the reserve armies left behind by the Occitanian barons would help him secure the capital. The eastern border realms of Narvon, Rhunia and Orrin would be conveniently pinned by a Thalamian incursion, and with the Lower and Upper Vallians out of the way on campaign there would be precious little to stop him seizing the crown.

Ivon allowed himself a vicious smile as he watched the crusaders put out to sea, amidst general fanfare as the common folk thronged the harbour to see the high lords off, like pigs at swill. Let Ragnar have his serpents and his toad-men and Abaddon knew what else – he was welcome to such eldritch cronies. By summer's end, Ivon de Vichy would be sitting on the Charred Throne – and all men but one would call him King.

Out Of The Cooking Pot And Into The Hearth

The second guard was nodding on his watch as Hari Yassin approached him stealthily, channelling air as he cloaked himself in shadows. The first lay unconscious where he'd felled him with a Fingers of Lightning strike; it wouldn't do to kill residents of Sha'iza'ar, they were going to be in enough trouble as it was. Gliding up to the guardsman, Hari allowed him just enough time to blink into surprised wakefulness, before he slammed a Hooded Cobra Rearing punch into his face. The guard dropped like a sack of oatmeal, but Hari caught him and lowered him soundlessly to the floor of the antechamber.

The keys to the cells were all on one hoop hanging off a hook in the wall, just as Hari had noted on their visit to inspect the Pangonian. Taking these up he slipped down the passage, channelling air and earth as he became one with its bricks, slinking past cells where gladiators lay snoring. A couple were busy in the act of love with slave girls: their monthly reward for success in the pits. He knew the Pangonian wouldn't be indulging himself: he always refused women, for some bizarre reason. He wasn't tempted by men or children either, his owner had said.

Reaching the cell, Hari peered between the bars of the door's single window. A rough shape on the pallet told his eyes the gladiator was sleeping, but his other senses said otherwise.

'Psssst!' he hissed, then whispered: 'Make no sound.' Taking the key he needed from the ring, he unlocked the door. He had noted that on his previous visit, too: habit of long years had taught him always to remember details such as which key a gaoler used.

Opening the door silently, he wasn't entirely surprised when the Pangonian lurched upwards and grasped him by the throat. Hari had seen enough of him in action to know that not even a trained martial artist like him could hope to win a straight fight between them: the man moved and struck with a controlled savagery Yassin had never seen before.

So he just let circumstances do his fighting for him instead.

'I'm here to give you your freedom,' he whispered, grinning in the faint light of the single torch that flickered in the corridor. 'But if you want this gift, you have to come with me right now. And not kill me on the spot.'

For an instant, he actually thought the gladiator would

refuse. That the brooding warrior would simply let him go and return to his pallet. Yassin's instincts told him this was a man who would be caged no matter where he went.

But it is one thing to be caged on the inside, and another to be caged.

The Urovian held his neck tightly for another second or two, his piercing grey-blue eyes never leaving Yassin's face. Then he let go of him and nodded.

Hari led the way, taking them past the two unconscious guards and out into the balmy night. Faint sounds of revelry indicated a handful of residents were still carousing, in a caravanserai not too far away. But a bit of ambient noise wasn't such a bad thing: another distraction to abet their escape.

The others were waiting for them, mounted on horses that were saddled and packed. The Bethlers had left immediately after the pit fight, taking their brother knight's corpse with them. Hari knew the Order well enough to know that a perverse sense of honour would bind them to their word – at least until they returned to Ushalayim and their Grand Master scourged said honour out of them.

That tiny bit of scruple gave them the opportunity they needed. It was just an hour past Wytching Time – they could make an excellent head start before the sun came up and their theft was discovered. By noon they would be across No Man's Land and into the sultanate. That of course would bring plenty of perils of its own, but hopefully the presence of a Sufieli would carry more weight there than it had here.

'One gladiator, safely freed from bondage as requested,' chirped Hari as they drew level with Horskram.

'He won't be safe until we're far from here,' replied the monk unsmiling. 'Get him up behind you ahorse, let's tarry not.'

Hari complied and the six of them nudged their steeds into a steady amble, so as not to make too much noise. As they passed the outer enclosures they urged them into a canter, increasing to a trot as they struck out across the moonlit wilderness. Only after a minute or so did Anupe risk lighting the taper she was holding. Then they spurred their mounts into a gallop, letting their horses' hooves eat up the miles of countryside.

Hari allowed himself a smile of satisfaction at another mission accomplished. It felt good to be a freebooter again.

The dawning sun was about an hour old when the Pangonian instructed them to halt. Adelko sensed something was on the man's mind, though clearly Horskram was too preoccupied to pick up on it.

'We don't have time for latrine breaks,' the adept said testily. 'We need to get across the border-'

'My pursuers caught up with me here,' said the gladiator, completely ignoring him. 'They paid dearly for my liberty, but not even one such as I could hope to hold off so many. I thought they would simply slay me and have done with it, but my brethren had crueller intentions. At least I managed to persuade them to bury my blade before they sold me to a slaver, so that it might not be used by another. A courtesy to my former high status, if you will.'

The pit fighter smiled sardonically.

Horskram's eyes narrowed. 'What are you babbling of? You're no ordinary captive or deserter – that's clear enough.'

The warrior did not reply, but pointed towards where a red rock jutted out of the dusty plain about a hundred yards away.

'Let me unearth her, and you'll have an answer to that question, master monk.'

Horskram nodded. 'I can't ask you to come with us, as our mission is dangerous,' he said. 'And there's no point freeing you only to abandon you in the wilderness alone and unarmed.' He sighed. 'Very well, but let's be quick about it.'

The soil around the rock was loosely packed. 'Some coincidence that we should come by the very place where you were captured and disarmed,' pointed out Hari, as the gladiator scrabbled away clumps of dry earth.

'There are no coincidences,' muttered the Pangonian, without looking up from his task. 'Only what Reus wills.'

Horskram exchanged a wry glance with Adelko. 'So you've found your piety then,' he observed.

'I found it a long time ago, master monk,' said the warrior, continuing to claw the soil. 'I found it by a dark and circuitous path, as you did.'

All wryness had gone out of Horskram's eyes as he glared at the gladiator.

The sun had shifted up another notch when he uncovered the weapon. It was a scabbarded greatsword, exactly like those the Bethlers wielded. Taking it up out of the hole, the Pangonian gazed at it with a look that was almost wistful. Then he unsheathed it. The orange sun caught its blade, running a seam of liquid fire down the fuller. As it cleared, Adelko caught an inscription at its centre. This close he could see it was written in Decorlangue.

Know Thyself.

'Gifted to me by Grand Master Hubert of Leon, when I first joined the Order,' said the warrior, just a hint of pride entering his voice. 'How glorious and full of hope those days seemed.' The familiar sadness settled back over him, a black shroud to blot out the sun.

This time Adelko remembered not to gawp like a dumb-struck novice, but the revelation was surprising all the same.

'You're a Bethler,' he said.

The knight favoured him with a nasty grin. 'Was,' he replied.

'And no ordinary Bethler at that,' put in Horskram. 'Inscribed blades they only give to the most illustrious members of the Order, and almost never to new recruits.'

The knight turned the sickly grin on Horskram. 'Hadn't you heard, monk? No one in the Order is illustrious, for we all but humbly serve the Almighty's will.' The sarcasm in his voice was hard to miss.

Horskram nodded gravely. 'Sir Azelin of Valacia, Pangonia's greatest knight, Wyrmslayer and lineal descendant of Sir Lancelyn of the Pale Mountain, Palom's anointed crusader and erstwhile commander in the Bethler Order,' he said. 'The apple has fallen far from the tree.'

'And straight into your lap, by the looks of things,' said

Azelin, using the baldric attached to the scabbard to sling it across his back. 'I hope you enjoy its taste.' Taking up the sword again, he sheathed it. 'I'll sharpen her later,' he said, patting the whetstone tucked into a pocket on the baldric. 'For now we should be getting on. Our friends in Sha'iza'ar must be awake, and old Haroun will be keen to recover his most prized possession.'

Adelko mulled over the sudden turn of events as they struck up another gallop, dust and dirt spraying in their wake. Arguably the greatest warrior in the Free Kingdoms had just been thrust into their path; and he was indebted to them for his freedom.

No coincidences, indeed. It was nice to know the Almighty still helped his servants on occasion. Considering they were trying to save the world from Abaddon, really it was the least He could do.

The days oozed by, brought to them on a sluggish tide of heat that seemed to grow more sweltering with every step south. Tipu steered them unerringly along paths that bent and weaved through the rocky wilderness of northern Nazharya, for he had travelled as widely as Horskram and knew the land well. Clusters of flies tormented Adelko day and night, and when they stopped to camp by a brook that emptied into a pool, he even followed suit as Tipu and Yassin and Anupe stripped and bathed.

'The flies are drawn to our stink,' quipped Hari, 'That's why after a few months in our country even *jhufa'ars* take to a good long soak!' Adelko was too busy trying to ignore Anupe's naked presence to respond. It was hard abjuring impure thoughts at the best of times, and he wasn't about to crack on account of the gnarled Harijan. Horskram turned his back on all of them as they splashed about in the warm waters, muttering stubbornly about bathing being bad for the constitution. But Adelko had to confess he slept more easily that night. Azelin for his part disappeared altogether, reappearing only later to take first watch. Adelko could swear the man only slept for a few hours every night.

'Soon we will be out of the wilderness,' said Tipu on their fourth day out of Sha'iza'ar. 'And then our journey becomes more difficult, for *fariz* are likely to patrol the richer hinterlands of the sultanate.'

'More difficult, or more dangerous?' inquired Anupe.

'Perhaps both,' replied the mystic. 'We are a day's ride north-east of Imanabad, perhaps two. If we take that route, the journey becomes very dangerous – for you at least. To reach the tombs you seek, we should therefore circumvent the city. But that will take us through more rough country, for the lands east of here rise steadily to meet the Abydos ranges. I hope you are ready for some slow and painful riding.'

The mystic looked as though that prospect did not bother him in the least. Did he ever get ruffled by anything, Adelko wondered.

'He has the right of it,' said Azelin. 'I've conducted many a sortie in these lands, and Haroun took me up and down the sultanate to fight in the pits. If its the Kishan Tombs you seek, our best way is due east. Once we reach the ranges we can follow them southwards.' He shot Horskram a suspicious glance. 'Though it seems passing strange to me that an Argolian should seek long lost riches.'

'Our Order needs money just as yours does,' said the adept. 'And some of the legends say the Kishan emperors of old were buried with entire libraries of papyrus scrolls. Such knowledge would be a treasure in itself to us.'

Adelko could sense his mentor's unease. Lying to the erstwhile warrior-monk was obviously difficult. For his part, the journeyman wanted more answers. Tonight he would try to get them out of Azelin, if he could.

Azelin was too busy sneering at Horskram to sense anything amiss. 'Ah, ever seeking to expand your knowledge of the world and all its doings,' he said. 'Take a good long look at these blood-drenched lands – that should tell you all you need to know about the world of mortal men.'

'I am sorry to find your cynicism so all-encompassing,' said Horskram stiffly.

Azelin sneered again. 'Is there any other kind of cynicism?' he asked. 'Spare me your sophistry, Horskram of Vilno, I've heard far too much of it from holy men in my time. I owe you my freedom. For that I'll see you to these precious tombs of yours and protect you, if need be – after that I go my own way. Is that understood?'

Horskram nodded sourly. Clearly the arrangement did not displease him. Adelko sensed his obvious dislike for the disgraced knight; he couldn't help but wonder if that wasn't a reflection of how the old monk felt about his own past.

~

On they pressed, the ochre ruggedness of wilderness they now hugged seemingly mocked by the verdancy of the rich grasslands to the south. In that direction Adelko could make out yak grazers gently droving their herds, the odd merchant caravan guarded by *taziqs*, and thriving villages surrounded by neat plots of sesame, millet and chickpeas and bare fields left fallow for the year. Without a doubt they were among the richest lands Adelko had seen on his travels – not that they'd be seeing much of them on this particular expedition.

'The peasantry prosper here,' explained Tipu when Adelko asked him about the Nazharyan farmlands. 'Free of the *kharaj* tax levied on Sha'abatians to the north by crusader lords, they are able to profit better from their labours.'

Adelko frowned. 'When we were staying with the Bethlers, one of them told me that in some places Sassanians are better off under Pangonian rule.'

Tipu smiled at that. 'I am sure that is what the warrior-monk told you,' he said, without a hint of irony or bitterness. 'It is not always the case that sultans rule wisely,' added the mystic, seeing the crestfallen look on the young monk's face. 'But Muqmurlish tek Nazar is by all repute a just sovereign. Some even say he is descended from the Kardin line of Enlightened Sultans, and has been sent by Ashanti to bring Sha'abatians out of the darkness into which they have fallen.'

From where he was riding pillion behind Hari, Azelin snorted. 'Another enlightened one, chosen of the Almighty! I think I've heard this tale before. It never ends well.'

'The Seven Sultans were not as other men,' Tipu went on, ignoring him. 'Abu'cuchaza'ar Kardin was the first ruler in Sassania to take Sha'abat's preaching into his heart. He appointed him as vizier and was rewarded with long life – the *Sassanic Reckonings* and our scriptures tell us he lived twice the three-score-years-and-ten of an ordinary mortal.'

'Twice the time to devote to conquest and bloodshed,' said Azelin. 'As I recall, the Third Sultan Zangid took Usha-layim from the Thalamians after a bloody siege that lasted years. Thousands were killed – many of them women and children. Isn't that when your prophet conveniently chose to ascend to heaven? Perhaps even he couldn't stand to watch what mortalkind was capable of doing in his name, eh? A pox on it, your religion's no better than ours when it comes down to it – serpent or wheel, holy symbols are just another weapon in the arsenal. Trust me, I should know.'

'But there was more to it than that,' insisted Tipu. 'As well as being granted long life and vigour, the Enlightened Ones could read men's minds. They were less susceptible to fear, hunger, anger, jealousy. Their mystic powers are the very ones my sect seeks to channel in doing Ashanti's bidding... and the powers of the Bethlers and the Argolians are not so very different.' The mystic paused to let his words sink in.

Azelin was unmoved, though Horskram looked trou-bled. 'I hear Grand Master Tobin has been using his special powers to rule wisely in Ushalayim,' the knight went on, his voice dripping sarcasm like an envenomed sting. 'Why don't you go back there and throw yourself on his mercy? I'm sure he'll be inspired by the Almighty to show clemency. Incidentally, why does the Grand Master want you all dead? I know why he despises me, but I can't see how a bunch of thieves and freebooters would concern him.'

Horskram related their cover story perfunctorily. Adelko could still sense the disquiet in him.

But Azelin apparently enjoyed the tale too much to doubt its veracity. 'Ha! I wouldn't put it past that old fanatic to get it into his head that you're all on a mission from the Fallen One. Honestly though, I'm surprised he didn't just let you do the dirty work to get the treasure, then have you killed so he could keep it and donate it to the cause. Never could stand the man, and when he was elected head of the Order, it was the final straw.'

'So you *are* a deserter then?' asked Adelko, spotting a chance to quiz the knight. 'That was why they came after you?'

'That, and other things,' replied the erstwhile Bethler. 'For some years I'd been questioning the wider crusade, our Order's doctrine. I had the temerity to display some conscience and remorse, so Tobin decided to eliminate me. He'd have had me killed one way or the other if I stayed, so I chose to desert. We've been straying from the path of Palom for generations now, and nowhere have we strayed farther or more quickly than in the so-called Blessed Realm.' He spat over the cantle of Yassin's saddle for emphasis.

'You'll get no disagreement from me there,' muttered Horskram. For once Tipu looked sad, and seemed at a loss for words. Yassin and Anupe just stared ahead, looking bored with the discussion.

The lands continued to rise, becoming ever more gnarled as Tipu steered them towards the mountains. Here the tumbling ridges were of a blood-red hue, as if the very earth itself bled. After a couple more hours they crested a basin to come upon a vast sprawling ruin of a city; its white marble villas crumbled back into inchoacy, its fractured squares overgrown with weeds and briars. Adelko marvelled, for surely a city of that size must have once held at least half a million souls. But there was something else, which set his sixth sense off: an invisible evil seemed to emanate from the place, and as Tipu took them past it, skirting a long dried-up river that would have watered the metropolis, his eye caught some broken statues lying in the rubble. Their loathsome forms, which seemed a hybrid of mollusc and human yet belonging to neither, reminded him immediately of the Warlock's Crown.

'These people were devil worshippers,' he gasped as Horskram made the sign.

'Behold Shamaria, sacked by Tycius and scourged for her sins,' said Tipu, making the sign of the Faith. 'She was the greatest city built by the Huryans, perhaps two thousand years ago. Today their descendants share the Ghorabi desert with the Halamites and other tribes, for they have returned to their nomadic existence of old, and their *sarakim* serve in the Sultan's armies. But in their spring they were a mighty people, and ruled all the lands from here to the Cerulean mountains.'

Azelin smiled grimly. 'The great civilising conquerors. Another story that never ends well.'

Anupe smiled a grim smile of her own. 'Let us look on the works of the mighty, and despair.'

The knight grinned at her. 'I like you, Harijan – you seem less deceived than most. I'm glad I spared your sisters in the pit two moons ago.'

'So am I,' breezed Anupe. 'It means I don't have to bother killing you in a blood feud.'

The disgraced Bethler laughed uproariously at that. The same harsh and grating sound, carrying little real mirth.

Adelko cleared his throat pointedly. 'I believe Tipu was telling a story,' he said crisply.

'Excuse me, master monk,' said Sir Azelin, with mock politeness. 'Pray continue, mystic.'

Tipu resumed his tale. 'The writings of sages tell us that by about a thousand years Before Illumination – that is the coming of the First Prophet – the Huryans had secured for themselves a mighty empire, covering most of present-day Nazharya, along with much of the hinterlands of present-day Kallandhar. Their lore waxed great, for the Hanging Gardens of Shamaria were once counted among the world's wonders.'

Adelko scrutinised the ruins, searching for signs of those fabled lush enclosures, where it was said a man could lose a day wandering and not notice. But naught more than sick weeds and thorny twigs rewarded his efforts.

'And many other grand cities besides Shamaria the Huryans wrought, for ancient papyri tell how the archangels visited their savants, just as they had done the Elder Wizards millennia before. And whilst the Unseen would not repeat their older folly and teach mortals sorcery, yet they conferred great learning upon the Huryan people. But alas, mortalkind will always seek a path to inevitable corruption, and that knowledge was destined to lead them into darkness.'

Azelin had slumped back into his brooding melancholy; Horskram stared silently ahead, his face set grim. Anupe and Hari continued to look bored.

'Go on,' said Adelko, when it was obvious no one else wanted to listen.

Tipu sighed gently. Then he said: 'Some two hundred years later, the Huryans turned to worship unclean powers. Always they had venerated Azazel, arch-demon of war, and through this worship they were gradually seduced by other servants of Iblis, whom you Palomedians call Abaddon. And so from worshipping Sha'jia, archangel of courage, whom you call Virtus, they turned to embrace his dark emanation, Zolthoth, avatar of wrath, who appeared to them as a terrible scarlet demon, with the face of a man contorted permanently in anger, and gigantic fists always sealed in a fearsome clench. Likewise they turned from Saramat, whom you call Stygnos, to his dark emanation Ta'ussaswazelim, arch-demon of cruelty, who appeared to them as a taloned, misshapen thing covered in horny hide, with wide grinning lips that told of ineffable depravity.'

The mystic made the sign again and grimaced, so caught up was he in his own storytelling.

He gives Master Horskram a run for his coin, thought

Adelko wryly. But he couldn't deny he was caught up in the tale, too.

'And these two Princes of Perfidy poisoned the cities and the lands of the Huryans, until they were cracked and broken as you see them now. Only Shamaria and her Hanging Gardens remained, their sacred power alone able to resist the Curse of the Two Princes. But even those were destined not to last, for when he conquered the Huryans and sacked their last city, Tycius destroyed everything he saw – in the name of conquest and righteous war.'

'I'll never understand why the Almighty uses such men as His tools,' sighed Adelko. 'It seems to me that all He ever does is allow us to fall into wickedness, then punishes us with even greater wickedness. I used to think it all made sense... now I'm not so sure. Sometimes I wonder if Reus even cares for us.'

'Do we care for ourselves?' was Tipu's answer to that. 'My sect teaches that the Unseen are indivisible from mortalkind – that they reside in our very souls, encased as they are in weak flesh. If we cannot care for one another, how can Ashanti possibly do so? He and we are one.'

Adelko pondered that. He half expected Horskram to interject, to tell them they were uttering blasphemy, but the adept said nothing.

It was only then that Adelko noticed the light had begun to wane; the summer sun set earlier this far south. Glancing back at the city, he felt as though its cursed statues were staring at them malignantly; even the ruined buildings seemed to possess a queer intelligence, as though things wrought could become imbued with the wickedness of the men that fashioned them.

Only it wasn't the wickedness of men they had to worry about.

Adelko could have sworn the sun began to move more swiftly towards the horizon as they jostled their steeds along the trail. The city continued to follow them with its invisible eyes. His sixth sense jangled painfully, he could sense it jarring against Horskram's – and Tipu's now as well. Without warning, their horses started to rear and panic. Their frantic whinneying was joined by an eerie cooing sound that rose up from the ruins below; as he struggled to master his steed, Adelko caught smoky forms coalescing up around the broken villas and mansions, seeming to drift up out of the lengthening shadows created by the shattered buildings.

'Ayee!' cried Hari. 'Let us begone from this place – it is but one big haunted grave.'

Reaching into his habit, Horskram produced a tiny phial that sparkled with a single dot of crimson. 'Have no fear, for I carry a relic of our Creed,' he said, sounding alive for the first time in a while. 'The undead can have no ingress past it.'

But Tipu's face was uncharacteristically anxious as he scrutinised the tenebrous forms solidifying about the city's shattered vaults and toppled columns. 'Those creatures are no undead,' he said.

'What are they?' asked Adelko as he struggled to bring his steed to bear. He could now see the solidifying forms were humanoid in shape.

'Ghouls,' said Yassin, his voice close to panic. 'I encountered them when I was a grave robber. We haven't even reached the Kishan Tombs, and already the Other Side comes to visit us!'

'We'll be lucky to reach them at all at this rate,' said Horskram. 'Come on!'

A hissing sound told of pursuit as they tried to spur their panicky steeds along the trail. But a profound terror had gripped their horses, and they would not consent to be ridden. Adelko's own limbs felt watery as he struggled to stay in the saddle, his own mount bucking and rearing and foaming at the mouth.

'The animal kingdom is more prone to the ghoul-fear,' cried Tipu. He himself sounded closer to panic than Adelko had ever heard him. 'We must abandon our horses and hope they are enough to satisfy their appetites!'

Looking down the slopes of the basin Adelko could see them now, leering in the twilight as they scampered up the rocks and ridges towards them. There had to be at least twenty.

'He's right!' yelled Horskram. 'Dismount and climb, it's our only chance!'

The six of them abandoned the saddle and began to scramble up the rocks. Risking a glance over his shoulder, Adelko could see the ghouls closing the gap between them at frightening speed, their gangly hairless forms slithering across the broken ground like hungry worms. Turning forwards again, he forced himself to keep climbing, wishing he could stop up his ears as the first of their horses started screaming.

Hari was the first to reach the top of the basin. Turning to look down past them, he shrieked: 'There's still a dozen of them after us! It's human flesh they crave!'

Muttering the Psalm of Fortitude only seemed to half work as Adelko tried to shrug off the fear and make the last part of the climb. It felt as though vinegar not blood flowed through his veins.

They joined Yassin at the basin's summit. Turning to look back down, Adelko realised with horror that the creatures had already closed more than half the gap between them. Not even the assassins in Ushalayim had moved so quickly.

'We can't outrun them,' said Azelin, drawing the greatsword from his back. 'Best to make a stand here.'

Adelko cursed his bare hands, and the Bethlers who had deprived him of his weapon. 'We're useless in a straight fight without our staves, Master Horskram,' he said. 'There must be some prayers we can use to help.' Even *Celestian's Compendium* was mostly silent on the subject of ghouls, said to be rare manifestations and even then limited to the wildernesses and deserts of the Hot South. They weren't creatures an Argolian would normally expect to fight.

'They aren't truly undead, nor are they entirely of the Other Side,' groaned Horskram as his own slender stock of knowledge came back to him. 'A ghoul is a mortal cursed by the Unseen for crimes of great wickedness. Child killers and the like.'

Through his fugue Adelko sensed a flare of pain from Sir Azelin, though he had no time to contemplate that as the ghouls surged up the rocks towards them. Hari and Anupe had drawn their own blades and taken up a fighting stance. Feeling utterly useless, Adelko rolled up his sleeves and hoped the few wrestling techniques Edemus had taught him would be good for something.

'In here, wayfarers! Come quickly!'

The words, spoken in Sassanic, came from around a rocky escarpment just behind them. Dashing around it, they saw a woman clad in a homespun garment in the manner of a hermit, standing at the mouth of a narrow cave. She was beckoning to them frantically.

The ghouls were almost upon them and they didn't need a second invitation. The hermit woman had retreated back into the cave's depths: a narrow passageway snaked down from the back of it into the bowels of the earth. At its far end Adelko thought he could discern a glimmering light. The hermit ushered them into the tunnel.

Down into its gloomy depths they stumbled, the dark making their movements awkward and clumsy. A few steps in and they lost their footing completely, tumbling down the passageway and landing in a heap at its bottom. Looking around, Adelko registered with surprise that they were in a room of some sort. From off this led several shafts, each supported by wooden beams. A sound from the tunnel alerted him – but it was just the hermit, following them down. With surprising strength she yanked a boulder across the rough entrance, pushing it firmly into place.

'That will keep the ghouls out,' she said. 'They don't care to linger below ground at night, for that is when they are free to roam the wide earth!'

They listened for scrabbling sounds of pursuit, but there

were none. Anupe was bleeding from a gash in her forehead where she had landed badly on the rock floor, but they were otherwise unhurt.

'What is this place?' asked Adelko, looking around. The light was coming from a couple of torches fixed to brackets.

'Disused gold mine, by the looks of things,' said Azelin. 'These hills used to be rich with it, they say.'

Tipu nodded. 'Part of the reason why the Huryans chose to found their greatest city here. The wealth of Shamaria was legendary.'

Horskram glared at the hermit suspiciously. Adelko's sixth sense was still jangling. She looked peculiar in the wan torchlight. She could almost have been considered handsome, after her own fashion: her swart face was full and round, with luscious lips and black eyes lustrous beneath a matted mane of black hair. Yet there was something strange about that face as well: the eyes were just a little too big, the mouth a little too wide...

It grew impossibly wider as she launched herself at him, a long tongue lolling between fangs that suddenly extended as she clamped taloned hands about his neck. She was inhumanly strong; her reeking breath wafted over him, and Adelko felt his limbs freeze up like ice blocks as the terror took him. Azelin threw himself on the she-ghoul, knocking her from the young monk while the others frantically scrabbled for their weapons. Azelin rolled on the ground as he grappled with the ghoul, who fought back with enormous strength. The knight cried out as the she-ghoul sank her teeth into his shoulder...

And then the mellifluous sounds of Tipu's flute filled the

dusty air. Rolling over onto his back, Adelko would have laughed if he could – of all the things to hear in a situation like this. The sweet notes seemed to expand and fill the mine, all but drowning out the she-ghoul's horrible hissing screams. The young monk was dimly aware of the thing bounding past him as she fled the chamber, darting down one of the shafts.

It took them all a while to recover. Tipu intoned a prayer in Old Sassanic, a guttural yet lilting tongue that seemed more complex and beautiful than its modern incarnation. As he let the mantras wash over him, Adelko felt the fear that had paralysed his limbs leaving him.

Azelin needed somewhat more prosaic treatment. 'A ghoul bite must be subjected to the fire,' instructed Tipu. 'Lest the victim succumb to the malady and become a demi-ghoul, forever in thrall to the one that dealt the bite.'

Azelin looked mournful. 'If it's child killers they curse as Horskram says, I wouldn't worry about any bite. I've killed just about everything that walked or crawled since I came to this wretched land.'

That silenced the company, until Anupe stood and reached for one of the torches. 'That may be the case,' said the Harijan. 'But I for one have had enough of ghouls. I do not wish to risk one joining our group.' The former Bethler nodded resignedly, picking up a rotting pick-axe handle and clamping his mouth around it.

This time Adelko found time to stop up his ears as Azelin gave vent to a muffled scream.

'So how did you know?' Adelko asked Tipu while Horskram bound up Azelin's shoulder. 'About the ghoul not liking music? We faced something similar in our lands.' And he told the mystic of their encounter with the Earth Witch's Golem, in the Argael forest the previous year. On that occasion Sir Braxus's harping had saved them, and not before time.

'Ghouls share their aversion to music with the spirits sent by the Unseen to curse them,' replied Tipu, nodding. 'These spirits take them away from the mortal plane by day, returning them here at sunset only to transform them into the hideous forms you saw. Possibly they are similar to those required to animate this Golem you speak of. In any case, I recalled the *Tale of the Three Wise Sages and the Exiled Princess*, one of the Ten Thousand Stories set down in our holy book. As an Argolian, I take it you are familiar with parts of it?' Adelko nodded perfunctorily. There was a copy of the *Litany of Sayings, Songs and Mantras* of the Faith in the library at Rima, so great in extent that half a shelf was needed to hold the entire set of scrolls. He hadn't had a chance to read any of it, but Johann had quoted from it often enough during their Sassanic tutorials. 'Very good, you know something of our holy scriptures at least,' said Tipu approvingly. 'But as I was saying, in the tale I am speaking of the Princess Myresha uses her skill on the barbat to save the sages who have been kidnapped by the wicked ghulah Ivrita. Myresha is rewarded by the sages, who bend the ear of Amin tek Abu, the Second Enlightened Sultan, and he marries her and takes her into his harem. Myresha enjoys great favour as a result, and is able to save her people from the warlord who exiled her from her homeland at the beginning of the tale.'

'A fine tale and a favourite in the brothels of Ushalayim and Ranishmend, not to mention many other cities,' commented Hari. 'I must confess I was too busy being terrified to recall its significance.'

Tipu smiled. 'It took me a little while to recall it myself – the ghoul-fear can easily rob a man of his wits.' Then he shook his head, the smile dropping languidly to a slight frown. 'And may I add that a brothel is no place to hear songs from scripture!'

Yassin smiled. 'Pray forgive me. I was raised in a brothel – well, for the early part of my childhood anyway.' He seemed about to say more but stopped himself. Instead he added: 'I travelled the sultanates far and wide in my days as a freebooter, and even a Sufieli mystic must understand that a man gets lonely on the road, from time to time.'

The smile reappeared on Tipu's face. 'I somehow doubt you have ever been lonely, as far as women are concerned.' He raised a finger in gentle admonishment. 'One can only hope you grow through such experiences, in the fullness of time.'

Hari laughed at that. 'In the fullness of time, yes!' He turned to the others. 'Are we ready? Something tells me our hostess will return soon enough.'

Adelko's still prickly sixth sense told him Yassin was probably right.

'We can't leave by the way we came,' said Horskram. 'Those ruins will be swarming with ghouls.'

'Speaking of which, why did the she-ghoul save us?' asked Anupe.

'Ghouls are greedy, the Sultana of Ghouls greedier still,'

said Tipu. 'The ghulah hoped to trick us and so feed on us exclusively. I don't think they get much human meat out here in the wilderness.'

'There's more to it than that,' said Horskram, frowning. He appeared deep in thought. 'Tipu, you know these lands as well as any – you would surely have known if the ruins of Shamaria were the lair of a ghoul pack.'

Tipu nodded. 'It has been in times past,' he confessed. 'But my sect has ever been quick to flush out the creatures whenever they reappear, and we had not had a manifesta-tion here for years. The spirits that inhabit a wicked man and turn him into a ghoul must be exploiting a widening in the Rent Between Worlds.'

'And that means somebody is using sorcery in the vicini-ty,' confirmed Horskram.

'It can only be Abdel Sha'arza, in that case,' said Hari. 'A wicked sorcerer, by all accounts! He lives in an ancient tower in the Abydos ranges.' He favoured Anupe with a reproachful look. 'If you won't trust me with a look at the Urovian lady's map I can't say for sure, but it's probably not far from the Kishan Tombs. An even more dangerous place than the one we are venturing to.'

Adelko could not stop himself shooting a guilty glance at Horskram. But the adept was still deep in thought. 'No,' he said at last. 'I don't think Sha'arza is behind this. If it was him-'

He was interrupted by a distant but clearly audible scut-tling sound from one of the shafts. Adelko's ears pricked up. No, not one of the shafts – several of them. They all froze, listening in the half-dark. Was that a faint hissing sound that could be heard as well?

Hari's face blanched in the torchlight. 'I think there may be more than one entrance to this mine,' he said, as the scuttling and hissing sounds grew louder.

CHAPTER 8
IN SEARCH OF A CLUE

Arik's face was drawn in the light of Hargus's taper. The pair of them were lurking in a cell adjoining one of the grand monastery's four cloisters. They could see their dormitory from where they were – and any journeymen on prefect duty who might happen by.

'I listened in on my mentor as much as I could,' said Arik. 'He was saying something about Johann being removed for further questioning, I didn't get the rest.'

Hargus felt anxiety tighten around his gut with strengthening fingers. He hated all this intrigue. What had Adelko been thinking, getting them embroiled in this daft investigation? Weeks of eavesdropping and rifling through gossip hadn't got them very far at all. In fact all it had done was to leave his nerves jangling, never mind his sixth sense. And to think he'd been overjoyed when their mentors had announced they would stay in Rima to continue their studies. Now he was starting to yearn for the simplicity of Ulfang.

'But removed where?' wondered Hargus aloud. 'The interrogation room below the inner sanctum is just that – why would they bother moving Prior Johann to somewhere else?'

Arik shrugged in that off-handed manner of his. That had begun to grate on Hargus no end. Normally he liked to be on good terms with everyone, but increasingly his haughty friend was making that difficult. No wonder he'd had a rivalrous spat with Adelko; Arik was increasingly far too sure of himself. Clever as he was, he wasn't *that* smart. Being enrolled to study for his journeyman examination had only stoked up his pride.

'I don't know,' said Arik after pausing in thought a while. 'But it certainly doesn't make sense. If I didn't know better, I'd suspect... foul play.' His dark eyes caught the flaring taper. Hargus didn't care for the effect, he was on edge enough as it was.

'Foul play? You mean, as in... murder?' The word should have no part in the monastery's doings, especially not here at the heart of the Order.

Arik shrugged again. 'Well that's usually what transpires when suspects are made to disappear abruptly, isn't it?'

Again the grating tone. Pushing his annoyance aside, Hargus said: 'All right, one more time. Let's review what we know. Adelko said he believes something horrible happened to one of the High Circle, some kind of possession that led to Wolaf dying. Another archmaster is on his death bed, a third is suspected of involvement in Wolaf's death.'

'No, Cathbad of Linfarne has been exonerated, I think,' Arik reminded him. 'Or that's what I caught my mentor saying the other day. He's been despatched quietly to some remote outpost.'

'He'll probably end up where we started out in that case,' quipped Hargus. Much as he was starting to miss it, windswept rain-lashed Ulfang certainly seemed like the end of the world from here. At least down south the weather was kinder: though it was near the Wytching Hour, he scarcely felt a chill.

'All right, so that's one suspect eliminated,' said Hargus. 'Adelko and Master Horskram believe Johann may have tried to have them murdered on the road in Vorstlund. Could he be behind Wolaf's death as well?'

Arik's raven eyebrows folded as he mulled that question over. 'It's hard to say for sure, but it seems unlikely to me. Johann hadn't been recalled from his monastery in Vorstlund when Wolaf is said to have died. What puzzles me more is who bound this demon to Wolaf and why... it seems strange that an undercover demonologist would use an entity that Master Horskram was already attuned to. Can we be sure Adelko has the right of this?'

Now it was Hargus's turn to shrug. 'We only know what the chap told us himself – and he gets his information from Master Horskram.'

Arik tapped his chin thoughtfully. 'No, there's something not quite adding up,' he said. 'If you were a warlock and you wanted to cause trouble in the High Circle, why would you use a demon that could be easily detected?'

'Perhaps this warlock didn't know everything,' suggested Hargus. 'Adelko himself told us they reckon it's some sort of conspiracy of mages they're up against.'

'A conspiracy of mages that can use Scrying to co-ordinate their actions,' countered Arik. 'No. This smells of a bait trap to me. I think whoever did the binding did so with the intention of their demon being found out.'

'But why do that?'

'I don't know.' Arik frowned. For all his cleverness he didn't have the answer to that question, neither of them did.

Hargus racked his brains. All they had to go on was what Adelko had told them, and their friend had only known so much: he'd learned of Wolaf's binding from Horskram. According to the adept, there had been a disagreement in the High Circle about what to do next, whether to seek out the other fragments or just sit on what they knew.

'All right, let's keep focusing on what we *do* know,' said Hargus. 'We know that eventually the High Circle decided to send our chum Adelko off south with Master Horskram...'

'... to seek the fourth fragment if it could be found. And another expedition party was sent north, to try to contact the keepers of the third.'

Their eyes met as their sixth senses intuitively filled the gap.

'It's a decoy,' gasped Hargus. 'Wolaf was set up to tell them not to act, then be exposed as a demon...'

'... so the rest of the High Circle would be persuaded to do just the opposite.'

Hargus felt the anxiety crawl up into the back of his tightening throat. 'That means whoever is behind Wolaf's binding wanted Horskram and Adelko out of Rima.'

Arik nodded gravely. 'And by the looks of things, their companions too.'

'But surely Horskram wouldn't fall for that,' protested Hargus.

Arik shrugged again. This time Hargus was too preoccupied to get annoyed. 'Don't be too sure of that! Adelko told us Master Horskram is far from infallible – he makes mistakes, too. And let's face it, he's had a world of troubles on his mind lately. It's possible he could have been blindsided.'

'But what about his sixth sense? Surely-'

Arik shook his head. 'You remember before he left, Adelko said something about the sense being cloaked here in Rima? I think he's right, Hargus – the more I study for journeyman, the more I feel it myself.'

'Well our sixth senses seem to have worked just now,' said Hargus, with just a hint of pride.

This time at least Arik had the decency not to shrug as he replied: 'True, but we're small fish, aren't we? Sometimes small fish slip the net.'

Hargus was just mulling that over when the sound of footfalls alerted them. He swiftly doused the torch, but wasn't quite swift enough. A few moments later an irate journeyman was standing at the entrance to their cell, a sour expression on his face. The monastery here was big enough that Hargus hadn't got to know all its residents yet.

'What are you novices doing up after curfew?'

'Sorry, sir,' said Arik, quickly channelling deference. 'I'm studying for journeyman, and I wanted to share a puzzle with my learned colleague here.'

'A puzzle that could easily have waited until study time tomorrow,' said the journeyman sternly. He peered at them in the light of moon and stars. The late spring night was clear enough, perhaps they shouldn't have bothered with the torch.

'You're Arik of Tjopkvist, aren't you?' asked the journeyman. 'Brother Helmo's second?'

Arik blinked in the moonlight, surprised to be recognised by a superior. The pair of them had been here for months, but at the Reverend Priory of St Argo novices were seldom known to journeymen by name unless they taught them.

'I am,' said Arik hesitantly.

'I've been hearing good things about you,' said the journeyman. 'You're making swift progress in your studies, or so they say. For that reason, I will not report this breach of regulations – just this once! But see to it in future that your progress is not at the expense of the rules of the Order.'

'Thank you, sir, I will,' said Arik, hurriedly rising and pulling Hargus up with him. The journeyman appeared to have forgotten all about him.

As they trudged back over to their dormitory, Hargus risked a whispered remark. 'You're rising in the Order – that's good, Arik! Might be you can get closer to the adepts, or even the archmasters – find out more about what's going on here.'

But Arik remained silent as they walked, his eyes fixed on the middle distance. Hargus sensed an elation within him, one he could have sworn wasn't altogether wholesome.

CHAPTER 9
OF WYRMS AND WYVERNS

The Vale of Penhalain was a surprisingly welcome
sight. An emerald strip of land carved from the
flanks of the Farfahailan foothills by the slow-moving
waters of the Bruach, its myriad blooms were a sight for Sir
Torgun's sore eyes. Hamlets that would not have looked out
of place in the King's Dominions of Northalde clustered its
banks, and shepherds grazed their goats on the gentle
slopes to either side of the river. The rocky highlands had
softened gradually over the past couple of days, becoming
grassy hills where a man might even plant crops. The mountains proper loomed in the distance, a moody grey etched
against blue skies, but the vale was by far the most lively
place on Skulla he had seen.

Its mistress, Ariadha ap Madrix, brightened visibly at
the sight of home. Pointing across the river to two hills, she
said something in her own tongue to Ianna and Fanwyn.
Torgun caught his breath as he registered what she was
pointing at. Straddling the hills, the fortress seemed to sit on

naught but the air betwixt them. At first Torgun thought it was fashioned of silver, then of glass, then of mist. As it glimmered and shifted before his confused eyes, he realised it was all of those things and none.

'Here in the Vale, the magick of the Old Time still endures,' said Morcant. 'In the days when the Moon Goddess smiled on us, our ancestors used gramarye to build forts and cities like this one. Intended as a last refuge was Nuallán – should earthly conquerors break past our coastal defences. Few armies would try and lay siege to a floating fortress, I'm sure you'll agree!'

Peering at Nuallán Hold with scarce believing eyes, Torgun fancied its tapering turrets were fashioned of moon-beams – though by his reckoning it was the middle of the day.

Wrackwulf scratched his beard. 'Are you sure that thing is habitable?' he asked suspiciously. 'I don't fancy bedding down for the night on a cloud.'

Morcant grinned. 'Never fear, sir knight! Once on the inside, looks and feels quite solid it does. You'll be perfectly safe.'

Joram scowled. 'More pagan sorcery,' he said. 'Perhaps one of yon hamlets will give me lodgings.'

The warlock inclined his head, seeming almost deferen-tial now. 'Whatever you say, master monk,' he said. 'Suffer me you will to go inside, though? 'Tis a long time since I sojourned at Nuallán.'

The scowl did not leave the adept's face as he replied: 'I'm in your country now, warlock. There's little I can do to stop you if you insist on continuing down the road to perdition. On second thoughts, better I come with you – that way I can keep an eye on you.'

The two knights exchanged meaningful glances. Joram hadn't showed any concern for Morcant's spiritual well-being when he'd wanted to execute him for his crimes in Thraxia.

Ariadha led them across a bridge of stepping stones broad and smooth enough to take their garrons; Torgun fancied their perfect forms were another product of the islanders' nature sorcery. The Marcher Lady led them up an incline towards the two hills. As they approached, a tendril of mist began to writhe down towards the ground from the underside of the floating fortress. Drawing closer, Torgun watched dumbfounded as it coalesced into a set of shimmering spiral stairs.

He had half a mind to seek lodging with a peasant himself, but found his hand drawn towards the sword fragment from the apparition. If he really was descended from an immortal, perhaps he shouldn't baulk at the idea of magic. And one way or another, he'd lived and breathed it for some time now.

Following the Westerlings, he dismounted and approached the shimmering stairs. At least he didn't have to ride the blasted mare any more.

The steps seemed to change colour from pink to blue to violet to cobalt and back again as Torgun took them one by one. The Westerlings seemed perfectly at ease, and Morcant hummed a cheerful tune as he ascended. The spiral stairs disappeared into a leaf-green circle of pulsing light; Torgun squeezed his eyes shut as he followed the mage through it.

When he opened them, yet another sight took his breath away.

The bailey walls, if you could call them that, appeared from the inside to be made entirely of sedge and moss. The floor consisted of what looked like the tops of shorn tree trunks packed tightly together. Instead of crenelations, gigantic intertwining briars rose up forbiddingly; but the central keep retained its ethereal facade.

The courtyard's occupants were strangest of all. Animals dressed in fustian livery walked about on hind legs: dogs, pigs, foxes, coneys, badgers and voles were just some of the more common creatures. They appeared to be conversing, and some even drank from miniature flagons clutched in paws that were oddly dextrous. Many wore hats of strange design, cocked at angles and triple-pointed.

Torgun and Wrackwulf simply stood and gaped.

'Don't look so befuddled, bold knights!' laughed Morcant. 'But myth-shadows are these – leftovers from the Old Time, when beasts held learned discourse with us long into the night. They aren't truly here, not any more.' Once again a sadness entered his voice. 'Only their former rulers, the hybrid Animal Kings you have already met, are permitted to linger on this side of the Veil nowadays.'

Blinking, Torgun looked again. Morcant was right. All he saw now were ordinary swine and goats behind pens.

'At least maybe there's a chance of getting some meat in this place,' muttered Wrackwulf, trying to make light of things.

The keep's double doors appeared to be fashioned from glowing crystal (though by now Torgun knew well enough not to believe anything his eyes told him). These parted in a rippling sheen that uncomfortably reminded him of the ice door that had shielded Andragorix at the Warlock's Crown. He felt a phantom pain from his burn wounds ghost across his chest as a retinue of servitors led by a proud-looking marcher lord came out to greet them. At least these looked to be normal men and women, if people here could ever be said to be normal. The marcher was a pale stocky man of about fifty winters with a greying beard, dressed in the same star-and-diamond sash as Ariadha. He muttered a curt greeting at her and favoured Ianna and Fanwyn with a cursory nod of the head.

They certainly don't stand on ceremony here, thought Torgun, watching as the ageing lord and Ariadha immediately fell to arguing in their own tongue. *Barbarians indeed, yet their magic works wonders.* He still felt unnerved by the floating fortress, despite Morcant's reassurances.

'What are they saying?' he asked the mage, trying to allay his nerves.

The warlock did his best to sound reassuring as Ariadha and the lord continued to bicker. 'Have no fear – the marcher lady is but making arrangements for our stay here. I don't think her Uncle Owyn approves of the decision to bring us here, but she's the one in charge! We'll rest and eat before we set out for Taras Cerawn on the morrow.'

'If she feeds us better than roots and leaves, I'll be content enough,' said Wrackwulf, eyeing one of the pigs.

Ariadha's uncle abruptly broke off the argument and beckoned impatiently for them to follow him into the keep. Torgun's skin tingled uncomfortably as he passed through the gateway. Once again he sensed the relic about his neck registering something like disapproval.

The main hall was almost predictable in its outlandishness. The floor repeated the design of shorn tree trunks, but the walls appeared to be made entirely of triangular shields dyed a multitude of colours, bound together like the scaly hide of a dragon. The ceiling was one vast shimmering pool of quicksilver.

'In times gone, the lords and ladies of Nuallán would lift their eyes and gaze upon the wide world through yon lens,' explained Morcant, the ceiling casting motes of light across his face as he spoke. 'Diminished is our present, and now we see in it but glimpses of the past.' The reverence in his voice was palpable.

'Your ancestors must have had terribly stiff necks,' observed Wrackwulf. 'Or did their magicks protect them from such aches and pains as well?'

'Who can say?' grinned Morcant, rising to the jest.

They were interrupted by Ianna, who announced in her halting Decorlangue: 'Servants show you to your rooms. Rest now before we eat.' Ariadha and her uncle had already left the hall, doubtless to continue their arguing in private.

Two servitors motioned for the guests to follow them. They had the same absence of deference as their master, despite their inferior status:

Is this what it means to be a free folk? Torgun wondered. He suddenly felt homesick.

Leading them through a doorway whose jamb and lintel were fashioned from antlers and horn, the servitors took them up an adjoining flight of stairs made entirely from animal bones. Torgun spotted an aurochs thigh, ribs of what looked to be a horse, and the skulls of dogs and wolves.

'You seem to venerate the animal kingdom, yet you use their remains more thoroughly than we do,' he pointed out.

'Far more sacred value than wood or stone an animal's corpse has to us,' explained Morcant. 'A great honour it is to use a beast's bones – for us and the creature.'

'So what about the shields in the hall then?' asked Wrackwulf. 'They use animal hide, yes, but also wood and iron besides.'

'Oh, those weren't shields,' said Morcant, smiling his sly smile. 'Dragon scales are what you saw. Taken from Wyrms our people slew in the Firedrake Wars.'

Torgun nearly tripped on the stairs. 'Your ancestors fought *dragons*?'

'Many times,' Morcant assured him. 'Long centuries passed before the firedrake threat was extinguished.'

Servitors showed them into a suite of spartanly furnished, rustic-looking rooms fashioned from oak beams and lime plaster the colour of autumn leaves. Upon these walls elaborate reliefs depicted scenes of the hunt. Looking closer, Torgun realised with a shock that the *animals* were chasing the *humans*, hunting them down with spears and bows as they fled naked through the wild.

'Some of us believe the Hour Of All's Ending will be a time of great reversal,' said Morcant, catching him staring. 'The beasts shall rise up and relearn the lore of the Old Time, whilst mortal men sink into the mire, becoming as beasts themselves.'

Torgun glanced at Joram, half expecting a pious rebuke,

but the monk was gazing blankly out of a horn-paned window thin enough to be transparent, lost in his thoughts.

'Never mind the bloody beasts,' said Wrackwulf, setting his things down by one of half a dozen cots in the room. 'I want to hear more about dragons.'

Ianna and Fanwyn had repaired to an adjoining chamber, leaving Morcant alone with the outlanders. Picking a cot for himself, the mage set down his things and sat down with a contented sigh.

'When first the Great World Serpent spawned the Wyrms on Hydrae, everywhere they were,' he said. 'The Elder Wizards slew many and drove the rest off, into high remote places where mortals venture not. Most sought refuge beyond the Fenris ranges in the Frozen Wastes, that we call the Mountains of Madness at the End of the World. Once or twice, the *Westerling Chronicle* tells, we even made compact with our age-old enemies the Northlanders, to see off the threat.'

Torgun thought about that. 'Our ancestors named the seas about Northalde the Wyvern, for that reason. But we have not had a dragonslayer in the realm since the days when Northalde was three kingdoms.'

'And largely thanks to us that is,' said Morcant. 'Though thank us for it you never have.' Before Torgun could reply to that, he went on: 'But one thing I believe you have confused, sir knight. For many believe "wyvern" to be but another word for wyrm or firedrake, yet this is not so. The wyverns that once troubled your seas were a lesser race of dragons, though still fearsome when encountered in numbers. Not born of Hydrae's primeaval union with the Great World

Serpent were they, but scales shed by him in his lair. The *Westerling Chronicle* tells how He Who Should Not Be Disturbed birthed the beasts, once every thousand years, in answer to the call of their greater kin.'

'No need to fear them any more then,' put in Wrackwulf. 'Since Sir Azelin of Valacia slew the last of the Wyrms, such monsters are thankfully gone out of the world.'

A queer light was in Morcant's eye as he replied: 'And yet our farseers and those of the Frozen Wastes have both prophesied a time shall come when the wyverns are reborn.' Looking at Torgun, he added: 'And such a time is when the power of Serpent-Killer will be needed again.'

Reaching into his cloak pocket, Sir Torgun pulled out the silver shard the apparition had given him. It seemed to catch the pale sunlight, intensifying its glow and becoming a thing of light rather than metal.

No man outruns his Wyrd.

CHAPTER 10
HOLDING BACK THE TIDE

Sometimes, prayers were answered. Stepping up to address the freemen of Strongholm one last time, Princess Hjala had prayed to her father's mighty spirit, for his words and strength to become her own. And so it had proved. With the Northlanders bringing a fleet of blades on a tide of ladders, grapnels and battering rams to the walls of the city, and darkness descending on the first day of the siege of Strongholm, she had found the words to inspire its citizens with the courage to resist.

Now that siege was a tenday old: in that time, more than a thousand strong men had joined the King's Watch and the White Valravyn. Wayns had been drawn up on the King's Thoroughfare and parked against the beleaguered gates, bales of wood and sacks of stone packed into them to shore up their defences against the relentless driving attacks of the Northlanders. From the lands about the King's Dominions, sorties of mounted knights had come and gone, each one repulsed by the invaders: the city was now ringed with palisades and ditches bristling with spikes. They wouldn't be enough to see off a larger army, but that larger army had yet to arrive and save the city. At least the realm's naval forces had showed up to the fight: on the Strang Estuary, Sealord Aesgir's warships had engaged the invading fleet three days past. Even now, from her room in the palace, Hjala could see them bucking and rolling on waves incarnadined with the toll of war.

She could only hope that was a decoy manoeuvre, a distraction to allow the muster at Vandheim time to reach the city by land and break the siege. There hadn't been a sortie for several days now: hopefully that meant the ragtag knights and bannerets from the outlying Dominions had realised the futility of small-scale assaults and joined up with the main relief army. Besides that, there should be another army marching from the south: but in the fledgling lords and knights of the former southron demesnes, Hjala could place but little faith. From what she'd heard, many of them were no more than jumped-up freeswords, men of dubious honour promoted swiftly to vassal status during the power vacuum created by the last war.

This war looks likely to last a lot longer, Hjala thought gloomily as she watched Aesgir's flotilla of galleys being driven off yet again by the Northland longships. Her brother Thorsvald had been unable to watch such spectacles: his yearning for sea combat and leal duty had become a torment to him, but his place was on the city walls with Visigard and Toric, leading the defence. Watching the blood-stained waves roil as injured sailors drowned and screamed was difficult for Hjala too, but for rather more prosaic reasons.

Turning from the window, she vomited into her chamber pot for the third time that morning.

Of all the times to get a bout of food poisoning. But then fresh provender was already becoming a thing of the past, and a besieged city had to eat what it could. At least the King's chirurgeon Yurik had assured her the case wasn't lethal, although Hjala was beginning to suspect the Angel of Death might choose another guise in which to visit her.

The rapping on the door was almost a welcome distraction.

'Come in,' she managed to gasp. She'd sent her ladies-in-waiting away – she preferred to be alone with her thoughts more often these days. Especially when those thoughts came to her over a sick bucket.

She wasn't entirely surprised to see her brother enter. He was dressed in mail, not the gilded sort befitting a prince, but a regular hauberk any bachelor might wear. The modesty became Thorsvald well.

He grimaced as his nostrils caught the stink. 'Still no better then? I came as quickly as I could, but duties on the walls kept me.'

Hjala waved a hand dismissively, pulling back her single braid and tightening it. She had kept her customary severe look, continuing to dress demurely in a simple gown, smock and stocks fashioned of rich but unadorned pale pink wool. She felt modesty became her too, under the circumstances: she was naught more than a princess under palace arrest, in a capital city that might not be a capital city much longer.

'Spare me your apologies and pour me a cup of physick, brother,' she said, indicating the silver flask and ceramic cup on her dressing table. Yurik had left it for her, a foul-tasting brew that made her feel almost as nauseous as the sickness it was supposed to remedy.

Thorsvald complied. He looked more in need of a cup of wine himself.

'So out with it, brother,' she said. 'You haven't come here just to see I'm in better health. Tell me news of the siege.'

Thorsvald's brow furrowed as he answered. 'We're still repulsing them, but they're getting closer every day. Last night we had to drive off a pack of berserkers who'd managed to scale the wall between the King's Gate and South Tower. They fought fiercely like the devils they are, we had to slay a dozen before the rest were beaten back.'

It was only then that Hjala noticed her brother's left arm was bandaged at the elbow. She'd been too busy with her own blasted pain to spot it before.

'It's nothing serious,' Thorsvald quickly assured her. 'Mail took the worst of it, but it bruised up nicely. I won't be using anything heavier than a buckler for a while.'

She knew her valiant brother well enough to know this wasn't the reason behind his troubled expression.

'That was last night,' she pressed him. 'What about this morning? I can see what's happening at sea well enough from here' – she winced inwardly at the pain in her brother's eyes, as he caught the retreating ships through her window – 'but tell me what's been happening on the walls today. Are they renewing the siege?'

Thorsvald forced his gaze away from the window and

back to his sister. 'They haven't, no. By the looks of things, they're building catapults.'

'Catapults? I thought Northland barbarians were ignorant of such sophisticated siegecraft.'

'They are, as far as we know,' sighed the prince. 'But the sappers and craftsmen they've captured from our coastal forts aren't.'

Hjala's face fell, along with her heart. 'So that rumour was true then.' She'd heard a sally-forth of Northland brigands had overrun the two forts flanking the Strang yesterday, but hadn't wanted to believe it.

Thorsvald's pained expression intensified as he said: 'There's just too many of them. Now the sorties from the Dominions have stopped, the Northlanders are able to range abroad at will. They've easily got enough men to do that whilst keeping the siege going. Every day, we manage to kill at least a hundred of them, but they just keep coming. Hjala, I've never seen savagery of its like! It's not just that they don't fear death, they seem to welcome it. One of the bastards I sent to Gehenna last night actually laughed in my face as he died on my sword.'

For the first time she could see how scared her brother was. Thorsvald had always assumed he'd die aboard a ship, on his beloved sea, not being caught like a rat in a trap. The manner of a man's death could unsettle him almost as much as dying itself, and the prince was no exception.

'If what you say is true, then we've killed a thousand of them already,' she said, trying to cheer him. 'That's a fifth of their fighting tally.'

'Aye, and you think they'll allow us another tenday, to do

the same again? We've lost men too, Hjala. Those stalwart lads you roused to their deaths in Trader's Square might be useful for hurling boiling oil and firing a crossbow, but they're naught but axe fodder once it gets to close quarters. We've less than a thousand trained men, and soon it'll be closer to five hundred. I don't give us longer than a week.'

Hjala was shocked into silence. Perhaps this war wouldn't last too long either, now it came down to it.

'Then we really are doomed – unless the King's Army gets down here. They surely must – Aesgir arrived three days ago, that means it must be almost a week since he sailed from Vandheim. The others can't be far behind!'

Thorsvald nodded. He seemed faraway and gloomy. 'Yes and when they do arrive, what then? I've been doing a reckoning of my own. The White Valravyn will bring four hundred knights and a like number of soldiers – that's at most I'd say, and with half the ravens deployed down south they won't all get here for a while. Add to that another five hundred knights with squires from the rest of the Northern Dominions, plus another three hundred soldiers. On top of that there'll be crossbowmen and archers, but it doesn't add up to nearly enough, Hjala – and you know it.'

'But there'll be the Efrilunders,' she reminded him. 'That's got to be good for another four hundred knights and squires and soldiers, more than a thousand fighting men in total. Archers too, on top of that.'

'Yes, we'll be closely matched in numbers,' Thorsvald allowed. 'But you're forgetting their defences – they've had time to shore up their position, they've tripled their barricades since they settled in for a siege. That means until the relief army can break past their outer layers, it won't get so much as a charge in with those blasted ditches and palisades. They've a good number of trained crossbowmen of their own, too. That's several more days before our men can really start to harry them – several more days that we don't have. Dammit, Hjala, barbarians they might be, but they aren't stupid. They've planned this well, this Shield Queen I'm hearing talk of knows her business!'

Hjala managed a wry smile. 'I would have thought Aunt Walsa and I would have convinced you of the cunning of women by now, brother.'

Thorsvald did not return the smile.

'But then we have the Southern Dominions to depend on, too. Oh I know' – Hjala raised a hand as her brother rolled his eyes – 'jumped-up freeswords and errants, but they'll come and serve if it means gain and glory.'

'Maybe,' her brother allowed. 'And who knows, perhaps even the Woldings and the Highlanders will be prevailed upon to join the fray as well.'

She did not care for his sarcasm. 'Well they bloody well did last time, Thorsvald! For heaven's sake, man, don't lose heart now.'

'There's more to it,' insisted the prince. 'Something you're overlooking. When Vaska went across the ice, he reported seeing well over a hundred Northland longships under construction. From what I can fathom, Aesgir's got little more than fifty on his hands. There's even more of them, sister. Maybe twice as many.'

That put her on the back foot. She'd been so ill she'd forgotten about Vaska's report.

'Ten thousand Northlanders? That is a mighty army for the Ice Thegns.'

'The mightiest seen since Ryøskil,' her brother confirmed gloomily. 'And just what are the other five thousand up to, I wonder? For all we know, they might have half our own troops pinned up and down the country, north and south! No, until I see banners streaming in the wind above men and horses, I'll not count a single spear to our name, sister.'

They said nothing more after that, and presently her brother bade her an awkward farewell before leaving to return to the walls. Hjala took another swallow of medicine and, fighting off returning nausea, shuffled over to the window. Aesgir's ships had gone. The Northland flotilla remained a forbidding chain of clinkered pine, preventing supplies and succour from reaching the city.

Her ample bedchamber suddenly felt very cramped.

CHAPTER 11
GRAINS IN THE HOURGLASS

The hissing noises didn't get louder as they delved deeper into the mine, but they didn't get fainter either. Adelko had a distinct sense that the ghouls were toying with them. Already he could feel the ghoul-fear returning to unman him. Tipu could keep the creatures at bay with his sacred fluting, but the holy magic in the notes was a reprieve not a cure: the mystic had said it might buy them an hour at most... and then the ghouls would come for them, drawn by their awful perennial hunger.

They had tried to leave by the way they entered, but the she-ghoul had cunningly wedged the man-sized boulder firmly into place: not even Azelin could shift it, and they didn't have time to keep trying all night. So that meant the mines, and a deadly search for whatever other entrances the ghouls had used themselves.

Azelin ranged ahead, clutching the torch he'd seized from the chamber. At least they had some light to see by: Tipu said ghouls could see better than mortalkind in the dark, but they also saw better by torchlight. Yassin brought up the rear, holding the other torch. By its light, Adelko could see numerous burrow holes dug by the ghouls over the years: when the music stopped, they wouldn't be short of ways to come at them.

Tipu's melody was still beautiful, but already after five minutes Adelko could hear his delivery was a little more strained, the notes a tad more stilted. Horskram walked just ahead of him as they shuffled single file through the tunnel they had picked at random. They could only hope their combined prayers and psychic powers would somehow be enough to guide them to another exit.

The first attack came sooner than expected. Adelko's sixth sense screamed at him before the ghoul did, but still it took all his combat training to fend off the horrible creature as it launched itself at him from a side tunnel. He was unarmed and forced to grapple with it, using the basic techniques Edemus had taught him. Like its queen, the ghoul possessed a terrible strength. Around him he was dimly aware of the others being assailed too, as the creature pressed its yellowing face up against his. Its breath carried the sickly sweet stench of a charnel house, its spittle seemed to burn as it spattered him. The loathsome thing reached for him with its tongue, seeming to shudder with pleasure as it tried to taste him...

The ghoul released him and clamped elongated hands over shorn ears, its distended tongue flapping wildly before it turned and scampered back off into the stygian darkness, hissing and wailing. As quick as they had come, the ghouls were gone again. Tipu continued to play steadfastly, though the notes trembled now in time with their maker.

Mercifully, the ghouls were less eager to try their luck after that. Adelko supposed they had decided simply to bide their time and wait for the inevitable. Tipu did not stop playing, but continued to break the dusty subterrene air with his plaintive warbling. It was almost as if the song itself were begging the Unseen to spare them a gruesome death; beads of sweat glistened on the old mystic's wrinkled forehead, catching the wavering torchlight in lucent pinpricks.

I know what he looks like when he's nervous now, thought Adelko grimly.

They walked on in leaden silence, ears straining for the telltale sounds of another assault as they wandered from one tunnel to another, searching for the delicious feel of fresh air that would tell of an escape route. Adelko found himself wishing Vaskrian were by his side. They had shared so much of this kind of danger together, first in Tintagael, then at Staerkvit, then the Argael and the Warlock's Crown and later the Draugmoors... somehow it felt strange to be stuck in this ghastly mine without the squire.

Vaskrian, I hope you're in better straits than I am.

The next stretch of mine had partially collapsed in on itself, and it took them a while to retrace their steps. Tipu's playing sounded increasingly manic. Adelko had half a mad urge to seize the flute and break it over his knee, though that would surely mean their deaths. Eventually they found their way to another passage; this one was wider than the others. In one direction it was blocked up with fallen earth where the mine had collapsed, but Yassin was confident that if they followed it the other way it would lead to an exit eventually.

'Look, see!' he said, pointing to a pair of parallel rusted iron girders running the length of the passageway. 'The Huryans would have used the railway to transport the ore in wagons from the mining site,' he explained. 'If we follow it we have a chance of getting out of here!'

'A railway?' quizzed Adelko.

'It's the name given to the system they used to transport yon wheeled wagons,' explained Horskram. 'The Thalamians used them as well, though no one is sure who invented them.'

'The Elder Wizards most like,' suggested Adelko, earning a dark look from the older monk. The journeyman cleared his throat nervously.

'Whoever invented it, I don't care,' put in Anupe. 'Let's just follow it and get out of here if we can.'

Adelko scarcely had time to marvel at the craft that had fashioned such cunning devices. The wagons they passed were in a state of ruin, but the rails themselves remained intact, their grooves perfectly straight in the torchlight.

'Tipu spoke truly,' said the journeyman to Hari, who was walking next to him on the other side of the tracks. 'They may be pastoral nomads nowadays, but these were a learned people once.'

'After their own fashion,' replied the rogue. 'The Huryan

Empire was a muscular civilisation, practical and strong-minded, or so I've been told. I've robbed a few of their tombs, and their booby traps are cunning enough, I can tell you! Doubtless the Kishan Tombs will be no different.'

'If we ever reach them,' muttered Adelko, momentarily forgetting that their cover story was just that.

'Be of some heart, young one,' said Hari, forcing a grin. 'If I'm right about these tracks, we'll-'

He stopped in mid-sentence, his face curdling in disgust. Adelko felt a giddy sickness unravel in his guts as he caught the stench a moment later. The others were coughing and spluttering too, reaching for rags.

'I am not sure this is a good direction to take,' mumbled Anupe from behind a piece of cloth.

Resolutely they pressed on, the stench seeming to drag them all into an invisible cloying embrace.

'Ayee, Ma'alfeccnu'ur has made a lair for himself down here, and no mistake!' said Hari. The pallor had not left his cheeks.

'Do not speak that name here!' admonished Horskram sternly, his face wan and drawn in the torchlight. Adelko's sense appeared to scream at him from a myriad directions now. Shutting his eyes, he focused, letting it guide his footfalls. All the while, the stench grew stronger...

He opened his eyes on to a new scene of horror as they emerged into a large cavern. Here most of the mining work must have taken place: massive grooves in the walls indicated where rich seams had long been carved out and picked clean.

The corpses piled up around the cavern had mostly

been picked clean too, but close to the top Adelko could see the fresher ones. Rotting organs peeped from ribcages caked with drying gristle, and bloody eyesockets encrusted with stale gore stared sightlessly at the new arrivals. The stench was coming from these semi-digested victims, of which there had to be several dozen; the older skeletons must have numbered in the hundreds.

Bending over, Adelko retched. Tipu's notes broke and fluctuated dangerously, but somehow he managed to keep playing, if you could call such a fractured melody playing.

He'd seen piles of corpses before. But that had been during wartime, out in the open air where at least a breeze might alleviate the stink of the dead. This was worse, somehow. As they gathered themselves together and moved among the wrecked wagons – now filled with necrotic flesh and bone – he could see that most if not all had been ordinary folk. Wayfarers, merchants, vagabonds, perhaps even pilgrims. Rusted mail shirts and tarnished blades told of freebooters here and there, but most had been the unwary, lured to a grisly doom. At least in a war you knew that death and destruction were coming.

'What fool would seek to rob the ruins of Shamaria?' gasped Yassin, his words muffled as he continued to press his silk neckerchief to his nose.

'The same kind of fool who would agree to help us rob the Kishan Tombs,' Horskram reminded him. 'In any case, I thought you'd encountered these creatures during your... career.'

'I have,' Yassin allowed. 'But only in twos or threes, in graveyards and burial grounds and suchlike. I've never encountered such a horde as this.' A queer light suddenly entered his eyes. 'But wait... ghouls like to hoard the treasure of their victims. Some of these men were wealthy, judging by their clothes. Oh yes, the horde might have a hoard!' His nausea had apparently dropped away, and he was leering at the mounds of bodies now.

'Quell your greed,' said the adept, making a disgusted noise in the back of his throat. 'Right now we have to concentrate on getting out of here alive. Judging by the sounds of yon mystic's errant warbling, we've less than half an hour left-'

'Look!' Anupe cried. She tugged at Horskram's sleeve. The monk pulled it away irritably, but glanced over at what she was pointing to. Adelko saw it too, and felt his gorge rising again. Over by an upturned wagon was what he took to be the most recent victims – their dismembered remains still raw and bloody. A cluster of flies was feeding on what the ghouls had left.

But Horskram's mind was on other things than his nausea.

'Yon flies had to get in here somehow!' he cried excitedly. 'Look around – we'll search this cavern top to bottom if we have to.'

Adelko grimaced. The prospect of burrowing around amidst the ghouls' victims did not appeal in the slightest, but it had to be done. There were several other shafts leading off from the cavern, all wide enough to admit railways. Moving towards the back of the cavern, he could sense a distinct breeze... but which of the passages was it coming from?

'Up there!' cried Hari. 'Look!' The rogue pointed with his torch. It was the height of some five men above them, on the edge of their circle of light, but they could just about make it out: an uneven hole in the rough cave ceiling, wide enough to admit several horses.

'It makes sense,' said Azelin, scanning the area just below the aperture with his own torch. 'There's a lot of rubble here, part of the cave ceiling must have fallen in.'

'And who's to say another part won't fall in?' muttered Anupe, frowning.

'I don't think that's the first of our worries,' said Adelko, fighting back returning panic as he saw hunched shapes crawling over the lip of the hole. He counted half a dozen of them, etched against the starlit skies. The all-too-familiar hungry hissing returned, as the ghouls began scuttling along the cavern ceiling. 'Those things can climb like spiders,' gasped the journeyman.

'They can jump like sand cats too!' cried Hari, but his warning came too late. No sooner had he spoken than the six ghouls let go of the ceiling, landing expertly in a circle around them. By starlight their ochre pallor looked even more ghastly, their grey distended teeth seeming to mock the moonlight.

Azelin handed Adelko the torch and unsheathed his blade, joining his two-handed sword to Anupe's falchion and Hari's scimitar. Tipu continued to play, the increasingly turgid strains making a mummer's farce of their brave last stand.

More hissing, this time from all around them. The rest of the ghouls were arriving to join the feast.

So this is it, thought Adelko. *After everything we've been through, all we've survived – we end up as food for half-human monsters. Thanks a lot, Reus Almi-*

Horskram nudged him severely. In his hand was a rusty scimitar, seized from a dead freebooter.

'Take this and take it quickly!' he barked.

Adelko complied confusedly. 'But I thought we're not meant to shed-'

'Ghouls don't count!' snapped Horskram, grabbing up another rusty sword for himself, this one with its point broken off.

Adelko clutched the weapon as the ghouls surged towards them. It felt awkward in his hand; all that Edemus had taught him suddenly seemed irrelevant as a ghoul lunged at him.

But when he raised the scimitar to parry, he saw just how relevant his training was.

You can't always fight on the ground of your choosing, with the weapons of your choosing, against odds in your favour, Edemus had told him time and again. *The one constant – the thing that doesn't change unless you're wounded or incapacitated – is you. Be your own odds, Adelko.*

The creature gave something akin to a roar as Adelko swatted its clawing attack aside, before sidestepping and striking it sharply across the back of the head. As fast as the thing was, the journeyman had anticipated its movements without even trying. Out of the corner of his eye, he saw Horskram had done likewise, bringing his ghoul low with a swipe of his stunted blade.

But there were still far too many of them. To make

matters worse, the ghouls weren't easily killed: Azelin had beheaded two in quick succession, yet still the headless bodies came on, clawing blindly at the warrior-monk as the heads snapped viciously at his heels. Anupe and Hari were in similar straits, fending off severed limbs as they tried to preserve their lives a little longer with whirling steel. In the midst of them Tipu piped on, but no one living or dead had ears for his music now. As Adelko repulsed a second ghoul with another swipe of his rusty blade, and the rest of the pack closed on them, he began mouthing a prayer he did not expect he would live to finish.

When the blast of heat and light came, he had to shield his eyes from it. For several seconds he couldn't even tell where it was coming from. The ghouls shrieked and wailed, as half a dozen of them went up like bonfires; the rest retreated, scampering back across the corpses and wagons. A shout alerted them to Hari, whose sleeve had caught fire; he was beating at it frantically when suddenly it went out like a snuffed candle.

A low chanting from above told of the fire's provenance. Seconds later, another coruscating sheet of flame shot from the hole in the cave ceiling: it swept up three fleeing ghouls, the magicked flames devouring them hungrily. In their wake, the other burning ghouls thrashed on the ground, as their mortified flesh charred and sloughed off blackened bone.

As the second sheet of flame cleared, a head poked over the lip of the aperture. A swart bald head, shining in the light of the burning ghouls... It took Adelko a couple of moments to recognise the stony features: it was the Zarumani priest who had watched them during the pit fight in Sha'iza'ar. In his hands was a length of rope, which he quickly fed down to them. It went taut, dangling a few handspans off the ground.

'Zaruman has sent his servant to aid you, for his cause and yours are joined as are wood and flame,' intoned the priest, 'but we don't have all night! I hope you are swift climbers.'

'I spotted him in Sha'iza'ar staring at us,' hissed Anupe. 'I don't think we should trust him.'

Adelko glanced at the ghouls, who had retreated to the corners of the cavern but now paused to eye them resentfully. Amongst them he could see the ghulah: she seemed much taller now, and had shed her robe. She looked robustly feminine, but it was a sickly parody of beauty that did little to test his devotion to Reus. Her eyes seemed disproportionately large as well, two yawning black pits of pure hatred and frustrated hunger.

'I don't think we have much choice, Anupe,' Adelko pointed out.

Hari was already climbing up the rope. Azelin wasn't far behind, and Horskram ushered Adelko forwards next. Tipu was gazing up at the Zarumani, a quizzical smile on his face. The Sufieli seemed to have rediscovered his serenity. 'When the worshippers of Zaruman aid the followers of Suf and St Argo, this is most portentous, yes most portentous indeed!'

Adelko shrugged. 'That's nothing, Tipu. We've had Fays help us on our adventures.'

Tipu frowned. 'What are "fays"?' he asked.

'Nature spirits, not entirely good and not entirely-'

Adelko was interrupted by Horskram urging him on impatiently. As if to emphasise the adept's words, a handful of the braver ghouls began to creep back towards them. Another sheet of flame quickly dissuaded them, but it was noticeably weaker than the last.

Hurriedly the journeyman pulled himself up the rope, gratefully abandoning the scimitar. Thanks to Edemus, his muscles were strong enough to make the climb a swift and painless one – battle fever boosted his strength, too. Tipu was the last to come up. Though older and weaker than the rest of them, he shimmied up the rope with ease.

'Well, he is light as a feather,' quipped Hari, but the rogue was glancing about him nervously as he spoke. The night air was surprisingly raw and chilly. The hole exited at another point just inside the basin cradling the city: its ruins looked even more forbidding beneath the black skies, the blasphemous silhouettes of the eldritch statues seeming to increase the darkness and suck light and life from the stars above.

When Tipu was up, the Zarumani pulled the rope after him hastily. He had tethered it to his horse, a sturdy-looking piebald gelding. That put Adelko in mind of their poor steeds, but he did not care to search for their remains. His mind flashed back to the demon on the Brenning Wold, half a lifetime ago, and the wet fragments it had made of their mounts.

Once the rope was lashed to his horse's saddle, the priest turned to address them curtly. 'The ghouls' hunger will overcome their cowardice soon enough,' he said. 'And fire weaving is not an inexhaustible art. We must go now.'

'You don't need to tell us that!' exclaimed Hari. 'But you'll have to ride slowly so we can keep up.'

'I will not ride at all,' replied the priest. 'A Zarumani shares the hardships of those companions that Mithras has joined him to.'

Without another word the orange-robed priest began marching up into the craggy hills, leading his horse by the reins. They followed him, all the while casting furtive glances back at the ruins, half expecting to see another tide of ghouls come pouring up after them. Mercifully, none emerged, and they left Shamaria unmolested.

They walked on through the night, fear galvanising their limbs and pushing all thoughts of sleep into a dark corner. Only when the sun began to gild the horizon in front of them did they stop to rest. The Zarumani fell to his knees and bowed his head towards it, intoning a prayer in a tongue that was foreign to Adelko. Several times during the chant the priest rose his head without breaking off the incantation; Adelko could have sworn he saw his eyes aflame.

Horskram shook his head as he sat on a rock wearily rubbing his legs. 'A disciple of Suf I can abide, but relying on help from paganers seems to be more commonplace by the day. Truly Reus moves in mysterious ways.'

If He moves at all on our behalf, thought Adelko disconsolately. He recalled the apocalyptic vision the Earth Witch had bequeathed him in her bower: how indifferent the Unseen had seemed to the plight of mortals, angels and demons alike ignoring the world and its doings. All except the Angel of Death, that was: Azrael never failed to interest himself in mortalkind. Adelko shivered in the cool dawn. No wonder he rarely allowed himself to think of that vision. He wasn't sure whether to thank the Earth Witch, or curse her.

Presently the sun hardened and warmth returned to the land. Safe from threat of ghouls, the weary adventurers stretched themselves out as best they could on the rough ground. Despite the absence of bedrolls, Adelko found himself drifting off quickly.

Once more he dreamed. It was an old dream this time, one that had recurred ever since he'd first had it in the Breka-wood, when he and Horskram had been on the run from Andragorix's demon. He was back at Ulfang, only now he was apparently in charge: all the monks there looked up to him and hung on his every word, as he lectured them before the evening meal in the refectory. Out of the corner of his eye, he caught the statue of St Ionus in his alcove, smiling at him: *I gave you the journey that you so desired, and you learned wisely from it,* the saint seemed to say. Someone nudged him in the ribs and Adelko turned back to address his congregation...

He awoke to find Hari nudging him with his boot. Annoyed at having so pleasant a dream dispelled, he sat up grumpily.

'What is it?' he mumbled. 'Surely we're not already off aga-' The words died on his lips as he registered the situation. He'd been too tired to notice before, but they had bedded down in a rock-strewn dell with cypress trees dotted about it and another rise of hills to the south. Cresting that rise were more than thirty mounted warriors. Taking in their swarthy complexions and oiled beards, black turbans and flowing mauve tabards, and exotic-looking hauberks fashioned of interlocking circular scales, Adelko judged them to be Nazharyan *fariz*. At their head were three more warriors, similarly attired but clearly of different provenance: Southrons, judging by their mahogany skins and broad strong features.

The Southron in the middle smiled thinly at the companions, who were by now all blearily awake.

'Now, this is a strange sight to behold!' he exclaimed, giving vent to a low whistle as he addressed them in Sassanic. 'Such a mismatched band of wayfarers, and the *djalis* have not even begun to sing.' His voice was deep and rich, suggesting the far-off beating of a distant drum. Another whistle, higher pitched and more mannered this time, and the cavalrymen under his command steered their horses down into the dell with graceful easy movements. Azelin was already on his feet, hand on the hilt of his sword, but Horskram motioned for him not to draw steel.

In less than ten seconds, a horseshoe shape of a dozen mounted *fariz* was slowly tightening around them, bright spears catching the late morning sunlight as they held them poised above their shoulders. Adelko doubted they would miss at this range.

As if reading his thoughts, the leader called out: 'I would not try anything foolish, if I were you.' He remained sitting on his horse at the crest of the dell, his fellow Southrons to either side of him.

The priest of Zaruman chose this moment to speak up. 'We are on urgent business that cannot wait. Bound for the Abydos ranges are we – no part do we take in the coming war betwixt Faith and Creed.'

The *fariz* leader arched a black eyebrow. 'Oh really? I will be the judge of that. Lay down your weapons, all of you. And don't try any of your sorcerous tricks, god-denier – I serve Muqmurlish tek Nazar himself, and the Sultan is not forgiving of pagans who cross him.'

The Zarumani looked angered momentarily, but was also cowed. 'The Sect of Light and Fire has no cause to anger the Sultan, or cross him in any way,' he replied deferentially. 'The four corners of the sultanate are his to command, and we but weave our fires upon its fringes.'

'Yes,' replied the Southron captain, 'so you do.' He did not sound approving. 'But there is more to you than that, I think,' he added, sweeping the band with his dark eyes. 'I will have your stories – all of them – before the new sun grows old. Lay down your weapons now, and submit to be bound. I would not shed blood without cause, but be sure I will not ask again.'

Reluctantly they did as they were told. Not that Adelko had a weapon to relinquish anyway, but he felt a bitterness he could not quell rise up in him as a Nazharyan dismounted to bind his hands. Always they were running from danger; always it caught up with them. Why couldn't they just fight sometimes? Right then he found himself wishing he had taken up the sword and not the book –

perhaps Rothgar and Danton and Tobin and their ilk had the right of it, and violence was a man's only way through life. He could fight. Give him fair odds and a sword, and he'd show these foreign devils his story all right-

He brought himself up short, shocked at the sudden tide of anger that had welled up in him without warning. The Sassanians were leading them back over the rise of hills now; off in the distance he could see a camp, where many more *fariz* were tending their horses and preparing the noon meal. What madness had he been thinking just now? He thought of his fight against Arik at the monastery in Rima, how he had longed just for a second or two to make an end of his old friend. What devil had Edemus unlocked in him? Was he destined to become a hothead killer like Vaskrian?

He pushed such thoughts to the back of his mind as their captors marched them into the camp. There had to be close on a hundred men in all; clearly they had fallen into the hands of a high-ranking captain. What that captain would make of them, travelling incognito behind enemy lines, remained to be seen: but the stares they received were for the most part sullen and hostile.

Adelko almost wished he were back in the mine with the ghouls.

CHAPTER 12
A UNION OF FAITHS

It wasn't long before the Southron captain called for them. Sat in the middle of the camp outside an elegant maroon pavilion resembling a gigantic turban, he appeared relaxed in a wicker chair. Flanking him and standing to attention were the two other Southrons: one now wore a smile that Adelko thought rather too cheerful for the circumstances, but the other looked more dour than ever. As their guards nudged them into the space between tents where their hearing would take place, his face dropped even further to a scowl.

All of them were still bound, save for Tipu who had been released once he declared his name and sect. The *fariz* captain addressed him now. 'Tipu Sulia, you are known to me,' he said, his voice still quiet yet strong, 'no doubt you will explain how you come to be in such outlandish company.' He indicated the rest of them with an elaborate sweep of the arm. Adelko could feel the cavalrymen boring holes in them with their eyes; but his sixth sense only tingled, telling him their captor was a just man after his own fashion. Perhaps they would be able to reason their way out of captivity. Perhaps.

'We are about the work of Ashanti,' Tipu replied in soothing tones. 'But before I speak further of this, may I know whom I am a thousand times honoured to be addressing?'

The captain smiled wryly. 'Ever the Sufielis have understood the virtue of courtesy,' he said. 'I am Zimri Sumanguru, of the Suman tribe in the Kingdom of Kushia, until but lately indentured as *amluq* to the Sultan Muqmurlish tek Nazar. My tenure of bondage being done, I now serve as a general in his army – that same army that will soon sweep the infidels back into the northern seas, whence they came.' He let his dark eyes fall on the three Urovians then, as if to add weight to his words.

Azelin had the temerity to speak up. 'A general with but a hundred troops under his command? It seems the Sultan does not trust his commanders as well as he ought.' The nearest *fariz* stepped forward to chastise him, but Zimri raised a hand to stay him.

'It is a fair observation, though clearly you are less well versed in courtesy than your guide,' he said sharply. 'But then the infidel Urovians have ever been crude of manners and speech.' Sneers and laughs from the Nazharyans showed what they thought of that. Even the scowling Southron lieutenant at Zimri's side cracked a smile.

But Azelin remained unfazed. 'Crude of speech is it?' he shot back. 'At least I have taken the trouble to learn yours. How is your Panglian, pray tell?'

'It is well enough,' replied Zimri in Panglian, before switching seamlessly to Decorlangue: 'But I believe it is the tongue of the ancient warrior-emperors of Thalamy that serves best, no?'

Azelin gaped, genuinely taken aback. Zimri only smiled. 'More to this Southron sworder than meets the eye, eh?' he said, dropping back into Sassanic. 'But I am clearly not the only one here who is not quite what he seems...' He turned his gaze back to Tipu. 'If you will continue, O Scion of Suf.'

The mystic told their cover story, and Adelko inwardly recited the Psalm of Spirit's Comforting. He sensed a disquiet in Azelin and Hari – were they beginning to suspect the lie for what it was? For his part Zimri sat silently, his strong jawline cupped in one hand as he listened. Many of the *fariz* stirred uncomfortably when Tipu mentioned the Kishan Tombs – Adelko could well guess what their reaction would be if they learned their true destination.

'Thieves,' Zimri said at last when Tipu was finished. 'That is what you claim you are, tomb robbers on a grand scale, and nothing more. A likely story! For when have the Sufielis ever coveted riches? And from what I have heard of the Argolians, they are not known for their avarice either...' He paused, as if deep in thought. Adelko expected Horskram to say something, but his mentor remained silent.

Then Zimri spoke again. 'Here is what I will do. Until sunset I shall give you, to come clean and tell me the truth. If I am not satisfied with your story as it stands by then, I will have no choice but to take you back to the Sultan's army for trial. And I warn you, Muqmurlish does not tolerate outlanders and lawbreakers in his domains.' He turned to look at Azelin again. 'Rest assured, *jhufa'ar*, I have many more men under my command – what you see here is but a sortie, the which I volunteered to lead. Crusaders I expected to encounter, not wayfarers out of *djali*'s song fleeing ghoulish apparitions... and Ashanti knows what else. Take them away! Feed them and guard them closely! I will see them again when the sun kisses the earth.'

Zimri turned away and muttered something to one of his fellow Southrons. The hearing was at an end. Their guards closed on them once more and escorted them through the camp to a tent towards its outskirts. The Nazharyans had already searched them closely; Adelko imagined Hari might be the type to keep a smaller blade up his sleeve, but they were otherwise unarmed – although at least their captors had the decency to untie their bonds.

The interior of the tent was dank and evidently used for supplies. Two guards came in with them; Adelko caught another giving orders to station four more outside. Even if they somehow managed to overcome their guard, they would have a hundred more elite warriors to contend with. Slumping back against a sack of provender, Adelko marvelled at the bizarreness of the situation his Wyrd had brought him to. It really was like something out of a song: two Argolians, a Sha'abatian mystic, a disgraced Bethler, a pagan fire-worshipper, a warrior-woman wanderer and a halfbreed rascal... Held prisoner by a Southron general in the Nazharyan army on the eve of another Pilgrim War.

When the bards put this into a lay, they had better be the best in the Free Kingdoms.

Presently Hari broke the silence. 'So, priest,' he said,

turning to the Zarumani. 'You saved our necks long enough that we might live another day at least – do you have a name?'

'I do,' replied the priest unsmiling. He did not turn to face Yassin.

Unfazed, the trickster tried again. 'If you won't divulge it, perhaps you might at least tell us why you helped us back there?' Horskram and Tipu remained silent but they were both paying attention. Azelin for his part remained sitting against a crate of supplies, staring off into the middle distance and lost in his own gloom. Anupe paced the tent restlessly.

The Zarumani tugged absently at his robes. He still did not meet anyone's eyes as he spoke: 'The two so-called prophets of Faith and Creed had not yet been born when Mithras came to Zaruman, whom we hold to be the one true prophet.'

'That is blasphemy,' interjected Horskram. Even Tipu was shaking his head. 'Your errors of belief are most egregious, my friend,' he said, more sadly than anything else.

The Zarumani was stolid as he replied: 'Have it howsoever you will, but we of the Sect of Light and Fire know the truth.' Behind him Azelin gave vent to a curtailed bark of ironical laughter. So he was listening, after all.

The priest ignored him too as he went on: 'Long ago, between the two Ages of Darkness, the peoples of Near Sassania followed their accursed Sendhéan cousins and turned to embrace unclean devils as their gods. The Assurians and the Huryans alike prostrated themselves before Shawa and Asu, bride and bridegroom of lust and greed, whom you of Faith and Creed both revile as archdemons. But worst of all were the Shemites, who conquered the lands east of the Abydos ranges that men today call the Sultanate of Halepo, and went on to build an empire straddling the northern shores of the Great Inland Sea. And the emperors of Kishai held commerce with the Sendhéans to the south, whose priest caste was founded long centuries before, in mimicry of the demon wizards who once ruled the Known World from the Forbidden Isle at the heart of those waters. And through them the Kishans became corrupted, learning the Left Hand Way, which all clean sorcerers abjure, taking demonkind into their hearts and bowing down before the Seven Princes of Perfidy, that we Zarumanis call the Seven Lords of Light's Extinguishing.'

'We are well versed in such lore,' interrupted Horskram. 'What has this to do with your pagan sect, or why you chose to help us?'

This time the priest did turn to favour Horskram with a look, if a far-off stare could be said to be a look. His eyes seemed to smoulder as he replied: 'Long have we weaved the fires, in our heartland beneath the mountains, and in return the flames have gifted us with glimpses of things to come. We know of your mission, the evil you seek to avert, and Mithras ordains that we help you – for He revealed Himself to Zaruman for the express purpose of fighting that same corruption that once held the lands of Sassania in its grip.' He turned to acknowledge Tipu then, nodding ever so slightly. 'True it is, that for a while the teachings of Sha'abat helped drive back such wickedness, just as his disciple Palomat did in the northern lands thereafter. But many centuries have elapsed since that time, the bloodline of the Enlightened Sultans has long since died out, and in the lands of Palomat even his foremost disciples are themselves corrupted and mistrusted.' He was looking at Horskram again. 'The fires have burned, and by their light we of Zaruman's teachings have seen – the Third Age of Darkness is almost upon us, and it will be the blackest of all if we do not stop the King of Night Unending and his Seven Lords from returning. To succeed in doing that, the Sunset Prophet must be stopped at all costs.'

Horskram shrugged. 'You aren't the most unlikely ally we've encountered on our quest,' he said. 'Even spirits and sorcerers fear Abaddon's plans, and rightly so! Yet how did you know where we were? Your arrival was most convenient, I must say.'

For the first time the priest smiled slightly. 'I have heard it said that the sages of Thalamy used to speak of 'gods in the design', when the Unseen intervened to turn the tale of mortalkind on its head. Perhaps there was some truth in what they said, though I believe they were originally referring to a poetic device used by their storytellers.'

'Don't let that spoil your argument,' sighed Horskram. 'As far as I'm concerned, we've been living an epic poem since we stumbled upon the first fragment theft.'

Adelko blinked, scarcely able to believe his ears. Catching his eye, Horskram sighed again. 'I think it fair to say the time for secrecy has passed. It's obvious that this doom has fallen on us all – everyone with an ounce of goodwill in them stands to lose everything they hold dear, schisms and politesse be damned. Perhaps I should have been quicker to recognise that.'

'A man cannot help but be set in the ways he has followed for a lifetime,' said Tipu kindly. 'Words of wisdom from our prophet – let them console you, Brother Horskram.'

Horskram inclined his head politely, though he hardly seemed consoled.

'To answer your question,' the Zarumani went on. 'My brethren despatched me immediately once the fires made clear you had arrived in the Pilgrim Kingdoms. We had glimpses of your possible fate, but could not be sure of the true outcome. I arrived in Sha'iza'ar posing as a lightfinder travelling with a caravan – my sect occasionally sanctions experienced members to seek employment in the outside world, for not even we can survive without coin, and donating to a pagan sect is punishable by death in the Sultanates. When I saw you arrive, I knew the fires had spoken true. Once you were out of town, I was able to follow you.'

'You might have helped us sooner,' said Horskram wryly. 'We almost didn't get to leave at all.'

'I might have,' allowed the priest, 'but blasting you out of trouble in Sha'iza'ar hardly seemed the best course of action. As for the ghouls, I had an inkling that they might be summoned to plague you, but didn't catch up with you until they had chased you underground. I had to consult another fire to learn of your precise whereabouts, and fire-divining is not an exact discipline. In any case, it seems apparent to me that your other companions have done their part in protecting you.' He indicated Tipu and Hari, whose face was pale with rage.

'Yes, I have done an adequate job of protecting you,' said the rogue, rising in anger. 'And it seems you have not been entirely honest with me in return. I was under the impression that we were on an expedition to the Kishan Tombs, not some sacred mission to deliver the world from evil!'

Horskram smirked and folded his arms nonchalantly. 'Yes indeed, it would appear that we have tricked the trickster.'

Adelko had to stop himself chuckling at that remark.

'You should not be so angry,' the Zarumani told Hari. 'If you have listened to half a word I have said, you will know that the witch-emperors of Kishai were in league with foul and dangerous powers. Their bourne is best avoided altogether.'

'I'll be the judge of that!' cried Hari. 'Do you have any idea what they'll do to me back in Ushalayim if I return empty-handed? If the Bethlers don't skin me alive, my rivals on the waterfront certainly will!'

'Oh, grow up,' snapped Horskram, losing his patience. 'Have you really not listened to a word that has been said? The Fallen One himself is bent on returning to cover all our heads in darkness, and you're worried about an assassin's knife.'

'You have been chosen to help,' said Tipu, favouring Hari with a beatific smile. 'It is a great honour that the Unseen bestow upon you.'

Hari was having none of it, however. 'Oh no,' he said, waggling a finger. 'I've heard enough of that kind of talk in my lifetime, I won't have it I tell you! I'll plead my case before the Sultan himself if I have to, but I'm staying out of this madness.'

'Interesting,' said Tipu. 'Where have you heard 'that kind of talk' before? I took you for a street thief who was raised in a brothel.'

'I am,' said Yassin. 'Ask anyone in the Mercadian Quarter, and they'll tell you just the same.' Adelko sensed the rogue's anxiety, skulking at the corners of his anger.

'Then why the strong reaction?' demanded Adelko. 'You act as if you'd spent half a lifetime being preached to by religious prophetic types.'

'Nonsense,' spluttered Hari, 'I just have a healthy aversion to prating talk of fighting the Fallen One – as any sensible person should. You've only to look about you to see what that kind of speech has done to these lands.' His words were well oiled, but Adelko's sixth sense picked up on the grating thoughts behind them.

'He's lying,' declared the journeyman.

'Of course he's lying,' muttered Azelin. 'Scurrilous rogues like him always do.' The apocalyptic discourse seemed to have moved him not at all, though he was clearly listening to every word.

'Why don't you tell us the truth, Yassin,' said Horskram, leaning forward. 'You know we're not after the Kishan treasure, now it's time you told us more about yourself, I think.'

'Pah,' Yassin snorted. 'I still don't know the half of what you're really up to. Why don't you tell me that first?'

Horskram glanced at the others and shrugged. 'Well, I did say just now the time for secrecy was past...'

The telling of the tale was a long one, and interrupted by their guards bringing them food. Adelko wolfed the delicious spread of dates, yoghurt, jasmine rice wrapped in palm leaves, cured lamb sausage and flat bread seasoned with cloves, washing it down with fruit juice that tasted like nectar from the Heavenly Halls.

At least they treat captives well, he thought gratefully.

Yassin clearly didn't share the journeyman's enthusiasm. He picked at his food and hardly ate, looking more and more sickly as Horskram proceeded with his tale, Tipu and the mysterious Zarumani interjecting occasionally to give their side of it.

'And this is what you drag me into?' Hari said, stunned, when the adept finally finished. 'Seven Princes, had I known, I would have taken my chances with the Bethlers and the Shirt Tails!'

'You already have taken your chances with the Bethlers – and lived to tell the tale,' Horskram reminded him. 'And it's the Seven Princes we're trying to stop, for Reus' sake. As for your gangland rivals...' Horskram made a dismissive gesture. 'I can't believe a rogue of your perspicacity would have pause before such riffraff, after everything you've faced.'

'I'm sorry... a rogue of my what?'

The old monk rolled his eyes. 'Palom's wounds, do you know your own language or not? Never mind that – you know our story now and that's what counts. Yes, we've tricked you, for the greater good I'm afraid. Now you know what we're about, it's up to you whether you continue to help us or not. I can't force you, though I will say we could probably use a man like you – much as it pains me to admit it.'

'We still don't know just what kind of man he really is,' interjected Azelin. 'A freebooter he may be, but there's more to him than that – as I believe he was on the point of telling us.'

'I am still here, you know,' said Hari petulantly. 'What is this "him" and "he" business?'

Azelin sneered. 'If you would be so kind as to tell us your story, master thief, we would be more than grateful.'

Hari grinned a lopsided grin. 'As it happens, I did have some... religious instruction in my youth, after fleeing the brothel my mother bore me in. Though, considering what I've been hearing, I think I will keep the details to myself for now.'

Everyone was looking at him askance now. Yassin appeared unruffled by their scrutiny. 'Of course it would be most pleasant to swap stories,' he went on, 'but if I am to be of service to you, I believe that a certain amount of... discretion as to my background will be of paramount importance. As a point in case, I might recall the Tale of the Scoundrel and the Three Wise Women, when Houdi the Lightfingered was better able to aid the hapless villagers of Nysore by concealing his true identity-'

Horskram waved him to silence impatiently. 'Have it your way, Hari Yassin, or whoever you may be. I can't compel you to tell us the truth of who you are, but at least my sixth sense is telling me you aren't dangerous to our cause, even if you are plainly lying.'

If Hari looked abashed at that, he hid it well. Tipu

merely frowned and shook his head, while Azelin sneered again.

'I think we're forgetting something more important right now, in any case,' said Adelko. 'We may have shared our story with Hari, but what about this Southron general holding us captive?'

Horskram nodded. 'When I said the time for secrecy was past, I meant it. We'll tell him everything.'

Adelko's jaw dropped. 'Everything? Are you sure, Master Horskram?'

'I'm not sure of anything, except that since this mess began to unravel I've been wrong as many times as I've been right. What good has keeping secrets done us so far? Why, it's blasted secrecy that's kept our mastermind concealed all this time.'

Adelko paused to reflect. His mentor was right. At least, this time he appeared to be.

Horskram turned to the Zarumani. The adept seemed more alert than he had been since Ushalayim, his mind working acutely again.

'One last thing,' he said. 'Just now you mentioned that you had an inkling about the ghouls... explain what you meant by that.'

The Zarumani's far-off look did not diminish as he replied: 'I told you fire-divining is not a precise art. The combination of Thaumaturgy and Scrying is an abstruse discipline to master, even for us. But the fires seemed to be saying that a warlock in the region might use sorcery to tap an ancient evil to send against you.'

'That would explain the sudden return of the ghoul pack,' said Tipu.

'And you are really set on seeking out this Abdel Sha'arza?' cried Hari. 'It's probably him that sent the ghouls to kill us!'

'I doubt that very much,' said the Zarumani. 'Though we do not countenance his left-hand ways and many in our sect would gladly see him cleansed by the fire, there is more to Sha'arza than you think. His mother was a priestess of our sect, abducted by his father Haziel, a notorious warlock and a scion of the Halpnese nobility. His position and his sorceries made him too powerful for us to oppose him, yet he was eventually banished from the sultanate of Halepo for his black crimes.'

Horskram nodded, exchanging knowing glances with Tipu. 'The rest of that tale is well known, I believe,' said the mystic. 'Haziel left with his young son and took up residence in the Watchtower of the Leviathan, after a months-long battle with the guardian demons bound to it by the Elder Wizards. After that he became only more powerful, passing on much of his learning to his son.'

'What happened to his mother?' asked Adelko.

The Zarumani's face darkened. 'No one knows for sure, and even the fires have been silent on the matter. More than a hundred years have passed since Haziel was banished from Halepo – some say she went with him and learned to love her tormentor, only to perish in Haziel's dark experiments as his mind became even more corrupted, others that she took her own life rather than live in bondage to a demonologist. For her memory alone do we tolerate her son, though many in my sect believe him to be an abomination nonetheless. But others, including me, believe that Abdel is not entirely corrupted, that the light of Mithras lives in him still, passed on to him by his mother. In that hope we must place some faith, that he will relinquish his seclusion and be persuaded to help us.'

Hari scoffed at that. 'Assuming it isn't *him* after these bloody fragments in the first place! If what you say is true, then Abdel has been alive for more than a century. I don't like to think what kind of methods he uses to preserve his immortality.'

'The fires have said nothing on that subject either,' rejoined the priest. 'Though the light of Mithras sometimes shines through a refracting lens.'

Through a glass darkly, thought Adelko, recalling the words of his own prophet.

'I do not doubt it is a risk,' allowed Horskram, 'for clearly Abdel is himself in league with dark powers, whatever the rumours say. Though he has never been known to covet such power as the reconstituted Headstone would command. If what you say of his background is true, it would explain why. In any case we have not found anything to link him to the plot to reunite the fragments.'

'What about his father?' asked Adelko. 'What happened to Haziel?'

The Zarumani shook his head. 'We do not know. He has been presumed dead for years, though for all we know he could still be alive, too. Any Necromancy the son knows for extending his lifespan would have been learned at the feet of the father.'

Horskram and Tipu made the sign of their respective faiths. Adelko was too wrapped up in his thoughts to follow suit.

We really are uniting against a common enemy. Palomedian, Sha'abatian, pagan... even some demonolators might not want to see the full powers of Gehenna unleashed. The thought gave him a strange comfort.

Just then the tent flap was thrown aside. In walked Zimri, flanked by his two lieutenants. Behind him a waning sun cast feeble rays inside; they had talked the whole afternoon away.

'I trust you have been well victualled and are sufficiently rested,' said the general. 'Now, are you ready to tell me the truth, or must I send you before the Sultan's justice?'

Horskram cleared his throat. 'We would fain break clean words with you, General Zimri, but alone if possible...' The old monk flicked a sidelong glance at Adelko that was almost awkward. Horskram just couldn't give up entirely on his old habits of secrecy.

Zimri's face was stern as he replied: 'These are my sword-kin, sworn to me since my youth to share blood and salt with me. Countless leagues have we journeyed together, and only we three remain of the two-score who set out from the Port of Lago many seasons ago. I will grant you a private audience as you wish, but what I hear they hear. Understood?'

Horskram nodded. 'Very well,' he said, 'but I would urge you to keep what you are about to learn to yourselves. Whatever you decide to do with us afterwards, this information must not be divulged freely. I am trusting your judgement in this.'

Zimri frowned. 'I did not think yours could be an ordinary tale of freebooting,' he said. 'Truly Ashanti's purpose shapes our ends, howsoever we may think the work is ours alone.' He made the sign of the Faith. 'Very well, come now! Let us away to my pavilion, I will hear your story in full whilst the earth cradles the sun in her arms.'

Zimri sat pondering long and hard after Horskram had finished his tale. If the adept was exhausted by having to tell it twice in a row, he showed no signs of it: his rhetorical flourishes had been as lively as ever. Surely the old monk would have been a troubadour if he'd been base born, and not chosen by the Almighty to live poesy rather than recite it.

'Well now,' said the Southron at length. 'That is *quite* a story. If it were not corroborated by a Sufieli and Zarumani both, I would scarcely believe it.'

Soldiers had been and gone, bringing them more food and stopping to light hanging oil lamps and tiny braziers filled with incense. The playful patterns created by the ornate lattice-work of the former combined with the heady fragrance of the latter to create a relaxed atmosphere. They had been in Zimri's pavilion for more than two hours, but silken bean bags made for comfortable reclining and brightly coloured rugs kept the cold rocky floor at bay. The low darkwood tables on which their food was served were inlaid with filigreed copper metalwork, featuring the archetypal serpent motifs of the Faith.

And this is just a soldiers' camp – I wonder what the Sultan's palace looks like.

'My story is quite true, every word of it,' Horskram was assuring the general, looking to the Zarumani and Tipu for agreement.

'My sect would not make common cause with antagonists of the Faith unless the emergency were dire,' put in Tipu. 'You have respect enough for us Sufielis not to doubt that much at least.'

Zimri nodded slowly. 'The Suman tribe from which I hail has ever cleaved to the Faith, and the Scions of Suf are renowned for their learning and wisdom,' he said. 'The Argolians I have heard of during my time in these lands, and they share your reputation. As for the cult of Mithras' – he spared a wry glance for the stoical orange-robed priest – 'I cannot say I trust pagan idolators, but the fact that your tales concord with one another's speaks volumes.' Horskram seemed about to say something more, but Zimri cut him off. 'However, your mission to consult a black-hearted warlock like Abdel Sha'arza smacks of folly to me. Do you not know that his enchanted fortress is guarded by a vast stone serpent? They say the monster uncoils from the base of his tower and devours all who dare approach it.'

'Not for nothing is it called the Watchtower of the Leviathan,' said Horskram dryly.

You certainly didn't mention that part, Master Horskram, thought Adelko. But the revelation hardly surprised him – after all he'd been through, he hardly expected the most powerful wizard in Near Sassania not to be powerfully protected. One of Zimri's lieutenants, the dour-looking one, leaned in and muttered something. He spoke in a singsong staccato tongue that Adelko did not recognise. Nor did any of the others, judging by their blank looks.

Zimri turned back to them. 'Kufa Sumanhiri says that Urovians are crude white-faced infidels, unclean in spirit and body. He says I should stake the three of you in the wilderness, and leave you for the carrion and the ghouls to feast upon. What say you to that?'

Adelko's sixth sense had moved up a notch, though it told him Zimri was unlikely to follow through on that suggestion. The other lieutenant, the one that often smiled, was looking at his compatriot with frowning disapproval.

Horskram was unfazed. 'I think your lieutenant has good reason to distrust Urovians, given the bloody rapine they have visited on these lands. But I can assure you we have nothing to do with the crusade – as you know, one of its chief architects is after us as well. As for our uncleanness of body, I can only say that bathing is not a custom among our people. At least yon incense should help alleviate the discomfort our presence causes you.'

A second of awkward silence. Then Zimri started laughing, along with his happy-go-lucky lieutenant. Kufa kept the scowl carved into his totemic features, but Adelko felt his sixth sense drop off. For now at least, they appeared to be in safe hands.

'Come!' said Zimri, rising. 'The night grows old, and we have dallied over long. The Wytching Time draws near, and we are accustomed to keeping the spirits from Beyond the

Veil at bay, with music and fire and laughter! You shall join us, as honoured guests. Tomorrow I shall decide what to do with you.'

The Southron ushered them back outside the tent. The starlit night was clear, the jewelled patina of the skies canvassing the earth gently, bringing no fierce winds to augment the chill. The *fariz* were gathered around a bonfire in the middle of the camp. Some were oiling and sharpening scimitars, others were bare-chested and scrubbing themselves with sand from kegs. Several had broken out exotic-looking wind and stringed instruments and were preparing to play.

Looking at them, Adelko recalled his childhood days in Narvik, listening to Ludo Sharpears and his brothers playing on feast-days. Ludo who had married Albhra Widehips the busybody, whom he would probably never hear again, whose simple way of life had once been his as well: a way of life he was fighting to preserve along with all others, if Horskram and Hannequin and the loremasters and prophets told it true.

He half expected to feel a pang of homesickness then, but no pangs came. Hearth and home had never been for him; like it or not he was a hero of sorts now. He saw clearly what Horskram had been trying to tell him all along: heroes tainted their souls in striving to make the world a better place. An ordinary man like his dead father Arun or brother Arik might live their whole lives and never change a thing, never so much as hurt a man; but a hero changed everything and killed thousands. The thought did not trouble him: instead Adelko felt a calm certitude that this had always been intended, whether by the Unseen or some other force, he couldn't rightly say.

As the Nazharyans struck up a tune that sounded halfway between ditty and dirge, and Tipu joined them on his flute and the Southrons came in with powerful baritones, Adelko shut his eyes and let the music seep into him. He had prayed for a dark miracle all his childhood, and it had been granted.

In his mind's eye he saw St Ionus, smiling down at him from the refectory wall in Ulfang.

Presently the music died down to a low murmur. The Nazharyans still seemed lively despite the late hour, chatting and laughing as they brewed the delicious coffee drink in small brass pans and chewed strange-looking orange nuts from leathern bags that they passed around. Zimri had broken off from his singing and took a nut for himself, biting into it gratefully. Adelko could see in the light of the fire that his teeth were a faint orange colour, too.

'*Ketel* nuts,' he grinned, catching the journeyman's stare. 'We often use them on the road to war. They are a stimulant to sharpen the mind and bestow energy – far better for a soldier than unruly wine!' He passed the sack to Adelko, who took a nut from it. Biting into it, he grimaced: the taste was bitter in his mouth.

Zimri laughed at his expression. 'You must chew it, and ignore the taste. I hear the rye beer that you jhufa'ars drink is an acquired taste, yes? Well this is no different!' He was speaking Decorlangue again: though he was technically their captor, the Southron showed the perfect manners of the gracious host. This close Adelko could see him to be a sleek, well-made fellow. His proud strong features were unlike those of any other man he'd seen, barring the hapless gladiator he'd witnessed in the pits. At Rima he'd glanced through Cuthbert's *Compendium of Lands Ancient and Far Flung*: the Arid Kingdoms were referred to as rich realms of fable, lying beyond the vast Zhosa Desert on the southern borders of Sendhé, its men and women said to be tall and dark of skin just like Zimri. Beyond that, the journeyman had a feeling he'd seen or heard of such people elsewhere, besides Sha'iza'ar. But where exactly? That question still perplexed him.

Zimri was eyeing him keenly in the light. 'You are a thoughtful young man, Adelko of Narvik,' he said, chewing on the rest of his *ketel* nut. 'What thoughts preoccupy you so, I wonder?'

'You speak our language well,' Adelko said. 'How does someone from so far away come to know the High Speech of Old Thalamy?'

A sad smile creased Zimri's broad lips, though his dark eyes burned with a lustre that seemed stronger than the flames reflected in them.

'My tale is a chequered one,' he began, taking another nut from the bag as Adelko passed it back. 'As I mentioned before, I was born to the Suman tribe in Kushia.' Passing on the bag and popping the nut whole into his mouth, he drew a curved dagger from his belt and began drawing a crude map in the dirt. 'My homeland is a mountainous region, well defended by the Copper Hills to the east, the Zhosa Desert to the north, and the Jungles of Ridwo to the south. To the west lies the Sea of Saraje – my people were converted to the Faith many generations ago by missionaries from Nazharya, who sailed down the Malabar Coast and made contact with us at our great trading port of Lago. We have long been a prosperous nation, well defended and benefiting from our mines of silver and gold and salt, and our coastal position that allows us to trade up and down the Saraje. I was born to a higher branch of the Suman tribe, for my father – may his name forever be exalted among the ancestors! – was one of the ruling Council of Princes that governed the realm. But originally it was my intention to follow in my uncle's footsteps and become an *ulama*, a priest of Ashanti, whom we call Uru, and a scholar of the teachings of his prophet Sha'abat.' Zimri paused to make the sign and Tipu nodded approvingly. Horskram's expression remained stoical, but he was listening. Anupe and Yassin had engaged in a game of dice with some of the *fariz*, while Azelin took himself a little way apart, squatting indifferently on the hard ground.

Zimri went on with his tale. 'So when I had seen but twelve rains, my father sent me to Djenna, the great City of Sages on the southern borders of the kingdom.' Zimri paused again and raised his eyes to the heavens, a beatific smile on his mahogany face. 'What shall I tell you of such a place? Its mud-brick temples are the size of many elephants, the shelves of its great library crammed with scrolls and tomes such as would take your breath away, learned as you are, Adelko of Narvik! Its caravanserai stretch for miles, for Djenna lies at a great confluence of roads, and its horse and camel markets are near as legendary as its temples and libraries. Four years I spent there, happily, learning at the feet of the greatest sages in the Arid Kingdoms.'

His face darkened again.

'So what went wrong?' Adelko knew by now when to spot an unfortunate twist to a tale.

The Southron grimaced. 'Our neighbour to the east and south is what went wrong, Adelko of Narvik.' He tapped his crude sketch of the Copper Hills reproachfully with the dagger. 'The ruling tribe of Ghanji and the empire they named after themselves has ever coveted our wealth. The hinterland provinces of the Arid Kingdoms that they rule cannot easily be counted, but always we had resisted them, denying them access to the sea. But in the time of Dyabe the Thrice-Cursed, their ambition waxed great and terrible again. The new Ghanji Emperor made pacts with the Copper Men, a race of pygmies who dwell in caves beneath the mountains and have long practised sorcery. And through them, his wazir Sani learned much that he should not have, becoming a storm wizard of great power. Through his control of the elements, he was able to move men through the Mungor Passes that we have always guarded, and thus began the invasion of my kingdom. I was recalled from my studies, and put aside the scroll, for sword and spear and bow. I had always excelled at athletic games in my youth, and took to my new martial calling well – yet I learned to despise my fate, for bloody slaughter of my own kind has never been my delight.'

He sighed and put the dagger back in its sheath, as if for emphasis. Out of the corner of his eye Adelko caught Sir Azelin's expression hardening. His sixth sense told him the knight was deeply troubled. It also told him Horskram struggled with his own conscience. Something about this exotic warrior had them all examining their hearts; as if by telling his own story he could draw theirs out into the open, too. Adelko exchanged meaningful glances with Tipu as Zimri went on.

'For years I led the Royal Maroon Cavalry to one victory after another. It took us seven years of bloody war, but at last we looked set to reclaim Kushia for our own, and recover what we had lost. But we reckoned without the powers of the wazir Sani, and the Three-Headed Serpent Goddess Wagada-Kali, a demoness of great power whom he had petitioned in his black sanctuary, aye and my cousin Zumu's even blacker betrayal!' Zimri paused to spit into the fire. 'For Zumu had come to covet not only our kingdom for himself, but the powers that Sani commanded. And so he treated with him, at first openly, pretending to sue for peace – but later we learned that secretly he had made pact with the Ghanjis. And when our guard was down, he led them via secret tunnels up to our capital of Mera, which is built upon a great plateau high in the plains, in the midst of our kingdom, impregnable to all who know not the route.

'They came upon us in the dead of night, and Mera's even-stoned ziggurats and pyramids they defiled with slaughter in their treachery, slaying all our nobility and many of our greatest warriors. I and less than half a hundred of my maroons escaped to Lago, whence we took barq to far-off Ulam, a mighty cityport on the western shores of Sendhé. But we would not stop there long, for it is an evil place, redolent of the very sorceries that corrupted my cousin. And so in time we came to Nazharya, and took indentured service for seven years as *amluqs* in the Sultan's army, serving as his shock troops as he consolidated his grip on power here. And well have I served, and well has the Sultan rewarded me! For Muqmurlish is more honourable and wiser than other men, and carries the blood of the Enlightened Ones in his veins. His Majesty has favoured my suit, and once he has crushed the infidels to the north, he will send me back to Kushia at the head of an army.' His eyes grew hard as diamonds. 'And then there shall be a reckoning, and my cousin Zumu who rules falsely as a puppet of the Ghanjis shall be overthrown, and the Faith shall be restored to my kingdom, the pagan idolators cast back across the mountains to where they belong! And then, Adelko of Narvik, and not before, I shall put aside the sword forever.'

Zimri made the sign again, casting his eyes to the jewelled heavens and falling silent. Behind them, Yassin yelled triumphantly as he won another round of dice.

'Good luck with that,' put in Azelin. 'You might find putting aside the sword more difficult than you'd bargained for. The taste of blood lingers on the tongue – try as we might to deny it, there is a sweetness to it that allures.'

Zimri became stern again as he turned to look at the disgraced warrior-monk. 'And what is your tale, Knight of the Bethel? How came you to be imprisoned in the pits?'

'I told you already, I deserted,' replied Azelin, affecting a bored tone that could not hide his sorrow. 'I tired of shedding blood for the vain and the rich. The Pilgrim Kingdoms are just another commercial colony, the Creed has nothing to do with any of it.'

Zimri smiled a thin smile. 'You will get no disagreement from me there, crusader. But tell me, for all your change of heart, why I should not have you clapped in irons and taken before the Sultan?'

Azelin shrugged. 'Do so if you wish. The Sultan is an honourable man, as you say, and respects gallantry in the field. He'll permit my family to ransom me.'

'I doubt that very much,' said Zimri. 'The Sultan is indeed honourable, deserters are not. Your kin dwell far away, and you have made some very powerful enemies amongst your own kind.'

Azelin shrugged again, seeming to lose interest in arguing his case. 'Think you that I lost my honour when I forsook my blood vows? I lost it long before then.'

'I too transgressed against the teachings of Palom, even as I made war in his name,' said Horskram. 'It isn't too late to turn aside from your iniquitous path.'

'And do what?' spat Azelin. 'Take holy orders, as you've done? You know what the inscription on my blade means, don't you? *Know Thyself*, as in: "When the powerful teacheth thy hands to make war, thou shalt know thyself for a wicked man or a righteous". Our very own prophet's words, may his peace be upon us all! Well I got to know myself, all right – and every man, woman and child I slaughtered in the name of the Almighty could tell you just what kind of man I am.' Getting up, he stepped over and kicked Zimri's crude map back into the dust. 'I don't care a fig for your homeland or its troubles, and I don't care what you do with me,' he told the general. 'I swore another oath, to see this lot safely to the Abydos ranges, but if I don't get to keep that one either, what of it? In truth it makes no difference.' His eyes looked haunted as he raised them to the cold skies. 'There's only one place I'm heading, and it isn't up there. What matter then what route I take?' Without another word, he stalked away towards their tent and out of the light.

'He carries a heavy burden and a terrible,' said Zimri, shaking his head. 'And yet methinks there is some virtue left in the man, somewhere.'

'If you would but give him leave to go with us, I think he may have chance to rediscover it,' said Horskram. 'Not for nothing did the Almighty put him in our path. He is one of Palom's tools gone awry – this is his chance to be put to good use.'

Zimri fixed Horskram with a sly look. 'And what makes you think I have decided to let you go, Horskram of Vilno?'

Horskram returned the stare. 'General Zimri, you yourself are a man of faith. I think you learned much in your years at Djenna, for legends of that great desert city of scholars we have heard. You know better than most what our mission portends, what the world stands to lose if we should fail. We cannot allow Ma'amun's wizardry to resurface in the world, it would be a calamity to eclipse a hundred crusades!'

And that was when it all came flooding back to Adelko. He *had* seen men like Zimri before, and not just in the fighting pits at Sha'iza'ar.

'The friezes in the Warlock's Crown! The men in them looked just like you, General Zimri.'

The *fariz* commander turned dark eyes on him, and for a moment Adelko feared he had misspoken. But then the Southron nodded, as though mulling something over. 'In Djenna, I remember holding discourse with one of the elder sages,' he said. 'For thousands of years, *djalis* have sung tales of the Juju Princes, exiled long ago from the Arid Kingdoms for using blood magicks. The legend has it that the Juju Princes journeyed far to the north, settling in a land beyond Sendhé, from where their powers waxed ever greater, so that in time of the Great Reaping, Uru Almighty punished their descendants, poisoning the seas and blasting the lands about them. And though we in the Far South were spared the worst of that cataclysm, yet we were affected too, for the Copper Men and goblin tribes were spawned of that curse, and other worse evils such as we are forced to practise juju ourselves to ward against.'

'But that doesn't make sense,' protested Adelko. 'According to our legends, the Varyans were taught magic by the Unseen *after* they settled on the Forbidden Isle. And our version says they only became corrupted later on, when Ma'amun was taught the Left Hand Way by Abaddon.'

Zimri frowned. 'I can only tell you the version of the myth that was given to me,' he said. 'But as the great lore-master Alziel Mustar of Imanabad once told me, there are many routes to the same truth.'

'How is Alziel?' asked Tipu, who had sat listening serenely throughout. 'It has been a while since I spoke with him, but then our sect is seldom welcome in the Sultan's capital nowadays.' He sighed.

That remark caught Adelko's attention. 'You as well? Our Order has problems back home, too.'

'The priesthood of the Faith is not so rigidly organised as that of the Creed,' explained Tipu, 'but even so the *ulamas* have much influence in the cities. Though we agree with many Orthodox interpretations of scripture, we also believe that the teachings of Sha'abat must be lived and intuited, and cannot simply be learned in theory. We derive our powers from this very embodiment. We are not considered heretics like the Unorthodoxers in Halepo and Murad, yet still...' His voice trailed off uncertainly.

'You are envied much as we are,' Horskram finished for him. 'Sufielis and Argolians have long made common cause and exchanged learning, though as you rightly say the experience of the Unseen must be just that, something learned empirically in the body and soul. Not for nothing are we aligned.'

Adelko's sixth sense flickered just a little. He knew well when his mentor was trying to manipulate someone.

'General Zimri, surely you have heard enough to persuade you that this is no ordinary alliance of men?' pressed Horskram. 'You have to let us go! Can't you see this is the Almighty's will?'

Zimri ran graceful fingers across his neatly trimmed beard as he considered. Then he nodded, as if acknowledging a self-evident truth. 'Very well,' he said. 'Tomorrow we shall strike camp, and I will escort you to the borders of the sultanate. Fresh horses you shall have from our remounts – and may Uru grant that you repay my generosity with success on your quest! But know that it is a dangerous thing you do, to seek the confidence of a sorcerer as powerful as Abdel Sha'arza.'

'We'll just have to take our chances,' said Horskram. 'This isn't the first time our duty has required us to do unsavoury things. I'd appreciate it if you'd let the Bethler come with us, too.'

Zimri frowned again, but nodded once more. 'I think right now he cares little for which way the wind blows him, so sure is he of final destination. Very well, Horskram of Vilno, you can have him, for I sense a higher purpose at work here.' The Southron clapped his hands together sharply with an air of finality. 'Now we rest, and tomorrow we ride.'

At his command the *fariz* rose to post watches and seek their bedrolls. The companions did likewise, all except the Zarumani priest, who remained silent and unmoving as he had throughout the night, eyes glazed over as they sought the mysteries of the flames.

Still he had not told them his name, yet Adelko fancied he knew more of the danger they rode to than any of them.

TO THE PLACE OF DOOM'S KEEPING

Wrackwulf's heart was oddly heavy as they left the Vale of Penhalain behind. They had sojourned there but a single night, yet already he had got used to the relative comforts of the enchanted fortress. At least Ariadha ap Madrix's servants had supplied them with a stout keg of mead to see them on their way. As they nudged their garrons deeper into the Farfahailan mountains, Wrackwulf found himself yearning for a taste of it. A thick mist filled the valleys and hollows as they followed the slender trail single file; it had a luminescence about it that seemed to turn it into a living thing, one that would have fain rubbed out all the lands about them and left the travellers floating forever in an endless fog...

Wrackwulf blinked spasmodically, inhaling deeply of the chilly air. This ensorcelled land was getting under his skin. He wondered if he would ever be quite normal after this expedition. Assuming he survived it, of course.

Ahead of him rode Sir Torgun. Small cheer of the young

knight's company could he expect: since his journey to the Valley of the Barrow Kings, the Northlending had become even more withdrawn. Once or twice Wrackwulf had awoken in the dead of night in the chamber they shared at Nuallán, to find him looking from the silver fragment to the Circifix of St Argo, mouthing silent words.

Wyrds and destinies were all well and good, but the last thing the freelancer needed was his one sure ally losing sight of the present. They'd not spoken a word about Joram, yet to Wrackwulf's mind the Argolian remained highly suspect. Throwing a glance over his shoulder that he hoped appeared nonchalant, all he saw was the monk's cowled face half in shadow. His dark grey habit looked almost black in the gloom; since they had left Penhalain first thing that morning, the weather had gradually resumed its typical character.

The freelancer cast his eyes to the cloud-blotched skies. The Unseen were living up to their age-old name: not a hint of anything did the archangels care to bestow upon them.

You might just give us half a clue, thought Wrackwulf resentfully. *After all, it's your work we're supposedly about.*

At the front of their column rode Ariadha; behind her went Ianna and Fanwyn. Besides Morcant they were the only islanders still with them: Ariadha's retainers feared to tread this far north. The trio had maintained their steadfast silence, all but ignoring them at table in Nuallán and leaving them to pick at a coarse evening meal of unseasoned pork, wild leaves, roots, berries and fungi. Wrackwulf had been on the point of breaking the silence, and not in a courteous way, but Torgun had shot him a warning glance and he'd reluctantly held his peace.

All in all, the miserable islanders were the most unfriendly folk he'd ever met. *They make the Pangonians look welcoming and the Thalamians seem cheerful,* he thought ruefully.

At noon they paused by a brook to water their horses and take some refreshment. Wrackwulf joined Morcant as he was washing his utensils.

'So where are we headed next?' he asked. 'Our guides don't tell us much.'

'To Lake Eidhannach,' replied Morcant. 'Where sits the lost city of Taras Cerawn, our age-old capital. Pass through it we must, if we are to gain access to the Place of Doom's Keeping. The High City of the Moon is the only way through the mountains, and only the Heir of Doom's Keeping can speak the words that will permit us entry.' The excitement in his voice was palpable. 'Many years have I longed to look upon it, for few of our folk travel this far north nowadays. A grand sight still it is, they say.'

'I don't suppose it's haunted?' Wrackwulf asked. 'I hope not, I've had enough of such things.'

'Never fear, sir knight,' said Morcant. 'Protected by its ancient sorceries is the High City, it will not corrupt for even now the Moon Goddess watches over it.' Again the sadness returned to him as he added: 'Tis for that very reason none may set foot in it, except in direst emergency such as this. We were found wanting, and now our brightest jewel is kept from us by Her who bequeathed it.' He stood and made to go back over to his garron. The others were already saddling up and preparing to rejoin the trail.

'Wait.' Wrackwulf caught the mage by the arm. 'What about... him?' He nodded over to where Joram stood with his back to them, tightening the girth on his saddle.

Morcant only shrugged. 'What more can I tell you, sir knight?' he asked rhetorically. 'I have said all I can say. In spite of everything, attuned to him I feel. A bond we share, whether I like it or not.' His eyes became fearful again. 'Best not to speak of it further just now.'

Without another word, the warlock went over to his own garron. Wrackwulf glanced from him to Joram to Torgun, but the Northlending was his usual brooding self, lost in his own thoughts.

Cursing inwardly, the freelancer went to see about his own horse. The three islanders were already mounted, waiting for them impatiently with stony stares.

Well Wrackwulf, old boy, it looks as though you're on your own.

The Farfahailans gradually increased in stature, like giants of rock and sedge slowly awakening from long torpor, their forms growing ever higher and sharper as the trail steadily unfurled its way into the heart of the island. The weather became even worse. On the afternoon of their second day out of Nuallán they were drenched by a tide of sleet, and Ariadha was forced to shelter them in a cave half a mile off the trail. That night they stopped at a huddled community of crofters, if half a dozen huts clinging desperately to the side of a mountain could be called a community. The seven of them crammed into the biggest one, as kilted clansmen and their wives broke out a mean repast of porridge and hard chewy bread. Not one of their hosts spoke, not even to their countrymen, choosing instead to defer silently to their visiting liege with food and lodgings. For her part, Ariadha ap Madrix remained taciturn, gazing into the firepit. Her eyes seemed to look upon something unpleasant that is faraway, yet still too close for comfort.

Later that night, a storm woke Wrackwulf. Above the sound of rain thrumming on the hut's flint roof, he caught the sound of whispered prayers. He turned, half expecting to see Joram, but saw Sir Torgun, clutching his precious relic and mumbling feverishly as he lay on his pallet. Looking around for the adept, Wrackwulf saw his pallet was empty.

It was then he noticed the door was ajar.

Stepping over to it, he edged it open. Joram was standing outside, his eyes turned to the roiling heavens. Another flash of lightning torched the skies; by its light Wrackwulf saw the moon, only it was a different colour now, tinged a golden red.

'What in the Known World is that?' he breathed, forgetting himself.

Joram did not start, though the freelancer was directly behind him. The monk answered without looking around. 'The Red Moon is what you look upon, illumined by the spheres beyond that make music eternal, the vibrations of which move the very firmament. All the signs are propitious.'

Wrackwulf gazed at him. He already knew the monk was odd, but now he was practically babbling. 'What nonsense are you speaking, Master Joram?'

He half expected an irritable rebuke, but none came. Joram just kept staring up at the lambent moon, still vivid even though the lightning had subsided. 'The skies shall be lit with colours no star can boast, as the spheres descend to those that have hearkened unto them. By their light a new darkness shall be exposed. All shall face a choice, to live or die by for eternity.'

The monk's voice almost trembled as he intoned the words. Wrackwulf wished one of the others were awake. Surely Morcant would make better sense of this than he could.

'Hardly the time for scripture,' said the knight, at a loss for anything else to say.

'Not scripture,' corrected Joram. 'Twas the Farseers of Norn who uttered those words, in the Frozen Wastes before the Creed was even born. Time is growing short.' At last the monk turned, making to go back indoors. 'We must rest. We'll need all our strength for the coming trial.'

Wrackwulf barred his way. 'You speak in riddles as oft as not,' he growled. 'I've come this far with you, now I'd have an answer to my questions.'

Joram peered at him from under his cowl, his half-shadowed face inscrutable. 'What questions do you have that I could possibly answer?' he asked.

Wrackwulf opened his mouth to speak, but nothing came out. Instead he just stood there, feeling keenly the foolish expression on his face as he stared at the monk.

At last some words came. 'I just don't understand what it is we are doing up here,' he faltered. 'One minute it seems as if we've simply come to warn these folk, the next it feels as though we're here for a more... ambitious reason.'

The monk's lips curled in a rare smile. His eyes remained lost in the shadow of his hood.

'I thought I had made this matter clear already,' he said. 'We are here to share information with the islanders. To inspect, and act where necessary. That is all you need to know, sir knight. If our plans should change, I will tell you.'

'And who says you're in charge? When your Grand Master despatched us, he said we were to reconnoitre with you – as an adviser.'

Joram laughed a hollow laugh at that.

'Then who *is* in charge, pray tell? Yon pagan sorcerer? Or perhaps it's your doom-laden Northlending companion, who scarcely seems to notice where he is half the time? Or is it you, the jumped-up freesword, that should lead us? The Grand Master does not act out of whimsy, Sir Wrackwulf – he sent you to me precisely so this mission would have a professional in charge of it! Or forgive me, are such eldritch matters as these no longer in Argolian remit? If you have such little faith in our acumen, why take up with us in the first place? For the coin? In that case, look to the things of this world, as is your wont – and leave me to worry about things of the other!'

One question after another, hurled at the freelancer like javelins. He had no answers for them.

'Is that settled?' snapped Joram, making to enter the hut again. 'Excellent. Now, if you'll excuse me...'

Glaring at the monk darkly, Wrackwulf stood aside to let him pass. When he was gone, the knight gazed back up at the skies, expecting to see the Red Moon again, but it had vanished behind the squalling clouds. Suppressing a shiver, he followed Joram back inside.

Ariadha had them up just before sunrise for a snatched breakfast of stale oatcakes and sour-tasting curds and whey, before harrying them all back into the saddle. The trail took them ever higher up into the mountains; far away to the east Wrackwulf could just make out the slender thread of a river. Up here the air was fresh and brisk; towards late morning the sun even managed to struggle free of its prison of cloud. Inhaling deeply, Wrackwulf at last began to enjoy the journey. The path bent around to the north-west underneath a knuckled overhanging of craggy rock; when they emerged from its shadow back into the light, the freelancer's jaw dropped at the new vista spread before him.

Directly below the path, the mountain ranges dropped steeply before rising sharply up again miles to the north, creating a deep valley with sheer sides. In the midst of this was a sparkling lake roughly the shape of a sickle moon. Studying it, Wrackwulf could see its surface glittered with hoarfrost. In the middle of the lake, just south of the river that fed it, stood a shining city of silver. Squinting against the bright light, he could make out soaring pinnacles and lofty towers; but where there should have been stone there was naught but metal, glistering in the noon sun.

'Taras Cerawn, I presume – you did not speak in jest,' he said to Morcant. Perhaps more out of a sense of civic pride than a need to rest, Ariadha had called a halt, allowing them to take in the spectacle.

Wrackwulf continued to squint at the silver city. 'Why not just go around it?' he asked.

'Look beyond the city, sir knight,' said the mage, pointing with a pudgy finger. 'The river that feeds the lake will suffer no fellow travellers on its course.'

Following his finger, Wrackwulf saw it was true: the mountain ranges rose steep and sheer to either side of the river. No fortress of men he had visited could boast walls half so high.

'And how does entering the city change that situation?' He had a sinking feeling he already knew the answer to that question, as Morcant grinned at him.

'The High City of the Moon obeys not the dictates of nature,' said the warlock. 'It is the only route through... assuming its custodians consent to let us pass.' He was about to say more when Ianna approached them.

'Go now down we must,' said the high priestess in her halting Decorlangue. 'Make camp for night by lake if move quickly we do.'

They resumed their journey. The trail that hugged the mountainside began to descend, bending and looping on its helter-skelter route down to the shores of Eidhannach. It took them the rest of the day, but by nightfall they had reached the southern fringes of the frozen lake. The dying sun revealed its colours, iridescent pinks and purples that nearly eclipsed the beauty of the city it supported. The tallest spires of Taras Cerawn could still be seen, glinting in the weakening light.

'Is that thing held up by naught but ice?' asked Wrackwulf.

'Tis said the lake has been frozen over since the Old Time,' replied Morcant. 'Children and animal spirits used to dance and play upon it, while the High Kings of old made merry and sported within the city walls. Yet even then the sun did shine, and the trees for leagues about were ripe with the Moon Goddess's bounty.'

Wrackwulf sniffed. 'Winter and summer at once? Moon gods bringing out the sun? Sounds passing strange to me.' The odd lone conifers scattered about the valley floor hardly conjured up images of plenty and prosperity.

Ariadha turned in the saddle and barked something over her shoulder, before urging her garron into a trot. Morcant sighed. 'We should hurry, she says, lest caught here at night we are.'

'What do you mean? I thought you said the city was safe.'

'It should be... provided the custodians take well to us,' replied Morcant. 'But Eidhannach itself is the denizen of frost wolves, or moon dogs as some call them. Find a cave and build a fire we must, to keep them at bay.'

'Moon dogs?'

'Told you before I did that in the Old Time we held discourse with the beasts of the earth, and they became more sophisticated as a result, just as we learned much of the natural order of things from them. When magick began to fade after the Wars of Kith and Kin, many of the spirits departed beyond the Veil and back to the Other Side. The

Animal Kings, half-castes born of beast and human, lingered as you have seen. But some animals there were, touched by the spirits, who remained changed forever. Such species are the frost wolves – part wolf, part elemental, they long to banish the cold from their bones. But they cannot, for fire is anaethema to them. So instead feed on flesh and blood they must, to warm themselves.'

'That doesn't sound so different to an ordinary wolf,' Wrackwulf pointed out.

'True, but 'tis said that when a frost wolf eats a man, he devours his soul as well, and so keeps the cold from his bones a little while. Moon dogs prize human prey above all else, for our refined souls remind them of the Old Time, when learned from one another we did. Of high intelligence they are, and long-lived: since the Second Age of Darkness have they roamed here. And rarely do they see mortalkind nowadays.' The mage's meaning was not lost on Wrackwulf, who found himself shivering for reasons besides the unseasonable cold.

'I think I see your point,' he said, urging his garron on.

Dusk had deepened into night by the time they found a cave large enough to shelter all of them and their garrons. Ariadha hastily chopped some branches from a nearby conifer and piled them in the middle of the cave; Ianna spoke a single word of power and these erupted into flame.

Her magick came not a moment too soon. The howling from off the lake had a strange timbre to it; he couldn't say for the life of him why, but to Wrackwulf it sounded metallic. Their garrons started to fidget and stir, but Fanwyn stepped over and muttered something, and they quieted.

'Horse-talking,' explained Morcant, catching the free-lancer's quizzical look. 'Much as I did with Scratcher.'

'I don't think I need know more,' said the knight. 'By the way, what ever did become of your... pet?'

A downcast look entered the mage's face. 'Ask him to come home with me I did,' he said. 'But he wouldn't have it. Said he would miss the forests of the mainland too much, so I let let him go. A long and fruitful association have Scratcher and I had, and I will not coerce a familiar.'

'I don't know why I even asked,' said Wrackwulf, shaking his head. 'You wizards are a strange lot, and no mistake.'

Morcant only smiled at that. 'From my point of view, a world without magick is the strangest thing of all.'

'Well, you're consistent in your beliefs – I'll give you that,' said Wrackwulf, turning to warm his hands at the fire. Magicked or no, the flames still brought comfort against the deathly chill of night.

The baying of the moon dogs intensified as they broke out rations and ate. Ariadha hacked off more branches from the conifer and tossed them on the fire, building it higher. She showed no signs of being afraid of the frost wolves, though her face looked taut as a bowstring in the shadowy light.

Ariadha felt as tense as she looked. She had enjoyed

returning home, but every step farther north only increased her sense of foreboding. The frost wolves didn't bother her – the flames would keep them at bay – but Joram still did. As for the two knights... the bushy-bearded fellow with the bent nose and broken teeth seemed affable enough, though she didn't care to talk to him, but the towering blond one with the huge frame had more the look of a Gygant than a man. And what had the Animal Kings wanted with him? Ianna had muttered something about an old prophecy, but refused to elaborate. Fanwyn had been just as tight-lipped, having hardly spoken since leaving Kell.

She knew the two of them were unhappy about the expedition, but the Druiding Council's vote was binding, and the three of them would be needed to get past the custodians of Taras Cerawn. The thought of that did nothing to allay her nerves; she had never been this far into her realm, and from what little she knew of the Guardians of the fragment, they were going to be even less happy about the intrusion than the keepers of Taras Cerawn.

She glanced at Ianna, who had come to warm her hands by the fire. The others were unrolling sleeping pallets towards the back of the cave, apart from Wrackwulf, who had lingered by the fire. He was ignorant of their tongue, so she decided to risk a conversation.

'You know I'm not happy about this either, Aspirant Ianna,' she said.

The high priestess sneered into the flames. 'You didn't give that impression at the All-Meet. Quite happy you seemed, to let strangers look upon that which it is your duty to guard.'

'And always guard it Clan Nuallán have!' she flared, getting a look from Wrackwulf. Moderating her tone, she continued: 'I'm not happy about it, but at the same time I recognise the need for alliances, aye even if they are with mainlanders. This is a calamity the like of which we've not faced in generations.'

The sneer did not leave Ianna's voice. 'Perhaps Connaer had the right of it, and you think yourself of druiding stock, to talk so.'

Ariadha kept her temper with some difficulty. The high priestess's haughtiness was maddening. 'I am no druid, but Ys is – and he it was who proposed we make common cause with the mainlanders.'

Ianna had nothing to say to that, but bit her lip fretfully as she contemplated the flames. Presently she spoke.

'There's a Red Moon,' she said, her voiced hushed. 'The first one in decades, and the first we've had in the spring cycle for centuries.'

Ariadha sighed impatiently. 'All right, Ianna, you've proved your point – I already said I'm no druid. Tell me what that means.'

The high priestess looked up from the fire and met her eyes. 'Our ancestors predicted a blood moon in time of spring would herald a new awakening, one of rapine and slaughter. Ys is wise, Ariadha, but he's not all-knowing – his judgement has slipped in this, I say.'

'So what, you're saying we shouldn't-'

Her words were interrupted by the renewed howling of the frost wolves. Twice as loud they were now. Fanwyn, who had stepped back over to the front of the cave to gaze out into the night, suddenly cried aloud and recoiled. 'The frost wolves! The Red Moon has them stirred! Ianna and Morcant – with me! We need to abjure them, fire alone won't keep them back now!'

Ariadha freed her spear from its sheath. It had a silver point, its hardwood shaft covered with embossed sigils from the Sorcerer's Script painted blue and gold; an eldritch heirloom from the Middle Time, when the druids had relearned the craft of their forebears and fashioned weapons using gramarye. It had been in her family for centuries, passed down from one lord to another. She'd only ever used it to hunt bear and boar in the wooded hills of Penhalain – Ariadha had managed to avoid war and skirmishing in her short reign, she had no taste for killing her own kind.

She stalked over to the front of the cave, hoping the glamours her ancestors had placed on the spear would work against the frost wolves. The mainland knight accompanied her, unsheathing his war axe. Ariadha still didn't like him over much, but she was glad of his strong right arm. The other knight had risen from his pallet and drawn his sword; together the three of them approached the cave mouth and peered out of it.

The moon had turned a gory crimson. By its light Ariadha could see the frost wolves: twice the size of an ordinary wolf, their blue-tinged fur had taken on a magenta hue. That wasn't the only effect of the Red Moon. As she watched in horror, their muscular forms warped and stretched, fur sprouting in ugly clumps and muzzles growing distended as a second row of fangs appeared behind the first. Their eyes were pitch black, and their tongues danced with flames that somehow seemed cold.

As one, the mutated wolves loped towards them, baying for blood and souls.

Ariadha caught the first one full in the chest as it crashed into her, driving the spear-point in up to the crossbar as she transfixed its heart. The beast's weight was still enough to bowl her back into the cave, where she landed hard on the rocky floor. The frost wolf's death throes wrenched the weapon from her hands, and a split second later another was on top of her. She could smell a bizarre combination of rain and burning as its serried jaws loomed large in her vision... The moon dog lurched to one side, Wrackwulf's axe buried deeply in its skull. Ariadha had no time to thank him, for just then another wolf leapt on his back, icicles melting off its slavering jaws as it bit into his light helm, which shattered as though turned to ice. The frost wolf howled as it caught a piece of helmet in the back of its throat; the knight wrestled free of it but had to drop his axe.

Desperately, Ariadha scrabbled for her spear, yanking it from the twitching wolf she'd killed. The blond knight was taking on a pair of moon dogs, his sword a blur as he sliced and hacked at the monsters. A third wolf already lay dying at his feet. There were many more, but they were skulking back now – why weren't they attacking?

The conjoined voices answered her question. She had heard her Westerling brothers and sisters use magick many a time, but straight away she knew there was something odd about this incantation. Turning she saw Joram and Morcant standing hand in hand, as they joined Ianna and Fanwyn with raised voices that sounded greater than the sum of their parts. The scarlet moon seemed to diminish then, to retreat and grow smaller and less vivid; as if responding, the frost wolves loped back out of range of the firelight. Ariadha could have sworn she saw the foremost regain their normal blueish tint before disappearing back into the darkness. A few moments later and they were gone altogether; not even their howling could be heard. Likewise the chanting died off. Her compatriots were gazing about them, bewildered expressions on their faces. But Joram simply stood stock still, gazing out into a night pregnant with horrors as though contemplating an ordinary pastoral scene. He didn't look in the least bit surprised by what had just happened.

Ariadha was distracted by a presence at her side. Looking up she saw Wrackwulf, standing wordlessly over her, proffering a helping hand. Grasping it, she allowed him to pull her up. Even if she didn't like the mainlander, he had probably just saved her life. That meant she could trust him – up to a point. Ariadha knew no word of mainland tongues; all she could do was meet his eye and nod her thanks. The knight seemed to comprehend, a smile cracking his ugly face as he nodded back.

'We should all get some rest now,' said Fanwyn, looking ashen-faced in the firelight. 'Abjuring the Red Moon is not something a druid has to do every day, and we'll need our strength for the journey tomorrow. Ariadha, if you would be so kind as to take first watch.'

The Marcher Lady of Clan Nuallán nodded sullenly. Though shaken she was unhurt, and the battle torrent still coursed through her veins: sleep would not come to her for a while. She settled down with her back to the fire and cradled the spear's runecrossed ashwood shaft in her hands, wondering what the morrow would bring.

They spent the next day crossing Lake Eidhannach on foot, drawing ever closer to Taras Cerawn. The windswept lake of ice was too treacherous for their garrons, which they had left in the cave. There they would be prey for the ice hounds, Sir Torgun knew, but what choice did they have? Despite his better instincts, he found himself gazing repeatedly at the ensorcelled city: ethereal and silvery, its dreaming spires seemed only half of this world. It appeared to be frosted over just like the lake, gigantic webs of ice shrouding its pinnacles and making it look like a giant's toy. He almost fancied he could feel the sword fragment vibrating empathetically, as though the same sorcery that had fashioned Søren's legendary blade had gone into making the city before them.

He didn't have time to pursue that thought further, for gazing up at its looming walls, he registered that they were within their shadow. Somehow he'd lost track of the time, he couldn't even say what hour it was. Directly before them stood two mighty portals, their lintels covered in arcane symbols that seemed to writhe and twirl maddeningly.

Ariadha motioned for the rest of them to stop, before approaching the gates with Ianna and Fanwyn flanking her. The Marcher Lady had fought well and bravely against the ice hounds, or whatever they were. In truth the encounter seemed faintly surreal to Torgun. Demons and draugar, witches and warlocks, had all tried to make an end of him... he'd faced worse than hellhounds in his time.

And would face far worse, before he was done.

Sir Torgun returned his eyes to the city as they stood and waited. Frozen in time, it gave nothing away; like the animal spirits of Nuallán, it seemed but a shadow of an age long past.

Like a dead hero's legend.

Imaginary butterflies that seemed all too real flittered through Ariadha's guts as they drew up to the city gates. She felt strangely light-headed. This close the gates put her in mind of her ancestral home: it could have been silver, or ice, or moonbeams that fashioned the vast doors barring their way, or all of those or none at all. Only where Nuallán was but a single fort belonging to the civilisation of the Old Time, Taras Cerawn had been its greatest city. She knew its magicks would be incomparably greater.

Ianna and Fanwyn were both looking at her expectantly. Taking a deep breath, Ariadha declaimed the words her father had taught her on his death bed:

Through sleep of centuries,
*   Evil lies dormant*
*   Until it awakes,*

To the Place of Doom's Keeping we go!

Through the long watch of years,
    The heirs of duty
    Help guard the marches,
    To the Place of Doom's Keeping we go!

At the final hour,
    The gods shall tremble
    As serpents uncoil,
    To the Place of Doom's Keeping we go!

The invocation had been set down by Caedmon seven hundred years ago, agreed with the custodians of Taras Cerawn. The words could only be spoken with effect by him and his heirs: not even druidkind could utter them and hope to gain ingress to the High City of the Moon.

They waited with baited breath. Nothing. And then... from behind a cloud, the Red Moon appeared. A single beam of crimson light shot from it, striking the portals dead centre and filling the gap between them. Without a sound, the gates opened inwards to reveal a shining cluster of buildings, a great thoroughfare leading through them. The ones nearest seemed to catch the rays of the Red Moon, which blended with their silvery surfaces to form a strange colour Ariadha could not begin to describe.

'The Farseers of Norn spoke true,' breathed Ianna.

'"When the High City of the Moon is stained with blood, the Hour of All's Ending shall draw near".'

Fanwyn looked at her disapprovingly. 'You would cite Northland prophecy, here and now?'

Ianna favoured him with a wry smile. 'Northlander and Westerling joined forces against the greater evil, during the Firedrake Wars, centuries after the Farseers lived and prophesied. Why should we not heed their words in darkest hour?'

Fanwyn frowned. 'Perhaps you are right, Aspirant Ianna.'

'Perhaps we shouldn't stand around debating theology,' said Ariadha, nodding towards the sparkling thoroughfare that beckoned them in. 'Heir of Doom's Keeping I may be, but I've no idea how long these doors will stand open at my behest. I've done my part – I hope you are both ready to do yours!'

Ianna turned her cold gaze on Ariadha. 'Rest assured, you will not find the Druiding Council slow to fulfil its obligations.'

'Of course I've no doubt of that,' returned Ariadha, just as coldly. *Not if it gives you another chance to take centre stage, you pompous slattern,* she added mentally.

Turning to the others, she motioned curtly for them to follow.

The spires looked even taller once they were among them, spiralling up to dizzying heights. Ariadha could see many walkways stretched from tower to tower, linking them to one another in criss-cross patterns and giving the city its look of being shrouded in a gigantic web. The spires themselves were of queerly alien form, whorled and twisted into shapes that were bizarrely elegant.

'It's nothing like the architecture of the Elder Wizards,' breathed Ianna, awestruck. 'Our ancestors built cities beautiful to mortal eyes.'

'And yet 'tis said by all our scholars that the Fays had a hand in their making,' Fanwyn reminded her. 'For what mortal could build such a city without help from beyond the Veil?' He frowned and shook his head. 'Our forebears stretched too far, Aspirant Ianna. Small wonder we were doomed to fall.'

'Is that what you teach the under-druids nowadays, Aspirant Fanwyn?' replied Ianna, the coldness returning to her voice. 'I had not realised you were given to such timidity of late.'

Fanwyn scowled at that, and was about to reply when they heard Joram chanting behind them.

Ianna rounded on him. 'Speak not the words of your benighted faith in this sacred place!' she cried. 'Would you anger the custodians before we've even met them?'

Joram broke off his litany with a sour sneer. 'I would first learn more of these custodians if I am to fear them,' he said. 'So far you've told us precious little about what to expect.'

Ianna gave a brittle laugh. It seemed to hang in the air: in here something strange happened to their voices, they had the same metallic quality as the howling of the frost hounds. 'I would have thought your monasteries would furnish you with ample knowledge on the matter,' said the high priestess, unfazed.

Her pointed remark silenced the surly monk. Beside him Morcant simply gazed at the vast webbed metropolis, his jaw hanging slack like a village idiot's. The two knights glanced about them shiftily, as though frightened to let their eyes linger anywhere.

The main thoroughfare took a meandering route that put Ariadha more in mind of a forest trail than a city street. The skies above seemed of the same mysterious colour as the buildings, and Ariadha could sense rather than see the Red Moon. She supposed it was evening now, but she had lost all track of time.

As such, she had no way of knowing how long they had been following the sparkling road when it terminated in a vast triangular courtyard. They had entered via the apex: its base was at the far side. Such a place might have been the site of a mighty keep or splendid palace, but all that stood at its midst was a fountain, albeit of gargantuan size. Ianna and Fanwyn took the lead now, advancing across the courtyard, which looked to be fashioned from a single colossal sheet of leaf-green crystal. Their boots disturbed a patina of hoar-frost, which seemed to rise up and become the lightest of mists as they followed the druids. All about them the whorled spires kept their eerie silence: so far they had not met a soul.

As they drew nearer to the fountain, Ariadha saw it was carved of white marble. At regular points about its rim rose twelve statues, of tall, impossibly beautiful men and women. The centrepiece was a swan fashioned of white gold; from its perfectly wrought beak a frozen spout of water arced, locked forever in the cold grip of long-departed aeons. The fountain's basin was filled to the brim with ice.

Ariadha found her eyes drawn to the swan's own, picked out with two sapphires, each of which would have filled a man's hand. Though apparently lifeless, there was a sadness in those gemlike eyes. Had the metallic fountainhead wept, she would not have been surprised.

'This is the spot,' said Ianna, as the rest of them drew level. 'It is here that we must petition the custodians.'

'And who are these custodians?' Joram repeated his question. 'Still you have not told us anything of them.'

'Hush!' admonished Fanwyn. 'You'll get the answer to that soon enough.'

As if on cue, the Red Moon appeared again. This time its beams were striated, one striking each of the statues. Ariadha felt her heart rise up into her mouth as they slowly came to life, cold colourless stone becoming warm flesh clad in elegant clothes of green and brown and yellow. Only now did Ariadha notice that each wore a crown of thistles. In petrified form they had faced inwards, but now all twelve turned to look at the interlopers with eyes that glowed a russet-red. Each one must have stood a full head taller than Torgun, though their limbs were in perfect proportion. They seemed even more beauteous than they had in statue form.

Ye gods, the old legends spoke true. Our ancestors really did wed Fays.

The Demi-Fays spoke as one, though their lips barely seemed to move:

. . .

We better brook the loss of ancient days
    Than such proud intrusion in latter time!
    Why dost thou tread within our sacred walls,
    Now barred to lesser men? For thou knowest
    The sins of thine ancestors, who defiled
    Moon Queen's holy ordinance; namely that
    The Left Hand Path eschewéd be, by all;
    Which Fada-Radharc broke of old, stirring
    Wars of Kith and Kin: and thus by his hand
    Were gates of moon's high city closed to all,
    We offspring of the Fays and kings of old
    Set here to guard, sometimes to guide, those few
    Whom fate sets on trammelled path anew.

Ianna and Fanwyn both knelt. Together they intoned:

O Demi-Fays, half of this world, half not!
    'Tis true we seek ingress through thy city,
    Not to despoil lost riches, but merely to
    Pass to Arat Ingor's innermost bourne
    And speak with doom's keepers, entrusted with
    Morwena's curse; so left-hand gramarye
    Might never be used again on our shores!
    Wise Caedmon's heir hath beseeched entry;
    Now true though lesser druids beg this boon
    In honest service to our mistress moon!

. . .

The half-faerie apparitions turned inwards again. No word passed between them, but Ariadha sensed they were communicating somehow. She spared a backwards glance for their companions... but they appeared to have traded places with the Demi-Fays, becoming as statues themselves.

Thus do we guard our secrets from outsiders, she thought. *I hope the Demi-Fays remember to turn you back, for your sakes.*

'What happens now?' she whispered to Ianna.

'How should I know?' the high priestess muttered. 'It's not as if I've done this before.'

'Hopefully this is just a formality,' put in Fanwyn. 'Our part we have upheld – an heir of Caedmon and two sitting members of the Druiding Council, one male, one female, beseech admittance. Those were the terms stipulated seven hundred years ago.'

'I'm supposing those terms said nothing about bringing outsiders with us,' Ariadha pointed out.

The two druids fell silent, while the Demi-Fays continued to debate their case wordlessly.

A low rumbling awoke Wrackwulf from his sleep. That was right... he'd fallen asleep, hadn't he? He scarcely had time to ponder that as he registered his surroundings. They were still in the bizarre triangular courtyard, standing before the fountain. Only something had changed, what was it? With a shock he realised the statues had gone.

That wasn't the only thing to have changed.

The ice within the basin had begun to crack; only then did Wrackwulf realise the rumbling was coming from deep beneath the crystalline floor, which was juddering frenetically. The ice exploded, shards melting as the Red Moon bathed them in its unearthly glow. A torrent of water surged upwards, the swan-like fountainhead cresting it as it spurted into the courtyard like a gigantic tidal wave. It was as if the entire lake below were rising up to claim the city.

He was distantly aware of Ianna yelling something. Morcant turned to them and translated at the top of his voice: 'The custodians have favoured our petition! Join hands we must, and stand fast for the swan!'

'This is favouring our petition!?' cried the freelancer. But he didn't hesitate to heed the mage's advice.

The water was surging up and up, filling the courtyard at an alarming speed. The fountain basin was entirely submerged now; Wrackwulf felt the waters lapping icily against his groin as they rose higher and higher. Somehow the seven of them managed to clasp hands: it was all they could do to avoid being bowled over, but they stood fast long enough to allow the swan to approach them. The fountainhead had been transformed into a longship of beaten gold, the swan's head and neck becoming its high white prow.

Desperately they clambered aboard. The water continued to gush upwards from the lake; its speed had gone from alarming to astonishing. With awe Wrackwulf registered that the city spires about them were half-submerged.

'What fell sorcery is this?' cried Joram. 'I had not expected-' But his words were drowned out by a roaring crash as the waters began to churn and froth, and for a while Wrackwulf almost fancied they were back on the Tyrnian Straits. The swan ship somehow stayed afloat as the waters, tainted crimson by the Red Moon, rose higher still, blotting out all sight of the city. Suddenly the vessel shot forwards, as though propelled by an invisible giant. It had no sails, and the seven of them clung on to the taffrail for dear life as it crested the scarlet tide at a sickening speed. The rumbling continued all the while, growing so loud that Wrackwulf thought he might pass out...

And then they were sailing up the river Eidhannach, the mountains that flanked its rushing waters towering on either side of them. Glancing back, Wrackwulf caught the lake behind them, its waters subsiding to reveal Taras Cerawn, unspoilt towers glimmering in the ghastly light of the Red Moon as though nothing had happened. Dropping his gaze to the river, he realised with a shock that they were moving against the flow, through white water rapids no earthly ship could have hoped to contend with.

'I begin to understand the strength of your defences,' he managed to gasp at Morcant. The mage just grinned weakly at him.

Snowflakes were falling along with the night by the time their magic boat beached them in a rocky pool at the bottom of a mighty waterfall that fed the river. No sooner had it done so than the entire waterfall and river abruptly froze over again.

'I will never understand the weather in this place,' growled Wrackwulf. 'Remind me, it's actually Growing Monath, yes? I didn't just fall asleep in some night-tripping faerie's arms and imagine winter's ending?'

Morcant grinned at him again. 'We don't celebrate Spring's Awakening in error, sir knight,' he said.

Wrackwulf did not appreciate the mage's jocularity. If anyone in the company was going to be jovial, it was him. And right now he felt anything but.

They had sailed (if you could call it that) through night and day, sleeping fitfully as the enchanted vessel took them into the highest part of the Farfahailans, penetrating deeper into the gorge as the wind rose to a stinging crescendo and skirled and tumbled about them. No settlements did they see, for not even the wretched islanders would be mad enough to try and live here. The vegetation gradually dropped away, leaving the odd gorse bush and evergreen to dot the slopes; the rest was a still silence of colour, naught but off-white.

Despite everything they had experienced at Taras Cerawn, not one of them had spoken during the journey.

'Marcher girl!' he yelled at Ariadha, trying to raise his spirits. 'It's getting dark. Any chance of another sojourn with some crofters? I'd so love to sample whatever piss it is they drink up here to while away their miserable lives.' Oblivious to his tongue, the Marcher Lady of Clan Nuallán ignored him. No one that could understand him laughed at his joke, but Wrackwulf was past caring.

Small chance of merriment in this godforsaken place, and I thought their lowlands were bad enough, thought Wrackwulf, gazing at the iron grey flecks that floated down and settled in his beard. *Even the snowflakes seem dull up here.* He turned his eyes to the frozen waterfall, strangely devoid of sound, feeling keenly the total absence of birdsong and other signs of life. A precarious trail snaked around the rim of the pool before disappearing behind the great wrinkled sheet of ice, which caught the expiring sun in myriad motes of scintillating light.

'What about the boat?' queried Wrackwulf, glancing at the vessel, which still gleamed brightly despite the late hour. 'I don't fancy trying the return trip without it.'

'Remain here it will for our return,' Morcant assured him. 'The half-faerie kings have guaranteed our passage back.'

They scrambled single file along the trail, passing beyond the waterfall into a large cavernous space: a womb of rock that beckoned them deeper in. Ariadha paused to light a torch.

'No gramarye?' inquired the freelancer.

Morcant shook his head solemnly. 'Not this close to the Guardians,' he said. 'Mislike it they will, if sorcery we use without their sufferance.'

In the flaring light of the torch, Wrackwulf could see the cave tapered back into a rough tunnel. Turning to the rest of them, the Marcher Lady of Clan Nuallán nodded and motioned for them to follow her into it.

For several hours it wound and twisted, but always heading due north as far as Wrackwulf could tell. The air never lost its dank chill. After a while they began slowly rising at an incline, gradual at first but then steadily steeper; Wrackwulf grunted and dug in for what he hoped was one last push. On they trudged, one foot in front of the other...

And then they were back out in the open, the night air raw and clear. The tunnel had exited onto another cave, this one set into the side of a mountain, giving them a panoramic view of a perfect circle of peaks enclosing a vast plain of rock. The star-spangled skies stretched a canopy of silvered purple above them.

Wrackwulf blinked as he gazed upon the Place of Doom's Keeping. In the midst of the plain was a thicket of gigantic plants. From the bottom they resembled uprooted trees that somehow remained upright, their snarled roots propelling them across the rocky floor; from the base trunk of each, masses of spiny tendrils writhed upwards and outwards, seeming to sniff out the new arrivals with an alien sense. Perhaps most unsettling of all was the gigantic stalk that crowned every one of them, a tapering proboscis that ended in a thick hood. From within the inky depths of these, faint points of light seemed to glimmer malevolently. Wrackwulf couldn't have said if such creatures had eyes, but he had the distinct sensation of being watched. An ominous click-clacking sound drifted eerily across the plain towards them, as a thousand stalks turned as one towards the new arrivals: Wrackwulf flinched before their cyclopean scrutiny.

The bizarre creatures formed a sort of a clearing at their epicentre. Much of this was taken up by a huge cairn of mighty granite boulders. Something about that cairn seemed to fill up the space around it, obviating everything: Wrackwulf had never been one to ponder the Other Side, but just then he felt like a cipher in the presence of an ancient evil, one that might swallow them all up where they stood. He was dimly aware of Torgun drawing forth the Circifix of St Argo: instinctively the freelancer pulled closer towards him, as a freezing man seeks the fire. Joram tried to mutter a prayer, but it died on his lips. Was the sturdy monk trembling inside his habit?

The four islanders stepped forward to the edge of a rocky platform abutting on to the cave mouth. No word was spoken, but worldly as he was even Wrackwulf could intuit some kind of communication was taking place. He made the sign, feeling the rareness of the gesture as keenly as the wind.

At length Morcant turned to address the outsiders. 'Told the Guardians of your purpose here we have. Down amongst them now we must go. Come.'

Wrackwulf exchanged one last glance with Torgun, who shrugged. *Too late to turn back now,* he seemed to say. Joram remained imprisoned in his silence, inscrutable as ever. But Wrackwulf fancied the monk still shivered in the night.

To one side, a long and winding set of steps carved into the side of the mountain led down to the enclosed plain below. The Westerlings were already descending. Taking a deep breath, Wrackwulf steeled himself, and prepared to enter the Place of Doom's Keeping.

CHAPTER 14
THE DARK SIDE BECKONS

'You were always the stronger of the two, in your heart you know this.' The words, soft and delicious in the gloom. Arik wanted desperately to believe them, but even now he wasn't sure.

'But he bested me in combat, and we were always so close in our studies...' He hated himself for the feelings of envy, rising like black bile, poisoning his heart and consuming all former thoughts of friendship. 'And then they made him journeyman, and him a year younger than me, too.' The bile washed over him, and suddenly Arik didn't hate the feelings quite so much. They seemed to feed him, as a man who loves wine too well is fed by the flagon.

The voice became stern in the darkness, the words sharp where they had been soft. 'I have already told you, the Master favours you. His promises to us all shall take us far beyond the petty offices of mortalkind. Was he wrong to trust you with this task?'

The words had sharpened to a point. Arik squirmed on

his stool, as though transfixed. The interrogation chamber was dank and cold, but that wasn't why he shivered. Despising Adelko was one thing, but what they were asking him to do...

'But Hargus has done nothing wrong,' he faltered. 'He's only doing what Adelko asked us to do, back before...' His voice trailed off. The chamber's single taper guttered. The older monk got up to light a fresh one.

'Hargus has been asking far too many questions,' he said, his voice now colder than the subterrene room they were in. 'You both have. But whereas you have been wise enough to see the validity of our great cause, Hargus is too weak-minded to do anything other than continue his fool's game, out of nothing more than blind loyalty to Adelko. He's been trying to find out why I was exonerated. Before long he will go to someone here with access to the High Circle, and blab what he thinks he knows. If he does that, Hannequin might have no choice but to reopen my trial, publicly this time. The Master cannot afford to have that happen at this stage of affairs. Your jocular little friend is every bit as impetuous as Adelko – he must be silenced.'

In the light of the dying taper, Arik's new mentor cut a grim silhouette, seeming to draw more darkness out of the shadows around them as he lit a new one. 'Did you really think it wouldn't come to the Master's attention, what the pair of you were up to? He has many servants here in the monastery besides me. I have made you an offer, one you were not slow to accept. Do you flinch at your first challenge? The Master will be disappointed.'

The torch was flaring into life and the room growing

brighter, but Arik felt as though the gloom were deepening. 'No... no!' he exclaimed. 'I'll do what he asks of me. I'm just... it was just a moment of weakness.'

The older monk sat back down on the bench opposite Arik. His sixth sense had begun doing strange things since his conversion more than a moon ago, but he thought it was telling him the monk was mollified. For now, at least. He didn't need any sense but common sense to tell him what had to be done to ensure he maintained his place in the New Order. Or what would happen to him if he didn't.

Reaching into the folds of his habit, the older monk produced a tiny phial and pressed it into Arik's trembling hand. The voice softened again, smooth as velvet and silk now it was. Deadly as a Shadowman's knife.

'Have your studies under me not progressed apace, young Arik? Are you not already learning to channel both paths of gramarye, and conjoin these with Argolian powers?' The voice hardened again, but this time it was stiffened with zeal. 'This New Order is meant to be, foreordained by powers only the Master can begin to comprehend! You are intelligent enough to understand our intentions – that fool Adelko and his even bigger fool of a mentor Horskram could never grasp the magnitude of what we seek to achieve. That – and your powers of spirit – is why you were chosen, and not him. This is a great gift, Arik – do not spurn it.'

Arik's hand closed and tightened about the phial. His new mentor's words made sense, and yet... if he had such great potential, why were they asking him to do such a dirty deed?

In tremulous tones he dared give voice to that thought.

His mentor sat back, making a disgusted gesture. His eyes glittered malevolently beneath his cowl. That malevolence both excited and repelled Arik by turns – since his conversion, he had been a roil of conflicting feelings. That wasn't uncommon prior to full initiation, he'd been told, but it agonised him nonetheless.

'I have told you already,' said his mentor, 'that in order to attain the pinnacle of mortalkind's potential, we must wade through crooked and murky ways. All of us must do things we would not ordinarily. Did you really think we would simply ask you to play along with Hargus and demand nothing more of you? You are but lately chosen – do not think you can seek to avert doing your share.'

The words and the mindset behind them were inexorable. Slowly but surely, Arik felt his inner resistance give way, and with it the last vestiges of his old decency began to slip. He had a vision in his mind's eye of himself toppling off a high cliff, the doppelganger's eyes that met his pained and innocent as they vanished into a yawning chasm...

Banishing the vision, he focused on the polished glass phial pinned to the middle of his palm. He met his mentor's glittering gaze, and his voice carried a leaden certainty as he said: 'It shall be as you say, Master Johann. I'll do it tonight.'

The erstwhile prior of Heilag smiled, a hairline fracture across his drawn face. 'Excellent. So the Master was right to place his faith in you, after all. The time is at hand, Arik. The Departure is nigh – you cannot yet fully appreciate what a great privilege the Master is bestowing upon you.'

Arik felt the lust for power harden in his heart. Far greater than the lust for women or wine or even knowledge that had burned in him since coming of age, it was a desire that would curse him forever. And yet he felt with all his heart that it was such desire that made him the essence of who he was.

Johann moved slickly on to practicalities. 'Azrael's Eye is swift and simple in its application,' he said in a voice that suddenly sounded hollow. 'A few mere drops upon his lips while he sleeps, nothing more. He will appear to all intents to have passed of natural causes, though none will be able to say for sure what malady took him.'

'Won't the apothecary know?' Arik's old quick wits were returning to him. Now he was resolved in his course of action, he felt better already.

Johann shook his head. 'Brother Jonas would have to be looking for poison to identify it, for which he would have to suspect foul play. Hargus has no enemies, so none will be suspected. Sometimes a man's heart is weak and gives out. Life under the Almighty's watch has always been cruel and capricious. We would change that forever, by the grace of the Fallen Angel.'

Arik stood and placed the phial carefully in the folds of his own habit. He felt stronger by the second. Johann was right. Truth to tell, he had no idea who this Master was, but he felt increasingly sure that his plans were in mortalkind's best interests. Adelko *was* a fool, and his stuffy mentor Horskram. Why, Adelko himself had almost finished Arik off in the courtyard, when they'd sparred in earnest during Edemus' class... who was he to act so high and mighty? He was just as fallible as any man. And he'd been unfairly promoted ahead of Arik.

But soon there would be a reckoning. Arik felt sorry for Hargus. He was genuinely innocent – but that same innocence had led him blindly to take Adelko's part in this. The part of ruin and folly, the part that would see mortalkind struggle on in pain, as it always had done.

Johann stood and placed a hand on his shoulder. 'I sense a great power in you, young one,' he said, the words soft and delicious again.

Arik nodded, allowing a slight smile to creep across his own face. 'I won't let you down, Master Johann,' he said.

Without another word, Arik turned and left the interrogation room. He had an old friend to murder.

CHAPTER 15
THE SORCERER IN THE TOWER

The jagged beauty of the Abydos ranges was almost a welcome sight after the rough monotony of the broken land they had traversed. The ochre peaks were limned with red as they cut the blue afternoon skies; twice as high as the Hyrkrainians, they were the tallest mountains Adelko had set eyes on.

Almost a welcome sight, but not quite. Indeed, how could they be in light of the shattered monstrosity that crowned them? Memories of fearful Tintagael came flooding back, recollections of the Warlock's Crown hard on their heels; Adelko mouthed a prayer and reached for his circifix – before remembering the Bethlers had stripped it from him when Tobin had taken them prisoner.

He'd be needing a rood a lot more than any Bethler, he reflected as he struggled to comprehend the ancient and vast edifice that seemed to erupt from the peaks. Octagonal in basic structure, just like its sister on the outskirts of Tintagael, it followed the same tapering form and was fashioned of the same irregular brickwork: irregular, yet somehow *perfect*. Following its lines with his eyes, Adelko searched the bizarre hotchpotch of gigantic stones for some fault, but found none. Like a mad god's puzzle, they fit together seamlessly.

And yet the Watchtower of Leviathan had proven vulnerable, to a power greater than all that mortal craft could ever muster. Adelko shivered in the sultry heat as his gaze tracked the tower all the way up to its broken summit; the thing in its present state was more than three times the height of Graukolos keep – how tall had it been before the Wrath of the Unseen shook it five millennia ago?

Next to him Zimri adjusted his turban fretfully. Beneath it, his normally rich dark skin looked pale and drawn. Only his two fellow Southrons – taciturn Kufa and his jocose compatriot, whom Adelko had learned was called Batu – had come with them on this final leg of the trip. The rest of the camp they had left just before dawn, for even a charismatic general like Zimri feared a mutiny if he brought his men here.

'Well now,' he said. 'I have done as you have petitioned me do, savants Tipu and Horskram. Though now I gaze on such fearsome ruins, I would not for all the world that I had.'

'Tis precisely for all the world that you have done so, much as it pains me to admit it,' said Horskram, his voice as hushed as the land about them. For nothing living cared to go within a country mile of the Watchtower; the ground that rose up to meet the slopes on which it perched was sere and brittle. Only grass survived, and that barely. Yet Adelko sensed there was something different about the Watchtower of Leviathan. It felt more lived in than the other he had seen, less... haunted?

The journeyman had to hope he was right about that.

'Our task done, we shall not tarry here,' said Zimri, motioning to Kufa and Batu. The two men gratefully wheeled their Kallandhari chargers around. The horses seemed nervous and skittish, decidedly keen to be off.

'We will take back our horses,' said Zimri. 'I hardly think they will consent to be ridden where you are going in any case.'

The seven of them dismounted. Wordlessly, the Zarumani gave his gelding to the Southrons to take: apparently he did not anticipate needing it again. A deathly silence had come over the company, and no one spoke. Zimri and his sword brothers took the horses' reins and began to lead them at an amble, back towards where the camp smoked distantly on the horizon as *fariz* prepared breakfast. Adelko found himself wishing he were going with them, though he was not hungry.

'I shall not wish you godspeed,' Zimri called over his shoulder, 'for if you are right in this, the Unseen already watch your movements, for better or worse. Farewell, strange travellers! Until we meet again – if there is a next time.' Without another word the Southrons rode off.

For a little while longer, the seven of them stood rooted to the spot. Adelko willed a bird to fly across the skies, to cut the awful static horizon, but none did.

Presently Horskram spoke. 'Adelko and I will recite the

Pslam of Fortitude on our way, to bolster our spiritual strength. Sir Azelin, join us if you still know how.'

The warrior-monk nodded. Curiously enough Horskram had proven correct in his surmise: for all his bluster about going his own way, the doomed knight seemed as happy to come with them as not. But then a man whose soul is already damned has little to fear from a black magician. Or perhaps it was simply Wyrd at work, driving Sir Azelin along the same path as the rest of them.

Tipu produced his flute. 'We have joined souls before in the great cosmic web,' he said softly. 'Ashanti grant that we may do so again.'

On they went. Adelko's voice sounded just as reedy in his ears as it had done when they'd banished Belaach from the girl Gizel, more than a year ago; Tipu's fluting sounded strained and harsh as it had when they were stuck in the ghoul mine. The Watchtower seemed to mock their efforts as it gradually filled up the horizon, swallowing everything around it.

And then a strange thing happened. Instead of drawing closer, everything seemed to reverse, and the panorama before Adelko grew immeasurably smaller; he saw in his mind's eye seven tiny figures approaching a vast pinnacle of stone built on a massive fluted pillar. And as the minuscule figures drew closer to the tower, he realised it wasn't fluting at all... Gradually the stone serpent began to uncoil, with a low cthonian rumbling that shook the earth; it extended towards them, two cavernous pits aglow with lambent fires staring at them atop a gigantic circular maw, lined with inwards-facing teeth that gave it a horrible puckered look.

Faster it came, faster, slithering along the shuddering ground with a terrible speed that belied its vastness. The seven figures seemed to stop moving forwards themselves, hanging suspended above the ground, though their limbs continued to move like puppets. Something in Adelko cried out then, that this was no illusion, but reality glimpsed from a darkened corner of the mind, and he found himself suddenly right back in the present moment, screaming alongside his companions as the serpent's maw opened wider, wider and still wider, until its stygian gullet blotted out all else...

Floating and falling at once, in a limitless darkness that constricted into a single infinitesimal point...

A sense of time being drawn out agonisingly, a second becoming a year becoming a millennium...

A silent mouth screaming infinitely into a single collapsible moment...

Adelko could not say to his dying day how long the unbearable sensation lasted – what dread length of alternate reality had been captured in that hidden bubble of time – only that mercifully it did pass.

And when it did, he found himself more than surprised by his surroundings.

The room they were in was covered in tapestries, rugs

and murals. Hangings festooned the ceiling. All bore abstract Sassanian artwork, though as well as the usual serpent motifs Adelko thought he saw stylised flames and other symbols. He and his six companions were sprawled across elaborately sequinned divans; the light came from hanging lanterns and the pungent smell of incense filled the air. The overall effect was that of a prosperous if somewhat gaudy southern merchant's dwelling.

In the middle of the room, on a chair of ivory carved to resemble a sitting man, sat a corpulent brown-skinned Sassanian. He was dressed in silken robes of blood red, bordered with black lace at the hem. His sleeves were wide and hid his hands. A comical expression was on his face, which looked almost jocular, although the glint in his black eyes told of one whose jests are sardonic as often as not. His curling hair was oiled, his triple-forked beard and moustachios lacquered. A high collar of cloth-of-gold hid his neck, and seemed to halo his head, upon which he wore a cylindrical tarbush. Pearly teeth flashed in a grin as he registered that at least one of his guests was awake.

'Good afternoon, I have been expecting you.' Catching Adelko's bemused stare, he added: 'Not quite what you were expecting, eh?'

Beside him the others were stirring, too. Horskram blinked and looked around. 'Where are we?' he asked.

'In my personal chambers, high in the tower,' said the man. 'So long as you do not stray from them, you've nothing to fear. Very few strangers who are swallowed by the Serpent end up here, so count yourselves most fortunate!'

Adelko blinked, scarcely able to believe what he was

hearing. 'You don't mean it actually...? I thought it was a vision.'

'And perhaps it was, after all,' said the man, giving a queer little giggle. 'Who can say? At any rate, here you are. Adbel Sha'arza, at your service!' The sorcerer stood and bowed floridly, removing his curious hat to reveal a shiny bald pate. He was as short as he was fat.

He looks funny enough, but I'll bet he laughs last and longest most of the time.

Just then a fluttering motion caught Adelko's attention. A tiny demon, humanoid in shape but sprouting disproportionately large wings, flew from a corner of the room to perch on Abdel's shoulder.

'Oh, don't mind my little Imp,' said the sorcerer. 'Helps me keep an eye on the place. He's quite harmless... most of the time. I named him Infidel.' Again the unnerving giggle. Having woken swiftly, Anupe put a hand to her falchion to show what she thought of the warlock's humour. Abdel muttered a single word, and the Harijan slumped back on the divan, snoring loudly.

'Don't worry, I've just put her back to sleep for a bit,' said the warlock, giggling again. 'Far too skittish around sorcery, the Harijans. But then they have lived near the Forbidden Isle for so long, one can understand their prejudices.'

'It is the Forbidden Isle we would have words with you about,' said Tipu. Getting off the divan, the mystic bowed his head to the carpeted floor. 'When he who follows the Mystic Way treats with the sorcerer in the tower, you shall know that the Final Hour is at hand. Thus spake Sha'abat.'

The Zarumani stood next, but did not bow. 'Long have

the fires weaved about the serpent, foretelling of the Great Transition. Mithras, Lord of Light and Fire, commands your role in it.'

Abdel Sha'arza chuckled again. Adelko began to wonder if his study of sorcery had driven him mad like Andragorix. 'Oh he does, does he? How nice to be visited by one of my dear departed mother's brethren. And you don't appear to want me lynched. You're nice ones for the formalities, aren't you...! Well, I have divined things for myself, and my own findings tell me your respective gods might be on to something.' He turned to look at Horskram and Adelko. 'And the Witch of the Forest told me to be on the look-out for two northern monks of the wheel-god, too. And so here we are, a merry little polyglot gathering, I must say...! But pray forgive me! You must be hungry and thirsty after your long journey. No one should take counsel on an empty stomach, yes? If you would be so kind as to follow me...'

A wall-hanging behind him suddenly furled up, revealing a passageway. Abdel was already walking over towards it, the Imp flittering about his shoulders in a manner that could only be described as companionable. An ebony cane had suddenly appeared from a voluminous sleeve; the sigils of the Sorcerer's Script writhing around it told of its true purpose.

'We can't just follow him!' hissed Hari. 'We'll be in trouble if we do.'

Abdel turned in mid-stride. 'On second thoughts, I'm not sure you really need to be awake right now either.' Another word, and Hari blinked before keeling over on to the divan, snoring loudly next to Anupe.

Adelko exchanged a wry glance with Horskram. He had not expected this encounter to be quite so comical. If his mentor shared his sentiments he showed no sign of it, shaking his head and muttering curses under his breath.

Blithely ignoring him, the warlock indicated the exit with a twirling motion of his wand. 'Come along, I'll see you fed and watered before we talk any further.'

Sir Azelin grinned his gallows grin. 'A hospitable wizard,' he said. 'Now I've seen everything.'

'They're generally quite good about that sort of thing,' said Adelko, trying to make light of things as he recalled the Earth Witch's bower.

The next room Abdel took them into was much like the first, except it had a horseshoe-arched window that looked out across the steepy ranges. Though opulent enough, the mundanity of the wizard's quarters seemed underwhelming. A long low table was laid with ebony jade-inlaid trays bearing a succulent array of spiced grilled meats on silver skewers, leavened flatbreads laced with garlic, salted aubergines and a filigreed silver ewer of wine with matching goblets.

'Pray excuse the simplicity of the repast,' said Abdel. 'My demon cook is being most recalcitrant today.' Seeing their horrified expressions, the sorcerer burst out laughing. 'Oh, but the looks on your faces! Please, indulge me – I so rarely get visitors up here. I can assure you I prepared this food myself, and I sourced the ingredients as any mortal would.' He motioned towards gold-webbed crimson cushions strewn about the table. 'Please sit, sit! In fact you'll find I'm quite the cook, even if I do say so myself.'

Smiling broadly, he began pouring them goblets of rich amber wine, while the Imp fluttered about him. It seemed anxious to give Horskram as wide a berth as possible, though; turning an off-white colour and fluttering into a corner of the ceiling as the old monk approached the table. Adelko guessed Infidel didn't welcome the presence of the Redeemer's blood.

The Zarumani was first to sit and speak. 'I am glad to find that the flames spoke true about you, Abdel tek Haziel. Many in the Sect of Light and Fire had feared your soul was damned forever.'

'Such a charming guest!' said Abdel, with his customary giggle. He handed the Zarumani a goblet as the others gingerly joined him about the table. 'But never fear – that is why you find me in such familiar surroundings. It's how I keep my mind from becoming polluted by this place.' His face took on a rare expression of seriousness. 'Believe me, there are some things on the lower levels you will not wish to see.' He took a sip of the wine, and the smile returned immediately. 'Ah, a fine vintage – being a powerful wizard does carry certain benefits, I must say! The Unseen know, my father was an impossible man to love, but he was richly rewarded in his heyday for his skills at sorcery.'

Adelko's sixth sense remained oddly cool. Not stifled as it had been at the monastery at Rima, more... subdued. He shrugged and accepted a goblet from the sorcerer. The rim had a disconcerting motif of tiny serpents chasing each other around it, but it seemed ordinary apart from that. The wine had a delicious caramely aftertaste. Abdel's worldly tastes at least were impeccable.

'You know what brings us here then?' queried the Zarumani. His face was as neutral as ever, but Adelko could guess at the tension in him.

Sha'arza nodded as he picked daintily at his food, tossing a morsel of meat towards Infidel, who screeched before catching it and swallowing it whole. Horskram made a disgusted sound, but Abdel merely laughed.

'Don't be so disconcerted, Master Horskram, merely a Fifth-Tier demon is Infidel! You've faced far worse in your time, no need to be afraid. I have him firmly under control – if it wasn't for that Palomedian artefact you carry, he'd be literally eating out of my hand!'

The adept's face curdled. 'Of all the dubious alliances my duty as an Argolian has behoved me to make, this surely ranks as the foulest. Abdel Sha'arza, your reputation justly redounds with notoriety throughout the Sassanian Sultanates, and far beyond. Let us not prevaricate or procrastinate any more, and get this odious business over with as swiftly as we can. I have not spent my life bringing your wicked kind to justice to sit here at meat with you and bandy words in presence of demonkind.' He made the sign and Infidel screeched, cowering further back into the corner as if to get as far away from the monk as possible.

Abdel smiled and dabbed at his fat lips with a bejewelled silk handkerchief. 'You Urovians are always so direct. The Witch of the Forest did warn me about you.'

'The Earth Witch is also wanted for crimes pertaining to her craft, and shall not escape justice either,' Horskram said sternly. 'But more important than both of you right now is who is behind the theft of the fragments. Not even a dastard such as you would be mad enough to covet its power, but someone is – and I mean to find out who, by any means necessary!' A fierce light burned in the adept's eyes now. Always irascible, now Horskram seemed to feed off an incandescent rage that burned within him. Just then Adelko wondered whose soul was really the darkest.

He's wanted this for so many months, the journeyman realised. *If he doesn't find out soon, it will surely drive him mad.* He felt a moment of sympathy for his embattled mentor.

'The monk has the right of this,' said Tipu softly. 'Not in an age of mortalkind has such disparate group of individuals come together. Every faith across the Known World points to a Third Age of Darkness arriving soon if we do not act.'

Abdel nodded, becoming serious again. 'I have peered through my scrying tool and looked upon the southern deserts. The Kardin tribes babble of a Red Moon at night, while livestock are born with two heads to ordinary herdsmen with not a whit of magick to their names. Sometimes I struggle to control the spirits that dwell here in this tower, I can feel them taking power from their age-old masters as never before. Beyond these mountains the Warlock Prince of Halepo is also afraid, for he sees the Great Inland Sea rising up higher than ever against the shores of his kingdom. In Sendhé the priest caste has redoubled its sacrifices, burning and slaughtering at the apex of its pyramid-temples from the Wytching Hour till dawn, in preparation for the Second Coming. The King of Gehenna would have dominion of the mortal realm, tired He is of bargaining with intermediaries such as me for a slice of influence here and there. And the spheres tell me He shall choose Varya as his point of re-entry, just as Ma'amun would have had it five thousand years ago.'

'And why, may I ask, would a black magician such as you be minded to oppose this?' asked Sir Azelin.

The smile did not return to Abdel's face as he acknowledged the question. 'In truth my father Haziel was a wicked man,' he said. 'The most powerful warlock of his age, some say since Ashokainan, his thirst for knowledge of both Ways knew no bounds. But over time his desire for power got the better of him, and he was banished – so he decided to seek mastery of the Watchtower sooner rather than later. After many months of struggle my father overcame the watchtower's defences, banishing the shades and binding the demons that have dwelled here since the Breaking. Once he had done so he brought my mother with him, against her will, may Mithras shine his light on her always!' Sha'arza's voice hardened as for the first time he became angry. 'My father killed her in the end with his depravity, giving her up to demonkind as part of his experiments with the magick of this place. But not before she had given him a son. And thus my fate was sealed, and I have spent my life here.'

The Zarumani's stoicism was shattered by the revelation. 'We never knew that for certain,' he managed to say. 'That is a dark evil to visit upon child and wife.'

'He had me under his thrall, and there was nothing I could do but watch and learn,' Abdel went on. 'The years went by and my father grew ever more corrupted, yet I learned at his feet – Demonology and Necromancy, yes, but it was Alchemy and its sub-discipline of artifice that delighted me most, and I only studied so much of the Left Hand Path as would appease him. In the meantime, he uncovered and deciphered the many tablets and tomes and other articles that this place guards, and pursued his own studies with ever more vigour. Over the decades I watched as he withered, as the Left Hand Path gradually destroyed him, body and soul.' The warlock actually shuddered now. 'But it was my father's knowledge of how to channel sub-avatars that horrified me the most.'

Tipu and Horskram both jolted at that. Adelko recalled the conversation in Hannequin's study a few months ago.

'The Grand Master of our Order mentioned sub-avatars to us before,' said Adelko. 'Demons clothed in mortal flesh, like a binding, only even harder to detect.'

'You recall correctly,' nodded Horskram. 'A sub-avatar is a demonic second that permits a more powerful demon of a higher tier to cross over to our world, through the medium of a less powerful demon, one small enough to pass through the Rent Between Worlds.'

'You understand perfectly,' said Sha'arza, nodding. 'This enables a sub-emanation of an archdemon if you will, not as powerful as an actual manifestation, but just as malevolent. Such entities can walk the mortal vale for years, if a wizard can keep them bound.'

'That sounds a bit like Belaach and Archmaster Wolaf,' said Adelko, frowning as he recalled Hannequin and Horskram's account of the binding.

Sha'arza raised an eyebrow over the rim of his cup. Horskram sketched an explanation of what had happened at the monastery. All pretence of secrecy had been dropped.

'Think more powerful still, Adelko of Narvik,' said Abdel when Horskram was done. 'Through the sub-avatars he conjured, my father was able to tap the essence of the First-Tier archdemons Sha'amiel and Azathol. The names those sub-avatars took in the mortal realm were Khartoun of Imanabad and Xamiel of Avalongne.'

Tipu lowered his gaze, while Horskram shut his eyes as though the revelation pained him. Sir Azelin merely laughed his bitter laugh.

'The Vizier of Ushalayim who counselled Sultan Jehan the Deceived to persecute visiting pilgrims of the Creed,' said Horskram, shaking his head in dismay, 'and the fire-brand Pangonian preacher who whipped up support for a crusade to conquer it in response. Many of us in the Argo-lian Order have long suspected demonkind had something to do with instigating the Pilgrim Wars, though until now we had no idea your father was behind it.'

Adelko frowned. 'Why would Haziel Sha'arza want to start a Palomedian crusade against people of the Faith?'

Abdel chuckled. 'You forget the Kallandhari and Nazharyan sultanates that bore the brunt of the Pilgrim Wars are Orthodox and revile sorcery. The Great Schism between Sha'abatians occurred after the rulership of the Enlightened Sultans was brought to an end at the Battle of Kurushan Heights. The Orthodoxers came to believe that Abu'cuchaza'ar Kardin and his descendants had been cursed for meddling in forbidden powers. But my father hailed from Halepo, where the Unorthodox interpretation of the Faith shows more tolerance towards sorcerers. It was once the heart of the Kishan Empire that the Shemites founded before the coming of the Faith, and our people have always been more at ease with magick.'

The wizard paused to refill his cup. 'But your question is a good one, Argolian. My father had other reasons for provoking the Pilgrim Wars. You see, in the course of his long studies he became a disciple of Abaddon, just as did Andragorix whom you fought.'

'You are well informed, it would seem,' said Horskram.

'What my own Scrying has not told me about your adventures, the Witch of the Forest has,' said Abdel. 'Like Andragorix, my father coveted the reunited Headstone, but also recognised that this was beyond his immediate power – three of the fragments were far to the north where his sorceries could not hope to reach, the fourth he could not find no matter how hard he looked. And so he resolved to bide his time and be bound, just as Andragorix was. Very likely the sorcerer you killed hoped one day to overthrow his master and reap the rewards of the recovered Headstone, becoming the Fallen One's right-hand man upon his return to earth. In a similar way my father hoped to pave the way for others to reunite it, so he could one day seize it for himself. His Necromancy would ensure him long life, albeit in most horrid fashion, so he could afford to wait.'

'That still doesn't explain why your father used demonic impostors to start the Pilgrim Wars,' pressed Azelin. A keen light was in his eyes now. Adelko sensed a needy longing in him too, to be reconciled with his own sins.

'Have patience, I am coming to that,' said Abdel. 'The real purpose of the Pilgrim Wars was to establish a foothold – in the form of an Urovian colony – in Sassania. This would enable a warlock in close proximity to the first three fragments to obtain those and seek the fourth here.'

Horskram was nodding thoughtfully. 'It makes sense. So the Blessed Realm is naught but a platform for the return of Abaddon.'

Azelin laughed grimly. 'How very appropriate – or is that ironic? I don't know if this makes me feel better, or worse.'

'Aren't we forgetting about one thing?' asked Adelko. 'What about the Grimoire needed to operate the Headstone? The Earth Witch said something about that when we stayed with her.'

'I was coming to that as well,' said Abdel. 'To obtain an original grimoire of Ma'amun's gramarye was one of the reasons why my father sought residence here. Only a very few are known to have survived the Breaking. Morwena was thought to have one, before Søren's intervention destroyed her Watchtower. The wizard Ashokainan was also believed to have a copy at his own tower in the Great White Mountains, also destroyed by Søren. A third was believed to be right here – this watchtower was once the lair of Cleops, a Sendhéan renegade who was Ashokainan's tutor. Like many other sorcerers, my father always assumed that the Grimoire had been left here by the Thalamian hero-mariner Antaeus, after he slew Cleops more than two thousand years ago.'

'Interesting,' said Horskram. 'The Earth Witch mentioned that Ashokainan tried to ensorcell Antaeus, so he could sail to the Forbidden Isle and steal the Headstone for him.'

'Just so,' confirmed Sha'arza. 'For by then master and pupil had become rivals, and Ashokainan wished to supplant Cleops and become the first to obtain it. But neither succeeded in bending Antaeus to their will, for he was a demi-god of even greater stature than Søren. In the end Antaeus destroyed Cleops, and left Ashokainan to be slain more than a thousand years later by Søren, whom some say was Antaeus reincarnated – another tool of the Unseen to counter the machinations of the Fallen One.'

Tipu frowned. 'But what about the Grimoire? None of the tales I have heard say anything about Antaeus stealing such a thing.'

'No indeed,' said Sha'arza. 'Antaeus did not covet sorcery. Whatever the purposes of the Unseen, as far as the hero himself was concerned, he was killing Cleops in revenge for unleashing Abeus the Hundred-Handed, greatest of the Gygants, upon the high seas and destroying half his fleet. And yet the Grimoire was not here, for high and low my father searched this place. This tower lay unmastered for hundreds of years after Cleops died, and it is possible that a powerful group of adventurers might have succeeded in recovering the Grimoire before my father arrived, though such a thing is unlikely.'

'Unlikely but not impossible,' said Horskram. 'Adventurers besides Søren have been known to raid even the Forbidden Isle and return to tell the tale, though all perished or lost their sanity afterwards.'

Sha'arza spread his hands, revealing long lacquered fingernails. 'Who can say? All I know for sure is that the Grimoire is not here. My father, greatly disappointed, bent the rest of his life to searching it out, knowing that the Headstone would be useless to him without its knowledge.

Doubtless Abaddon was only too keen that he succeed in this mission, for obvious reasons.'

'So how come he never succeeded?' asked Adelko. 'In finding the fourth fragment or the Grimoire?'

'Doubtless he would have, in time,' said Abdel. 'But before he could, I grew powerful enough to stop him and avenge my mother. I confronted him one night, high in his observatory at the broken summit of this tower. His energies were sorely taxed, given over to keeping the demons here bound and maintaining the puppet demons Xamiel and Khartoun. Even so, it was a terrible battle, and our thaumaturgies raged day and night for a week before I finally smote him down. Once he was dead, I was able to send the two sub-avatars back to Gehenna, and with them the essence of their archdemonic masters.'

'Hence the legend of Xamiel's glorious ascent to heaven,' put in Horskram. 'Oh, what blasphemous irony!'

'Not to mention Khartoun's mysterious disappearance,' added Tipu. 'It was always thought that the Vizier was assassinated by rivals of Jehan the Deceived, who blamed him for bringing the crusaders down on their backs.'

Abdel drained his cup and immediately refilled it. Clearly recounting his patricide and the disastrous events leading up to it had unnerved him.

'I did what I could to put right the evils my father had done,' Abdel went on. 'Such notes as he had compiled on the possible whereabouts of the Grimoire and Headstone fragment I destroyed. I did not dare even to consult them, for fear I might be tempted myself. But I could not reverse events. By then Rayonde the Scourge had conquered Ushalayim, and the Pilgrim Kingdoms were a reality. I knew then it was just a matter of time before the Author of All Evil steered events further towards his ultimate goal. And so it proved, for by then the false prophet Xamiel had taken on an understudy.'

'Abelard of Montrevellyn,' said Adelko and Horskram in unison.

'Just so,' said Sha'arza. 'I believe he is known very well to the Argolians.'

Adelko mulled things over in the gloomy silence that followed. So the fanatic perfect responsible for the Purge really had been an apprentice to Xamiel, himself an incarnation of the archdemon Azathol. But something else occurred to him. 'Wait... Master Horskram, didn't you say that the Supreme Perfect was chief inquisitor during the Purge? And he's the one behind the next Pilgrim War...'

Horskram stroked his beard thoughtfully. 'Cyprian was a notorious enemy of the Order, but was never found guilty of colluding with Abelard in his black sorceries. Though undoubtedly he was influenced by him, and to this day carries hatred of our Order.' The adept hadn't touched his wine, but now took a good long draught of it. 'Circles within circles within circles... this conspiracy outstrips even my darkest fathomings.'

'I fear there is more left to be uncovered,' said Tipu. 'We still do not know the whereabouts of the Grimoire. Or the fourth fragment, for that matter.'

'The Grimoire I cannot help you with,' confirmed Abdel. 'As I have said, I have no wish to seek out such a thing!

Better that it is left unfound. As for the fourth fragment...' His voice trailed off awkwardly.

'What?' pressed Horskram. All of them were staring Sha'arza now.

The sorcerer giggled again. 'I might just know something of its whereabouts...'

CHAPTER 16
THE GUARDIANS

It felt as though gleaming eyes glared at them from all sides. A dozen of the plant monsters had formed a ring about the interlopers, as impregnable as a curtain wall. Torgun had looked on many beasts fell and strange, but the Guardians were in some ways the most unsettling of all. Nature spirits, Morcant had called them. They weren't demons, as far as he could tell. Yet they shambled about on their roots in a way that was blasphemous to the natural order of things. This close, he could see their sprouting tendrils were covered in needles each the size of a man's forearm. These seemed to writhe like morasses of snakes as the creatures shuffled about; they never stopped moving, though the ring about them remained firm. The hooded stalks that passed for their heads were pointed down towards them; the points of light they had made out from the rocky shelf seemed to come from hideous luminous organs that quivered within their plantular cowls.

Ianna and Fanwyn were addressing the largest one,

which was the size of a pine tree. Torgun supposed this must be the leader, if such creatures could be said to have leaders. When the chieftain responded, all he heard were groans and snaps like wood being pressured and broken. He hoped that wasn't what the Guardians planned on doing to them. To make matters worse, the rest of the creatures continued their ominous click-clacking, as though registering displeasure at the intrusion.

The knight edged closer to Morcant. 'What are they saying?' he hissed.

'Not pleased are they,' the warlock whispered back. 'Never before have outsiders been brought to Place of Doom's Keeping. Ianna and Fanwyn are explaining, but slow to grasp new things are the Guardians. Confused they are by our arrival.'

Torgun suppressed a sigh of dismay. Even in these strange circumstances, it behoved an emissary to be polite. He flicked a sidelong glance at Joram. The monk had remained steadfast behind his invisible wall of inscrutability, but over its parapets he peered keenly at the monsters. He appeared to have mastered his fear.

'Any idea what's on his mind?' Torgun asked Morcant.

'I think he wants to get a look at... it.' The mage paused meaningfully, then swallowed hard. Torgun had never seen him so nervous. Even in the fearful presence of the Guardians, the knight could sense a far greater evil. It set his hackles rising, on unseen stems that seemed to burn the back of his neck with a prickly heat.

Torgun was more unsure about their mission than ever. It had been clear enough at the outset: get to the Westerling

Isles, warn the keepers of the fragment, and assess their defences. In the last resort, try to take it back to the monastery at Rima for safekeeping if necessary. Only now, letting Joram anywhere near the fragment didn't seem like such sound counsel.

And yet, what had the adept really done to arouse their suspicion? Torgun shifted his eyes to Wrackwulf. The freelancer was watching Joram like a hawk, as if daring him to make a suspect move. Beside him, Ariadha looked on uneasily as the two druids continued to debate with the chieftain in the strange tongue of wizards.

We're all watching one another, but we don't have a clue what will happen or what to do next.

The conversation – if you could call it that – grew more heated. The chieftain had begun to sway in obvious agitation, looking ever more menacing as it loomed above Ianna and Fanwyn, its tendrils writhing angrily. Its clicking and creaking was louder now, and more strained: it set Torgun's teeth on edge. Ariadha began yelling at the druids in the Westerling tongue. Ianna held her hand up in her face, motioning for silence, while Fanwyn continued to argue with the chieftain. The other Guardians had taken their own click-clacking up a notch as well: the cacophony was becoming unbearable.

'What's going on?' Torgun yelled over the noise.

'They say we are cursed,' said the mage, his voice frantic now. 'That we have brought a great evil by coming here. Some of them are saying we shouldn't be allowed to leave alive!'

'But that makes no sense!' cried Torgun. 'We're here to prevent evil, not-'

The chieftain emitted a great tearing sound, like an oak tree being felled. Before any of them could react, it picked up Ianna and Fanwyn in two of its tendrils, which curled about them horribly like giant snakes. The druids screamed as the spines pierced them; two other Guardians lurched forwards and dipped their hooded heads with frightening speed. The pulsing organs within them flared, growing outwards like gigantic blooms as they latched on to the Westerlings. The next tearing sound was decidedly flesh-like as the plant monsters decapitated their victims, swallowing their heads whole. The chieftain tossed the spurting corpses at the rest of the Guardians, who clacked hungrily as they fed on the remains. Within a minute there was no evidence that the druids had ever existed.

Torgun and Wrackwulf drew their weapons as the monstrosities began to contract around them. He fancied their glaring organs now looked murderous as they shuffled inexorably forwards. At least they moved a lot more slowly than they struck; their gait was awkward and clumsy, but taking in their tough leathery bodies and sheer size and numbers, Torgun did not doubt who the victor would be.

Grimly the two knights closed together in formation, and prepared to make a last stand. Joram had begun to mutter a prayer as Morcant mouthed a spell in a voice that wavered, but against so many of the monsters Torgun knew psalmody and sorcery would be about as much use as a sword.

'We should never have come here,' he said, calm in the

face of death. 'This was a mistake.'

The ring of Guardians drew ever tighter, their hooded stalks eating up the starlight as they clacked and clicked towards them. Joram raised his hand, which was clenched in a fist. Something in the monk's litany jarred momentarily, but Torgun couldn't make it out above the din. Joram seemed to yell in pain and suddenly nurse his hand. The clacking was as loud as ever, but the Guardians had stopped dead in their tracks, their roots scratching frantically at the rocky ground. Beyond the jarring noise of their awful voices Torgun caught something else, a hungry keening sound.

And then he felt it. A wind. Not a brisk breeze one would expect this far north, but a hot gust. One that carried the taint of hell.

Morcant screamed as he sank to his knees. The Guardians raised their click-clacking to a horrible pitch now, and Torgun dropped his sword and clapped hands to his ears. He was dimly aware of Joram bent over double, vomiting up bile. He could positively feel the relic about his neck protesting, as though St Argo's shade was screaming at him from the Heavenly Halls. The rood was shining brightly now, a reflection of the vanished starlight: the skies had turned as black as Azrael's wings. Torgun could feel the hellish wind gathering, the heat intensifying as it closed around them with a smothering grip that a thousand Guardians could not hope to match.

The click-clacking became a crackling sound as yellow light washed over them. The plant-things were burning. Not as one might expect at touch of fire: it was as if the wind itself consumed them. Thick smoke roiled about them as hundreds of the creatures went up like giant torches. It carried the sweet stench of the charnel house. But beyond that was another smell, far more horrid: it put Torgun instantly in mind of the ravening demon they had fought at Staerkvit. The wind blew harder as the knight braced himself for the end, wondering what the apparition's prophecy had been all about after all...

A great *crack* seemed to split the rocky plain in two. The ground shook and rocks and boulders began tumbling off the sides of the mountains. Torgun was dimly aware of an eruption, of sharded granite and sloughing fragments of stinking plant cartwheeling high into the air... And then everything began suddenly to subside: the crackling, the burning, the keening, even their own screams died in their mouths as a velveteen darkness settled over them, like a giant hushing hand. Torgun felt that dark hand penetrate inside his skull, questing for his fevered brain, stroking it with fingers that were gentle yet sinister.

The darkness engulfed him, and Torgun resigned himself to oblivion.

He came to, opening his eyes to pale bleak sunlight. Jerking upright, he reached instinctively for his sword, but quickly realised no blade could help him here.

The scene was one of pandemonium. The Guardians, or what was left of them, were scattered about the valley, their husks telling blackened tales of annihilation. Some were still just about alive: bereft of stalks and tendrils, their mutilated trunks limped obscenely on what few roots they had left. The stench was awful: burning plant had mingled with the preternatural reek of whatever hellish denizen had wiped out the Guardians. In amongst the steaming piles of plant remains, Torgun could make out other more hideous substances: globules of orange-tinged miasma that seemed slowly to reduce in the light. Whatever form it had taken, the Guardians' antagonist had clearly paid dearly for its victory.

Yet a victory it had won nonetheless. In the centre of the plain, where the cairn had been, sat a crater that smoked and smouldered, blasted pieces of charred granite flung about it. The aura of evil still emanated from its depths.

Morcant was sat nearby, gazing blankly around him as though stunned out of his wits. Looking around for the others, Torgun saw Wrackwulf pinned under a dead Guardian. The freelancer was just coming to, groaning and grimacing as he tried to prise the thing off. Staggering over to him, Torgun pitched in, and with some effort the two men managed to haul it off. Helping Wrackwulf to his feet, Torgun saw with some relief that he had escaped with minor cuts and bruises.

'We need to find the others,' Torgun told him. 'They could be anywhere under this mess.'

It took the rest of the sunrise to uncover them. Ariadha was alive, though she appeared to be in shock and would speak to no one, not even Morcant. As for Joram, they found him being violently ill beneath the chieftain, who had fallen across him. Its charred and sloughing husk was only recognisable by its sheer size. Joram had broken several ribs and an arm and gashed his head badly, but that didn't appear to be connected to his sickness.

Last of all they dared to inspect the crater. Whatever had been kept there was now gone: the reek of brimstone was strongest here, all that remained to suggest the smoking black hole had been the keeping place for a thing of ancient evil.

Morcant raised his eyes to the heavens, but the watery firmament told them nothing. 'Gone it is,' he said mournfully. 'You were right, Sir Torgun – coming here was a mistake.'

'You think we led... whatever, whoever... here?' asked the knight. 'But I thought it widely known that the druids guarded the fragment – why wait until now to strike?'

But the wizard had no answer to that question. 'I've never witnessed such magic as I saw last night,' he said. 'Thaumaturgy it was, crossed with Demonology...' He shook his head. 'Nothing I've ever studied or conjured even approaches such dire incantation.'

Wrackwulf glanced behind them. 'Joram's in a bad way still, coughing up bile from who knows where. I don't think we're going to get an Argolian's wisdom on the matter.'

Torgun sighed wearily. Though the worst of the sorcery appeared to have abated, he felt on edge and enervated. 'There is no point in tarrying. We'd better make a stretcher for Master Joram and get out of here, while we still can. Is the Marcher Lady of Clan Nuallán able to walk?'

Wrackwulf glanced sympathetically to where the clanswoman sat stupefied next to Joram. 'I've seen her in better fettle, but I think she'll be all right to walk and climb.'

'Good,' said Torgun. 'We'd best make hurry now, and pray our magic boat is still waiting for us.'

They went about it as swiftly as they could, and by mid-morning they were lifting a stretcher with Joram on it. The monk had lapsed into some kind of strange fever. It put Torgun in mind of the draugbreath; he gathered Wrackwulf was thinking much the same, though neither man cared to broach the subject. Morcant gazed at the monk with concern graven on his weaselly face. That, and confusion: as though he could not fathom why he felt that way about someone who had wanted him dead a few months ago. Ariadha appeared to have recovered her wits somewhat, though her face was ashen as she led them from the devastated valley.

The two knights were just setting off in her wake, carrying Joram, when Wrackwulf grunted and motioned for them to set down the litter. Bending down to inspect his boot, the freelancer took a stone and used it to prise something off the underside, holding it up to the light. Peering at it, Torgun saw it was red and sticky. For a moment he feared Wrackwulf had accidentally trodden on a globule of demon flesh, but then he realised what they were looking at.

Taking it from the stone, Torgun rolled the glob between his fingers. He had seen such a thing many times, in his father's study at Vandheim, but it was strange to find it out here in a forsaken cursed wilderness.

Sealing wax...?

CHAPTER 17

FROM HELL TO HEAVEN

Adelko virtually held his breath as Abdel Sha'arza led them from his suite of chambers. He'd already looked upon the architecture of the Elder Wizards, but this was the first time he had been inside one of their mythical watchtowers. He felt a sense of trepidation as Sha'arza led them through a sucker-shaped exit, twice the size of a man, its alien stone writhing with conjoined friezes of demons and angels that seemed to mock them as they stepped through it.

Azelin, Anupe and Yassin stumbled along as if in a trance; a necessary precaution to preserve their unsanctified minds from insanity. The ruins of the Warlock's Crown had been bad enough, but here all the most potent sorceries of the Elder Wizards would be concentrated. Few places besides the Forbidden City itself would hold such elan, and for an ordinary soul to gaze on it would profane the psyche beyond repair.

They emerged on to a round stone gallery that over-looked a sheer drop. The circumference of the tower was covered with multicoloured friezes that seemed to come alive in the magic puffball of light that fluoresced above Sha'arza's head: gazing on the queer-looking stone, Adelko fancied it was almost alive. The sorcerer reckoned the Elder Wizards had constructed the tower from a meteorite they had conjured to fall to the earth for that purpose, when they had communed with the spheres and conducted their heav-enly music to their own ends.

The journeyman shuddered with renewed vigour as Sha'arza led them along the gallery walkway past the impos-sibly detailed and lifelike sculptures: in amongst the demons and angels and elementi and other spirits of the Other Side, Adelko thought he discerned gibbering monkey-like figures, grotesque parodies of mortalkind. Some of these were leashed to the sculpted depictions of the Unseen; mere pets and playthings for what the pagans called gods. In amongst them strode the Varyans, taking the leashes from angelic and daemoniacal hands, ebony skins and braided hair stark against their flowing white robes. Tall and proud and erect, the Priest Kings seemed to nod in acknowledgement to the Unseen, as they led their lesser fellow mortals towards high-pinnacled cities and onion-shaped temples.

Adelko gasped as he grasped the meaning.

'The Varyans,' he said as Abdel led them along the gallery walkway. 'They just took over from the Unseen, didn't they? In ruling mortalkind, I mean.'

Sha'arza chuckled slyly.

'Perhaps that is what *you* see, Adelko of Narvik,' he said. 'For the watchtower is all things to all men. But how curious that an Argolian should see the Varyans as custodians and leaders of humankind, and not gross idolators...'

'I've learned they were both during their thousand-year reign,' said Adelko, somewhat too defensively for his own liking. Now they were in the watchtower proper, he felt thoroughly unnerved. It wasn't just the blasphemous sculptures and what they suggested; the very dimensions of the place seemed to confound the eye. One moment he was sure the tower was even bigger on the inside than it had looked from without, the next he felt it was claustrophobically cramped. Likewise the cityscapes and deities and demons seemed to change perspective and size all the time; more than once he felt as though he would stumble and topple off the walkway into the dizzying depths below.

The depths below... they were even worse somehow. One second all he saw was stygian darkness that seemed to negate everything that tried to look upon it; the next a red inferno that roiled and multiplied into hybrid faces that grinned at him; after that he caught a glimpse of what looked like sylvan angelic figures, silvery and laughing, as fresh as an early morning mist, who beckoned him to come down and cavort with them forever... and then he was looking at stars in the sky. But wait – was he still looking down, or staring upwards now through the summit of the tower?

Abruptly, Adelko came back to where he was. His

mentor was talking, replying to what he had said seemingly ages ago.

'That is the account of the Elder Wizards given in the *Codices of Zhorrah*,' said Horskram, reiterating what he had told Adelko in the cave above the Brenning Wold, when their adventure had barely begun. 'Though those texts were written down by the priest-caste of Sendhé, themselves but apprentices who survived the destruction of Varya. I would not believe any people that claims right of rulership over mortalkind, for 'tis naught but hubris that guides them. I see in these loathsome sculptures the very archdemons who placed such ideas in the minds of men in the first place.'

As they followed the gallery around, Adelko saw it was true. An impossibly gorgeous succubus, Invidia leaned down, beckoning to the proud priests of Varya, pointing to unconquered lands and cities and urging them to take what was not theirs by right; while at her side Azazel pressed cruel weapons of war into the hands of soldiers and ushered them onwards in their wake. Just behind Azazel leered Zolthoth, who bore even crueller implements of torture such as Grand Master Tobin would have envied, and beyond him Ta'ussaswazelim beat two vast cymbals together, stirring up the arming soldiers into a rage with his clangour. Adelko could have sworn he could hear the cymbals clashing like the bells of hell, the mounted cavalry giving vent to war-cries in anticipation of the coming bloodshed. And yet in other parts of the gallery, the archdemons had their glorious opposites: Ezekiel and Stygnos in gilded form, leading a host of winged paladins in beautifully scroll-worked armour, nobly preparing to defend the cities about to be attacked.

'You cannot have good without evil, nor evil without good,' Sha'arza reminded him. 'Thus it was in your vision in the Witch Queen's forest – a world without the Unseen to watch over it will be a bleak one indeed. And yet that is just what we are striving towards, I fear.' The sorcerer actually sounded sad now.

'You know about my vision?' Adelko had tried to forget what he had seen in the Earth Witch's bower a thousand times, even though she had obviously been trying to help him.

'The Witch of the Forest and I share certain things,' said Sha'arza, 'the vision bequeathed you by her magicks being one of them. According to one truth, the Third Age of Darkness is at hand. But according to another, the time of magic and miracles has nearly run its course. Or to put it another way, in order to avert the Second Coming of Iblis, one cannot simply defeat evil, because as I have just said evil cannot be overturned without overturning good as well, and it is impossible to have a world of sentient beings where neither one exists. No self-conscious being can live in a perpetual state of concordant-opposition – a world without good and evil would be an inhuman place.'

Sha'arza paused to let his words sink in. Adelko had a sense that they weren't even walking any more, just suspended over a vast space as they talked.

'So what must be done, in your opinion?' asked the journeyman.

'The evil must be channelled elsewhere – and with it the good. According to one of the truths I have been recounting, that would mean no more magic, and no more miracles – all of these deities you see here will turn their backs on this plane, if this truth comes to pass.'

'I saw something that suggested that in my vision, but what will that mean exactly?'

'What that will mean is that good and evil, its constitution and distribution throughout the world, will become an entirely human affair.'

Glancing again at the writhing walls, Adelko saw that all of the Unseen – demonic, angelic and un-angelic alike – had abruptly vanished. Instead the human figures had multiplied, only now their leashes were gone. Instead they held strange devices and operated machines that looked simple yet complex. Behind them loomed smooth straight towers of glass, great metallic dragons flew through the air, and the sun and stars in the skies beyond grew smaller and weaker... In amongst them he saw Kaia, personified as the moon, her round face weeping as it grew sickly and pock-marked.

Adelko felt his mouth go dry as the full significance of the Earth Witch's vision flooded his mind.

'We'll become as gods ourselves,' he breathed, 'but we'll be our own demons, too.'

Sha'arza smiled. 'I think you understand much, Adelko of Narvik. You are without doubt a tool of the Unseen.'

With a shock Adelko realised that he and Sha'arza were alone on the platform.

'The others!' he gasped, reaching for a quarterstaff that was not there.

'Are safely transmitted to the summit,' said Sha'arza, smiling and indicating another sucker-like entranceway they had drawn level with. Just beyond this was a thick beam of coruscating light, disappearing up and down a shaft as far as the eye could see in both directions. Adelko thought he could just make out the images of his companions vanishing upwards.

'You're using magic to transport us to the top of the tower?' baulked Adelko. 'How did you convince Master Horskram to agree to that?'

Sha'arza's smile broadened, making his mouth look unnaturally wide. 'I didn't give him a choice in the matter. Not even a hierophant of your Order can withstand my powers, when I draw them directly from the stones that the Magi laid. Your mentor is himself a tool of the Unseen and a force to be reckoned with, but he is stubborn and set in his ways, and I do not have time to argue with him.'

'And what about the others? Tipu and the fire priest, they seem to know a lot as well.'

'Tipu's heart is as pure as yours, and his powers you have already seen demonstrated, but he is too diffident, too serene to be instrumental in this. His kind are inclined to accept victory and defeat as fated. Heroes must strive. As for the rest of your companions, near and far, they have their parts to play, but they are just minor craftsmen in the great design we are fashioning.' The sorcerer's eyes seemed to deepen to infinite pits of night as he scrutinised Adelko in the fey lighting. 'Adelko of Narvik, you alone have the power and purity in both measures to see this through.'

'See what through exactly? I've only just been made a

journeyman of my Order. It's hardly down to me alone to stop the Headstone from being used to summon Ma'amun back to the world.'

'Your modesty does you credit, Adelko of Narvik,' said Sha'arza, still smiling broadly. The sorcerer motioned for Adelko to step into the shaft of light. He was not using magic to compel him: unlike his companions, Adelko was being invited to do so willingly.

'If the truth I have been alluding to is the one that comes to pass, then this quest for the fragments is but the beginning of the Great Transition,' Abdel went on. 'The tools of the Unseen are many – some sharp and dangerous, others canny and crafty, others still ingenious and subtle. All fit for differing purposes, to craft good and evil of different kinds. I believe you are fated to craft something that will last far beyond your mission.'

'You mean we're destined to succeed in stopping the Headstone being reunited?'

'I did not say that. Perhaps a reunited Headstone is an essential part of this grand design I have been referring to.'

They had both stepped into the column of light. Adelko suddenly felt strangely euphoric and giddy. His body tingled all over, and a glitter of sound he fancied he could see rather than hear all but drowned out his senses.

'Wait!' he cried as he felt them both starting to fade out of existence. 'Tell me more! What happens after the Headstone?'

But Sha'arza simply continued to smile. He was mouthing words now. Adelko wasn't sure if they were in the sorcerer's tongue, but he heard other words that he could understand, whispering in his inner ear.

'Many routes, Adelko of Narvik, and many truths...'

When his body reconstituted itself, he found himself standing in the open air, beneath a strong late afternoon sun. Blinking, he looked about him. His companions were all there, looking similarly nonplussed as they gazed upon what must be the shattered summit of the tower. The broken walls loomed about them, their serrated tops putting Adelko in mind of the Warlock's Crown. Similar in stature, the stones here seemed to radiate an even more potent power. At least here there were none of the mind-boggling friezes. They appeared to be standing in what would have once been a vast chamber, several times the size of a great hall of latter-day men. Sha'arza, who seemed perfectly at home, pointed towards a shattered doorway with his wand.

'This is the one we want,' he said cheerfully. 'Try not to look at anything more if you can avoid it, and above all don't touch anything! I'm doing my best to protect you from this place.'

'Have no fear,' said Horskram, who appeared to have no recollection of being transported. 'I have no wish to linger in this foul place, and none whatsoever to study its black evils.'

'I'm glad to see our little jaunt through my home has not diminished your manners,' replied Sha'arza with his customary giggle. 'Come now, brave companions, please follow me!'

'You have been chary of revealing details,' pressed Horskram as they did. 'You claim to know the whereabouts of the fourth fragment, though you are not its keeper. What of the boy Cael? Have you found his shade?' Age-old rumours of the Westerling lad who had been entrusted with the fragment, only to fall foul of its curse and spend centuries wandering undead through the Ghorabi desert, were myths that few if any could verify.

'So impatient!' said Abdel, as he led them along a corridor that zigzagged maddeningly and for no apparent purpose but to satisfy the whim of a no less mad architect. 'I told you already, I know nothing for certain. But a contact of mine... it is rumoured that he came by an artefact of great power, a stone is what I heard. Who can say if the spirits spoke truly? They mislead as often as not.'

'So that's it?' protested Adelko. 'This is why we've come all the way here to see you, for a rumour from the Other Side?'

They had passed into another oblique-angled room. This one abutted on to the tower's edge, and through a great fissure in the ruined wall the westering sun glowered at them, forcing Adelko to squint.

Sha'arza abruptly stopped and fixed Adelko with a squint of his own. 'Do you have any better leads?' he asked pointedly.

For once Horskram was placatory. 'We'll visit your contact, Sha'arza,' he said. 'Though why you have brought us to the top of your tower is beyond me. Know that if you intend to trap us, we will resist you with every power at our disposal.'

The Zarumani and Tipu had held their peace, but now closed ranks with Horskram.

Sha'arza only giggled at that. 'You might try!' he exclaimed. 'But have no fear, for as I keep telling you, a larger fate brings us together. This common enemy must be opposed at all costs.'

The sorcerer sounded sincere, yet Adelko could not shake the words he had just told him.

Perhaps a reunited Headstone is an essential part of the grand design.

'Many routes and many truths,' Adelko muttered to himself, as Sha'arza spun on his heel and pointed to a flight of stairs at the far end of the chamber. The Imp fluttered about his shoulders, and seemed to grow more excited as they advanced towards the pitted stairway, though it still made sure to give Horskram a wide berth. Adelko glanced over his shoulder at the rest of his companions, but Yassin, Anupe and Azelin appeared to walk vacantly as if in a deep sleep.

Adelko soon found reason to envy them. Climbing the stairs was a sickening experience, for they seemed to double back on themselves continually, and at one point even seemed to turn upside down, an unseen force keeping the wayfarers glued to their cracked stone surfaces. Adelko screwed his eyes shut, trusting reluctantly to Sha'arza to guide them.

When he opened them again, they were all standing on a raised platform. The highest surviving part of the tower, it looked out over the shattered upper level, a warren of honeycombed chambers through which they had just passed.

Sha'arza banged his walking-stick wand on the jigsaw-patterned flagstones for emphasis as he cried: 'Behold, the *Chariot of the Sky!*'

Turning to look across the platform, Adelko blinked in surprise as he registered...

... a ship?

At least that was what it looked like. Its stern and prow were clearly discernible, likewise its huge triple masts put the journeyman in mind of the pilgrim ship they had travelled in to Ushalayim. But where that vessel had been fashioned of pine, this was metalclad – not a single grain of wood could be seen beneath the smooth, sleek panels that covered the ship from keel to freeboard. The figurehead that seemed to bleed up out of the prow was likewise fashioned of the same dark metal: the androgynous winged figure that spread its arms to the heavens could have been angel or demon, perhaps both.

Sha'arza's trance spell had clearly expired, for everyone was staring at the ship, parked on four vast blocks of stone seemingly hewn for the express purpose of holding its gargantuan bulk.

Yassin's eyes widened as he took in the vessel. 'You must be joking,' he gaped. 'I thought I'd dreamed everything, perhaps I am still dreaming.'

'All of mortal life is but a dream,' Tipu interjected. 'He who sees through the illusion is truly awake. We are still dreaming, all of us.'

Perhaps we won't be for much longer if Sha'arza's truth comes to pass, thought Adelko. *Not that a waking nightmare sounds much better.*

He pushed that thought to the depths of his mind, as Abdel ushered them across the platform towards the ship. The *Chariot of the Sky* was even bigger than the *Pilgrim's Passage.* Windows were embedded along the length of its hull; like those of the tower it rested on, they were a myriad of confusing shapes. What should have been the rudder and forepeak were coated with strange clustered growths of crystalline carbuncles.

'I told you earlier, my greatest delight of the Seven Schools and their sub-disciplines was artifice,' said Sha'arza excitedly. 'Long and hard have I studied the eldritch machinery of the ancient wizards, many decades it took me to refashion this beauty!' He pointed at the iridescent crystals just behind the ebon figurehead. They swirled with a faint gaseous mist. 'More than a hundred Aethi are bound to this vessel – once we are aboard, they shall take the *Chariot* to the skies where she belongs.'

'This hellish contraption beggars belief to look upon,' said Horskram. 'I shudder to think what devilish entities of the Other Side you consulted to relearn such craft.'

Sha'arza favoured him with a sidelong grin. 'Oh don't worry, master monk, I can assure you every man I sacrificed to consult the spirits of the Other Side was himself a fiend in human raiment, and thoroughly deserving of his fate!'

The adept made the sign of the Wheel as if to ward off the warlock, prompting a venomous screech from Infidel. Even Tipu, normally so tranquil, appeared to have paled as he contemplated the ship. Peering more closely at it, Adelko could see the sheets of metal were night-black and impossibly seamless. He'd seen metal like that before – at the Warlock's Crown.

'Ebonite,' he gasped. 'This thing is coated with ebonite!' No one living today knew how to smelt the near-indestructible metal, though many ancient and disused mines were dotted across the Known World. So far as anyone knew, they had lain dormant since the Breaking – not even the Thalamians or the priest-seers of Sendhé had relearned how to smelt it.

'Just so,' nodded Sha'arza when he pointed this out. 'Weapons and tools made of it all but disappeared after the Wrath of the Unseen. Nowadays one will find just a few scattered remnants in the watchtowers, and other structures built by Them – the Colossean Shelves that lie on the eastern fringes of the Sundering Sea, and of course the Forbidden City itself.'

'I always just thought of weapons and tools and the like,' said Adelko. 'It never would have occurred to me to reinforce a flying ship with ebonite.' He paused and scratched his head. 'Then again, it wouldn't have occurred to me to build a flying ship in the first place.'

Sha'arza winked at him. 'The Elder Wizards thought of a great many things,' he said. 'Things that we of the so-called Silver Age have long forgotten in our ignorance. Even the mighty civilisations of the Golden Age fell far short of their learning.'

'This is all well and good,' said Hari. 'But you still haven't said where you are taking us.' The trickster's face looked even paler than Tipu's. Adelko guessed he would be a long time in forgiving Adhelina for deceiving him into joining their madcap adventure.

'Let us board first and get started, then I will explain everything,' said the mage. Sha'arza tapped the side of the hull with his wand. There came a sound like many portcullises being raised. A section opened out from the side of the hull, becoming an unfolding set of stairs. The sorcerer began to ascend the steps, surprisingly lightly for a man of his girth.

The companions exchanged a last look. Then Horskram sighed and motioned them forwards. They had come this far – they could hardly turn back now.

The ship's deck was fashioned of a rich dark teak. Catching Adelko looking at it, Sha'arza giggled again and said: 'Can't risk passengers breaking every bone in their bodies if they fall on pure ebonite, now can I?'

'What about the crew?' asked Adelko, looking around at the empty main deck. The mizzen, main and foremast loomed above them, higher than turrets, cream-coloured sails hanging dormant. Adelko couldn't say for sure, but he had a feeling they weren't made of ordinary canvas.

'No need for sailors,' said Sha'arza, striding over to the stairs leading up to the forecastle and taking them two at a time. Adelko followed him without even thinking twice about it: the incredible ship had his natural curiosity stoked up like a bonfire. The forecastle was crowned with a large spherical crystal set atop a podium of ebonite chased with gold filigree. Touching this, the sorcerer muttered a few words. A white light ignited deep within the crystal, and a great juddering ran the length of the vessel. 'Better hold on to something!' cried Sha'arza above the rumbling. 'In my experience, those who have never travelled by air are as likely to get sick as those who haven't got their sea legs!'

Sure enough, Adelko's stomach shot into his gullet as the mighty ship lifted clear of its holding blocks. The sails unfurled of their own accord from the three masts, while two more appeared from hatches on the port and starboard sides of the hull, sails sprouting from these to make the *Chariot* look like a gigantic bird. Down on the main deck, Horskram and Tipu made the signs of Faith and Creed, mumbling prayers in shaky voices as they clutched the taff-rail feverishly. Yassin and Anupe were already being sick over the side, while Azelin and the Zarumani stared sight-lessly out across the panoramic vista. Adelko followed their dazed gaze, forgetting prayers of his own: never in all his childhood daydreams had he thought this would happen to him. Not ever.

The *Chariot* lurched upwards at dizzying speed. Already the tower was receding at an alarming rate. The Abydos ranges stretched out beneath them like a great orange spine; the cracked plains to either side could have been the flanks of Aurgelmir the Father of Giants himself. The wind whis-tled fiercely in Adelko's ears, becoming surprisingly cold and raw as he clutched the forecastle rail with white-knuckled fingers.

'Altitude makes a difference to temperature,' explained Sha'arza, yelling to be heard above the wind. 'But have no fear – Aethi are not the only elementi bound to this ship.' He banged down his wand again and lamps hanging from the shrouds flared into light, radiating a heat that offset the chill perfectly.

Touching the pulsing crystal again, Sha'arza furrowed his brow in concentration. Sails creaked as the skyship's five masts adjusted position. The *Chariot* gradually stopped ascending and began to move horizontally in a southerly direction.

'The sails tap the winds for steering, while the Aethi keep the ship afloat,' explained Sha'arza. 'Truly a wonder of the Platinum Age, the *Chariot of the Skies* combines science and magic to achieve something miraculous!'

Adelko felt queasy in spite of his excitement. Miraculous wasn't quite how he would have put it. 'How many of these ships did the Elder Wizards build?' he asked.

Sha'arza did not look up from the crystal as he replied. 'The *Codices* say they had an entire fleet of them, and used this to conquer the Known World and subdue the dragons. Tens of thousands of soldiers would have been transported across vast distances in a short time – it's said the Varyans took less than a hundred years to conquer all of the Known World, from the Westerling Isles to the Great Eastern Wall that guards the fringes of the Urovian New Empire, everything between the Fenris Mountains to the far north and the Zhosa Desert that lies on the fringes of the Arid Kingdoms! But legends tell they met their match at the Steppes of Koth, for something dwelled in those wastes that even the Elder Wizards feared to confront. So they built their wall and patrolled the lands about it, accepting that even their empire had reached its limit.'

That got the journeyman's attention. 'Really? I never knew the Elder Wizards feared anyone or anything.'

'No one knows for sure what power it was that checked them,' replied Sha'arza, staring at tendrils of cloud that now appeared disconcertingly at eye-level. 'But all agree the Priest-Kings stopped at the steppes. For that reason the kingdoms and empires of the Uttermost East were left to flourish and fall of their own accord, and the people there are different in their customs. Their magic is said to be different too, more subtle and less potent than ours. Sometimes the Easterners sail up the Vindus river in merchant parties, to trade strange goods with the Khedivates and the Free City of Aratheny, but-'

He was interrupted by Horskram arriving on the forecastle next to them. The monk's face was as pale as the sails, but he appeared to have recovered his fortitude. 'Enough history for now,' said the adept. 'I think it high time you told us of our immediate future instead, namely where we are going.'

Sha'arza nodded. 'Very well. The *Chariot*'s course is set, and I can leave her to follow it. Let us go below decks and get out of the wind. I think some refreshments are called for.'

Heading back down to the deck, he led them over to a circular hatchway between the mainmast and mizzen. The *Chariot* lurched and creaked like a giant bird, putting Adelko in mind of the legendary Roc, slain by Antaeus on one of his many voyages across the Great Inland Sea. Had the Elder Wizards used their magic and loremastery to defeat such creatures too, he wondered?

Sha'arza touched the ebonite hatch with his wand and muttered a word. A series of concentric overlapping spirals slid open to reveal a ladder leading below decks. Another word, and a refulgent glow sprang up out of the dark. The wizard began climbing down, Infidel flittering and screeching about him.

'Well don't just stand there,' he grinned, just before his head disappeared. 'I'm not going to waste energy teleporting you everywhere.'

'The things the Almighty bids us do,' said Horskram, a sickly look plastered across his face. But he followed Sha'arza down into the bowels of the strange ship.

Below decks it was reassuringly normal. Decorated in similar fashion to Sha'arza's private suite, the cabins they passed through were well-appointed and opulent. And silent. Not so much as a whisper of wind penetrated, and glancing at the hotchpotch windows as they followed Sha'arza, Adelko realised they were airtight.

The wizard stopped when they got to a cabin larger than all the others they had passed through. Half of this was given over to a laboratory of some kind: Adelko had seen such when they had destroyed Andragorix's after defeating him, and the Sea Wizard's too. But those apparati seemed like the mean triflings of hedge witches compared to the conjoined and convoluted web of tubes, phials, vials, decanters, tripods, dishes, retorts, aludels and other para-phernalia that rested on the heaving table. Brightly coloured liquids of all hues sat distilling, and some bubbled as a miserable-looking Saraphus caged beneath a grill kept them heated.

'Never mind my potions,' said Abdel, breezing over towards an ornate shelf of ivory and mahogany filled with rhytons and decanters. 'I prefer to keep a laboratory to hand when I go on my little jaunts.'

'You must terrify the locals,' observed Tipu dryly. 'I am surprised they have not called on my sect more often, thanks to you and your jaunts.'

Sha'arza only laughed at that. 'Unlike my erstwhile apprentice Hakan Göker, I fly high enough so as rarely to be seen,' observed the sorcerer, picking up a decanter full of amber-coloured wine and placing it on a low table surrounded with cushions. 'The Sultan of Halepo is in the habit of keeping his subjects in check by terrorising them with that winged wooden horse of his. I sometimes wish I'd never taught him how to fashion the thing!'

'What allegiance will His Majesty owe in the coming war?' It was the first time the Zarumani had spoken in a while. 'The fires have been somewhat confusing on the matter, though my sect would fain learn which way he will lean in the coming conflict.'

Sha'arza shrugged as he set down a tray of silver rhytons next to the decanter, bidding them all sit. 'I cannot say for sure. I think the Sultan of Halepo is biding his time and scrying as much as he can to find out which way the wind blows strongest. I will keep an eye on my former pupil, don't you worry! Now, it behoves us I think to discuss a matter of more immediate concern.'

'Yes it does,' said Horskram pointedly, squatting on a cushion and taking a slow sip of wine. His eyes did not leave the sorcerer as he did so.

'Very well,' said Sha'arza, raising his rhyton in a toast before taking a sip. 'The *Chariot* is taking us to the Cerulean Mountains that border the Hierocracy of Sendhé. As most of you will know, in the midst of those ranges sits Ortiz, the Fortress of Perpetual Forbidding, which for a hundred years has been home to the Old Master of Time's Arrow and the Order of the Silver Shadow he commands.'

Horskram almost dropped his rhyton. 'Are you mad?' he gasped. 'We were nearly assassinated by Shadowmen in Ushalayim!'

Sha'arza raised an eyebrow at that. 'Any idea why?'

The adept shook his head. 'With everything that has happened to us since, I've barely had time to give it any thought. All I know is that assassins tried to kill us during our sojourn at the Bethler headquarters, and Grand Master Tobin had us imprisoned pending execution directly after that. Were it not for friends of ours in the Holy City, and the efforts of Hari Yassin here, we would be seeking the Judgment of Azrael by now.'

Azelin's brow was furrowed. He appeared deep in thought. 'The Bethlers have long had contacts with the Order of the Silver Shadow,' he mused. 'The Old Master's followers cleave to the Unorthodox Faith, so they are natural allies against the Nazharyan and Kallandhari sultanates. Strange indeed that the Silver Shadow would invade the sanctity of the Bethel's headquarters.'

Yassin stood and made a sideways slashing movement with his arms. 'You're taking us to Ortiz?' he exclaimed. 'Absolutely not! I've had enough of this madness. You can bloody well land this thing and put me down, I'm not going!'

'I had not realised you held the Order of the Silver Shadow in such aversion,' said Sha'arza mildly.

'Don't be too surprised,' said Horskram dryly. 'I doubt the Old Master would give warm welcome to a renegade.' Hari turned to look at him, but Horskram brushed off his incipient protests. 'No need to dissemble, I worked it out when we were being held at General Zimri's camp. Your protests against fanatical religious types gave you away. Besides that, I had been wondering where you learned your craft – no ordinary street thief could have done what you did to save us from Tobin.'

Adelko wasn't surprised by the revelation either. His sixth sense had been telling him Hari was more than he seemed for a while, too.

'I won't do it!' Hari persisted. 'It's my neck if you take me there – I'd sooner take my chances back on the waterfront with the Shirt Tails and the Bethlers. Or the bloody Ghorabi desert, for that matter. Just let me go, I won't breathe a word of your quest to anyone!'

Horskram turned to look at Sha'arza again. 'I must say, I'm inclined to agree with yon rogue, albeit for different reasons. Are you quite sure the Old Master of Time's Arrow knows anything of the Headstone fragment? We still don't know why he tried to have us killed – possibly he learned of our quest and wishes to protect what he knows, or even the fragment itself if he really has come by it.'

Abdel tugged at his moustachios as he pondered that.

'Perhaps all the more reason to seek him out,' said the sorcerer. 'Persuade him that you have no designs on the fragment.' He narrowed his eyes. 'I assume you have no designs on it, of course.'

Horskram frowned. 'That depends. I will confess that initially I was minded to try to bring it back to our own Order's headquarters, for safekeeping. But if the Old Master is holding it and has no intention of using it, that is a different matter. Ortiz is well guarded, by worldly means and others. In all honesty, I can scarce think of a better resting place for it – but we must be sure of its safety all the same.'

'But that's just it,' put in Adelko. 'We can't know for sure whether this Old Master isn't the one behind the Headstone plot.'

Tipu shook his head. 'The Old Master is known to me,' he said. 'For his sect and ours have had some dealings – purely in matters of the spirit, I assure you! I do not think he would ever wish to see the Headstone reunited – he is a devout Unorthodoxer and considers himself a blood descendant of Alamuz, great-grandson of Abu tek Jahib, last of the Enlightened Sultans. His Shadowmen use violence that we Sufielis cannot hold with, but they have never been friends to demonkind.'

'Unlike our sorcerous host,' said Horskram, indicating the Imp cowering behind the laboratory with a disgusted gesture. 'I am beginning to wonder if we were not foolish to trust you, Abdel Sha'arza. Is this some sort of a trap?'

Sha'arza spread his arms in a helpless gesture. 'Why would I tell you where I'm taking you if that was the case? I had no idea Shadowmen had tried to kill you – even with my Scrying, I cannot see everything that happens!' He shook his head in puzzlement. 'No, I am as surprised as you that the Old Master wanted you dead. Truly it makes no sense.'

'Unless, of course, he was commissioned to do the job by the Bethlers themselves,' put in Azelin. 'It's obvious Tobin wanted you both dead. It seems to me that he used his own fanaticism as a cover, to order your execution once he realised his first attempt on your lives had failed.'

Adelko and Horskram exchanged knowing looks. 'We did wonder why he was going to such lengths to kill us,' commented the older monk dryly. 'Though Tobin's fanaticism alone is enough to make him a dangerous enemy.'

'But you're suggesting Tobin's wish to see us dead and the Shadowmen's attempt to kill us are directly connected?' said Adelko.

Azelin shrugged, before draining his rhyton. 'I wouldn't put it past him. Tobin is as corrupt a potentate as any, and a schemer to boot. He'd gladly see the Pilgrim Kingdoms and the rest of Sassania cleansed of Sha'abatians, he doesn't care about the means so long as the ends are achieved. Perhaps this secret wizard you're hunting offered him what he wants in return for getting rid of you.'

'It makes sense,' said Horskram, nodding thoughtfully. 'It's likely our mastermind has recruited powerful allies by promising them the thing they desire most. There's no reason why a power-mad fanatic like Tobin wouldn't succumb to such temptation. Thus have the Fallen One and his servants worked since the beginning to corrupt the hearts of men.' He sighed. 'So it looks as though we can add the Grand Master of the Knights Bethler to our list of conspirators.'

'I think we should press on and consult the Old Master at Ortiz in that case,' ventured the Zarumani. 'By the sounds of it, he will have the answer to many questions.'

'He may also have all our heads,' protested Hari. 'Mine for certain! I bought my freedom from the Order many years ago, but was sworn never to return to the Fortress of Perpetual Forbidding on pain of death.'

'You don't have to come with us when we arrive,' suggested Sha'arza. 'You can stay here aboard the *Chariot* – but try pinching anything and I'll know. Then you'll wish for the Old Master's justice!'

Hari narrowed his eyes and folded his arms defensively. 'What would I want to go stealing from a sorcerer for?' But Adelko sensed the wizard had fathomed the rogue.

'That settles it then,' said Horskram, 'we continue on as planned, and put our lives in the hands of Ushira. May the archangel of good fortune smile upon us.'

Sha'arza nodded as though satisfied with the outcome of the discussion. Hari shifted and scowled, before getting to his feet. 'I think I'll take some air, if you don't mind,' he said. 'By the looks of things, I'm going to be cooped up below decks for some time.' He stalked towards the exit and Abdel motioned for them all to rise.

'You may as well accompany him,' he said. 'I can assure you, watching the sunset from this elevation is quite spectacular!' The sorcerer was doing his best to sound cheerful, but Adelko sensed great foreboding in the company. Their sentiments mirrored his own.

He felt his spirits rise once they were back up on deck. The ball of fire that was the setting sun shone with all the powers that Solus could muster: the pagans had held him to be embodied in the sun itself, with Palomedians and Sha'abatians countering that Solus was in fact an archangel who controlled the sun remotely.

Of course, nowadays Adelko couldn't be sure of anything.

Anything theological that was: he was quite sure his natural senses were telling him the vista spread out before and beneath him was beyond magnificent. The quilted lands of Nazharya lay thousands of hands below them, their farms and orchards and cities all but invisible to the eye. The *Chariot* was moving at a rate of knots that would have made a Northland longship spurred by the Sea Wizard's sorcery look slow; the taffrail came up to chest height, presumably to avoid any accidents in the high winds. The lamps kept them warm, their orange glow reflecting the sun's as the fiery orb sank down towards the incarnadined plains. The skies were gradually bleeding out of colour, cobalt becoming pale blue becoming light yellow to the west.

Sha'arza was back on the forecastle, his hand on the crystal as he steered the flying vessel south-south west. Adelko decided to go up and join him again.

'How long until we reach Ortiz?' he cried above the wind.

'At this speed, we should make the Fortress of Perpetual Forbidding by dusk tomorrow,' Sha'arza yelled back. 'And when we do-'

A flurry of motion distracted them both. Adelko felt his heart leap into his mouth again – but it was just a golden eagle, perching on the forepeak, its wings flapping as it gazed at them with beady eyes.

'Probably from an eyrie in the mountains,' said Sha'arza, nudging his head towards the Abydos ranges that now lay to the north-north east. The eagle continued to regard them with its black eyes. Adelko suddenly felt his sixth sense flare.

With a malevolent squawk, the bird launched itself at the forestays, tearing at the sail with its razor-sharp beak and claws. Abdel Sha'arza barely had time to curse before another eagle flashed into view, its golden crest catching the sunlight as it joined its brother. Yells from down on the main deck turned Adelko's gaze. More eagles had arrived to ravage the shrouds and topgallants that sprouted from the fore and main masts. Some plucked at the lamps, tearing them from their fixtures and casting them overboard.

Looking towards the mountains, Adelko saw yet more eagles were coming. Many more eagles.

'They'll cripple the ship,' cried Sha'arza, cursing again and taking up his wand. A bolt of blue lightning forked from it, frying the first two eagles to cinders, but hard on their wings came half a dozen more, clustering about the sails and rigging.

Adelko cast around, looking for something, anything, to take up and use as a weapon. Nothing, not so much as a belaying pin to be seen on the enchanted vessel. More blue cracklings, followed by squawking and the stench of frying flesh, told him Sha'arza was not idle. But there were too many of them: hundreds of eagles now swarmed about the ship like parasites. Some began to attack them, too: Adelko yelled as a couple fastened on to his habit, one trying to pluck out his eyes while the second clawed at his face. Nothing Edemus had taught him could prepare the journeyman for this kind of fight: with a blind instinct born of desperation, he seized the eagle pecking at his eyes by a leg, dashing it against the taffrail and smashing its skull. A flare of light nearly took his head off, singeing his hair... the other eagle fell from his shoulder, a twitching mass of charring feathers. Sha'arza was bleeding from several cuts to his face and arms too, but his magic seemed to have got the best of the creatures on the forecastle.

Glancing back down at the main deck, Adelko saw Hari, Anupe and Azelin hacking at birds on the left hand and the right; for every one of the maddened creatures they cut down, another appeared just as quickly to menace them. A pirouetting crescent of fire from the Zarumani sent three flaming eagles spiralling over the side of the ship, but his fire-channelling had set the main stays on fire as well. Yelling another curse that segued effortlessly into the sorcerer's tongue, Sha'arza sent a rivulet of water spurting from his wand; smoke hissed up into the darkening skies as the opposing elementi neutralised one another.

Once again Adelko cast around, this time looking for Horskram and Tipu. They had retreated to the poop deck, and a melodic fluting mingled with a sonorous voice told of their sacred music. Horskram was singing the Psalm of Gramarye's Quenching; Adelko joined his own voice to the psalmody, made all the more beautiful by Tipu's piping.

All around him the fight seemed to recede in a kaleidoscopic whirl of smoke and steel and fire and lightning; letting those things drop away, Adelko focused on the holy words, each one seemingly given wings by the fluted notes... He felt in that moment that all was conjoined and reconciled, all faiths and creeds and kingdoms united; even demonkind and angels cast aside their weapons and embraced one another, just as they had done in the Elder Wizards' friezes...

The Elder Wizards. No. It cannot be. They cannot have been right. Adelko felt a knot of resistance in his gut growing tighter, as invisible hands pulled on it with a monstrous strength.

Question everything. The Earth Witch gazing at him inscrutably under moonlight in her bower...

Many routes and many truths. Abdel Sha'arza smiling at him as he grinned in the coruscating beam of light...

Gloom gathers on the road ahead, not all shall take an open road. The Fay princes, gifting him with prophecy, unlikely allies who had most likely saved his life...

The war of the worlds is coming, which side will you be on, my clever friars? The demon Belaach at Rykken, feeding him with twisted words designed to poison...

And then he saw someone smiling: a person he thought he recognised, someone he could trust. But when he looked closer, the smile curdled on the figure's lips, and the eyes became great gaping mouths that sought to devour him...

~

Adelko lurched upwards with a sharp cry. His companions were gathered about him, anxious looks stamped across their faces. Taking in the weakened glow of the remaining lamps hanging from the shrouds, he realised it was dusk.

Looking around him, he blinked. 'The eagles...?' he murmured.

'Gone,' said Sha'arza. 'That is quite a power the three of you conjured up. It was enough to break whatever infernal bewitchment compelled them to attack us.' The wizard scratched his tripartite beard thoughtfully. 'A clever trick, I must say – crossing the schools of Enchantment and Thaumaturgy to control creatures of the animal kingdom. Your quest has earned you some resourceful enemies.'

'Enemies, yes!' exclaimed Adelko excitedly. 'I saw... I saw...' He felt confused. What had he seen?

Tipu rested a gentle hand on his brow. 'Rest,' said the mystic kindly. 'You have taxed yourself over much. I will play the melody to the Shura of Spirit's Rejuvenation, it will expedite your healing physically and mentally.'

'I've a brew or two that will help with the cuts from the eagles,' said Sha'arza. 'We should away below.'

Adelko felt his forehead. It was badly gashed, with congealed blood down the side of his face, though that wasn't the first time he'd taken a head injury. Nor probably the last, he reflected wiwincingly. Anupe and Yassin had both taken light wounds of their own, though Azelin's peerless skill had been too good even for the swift and savage eagles. Not that he looked any less melancholy for it.

Adelko surveyed the *Chariot* frowningly. About half the lamps were gone, leaving the main deck where he supposed his companions had brought him half submerged in gloom. The main stay was a blackened remnant where the Zarumani's sorcery had set it afire, and many of the other sails were torn; the ship was still moving, though more slowly than before. It was then Adelko noticed the Imp, screeching resentfully as it flitted from one sail to the next, huddling over the rents and spitting green sputum on them before sealing them shut with its tongue.

'As you can see, Infidel has his uses, besides being my eyes and ears!' giggled Sha'arza. 'It will take him all night, but he will have us airworthy again.'

'I can't help but notice that your eyes didn't spot a ravening flock of eagles bent on tearing us from the skies,' offered Hari, nursing a vicious-looking cut to his upper arm.

Sha'arza's elaborate brows furrowed at that. 'Indeed. Part of the Enchantment must have been used to cloak them until they were near. As I said, you have some resourceful enemies. But never you mind that for now! Let us go below, and I will treat your injuries. Then you must tell me more about your journey, I want to hear more of this ghoul pack in particular.'

Horskram and the Zarumani exchanged glances at that. 'We had also been wondering who might be behind them, seeing as Tipu's sect supposedly cleansed the ruins of Shamaria not long ago.'

'You think the eagles and the ghouls might be linked to the same sorcerer?' suggested the fire priest.

Sha'arza laughed at that. 'I think it safe to say, gentlemen, that many more incidents than that are linked to the same sorcerer.'

Without another word, the wizard led them back down below hatches, leaving Infidel to his laborious work. Adelko was last to go down, pausing briefly to take in the vanished sun's afterglow. His latest vision swirled around in his mind, an ephemeral abstract jigsaw puzzle that teased the edges of his consciousness. But try as he might, he still could not quite piece it all together.

CHAPTER 18
TO THE FOUR WINDS

The lights of Kell looked mean in the mist as the weary travellers approached it. Sir Wrackwulf felt little cheer at the sight, despite the arduous days they had spent making the return journey. The swan boat had been waiting for them by the waterfall, and the river had unfrozen no sooner had they boarded it, carrying them swiftly back towards the lake. This time they'd had no trouble getting past Taras Cerawn, skirting it effortlessly to reach the far shore. No sooner had they disembarked than the boat had vanished, the lake waters freezing over again. Seeking shelter for the night in the same cave, they had found to their great surprise that their garrons were alive and whole; Morcant had hazarded a guess that the Demi-Fays had called the moon dogs off. The Red Moon itself had vanished, and the night in the cave had been eerily silent.

Ariadha still rode with them; as sole survivor of their escort, it was her duty to report back to the Druiding Council. They'd spent a brief night at Nuallán Hold: the following morning the entire household had gathered to see her off with sorrowful eyes, Owyn shedding tears freely from his. Wrackwulf guessed the punishment for islanders who failed to keep to their ancestral pledges was harsh. Despite that, the warrior-woman had not favoured Penhalain valley with so much as a backwards glance. He had to admire her stoicism.

So similar to Anupe in so many ways, he reflected. *Those two would probably get on.*

Slowly the travellers descended the last of the broken hills towards the shoreline, taking the same snaking path they had a handful of weeks ago. A couple of retainers from Nuallán carried Joram in his stretcher; despite having his wounds treated at the magic fortress, the monk had done little but mutter and rave in his fever, speaking of dark kingdoms to come and angels who could kill with their beauteous looks alone. Wrackwulf shivered as the adept started up again; more than once he had thought of putting him out of his misery.

Sir Torgun had offered scarce little more in the way of cheer. The knight had perfected his thousand-league stare, absently stroking the Circifix of St Argo and wondering aloud why it had done so little to ward off the spirits that had come for the fragment and destroyed its protectors. Morcant had ventured something about hybrid magick that wouldn't be affected by a relic; and besides that the elemental spirits hadn't attacked them directly. He'd also hazarded a guess that the Guardians themselves had become corrupted by their long association with the anti-relic they had guarded for centuries, resulting in their unbridled hostility. Wrackwulf didn't rightly understand a word of it, and besides that the mage had done little to elaborate on his theories. Joram's affliction seemed to have affected the mage, too: Morcant looked even paler than usual, and hovered fretfully around the monk whenever they set him down.

Every single thing about this damned mission has been stranger than the last, thought the freelancer for the umpteenth time as they drew closer to Kell. *How I long to be off this cursed rock of an island.* Thoughts of his strongbox of coin in the palace at Ongist, and wenches he wanted to swyve, and mead that tasted good, and wholesome food that was appetising, and music he could understand, called to him more loudly by the minute.

I just hope the islanders don't see fit to punish us for our failure, too.

More lights winked into view as they approached the ramshackle curtain wall surrounding the city. Glancing up at the tower where they'd been held under house arrest, Wrackwulf scowled and reached towards the haft of his axe. If the islanders were going to try that again, he'd give them a sharp response this time.

As it was, a shabby-looking guard simply waved them through the crumbling gatehouse. Its flint stones seem to point at them accusingly as they rode into the outskirts of Kell. The mean thatched roofs and daub-and-wattle walls looked at odds with the dotted ruins of the grander houses from the Old and Middle Times; the bleak country his Wyrd had brought him to was even sadder after glimpsing the glory of its heyday. Already the silver spires of Taras Cerawn seemed a thousand miles away.

At least the wooden buildings became sturdier and straighter as they neared the city centre. This was a big muddy square where hawkers and craftsmen crowded every day to ply what meagre trade they could. Many were still there now, despite the late hour; nearby a couple of drunks rolled and grappled in the thick mud, screeching at one another dementedly.

And they consider exile from this place a punishment? That's a penance I'll gladly serve.

Hardly anybody paid them any mind as they rode through the square towards the waterfront. Wrackwulf guessed the All-Meet hadn't been candid with the lower orders about what had been discussed.

So much for being a free and open society. As always, freedoms only stretch so far in the end.

Surveying the half-starved townsfolk, Wrackwulf wondered how many of them would care even if they did know. Their daily lives seemed harsh enough without worrying about the end of the world.

Malhavern's Point rose up forbiddingly as they made their way out of town, punctuated by the multicoloured lights of Skelnaervon's grotto. Beyond that, the surging seas began to take on a tarry look as the sun died its slow death once more. Atop the cliffs, Aurgelmir's Teeth jutted up against the vanishing skyline, and for an instant Wrackwulf wondered if they hadn't all been swallowed up by the Great World Serpent. There was something premonitory in that fancy that made the freelancer shiver again.

He wasn't entirely surprised to find them waiting on a strand of shingle beach that ran between Kell and Malhavern's Point: the seven remaining chief druids, or whatever they called themselves, and the highest-ranking marcher lords and ladies from the All-Meet. A more welcome sight was their little sloop, bobbing up and down in the sea a few strides beyond the pebbles, Garhan and his scurrilous crew skulking furtively aboard.

So they do mean to let us go, after all. Wrackwulf couldn't deny he felt relieved. Next to him Sir Torgun put a brawny hand on the hilt of his sword, but the freelancer stayed him.

'Nothing too hasty, comrade,' he said in a low voice. 'I don't think they mean to harm us.'

At least I bloody well hope they don't. After all they'd survived, being lynched by a mob of islanders wouldn't go down as the most heroic of deaths.

They stopped awkwardly at the shoreline, squaring off against the assembled lords and druids. Ys looked as stern as ever, his black-ringed eyes firing invisible darts at them, the myriad eyes in his mantle doing something similar. But his tone seemed calm enough as he began to address Ariadha. She shook her head sadly, answering his questions in a low voice. The Grand High Druid continued to question her, his face by turns sad and angry. But fearful most of all.

When they were done, Ariadha knelt on the stony strand and presented her neck. To Wrackwulf's surprise, Morcant followed suit. A marcher lord with bow legs and heavily muscled arms stepped forwards, a drawn sword in his hand; but another lady, a girl of no more than fourteen summers sporting stylised black and white dragon's teeth on her sash, stepped forwards to bar his way.

Torgun and Wrackwulf exchanged uneasy glances as the marcher lords fell to bickering again. Behind them a crowd of ordinary townsfolk had gathered at Kell's outskirts to watch the unfolding drama.

Sir Torgun's face was stony in the greying light as he said: 'I don't care a fig for their benighted customs, I'll not let them execute two companions who've shared the road with us.' So saying, the knight slowly drew his sword and stepped forwards, eyeing the lords meaningfully.

With a sigh, Wrackwulf unsheathed his axe and joined him.

We'll take a few marcher lords with us, perhaps it won't be such an ignominious death after all.

Into the midst of the babbling fury stepped Ys, raising his staff. The eyes in his mantle seemed to blaze with a green light, blinding everyone. The Grand High Druid raised his ram-head staff, declaiming something in his high fruity voice; as his vision cleared, Wrackwulf saw Ariadha and Morcant getting to their feet. The mage looked plainly relieved, though the Marcher Lady's face still looked drained of joy. The younger lady stepped over to embrace her, tears darting from her eyes beneath a mop of ginger hair; the muscular marcher lord with the bow legs had sheathed his sword, but was muttering and shaking his head.

Wrackwulf seized Morcant by the arm. 'Would you mind telling us what in Five Hells is going on?'

'Agreed to commute our sentence have the Druiding

Council – exile not execution to be our punishment. Failed in her lineal duty has Ariadha ap Madrix, to guard the fragment that Caedmon took upon himself and his descendants to protect, but Ys can find no evidence that she was responsible for the Doom's theft.'

Wrackwulf raised a bushy eyebrow. 'It's hardly her fault then. Seems like a harsh penalty to me.'

The mage shrugged and gave Wrackwulf one of his sly looks. 'Are not mainland laws often harsh?'

The freelancer frowned. 'I suppose you've got me there,' he allowed. Besides, he couldn't deny part of him was pleased the fierce islander was coming with them. 'Fine, we've space in the boat after we lost crew on the journey here,' he said. 'But why are they banishing *you?*'

Morcant's eyes flittered uneasily about the darkening shore as he replied. 'Tainted they say I have become, by my travails on the mainland and...' His eyes settled momentarily on Joram, still moaning feverishly on his stretcher.

Wrackwulf shook his head. 'I tell you, this has without a doubt been the most outlandish adventure of my bloody life. Why you've any affinity to a man who wanted you dead is beyond me, but it doesn't seem as though you've much choice in the matter. All right, let's get your bosom companion aboard, and get ourselves out of here!' That it was approaching night-time barely occurred to him; he'd seen enough of the Tyrnian Straits and the land they guarded to know sailing against the tide probably meant nothing out here.

The assembled druids and lords watched them impassively as they loaded Joram onto the sloop. Ariadha finished brief farewells, before taking down a laden pack from her garron and slinging her rune-embossed spear across her back. As at Nuallán, she did not favour Kell with so much as a backwards glance as she joined the rest of them in the boat. Garhan was already barking orders at his men, who pushed the sloop farther out into the eddying waters before jumping aboard.

As Wrackwulf had fathomed, the straits took a lenient hand with them. The waves seemed to change direction, pulling their little boat out into the seas. The freelancer fancied he could see dozens of watery hands clutching the keel as the last of the sun expired, pulled down to its diurnal grave by the Great Western Ocean. Presently all that could be seen of Kell and Skelnaervon were glimmering points of light, and before long even those were swallowed up by a darkness pierced by just a handful of stars.

Feeling suddenly very tired, Wrackwulf slumped down in the bow and shut his eyes. The sleep that took him was blacker than the skies above.

Ariadha lost count of the days they spent at sea. Too wrapped up in her gloom, she scarcely noticed as the skies became clearer, the sun warmer. The ghostly protectors of her lost homeland did not harass them, but seemed instead to stare at them with a queer respect in their spectral eyes. Morcant did what he could to console her, teaching her the rudiments of Thrax. It wasn't completely sundered from her native Gnáthtéanga, and learning it was something to occupy her mind. But try as she might, the erstwhile Marcher Lady of Clan Nuallán could not get Ys's final words out of her head.

A curse you have birthed unwittingly upon this land, and it can bear you no longer. By universal consent of lords temporal and druiding, I strip you of all title and claim to lands, and name you exile, for the term of your natural life.

The term of her natural life. The years seemed to stretch before her, barren and bereft of hope. Where would she go, and what would she do? At least she had Morcant as a guide – for now. The ugly knight also tried to make conversation, frequently proffering her the watery mead her folk had packed on the ship for their journey. He grinned and nodded a lot and seemed friendlier than his saturnine comrade-in-arms. Perhaps the mainlander had taken a shine to her; perhaps she could put that to use, where they were going.

The sight of the Thraxian coast stirred up some feelings in her, for Ariadha had heard bards sing many tales of the Middle Time, when her ancestors had traded with the Four Old Kingdoms, before the greed of Ifwyn Gold-blind and the Forty Years' Kin Strife had broken those ties for good. That had been hundreds of years before Morwena and the coming of Søren, and the bringing of the Doom to their shores.

We should be rejoicing, now our share of the burden is finally gone, she thought bitterly. *Such a thing never belonged on our shores in the first place.*

The Rundle brought Ariadha briefly from her melancholy; she had never looked upon a river so wide. Likewise the sunlit fields and hedgerows impressed her with their abundance, though Morcant had told her Thraxia was considered a poor kingdom.

Once upon a time we enriched the mainland; now we languish in its wake.

Only when their sloop pulled into teeming Ongist did she feel a small sense of satisfaction; though it was several times the size of Kell, its citizens seemed no more prosperous.

'Still not recovered from civil war and misrule have the mainlanders,' explained Morcant as Garhan and his crew expertly slunk in amongst the bigger ships towards a space on one of the docks. A pole-wielding longshoreman was about to push them back and appeared to be telling them to wait their turn, when Joram produced a bronze badge that flashed in the pallid sunlight. The monk's fever had broken a couple of nights ago, and though too weak to do much more than sit up, he appeared to have recovered his awareness.

'What's that?' asked Ariadha, eyeing the glinting metal in his hand. Whatever it was, it appeared to have the desired effect, for the ruddy-faced longshoreman permitted them to dock immediately.

'Joram bears the King's insignia,' explained Morcant. 'Permits us free conduct through his domains.'

The Westerling woman nodded perfunctorily. The ways of mainlanders seemed curiously formal.

Ariadha attracted no few stares as they exited the sloop. Garhan tied the boat up before turning to bid them farewell. Without a backwards glance, he and his men turned and disappeared into the throng of people on the wharf.

Ariadha watched him go with little interest. She could feel the stares on her. She bared her teeth in a grimace at the nearest one, a well-dressed man whom she took to be some sort of trader or dignitary. He didn't look so dignified when he turned away fearfully.

Wrackwulf parked a meaty hand on her shoulder. She shrugged him off irritably, but took his meaning. Reluctantly she lowered her gaze, and allowed her unlikely companions to walk her from the docks, one knight to either side. She hated being cossetted by men like that, and foreigners to boot, but at least no one had tried to put her in chains yet. She'd heard that's what happened to Westerlings who ended up on the mainland nowadays, and Morcant's experiences seemed to tell the same tale. She glanced at the mage, who was helping Joram through the crowds towards the ramshackle buildings lining the waterfront. Many of these were selling ale – and other things, judging by the scrawny scantily clad women who lifted their grubby skirts enticingly at passers-by.

Everything the elders ever told me about the mainland is true, it seems. Ys, my punishment is more than I deserve.

They chose the least wretched-looking hostelry and entered its low cramped interior. Weak tapers burning in rusty sconces did little to augment the narrow beams of light shining through cracks in the crooked shutters. Torgun sighed inwardly, reminding himself that soon he would be homeward bound. Wrackwulf wasted no time in stepping over to the counter and ordering them tankards of frothy mead. Torgun joined him at the unvarnished oak board and quaffed gratefully; mainlanders certainly did a better drop than their island cousins, though he would fain have had wine instead. Morcant helped Joram sit down on a bench, while Ariadha stared about her with the same bewildered expression she had worn since they docked.

Wrackwulf slammed his empty tankard on the counter and beckoned to the hunch-backed innkeep for a refill. 'One more, then we'll head up to the palace,' he said. 'I'm sure the King will give us a right royal welcome, he cares little for... our wider mission. And the way I see it, Cadwy still owes us a boon for saving his kingdom.'

'You might want to apply those realm-saving skills closer to home, outlander.'

The voice was trim, well educated. Glancing over at the speaker, they saw a black-frocked mendicant perfect, his pungent perfume at odds with the reek of the common room. He was sat in the corner nearest to them, surveying them coolly over his tankard with heavy-lidded eyes.

'And what mean you by that?' queried Wrackwulf, eyeing the priest suspiciously.

The perfect made the sign, raising his eyes piously to the heavens. 'My calling takes me hither and yon, begging groats and pennies and coppers in the Redeemer's name. The dust of all the Free Kingdoms is on my boots, the spray of all her seas upon my lips.'

Wrackwulf gesticulated at him with his refilled tankard.

'In Palom's name man, spare us your rhetoric! Tell us what you mean to tell us.'

The perfect shifted his dirty frock and adjusted his travel-stained cloak. His closely cropped dark hair and tanned skin spoke of a southerner, though his perfect Decorlangue could have been learned at a priory or temple anywhere in the kingdoms.

'I just lately arrived in Ongist, having taken ship from Gorleon province in Pangonia,' said the perfect. 'Did you know they have invaded Vorstlund?'

Wrackwulf nodded impatiently. 'Aye, I did, and you've guessed right, I am a Vorstlending,' he said. 'But I'm a free-lancer first, and I go where the fattest purse jingles. I care little for the wider wars of great men, unless great men choose to pay for my services. So how goes Carolus's little invasion?'

The perfect smiled thinly. 'Not as well as he'd hoped. The Prince Regent Franz and his mother Utha have brokered an alliance, bringing together the Council of the Nine. The northern baronies have ceased their civil war. All are flocking to the Westenlund banner, while Thalamy has made common cause with the Pangonians. Plenty of work for a veteran of the recent wars here, especially now the blockade of Westerburg has been compromised by the Eorl of Dreylund's warships.'

Wrackwulf licked froth from his bearded lips thought-fully. 'I begin to see your point, priest,' he mused. 'Thalamy has invaded too, you say? They'll be hiring every spare blade they can get if they've got two attacking nations on their doorstep.'

'And paying well, from what I've heard,' rejoined the mendicant.

Wrackwulf turned to look at Torgun. 'Fancy a little jaunt back to Vorstlund once we're done here? Plenty of work for a strong sword arm like yours, too. Be nice to do something normal, for a change.'

Sir Torgun shook his head. 'I'll away up to the palace with you, pay my respects to King Cadwy and collect my things. Then I shall take Hilmir from the royal stables, and ride him hard to the east. I shall not cease until I have crossed the mountains and look upon Northalde again.'

His grandiloquent cast of speech mirrored his mood. Torgun had always been a serious man, but now he felt his Wyrd calling to him more loudly by the day. The apparition on Skulla had shown him a brief but lucid glimpse of his fate. He had to get back home.

The priest chose that moment to speak up again. 'You'll have your work cut out for you in Northalde as well, sir knight,' he said. 'For your homeland has also been invaded.'

That did catch Torgun by surprise. Thanks to the apparition's vision, he had an inkling war was coming again to his country, but hadn't expected it to arrive this soon. 'Pray explain yourself, father,' he said, nodding respectfully at the perfect.

The priest languidly stroked his money pouch as he answered. Plainly he expected alms to be given in return for his news, but Torgun didn't mind as long as he told him what he needed to know. 'I heard it just this morning, from the captain of a merchantman out of Strongholm. He said he only just managed to leave before a great fleet of reavers arrived, from the Frozen Wastes. The Ice Thegns are united, under one queen they say. She means to carve out a mainland empire such as has not been seen on the coasts of Northalde in centuries.'

'More details, man,' insisted Torgun impatiently. 'Where exactly have they landed, how strong are they?'

The perfect raised his spidery hands apologetically. 'I only know what I was told, sir knight. Strongholm is invested and the lands about sore pressed. There are rumours of other incursions farther down the Northlending coast, with much laying waste and slave-taking. Some are talking of a hundred longships of great size, others say twice that and more.'

Torgun put down his tankard and fished into his money pouch. 'For your trouble,' he said curtly, tossing a few silvers on the perfect's table. He turned to his companions and favoured them with a half-bow.

'Comrades, I must leave you now. It has been an honour to share the road with you, but duty calls me back home. May Ezekiel and Stygnos watch over you all.'

Without another word, Sir Torgun stalked across the common room back towards the door. A grinning harlot made advances but he shook his head grimly, not breaking his stride. He scarcely noticed the disappointed look on her face as he flung open the door.

'Wait!' cried Wrackwulf. 'You haven't even finished your-' The freelancer's words died as Torgun slammed the door behind him, striding purposefully through the crowds towards the Palace of Bending Branches.

As he did a feeling of elation, so long missed, crested the

gloomy mood that had become so normal to him. Let the Unseen doom him howsoever they chose, but he was done with Argolians and sorcerers and monsters and questing abroad. It was time at last for Sir Torgun to go home where he belonged, to do what he did best, and fight for his country.

The smile that raised his rugged face had never felt more welcome.

'-mead,' finished Wrackwulf lamely, eyeing the half-full tankard on the rough oak counter as Torgun banged the door shut behind him. 'Ach well, it was nice knowing you, too.' He raised his tankard in a toast to his departed friend. The stringy harlot switched her advances to Wrackwulf. He wouldn't have minded, only Ariadha was gazing at him over her stoup, an inscrutable expression pinned to her savage face.

'He's off home,' said Wrackwulf, not even sure if she understood him.

Ariadha turned to Morcant and began addressing him in their native tongue. Joram joined in perfunctorily, before getting weakly to his feet.

'We should be getting along to the palace ourselves,' said the monk, grimacing with every word and adjusting the sling that held his broken arm. 'I needs must give an account to King Cadwy, after that he'll commission us berths on a ship to Rima.'

Wrackwulf shook his head. 'I'm not going back. Didn't

you hear just now?' He nodded towards the priest in the corner. 'There's a war on in Vorstlund. I'm done with Argolians and their games. I yearn for a foe I can fight properly.'

'As you wish,' said Joram, his face still horribly pale. 'Though you'll have trouble getting to Westerburg by sea if there's a naval war being waged in its waters.'

'Yes, well... I've an idea about that,' said the freelancer. 'First I'm going to finish this stoup, then I'm going to find Garhan. He'll take me at least as far as Cobia – I should be able to get into Vorstlund travelling overland from there.'

Joram nodded absently. He seemed more distant than ever, if that was possible. After his fever had broken, they'd told him what had passed at the Place of Doom's Keeping, but he had given little indication of how he felt about it. To be fair, the monk had broken bones to nurse, but Wrackwulf thought it passing strange their mission's abject failure had made so little impression on him.

But though his suspicions about Joram remained, honestly what more could he do? He'd held up his part of the bargain in good faith: the Argolians had paid him to fight and protect, not intrigue. And one way or another, the fragment that the islanders had guarded for centuries was gone. Let those best qualified to deal with such a problem concern themselves with it.

His reverie was broken by Joram wincing as he tried to sit back down unaided. Morcant scurried over and grasped him by his good arm, easing him on to the bench.

'I'll head up to the palace myself,' said Wrackwulf with a sigh. 'I'll get the King to send some men to help you. I'll arrange for his chirurgeon to tend your wounds too, while we're about it. I don't trust foreign medicine.'

Joram nodded again, proffering him the King's insignia. Taking it, Wrackwulf downed the last of his mead and left the harbourside tavern, wondering if anyone would ever truly fathom the enigmatic monk.

Ariadha watched the second knight leave, and loosened her spear in its sheath on her back. She cast furtive eyes about the common room, but none of the patrons seemed like fighting types. The mainlanders were effete, softened by their civilisation. That would serve her well now her body-guards were gone.

She finished off her mead in silence. Even the Moon Goddess seemed more inclined to favour these folk – the drink here was less watery, more full in its flavour. Beckoning to the innkeeper, she motioned for him to refill her cup. He scowled at her until she scowled back, then did as she bade him.

Sipping on it gratefully, she leaned on the counter and pondered her options. From what Morcant had told her, their destination lay far to the south, in one of the great cities of the Free Kingdoms, a place to make Ongist look like Kell. Ariadha didn't like the sound of that. Already she yearned for the dales and dells of her homeland: rough hewn though they were, they'd always been home. The last thing she needed was being cooped up in a stinking city, nothing more than a curiosity for idle and decadent main-landers.

'Give me a clear vista, island brother,' she said to Morcant. 'Where do the four winds take us now?' She hoped her weaselly compatriot would speak the Moon Goddess's truth.

'Sir Torgun rides east, to the kingdom of the Northlendings and war,' said the mage. 'Sir Wrackwulf shall head south with Garhan, to the land of the Vorstlendings' – he smiled wryly – 'and war.'

'It seems the mainlanders think of little else,' said Ariadha.

Morcant's expression became uncomfortable. 'War shall engulf us all, I fear. The loss of the third fragment portends disaster.' Next to him, Joram appeared to have lapsed back into his fever, leaning back against the plastered wall and muttering to himself, eyes half closed.

Ariadha took a deep breath, feeling even more grateful for the strong mead. 'So it would appear. But if the Hour of All's Ending draws nigh and I cannot face it on our native soil, I'll be night-damned if I'm spending it stuck in a city. Tell me, do any of these mainland lords employ foreigners as mercenaries?'

'All the time,' Morcant assured her. 'Though 'tis probably best to conceal your sex in this backwards region.'

Ariadha almost smirked at that. Her contempt of main-land morals aside, she didn't have all that much femininity that needed hiding.

'You have sown many years in the furrows of mainland soil,' she went on. 'Which of these lands should I ride to?'

Morcant reflected on that for a while. Then he said: 'From what I know, the Principality of Westenlund is among the richest provinces in the Free Kingdoms. Probably pay better they will, and have more money to commission freeswords. So to head south with Wrackwulf and Garhan is probably your best bet. Different is the Vorstlending tongue though, so I hope you're up to learning more languages!'

Ariadha frowned. She'd scarcely thought about that, but what choice did she really have? She suddenly thought of Lyna ap Fadwyn, a dear friend she would never see again. Lyna, wise beyond her greening years: what would the young Marcher Lady of Clan Draghain tell her to do? Lyna would tell her to stay quick of mind and sharp of eye, and go wherever the wind blew strongest.

And right now, the wind was blowing towards the land of the Vorstlendings.

Turning back to lean against the counter again, Ariadha sipped her mead, and waited for Sir Wrackwulf to return.

CHAPTER 19
A MYSTERY UNRAVELLED

Thousands of spans below them, the sands stretched and shifted, a great golden blanket that rippled in the wind. Even had he not been viewing the Ghorabi Desert from a flying ship, Adelko felt sure his first glimpse of it would have taken his breath away just the same.

Despite Infidel's best efforts the eagles had taken their toll, and with the sidegallants and stays also damaged steering was more difficult. Their second day at sky had brought them to the fringes of the great southern desert; their third would bring them to Ortiz. Evenings had been spent pondering who was behind the most recent attack on them; whoever it was had probably also been responsible for stirring up the ghoul horde at Shamaria. One more warlock sent to despatch them, using clever tricks to circumvent the protection afforded by the Redeemer's blood that Horskram carried. For his part, Infidel seemed increasingly discomfited by its presence, looking positively sickly whenever the adept came near him.

Other more prosaic concerns had presented themselves. On the second morning of their airborne journey, they had spotted a vast host shadowing the plains of central Nazharya; doubtless one of Muqmurlish's armies answering his call to war. Now high summer had come upon the earth, it wouldn't be long before it was soaked in blood.

That thought dimmed Adelko's enjoyment of the journey as the Cerulean mountains began to glimmer into view on the southern horizon. Their beautiful blue-white tips did little to allay his troubled thoughts as he wondered how the wars up north were going. Sha'arza had scryed and told them of the invasions of Vorstlund by Pangonia and Thalamy, and though Thraxia seemed to have attained an uneasy peace, conflict still raged in its highlands: a lowland lord with auburn hair rode at the head of a grizzled company, burning and slaying and laying waste on the left hand and the right. It sounded disquietingly like Braxus, though Adelko didn't want to believe his affable comrade had turned into such a bloodthirsty killer.

Worst of all, Northalde was under invasion, by a mighty fleet of Northland reavers. But when Sha'arza had tried to scry on the Frozen Wastes, a great darkness had come upon his vision; beads of sweat stood out on his forehead as he recounted some hideous power being channelled, so potent his scrying tool had winked out when he tried to look upon it.

Hearing all of this, Adelko thought fretfully of his brother Arik, and his companions Vaskrian, Torgun, Braxus and Wrackwulf, caught up in a storm of steel. Twice he'd asked the sorcerer to scry on the monastery at Rima, to give him some inkling of his friends there too, but Abdel had shook his head frowningly and said his magicks were hazy around the Reverend Priory of St Argo.

As he mouthed a psalm and watched the Ceruleans grow taller and wider, Adelko let such troubled thoughts wash over him and pass away, lulling himself into a meditative state. Higher even than the adjoining Abydos ranges, the mountains rose up from the southernmost fiefs of Nazharya, on the far fringes of the Ghorabi. Sparing a glance for the desert far below, Adelko caught glimpses of caravans and other pinprick riders wending their way towards the desert city of Tesh. It seemed a short time after its myriad oases vanished from sight that they were leaving the Ghorabi behind; golden sands became brown scrublands, before turning into green fields that stretched towards the foothills of the mountains.

Sha'arza muttered an incantation and began steering the *Chariot* diagonally downwards, the top and sidegallants creaking noisily as they adjusted to the new angle. The warming lamps dimmed accordingly as they descended; after the eagle attack the wizard had been forced to concentrate these on the forecastle, rendering the rest of the deck uninhabitable at high altitudes.

'Let me bring her down lower,' he said. 'When it's safe for you to leave the forecastle, you can go below and tell the others we are almost there.'

The peaks were lurching up towards them at an alarming rate now, the range yawning wide to take them into its stony maw. Adelko shut his eyes as visions of the great serpent at the base of Sha'arza's tower came flashing back into his mind. He seemed for a moment to glimpse another serpent, much larger, its coils shattering kingdoms as they unwound...

'Adelko!' He felt Sha'arza's hand gripping his shoulder tightly. The warlock's fingernails were longer than a harlot's and twice as sharp.

The journeyman shook his head, meeting Abdel's concerned gaze.

'Sorry,' he stammered, glancing again at the mountains, which now loomed all around them. 'I'll go and fetch the others.'

Hari Yassin gazed on Ortiz and knew dread. His time with the Order of the Silver Shadow had not been an easy one. The Old Master's cult had taught him many useful things, but its stern regime had been too much for a lad of fourteen to endure any more. He had paid his *diyah* years ago, but that wouldn't necessarily stop a disgruntled zealot slipping a poisoned knife between his ribs if he got too close to the Shadow again.

And now here he was, speeding towards its age-old headquarters on a flying ship.

Ortiz had not changed a whit. A citadel of spired towers, it perched atop a tapering pinnacle of rock that thrust upwards from a ravine so deep as to be virtually a chasm. No bridges connected the rock on which the citadel sat to the lip of the ravine; the ways into and out of Ortiz were closely guarded secrets, as much mystical entranceways as physical ones. Yassin caught the once-familiar sight of Shadowmen sparring in the diamond-shaped courtyard as they flew ever closer. From its centre rose a single slender spire, its needle-like structure stabbing the skies. From the summit the Old Master could survey all his holdings: the barracks and granaries, the gymnasia and villas and pleasure gardens. The Apostate's Gate, from which traitors to the Order were hurled into the chasm. Hari shivered, and hoped that wouldn't be his fate.

'How many live here?' asked Adelko, tiptoeing so as to get a better view over the taffrail.

'A thousand men and boys of the Order, plus thousands more to serve our needs – cooks, craftsmen, garden women and the like.'

'Garden women?'

'Whores, if you will – exclusively for the use of Shadowmen who please the Old Master.'

Adelko looked a little abashed at that, so the wryness of his response surprised Hari. 'And you chose to leave?'

Hari grinned a lopsided grin. 'My mother was a harlot, in Ushalayim. I spent the first seven years of my life in a brothel, and such things hold little appeal once you have seen them on the inside. In any case, there weren't any garden women for initiates, let me assure you! No, seven years was enough and I longed for the open road, to travel back to my native city and see more of the sultanate on the way.'

'How did you escape?' Guards on the walls were pointing and shouting as the *Chariot* hovered above them. Several discharged bolts from crossbows, but these glanced harmlessly off the ship's ebonite hull. Adelko and Hari ducked back under the taffrail.

'I absconded during a training mission, and never came back,' explained Hari. 'I spent the next five years on the run, carving out a living wherever I could before I returned to Ushalayim. Once I established myself there, I was able to pay the Order my *diyah* – the blood price for deserting. But the cost of that set me back financially, and always I am running to stand still.' He sighed. 'Truly it is said by the Wise One that thievery pays the thief less than it takes from him, over time. But such choices have I made, Adelko of Narvik.'

'But why are you so nervous about coming back here? You said you'd paid off the Order.'

Hari grimaced. 'My mother was raised in the Unorthodox Faith and traced her bloodline back to the Alamites, long before her branch of the family fell on hard times. For that reason alone was I able to secure *diyah*. But many in the Order would happily see me hurled from the Apostate's Gate regardless, for usually the penalty for my crime is death.'

'Sounds as though they're quite keen to kill us as it is,' said Adelko, as more crossbow bolts rattled off the *Chariot*'s hull.

'I can only hope our sorcerous guide knows what he is doing,' said Hari. 'I for one will not be parlaying with the Shadowmen!'

Sha'arza must have heard them. Clutching a whitestone amulet and holding it to his lips, he began speaking into it. The rest of them continued to cower behind the taffrail, but the zinging of bolts soon stopped.

'I have made contact with the Old Master,' said the wizard. 'We can land safely now.'

Several dozen black-garbed Shadowmen clustered about them as Abdel berthed the ship, its keel hovering just a handspan above the flagstoned courtyard. Hari slunk down below hatches, muttering to himself, as Sha'arza activated the mechanism to open the stepped gangplank.

All the Shadowmen had donned masks by the time they descended from the *Chariot*, and many had crossbows trained on them. Not a word was spoken as the faceless assassins closed around them, but Adelko's sixth sense remained cool – he hoped they were under instructions to do them no harm unless attacked.

After a long-seeming minute, the assassins parted to reveal a small man. Dressed in a brown leather jerkin and cobalt pantaloons with grey upturned shoes, he looked at odds with the assassins. His beard and hair were lightly oiled, and black eyes twinkled in an ageless face as he favoured Abdel Sha'arza with an elegant half-bow.

'Wishing you a bountiful al'Nurë, O master warlock of the Sha'arzan House,' said the man. 'It has been many a High Heat since you chanced to visit Ortiz in your skyship – I fear some of my younger disciples were panicked by your arrival.' His voice was soft and smooth; Adelko had never heard the guttural Sassanic tongue sound so gentle.

Sha'arza returned the bow, saying: 'A thousand apologies for failing to inform you, O Scion of the Alamites and

Keeper of the Kardin bloodline, a hundred-times-blessed descendant of Abu tek Jahib, last of the Seven Enlightened Ones! Time has been most pressing of late, and quite driven me to distraction.'

So this is the master assassin who tried to have us killed, thought Adelko. *Our enemies are so rarely what we expect them to be. And he's supposedly heir to a long-lost kingdom too, if I've just heard right.*

The Old Master beckoned for them to follow him with a sweep of the arm. 'You had best bring your companions inside,' he said. 'In truth your coming here was not entirely unexpected, but I would learn more in privacy.'

Without a word of command being spoken, the Shadowmen formed a human corridor leading to the central spire of Ortiz. Beyond those men, not one of the citadel's occupants had come to look at the new arrivals, and the heart of the forbidden citadel was eerily silent. Approaching the central spire, Adelko could see it was fashioned of dark grey stones, each one perfectly arranged so as not to vary in size or angle. The precision was breathtaking.

'Built by the Kishans of old,' said Tipu in a low voice, catching the expression on his face. 'Unlike their forebears, they sought to use magic to order their world, rather than embracing the inherent entropy of the universe.'

'Which of them do you believe was right?' asked Adelko on a sudden impulse.

Tipu only smiled as they drew towards the gatehouse, carved to resemble a gigantic human face, its mouth agape. 'I believe in many truths, Adelko of Narvik.'

The journeyman felt a sense of unease as Sha'arza shot

the mystic a knowing glance. He suddenly had the feeling that his new companions knew each other a lot better than they let on, though that could have been his mind playing tricks on him.

The sculpted face looked to be a Sassanian of some kind: it was fat and puffy, the eyebrows tapered in exaggerated fashion like Sha'arza's. Its side-beard was fashioned of slate tiles, making it look more like a coat of mail than hair. And yet something about the eyes was different, the broad features carried a hint of those of the Elder Wizards...

As if sensing his curiosity, the Old Master spoke without turning around as he led them up a ramp and into the mouth. 'According to the *shuras* of the Faith and the *Codices of Zhorrah*, Ortiz was built by the priest rulers of Sendhé for their great warrior caste, to guard the northern flanks of their empire against Huryan desert raiders. But in time, the warrior caste rose up and rebelled against the priest caste, and the Deist and Monarchist factions fell to warring against one another for mastery of the hierocracy. During that conflict Ortiz was sacked and fell into disuse. Its gramaryes protected it from further despoiling for long ages after that, for no one unversed in the dark arts could approach it.'

'Untrue,' put in the Zarumani. 'Zaruman himself braved this precinct, cleansing it of much of its foul taint.' As if responding to the fire priest's words, the torches in their sconces seemed to flare a little more brightly.

'I was coming to that,' said the Old Master. 'It was indeed thanks to Zaruman that I was able to take up residence here centuries later, once I had learned the interstices by which I might gain entry to the citadel.'

'And how do you get all the ordinary folk in here?' asked Adelko.

'We capture them in raids and bring them here blindfolded, using the ways I rediscovered,' explained the master assassin. 'At first many baulk, but once they witness the palatial delights in which they might live, few choose to leave by the Apostate's Gate.'

His final words hung heavy in the silence of the corridor leading into the keep proper. Their meaning was not lost on any of the visitors.

The corridor terminated in an octagonal antechamber. It put Adelko uncomfortably in mind of the basic structure of the Elder Wizards' watchtowers, but then he supposed the Sendhéans had been influenced by them. Seven other archways faced them, one in each wall. The chamber was devoid of embellishments. Looking up, Adelko saw there was no ceiling; the vault simply disappeared into stygian blackness.

'Please follow me,' said the Old Master, motioning towards the archway in the opposite wall. As if in a dream, they entered the entrance one by one, all of them muttering prayers to their varying gods as they disappeared...

... only to find themselves in a capacious chamber high in the spire, one of its walls entirely open to the darkening vista of the citadel below and the mountains beyond. This room was far more ornately appointed. Burnished pillars of brass caught the light from hanging braziers in the ceiling, burning scented oils that filled the room with a pungent odour. The ceiling was covered with serpent and knife motifs, picked out in gold filigree. Betwixt the pillars, virtually unnoticeable, Shadowmen stood to attention, awaiting their master's orders.

'Quite the view, is it not?' The Old Master spoke from behind them. He was sat cross-legged on a simple mat of woven reeds; behind him a great serpent effigy of brass coiled upwards, splitting into two heads, topaz eyes glinting dully as they glared over his shoulders at the new arrivals.

Serpents everywhere, thought Adelko. *Here in the lands of the Faith, in the towers built by the Elder Wizards and their apprentices, even in my dreams of the north...*

'The serpent is everywhere,' said the Old Master, again giving the unsettling impression of having just read his thoughts. 'Do the pagan barbarians of your hinterlands not speak of a Great World Serpent, whose uncoiling shall bring about a Second Breaking of the World?'

'That myth is well known to us,' Horskram allowed. 'Though we prefer to think it the archangels who destroyed the world, as just punishment for the Elder Wizards' transgressions.'

The adept's turn of phrase and tone were almost deferential: gone was the firebrand monk Adelko had known for years.

'It is the Elder Wizards and their transgressions that bring you here,' the Old Master went on. 'Now we are alone, we may speak of such things.'

A glance at the alcoves between the pillars told Adelko that the Shadowmen had vanished. Had they even been there in the first place, he wondered, not knowing whether to trust his senses any more.

'Such things – and a few others besides,' said Horskram. 'Why did you try to have us killed in Ushalayim?'

The Old Master brought his fingertips together, keeping his elbows perfectly still just above his knees. If he was apologetic, he gave no sign of it. 'For many years now, the crusaders have been our sometime allies against the Nazharyan sultanate, for we revile the apostates of so-called Orthodoxy even more than the crude infidels from the north. As such, when the Grand Master of the Knights Bethler commissions our services for a handsome fee, we seldom ask too many questions.'

They all exchanged looks. 'It seems as though you were right, Sir Azelin,' said Horskram.

'Being right doesn't usually satisfy me,' said the disgraced Bethler.

'And yet it isn't all that often the Knights Bethler ask you to kill men of the cloth on their own sanctuary, is it?' pressed Horskram.

The Old Master inclined his head. 'True, this assignment was unusual – but not as unusual as you think. At the time, I simply assumed you were religious rivals of the Bethlers. However, it did surprise me that Grand Master Tobin wanted you assassinated on his own grounds. But as I said, our agreement with the Bethlers has always been not to ask too many questions, so long as they pay gold promptly for our services.'

'And have they?' asked the adept pointedly. 'Here we are, alive and in your power... why not simply finish the job?'

The Old Master smiled. That smile looked almost as serene as Tipu's – and was all the more sinister for it. Adelko could sense that the master assassin really was contemplating whether or not to do as Horskram had suggested. He also sensed the vanished Shadowmen weren't very far away at all.

Master Horskram, I hope you know what you're doing this time at least.

'Again, you have struck close to the heart of the matter,' the assassin went on. 'I could simply execute the pair of you, deliver your heads to Grand Master Tobin, and claim the rest of my fee. However, when my acolytes reported the failure of their mission, I realised from their account that there was far more to the pair of you than at first might seem. I have never had reason to trust the Bethlers, though it is true we do find mutuality in our causes on occasion. That was when I decided to contact my ally Sha'arza here, and told him to keep an eye on your movements.'

'That was how I knew to expect you,' put in the sorcerer. 'I had been watching you both since you left Ushalayim.'

'Well, that is one piece of the puzzle in place,' said Horskram. 'But there are more to come, and you hold them, Supreme Scion of the Shadowmen. You know what brings us here by now – I can sense that much at least.'

The Old Master let a single drawn-out breath escape his thin lips, more of an exhalation than a sigh. 'Some ten years have passed since I found the boy's shade, wandering through the Ghorabi. I used to take myself into the desert, relishing its solitude, for a master of the Way of the Shadow need never fear thirst or hunger. A pitiful and forlorn wretch was he, neither truly living nor truly dead, and immediately I laid eyes on him my heart was moved. When he begged me to take his burden from him, I complied, thinking it Ashanti's will that he should come into my path. For so many centuries he had borne that stone, yet not one person had been able to lift its curse.'

'You've had it all this time?' said Adelko. 'How have you managed to keep it secret?'

For the first time since their meeting the Old Master frowned. 'You are no apprentice, to talk out of turn so!' he admonished. Adelko felt abashed then, for though unprepossessing in appearance, the master assassin had an aura of greatness. 'But no, I sense great thirst and power in you,' the Old Master continued. 'And your question is an astute one. In point of fact, I have not been able to keep it such a secret, for your guide here has known of my encounter with the undead boy for some time now, and I fear one who covets the thing I keep is increasingly close to the truth of its whereabouts.'

Horskram flicked a glance sidelong at Sha'arza. 'We fathomed as much with regards to Sha'arza, but who is this other that you speak of?'

'I was hoping you might be able to help me answer that riddle,' replied the Old Master. 'For I am fairly certain the Grimoire needed to operate the Headstone of Ma'amun was taken from these lands a few years after I came by the fragment.'

That had them all surprised, even Sha'arza. 'You are full of surprises, old friend,' he said. 'I thought the Grimoire's whereabouts were a secret since I destroyed my father's notes.'

Horskram's voice became sharp. 'You knew of the Grimoire's whereabouts, too?' he demanded of the sorcerer.

Sha'arza rolled his eyes. 'You think my father would not have known of such a thing? You should be thanking me that I put an end to him before he could mount an attempt on it. I kept the knowledge hidden from you, as insurance if you will – I was not prepared to divulge all my secrets at once, not until I could be sure you were trustworthy your-selves. You of all people should be able to appreciate that.'

Horskram gestured irritably. 'I suppose it's a moot point now, by the sounds of it.'

'I have guarded secrets too,' interjected the Old Master, looking at Sha'arza. 'I told you nothing of the Grimoire's subse-quent theft, for you had told me how much you feared being tempted by such knowledge. I myself had only known of its existence for a short time, for it was not until the boy Cael gave me his burden that I began to take an interest in the artefacts of the Elder Wizards. I managed to trace the Grimoire to a fortress in eastern Kallandhar, close to the border of the crusader kingdom of Keraka. Nowadays that region is a dismal place, the site of internecine skirmishing betwixt Faith and Creed. As such, I was not surprised to learn shortly afterwards that the fortress had been sacked by a sortie of Knights Bethler, its entire garrison put to the sword. Even then I did not greatly fear, for what would a religious order want with such a thing? At first I simply assumed the motive for the siege had been military, that the attack had been a coincidence. But when I sent my acolytes to inspect the ruined fortress after the raid to be sure, I found the crypt below had been ransacked too.'

'Wait,' interjected Horskram. 'Explain yourself. What crypt?'

'The fortress was built on the site of a much older structure, one that belonged to an archmage who practised sorcery in the time of the Assurians, when the Shemites were carving out the Kishan empire and the Huryans were building Shamaria. This was in the Second Age of Darkness, before the True Prophet's Coming, and many of our ancestors were given up to dire rituals, and worshipped demons openly as gods. This archmage, also an influential noble, managed to learn of the Grimoire's whereabouts and sent a party of adventurers to recover it for him. This they did, but fortunately the archmage died before he could unlock its secrets or learn anything of the fragments it controlled. He had himself buried with the book, so no one else might use it, laying magical traps and locks on it such as were enough to confound all seekers for centuries – even your father Haziel had pause before such obstacles.'

Abdel nodded thoughtfully. 'He was close to mounting an assault on it though, I fathomed that much. That was why I destroyed all his notes on the subject, fearing lest I became tempted by his well-laid plans.'

'More to the point,' said Horskram. 'How in Palom's name did the Bethlers learn of such a thing? And how did they manage to take it? Frankly I am surprised you didn't try to do so yourself,' he added, looking at the Old Master suspiciously.

'If you think I would ever covet such a thing, you have misjudged me,' said the Old Master. 'It was only for pity's sake that I took the fragment from the boy Cael, so that his shade might finally be freed. I had no wish to come by a second portion of Hell's Portal – in fact once I learned of the Grimoire's location I was content to leave it there, instructing my men to monitor the fortress. Little did I suspect that someone would come to claim it, someone powerful enough both to overcome the fortress's military defences and the sorcerous protection of its hidden under-world. But come he did, and perhaps it will not surprise you to learn that this man's name was Brother Sir Tobin, then a superior commander in the Knights Bethler.'

Horskram gaped. 'And you still did business with him? Knowing that he had successfully recovered one of the most dangerous artefacts in the Known World?'

The Old Master frowned. 'I have my own destiny to follow, master adept,' he said sternly, 'and the Unseen guide us in mysterious ways. Know that we intend to do away with the so-called Orthodox apostasy that has blighted the lands of the Faith for too long, and restore the bloodline of the Enlightened Ones! For that to pass, we needed Tobin and his ilk. I cannot be a midwife to every cause in the Known World.'

Adelko felt his sixth sense like a lump of ice being run along the length of his spine.

Sheer madness, all of it. One good cause conflicts with another, and we never unite against the greater evil. What chance do we have of averting it if we're always carrying on like this? He thought of the monkey-like friezes on the inside wall of Sha'arza's tower, and suppressed a shudder.

Horskram was shaking his head in sheer exasperation. 'You do realise that this means Grand Master Tobin himself is likely a magician of some potency? Perhaps as great as Sha'arza's father Haziel, or at the very least possessed of some damnably powerful tools to get past those sorcerous traps you just mentioned!'

The Old Master simply shrugged. 'He would not be the first warlock I have allied the Kardin cause to.'

'Never mind,' Horskram sighed. 'At least you had the sense to call off the attempt on our lives.'

'Speaking of which, that is another riddle we may have solved,' said Tipu thoughtfully. 'For it would have taken an accomplished sorcerer to raise up the ghoul horde against us at Shamaria.'

'Not to mention summoning the flock of eagles that nearly made ruin of my ship,' added Sha'arza, a hurt expression on his face. 'I had no idea this Bethler Grand Master was such a powerful enemy.'

'We need to know more about him,' rejoined Horskram. 'Scion of the Shadowmen, when did this raid on the crypt and fortress take place?'

'Three years ago,' replied the Old Master, 'shortly before Tobin was promoted to Grand Master of the Knights Bethler and moved from Keraka to Ushalayim.'

'That makes sense,' mused Azelin. 'I recall Tobin mentioning that he'd sacked a key outpost in Kallandhar not long before he took up his post in Ushalayim. He didn't say anything about an underworld or a grimoire, of course. I can't say I'm surprised by the revelation that he's a warlock though.' The warrior-monk grimaced as though he'd just drunk sour wine.

'I had Tobin put under close watch after the siege,'

continued the Old Master, 'for we have eyes everywhere in the lands of the Faith. A few months later they reported Tobin meeting with an official – some kind of clerical authority we believe – and passing him a casket that may or may not have contained the Grimoire. My spies say this official was received personally by Tobin, and stayed in the guest wing of the Sultan's former palace, as you did. They met in Tobin's solar, but spoke too softly to be overheard. The following morning this official was seen leaving the Bethler headquarters with the casket.'

The Old Master's face suddenly became grave. 'These were some of my best acolytes, trained in the psychic arts. Both said they sensed a thing of great evil lay within that casket, though they did not feel sure enough to try to take it from this official. In truth, I think they feared to go near such a thing, and were only too glad to let it pass from these lands. At any rate, they never got a look inside. The official took the casket and boarded a pilgrim ship bound for Pangonia. After that, our trail goes cold.'

'What did this clerical official look like?' asked Horskram.

'He was dressed much as you are, though his habit was black not grey,' said the Old Master. 'He wore his cowl pulled up, but my men say everyone seemed to defer to him. Because no one but Tobin interacted closely with him, we could not learn of his identity. In fact I cannot say for sure if he was even a member of your Order, for Argolians seldom visit these parts.'

'But when they do, it's the Bethlers they stay with,' mused Horskram. 'That's why Hannequin sent us with a

letter of introduction to Grand Master Tobin in the first pl-
'

The words froze on his lips.

Adelko's surroundings seemed to drop away from him then, and he was back at the Warlock's Crown, staring down at Andragorix as he died.

Tell us who you serve!

Standing over the mad warlock, demanding to know who his master was.

A dying man is bonded to no one but the Angel of Death. Tell us who you serve!

Andragorix's lips desperately trying to form words, as the final dregs of life ebbed out of him...

He-

They'd been so close to learning the truth back then, so close...

The flashback receded as quickly as it had come on, and Adelko was back in the Old Master's solar. Horskram's face had gone white. Had he just had the same vision? The others were staring at them, confused.

And then Adelko knew. He could not say how, but he just *knew*.

Andragorix's last word hadn't been *he*. It had been a man's name, cut short by Azrael's scythe. Horskram's lips barely seemed to move as he finished it now.

'Hannequin...'

CHAPTER 20
HIDING IN PLAIN SIGHT

From behind the multicoloured glass wall of the observatory, in the dome at the summit of the inner sanctum, the Grand Master of the Order of St Argo watched as his last disciple entered through the gatehouse. He wasn't entirely surprised to see Joram had the warlock in tow; his disciples were exploring new powers, and in fusing themselves to other magic users they could experience all sorts of unusual psychic attachments.

Have no fear, brother, I'll soon part you from your dupe, he thought.

Twenty years he'd waited for this moment. Twenty years to study and plot and scheme and seduce. Had he been marked out by the Unseen the day he'd torn the covers off the spellbooks belonging to Abelard, substituting ordinary tomes and burning those – along with their owner – in full sight of Pangonia's ruling class in the main square of Rima? Or had he been singled out by the King of Gehenna long before, to be the torchbearer after Abelard passed?

Hannequin rather fancied the latter.

In his mind's eye he saw them stretched out, links in an infernal chain of hellish bliss: the Fallen One Himself, his first prophet Ma'amun, then in turn many other sorcerers and demons down through the ages: Cleops, Ashokainan, Morwena, Haziel Sha'arza, Xamiel and Khartoun, Abelard, and finally Hannequin himself.

Long has Abaddon plotted and schemed, to take back what is rightfully his, and I shall be the one to usher in the long-awaited new era. The Grand Master of the Order he would soon destroy seemed to feel rather than see the world swallowed up by a delicious darkness, warmed by fires that burned unending. An end to war, famine, disease and the rest of mortalkind's petty follies, as all writhed in blissful bondage to the Elder Ones.

But that was some way off yet. For now it remained to hold steady, to hold one's nose and enact the very games He would soon put an end to forever. It took a Jedrez player to manipulate mortalkind into doing one's bidding, to see many moves ahead to the ultimate toppling of thrones. And Hannequin was a master Jedrez player.

He sensed the presence of Johann before he entered the room.

'Are the brethren all here?' he asked as the former prior of Heilag bowed, inverting the sign of the Wheel.

'All accounted for – bar Joram, that is.'

'Brother Joram has arrived and will join us shortly. The others are gathered in my private chambers?'

Johann nodded, half bowing again. 'They are below, waiting for you.'

His obsequiousness did not go unnoticed. Since Hannequin had quietly dropped the charges against him, Johann's deference had only increased. He had slipped up badly at Heilag, giving Horskram wind of his involvement and subsequently failing to have him and his troublesome apprentice killed. But he'd redeemed himself by refusing to buckle under investigation, distracting the Order long enough for Hannequin to put the final phase of his plan into action. And his role in getting rid of the irritating novice Hargus had also been useful: at this late hour, the smallest fly could ruin the ointment.

The Grand Master turned once more to survey the monastery he would soon abandon forever. Its concentric circular walls with their domed turrets and covered walkways were slowly turning crimson in the dusking light. Would he miss its cloistered walks, its shady groves and cool, elegant halls? Unlikely – Hannequin now went to a place of far more magnificent beauty, for those that could comprehend it without going insane.

Joram was being escorted into the middle enclosure now, towards the sanctum, where torches were being lit to welcome the twilight as the early summer's day drew to a close. The sorcerer was still with them, but they would shortly be parted: cold links of iron and the interrogation chamber awaited the warlock. Let him fall victim to those zealous members of the Order left behind, who would be only too happy to have a scapegoat once Hannequin and his true brethren were gone. Joram, his most active agent to date, would be ushered upstairs to give his report: he had lost his scrying tool when Kilucan monastery was razed by

Abrexta's forces, and using his own to keep tabs on him had been difficult thanks to Morcant's counter-scrying talisman.

Not that Hannequin needed to know much more concerning the mission he'd sent him on, for it had been a resounding triumph.

The transporter demon had winged its way silently to the observatory in the dead of night, flying under a cloak of invisibility. The third fragment had given off the same intoxicating aura of subdued but incalculable power as the other two: as with the pieces from Ulfang and Graukolos, he had been prepared for its arrival, quickly banishing the demon and hiding the fragment with its brothers in his laboratory.

To this room Hannequin now went, leaving the giant brass contraption he'd used to learn secrets from the stars with a congenial pat. Silently Johann followed him from the observatory. The laboratory adjoined it: like all the chambers given over to Hannequin's decades-long study of the arcane arts, it was located within the dome of the sanctum itself, directly above his personal quarters.

In fact, *former* laboratory would be nearer the mark. Everything was packed and ready for the Departure. The only apparatus that remained in place were Hannequin's scrying tool and, of course, the astral portal. A master work of Thaumaturgy, Scrying and artifice, it had taken him years to fashion. The far wall had been inscribed painstakingly with hieratic symbols: birds of flight, gateways opening, and a humanoid figure disappearing were just some of the abstract sigils picked out in rare paints on the stones, forming a virtual gateway.

But what drew the Grand Master's attention was the

mighty casket of iron in the middle of the room that contained the things he had worked so hard to obtain.

Hannequin permitted himself an ironic smile as he looked at the scriptural writings in Decorlangue he had etched on its surface. It had taken all of the Redeemer's good words to contain the evil presence of the fragments, to stop others in the monastery detecting them.

Good and evil, such trite terms, he mused. *How abjectly mortal tongues fail to describe the nuances of the Universe that the Unseen fashioned. O Reus, thou false king, where are your injunctions now? I shall use all the powers at my disposal to make a better world.*

Surveying the assembled caskets and chests, he nodded in satisfaction. 'It is well,' he said. Not all his possessions would be able to go through the portal, but the essentials would come with him and his handpicked cabal. Stepping over to another casket, this one bound in bronze, he rested a hand on it. Tobin had served him well in obtaining the Grimoire, though of late his understudy had been less than successful in carrying out commands.

Horskram and Adelko, so very hard to kill. Perhaps you do still take some interest in the world you think is yours by right, O Heavenly Usurper. Your agents are resourceful and resilient, granted – but I know them better than they know themselves.

Indeed, Horskram's persistent survival had furnished him with one bonus: it had confirmed the whereabouts of the final fragment. The Old Master of Time's Arrow's defences in Ortiz would be formidable, but he would find a way past them, just as he had with the druids on the Westerling Isles. Getting an agent within their closely guarded bourne hadn't been easy, but Brother Joram had served him well.

The sound of the secret door grinding open alerted him to the monk's arrival from the dungeons, where he'd just left the hapless Morcant. The shaft had been constructed by the Thalamians, when the sanctum had been a pagan shrine; their engineering craft had almost begun to approach that of the Varyans. The pulley-operated lift that ran the length of it allowed a Grand Master of the Order swift access to suspects in the rooms below; it also conveniently allowed Hannequin to ferry whomever he pleased to his quarters without alerting anyone else in the monastery.

Joram entered and managed a quarter-bow. His injuries had healed somewhat on the two-week voyage from Ongist, but he still bore them. It mattered not – once their next task was complete Hannequin would see to them in little time.

'Grand Master,' Joram said reverentially. 'I trust the rest of the mission was a success.'

Once again Hannequin permitted himself a smile. 'Quite the success, I assure you,' he said, in the manner of a tutor praising a student for excellent work. 'Once the artefact concealed inside the sealed message I bade those fool knights bring you was activated, it was an easy matter to conjure a transporter demon to reconnoitre with our hybrid friend and complete the job.'

Joram rose, smiling darkly. 'You were right in what you said in the message – at close range the spell was devastating, though the artefact nearly took my hand off when I acti- vated it. Not even the Guardians could withstand a Third- Tier demon fused with Saraphi and Aethi. Truly nothing of the like has ever been seen in this age.' The smile curdled into a frown. 'Though I must say, Grand Master, placing such a powerful item within the message's seal was risky in the extreme.'

'Silence!' interjected Johann. 'You dare question the Grand Master?'

Hannequin raised a hand. 'Brother Joram has served me better than anyone here to date,' he said pointedly. 'He is entitled to divulge the contents of his mind.'

'The knights were not so foolish as you thought,' Joram went on. 'A good thing Lord Braxus was distracted by his ancestral duties, I fear he would have been difficult had he come with us to the islands. As it was, the freelancer Wrack-wulf suspected me from early on, and even that prating dolt Sir Torgun was on my spoor towards the end. And any one of them could have opened that letter before they even reconnoitred with me in Thraxia.'

Hannequin scoffed at that. 'Really? And broken all forms of protocol? I doubt it, Brother Joram. Besides – they can barely read, if at all. No, the plan worked admirably – by no means could I deploy such innovative and powerful magicks at long range, I had to have an agent trained in the arts who could get close enough to activate the artificed glyph containing them.' He clapped his hands together in satisfaction. 'A capital success, then. Now, Brother Joram, tell me of the remainder. I see you did not escape unscathed – how did the others fare? For I have not had the elan to spare to keep tabs on them.'

Joram made a dismissive gesture with his good arm. 'Lord Braxus you know of. Sir Torgun and Sir Wrackwulf decided to return to their respective homelands, I parted company with them a fortnight ago. With the freelancer went Ariadha ap Madrix, an exiled Westerling chieftain punished for failing to guard the fragment. That is all I know, for Morcant and I took ship for Rima as soon as we could.'

A pained look crossed Joram's face as he mentioned the mage. Even without that, Hannequin could sense the extent of his attachment.

'I did warn you what to expect,' he said. 'When my message instructed you that we were switching allegiance from Abrexta to the Crimson League and I told you to spare the warlock and use him to get close to the druids, I said your alliance with him might lead you into psychic bondage.'

Changing allegiances like that had been another risky move – but with Rowena rallying support for her cause and Abrexta overusing her magic to plunge her half of Thraxia into misrule, the original invasion plan of the Westerling Isles had seemed less likely to succeed. It had been a gamble, but one that had paid off in the end. A good Jedrez player must be willing to change tactics and make sacrifices at any time. The conquest of the Island Realms had only ever been a means to an end – pour honeyed words of a return to the Old Time into Abrexta's ears, and she had been willing to go along with anything. But her usefulness had come to an end.

Hannequin could still sense Joram's confused roil of emotions. Like the rest of his cabal, the adept was a pioneering entity – half monk, half mage. But unlike most of the rest of them, Joram had been used in the field far more often than not. Some confusion was natural under the circumstances.

'Andragorix was different,' muttered Joram. 'When you sent me to apprehend him after Horskram and Belinos maimed him, we fought against one another and I overcame him – but Morcant and I, we fought *together*. That changes things.' He fixed Hannequin with a plaintive look. 'There's no way we can...?'

Hannequin shook his head gently but firmly. 'Andragorix was already deeply corrupted, an easy pawn to use in our great game. I had no trouble enthralling him once you had brought him back here that moonless night. But Morcant has rather too much of the Right Hand Way about him, I'm afraid – he'll never consent to be bound. Such an attempt would, in fact, kill him.' He laid a firm hand on Joram's uninjured shoulder. 'Better to let the less enlightened brethren deal with him, once we are away from here.'

Joram grimaced, but Hannequin sensed him mastering his emotions. Slowly, he nodded. 'It shall be as the Grand Master wills,' he said, not without reluctance.

Hannequin smiled. 'Good. Now if that is all, brothers, I believe the rest of the cabal are waiting for us...'

There were some forty of them, crammed into Hannequin's study. The same study where he'd sent Horskram on his mission, hoping to spell an end to him. Thinking on that, Hannequin felt a flickering of rare doubt – would the pair still be able to make trouble for him? Horskram was old and set in his ways, but the journeyman hierophant Adelko was powerful beyond his own reckoning, and too pure of heart ever to be truly corrupted. For only those willing to embrace personal corruption could ever truly change the world for the better: that was the way of things, never mind the legends and the lays.

The Grand Master quelled such thoughts as he faced his cabal. Most were adepts, with a sprinkling of journeymen – and one novice. Arik, sullen-faced, stood at the back. Murdering his friend had poisoned his soul forever – that would only make him easier to control, of course. But Hannequin sensed great power in the young apprentice, too – the negative to Adelko's positive perhaps.

Send your minions against me, Reus, and I shall send them back doublefold. For too long have you and your archangels mismanaged the fate of men. If we must align ourselves to devils to thrive, then so be it.

Foremost among the cabal were the three surviving archmasters he had won over to his cause. Adamantus stepped forward, his dignified leonine features indicating nothing of his betrayal of the Order. But Adamantus had ever been a cunning man, and a tactician. This was the cunning move, the tactician's move.

'High and proud the walls of Varya loomed,' he intoned. 'Let them shine in splendour again, for all the world to see. We stand ready, Grand Master.'

Next came Gabrien. Still of spiteful mien, petty, overweening and vindictive – and yet he had his uses.

Hannequin knew how trifling those were, in the overall scheme of things. But a pawn was still a pawn for all that.

'Long the music of the spheres sang to the Priest-Kings of old. Let their sound be heard again, by all the realms of the world. We stand ready, Grand Master.'

Last was Edelmir. Dashing Edelmir, blond and handsome, Horskram's erstwhile understudy. And yet the flamboyant Pangonian had been easy enough to seduce. For he had courted Azathol in his vanity from a young age, scarcely even knowing it.

'Vast was the shadow cast by the Forbidden Isle across the face of the earth. Let that shadow rise and stretch again, that all mortals might seek its shade and know peace. We stand ready, Grand Master.'

Looking at each of them in turn, Hannequin nodded with quiet satisfaction. Joram and Johann had joined the congregation. Outside, beyond the closed shutters, night was falling. The sun would rise again tomorrow: but it would shed light on the beginning of a new era.

A new era, to mark the end of the old.

'It is well,' declared Hannequin. 'All that remains is to offer thanks to our dear departed brother Wolaf, who willingly consented to be bound to Belaach for the greater good...' – he paused – '... or the greater evil, depending on how you choose to look at it.' A few wry chuckles about the dimly lit study. Hannequin's smile belied how risky that move had been as well. Duping Horskram into suggesting the expedition mission to the Westerling Isles had been his most delicate ploy to date. Setting up Wolaf to counsel inaction, and subsequently exposing him as demonbound, had been enough to persuade him they should do the opposite of what the archmaster had suggested.

The oldest trick in the lays, and it has kept you off my scent for long enough, Horskram of Vilno.

Hannequin reached for his quarterstaff where it stood in a corner. Muttering a word of power, he pictured two sigils in quick succession, a candle being snuffed out and a torch being lit. As the tapers and lanterns in the study winked out, a single point of light appeared atop his quarterstaff.

'The hour is here, brethren,' he said. 'We shall not meet it by the unsteady light of mortal fire.'

Without another word, he turned and led his disciples from the study.

Back in his former laboratory, Hannequin paused before the polished quartz disc hanging from a bronze chain nailed to the wall. Plain and unadorned, nothing about his scrying tool suggested its true use. A hawk, an ear and an eye passed across his mindset as he murmured the words. Ivon's svelte features appeared before him, though they shimmered ever so slightly: even now, with all the power at his disposal, Hannequin had to conserve elan for the coming effort.

The Margrave of Vichy was bereft his usual facetious humour. His face looked taut, though his expression was outwardly composed and Hannequin could sense he was ready.

'The Departure is nigh,' said Hannequin. 'I trust you are

ready to assume command of the rest of the brethren in my absence?'

Ivon nodded. 'All is in place,' he replied. 'By the time you stand with an army of draugar and demonkind at your back, half the Free Kingdoms will be conquered – perhaps more.'

Hannequin frowned. 'Not what I have been hearing. Yet still, as long as you keep the realms of men occupied fighting one another that will be enough. Once the Headstone is complete, I will take care of the rest. Stand by for further instructions, I shall be in touch again presently.'

He murmured another word and the quartz went dark, before repeating the spell, questing much farther south this time. It took a while longer, but Grand Master Tobin's granite face appeared, flickering and uneven.

'From one Grand Master to another,' said Hannequin, inclining his head respectfully. 'And yet you have proved rather less effective than usual, of late.'

Tobin's face darkened. 'Horskram's friends proved more loyal and resourceful than I could have fathomed,' he said. Hannequin could sense the rivalry in him: his fanaticism and lust for power had made him easy enough to corrupt, but the man's hubris made him a dangerous tool.

'No matter,' Hannequin assured him. 'They haven't been eliminated, but we have them very much on the back foot.' Tobin was no pawn – best to treat him with due respect, for now. If Ivon was his queen, Tobin was knight and bishop rolled into one. Hannequin hid a wry smile at that thought, which amused him on more than one level.

'Everything else speeds as you intended,' Tobin assured him. 'The Fourth Pilgrim War will cleanse Sassania of its

Sha'abatian scum once and for all, and pave the way for the Second Coming.'

Tobin was the kind of man who was so consumed by gut prejudice he could not believe certain peoples would ever share in Abaddon's glory. How parochial and pathetic his bigotry was – what mental contortions he must go through to justify his own position to himself, Hannequin could scarcely guess at. But he would undoubtedly be useful in the Sassanian theatre of operations. What Tobin failed to realise was that his precious crusade would be but a distraction, allowing the real victory to be won elsewhere.

Not for the first time, Hannequin wondered how intelligent men could be so stupid.

'I am glad to hear it, Grand Master Tobin,' he said, smiling affably. 'I shall of course be coming to your aid – in good time.'

Tobin's face betrayed a rare uncertainty. 'To be sure it is a great risk, employing the Fallen Angel's very own servitors to expunge evil and bring about heaven on earth. But, as I have often mused, any agency may be legitimately employed in the service of the Almighty.'

Next to him Adamantus was on the point of scoffing openly. Hannequin silenced him with a surreptitious flick of the hand.

'You understand perfectly,' said Hannequin, the smile not leaving his face.

You understand nothing, you sententious zealot. For all that you proved passing quick at learning the very gramarye you once affected to despise.

'Farewell for now, Grand Master Tobin,' he purred,

keeping his thoughts to himself. 'Put your recent failure behind you, and concentrate on the coming crusade. You shall hear from me presently.'

Before Tobin could say anything else, Hannequin closed the spell and the quartz went dark again. He motioned to a couple of journeymen, who lifted it off the wall and added it to the pile of paraphernalia.

'I still don't see why we need to bother with all these temporal wars,' said Adamantus. 'After all, the power of the Headstone...'

'... will be used sparingly,' Hannequin cut him off. 'I have no intention of provoking a second Breaking of the World, Adamantus. One piece at a time, remember – as in a game of Jedrez. It is the King of Gehenna's will that this thing be done gradually. The Betrayed One would not have a smoking ruin to rule over, and neither shall we.'

The elderly Thalamian inclined his head deferentially. 'Forgive me for speaking out of turn, Grand Master.'

'Speak all you wish,' said Hannequin, almost sounding his usual kindly self – the kindly self he'd used to fool Horskram and so many others, for so many long years. Learning to obfuscate the highest concentration of sixth senses in the Free Kingdoms had been one of the most potent acts of Enchantment he had mastered. 'I have ever welcomed frank counsel from those who serve me. That is how we shall triumph, brothers – by pooling our superior intellects.'

The archmaster nodded again. Hannequin sensed that his respect was genuine, as it should be.

The rest of the cabal had gathered around, in readiness

to take up chests and caskets when the portal was activated. Mean work for the future masters of the world, but needs must for now – no ordinary servants could be expected to withstand the presence of Varya, Forbidden City of the Elder Ones. But see this thing through, and they would have more servants than any emperor had ever commanded.

One last time, Hannequin turned to address the nucleus of his new world order. Together they would make up a synod of ruling priest-kings – the first since Ma'amun had held sway over the city of Varya, five thousand years past.

'Three of the four fragments are in our possession, along with the Grimoire needed to operate the completed Headstone. For many long months we have pored over that tome, learning its eldritch lore and the gramarye needed to survive the perils of the Forbidden City. Now we are prepared and can journey via the cosmic interstices to Varya, our aeons-heralded birthright. The fourth fragment will be in our grasp shortly – now we have everything else we need, we can focus our energies on conjuring up an army to take Ortiz.' His hand clenched in determination. 'Not even the Old Master of Time's Arrow will be able to resist the One-Eyed General-King, when I raise his host from its spectral haunt in Varya. For so it was foretold.'

The cabal pulled cowls over heads and murmured their assent in sussurant voices. Hannequin sensed their elan, conjoining across the interstices that separated the left and right-hand paths of sorcery, straddling the psionic powers of the Argolian Order. This was evolution: mortalkind must adapt, or perish. Once more, he let a smile divide his aristocratic features. And to think the scions of his noble house had tried to discourage him from seeking a career in the Temple. But thanks to the choices he had made, all the world would soon be one house – and he would sit at its high table with the True King.

That thought bolstered him as he stepped up to the portal. Gathering his elan, Hannequin prepared to cast the spell that would take them to the city of the Elder Wizards.

GLOSSARY OF NAMES

Here follows an overview of some of the more common names relating to legends, geography, history, religion, magic and supernatural entities that feature in this book. It is not intended to be exhaustive but may be used as a reference to guide the reader.

Abaddon: Foremost among demonkind; led the revolt against **Reus** and the loyal angels and **archangels** during the Battle for Heaven and Earth at the Dawn of Time. Was condemned to languish in the Kingdom of **Gehenna** on the **Other Side**, but has been influential in the affairs of mortalkind ever since. Corrupted **Ma'amun**, foremost among the **Elder Wizards** of **Varya**, by teaching him the **Left Hand Path** of sorcery. Also known as the Fallen One, the Dark Angel, the Author of Evil, and the King of Gehenna in mainland **Urovia**; known as Sha'itan, Loth, **Logi** and the Cloven-Hoofed God in other cultures.

Abelard of Montrevellyn: Firebrand preacher who whipped up support for the **Purge** against the **Argolian Order**, later discovered to be a secret disciple of **Xamiel of Avalagone**, a demonic sub-avatar responsible for starting the **Pilgrim Wars**. Abelard was subsequently executed in sight of all in Rima, his dastardly tomes on magick burned along with him on the orders of Hannequin, later to become Grand Master of the persecuted Order of St Argo.

Acolytes: Palomedes' seven closest advisers and disciples who afterwards were instrumental in spreading the **Creed** – a religion based on his teachings and life examples – throughout **Urovia**. Generally heralded as bringing spiritual salvation to benighted peoples, though dissenters argue that their teachings were flawed interpretations of the **Redeemer**'s beliefs and practices.

Alric: Most holy of the knights of the **Purple Garter**; saved King **Vasirius** from the curse of the White Blood Witch using a drop of the Redeemer's blood.

Alysius: One of the Seven **Acolytes** of **Palomedes** the **Redeemer**; brought a phial containing His blood to the shores of **Northalde** shortly after the prophet's execution in Tyrannos.

Ambelin: Ruling royal house of the Kingdom of **Pangonia**. Its present incumbent is Carolus III, a scheming and self-serving monarch who has alienated many of his barons with high taxes since ascending the Charred Throne. Ambelin has held power for more than a hundred years since it emerged victorious from the Fourth War of the Royal Succession, fought after the reign of King **Vasirius** was brought to an end at the Battle of **Avalongne**.

Ancient Thalamy: Also known as the Thalamian Empire, a **Golden Age** hegemony that straddled the Sundering Sea and incorporated the modern kingdoms of Thalamy, **Pangonia**, Mercadia, the southern reaches of the **Urovian New Empire** and northern **Sassania**, lasting for several centuries until its destruction by Wulfric of Gothia. It most notable potentates include Vaxus, who first unified the warring city-states of Thalamy, and Tycius, the gifted general and warlord who sacked **Shamaria**.

Antaeus: Legendary mariner and adventurer belonging to the **Golden Age,** said by some to have been the son of the **archangel** Aqualcus, worshipped as a god in pagan times before the coming of the Faith and the **Creed**. Hailed from **Ancient Thalamy** in the Era of Warring City-States before the empire was consolidated. His exploits against **Gygants**, Ifriti, Seakindred, **Wyrms**, **Wadwos**, warlocks and other supernatural foes are celebrated in song and poetry throughout **Urovia**.

Anti-angels: Demonkind or evil spirits; angels who sided with **Abaddon** in the Battle for Heaven and Earth at the Dawn of Time. Known by different names in various cultures, for instance Ifriti in the **Sassanian Sultanates** and Juju in some parts of the **Arid Kingdoms**.

Aquitania: Most powerful of the southern margravates of **Pangonia** and foremost participant in the **Pilgrim Wars.** The scions of the Kingdom of Keraka in the **Blessed Realm** are descended from its ruling house.

Archangels: Most powerful of the angels who stayed loyal to **Reus;** foremost among them are the **Seven Seraphim.**

Archdemons: Most powerful of demonkind along with **Abaddon** himself; foremost among them are the seven **Princes of Perfidy.**

Argolian Order: Founded by Saint Argo five hundred years ago, this learned order of monks and friars is tasked with fighting evil spirits and hunting down witches and warlocks throughout the **Free Kingdoms** and **Pilgrim Kingdoms.** It is also celebrated for its learning.

Ashokainan: A legendary left-hand wizard who reputedly lived for hundreds of years until **Søren** slew him seven centuries ago. One of the most powerful warlocks to walk the Known World since the demise of the Priest-Kings of **Varya.** Believed to have been understudy to Cleops, another Golden Age sorcerer of immense power, before becoming his rival.

Assurian Empire: This once-powerful tribe controlled a maritime empire that straddled the entire coast of Northern Sassania on the Sundering Sea during the Second Age of Darkness; in keeping with many of the peoples of that benighted era, the Assurians turned to unclean devil-worship, venerating **Seven Princes** as deities.

Avatar: A collective name intended to summarise a complex terminology that covers all supernatural entities regarded as a manifestation of **Reus Almighty** (i.e. a direct extension of His being). This includes **archangels**, angels and their demonic opposites; the word is also commonly used to describe such entities sent to earth in mortal form to guide mankind for good or ill. The term can also be used to describe a saint who is rewarded for a virtuous life by being exalted to the ranks of the **Unseen** upon death. Most religious scholars across the Faith and **Creed** agree that the **Two Prophets** fall into the former category of avatar (i.e. that they were angels or archangels sent to earth to help mortalkind), though some cleave to the second interpretation (that they were mortals rewarded in the Afterlife for their service to mankind).

Azrael: The Angel of Death, tasked by **Reus** with judging the souls of the dead, determining whether they go to **Gehenna** or the **Heavenly Halls**. Known by many different names across cultures throughout history, including Orcus, Osirian, Mortis, Mahatsu and Imraan.

Battle of Avalongne: Decisive battle fought a century and a half ago that brought about the end of King **Vasirius** and his reign. Even though his forces were victorious, it ultimately proved a pyrrhic victory as most of the Knights of the **Purple Garter** and his loyal nobles were slain; this created a power vacuum that prompted the Fourth War of the Royal Succession. For this reason the Battle of Avalongne is still mourned by loremasters and troubadours alike as heralding the end of the halcyon era of Vasirius' just rule.

Battle of Kurushan Heights: This battle finally brought to end the era of the **Seven Enlightened Sultans**, when their last scion Abu tek Jahib was slain by Muhmet Iron Breaker, a rival warlord. However, many of the Unorthodox **Faith** believe the Kardin bloodline did in fact survive, when Abu's grandson Alamuz was spirited out of **Ushalayim** before Muhmet's forces seized the city.

Knights Bethler: Elite military religious order of

warrior-monks, charged with defending the **Pilgrim Kingdoms**. Said to be the most formidable warriors in the Known World, believed by many to be able to channel a sixth sense akin to that of the Argolians to fight better. Founded by the Seven Paladini, knights who took the Wheel and distinguished themselves during the First **Pilgrim War**.

Blessed Realm: Common name given to the **Pilgrim Kingdoms**.

Breaking of the World: Cataclysm visited on the Known World by **Reus** and the **Archangels** five thousand years ago as punishment for **Ma'amun**'s attempt to open the gates of **Gehenna** at the behest of his master **Abaddon**. Resulted in the destruction of the **Varyan** civilisation and substantially altered the geography of the **Urovian** and **Sassanian** continents. Ushered in the **First Age of Darkness**, during which nearly all the vast learning of the Varyan Empire was lost.

Cael: A learned youth from the **Island Realms** tasked with taking the fourth fragment of the **Headstone of Ma'amun** to **Sassania** after it was broken by **Søren**. Disappeared with the fragment centuries ago, though since rumoured to have become one of the undead, wandering the Ghorabi desert in southern Nazharya.

Cierny: Ruling royal clan that holds the throne in **Thraxia**. Current incumbent is Cadwy, a weak ruler widely rumoured to have been ensorcelled by the witch Abrexta the Prescient.

Creed: Monotheistic religion founded by the **acolytes** of **Palomedes**, one of the **Two Prophets**, who opposed the tyranny of the **Thalamian Empire**. It falls into two mainstream churches: the Orthodox Temple in the **Urovian New Empire** and the **True Temple** in Western **Urovia** and the **Pilgrim Kingdoms.**

Draugar: Undead race of warlock kings who are believed to have served the **Elder Wizards** as vassals. It is not known if they were themselves **Varyans**, subject peoples who were rewarded with great power by the Elder Wizards for their service, or a mixture of the two. Draugar are reputed to occupy certain remote areas, including the Draugmoors in central **Vorstlund** and the Valley of the Barrow Kings in the **Westerling Isles,** and have numerous powers including shapeshifting and draugbreath, a curse that afflicts victims with the preternatural Rotting Sickness.

Dulsinor: Lands in northern **Vorstlund** ruled by the House of Markward, until Eorl Wilhelm Stonefist was treacherously murdered by the rival Lanraks. The Eorldom is one of nine principal states that compose the Vorstlending realm.

Elder Wizards: Ancient race of warlocks who ruled over the Known World from their island homeland of **Varya** for a thousand years until the **Breaking of the World**. Foremost among them was **Ma'amun**, who became corrupted by **Abaddon** after he learned the **Left-Hand Path** of black magic at his feet. Known by various other names throughout the Known World including the Priest-Kings of Varya and the Magi.

Elementi: Race of spirits belonging to the **Other Side** corresponding to the four elements: Terrus (earth), Aethi (air), Saraphi (fire) and Lymphi (water).

Faith: Principal and monotheistic religion of **Sassania** based on the teachings of the Prophet **Sha'abat**, who preceded the coming of **Palomedes** by several generations. Unlike Palomedes, Sha'abat was never a warrior and always counselled peaceful resolution of conflict wherever possible. However, this has not prevented adherents of the Faith from making war in his name. The Faith is divided into two principal camps: the Orthodox adhered to in the Sultanates of **Nazharya** and Kallandhar; and the Unorthodox branch cleaved to in **Halepo** and Murad. The Unorthodox branch still believes in the bloodline of the **Seven Enlightened Sultans**, and is more tolerant of mysticism and sorcery as such.

First Age of Darkness: A thousand-year period of backwardness and strife directly succeeding the **Breaking of the World**; few civilisations if any flourished during this bleak era.

Firedrake Wars: Series of conflicts between the **Westerling Isles** and the **Wyrms**, foremost of whom was Erebon, which straddled the **Middle Time** between the **Wars of Kith & Kin** and the subsequent Latter Time. The **Northlanders** also suffered greatly due to Erebon's depredations, leading the two peoples to make common cause. The Firedrake Wars came to an end when the Northlandic hero **Søren** slew Erebon and his wife Antelywa, crippling their son Anglaurang. After this the Wyrms went into terminal decline; Anglaurang was slain by Sir **Lancelyn** of the Pale Mountain centuries later, and when Sir Azelin of Valacia slew his son Baphomet, their race became extinct.

First Clarion: Marked the Dawn of Time and the

creation of the Universe by **Reus Almighty**, who set his angels to work creating the galaxies, solar systems and planets thereafter. Scholars dispute over what timeframe this occurred, with estimates varying between a few hundred years to aeons in mortal reckoning.

Free Kingdoms: Collective name given to the six principal realms of Western Urovia: **Northalde, Thraxia, Pangonia, Vorstlund**, Mercadia and Thalamy. The epithet 'free' comes from the fact that slavery was abolished throughout these realms with the coming of the **Creed** – although serfdom and other types of feudal bondage still persist.

Frozen Principalities: Name given to a string of petty kingdoms belonging to the Northlanders, barbarian tribes who still worship angels and demons as gods and cling to their age-old customs. Also known as the Frozen Wastes, these lands are ruled over by the Ice Thegns and their seacarls and housecarls – fierce warriors who pledge fealty to their liegelords. Recently the Ice Thegns have become united under one ruler - Magnhilda, Shield Queen and Magna of the Frozen Wastes.

Gaellentir: Stretch of lands in northern **Thraxia** once ruled over by Clan Fitzrow, recently conquered by highland rebels. Its principle seat is Gaellen, a fortified town and castle.

Gehenna: The island prison on the **Other Side** to which **Abaddon** and his demonic followers were banished by **Reus** after the Battle for Heaven and Earth was lost. At its heart lies the City of Burning Brass, divided into Five Tiers – the first and highest of these is reserved for **Abaddon**

himself, the **Seven Princes of Perfidy** and other archdemons.

Golden Age: New era of civilisation that flourished after the end of the **First Age of Darkness** some four thousand years ago and lasted for three millennia. During this time the civilisations of Sendhé and Ancient Thalamy flourished; much lore was relearned or rediscovered, though the glory of mortalkind never attained that achieved during the apogee of the preceding **Platinum Age.**

Grand High Monastery: Informal name given to the headquarters of the **Argolian** Order just outside Rima in **Pangonia.** Its proper name is the Most Reverend Priory of St Argo, and it is the first chapter of the Order founded by the saint of that name five hundred years ago.

Great World Serpent: The first of **Reus Almighty's** sentient creations along with Aurgelmir the Titan. Fathered the race of Wyrms with Hydrae the Many Headed (whom **Søren** slew on his Seventh and final Deed). According to legend, the Great World Serpent's body was used to create the world when Reus crushed him and Aurgelmir together to stop them destroying the Universe with their constant fighting. The same legend states that the World Serpent lies coiled at the centre of the earth, surrounded by the flesh of Aurgelmir; should he ever be woken from his slumber the Known World will fall apart and be destroyed. As such, the Great World Serpent is also referred to as He Who Must Not Be Disturbed, particularly among the Northlanders of the **Frozen Principalities.**

Gygant: A race of giants, believed to be **Reus'** first attempts to fashion mortalkind from the rock and clay of the earth (itself created from Aurgelmir the Titan, who is thus also known as the Father of Giants). Many times larger than their human descendants, though extremely violent and stupid, Gygants terrorised early human settlements until the **Elder Wizards** slew most of them and enslaved the rest.

Halepo: Sassanian sultanate that lies along the western shore of the Great Inland Sea; of the Unorthodox branch of the Faith, its scions have long been more tolerant of sorcery than its neighbours. Once the centre of the **Kishan Empire**, ruled by a race of sorcerer-sultans in the **Golden Age**, the realm has a strong heritage of magick. More prosaically, it is also noted for its spicy stews.

Headstone of Ma'amun: Tablet of incalculable power wrought by **Ma'amun** five thousand years ago; inscribed with hieroglyphic writing said to represent additions he made to the Sorcerer's Script under the tutelage of **Abaddon.** It is said to contain the power to break the hold placed on the Fallen One by **Reus** and summon him and his followers back to the mortal vale. It is not clear whether Ma'amun sought to control Abaddon or serve him, and as such whether the Headstone will enable its user to bind him to his or her will.

Heavenly Halls: The Kingdom of **Reus**, where the **Seven Seraphim** sit at his side and the rest of the **archangels** and angels dwell. The most splendid of the island realms of the **Other Side**, where the souls of those judged fit by **Azrael** are sent to reside until the Hour of All's Ending and Judgment Day.

Hierophant: A member of the **Argolian** Order who has attained exceptional psychic powers, outstripping those of even the most accomplished adepts. In this era there are thought to be three: Horskram of Vilno; Hannequin, current Grand Master of the Order; and Malthus of Montrevellyn, who left Rima years ago on a secret mission and is rumoured to have sought audience with the **Fays** of **Tintagael** before vanishing into the uttermost north. Adelko of Narvik, a novice seconded to Horskram for further training, is also believed by him to be a potential fourth hierophant.

Huryan Empire: The Huryans are a warlike tribe that today dominate the Ghorabi desert, centring on its city of oases Tesh; but in the **Golden Age** they founded a mighty empire straddling much of central **Nazharya**, building the fabled city of **Shamaria** and learning many other crafts and trades long since forgotten. They fell to unclean worship of demonkind in the Second Age of Darkness, which ultimately proved their undoing and culminated in the sacking of Shamaria by the Thalamian warlord Tycius.

Ingwin: Ruling royal house of the Kingdom of **Northalde**; current incumbent is Prince Wolfram who rules as Regent. Coat of arms is two rearing white unicorns facing each other on a purple background.

Island Realms or Westerling Isles: Series of islands, the two principal ones being Kaluryn and Skulla, ruled over by the Marcher Lords and Druids, lying in the Great Western Ocean. The most westerly known civilisation, the Island Realms cling steadfastly to their ancient beliefs, having been visited by Kaia the Moon Goddess during the **First Age of Darkness** and taught the **Right Hand Path** of magick lost to man when the **Varyan** Empire was destroyed at the

Breaking of the World. Also known as Druidsbourne and the Islands of World's Ending.

Kardin: Name given to both the ancient tribe and the bloodline they founded when Abu'cuchaza'ar Kardin became the first of the **Seven Enlightened Sultans** by taking the teachings of the Prophet Sha'abat into his heart. The tribe still exists today, albeit in greatly diminished form; its leading figure is the Sultan of **Nazharya**, Muqmurlish tek Nazar, who is of Kardin ancestry on his mother's side.

King's Dominions: Stretch of rich lands between Efrilund to the north and the Southern Provinces ruled directly by the **Northlending** King. Here royal law is strongest; consequently this is the wealthiest and most stable part of **Northalde.** Recently it was extended to include the Southern Provinces after a successful war against southron rebels.

King's Fold: Northern half of Umbria in **Thraxia,** ruled directly by the Royal Clan **Cierny.** The rest of the ward is parcelled about between several barons.

Kishan Empire: Founded by the **Shemite** tribe during the **Golden Age** of **Sassania,** this maritime empire once straddled the Great Inland Sea and included modern-day **Halepo** and the Khedivates of Rawalpinda, Zingoul, and Shamara. Its foremost scions were accomplished warlocks, and the treasures buried with them in their tombs have become legendary, likewise the traps set to guard them.

Lancelyn: Greatest of the Knights of the **Purple Garter,** most renowned for slaying the Great Wyrm Anglaurang in the time of King **Vasirius.** The latter's skull he brought back to court at Rima, where it was used to fashion the Charred Throne where the Pangonian king sits to this day.

Laurelin: Ruling house of Vichy, a prosperous margravate close to the heart of **Pangonia**. Its present incumbent, Lord Ivon, is a wily politicker of notoriously dissolute appetites, often connected to intrigue at the court of King Carolus. The House of Laurelin is one of the oldest and most prestigious in the kingdom, and has ties to the Ruling House of Rius from the time of King **Vasirius**. Some of its elder scions are also rumoured to have practised sorcery.

Left Hand Path: Black magic, derived from the teachings of **Abaddon** to **Ma'amun** more than five thousand years ago. Comprises Necromancy and Demonology, the two **Schools of Magick** most closely aligned to the Left Hand Path. However, some sorcerers who practise left-hand magic claim it is not necessarily wholly evil of itself, for instance those who use it to ask the dead for advice.

Logi: Name given by **Northlanders** to **Abaddon**, reviled by them as a trickster god.

Lower Thulia: One of the nine major baronies in Vorstlund, the Dukedom is perhaps the most powerful in the realm along with the Principality of Westenlund and the Dukedom of Stornelund. It is ruled by the House of Alt-Ürl.

Lower Vallia: Old name given to the southern margravates of **Pangonia**, of which **Aquitania** is the most powerful. Its inhabitants have a distinctive identity and are on the whole more zealous in the **Creed**. As such they have a proud tradition of crusading and have contributed many knights and soldiers to the **Pilgrim Wars**.

Ma'amun: Most powerful of the **Elder Wizards**, became

corrupted by **Abaddon**, who taught him the **Left Hand Path** and encouraged him to extend his powers. Ma'amun was slain along with all the other Magi at the **Breaking of the World**, when the **Unseen** punished him for perverting the Gift of Magick and daring to challenge the Laws of Reus. His shade is believed to be trapped in **Gehenna**, where he languishes in the City of Burning Brass ruled by his erstwhile teacher along with all the other souls of the damned.

Mercadia: Most southerly of the Free Kingdoms and arguably the most wealthy; a former province of the short-lived Muradi Empire, its people have absorbed many customs of the Sassanians including a lively respect for trade. Less feudal than most of its Urovian neighbours, Mercadia has nevertheless thrived by providing shipping to crusaders in the Pilgrim Kingdoms.

Middle Time: In the Westerling reckoning, this is the era that spanned the ending of the Nine Pestilences (Kaia's punishment for the folly of the **Wars of Kith & Kin**) and the Forty Years' Kin Strife. Something of an 'electrum age' for the Islanders, it was marked by a renewal of contact between the **Island Realms** and the Four Old Kingdoms of **Thraxia**, that saw both sides enriched by trade in goods and ideas. During this era, which lasted around two centuries, magick revived somewhat and nearly approached that of the fabled **Old Time**. For this reason it is recalled fondly by many in the Island Realms and Thraxia, which greatly benefited from contact with its ancestral motherland.

Morwena: Beloved of **Søren**; a sorceress of fearsome repute who hailed from the **Island Realms**. Ensorcelled the great hero and sent him on his Seven Deeds, which were ultimately purposed to recover the **Headstone of Ma'amun** from the Forbidden City on the Island of **Varya**. Slain by Søren after she spurned him on completion of his Final Deed, in which he brought the Headstone from Varya to the Island Realms.

Morwena's Doom: Name given by folk of the **Westerling Isles** to the **Headstone** of Ma'amun.

Narborg: Centring on the Cauldron, a shrine to the **Great World Serpent** leading all the way down to its lair at the heart of the earth beneath the waves, Narborg is a town built on a group of islets linked together by platforms and walkways. Currently controlled by the **Northlanders** of the Skjel Isles, it was built by the **Elder Wizards** and was once a mighty city; today its magicks still redound, and though it is a great trading entrepot in the Valhalla, few stay there long after transacting their business.

Nazharya: Greatest of the sultanates of **Sassania**, named after the house of Nazhar that founded it shortly after the **Battle of Kurushan Heights** that brought to an end the rule of the **Seven Enlightened Sultans**. Has suffered as a result of the **Pilgrim Wars**, losing territory to the encroaching **Pilgrim Kingdoms**, though it looks set to recoup some former glory under its new ruler, the Sultan Muqmurlish tek Nazar, who has reunited the realm.

Northalde: One of the **Free Kingdoms**, settled by Northland reavers from the **Frozen Principalities** seven hundred years ago. Comprises the lands north of the Argael and west of the Hyrkrainian mountains that divide the north-west peninsular of Western **Urovia** between it and the kingdom of **Thraxia**. **Northlendings** are famed for their skill in warfare, horsemanship, shipwrighting, armoury and castle-building.

Northlander: Inhabitant of the **Frozen Principalities**, whose ancestors founded the mainland colonies that would eventually become the Kingdom of **Northalde**. Northland raiders also settled the coasts further south and such many Vorstlendings can also trace their ancestry back to the Principalities.

Northlending: Inhabitant of the Kingdom of **Northalde** in north-western **Urovia**; not to be confused with **Northlander**, an inhabitant of the **Frozen Principalities**.

Occitania: Western peninsula of **Pangonia** comprising more than half a dozen margravates. Occitanians are fiercely independent and have historically caused the crown trouble. Its foremost powers are probably Gorleon, noted for its maritime tradition, and Vichy, which has access to vital trade routes with the northerly Free Kingdoms via the city of Broullion. Armandy province is also widely celebrated for the quality of its wine.

Old Time: In the reckoning of the Westerling calendar, this roughly corresponds with the early Golden Age, between the Coming of the Moon Goddess to the **Island Realms** at the end of the **First Age of Darkness** and the Wars of Kith & Kin two thousand years later. A halcyon era for the islanders, when the right-hand druiding way was at its peak and folk enjoyed greatly increased prosperity and longevity.

Other Side: Collective name given to all the dwelling places of spirits, **elementi, fays,** demons, angels and **Reus Almighty** Himself. Said to be an endless sea of vapour punctuated by islands, including the **Heavenly Halls**, **Gehenna**, and the Place of Judgment where **Azrael** dwells. All supernatural beings hail from the Other Side, and this is consequently where warlocks of all bents derive their powers using the Language of Magick and the Sorcerer's Script.

Palomedes: Second of the **Two Prophets**; inspired the **Creed**, the major religion of **Urovia**. Born to a soldier in Ushalayim about a thousand years ago in what is now the **Pilgrim Kingdoms**. Initially intended to follow his father into the Thalamian Legions but began hearing the Voice of **Reus** shortly after coming of age at fourteen. Resolved to use his martial skills to lead a revolution against the tyrannical Thalamian Empire and acquired a great following, but later forsook the sword and led his supporters in a campaign of passive resistance. Was finally apprehended by the Thalamians after being betrayed by his former lieutenant Antiochus the Red-Handed, taken to Tyrannos and broken on the **Wheel** at the Emperor's command. Also known by his abbreviated name, Palom (which becomes Palomat in the lands of the **Faith** by way of derivation), and his most common epithet, the **Redeemer.**

Pangonia: Most powerful of the **Free Kingdoms**, though its influence has waned somewhat since its apogee under the Chivalrous King Vasirius, who ruled some two centuries ago. Its capital Rima is also the headquarters of the **True Temple** and the **Argolian Order.** Currently ruled by King Carolus III of the House of Ambelin, a scheming, ambitious monarch known also as the 'wily' and the 'greedy' for heavy taxes imposed on his barons.

Pilgrim Kingdoms: Collective name given to northern **Sassanian** territories carved out by **Urovian** crusaders a century ago, consisting of the **Kingdom of Ushalayim**, named after its principal city, where **Palomedes** the **Redeemer** was born, the Kingdom of Keraka and the Kingdom of Ranishmend. Also known collectively as the **Blessed Realm.**

Pilgrim Wars: Series of crusades – holy wars against the heathen **Sassanians** sanctioned by the **True Temple** – begun more than a hundred years ago that recaptured the holy city of Ushalayim where **Palomedes** the **Redeemer** was born. Many factions besides the victorious crusading dynasties have profited from the Pilgrim Wars, most notably the merchant houses of Mercadia, most southerly of the **Free Kingdoms.** However, the Pilgrim Wars have not been endorsed by all Palomedians: the Orthodox Temple in the **Urovian New Empire** has openly voiced its disapproval, whilst the **Argolian Order** has refused to condemn or condone them. And few knights from the northerly Free Kingdoms of **Thraxia** and **Northalde** have taken the **Wheel**, with most crusaders originating from **Mercadia, Vorstlund, Pangonia** and Thalamy.

Platinum Age: A thousand-year epoch during which the **Elder Wizards** ruled all of the Known World from the Island of **Varya**; during this time mankind, though in bondage to the Priest-Kings, reputedly lived in a state of ease, comfort and luxury unparalleled in mortal history. According to some scholars the average lifespan exceeded a century and even the lowest of birth were well educated and literate. This era came to an abrupt end some five millennia ago when the **Unseen** punished **Ma'amun** for daring to challenge their authority by destroying Varya and much of the Known World, laying waste to the great civilisation it had built.

Princes of Perfidy: Collective name given to the seven most powerful **archdemons** who serve **Abaddon**: Sha'amiel (**avatar** of greed and bigotry); Azathol (vanity and hubris); Zolthoth (wrath); Ta'ussaswazelim (cruelty); Chreosoaneuryon (gluttony); Satyrus (lust and sexual depravity); and Invidia (envy). The Seven Princes are themselves dark emanations of the **Seven Seraphim** and thus have their celestial opposites among the **archangels**, whose virtues they seek to corrupt and subvert.

Purge: Calamitous event a generation ago that saw the **Argolian Order** falsely accused and tried for witchcraft by clerics of the mainstream **True Temple** in Rima. Many Argolians were tortured and made false confessions which they later retracted. The Order eventually succeeded in refuting the charges and even turned the tables on their accusers – a divination led by Hannequin, Grand Master of the Order, revealed many of their accusers including the Supreme Perfect to have been themselves acting under the influence of the **archdemon** Sha'amiel. The guilty perfects, led by **Abelard of Montrevellyn**, were burned alive in the main square at Rima. However, in another twist, since then the Temple has been held to be itself 'purged' of all wrongdoing, its traitors having been brought to justice, whilst much suspicion continues to fall on the Argolians, whose psychic and spiritual abilities are held by many to be akin to sorcery itself.

Purple Garter: Also known as the Crescent Table, this elite Order of thirty knights was founded by King **Vasirius** and is supposed to comprise the flower of Pangonia's chivalry. Nowadays it is more a political tool, used to keep more powerful nobles in check by appointing their younger brothers to key posts of state.

Redeemer: Common epithet by which **Palomedes** is referred to among believers of the **Creed**.

Rent Between Worlds: The name given to the gap between the mortal vale and the **Other Side** that wizards of all kinds use to draw upon the supernatural powers essential to sorcery, using the Language of Magick and the Sorcerer's Script. This gap was greatly widened during the **Platinum Age** when the **Elder Wizards** ruled the Known World, and is said to be responsible for all manifestations in the mortal vale, be it **elementi**, demonkind, **Fays**, **Gaunts** or other supernatural entities. The Rent widens in accordance with how much sorcery is being used; hence if a warlock is particularly active in one area, the Rent there will be widened, increasing the likelihood of possessions, hauntings and other apparitions.

Reus Almighty: God; responsible for the creation of the Universe and everything in it, including the Known World, the **Other Side, archangels**, angels, spirits, **elementi**, mortalkind and the animal kingdom. Sages differ on whether His power is truly infinite or simply incalculable according to the reckonings of mortalkind. The Almighty was unknown to pre-Faith mortals, who worshipped the archangels and **archdemons** as gods in their own right during the **Platinum** and **Golden Ages**.

Right Hand Path: More benign white magic originally taught to the **Varyans** by the **Archangels** to help them fashion their civilisation during the **Platinum Age**. Some thinkers, the **Argolians** among them, hold that all magic is a mistake, and that even the Right-Hand Path can be used to do evil in the wrong hands. Others such as the pagan followers of Kaia The Moon Goddess – who retaught aspects of white magic to the folk of the **Island Realms** during the **First Age of Darkness** – disagree on this point.

Ryøskil: Treaty signed by the **Northlanders** several generations ago forcing them to stop officially raiding mainland **Northalde** (though clandestine raids have continued sporadically). The Northlanders were brought to the treaty after being defeated decisively in battle by the **Northlendings** under King Aelfric III.

Sassania: Lands of the hot south lying beyond the Sundering Sea that comprise the Four Sultanates, the **Pilgrim Kingdoms** and various other petty principalities. Principal religion is the **Faith**, founded by the First Prophet **Sha'abat** several generations before the coming of **Palomedes**.

Second Age of Darkness: Another period of decline marked in Western **Urovia** by the destruction of the Thalamian Empire after Tyrannos was sacked by Wulfric of Gothia more than nine hundred years ago. It is generally agreed to have ended with the consolidation of barbarian petty kingdoms into the six **Free Kingdoms** more than three centuries ago, ushering in the advent of the present **Silver Age**. Note that other cultures differ in their reckoning of the Second Age of Darkness; for instance the **Urovian New**

Empire dates its ending with the completion of the Hundred Years Conquest slightly earlier, while the **Sassanians** date it from the demise of the last of the **Seven Enlightened Sultans**, two generations after Wulfric sacked Tyrannos.

Second Sight: A mystic gift, conferred only on women, that allows them to experience visions of the future (both their own and that of others they may be connected to). Like the **sixth sense** cultivated by the **Argolian** friars, it is not a precise craft.

Seven Enlightened Sultans: Gifted bloodline of the first rulers of the Sha'abatian world, established when Abu'cuchaza'ar Kardin took the teachings of the First Prophet into his heart; believed by the Orthodox branch of the **Faith** to have been wiped out at the **Battle of Kurushan Heights**, when the last of the Seven Sultans, Abu tek Jahib, was slain. However, many Unorthodox sects, including the **Sufielis** and the Order of the **Silver Shadow**, believe the bloodline survived this calamitous defeat, which brought to an end the halcyon era of wisely guided sultans in Near **Sassania**.

Seven Schools of Magick: The core disciplines of sorcery practised by warlocks and witches of varying bent and aptitude throughout the Known World. These are: Thaumaturgy, Transformation, Enchantment, Scrying, Alchemy, Necromancy and Demonology. The first five are broadly classified under the more benign **Right Hand Path;** the last two belong to the darker **Left Hand Path.** Many subdivisions of the major schools also exist; for instance *artifice*, which is a sub discipline of Alchemy and involves the manufacture of various magical charms and other items.

Seven Seraphim: Foremost among the **Archangels**, those that sit at the right hand of **Reus Almighty**. They are: Logos (**avatar** of prosperity and tolerance); Siona (grace and dignity); Virtus (courage); Stygnos (stoicism and fortitude); Euphrosakritos (merriment); Luviah (love); and Aeriti (aspiration). The Seraphim are opposed by their dark emanations the **Princes of Perfidy,** who represent twisted or corrupted forms of the virtues they embody.

Sha'abat: First of the Two Prophets, an avatar of the Unseen who manifested somewhere in the Zhosa Desert region beyond the Hierocracy of Sendhé more than a century before the coming of **Palomedes.** Sha'abat preached in Sendhé but was exiled by the Priest-king Pankott, who felt threatened by his enlightened doctrine of peace, yet could not undo him with his sorcerous powers. Sha'abat was eventually taken on as vizier by Sultan Abu'cuchaza'ar of the Kardin tribe, who went on to found the line of the **Seven Enlightened Sultans.** Today adherents of the Faith across Near Sassania cleave to the teachings of Sha'abat, though since the Great Schism there has been a violent split within the **Faith.**

Shamaria: Legendary city built by the Huryans shortly before the **Second Age of Darkness;** famed for its splendid gardens, said by some loremasters to have been conjured by right-hand sorcerers using Thaumaturgy to amplify nature. The last outpost of the **Huryan Empire,** the city was sacked and destroyed by the **Thalamian** warlord Tycius.

Shemites: An influential and subtle tribe from the Ghorabi Desert in what is now southern **Nazharya;** of all the Sassanian tribes of the **Golden Age,** they were the most conversant with sorcery, second only to the Sendhéans, occasionally straying towards the Left Hand Path. The Shemites went on to found the **Kishan Empire** east of the Abydos Ranges after being driven out by the rival **Huryan** tribe. Today it is thought their descendants still dwell in the Ghorabi desert, in the form of the reclusive Halamite tribe.

Silver Age: The present age; regarded by most Western **Urovians** as beginning with the consolidation of the **Free Kingdoms** some 350 years ago. Distinct from the previous **Golden Age** in that it is an era in which **Reus Almighty** has made Himself known to mortalkind – yet civilisation in Western Urovia is acknowledged by the learned to lag far behind that of the preceding epoch.

Silver Shadow: Elite order of adepts trained in both the psychic arts and assassination. Established by the Old Master of Time's Arrow more than a century ago, this Unorthodox sect of the **Faith** claims to derive its supernatural powers from the **Seven Enlightened Sultans**, of whom the Old Master claims to be a lineal descendant. Based at his fortress stronghold of Ortiz in the Cerulean Mountains, the Old Master and his sect have long been a thorn in the side of the Orthodox sultanates of Kallandhar and **Nazharya**, sometimes even allying with the crusaders (most notably the **Knights Bethler**) against their common enemy.

Sixth Sense: Special talent particular to the **Argolian Order**, honed by years of prayer and meditation. Its abilities are somewhat vague and thus difficult to define, but broadly speaking they allow a monk of the order to detect the following, with varying degrees of accuracy: when a person is lying or concealing something; when danger (particularly supernatural danger) is near; past pain or sorrow that continues to plague a victim; the presence of a warlock or witch and the type of magick being used; and a demon's psychic spoor. Other mystic orders including the **Knights Bethler**, the **Silver Shadow** and the **Sufielis** are thought to have cultivated similar powers of varying degrees of potency.

Sjórkunan: Foremost deity of the **Northlanders**, revered for his mastery of the waves and said to preside over the Halls of Feasting and Fighting below the Sea of Valhalla, the Northlandic equivalent of the **Heavenly Halls**. Known as Aqualcus, Baha'muhit and the Salt King in other periods and cultures. Believed by the Northlanders to have been the true father of Søren.

Søren: Legendary hero who hailed from the **Frozen Principalities** and came over with the First Reavers who began conquering and settling what is now **Northalde** seven centuries ago. Reputed to have been fathered on a mortal maiden by the archangel Sjórkunan, Lord of Oceans, whom the Northlanders worship as a god. Is most famed for his adventures thereafter, when seeking the westerly **Island Realms** in his magic ship Jürmengaard he stumbled upon the sorceress **Morwena**'s lair in the ruins of one of the **Watchtowers of the Magi**. She ensorcelled him into performing his Seven Deeds, the last of which saw the **Headstone of Ma'amun** recovered from the Forbidden City of **Varya**. Søren subsequently slew Morwena and broke the Headstone into four pieces, before taking his ship and sailing out across the Great Western Ocean, never to be seen again by mortal eyes. Has gone by various epithets during and after his lifetime, including the Doomed, Irongrip, Wavetamer and Wyrmslayer.

Sorcerer's Script: Hieratic script taught to the **Varyans** by the Archangels and used to express the Language of Magick. It is used to store and communicate spells and incantations of all kinds. Like the Language of Magick, its darker modes constitute the Left Hand path taught by **Abaddon** to Ma'amun.

Stornelund: One of the richest of the nine baronies that compose the realm of **Vorstlund**, neighboured by **Dulsinor** to the west and Ostveld to the south. Ruled over by the House of Lanrak; the current Herzog is Lord Hengist – a vain, inept and bibulous man unworthy of the title. Most believe his steward Albercelsus to be the true power in Stornelund.

Sub-Avatar: A secondary avatar or host body that allows a greater demon to bridge the gap between **Gehenna** on the **Other Side** and the mortal plane, inhabiting this human form (often at a powerful demonologist's behest). This enables a greater demon to operate on the mortal plane, albeit with limited powers. The most notorious examples of sub-avatars are **Xamiel of Avalogne** (the archdemon Azathol), and the Vizier Khartoun (the archdemon Sha'amiel), who are believed by some to have jointly provoked the **Pilgrim Wars**. It is not known whether archangels have ever made use of sub-avatars, though some theologians claim that the **Two Prophets** were in fact just such, hosting angels of unknown identity.

Sufieli: A sect loosely affiliated with the Unorthodox branch of the **Faith**, widely respected (despite their perceived heresy) throughout the Sha'abatian world for abilities to combat evil spirits and lift curses. In their learning and ascetic wisdom they of all sects in Sassania most closely parallel the **Argolian** Order, with whom they have had some contact since the **Pilgrim Wars**. Where Argolian friars rely on chanted psalmody to fight demonkind and the undead, the Sufielis tend to use sacred fluting and main force of will to accomplish the same effect. They take their name from the savant Suf, who founded their order several centuries ago.

True Temple: The church of the **Creed** that holds sway in Western **Urovia**, with the Supreme Perfect headquartered in Rima, the capital of **Pangonia**. Its name differentiates it from the Orthodox Temple, which administers the Creed in the **Urovian New Empire** east of the Great White Mountains. The True Temple was created by a schism, known as the Sundering of the Temple, six hundred years ago.

Thraxia: One of the **Free Kingdoms** of Western **Urovia**, composing the lands west of the Hyrkrainian Mountains that divide it from **Northalde**. Originally settled by clans fleeing the **Island Realms** after the Wars of Kith and Kin two thousand years ago. The last of the kingdoms to embrace the **Creed**, Thraxia has somewhat more tolerance for right hand magic than the other western kingdoms, although the **Left Hand Path** is punished severely. Thraxians are famed far and wide for the excellence of their poetry and music, and their greatest bard **Maegellin** is celebrated throughout the Free Kingdoms and beyond. Their skill at hunting and their fine mead are also noteworthy.

Tyrnor: War god worshipped by the **Northlanders**.

Reviled in Palomedian culture as Azazel, the archdemon embodying war.

Upper Vallia: Ancient name given to the northern and central margravates of **Pangonia**, including Rima where the royal seat is. Besides the capital its foremost provinces is Gorlivere, long rich in arable lands, vinyards and iron ore. Its smiths are renowned for their smelting skills, and the fineness of its wine is surpassed only by that of Armandy province in **Occitania** and Aquitania in **Lower Vallia**.

Two Prophets: Collective name given to the **avatars**, **Sha'abat** and **Palomedes**, whose teachings inspired the **Faith** and **Creed** respectively and brought the knowledge of **Reus Almighty** to mortalkind. Due to religious conflict, particularly the **Pilgrim Wars**, adherents of both religions respectively call the prophets 'true' and 'false' – though some loremasters acknowledge both. Note that the term 'false prophet' is also used to describe those possessed or impersonated by **archdemons** in order to lead mortalkind astray.

Upper Thulia: Lands adjacent to Dulsinor ruled by the House of Ürl, long hostile to the House of Markward. Its ruling Eorl was crippled by Sir Balthor during the last war between the Ürls and Markwards, and has nursed a bitter grudge against them ever since.

Un-angels: Collective name given to 'neutral' entities that are considered neither angels nor demons. Foremost among them are **Azrael**, judge of souls; Kaia, worshipped as a nature goddess throughout pagan communities in the **Island Realms**; and Nurë, the archangel of fire, prayed to by smiths of all kinds. The **Fay Folk** are also considered by many loremasters to be lesser un-angels, being far from good but not truly evil.

Unseen: Collective noun given to all inhabitants of the **Other Side** after the **Breaking of the World**, when angels and other supernatural entities ceased to walk openly among mortalkind. Throughout the **Golden Age** they are said to have reappeared occasionally, though with diminishing frequency, and by the advent of the **Silver Age** such manifestations had become virtually unknown. Note that demonkind will manifest in the form of possessions and in response to summonings by a demonologist meddling with the Other Side using the **Left Hand Path**.

Urovia: Name given to all the lands lying north of the Sundering Sea and the Great Inland Sea, as far the Steppes of Koth that lie beyond the Mercenary Kingdoms to the east of the **Urovian New Empire**. Nowadays Urovian culture is usually associated with the **Creed**; but note that the Three Emirates lying directly south of the Mercenary Kingdoms and Koth are considered **Sassanian** by virtue of their religion and culture.

Urovian New Empire: The most powerful and technologically advanced country of the **Silver Age**, a land empire comprising seven former kingdoms that were consolidated four centuries ago by the House of Usharok during the Hundred Years' Conquest. Protected by a string of fortresses in the Great White Mountains to the west and the Great Wall to the east, the Empire guards its secrets jealously and trades selectively with its neighbours. It is said to have preserved or relearned much of the lore of **Ancient Thalamy**, and former outlying provinces of that fallen empire are now part of the New Empire. Its capital, Illyrium, is said to be the greatest **Urovian** city since Ancient Tyrannos, and is the seat of the Imperator, the Ruling Senate, and the Orthodox Temple.

Ushalayim: The Holy City, consecrated by virtue of being both the birthplace of **Palomedes** and the site where **Sha'abat** ascended to heaven when he was recalled by the Unseen after serving mortalkind. Nowadays it is the heart and soul of the **Pilgrim Kingdoms**, though the realities of politics and war mean it is also a colonised city, ruled by Pangonian occupiers often at the expense of the native Sha'abatians.

Varya: Name given to the civilisation and the island city that spawned it more than six thousand years ago in the midst of the Great Inland Sea. Inspired by the **Archangels**, who regularly visited them and taught them the Language of Magick among many other arts and crafts, the Varyans founded an empire that covered the Known World, from the **Island Realms** in the West to the Steppes of Koth in the East. They were ruled over by the Synod of **Elder Wizards**, said to number some five dozen warlocks of power unsurpassed before or since. This empire lasted about a thousand years until it was destroyed by the **Unseen** at the **Breaking of the World,** by which time it had fallen into demonolatry, decadence and corruption thanks to **Ma'amun**, foremost among the Elder Wizards, who was seduced by **Abaddon** during his astral wanderings through the **Other Side.** Varya is also frequently referred to in texts as Seneca, the name given to it in Decorlangue, the language of **Ancient Thalamy.**

Valley of the Barrow Kings: Site of the **Watchtower** of the same name, which was where the enchantress **Morwena** made her lair and her thrall the hero **Søren** brought back the **Headstone** from **Varya** and broke it, after slaying his fickle mistress. From this piece of history it takes its alternative name of the Vale of Shadow's Lingering. Its more common name derives from the hundreds of **Draugar** that lie in wait for the Second Coming, when the power of the **Elder Wizards** shall be unleashed again.

Vasirius: Also known as the Chivalrous King, lauded by poets and loremasters alike for his uncommonly just rule, he was the Scion of the House of Rius who ruled Pangonia more than a hundred years ago and instituted the Code of Chivalry, designed to reform knighthood and rein in its worst excesses. Since Vasirius' death at the hands of the Traitor Prince Ancelet at the Battle of **Avalongne**, the code has waned in influence, though it still attracts adherents among idealistic young knights across the **Free Kingdoms.**

Vorstlund: Formerly a kingdom until the Partition Crisis that sparked the War of the Four Kings some two centuries ago, Vorstlund is now a loose federation of nine baronies, although it is still classed as being one of the **Free Kingdoms.** Vorstlendings are known for their gluttony and generosity, but can also be quick to anger and are doughty fighters.

Wars of Kith & Kin: Tragic series of conflicts between Kaluryn and Skulla, the two principal isles of the **Island Realms.** It ended two thousand years ago with the defeat of Kaluryn, and saw the Exiled Tribes found the early kingdoms of **Thraxia** on the mainland. It also marked the beginning of a long and steady decline of Westerling civilisation, as magic began slowly to fade from the realm.

Watchtowers of the Magi: A series of huge towers built by the **Elder Wizards** to watch over their vast domains across the Known World. Many were destroyed during the **Breaking of the World**, but some survived partially intact, including the Watchtowers of the Leviathan in the Abydos mountain ranges, the **Valley of the Barrow Kings** in the **Island Realms**, and Mount Brazen in the Great White Mountains that divide the **Free Kingdoms** from the **Urovian New Empire**.

Westenlund: Richest of the nine major baronies of **Vorstlund**. Ruled over by the House of Drüler, which insisted on retaining the title of principality after the kingdom was broken up two centuries ago, on account of its scion Aelle being the last king of a united **Vorstlund**.

Westerling: Name given to an inhabitant of the **Island Realms**.

Wheel: Chief symbol of the **Creed**, derived from the execution of its prophet **Palomedes** on a torture wheel in Tyrannos a thousand years ago. The sign of the Wheel is made by first touching the forehead and then splaying the fingers of the hand across one's chest, in representation of the spokes the **Redeemer**'s limbs were broken on.

White Valravyn: Chivalrous order founded by the Hero King Thorsvald of **Northalde** a hundred years ago, in memory of the warrior saint Ulred; charged with upholding Royal Law throughout the **King's Dominions** and bringing justice to all during peacetime, defending the realm in times of war, and the King's personal security.

With-Y-Passes: Ancient name given by **Westerling** settlers to the Hyrkrainian Mountains that divide **Thraxia** from **Northalde.** The name is still commonly used in the former kingdom.

Wyrm: Also known as dragons and wyverns; the ancient offspring of the **Great World Serpent** and Hydrae the Many-Headed. Now an extinct species, after the last of the great venom-spitting reptiles was slain by the Pangonian knight Sir Azelin of Valacia some years ago. A weaker but more numerous sub-species (known as wyverns) are believed by some loremasters to have once existed too, although this is disputed.

Xamiel of Avalogne: Firebrand preacher who whipped up support for the First Pilgrim War, launching the era of crusading that led to the establishment of the **Pilgrim Kingdoms** in northern **Sassania.** Rumoured by some to have been a **sub-avatar**, channelling the **archdemon** Azathol.

Yathaga the Three-Eyed: Westerling renegade, who fled her homeland after studying the forbidden **Left Hand Path** and eventually became the latter-day witch Abrexta the Prescient's tutor. Yathaga believed that the enchantress **Morwena** was doing the Moon Goddess's will by trying to unlock the **Headstone**'s powers, and constantly meddled in the affairs of mortal men in an effort to reunite the fragments. During one battle Yathaga was branded by St Meath, earning the witch her epithet, but managed to escape and go into hiding. A necromancer of some repute, she was eventually apprehended by the **Argolian** Order and burned at the stake in Ongist for her crimes.

Zaruman: The so-called 'little prophet' who took the

conjoined entity of Mithras into his heart and founded the Sect of Light and Fire. Mithras is believed by his cultists to have been a unique fusion of the archangel Solus (worshipped by pagans as the god of the sun) and the un-angel Nurë (fire). Originating before the time of the **Two Prophets** in Near **Sassania,** the sect still survives in the present day, practising in its secretive lair in the foothills of the Abydos ranges in the Sultanate of **Halepo.**

ACKNOWLEDGMENTS

First and foremost, thanks to the Four Betas for continued advice, feedback and support – no writer should ever be without a second pair of eyes, and thanks to Cris, Moonika, Timy and Sam I have that in spades.

I'd also like to extend a heartfelt thanks to fantasy vlogger Kitty Gray – had it not been for her timely reviewing during the 2017 SPFBO competition, far fewer people would be reading these words now. I hope this latest instalment of the Broken Stone Chronicle continues to enthral you! Likewise a shout-out to all the folks who took a punt on this first-time author's hugely ambitious project, and helped me to turn a long-held dream into a reality.

And finally, a big thank you to my partner, my mother and my friends, who have been so supportive and encouraged me to believe in myself – I hope this repays your confidence in me.

I'll sign off with one small but significant request. Reviews are vital to growing any fan-base: to that end, I'd be enormously indebted and grateful to anyone who puts a rating/review up on Amazon and Goodreads. Let's try to grow the Broken Stone cult a bit more!

Much love,

Damien Black

London, July 2019

@TheDevilsFriar

www.facebook.com/brokenstonechronicle

https://www.goodreads.com/author/show/

6432407.Damien_Black